EXPERIMENTAL HEART

EXPOSED

BOOK 4

SHANNON PEMRICK

Exposed
Experimental Heart | Book Four

Copyright © 2017 Shannon Pemrick
www.shannonpemrick.com

Cover Illustration by Jackson Tjota
Cover Typography by Amalia Chitulescu
Editing by Sandra Nguyen and Cody Anne Arko-Omori

ISBN 978-0-9984464-1-7 (paperback)
ISBN 978-0-9984464-2-4 (hardcover)
ISBN 978-0-9984464-0-0 (e-book)

To my parents
For supporting me and teaching me to never give up on my dreams.

And

To Sammie, Taryn, and Frank
Without you three, this story would have never been so exciting.

BOOKS BY SHANNON PEMRICK

EXPERIMENTAL HEART
Destiny
Pieces
Secrets
Exposed
Surrendered

ORACLE'S PATH
Prophecy of Convergence

Prophecy Tested
Prophecy Chosen

LOOKING FOR GROUP
Spellbinding His Ranger
Protecting His Priestess
Summoning Their Elementalist

The clanging of metal boots rang through my ears as soldiers dragged my limp body down the hall to my holding cell. I was bloody, bruised, and weak from the torture I'd endured. But just as the other times they had interrogated me, I hadn't cracked. I wasn't a rat.

They threw me onto the floor of my cell once we arrived, and locked the door behind them. My eyes didn't want to stay open and my brain told me to stay put, but I didn't want to just lay there. My comrades moved to assist me, but I wouldn't accept it. It wouldn't be right. It was my fault they were here, and I didn't deserve their help.

Slowly, I pulled myself over to my corner and curled up. I refused to ingest the slop we were to call food. Not even when the others insisted I eat something. I refused to accept a healing session. My body deserved this punishment. I wasn't worthy of their kindness for what I'd done.

The only thing I deserved was to relive the events my poor judgment caused. My eyes closed from exhaustion. Reliving that through my dreams was inevitable.

TWO WEEKS

1
CHAPTER

wo weeks. It had been two weeks since I had sent Raikidan away. It took a little adjusting to his absence, but
now everything was back to normal. I flipped a page in
my Library book. *Back to normal.* Right. Who was I trying
to fool? Myself… that's who.

It was hard for me to adjust, but I was getting there. I just needed
time. I'd think about him from time to time and wonder what he was
up to and how he had felt when he woke up in that cave. And that was
okay to think about, nothing wrong with it. It wasn't like it stopped
me from doing my job in the rebellion or anything.

"You don't need him." It was the malicious voice in my head that took
delight in taunting me.

"Get lost." I concentrated on my research.

Someone knocked on my doorframe. I looked at the short, buxom,
brown-haired woman standing in my doorway. "Hey, Ryoko, what's up?"

She smiled at me. "Genesis has an assignment for us."

I shut the book. "Good, I need something productive to do."

Her lips twitched before nodding and leaving. *Strange.* It was if she
were upset over something.

I slid off the bed and entered the living room. A slim woman with
pale skin and dark hair and a tan man with white hair were sitting on

the large couch. Both Genesis and Rylan appeared content, so why had Ryoko not?

"Hey," Rylan greeted, a little too cheerfully.

My brow row. "Um, hi?"

He chuckled. "You've been secluding yourself all day, so this is the first time I've been able to greet you."

"I haven't been secluding myself." I tossed my thumb behind me. "My door was open."

Rylan opened his mouth, but Genesis intervened. "We don't have time for this. Where is Raikidan?"

Ryoko and I passed each other a glance before Ryoko answered, "Uh, Gen, Raikidan is gone, remember?"

"What? Oh, right." She rested her forehead on her hand. "Shoot."

"What's wrong?" Rylan asked.

"I had accepted this assignment thinking he was here." She sighed. "I okayed Zane to take the boys to the shop to work on a big-income project because I thought we were all set."

"Tell us the mission and we can decide if we can pull it off," Ryoko said.

"The mission is to infiltrate two buildings at a command post," Genesis explained. "We have intel that alludes the military has paper filing rooms with some information on potential new supply locations we could infiltrate, as well as troop movement outside the city and numbers residing here that could help us."

Ryoko cocked her head, her brow knitted. "That's weird. Why would they store paper files at a command post?"

"Probably because they know few would suspect them to store the files there, as it would be rather illogical," I said. I focused on Genesis. "We can still pull this assignment off. Rylan and Ryoko can go into one building while I go into another. Nothing to it."

"You sure?" she asked.

I nodded. "Yeah, of course. I don't need someone to help me. Sure, it'd make it easier, but I'm used to working on my own."

I could tell Genesis doubted my words, but she nodded instead of voicing an argument. "All right, we'll continue with the plan, then. Get ready, and I'll send the coordinates to your communicators."

The three of us nodded and readied ourselves quickly before heading out.

The window didn't want to budge as I tried to open it, but I was going to be just as stubborn. It finally gave in and I slipped into the filing room of the building. The room was dark, but there was enough light from the windows to allow me to see. I crouched under the window and listened. I could hear someone moving around, but couldn't pinpoint where.

Keeping my movements slow, I made my way over to the filing cabinets and pulled open a drawer as quietly as possible. While it wasn't smart to send a common illiterate person to grab files, Genesis only expected me to grab anything I could manage. We'd find out later if they were of any use.

My backpack was about half full when the air in the room changed. I froze and listened. When I heard unfamiliar, heavy breathing, I spun around and narrowly dodged a soldier who had been sneaking up and attempted to grab me. Acting quickly, I grabbed onto him instead, and smashed his head into the metal filing cabinet. He fell to the floor, out cold.

"Raikidan, what the hell? You're supposed to watch"—I looked around and realized I was alone—"my… back…" I sighed. *Right… Hard to watch my back when you're not actually around.*

"Fool."

There it was again, that same harsh voice in my mind. Yet it was right this time. I was stupid. I did exactly what Genesis had done. I knew he wasn't here. I knew I had to rely on myself. I was used to relying on myself. So why had I not been able to do it? Why had I failed the easiest thing for me?

I grabbed a few more files before shutting the drawer and headed for the window. It didn't matter. I needed to leave, now that I had incapacitated the soldier. His comrades were sure to come looking for him soon with the ruckus I caused.

Sliding the window shut, I slipped into the shadows and sent a signal to Ryoko and Rylan before heading to an area where we could meet up and head home. As I did, a thought about Raikidan popped into my head, but this time, I pushed it away. *He's gone and I need to move on. That's just how it is.*

ONE MONTH

2
CHAPTER

One month. It had been one month since I had sent Raikidan away. By now everyone had gotten used to him being gone. It was easy once you allowed yourself to accept he wasn't going to magically appear when you woke up the next day. Even I was fine now. Really. I was.

I inspected my finished carving and nodded in approval. This was the seventh one I'd completed today, and I was due for a break. With today being a day off from the club, and Zane not needing my help, I needed to find something to keep my mind occupied until Genesis came up with another assignment.

Slipping my tools into their protective case, I slid off my bed and went about cleaning up. When I finished, I thought about what else I could do, and figured my daggers needed some TLC. Grabbing them from my dresser, I surveyed each blade and hilt to assess what needed to be done to them. Then I went looking for supplies to clean them up, and a whetstone to sharpen two of the blades. Tracking down my cleaning items was easy. The whetstone… was another story.

I searched high and low for it, but couldn't track it down. Growling in frustration, I spun around and looked toward the window. "Raikidan, have you seen"—I stopped and then released a slow breath—"right. You can't know where something is if you're not around."

Slamming my dresser drawer shut, I abandoned my quest and decided to take a bath. I wasn't in the mood to clean my daggers anymore.

Snatching a towel from the top of my dresser that I had yet to put away, I went to open my bath door but stopped when I caught my reflection in my long mirror. I put my towel back down and stood in front of it to look myself over.

I looked like a bum. I was still in my night clothes, and my hair had been roughly thrown up. I could also use some extra sleep, but that was because the nightmares had returned with a vengeance mere days after I sent Raikidan away.

"You look pathetic." The voice was right yet again. I looked terrible.

I missed the way he made me laugh. I missed the slight gravel to his voice—missed that stupid grin of his. And I missed... *him*. I couldn't lie to myself anymore. My life felt... emptier. This was the exact reason I had told myself from the beginning not to make any connections. He just made it hard not to...

I touched the necklace he had given me and pain twinged in my chest. I stared into the mirror and I thought I could see him reflected behind me. I whipped around but I was alone. *Stupid.*

I released a sorrowful sigh and removed the necklace. I couldn't wear this anymore. I needed to get over this. He wasn't coming back. He couldn't come back, that was that. I carefully tucked the necklace away. It was best if I removed all reminders of him. It was the only way I'd be able to move on.

I picked up my towel again and went to take a bath. Maybe that'd help. *Doubt it.*

CHAPTER 3

I opened my bleary eyes; the sweet smell of pines and damp earth, and sounds of birds trilling morning tunes enticed me out of my slumber. Except, I'd fallen asleep in my bed—in a city. Panic set me on alert, and I sat up. Sunrays filtered through the thick canopy above, and foliage rustled in the light breeze. *Where am I?*

Pulling myself to my feet, I peered around to get a sense of my surroundings. Nothing came off as familiar, but I couldn't shake the feeling I'd been here before. The distant sound of a babbling brook drew me out, and I set out on a mission of exploration. I wouldn't get answers sitting around.

Leaves crunched underfoot as I explored. Occasionally a bird flew from its perch, or some other woodland critter would run away, disturbed by my presence. Yet no matter how much I tried, I couldn't figure out my location, or how I got here. I also didn't seem to be making any ground in finding the water source. Swiveling my head and putting my nu-human hearing to work, I determined I hadn't gone any further from the brook, but I was also no closer. *What is going on?*

I stopped when leaves of the underbrush rustled behind me. I took a good whiff to get some sort of indication of what might be beyond my sight, but the heavy petrichor masked anything that could be hiding. I decided it would be best to keep moving, but upon trying to continue on, my feet remained planted. *What?*

The bushes rustled, as if something were moving just beyond them, and then, a figure stumbled out into my path, twigs catching his pant legs. My heart stopped at the sight of the recognizable man, his familiar strong scent crashing into my nose moments later. Black hair with a red stripe down the center, black goatee, muscular build, and tan skin. *It can't be...*

The man righted himself and then stared at me, his sapphire blue eyes going wide. "Eira?"

That voice... Low-pitched, gravely, and familiar. Just how I remembered it.

His presence shocked me so much, I almost wasn't able to say his name. "R–Raikidan?"

The two of us stood there, staring, mouths agape. Suddenly, Raikidan took a few steps toward me, his fingers outstretched—his eyes showing the fear I felt—that he wasn't really there. My feet refused to move. All I could do was reach out for him. Our fingertips touched and my heart skipped. He grabbed hold of my hand and held my gaze. *His hand is warm... strong, just like I remember it...*

Raikidan reached out with his free hand and cupped my cheek. His thumb caressed my skin. "It's really you... You're really here."

Before I had the chance to respond, his hand slipped behind my head, curling over the back of my neck. He yanked me closer, my feet finally finding movement, and his lips crashed into mine. A jolt ran down my spine and my heart pounded in my chest. His scent and his taste overtook my senses. *Just like I remember.*

But just as suddenly, he pushed me away. "Look out!"

I fell back, and a gunshot rang in my ears. Raikidan cried out in pain. The forest darkened, and all normal sounds disappeared. I hit the ground with a *thud* and immediately turned to look at Raikidan. He lay on the ground, convulsing. "Rai!"

I scrambled to his side to find him going into shock, his body tense with convulsions, and his pupils dilated. I touched his chest, only to retract when a slimy substance slipped over my skin. A silvery metallic liquid dripping from my hand. *It can't be!*

I watched helplessly as Raikidan's life faded before me. *No...*

Strong hands grabbed me and I gasped. I struggled against the hold and shut my eyes. Finally, I broke free and pushed forward, my eyes snapping open—the forest gone. *My room?* I looked around as I sat in bed. *A dream?* I gazed down at my hands and then touched the side of my face. *It felt so real…*

I tipped my head up toward the skylight; night still clung to the sky. Slipping out of bed, I stood in the center of my floor, where Raikidan used to sleep. *I was so sure…*

My knees felt weak, my heart heavy. I sat down on the floor and then curled up on my side, my hand pressed against the wood. *Cold.* I didn't know what else I had expected to find. Raikidan hadn't slept here for nearly a month and a half. I rubbed my fingers together, remembering the silver liquid coming out of his chest.

Please let that all have been a bad dream… Gods please, be safe and happy as you should have been had you not crossed paths with me…

ONE AND A HALF MONTHS

4
CHAPTER

O ne and a half months. It had been one and a half months since I had sent Raikidan away, and things hadn't changed much...

I peeked around the corner of the wall before diving behind a crate. Ryoko rushed to my side after she made sure it was safe to join me. Sirens blared outside the warehouse.

Genesis had sent Ryoko and me on this assignment, alone, to a Quadrant Four compound with rare weapon supplies, thinking it would be easier for the two of us to get in instead a group of us, due to the high security. And it would have been easier, had it not been for me being unable to concentrate. It had been my fault the wire had tripped and my fault we were stuck in this warehouse; I couldn't focus. My mind kept going to Raikidan.

"Because you're a fool!" The voice was relentless, but again, not wrong.

Stupid. How could I allow my mind to wonder on an assignment? I couldn't stop thinking about him. I wondered how he was doing, what he was doing, and what he would do in certain situations. I wanted to just forget him, but nothing I did allowed me to.

Ryoko nudged my arm and headed over to another crate. I exhaled and peeked around the crate, but pulled myself back as fast as I could. Soldiers came our way, and I had no idea how Ryoko managed to not be seen. She shot me a questioning glance, and I jerked my head toward the direction of the soldiers. She nodded and pushed herself farther back so they'd be less likely to spot her. I did the same, but luck wasn't on my side—not that it had been for some time.

The metal crate smashed behind me, and I whirled around to see a large Brute-soldier grinning down at me. It took me less than a nanosecond to move away from him and his hand as he tried to grab me. It was quite apparent they had seen Ryoko previously, and now I was reaping the consequences.

The soldier went to chase me, but Ryoko shot at him with her railgun, giving away her position. The other soldiers who had been hanging back were now going after Ryoko. *A trap to separate us. Great.*

I threw fire at the soldiers to give her a hand, but as I went to run, the Brute grabbed me and threw me into a metal crate. All the air in my lungs escaped, and I gasped for breath as I fell to the ground. I tried to move, but I was too winded to do much. I could, however, scream, and that's just what I did when the Brute stomped down on my leg.

The soldier chuckled and grabbed me by the throat. "Traitorous scum. You'll get exactly what you deserve."

"I fight... for a real purpose," I managed.

The soldier scowled and tightened his grip. I choked and struggled, but it was no use. Ryoko was off somewhere trying to stay alive, and I was on my own. I just hoped she'd get out safe. My life didn't mean as much as hers. She had someone waiting for when she got back...

"Let her go!" a male voice shouted.

I blinked. That voice sounded eerily familiar. Before I could think on it, my assailant dropped me when a body collided with him. As I fell to the ground, I took in the features of my rescuer. Tan, muscular physique, and black hair with a red stripe down the center. *Raikidan? No, it can't be him.*

My gaze flicked away when someone knelt next to me. He had golden eyes, and forest green and ebony hair, shaved in the style of a mohawk, but unstyled. His tan body rippled with toned muscles. I reached for the dagger strapped to my leg, but the man held up his hands. "Easy, I'm here to help."

"Don't trust him."

I eyed him. An air of familiarity emanated from him, but I had no memory of meeting someone with his appearance. *Or do I?* I didn't get the chance to ask him anything. A pair of strong arms grabbed onto me and I almost retaliated, except my surprise froze me in place. I blinked to be sure I wasn't seeing things, and when I opened them, sure enough, my rescuer had been Raikidan.

Recovering, I hissed at him, "What the hell are you doing here?"

He grunted and hauled me into his arms, wrapping me in his familiar scent. "Saving your ass."

Pain shot through my leg and I screamed in agony.

"Raikidan, be careful with her!" The mystery man's eyes bore into my dragon friend. "That leg of hers is mangled."

"I'm trying!" Raikidan bared his teeth. "This isn't as easy as it looks."

The echoes of a railgun's magnetized bearings rang out near us, and Ryoko appeared. "Will you two ladies quit yer bitching and start moving? I'm running out of ammo, and Laz needs medical attention, like, yesterday."

Raikidan grumbled and carried me to the back part of the warehouse. "Corliss, I need you to make a door."

I looked at the man Raikidan brought with him. No wonder he had an air of familiarity. Corliss nodded at Raikidan's order, and took a deep breath before projectile spitting out some strange, translucent green liquid. My eyes widened when the liquid dissolved the metal wall on impact. I had thought all dragons breathed fire. Apparently, I was wrong.

Corliss spit a few more times to speed up the corrosion process. When Raikidan determined the hole was big enough, he shot out into the open. It was reckless, given he couldn't be sure it was safe, but this wasn't the time to reprimand him.

Ryoko rushed out of the building with Corliss, and she pulled out her emergency grenade. Pulling the pin, she tossed it into the warehouse and pushed us to move faster. The grenade detonated, and we pushed harder as other warehouses filled with explosives; were caught up in the chain reaction.

Ryoko directed Raikidan where to go until we came to the break in the fence we had made when coming in. Ryoko pulled the chain link back to allow Raikidan to slip through with me with ease. She then motioned to follow her when she slipped through herself. The two dragons followed her through alley after alley until we came to the back door of a safe house and slipped in.

Ryoko opened a secret passage and rushed through. Raikidan didn't hesitate to follow, but Corliss stood still, marveling in amazement. That is, until the door started closing on him. Ryoko jumped down into the sewers, and then growled at Raikidan when he carelessly followed suit and shot pain through my leg. He ignored her, though, pushing past her and nearly knocked her into the sludge below.

"Watch it, Raikidan!" she hissed. "And to think I missed having you around."

Raikidan continued to ignore her and kept at his fast pace. I was quite interested in this behavior. It wasn't like him to be so rude to Ryoko. One of the guys, sure, but the women, not a chance.

Ryoko ran ahead of us and opened the secret door to our house, and Raikidan picked up his pace. Corliss, not wanting to be shut in this smelly place, matched Raikidan's pace. Ryoko ushered us inside, and Raikidan spared no glances to the basement as he rushed upstairs. I tried not to make a sound, but the pain he caused was becoming unbearable.

Before he could even think to open the door, it flew open and Seda stood in front of it. "Get her on the couch, now."

Raikidan nodded and moved around the couch to set me down. Shva'sika rushed over to me, barely containing her laughter as she got one good look at me. "Why can't you, just once, do something that doesn't nearly cripple or kill you?"

I chuckled. "Because I need to give you something to do."

She shook her head and examined my injury. Raikidan moved away, much to my relief, and positioned himself behind the couch. I wanted to mentally prepare myself for what was going to happen between the two of us, but the pain wasn't allowing that to happen.

Seda hovered over the back of the couch. "Elarinya, I'm going to set everything back in place before you heal her, to make sure everything goes back the way it's supposed to be."

"A shaman's healing ability would ensure such a new break would heal properly," Shva'sika explained. "And I'm more worried about Laz's pain levels right now. She may be able to handle a lot, but too much could cause her to pass out."

"I'll block her pain receptors. She could use the reprieve anyway."

Shva'sika nodded. "All right, let me know when to heal her up."

Seda took a deep breath and then held one hand up toward my head and the other to my leg. The pain melted away, and I exhaled with relief. The lack of pain felt so good, I relaxed enough where I didn't notice Shva'sika had begun to heal me. Corliss became visibly curious, but remained quiet as he observed.

Genesis approached me. "Safe to assume you weren't successful on grabbing anything?"

I shook my head. "Sorry. I take full responsibility for the failure."

She nodded. "We'll debrief later. I want you rested after what you've gone through."

"Thank you."

Shva'sika pulled away when she finished. "All right, all done. Just lay there for a bit, and—or you could move against my better suggestion, that works too."

I chuckled as I pulled myself up into a sitting position. It wasn't like I planned on standing up just yet.

Raikidan leaned over the couch. "You should listen—" He stumbled backward when the palm of my hand collided with his face. He rubbed his cheek. "What the hell, Eira?"

"What the hell? What the hell are you doing here, is a better question!" I seethed.

Everyone in the room backed away, knowing full well what was about to happen.

"Eira, I—"

"Do you have a problem with listening or something?"

"Eira—"

"Do you just not give a shit?"

"Eira, please—"

"Will the two of you just shut up?" I stared at Corliss. He was ballsy. He looked at Raikidan. "We really need to work on your communication skills." He pulled out a folded up piece of paper from his back pocket and wandered over to me. "I saved this just in case something like this would happen. Read this line here."

"That's in your tongue, you realize that right?" I said.

He stared at me for a moment and then laughed. "Oops, sorry. I guess I'll just tell you then. It's safe for Raikidan and me to be here because we're half-colors."

My brows knotted in confusion. "I don't understand."

"This treaty specifically states colored dragons can't step foot here, but in our society, half-colors are something completely separate. We're not considered a colored dragon. We're half-colored."

I shook my head. "It's not seen that way in this human society, however. A dragon is a dragon."

"Except it would have been made clear when the treaty was crafted and signed."

I sucked in a deep breath and tried to think of a way to continue arguing. This guy was smart. Too smart for his own good.

"Besides, there are other dragons here in this city," Corliss said. "I could smell their temporary territory marks. They're red dragons, and have made it clear by the marks, they're here for a reason."

I shook my head. "They have to be old then. I sent the same letter to Zaith's clan."

Leader of a large red dragon clan from the Velsara Wilds, I'd made a tenuous alliance with Zaith in order to help our position on dealing with Zarda. His clan had proven useful, though I made sure to keep minimal contact with Zaith himself before sending his clan away due to... an unwanted offer he made me.

"These are fresh and well maintained. They obviously didn't listen, and kept a low profile if you don't know."

"That doesn't make sense. Why would they take the risk?"

"Why do you take risks?"

I opened my mouth, but failed to come up with a comeback. That was too good of a point. Ryoko began to squeal when I remained silent, and Rylan, who had been hanging back, laughed at her excitement.

"Does that mean they can stay?" she asked.

I sighed and pulled myself onto the back of the couch. "They can do what they want."

Ryoko squealed again and everyone laughed at her. Corliss backed away from me as I swung my legs over the couch and headed for my room.

"So that was supposed to be a yes?" Corliss asked.

Shva'sika laughed. "That's Laz's way of saying, welcome to our dysfunctional family."

"Very dysfunctional," Ryoko added.

Corliss chuckled and nodded.

Raikidan followed me to my room. "Eira, I still need to talk to you."

"No, you don't."

"Eira, just let me talk."

"Just go to your room and go to bed, Raikidan."

"I'm not doing anything until I talk to you."

I tried to close the door on him, but he forced his hand in the way and tried to push his way in. "Go to your own room!"

"Are they always like this?" Corliss asked.

"It's common for them to bicker," Seda said. "It's how we know they're getting along. But I'm afraid this isn't one of those times…"

"Should we do something?" he asked.

"No, it's best they sort it out themselves. Follow me. I'll show you to your room. Once you're situated, I'll help you contact your mate so you can tell her what's going on."

"How did you kn—"

"We've learned Raikidan isn't the type to give warning before he does something. And I'm psychic, so I've caught glimpses of some of your thoughts."

"All right, I'll give you that."

Raikidan forced his way into my room and slammed the door shut. "I deserve an explanation."

I turned to face him. "I gave one to you. It's all in that letter."

"I deserve better than that!" he shouted. I flinched. "I deserved to have a say."

"There was nothing to discuss, Raikidan." I tried to stay calm. "Based on how it was written, the only interpretation could be what I had concluded. I knew you'd try to fight me on the decision to send you away and I couldn't have that. I couldn't allow my selfishness to put your race at risk."

"I had a right to a say in all this. I could have told you the actual meaning!"

"Oh really? Is that why it took you almost two months to come back?" He hesitated and I snorted. "Exactly. You would have thought the same. You're just pissed off because you didn't have a say."

"Yes, I am angry, Eira. I had a right to have a say in all of it! But you didn't care. That's why you're not wearing the necklace I gave you."

I stared at him in disbelief. "Are you kidding me? You have no idea what that choice did to me. How much that hurt"—I took a deep breath through my nose, my hands flexing out—"You know what, forget it. You don't really give a shit. You never have, and you clearly only care about your own feelings. Why did you even bother coming back? Just get the hell out of here."

Thoroughly disgusted, I spun on my heels and went into my closet. I sighed and sat down on the circular couch just as my door slammed shut. My fingers ran through my hair and then my hands slid over my face. I couldn't believe him. I could understand his anger for being sent away, but to accuse me of not caring...

"You don't need him. He's just like the others. Selfish. A liar. He doesn't care about you. You're better off without him."

I knew this *friendship* he claimed to want with me was too good to be true. Dragons and humans just couldn't coexist, and I shouldn't have allowed myself to get so close. When he had told me he was promised to someone, I should have gotten my heart under control. That was the first sign. *I knew better than to think—*

I shook my head and changed my clothes. No point dwelling on it. My heart proved once again it was stupid and should remain caged up and forgotten about. And that humans and dragons should remain apart. Why he came back was beyond me, but he'd leave on his own free will in time, and not look back, and I'd need to learn to do the same.

5
CHAPTER

I flipped through the reports on my planner and felt my mood souring by the minute as I read them over. There was nothing good in here. It was all negative test results, and the conversation with its test taker was not going to be a pretty one. But as I thought about what to say to him, I drew a blank, and this frustrated me more.

The communicator crashed down onto the coffee table and I paced back and forth in front of the TV. Everyone's attention focused on me, but it was a little while before anyone said anything.

"Laz, you wanna share with us what's got you all worked up over there?" Ryoko asked. I didn't exactly hear her, as I continued to pace and chew on my lip as I thought. What was I going to say? "Laz!"

I looked up and blinked. "What?"

"Tell us what's bugging you. We might be able to help."

I sighed and rested my hands on my hips. How could I word it for them to help? "How... how do you tell a fighter he can't fight anymore?"

"This is about Zenmar, isn't it?" I nodded and her shoulders slumped. "He's not doing well, is he?"

I shook my head. "He's barely able to walk with the prosthetic with a cane. There's no way he's going to be able to get better soon enough to fight again."

"So Raynn is going to find him completely useless," Raid said. "Well, most teams will, to be honest."

I nodded. "I'm… I'm not sure what to do."

"Why not request to transfer to this team?" Shva'sika said. "I mean I'm considered a part of it and I don't do much, but that's not to say we couldn't put him to good use."

"We could assign him to casual spying assignments," Argus suggested. "They're not fun, but at least he'd feel a little useful, instead of us just saying, 'Go home and wait for it all to be over.'"

I took a deep breath and nodded. "That might just be the only option we have."

"We might as well bring it up with the Council," he said. "It was Raynn's fault, after all. They might be able to do something to him while we're at it."

I grunted. "They should do something about it."

"I'm glad you feel that way." My gaze turned to Genesis as she walked into the room. "The Council already knows about the results, and just called me. They want a meeting. Now."

I took deep, slow breaths and I waited on my platform. The air was tense and the quiet murmur from other rebels in the large room filled my ears, although I did my best to block it all out. I needed to be on the top of my game. Raynn would be sure to cause an uproar, and I wasn't sure where the Council would stand as a whole.

A tall, light-skinned, white-haired and crystal-eyed man, Elkron, started the meeting. "Eira Risryn, Raynn Larken, please step forward." I jumped from my platform down to the main one and waited for Raynn to join me. He was much slower to react, and it made me wonder if he knew what was going to happen.

"As everyone here knows, we are here to discuss the results of Zenmar's few months of therapy after his unfortunate accident. Eira, seeing as you had direct control over the therapy, please provide us with these test results."

"They're not good." I knew Zenmar was here to witness this, but I wasn't going to beat around the bush on this one. I used the room's strange nature to my advantage and had it display different charts and test results. "There isn't enough time for Zenmar to use the prosthetic properly to be effective in battle if they come about. We are on a time frame, and that time frame isn't accommodating to many. This is one of those times."

"So are you saying he needs to be relieved of duty and stay hidden until this is over?" Hanama questioned.

"No."

She titled her head. "Then was do you suggest?"

"I'd like to make a request. A transfer, more specifically. While some won't find use for him in his state, my team does. We would like Zenmar to join Team Three, and have the one responsible for this whole issue held accountable for not only Zenmar's injuries, but for the injuries and deaths of others as well."

"What are you saying there, pipsqueak?" Raynn shot.

"You know what I'm saying. You screwed up far too many times," I accused. "You've abused your power since you became a general in the military, and you've thrown away everything it means to be one. You've only ever looked after your own ass, and couldn't care less about those you've gotten killed or injured in your own greed and self-preservation. You would have left Zenmar to die in that battle. You ran like the coward you are, instead of going back to aid him. Now he suffers for your incompetence."

"I told you to leave him. He wouldn't have any problems if you had."

"No, he would have just been dead." I spat on the ground. "You have no loyalty. You have no honor. You don't deserve your rank, and you don't deserve your team. I ask the Council to strip Raynn of everything he is. I ask he no longer be regarded as a former general, no longer be able to order a team, no longer be a part of a team until he learns what it means."

Raynn bared his teeth. "How dare you!"

"I vote yes!" a man called out.

"Ven, I hope you have a good reason to speak out of turn," Eldenar scolded.

I shifted my gaze to a tall man with dark skin and dark eyes just as he nodded at Eldenar's words. "I believe this decision goes beyond just the Council. There are many of us who have been affected directly by Raynn's incompetence, and the rest have witnessed it. A blind eye has been turned for too long. Raynn is far too incompetent to be trusted any further. I agree with Commander Eira and vote yes."

I listened as murmurs of agreement sounded throughout the room. At least I had backing. Although it wasn't a secret many didn't like Raynn, losing a team leader was hard. Teams weren't just assigned new ones on a whim, so other measures would have to be taken, which caused more problems in the end.

"I, too, agree," Seda voiced.

My brow rose with interest. *What is she up to?*

Enrée took great interest in her. "Seda, you never speak out of turn. What drives you to do so now?"

"As psychics, we see things and feel things no one should. What Raynn has done, the toll his actions have taken, they are much deeper than many realize. It would be unwise to tolerate such actions any longer."

"You all can't be serious!" Raynn bellowed.

"Quiet, Raynn!" Hanama barked.

His face reddened in anger "The hell I will. I have a say in my surprise trial."

"It shouldn't be a surprise," Hanama said. "We've kept a close eye on you for a long time, Raynn. Due to issues with your removal, we just hoped you'd smarten up. We've been keeping tabs on Zenmar's progress since the incident. We received all reports before Commander Eira."

"We gave her a chance to prove herself as a worthy leader, which she has done and more with spearheading Zenmar's recovery. And even though we did not expect her to propose this, it should not have come as a surprise either. I do not need to hear anything more. You could not prove yourself before, and you won't get a second chance in my eyes. I vote yes to her request."

"I, too, vote yes," Adina said.

"Yes," Elkron agreed.

"Yes," Enrée and Akama agreed together.

Eldenar nodded. "This notion has my support."

"Then it is decided," Genesis announced. "In a unanimous decision, Raynn, you are hereby stripped of your standing rank, and for the time being, Team Seven will be disbanded. Appropriate accommodations for those who are unfortunately involved will be made if requested."

Mocha's quiet voice echoed through the room. "What are the terms of our team coming back?"

Elkron gazed at her sympathetically, much to my surprise. "If Raynn can prove he is capable of change and shows traits and actions of a true leader in a timely manner, then we will revoke our call. If he cannot, we will call a meeting to discuss future plans for more permanent actions."

"How long is that?" she asked.

"It depends on the progress. If there isn't any, a few weeks. If there is some, a few months."

"Okay." There was something in Mocha's voice that interested me. She sounded scared, a trait their little group went out of their way to hide.

"This meeting is now adjourned," Eldenar announced. "There are many preparations to be made, and little time to do so."

I spun on my heels and headed for the exit, not even passing a glance at Raynn. He wasn't my problem, and I had someone more important to talk to.

Hopping off the platform transporting me to the other side of the room, I swiftly moved through the hallway and ignored anyone I passed. Once I reached the virtual training room, I looked around. Noticing Zenmar and his girlfriend sitting alone, I advanced toward them.

Zenmar struggled to his feet when he saw me. "Commander."

"Just Eira, please."

"All right, Eira, are you sure you want me? I know how terrible I am with this leg. I'm of no use to you."

I sat down next to his girlfriend focusing on her. "Do you need new living accommodations?"

She shook her head. "No, we have our own place. Zenmar has been having some trouble using the stairs there, but I think it'll be good for him so I have no quarrel with staying where we are."

"Okay, now for you specifically. Were you a part of the same team? I didn't factor that in."

She nodded. "Yes. That's how we met."

"Then you'll be transferred to Team Three as well. I will have the Council informed of this decision so there isn't any confusion."

She smiled. "Thank you."

"Just let us go," Zenmar insisted. "Between work and taking care of me, Lena doesn't have any time for assignments, and I'm going to be of no use!"

"Zenmar, stop it," Lena scolded. "Be grateful she believes in you."

"It's pointless!"

She only frowned at him. It was obvious the two fought over this a lot.

"Our team is in need of spies," I said. "It's a greater need than I'd like to admit. I could use you both on this."

Lena smiled. "I'm fine with doing that. To be honest, it's the best way I can help. I'm not good at any of the more... labor intensive work. I'm just a civilian, after all."

I regarded her for a moment. "I had no idea."

She smiled. "Well, that's good. I always felt it was easy to tell."

I chuckled. "Civilians aren't much different from those of us who are tank-born. Only a little."

Zenmar frowned. "She may be okay with this, but I'm not."

"Well, you don't have to be," I said in an authoritative tone. "It is what it is, and you're going to do it, do I make myself clear?"

He sighed. "Yes, ma'am."

Lena looked at me with a raised brow, and I leaned in to whisper to her. "It will be some time before the mental scarring from this accident fades. There will be times he needs a gentle hand and others you will have to be firm. It won't be easy, but you can't give up on him. You two need each other to get through this."

She smiled. "Thank you. That's something I needed to hear right now."

I stood. "I should leave you two alone now. I don't have anything else to tell you."

Lena nodded. "Thank you, Commander, and not just for the advice."

I smirked. "Just call me Eira."

CHAPTER 6

Glasses clanked and plates rattled as I carried them to the kitchen. Today had been busy, and I couldn't wait for it to be over. I had forgotten to let Azriel know Raikidan had returned, and when we got back here, I thought Azriel would have been mad, but I was surprised at how happy he was. He immediately put Raikidan to work bouncing with Orchon, and it wasn't until later that evening that I realized why Azriel was so happy. Although Azriel had filled Raikidan's bartending position only a week after I sent him away, we had lost a bouncer last week due to pay disagreements, so that meant Raikidan would be a full-time bouncer, making my job a lot easier—sort of. Since we still weren't on speaking terms, I couldn't be sure how often he'd watch my back.

A week after I sent Raikidan away, I just about quit on the spot. Zo and his goons were relentless, and Genesis had forced me to go out on another date with him two weeks ago. Zo had asked about where Raikidan disappeared to, and acted all too happy to hear Raikidan had to go back to our home village for a while. I knew he figured Raikidan wasn't coming back, but today proved fruitful, as Zo's hopes had been crushed the moment he spotted my dragon friend and he had pretty much left me alone all night.

Leaving the glasses and plates on the counter next to an already-started pile, I left the kitchen and headed down to Azriel's office to complete my next task. I came to a halt when I heard a strange noise. It sounded like wood clanking together and some sort of liquid being poured. Curious, I forgot about my trip to the office and walked down a new hall in hopes to locate the source of the strange sound.

As I walked down the hall, a thick, acrid odor wafted into my nose and my instincts told me not to continue on. *What is that?* My eyes widened, and against my instincts' wishes, I picked up the pace when I realized what the smell was. Taking another corner, I skidded to a halt as I met with a wall of fire. The club was on fire. I needed to warn Azriel. There was too much fire for me to try to force down.

"Behind you!" Despite being a pain in my ass, I'd learned to heed the voice's warning.

I spun on my heels and sprinted down the hall, but someone latched onto my arm when I had only managed to make it half way. I turned to face my assailant and was taken aback by the man staring me down. He was tall, with white hair, and pale eyes. His skin was so fair, blue veins were visible underneath. The man looked like he belonged on the spiritual plane.

"I'm afraid I can't let you warn them."

He came at me with surprising speed that rivaled my own, and before I could react, he grabbed me by the throat and slammed my head against the wall. A pulse of pain rushed through me and then my vision failed me.

My head spun and my body felt heavy. The place I was in was warm, and it was hard not to just stay still and be soothed. Several moments passed before I was able to open my eyes, and even then, my vision was a blur. My memory came back to me just then, and I began to panic. How long had I been out?

I pushed myself up, my eyes darting around. When my eyes finally cleared, I realized I was in a utility closet. Pushing myself to my feet, I stumbled to the door but I hesitated to grab the knob. The door felt warm. Instead of grabbing the knob, I rested the back of my hand against the door and instantly pulled it away. *That's scorching!*

Taking a deep breath, I kicked down the door and was met with a wall of fire. I narrowed my eyes. Whoever that man had been, he had to have set the fire, and then tried to trap me in here. Feeling out the strength of the fire, I forced it away and moved into the hall, although I wasn't sure if that had been the best idea to do. The hall was even hotter than the utility closet, and everything was ablaze. The smoke in the air was thick and suffocating. I coughed violently and tried to cover my nose and mouth as best as I could as I made it down the hall, moving any flames in my way.

My body grew weaker by the moment from the smoke and I wasn't even to the end of the hall, let alone close to the main part of the club. I collapsed on the floor when I reached the end of the hall but forced myself to get back up. I needed to get out of here. I took a few more steps down the hall but jumped back when the roof caved in. I tried to look over and around the pile of rubble to spot a way out, but couldn't. There was no way around this barricade and I feared I was now trapped.

I turned and searched for another way out. There had to be one, but my body had other ideas. I collapsed once more and coughed violently. I had inhaled too much smoke, and the fires were too wild for me to control. I wasn't going to make it out of here alive. I knew that. There was no reason to believe otherwise.

"Eira?"

I coughed and weakly looked around. "Rai?"

I had to be hearing things. There would be no way he'd be stupid enough to run blindly into a burning building, right?

"Eira? Eira, where are you?" I blinked slowly. It really was him. "Eira!"

What does he want? It's not like he cared about you.

"Give it up." Zo's voice came. "She's not here. She has to be outside somewhere."

"No, she's in here and I'm going to find her," Raikidan said. "I won't give up on her."

"Are you mad? This place is about to collapse. We need to get out of here."

Raikidan coughed. "Then go. I'll look for her myself."

"Rai…" I managed.

"Eira?"

I tried to move closer to the fiery barricade blocking me in, even if it meant dragging myself, but I just fell over in a crumpled heap. It was too late.

"Eira, hold on. I'll get you out of here."

"Why does he want to save you?"

"Rai… go…" I coughed. "Get out of here…"

"Hold on," Zo told Raikidan. "My armor is fire resistant. I'll be able to break this down."

"Fine, just do it fast."

My eyes hooded and I wished they'd just leave before it was too late. They wouldn't be able to get through—

Instinct kicked in and I threw my hands over my head when the barricade burst. A gloved hand touched my shoulder. I lifted my gaze to see a helmeted soldier, who I assumed was Zo, hovering over me. But he didn't stay there long. Raikidan pushed him out of the way and knelt beside me. I couldn't help but smile. He would be that rude.

Raikidan whipped his shirt over his head and placed it over my nose and mouth. "Hold that there. I'm getting you out of here."

I weakly held his shirt to my face and he lifted me up into his arms. Once secure, he set a quick pace for the exit, not caring whether Zo was behind him or not. *Why is he saving me?*

"Maybe he's not all bad. He's making it so you'll live. But it could be a ruse."

Cold air rushed over me when we burst through the front door, and I began to shiver from the temperature drop. Raikidan held me closer and I watched him frantically look around.

"Ray? Ray, did you find her?" *Ryoko?* What was she doing here? I heard her gasp and she came into my blurry vision as she rushed over. "By the goddess! Eira, are you okay?"

I coughed in response.

Ryoko turned away and searched the road. "Medic! Medic!"

Heavy footsteps ran over to us. "What's wrong, Ma—by Gina's holy heart, you found her! Follow me. We need to get her oxygen, now."

I watched as the world around me started moving again and people came in and out of my limited vision. I coughed more and it hurt my raw throat. I wished it'd stop hurting. It was the only part of me that really hurt. Sure, my head hurt, but that was because it had been smacked against a wall.

Raikidan knelt and gently rested me on the ground. He then moved behind me and positioned my head on his legs. The cold ground caused me to shiver more. Raikidan removed his shirt from my face and laid it out over me as a pseudo-blanket, but it didn't help.

The medic who had brought us over placed a mask over my mouth and nose. "Just stay calm and try your best to breathe evenly. This will help, I promise."

I reached up and held the mask as clean oxygen rushed relief to my lungs. I made sure my breaths were long and deep. I coughed several times, each as painful as the last. I smiled when Azriel suddenly appeared at my side. He looked like a frantic mess, but I was glad he was okay.

"Eira, I'm so glad you're okay." He touched my bangs and then my eyes as his training started to take over. "I am so sorry."

"Az..." I whispered.

"I really didn't think you were inside when we evacuated."

"Az..."

"If I had known you were still inside—"

"Azriel."

He blinked. "Yeah?"

"Shut up."

He chuckled and others around me did as well. "All right."

My eyes felt heavy and I was going to let them close, but a helmeted soldier knelt next to me. Zo pulled his helmet off and surveyed my condition. "Eira, I know you're in no real shape to talk, but I need to ask you a few questions."

Azriel's mouth fell open. "Are you kidding me? She's barely out of a burning building for ten minutes after being trapped inside, and you're asking her questions?"

Zo rubbed the top of his head, trying to think. "I know I shouldn't be, but we need answers."

"Sir, I have to object. She's in no condition to be talking," the medic told him.

"We need answers now. She was the only one to not evacuate when the fire started. Furthermore, she has no burns on her and we found her in a burning hallway."

"She's still in poor condition." Raikidan's lip curled as he nearly growled out the words. "You'll get your answer when she's better."

I just watched as the four bickered. It was amusing in a way, seeing the different sides justify their stance, but the reality was, I did need to tell them what happened.

"Hey, guys?" Ryoko said. The men ignored her and continued to argue. "Guys." Again she was ignored. "Hey, meatheads!" They immediately stopped and looked at her. "I think Eira wants to say something, regardless of what you all think."

Azriel shifted his focus to me. "All right, Eira, what do you have to say?"

I would have answered him, had someone not caught my attention. His pale complexion was unmistakable. I pointed. "Him…"

Azriel blinked. "What?"

"He… did it." I coughed. It hurt to talk. "He set… the fire."

Zo shook his head. "That's ridiculous. He's one of us."

I glared at him. "Slammed… head… into wall. Shoved me… in… closet."

I cranked my neck and Ryoko cocked her head. "What are you looking for?"

"Something… to hit… him with."

She smirked and picked up a rock. "Allow me."

Ryoko flung the small object at him and it bounced off his uniform. The man blinked and swiveled his head. He froze up when he saw me. I glared. He swore under his breath and ran.

"Men, stop him!" Zo ordered.

I blinked when Raikidan rested me on the ground and took off. I looked at Azriel in hopes of getting an answer, but he only chuckled, confusing me more. I gazed up at Ryoko but she merely smiled. What was I missing? I closed my eyes with a sigh and continued to take in oxygen. I'd never know, so it was pointless to wrack my brain over it.

I cracked my eyes when I heard approaching footsteps. Raikidan crouched back down by me. He appeared content for some reason. What did he do?

"Did you get him?" Zo demanded.

"Yes, sir, he's in our custody." I shifted my gaze from Raikidan to the small squad of soldiers who were now with us.

"Well, where is he?"

"With the other men, sir," the soldier informed Zo. "They're waiting for him to come to so he can be questioned."

Zo's brow rose. "Excuse me?"

The soldier pointed at Raikidan. "Ask him, sir."

Zo looked at Raikidan but he only grunted. "Just be glad I didn't go the less legal route."

"I approve of his choice, though the less legal route would have been better."

I stared at him. I couldn't believe what I was hearing. *I don't understand… if he hates me so much, why is he acting like this?*

Raikidan slipped his arms under me to scoop me up. "Now let's get you home to rest."

"Are you kidding me?" The medic attempted to stop him. "She needs to go to a hospital."

Raikidan glared at him. "We don't use your medical facilities."

"She needs professional medical attention."

Raikidan rose with me in his arms. "No."

The medic held his ground. "I'm not letting you take her home. She needs proper attention."

I shook my head. "No hospitals…"

The man blinked. "Ma'am, please—"

I shook my head again. "No hospitals…"

"Ma'am—"

"I'll take care of her," Azriel interjected.

"You ca—"

"I will. They have their reasons for not wanting to go, and Eira needs attention. I'm more than qualified, and I'll need something to do while this mess gets cleaned up. If she gets too bad, I'll just have her stay at my place so I can monitor her around the clock."

The medic sighed. "All right. I guess I have no choice, since you're all refusing my recommendation."

Raikidan shifted me in his arms so he had a better hold on me. "Good. Now let's get you home, Butterfly."

I smiled at him and then Azriel when he stood and handed me my portable oxygen canister.

"I'll go get the truck," Ryoko said before running off.

I exhaled when Raikidan held me closer to him. His warmth enticed me to melt in his arms. I needed the heat, but I knew it was wrong to just curl into him like his… *Don't think it, Eira.* My eyes slowly closed as the excitement of the night died and my body's growing weariness grew. I needed to rest. Otherwise, I'd never be back at one hundred percent effectiveness.

7
CHAPTER

From my position on the couch in the living room, I watched
Azriel speak with Shva'sika, my breath coming out in
shallow rasps. They finished their conversation about my
condition, and he then left to rest at his place. It had been
three days since the fire at the club. In that time, several more buildings had been victims of arson, though none so far had any common
connection besides being places of popular non-exclusive client business. My condition also hadn't improved much. I struggled to speak,
most times my voice coming out in painful rasps, and moving hurt
even more.

Shva'sika's healing wasn't working like it should. She blamed her
inexperience, and she wouldn't listen to reason when I attempted to
explain to her how it was nowhere near her fault. Raikidan was even
less help. He didn't want to come anywhere near me, let alone give
me healing fire.

I didn't get him. One moment he wanted me alive and protected,
and the next he allowed me to suffer.

"It's because he doesn't really care."

Still, it had gotten to the point where Azriel had mentioned the
thought of having me stay with him for a while. While I was grateful
for his help, and staying at his home wouldn't be a terrible thing, I

wasn't too thrilled with the idea. It had been hard enough allowing the others to go out on assignments without me, but to be sent away to heal and not know what was going on at all, that didn't settle well with me in the least.

It didn't settle well that I was still like this. I should have been able to take out that soldier, not the other way around. I felt so pathetic. I wasn't even allowed to move much. I was to *rest* to make sure I didn't put too much strain on my lungs. I wasn't sure what was so strenuous about walking from one room to another, but if both Azriel and Shva'sika said it was, then I knew not to fight them.

Rylan and Genesis caught my attention when they came into the living room. She handed him a cloaking watch and finished speaking with him, her voice too low for me to catch in my state. He nodded and used the watch to change his features and to hide his chains. *What is he doing?*

Rylan slipped down into the basement and Genesis looked at us. "Rylan is being sent on a spying assignment. Let me know when he gets back."

I blinked. Since when was Rylan sent on solo spying assignments? Sure, I was out of commission, but Rylan would have opted to have someone go with him. What was Genesis thinking?

Shva'sika came over to the couch with my library access book. She handed it over, and I smiled in thanks for her thoughtfulness. I read up on various things until the sun began to set. I only stopped reading because I was starting to feel weird, in a bad way, and it concerned me.

Raikidan looked up from where he sat at the kitchen bar eating. "Eira, what's wrong?"

His concern alerted Shva'sika, who rushed over to me. "Laz, what is it?"

"I'm... I'm not sure..." I took a deep breath as the sensation worsened. "Something... isn't right."

"Do you need me to call Azriel back? I doubt he'll mind com—"

I shook my head. "It's not that. It's... something else."

My eyes widened when sudden pain shot through me. I screamed and my body jerked as if it were trying to get away from the pained areas. Shva'sika and Raikidan jumped and stared at me in shock, and Ryoko rushed over to me from her position on the couch. "Laz!"

I cringed as more pain shot through me. "It's... it's Rylan..."

"Laz, what's going on?" Ryoko demanded. "What's wrong with Rylan?"

I screamed in agony again instead of replying. I wasn't even sure if I could say what was going on even if I hadn't screamed. I had never felt this kind of pain from our bond. Seda, Raid, and Genesis rushed into the room just as Raikidan ran over to the couch. I squeezed my eyes shut as another spasm of pain rushed through me.

"Rylan's been caught," Seda informed. "We need to get to him now."

"But what's going on with Laz?" Shva'sika asked.

"The bond she and Rylan share allows them to be aware of each other's presence, as well as how they're feeling. Unfortunately, in her weakened state, Laz has more than just awareness. She's experiencing his pain."

Ryoko's hands flew up to her mouth. "They're torturing him?"

Seda nodded. "I need all of you to come with me. We're going to need everyone on this, including you, Shva'sika, and you, Corliss."

"But what about Laz?" Ryoko asked. "She can't be left alone in this state."

"I'll be watching her," Genesis said. "Now, get going."

Shva'sika and Ryoko looked at me in concern before leaving, but Raikidan didn't move away. Instead, he did the opposite. He sat down next to me, and I would have sighed had I not been cringing in pain. He had no intention of leaving, and I couldn't understand the flip-flop actions.

"His intentions are shrouded in darkness. Don't trust him."

"Rai... go with them." He stared at me. "They need... you... and the sooner"—I cringed as a painful spasm shot up my spine—"the sooner you get Rylan... the sooner I'll be okay."

Raikidan hesitated, and I touched his arm only to spasm again and startle him. Genesis knelt next to him. "Raikidan, go with them. I can handle this. They need you more right now."

Raikidan's eyes shifted between us several times as if he was trying to calculate the best choice. Eventually, he made up his mind and joined the others.

"Ryoko, can you grab something Rylan has worn recently?" Raid asked her. "I might need to use it if Seda can't locate him."

"Yeah, I'll grab his work shirt."

I closed my eyes and tried to will the pain away. I hoped it might help Rylan too, but I doubted it would help either of us. As my body spasmed and cringed, I listened to everyone leave. It was quiet now, except for Genesis' quiet breathing.

I cringed in pain, but this time I forced myself to roll over as I coughed up blood. Genesis offered me a towel when my fit ended. "Here. Seda told me you might need this."

"Thank you," I rasped as I took it.

"Eira... I'm... I'm sorry... I shouldn't have sent him out to do this, knowing you weren't feeling well."

"Gen, it's all right. You didn't know it would... end up like this. Hell, I didn't even know I could feel... this kind of pain from the bond."

"I shouldn't have asked you to rekindle the bond when you returned to us back in the spring. I never imagined this could happen. I didn't think to ask what it really meant for you two to have it, and for that, I'm sorry."

"Gen, I told you... it's all right."

She shook her head. "I'm just trying to be useful. I'm not like you guys. I don't have any real skills. I can't even use my necromantic skills properly, given the chance. I can only look at offered assignments and determine if all of you would be good at them or how beneficial they'd be to pursue. I didn't even want to take this one, since you were the best choice, but no other team would take it, and completing it would really help us. That's why Rylan offered. He overheard me talking to myself about it."

I frowned. That would explain why he went alone. "Gen, listen... to me. You are useful. You choose... the best assignments for us. You take all the heat... if we mess up. You have to deal with the rest of the Council and discuss... with them what you all believe... is right for us as a whole." Genesis gazed at me with curious eyes. "Just because you're not... doing the same stuff as us, doesn't mean you're not pulling your own weight. Even Shva'sika and Zane pull their own type of weight, even though they don't... normally join us on assignments."

She sighed and focused her eyes on the floor, the conflict raging inside her evident. I didn't see why she wanted to be in the thick of the battle. It wasn't anything great, or glorious for that matter.

Maybe if I could connect with her in some way, I could figure her out. "Gen, can you explain your abilities… better to me? You've always… skirted around an explanation."

"Well, that's because I'm not sure how to describe it in a way others can understand."

"I talk to dead people. If anyone… will understand, it's me."

She giggled. "I supposed you're right. Well, the ability is rare and is a naturally-occurring skill. It allows me control over bodiless souls, like the way you have control over fire. Some books have touched on it, though they don't delve deep into it, but necromancy is believed to be similar to elemental control."

"Thank you… for being open… with me," I said. "That isn't… an ability that should be taken lightly. Be aware of that. But if that is something you can do… then maybe I can come up with something that will make you feel useful." I chuckled. "But as a shaman, I can't… be fully supportive of such… a skill and what I come up with will not utilize said skill. And trust me… we appreciate you dealing with the rest of the Council… like you do. They're not exactly… the easiest people to deal with. Now, do you mind helping me to my room? I think… it'd be best if I rest in there."

She nodded. "Sure."

I cringed as she helped me up. She continued to apologize to me, even though she wasn't the source of my pain. Moving was actually helping in some way. We were almost to my room when Genesis gasped and her presence left me. I turned as best as I could, only to see her tossed away from me like a ragdoll and her assailant coming at me.

He grabbed me by the throat and slammed me against the wall. My eyes widened when I realize our assailant was the man who burned down the club.

"You fucking bitch. You ruined everything!" he growled. I choked and struggled, but he had too tight of a hold on me. "The shamans foiled our first infiltration. But we used it to our advantage. While the military was busy following loose ends and false trails, we spent time weaseling our way into the military. We spent so much energy proving our fake loyalty so we could get the information we needed. So much time you just tore apart!"

"You shouldn't have… burned down… my club."

"Let her go!" Genesis screamed. She tried to attack him but he grabbed her and threw her against the adjacent wall. She hit it with a sickening thud and slid to the floor.

The man's grip tightened. "You're going to regret getting me thrown in jail. You're going to regret—"

"You're going to regret hurting her!"

The man was pulled away from me and thrown into the TV. I slid to the floor and weakly looked up to see Raikidan taking a protective stance in front of me. Someone knelt next to me and I lifted my gaze to see Corliss. My head hurt, and I was so confused. What were they doing here?

"C'mon." Corliss helped me up. "We need to get you and Genesis somewhere safe. We don't need Raikidan accidentally hurting either of you as well."

I nodded and shuffled my way into my room, Corliss guiding me. He left to retrieve Genesis. I gave her a once over when he placed her unconscious body on my bed. I was concerned Genesis may have been right in some way. She really had been useless. She hadn't been able to defend herself or make a decent attempt at saving me.

"She's going to be okay," Corliss said. I nodded, turning my focus on the shut bedroom door. He chuckled. "Raikidan is going to be fine too." I slid off the bed and grabbed a dagger. "Whoa, you're in no shape to help him."

I held out the weapon to him and coughed a few times. "Not for me. Give it to Raikidan."

Corliss nodded. "It might be too late now, but we'll see."

I sat back down on the bed when he left, and I waited. There was nothing else to do, except cough up my lungs some more, and I was getting tired of that. I checked Genesis to make sure she was still doing all right, and I waited some more. I couldn't hear what was going on out in the living room, which was weird. It was like nothing was happening out there.

I looked at the door when it finally opened. My brow twisted when Azriel strolled in, the two dragons behind him. "Before you ask, Seda told me something was up, so I came by to check on you. I haven't been here long."

I nodded and pointed to Genesis. He'd give me flack if I tried to talk. I watched Azriel checked Genesis over and nearly jumped out of my skin when someone gently touched my neck.

"Easy," Raikidan murmured. "I'm just checking."

I remained still so he wouldn't hurt me. My neck was tender from the attack, and if he or I made a wrong move, it was going to hurt more.

"Don't let him touch you. He's not safe."

"Genesis is going to be all right, so I'm going to go wait in the living room until the military gets here to clean up the mess we have in there," Azriel informed.

Why isn't he insisting on checking on me? That wasn't like him. Sure, Raikidan was just finishing his check, but he was no medic, or healer. He was acting weird again. *Both of them are.*

Raikidan brushed my bangs, getting my attention. "You should rest. You look to be in far less pain so you may be able to get some."

I took a moment to feel out the bond and found he was right. It had returned to its normal state. The incident had distracted me from the pain the bond had caused, keeping me from realizing when Rylan had finally been rescued.

I yawned loudly and then grabbed my neck when it throbbed with pain. I needed a lot of rest. I knew the soldiers would want to talk to me when they got here, and if Genesis was conscious by then, they'd want to talk with her as well. Laying down, I yawned once more before settling down for what I hoped would be a restful sleep. Raikidan rested his hand on my head briefly before leaving us to rest.

I exhaled and listened as the soldiers finally left. They had reamed me with questions on what happened to make sure my story was right, and now my head hurt. They had even drilled Genesis unnecessarily when she woke up. I didn't know what their problem was. It wasn't like we made a habit of getting attacked in our own house, or of killing people in our living room, but they sure acted like we did.

Luckily their reaming stopped when Ryoko chewed them out. Once she pointed out how it had been their fault in the first place that he'd escaped custody, all they wanted was to leave and escape their embarrassment.

I looked up when someone rapped on my half-opened door. "Hey, Ryo."

She smiled and came in. "How you feeling?"

I bobbed my head back and forth as I thought about her question. "All right, I guess."

"You sound less hoarse than before," she said as she sat down on my bed.

"It still hurts to talk, but it's a lot easier, now that I've had more rest—and Shva'sika gave me a healing session the moment the soldiers left the room."

"Well, that's a relief. I was worried that guy had screwed up your healing time."

I chuckled. "He didn't have much time to do a lot of damage. I'm more worried about Genesis, to be honest. He hit her pretty hard."

"Both Azriel and Danika say she's going to be fine, so don't sweat it too much."

There she went, calling Shva'sika Danika some more. I understood that was the human equivalent to Shva'sika's elven name, Elarinya, but a part of me wished Ryoko would attempt the elven or shaman name. Everyone else used her shaman name, and even my uncle had managed to get better at Shva'sika's elven name.

Ryoko placed a finger on her lips. "That reminds me, for some reason—did Raikidan tell you how he knew you were in danger?"

I blinked. "What are you talking about? I thought Seda told him and rushed back here."

Ryoko shook her head. "No. He stopped running with us, and before I knew it, he was saying your name to himself and running back the way we had come. Seda didn't even know you were in trouble until a little bit after, and that's when Corliss ran back to catch up with Raikidan."

My brow furrowed. "That's weird."

She nodded. "Corliss is avoiding my question, so I thought maybe you knew."

"No, but now I want to know. I'll figure it out."

She slid off my bed. "All right. If you do, let me know so I can let my poor brain rest."

"Okay." I leaned back and thought about what she said when the door shut. Something wasn't right here. How would he have known I was in trouble?

My door opened, taking me out of my thoughts, and Corliss poked his head in.

"You won't find Raikidan in here," I said.

"I know. I'm here to make sure you're doing okay," he replied.

"Oh, I'm a little better, thanks."

"I'm guessing Raikidan hasn't been in to check on you?"

I snorted. "It will be a while before he steps foot in here again. I've been given the a-okay, so he isn't obligated to be near me."

Corliss shook his head. "He's an idiot. Don't let him get to you."

I shrugged. "He can think and do as he pleases. I don't care anymore."

Corliss frowned. "Well, since you're okay, I'll leave you to rest."

"Before you go… do you know how Raikidan knew to come save me?"

He shook his head. "He won't talk to me about it."

"You have a guess, though."

He smirked. "You're too observant. Yes, I do have a guess, but until I have proof, I won't say, because if I'm right, it's a delicate situation for us dragons."

I lay down. "All right, thanks anyway. And thanks for being considerate enough to check on me."

"Sure."

He left and I closed my eyes to sleep. If Corliss didn't know for sure how Raikidan knew, and couldn't get it out of him, then there was no way in hell I'd find out. Even if we were on talking terms, I doubted he'd tell me. *Raikidan has his secrets, just as I have mine.*

8
CHAPTER

I stared up at the ceiling as I laid on the couch. There wasn't much to do, thanks to the military and my condition. They had made a public service announcement over the TV and radio stations of a mandatory house arrest until further notice. They hadn't given a reason for the detention, but we listened anyway, knowing the consequences if we didn't.

I sat up when we heard a knock at the door. *Who could that be?* With everyone under quarantine, no one should have been knocking at our door. Curious, Ryoko trotted down the steps to see who was here. "May I help you, Officer?"

I blinked. *What is the military doing here?*

"May we come in, ma'am?" the officer asked. "What we have to say needs to be relayed to all residents of this house."

"Um, all right." Ryoko came back upstairs with a small squad of soldiers behind her. I became concerned when I noticed two of them were psychics. Only one psychic had ever shown up in a team in the past. Something was up. "Everyone needs to be in here, I guess."

"I'll go get the boys," Shva'sika offered.

"Rai and Corey are down in the garage, last I knew," I told Ryoko.

She nodded and headed downstairs to find them. It was weird calling Corliss by his cover name. He had come up with it on his own last night when the soldiers had interrogated him about the incident, and I had to admit, it wasn't a bad one.

The soldiers fanned out and blocked the front door. My eyes narrowed. *It's like they expect someone to run. What is going on?*

Ryoko returned with the two dragons behind her and, soon after, Shva'sika came back with the rest of the boys. Once everyone was assembled, we waited for one of the soldiers to speak—but they remained quiet.

"Are you guys going to tell us what this is about, or can we go back to our daily lives?" Rylan demanded.

The general cleared his throat. "My apologies. I was just making a head count."

Rylan grunted. "I'm sure."

"I'm not going to lie to any of you. None of you are going to like what I have to say."

"Just come out with it, man!" Zane said. "Some of us aren't getting any younger."

"We're here to find out the intentions of the residents of this house."

Ryoko placed her hands on her hips. "Isn't that what your stupid inspections are for?"

"They're not here to search rooms." A few of us looked at Corliss as he spoke. He crossed his arms, his lip threatening to curl. "They brought these psychics here to probe us."

The sudden tension in the air tightened my chest as everyone focused their attention on the soldiers again. *This isn't good.*

Ryoko glared at the general. "Excuse me? He had better be wrong."

"I'm afraid not, ma'am."

"How dare you!" she screeched. "What right do you have?"

"Due to some… unfortunate circumstances this past year that we cannot disclose to you at this time, we are forced to take extreme measures to eliminate any threat that may still be lingering."

Rylan crossed his arms. "So why are we targets?"

The soldier held up his hands. "No one is being targeted. All citizens will undergo this check."

"Well, seeing as we have nothing to hide, we might as well get this done and over with," Zane said. "Who do you want first?"

"Right now, our orders are to check immigrants only," the general informed. "More correctly, immigrants who have arrived in the past two years."

"You just said you had to check everyone in the city." Ryoko pointed at him. "Singling out groups of people isn't everyone!"

"Stay calm. We will be checking everyone," the general defended. "We are just required to check out immigrants first and then check long-term civilians after." He turned and focused on me. "We'll start with you."

Raikidan snarled. "Like hell you will."

The general narrowed his eyes at him. "Excuse me?"

"He's right," Rylan agreed. "Eira is in no condition to have a psychic enter her mind. Or did you forget about the fire at the club?"

"Or the fact that she was attacked recently by the guy who set the fire after he escaped your custody?" Ryoko said.

"Or that it has been noted on her records she is still recovering from amnesia?" Blaze also added.

"Sir," a soldier whispered to the general. "With that bit of information, I have to side with them on this. Those afflicted with amnesia are hard cases, and this information search could severely harm her."

"Order are orders," the general stated.

"As a medical professional, I can't allow you to do this."

"Our orders are to check everyone, regardless of health. You know that."

Raikidan growled, but I stopped him by speaking. "It's all right, I'll do it." My housemates watched me as I struggled to pull myself onto the back of the couch. "I don't think it's going to do any harm."

My body lifted into the air, and I looked at the psychic closest to me. *"I thought you could use a hand."*

I blinked and pretended to be new at thought speaking. *"Um, thank you."*

He walked closer to me and lightly touched my face with his hands. *"I promise this will not hurt."*

I only blinked in response as I made a silent prayer he wouldn't see anything he wasn't supposed to. The psychic moved his fingers so they were on specific parts of my face, and it confused me. Seda never needed to have her hands in any specific position when mind reading, not that she needed to use her hands at all.

My gaze wandered, and I noticed the other psychic doing the same to Raikidan—and I began to worry. Raikidan wasn't made. He didn't have a safe block we experiments had. If that psychic saw anything he wasn't supposed to, we were done for.

"You need to relax," the psychic messaged. *"You are far too tense."*

I took a deep breath and relaxed, closing my eyes to help. I couldn't worry about that. I had to have faith that Seda may be able to throw a twist into this situation without getting caught.

Uncomfortable pressure filled my head as the psychic entered my mind. He worked his way to my memories, and I waited with bated breath. A new pressure pulsed in my head, and then a searing white light invaded my vision. No amount of preparation could have prepared me for what I saw next.

Bright images flashed through my mind. They weren't in full color, but the color that did show up was bright. People came and went, but a young boy with two-toned hair and girl with unruly, long hair stayed throughout. They played and laughed as the memories changed sporadically. The girl didn't laugh all the time, though. Those memories—her eyes—gave away sadness.

A man, who I could only assume was her father, left daily for long hours and would force her to stay home. A woman, who I assumed was the girl's mother, would try to engage the girl in activities such as sewing and cooking, but the girl wanted nothing to do with those activities. Instead, she stared out a window and watched the two-toned-haired boy and another boy playing outside or leaving the village with their fathers. The second boy appeared similar enough to her that I figured he was her older brother.

The girl didn't have any friends. She spent her days alone, or with her brother or younger sister inside. She rarely went outside, and when she did, she wasn't allowed to venture far from the house alone. It made me wonder what was wrong with her.

It wasn't until she grew up a little that I knew who she was and why she was alone. The girl was me, the two-toned-haired boy was Raikidan. Village customs dictated I stay inside and learn how to be a good wife, ignoring any dreams I had. I didn't like the customs. I disliked them enough that I taught myself how to use a bow and how to rely only on myself when the time came. I'd sneak out in the dead of night to teach myself so no one would know. But as the memories passed, there was someone who did know.

Raikidan. He was around all the time because of my fake brother. They were friends, and he'd watch me, knowing full well I was unhappy. The memories flashed and became almost unreadable, as if they weren't meshed together like a normal memory should be. The bits showed Raikidan confronting me and the two of us arguing. It showed my father finding out what I was doing, and the two of us fighting. It showed me running away, of Raikidan finding me, and then of him convincing me to come back home.

Then the memories changed suddenly. We were older, much older. There was a giant gap between these new memories and the past ones. Raikidan was a skilled hunter, as was my brother. But they weren't the only ones—I was, too, and I didn't have to hide it anymore. Something had changed as the memories skipped, but my memories weren't going to dwell on it. Instead, it focused on Raikidan and me. We were closer now. We did just about everything together. Raikidan even hung around me more than he did with my own brother, but in any of these memory clips, my brother didn't seem to mind.

Some memories showed me watching other young women in the village from a window as they worried about how they looked, and how I reacted when I gazed at myself in a mirror. Doubt. Lack of self-confidence. But that disappeared when Raikidan was around. I acted like it didn't matter because it didn't matter to him, either. Some of the women I watched from time to time would fawn for his attention, but he paid them little mind. He just followed me around, much to the other women's distaste.

Then the memories changed dramatically again, and this time they weren't so peaceful. This memory came in quick blips, and was quite disturbing. Flames—running—fiery wooden beams falling—the memory wasn't clear, but I knew this was the fire I had made up. The fire that caused my supposed memory failure. Then, just as suddenly as the bits of memory had come, they disappeared, and a new one of me waking up in a bed replaced them. Bandages covered me from head to toe, and Raikidan sat on a chair close to me. I was smiling at him and I saw relief flash through his eyes as he smiled back.

The memories changed again, at a quick pace. They showed me

trying to recover, and Raikidan's decision to move us elsewhere. They showed us entering the city and meeting up with Zane. The memory went to change, but I didn't get to see the memory play out. The memories slipped away and my eyes fluttered open. The psychic had retracted his touch.

I didn't pay attention to his reaction. I found myself too preoccupied with the turmoil raging inside me. "Please... excuse me."

I walked around the soldiers and stared at the floor. I barely heard my door click behind me before I lay on my bed and pulled my legs up to my chest. My failsafe had never needed to be used in my life, but never had I imagined something so... nice. To a normal person, some of those memories may have been harsh, but to me...

My door creaked open. "Eira?"

"Go away," I mumbled. "I want to be alone."

Raikidan sat down on the bed. "Eira, talk to me."

I slapped his hand away when he tried to touch my shoulder. "I said go away! I don't want to deal with you and your bullshit right now."

He sighed and grabbed me by the shoulders, pulling me into him. "Come here."

"Don't let him do this. He can't be trusted."

I struggled against his grip as he laid back and held me against his muscular chest, but then stopped when he stroked my hair. The action soothed me, although the pain remained, as well as the desire for those fake memories to be real.

"Thank you," I murmured when the pain finally started to ebb.

He hushed me. "Don't talk unless you're feeling better."

"I am feeling better."

"Enough to talk about it?" I shook my head and his chest rumbled. "All right, then are you up to explaining how I saw what I did when that psychic probed me?"

"It depends. What did you see?"

"You, me, your fake family, and my real one, but as humans."

I chuckled. "You need to be a little more specific than that."

"I don't know how else to say it. My life wasn't the one I know. You were in it the whole time. My family stayed in it for most of the time—except it played out in bits and pieces."

"My guess is, Seda was able to sneak my memories into yours without the psychic noticing."

"How is it you can control those kinds of memories while a psychic is present?"

"I can't."

"I don't understand."

I worked my jaw. "All experiments are designed with something we call a failsafe memory bank. It's used for is situations like this. Many of us don't have to use it, but if we're captured during an assignment, or some other situation arises where it's needed, it helps to present us as innocent."

"But these memories had the two of us in it. They had that fire you made up. How would it create those before we met?"

"If the failsafe is never used, events during the experiment's life will alter its potential output until used. So my lies triggered my failsafe change, and now that a psychic has viewed it, it will remain like that."

"That's incredible."

"For some, it would be…"

"You want them to have been true, don't you?" I tensed, the pain creeping into my chest again. Raikidan's grip tightened. "I'm sorry. I shouldn't have asked that."

I didn't respond. I couldn't. I was too busy fighting the pain and desire for it all to be true.

9
CHAPTER

A chess piece wobbled as I tapped the board in thought. I wasn't any good at chess, and Argus made this game just about impossible to win. I'd make a move, and he'd counter it every time flawlessly, as if he had figured out every possible move before I could even think about what piece I wanted to move. But that's what he was best for. He was a thinker, not a fighter.

I looked up when a door swung open and someone's footsteps thumped down the hall. Seda stormed around the corner and sat down on the couch next to Argus. She rested her cheek on her fist and moved one of my chess pieces. "Your move, Argus."

I regarded her state for a moment. "You okay, Seda?"

"I need a distraction," she muttered. "I'm playing for you."

Argus leaned back. "What's eating you?"

"Blaze. Now can we play this game?"

My eyes narrowed. "He's at it again?"

She hid her face in her hands with a sigh and nodded. "He's always purposely thinking about something to get to me, but today is the worst. Usually I can convince him to stop, but he's getting extra enjoyment out of it this time." Her hands slid into her hair and clenched. "I just want it to stop! For a single moment I don't want to have to"—she turned her focus to Argus when he jumped to his feet and stormed off—"Argus?"

My brow creased. I had watched his features go from concern to anger within seconds, and then he stormed off without a word.

Shva'sika knelt in front of Seda. "Don't worry about him right now. Let's see if we can block out any of those thoughts with some spirit energy."

"I don't think that'll work, because I'm psychic," Seda voiced.

Shva'sika rested her fingers on Seda's forehead. "It's worth a shot. Now relax."

Seda let out a slow breath and her shoulders sagged as she relaxed. Shva'sika's eye began to glow, but after several moments, Seda sighed and removed Shva'sika's fingers. "It's not working, they're sti—"

Her sudden silence interested me. "What is it, Seda?"

"His thoughts suddenly changed to confusing, fearful ones. They're not even complete thoughts."

"But you can block them out now if you wanted?"

"Well, yes, it would be easy now."

"Then don't complain."

She chuckled. "I suppose I shouldn't, but I'm curious."

"Well, you might get an answer," Ryoko murmured, peering down the hall. "You all right, Zane?"

Zane grunted as he stepped into the living room. "Can someone explain to me why I had to prevent Argus from beating the living daylights out of Blaze just now? I've never seen him like that in all my years of knowing the kid."

Ryoko and I exchanged a glance. That was very uncharacteristic of Argus.

"I'm not sure, Zane," Ryoko lied. "He seemed okay when he left the room. But that reminds me, Laz I need to talk to you in my room."

Zane's face scrunched in confusion. "How does that remind you of that?"

I chuckled and headed for Ryoko's room. "You know not to question those things, Uncle."

He nodded. "True."

Ryoko latched onto my arm and yanked me into her room. I cringed when the door slammed behind me. "You need to calm down."

"I can't," she admitted. "Now I know for sure there's something between those two."

"Between who?"

Ryoko placed her hands on her hips. "Don't give me that. You know who."

I shook my head. "Ryoko, stay out of it. It isn't your business to get involved."

She gave me a long, hard look. "Oh? Coming from you, who got involved when it came to me and Rylan?"

"Two words. Sixty-five years."

She crossed her arms and grunted. "Fine, I'll let that one slide, but I think we should do—"

A small rap on her door came, cutting her off, and Seda slipped in. "Can I talk to you two?"

"Uh, sure," I replied.

Ryoko waved her over. "Yeah, come sit down."

She complied and we all sat on Ryoko's bed. She was quiet for a few moments before she ran her fingers through her hair. "I don't know what to do."

"You like him, don't you?" Ryoko guessed. Seda nodded. "But you don't know how he feels?"

It was a strange question since Seda was psychic, but there were many things we didn't know about her or them.

Seda chewed her lip. "There is one thing psychics can't see. If anything has to do with us, it's unreachable. We can't see our futures, or thoughts and feelings anyone has about us directly."

"So you can never see someone else's thoughts about you, ever?" Ryoko questioned.

"Well…" Seda wrung her hands together. "Once you share your life with someone for a long period of time, that changes. The two minds are always connected. Otherwise, any thoughts about us are generally hidden from us. As a Psychic with some unusual gifts, I have caught quick glimpses of what others have thought about me by accident, like Blaze"—she giggled—"He once thought I had one eye, and Zane once thought I had three, but I never saw anything major."

"So what you're trying to say is, you're scared," I said.

She nodded. "We psychics deal with a lot of prejudice, and due to our… unique physical traits, we are often met with fear, hatred, and rejection. I watched this happen to my brother and a few others. It's why my brother acts the way he does now. He was a pain before, but the situation made him worse."

She sighed. "I've only been with one man in my life. It pained me when he died. I had never experienced such a deep connection with another person before. Until Argus. Getting to know him as a friend, I found myself connecting with him on a level I never thought possible. But…"

She wrung her hands together. "I'm afraid. Argus' mind is closed to me, unlike my past lover. Lately, he's done some things that are out of the ordinary in regards to me, which could point to where he stands. But I don't know how he'll react to the truth. I don't want to go through what my brother did."

"But that's what being human is all about," Ryoko said. "We take chances, knowing there is a positive or negative consequence attached."

I placed my hand over Seda's. "Just take the chance. You might not know what'll happen, but if you don't take it, you'll have those type of regrets, and always wonder about the 'what ifs.'"

Seda smiled. "True. Worst thing that could happen is that I'm wrong, right?"

I chuckled. "Not the most positive way to see it, but yes."

"But that also means if you are wrong, you can stop wasting your time on him and look elsewhere," Ryoko added.

Seda continued to smile. "Thanks, you two. Can I ask you both to be there while I do this? Well… not physically, because that'd be weird, but…"

I chuckled. "We get it."

"And to answer your questions, yes, we'll be there for you," Ryoko said.

"Thank you." She puffed out a quick breath and slipped off the bed. "I'd better get this over with."

Ryoko smiled and stood next. "Stay positive."

Seda nodded and then headed out. We didn't follow her immediately, so that no one would ask too many questions.

Ryoko nudged me when we reached the door. "Take a chance, eh? Maybe you should take your own advice."

I rolled my eyes and pushed her. She only laughed in response.

"Everything okay, ladies?" Zane asked as we sat down on the couch.

"Yep, everything is fine," I replied. *I hope.*

I hoped Ryoko and I weren't wrong. Seda was right, Argus did go out of his way for her lately, but that didn't guarantee he'd be able to handle a psychic. I relaxed on the couch and closed my eyes as Seda tried to show me something.

I saw the hallway in a fixed view, as if I were following her. She bit her lower lip and wrung her hands together. I couldn't blame her for being nervous, but I knew she'd be more so had she been doing this alone.

Her pace didn't slow as she passed Zane's room and then Blaze's. She didn't stop to second guess herself as she passed the laundry room. She headed straight for Argus' room with determination in her step, as if she knew, without a doubt, that's where she'd find him.

Much to my surprise, she didn't knock on the partially shut door. She walked in and honed in on Argus, who stood by his clothes basket with his shirt in his hands.

"Blaze, I don't want—" Argus turned around and blinked in surprise. "S–Seda. I–I'm sorry. I thought you were Blaze. That's not to say that, uh—"

Seda giggled. "It's okay, Argus. I know what you mean."

He gave an inscrutable smile. "Uh, well, what can I help you with? Do you guys need me or something?"

"No, I'm here for a more… personal reason." I could feel her nervousness growing.

Argus' brow creased. "Um, okay. What's u—"

Seda reached up and unbuckled the back of her mask. I watched as Argus dropped his shirt and stared at Seda with wide eyes as she pulled the mask away from her face. My heart sank. *Not the right way to react, Argus.*

Seda didn't give him much time to even try to adjust his reaction. "I'm… I'm sorry for bothering you. I'll leave you alone now. Please excuse me."

The sadness in her voice hurt. Her worst fear had come to fruition, and Ryoko and I had encouraged it all. We shouldn't hav—

Argus composed himself and grabbed Seda by the wrist. "Don't leave."

Seda stopped, but didn't look at him, so Argus grabbed her lightly by the hip and turned her around. The hand he had used to grab her wrist let go and reached up to touch her face, his eyes soft, conveying a completely different emotion from his first reaction.

"I'm sorry. When you said personal, I didn't think you meant this personal. I never thoug—"

Seda tried to push him away. "Argus, you don't need to make up excuses. I—"

When Argus' lips touched hers, all arguments became invalid. Seda's grip on her mask loosened, and it crashed to the ground, my vision following it. As if telling us we were not welcome, the door closed in front of me, and my vision darkened with it.

I kept my eyes closed for a few moments, and then slowly opened them. Ryoko grinned ear to ear, and I couldn't help but smirk as well.

"What are you two smiling about?" Zane questioned.

I relaxed in my seat. "Nothing."

"And I was born yesterday. You two look like you committed a murder."

Shva'sika gasped. "You didn't have Seda do something to Blaze, did you?"

I laughed. "No, Blaze has nothing to do with this, though that's a great idea."

"Then spill the beans already," Raid begged.

I picked up a chess piece belonging to Argus with my toes and moved it. "You'll find out soon enough. Now, who wants to help me finish this game?"

"Fascinating," Corliss mused. "I've never seen a human pick something up with their toes."

"That 'cause Laz has monkey feet," Ryoko teased.

I glared at her. "I do not."

"Do too."

"Do not."

"Yeah you do," she continued to insist. I grunted and tried to grab her face with my feet and she squealed. "Laz, stop it! That's gross."

I chuckled and then sat up when Shva'sika sat down on the opposite side of the coffee table to join my game. Her brow creased when she scrutinized the chess pieces at her disposal. "Laz, dear, you suck at this game."

I chuckled. "Yeah, I know."

"Then why do something you're not any good at?" Corliss questioned.

"Because it makes life interesting," I said as I countered Shva'sika's move.

"It's a human thing," Ryoko said. "It's just something we do."

Corliss chuckled. "All right, I won't question it, then."

I hesitated on making my next move when I heard a quiet thump. It sounded like something hitting a wall, but I couldn't be sure, so I ignored it.

I looked up from my game when someone came down the hall. Blaze entered the room, holding his face and muttering to himself. His muttering was mostly incoherent, but there were enough intelligible words to get an idea of what happened.

Ryoko held a hand over her mouth and kept quiet until he shut the basement door. "Did he just say something about walking in on them?"

I sputtered on a laugh. "Serves him right."

"That would explain the sound of something breaking," Raikidan said.

Shva'sika's eyes shifted between Ryoko and me. "Is that what you two were hiding?"

I nodded. "Told you you'd all find it out soon."

"What?" Raid blinked. "What am I missing? Who was Blaze muttering about? What do you guy know that I don't?"

Ryoko sighed. "Argus and Seda."

He turned his head, still not getting it.

She let out an exasperated sigh. "You're so clueless." She then put her two index fingers together. "The two are together now."

"Since when?"

"Since"—I picked up a communicator lying on the coffee table and checked the time—"ten minutes ago."

Raid held his head. "Forget I asked. I'm better off being clueless."

Ryoko and I laughed at him. When my laughter quieted down, I went back to finishing my game against Shva'sika that I was now losing—again.

10
CHAPTER

The colored thermal outline of soldiers moved about the dark blue space of my heat sense ability. Ryoko sat next to me with a set of night-vision goggles, and Rylan sat on a far-off building with his sniper scope. Raikidan and Corliss flew about the compound below in the forms of owls, and Raid ran around in his dog form, both parties getting a closer look without raising any alarms.

My painful game of chess had been interrupted by this assignment, not that I was complaining. Recon assignments cycled through the teams, and were an important step to plan out other assignments for the reconned location. This facility, Radar Technics, was a military-run research facility specializing in state-of-the-art robotics. Or so they told the public.

This sprawling three-block compound had some of the tightest security around. Because of this, many would question what they were really hiding inside. But for curious minds who wanted to find out, they had to get past the outside security of fencing, cameras, and soldiers, let alone whatever security they had inside.

I closed my eyes to deactivate my ability, and opened them again. "Okay, I'm going to move in closer."

"Be careful," Ryoko said.

I nodded and slipped down a rope we had secured to the building. Once safe on the ground, Ryoko pulled the rope back up to hide her position. Keeping low in the shadows, I snuck along the walls, stopping and hiding when any movement caught my eye. When I made it to the fencing, I followed it, looking for weak points and reinforced areas. With each change, I wrote down the details on a digital display resembling a clipboard, careful to keep the light it emitted hidden. *Thank you, Team Six and Argus.*

They had created a few of these prototypes for these recon assignments. I found the light to be a hassle, but the real map to make marks on, and the ability to send it to Aurora to compile all our separate notes, outweighed that one drawback.

A camera attached to a nearby building swiveled my way, and I pulled back, hoping it didn't spot me. I waited, listening for any signs I had triggered a defensive response. Minutes passed and nothing from the compound changed, but a scuffling sound from behind me caught my attention.

"Be careful."

Tucking the digital display away, I readied a weapon and moved closer to the sound. I couldn't take any chances.

I pressed myself against the wall when I reached the corner of the building and listened. *Scuffling is… footsteps. Male. Average size feet. Semi-muscular build; a bit top-heavy—could stand to not skip a few legs days. Approaching my direction.* I readied myself, and when the footsteps were upon me, I sprung.

The man wasn't armed, making it easy to disable and pin him to a wall, only to find out my mistake. My brow rose at the sight of the partially shaven, blue-haired, and punky clothed man I had apprehended. "Doppelganger?"

"Uh, yep, last I checked," he muffled out, his face well squished into the brick.

I let him go and continued to keep my voice low. "What are you doing here?"

He wound his arms around to loosen his shoulders. "I heard there was a party nearby and thought I'd check it out. Got jumped by a chick instead." I crossed my arms and my brow rose again. He sighed. "I came to give you a hand, okay?"

"Don't trust it. Too suspicious."

"Why?" I asked. "Unless it's Council's orders."

"No"—he rubbed the back of his neck—"I came on my own. Thought my abilities would be helpful for this."

"Well, I'm not going to say no to help. This place is pretty big. And you're right about your abilities. But I'm not sure why you want to help."

He wouldn't look at me. "I have my reasons, okay?"

I shrugged, knowing pressing wouldn't help. "All right." I pulled out my digital clipboard and marked off where I found the security camera, as well as notes on its movement ability. "I have this marked-up map, if you'd like to take a look. It's only my not—"

An owl swooped down and quickly changed shape. I nodded to Raikidan as he approached, but Doppelganger's posture changed to indicate his agitation. *What is up with him?*

"Here to check in?" I asked Raikidan.

He nodded. "Corliss is checking in with Ryoko. Keep the suspicion level down."

I handed him the digital recording device. "Good call."

He went about making marks. My curiosity got the better of me, and I peered over his shoulder, only to be impressed by the information he could give. And I didn't doubt that Corliss' were as good. At this rate, we wouldn't need to be here for much longer. I did notice something important missing, though. "No weak points for entry seen?"

He shook his head. "Not yet. But we're looking."

I nodded. Raikidan finished up and then took notice of Doppelganger, but didn't say anything. He shifted into an owl again and took off.

Doppelganger chuckled. "What, no kiss goodbye? Or is it because I'm here?" My narrowed my eyes and he shrugged. "Rumors."

I crossed my arms. "Yeah, well, believing rumors gets you into trouble. Raikidan and I, not a thing." *Still don't even understand why he bothered coming back...*

He shrugged. "Shame, seems like your type."

"If he were more trustworthy... the punk wouldn't be entirely wrong..."

I rolled my eyes, at both him and the voice, and held out the digital display. "Take a look, so you know what you're up against."

Doppelganger accepted the device and mulled over the map and notes. He then handed it back to me. "Three copies of myself should be good for this."

I nodded. "I'll let the others kn—"

"Actually," he said. "I'd like it if they didn't know I was here."

I cocked my head. "Why?"

He gaze flicked elsewhere. "Because I don't want them to. I have to deal with Raikidan knowing since there's no changing that, but the others, I don't want to know."

"They're scoping the place out," I said. "They're going to notice you."

"That's fine. Just don't tell them until that happens."

I sighed and shook my head. "Fine, we'll do it your way."

I didn't understand what his problem was, but we were wasting time arguing about it. Doppelganger smiled his thanks and then went about making copies of himself; the sight of another version of him slowly pulling away was rather disturbing to see. I chose to go scout ahead and be productive, instead of standing around watching.

"I guess he'll be helpful to us. Just watch your back."

Several more cameras came into my view, a few outside the fence line. *This is going to be one hell of a tricky outpost.* I hoped the secrets inside would be worth all the hassle we had to go through. It would be just like Zarda to put in the extra effort to throw us off.

Doppelganger came up to me, one of his copies with him. "I sent the other two in different directions to cover more ground. This one will go ahead of us to scout a side I noticed we hadn't touched yet."

On command, the copy of him moved on and disappeared behind a building.

"Smart move," I said. "The quicker we finish here, the better."

The two of us proceeded with caution, taking notes where needed. Occasionally, Doppelganger stopped walking and closed his eyes. When he reopened them, he took my display board and wrote notes.

After the third time he did this, I decided to ask. "Are you checking in on your copies?"

He nodded. "My copies are far more than illusions. For all intents and purposes, they're non-permanent clones. This means they each have their own memory. To access this memory in full, I have to physically re-absorb them. If they disappear or die prior to absorption, the memories I can recover will be patchy. But this connection also allows me to tap into portions of their memory remotely from time to time."

"That's handy."

"Yeah, but they're a liability, too," he said.

I tilted my head. "How so?"

"Let's hope you don't have to find out." He moved on down the alley we were in.

I found this behavior peculiar. Well, his being here on his own terms was peculiar, too, but I suspected I knew what his reasonings were. I continued on after him. *Maybe they're connected.* It made sense—a lot of sense, when I thought about it. He wasn't comfortable enough around me to tell me everything about himself, but he was trying to be a decent person. I respected that.

I continued on, keeping an eye out—especially behind us. You never knew when a patrol would come by and surprise you with a bullet in your back. And it was lucky I did. When two pairs of footsteps echoed through the alley behind us, I grabbed Doppelganger by the back of the jacket and yanked him behind a dumpster.

We held our breath as two armed men passed us and disappeared into the night. I took a deep breath and activated my heat sense, watching the thermal images of the two soldiers as they continued on their path.

"We're good," I whispered when they turned a corner.

"How can you tell?" Doppelganger asked. I turned to look at him and he jumped. "Whoa, what's up with your eyes?"

The thermal sense didn't only change what I saw. It changed how my eyes appeared, and others noticed. The gold ring round my pupils spread, and my pupils became oblong. A slight orange glow could be seen sometimes, although not everyone noticed it.

I grinned at him. "It's an ability I have. I'll be keeping it up for a bit longer, so there's your warning. This helps me see heat signatures. Problem is, it sometimes doesn't work around small electronics, so I'll be relying on you to warn me about cameras and such."

He nodded. "Good to know. Do you struggle to see people at any point?"

I rocked my head side to side. "A standard person, no. They give off heat signatures all day long. Armor, though, is another story. There's armor out there that masks a person with a faux ambient temperature. That's the dark temperature signature on a scan. It means there's little to no heat coming from that area. Assassins use this technology in their armor, as well as high-ranking military personnel. But the average soldier doesn't get that luxury."

"Interesting…"

"Why?"

He shook his head and motioned for me to follow. "Chameleon said once he can't be picked up by thermal scans. Wasn't sure if he was pulling my leg or not."

I kept close to him. "He's telling the truth on that one. He's the only one I can't pick up."

He looked surprised, but nodded and focused on the job at hand, though I found myself thinking about the topic some more. Since he'd been the only one I'd come across like that, I had almost forgotten those types of scans couldn't pick up Chameleon. But with how many decades had passed since his creation, and the rate technology had advanced inside that fortress, could more soldiers have been created like him? Scary thought for sure. That would eliminate the need for the special armor, and make these soldiers even more lethal.

I stopped walking when new sounds caught my ears. My head swiveled back and forth, but nothing caught my attention. The scent of a new person passed my nose, but still, I saw nothing. *Something's not right…*

"Hide!" the voice in my head hissed.

Before I could react, Doppelganger grabbed my arm and dragged me into an alcove. I knew better than to protest, and thanked the gods I didn't when someone ran past our location. I barely caught the movement in all the ambient color, but I knew I'd seen something.

Doppelganger crept away and returned. "He's gone. What happened?"

I chewed on my lip, thinking about what happened. "What did the guy look like?"

"Standard soldier to me. Usual armor and all."

I nodded. "I don't think Chameleon is the only one who can't be picked up anymore."

Doppelganger glanced back again, then focused on me. "Seriously?"

I closed my eyes and shut down my ability. "I didn't see him at all. Even when he ran past us. Had I not been focusing on that location as hard as I was, I wouldn't have caught his slight movement."

Doppelganger watched as I wrote down notes about this phenomenon. "So, will you continue to use the ability?"

Before I could respond, he cried out in pain and stumbled, slamming into the wall. I reacted immediately and checked him, but there wasn't any sign of a wound. Then, an alarm blared, and the entire compound came to life.

"They spotted and shot one of my copies," Doppelganger said through clenched teeth.

"You idiot," I hissed as I grabbed him and slung his arm over my shoulder. "You should have told me you experience your copies' pain."

He chuckled. "Yeah, well, like you said, I'm an idiot."

"Laz, what happened?" Rylan called in through my communicator.

"We had some extra help that came in but were caught," I said.

"Are they okay?" he asked.

"He will be," I said. "Get out of the vicinity."

I did my best to get us out of there as quick as possible. Doppelganger clutched his chest and struggled to keep up my set pace, but I didn't let him lag behind.

"Leave me behind," he said. "I'll manage."

"Like I said, you're an idiot," I said.

We slipped into a side alley, and not a moment too soon, as several pairs of feet rushed down the street we had just come from. Doppelganger clenched his teeth and clutched his chest tighter, trying to stop himself from crying out in intense pain.

"Another one gone?" I whispered.

He nodded. "L—last one is off their radar..."

I pushed on. I needed to get him out of here. Even with the last copy safe, he wasn't. His body could only take so much. I gasped when two men ran around a corner, but relaxed when I realized it was Corliss and Raikidan.

Corliss pointed to our right, down another alley. "Go that way."

I nodded and we changed directions, Corliss giving me a hand with Doppelganger. Raikidan took point and zig-zagged us through alleys and streets, sometimes forcing us to backtrack due to soldier activity. When we came to a dead end, I helped lean Doppelganger against a wall and caught my breath. Corliss and Raikidan took positions near the entrance to keep an eye out. We hadn't made it out of the hotspot yet, but I needed a breather, as did Doppelganger. *He needs a medic, really.*

Our rush to get out of there wasn't helping him recover, not that he'd have an easy recovery from an invisible bullet wound in the chest. I was honestly surprised he hadn't died.

I gasped and drew a weapon when something large moved behind me by the wall. A man with bismuth hair and kaleidoscopic eyes still half sticking into a wall held up his hands. "Easy, it's just me. Not your favorite person, but not a threat either."

I lowered my guard, my brow raised. "Chameleon, what are you doing here?"

He pointed to Doppelganger. "To get him. I saw what happened to his copy. You were efficient enough in your extraction where it was hard to intercept to take him."

"How did you see that happen?" I asked.

He held out a digital display board. "I was doing work of my own."

I took the tech and scanned at all the notes he had marked about the inner workings of the compound. "You were inside there the whole time?"

"I was the only one of us who could, without being seen." He held out his arm. "Now hand him to me. I can get him somewhere safe."

I helped Doppelganger over and then gave the device back to Chameleon. "Don't forget this."

"Why aren't you taking it?" he asked.

"One, because Doppelganger needs to input his notes from his copies, when he's done being half-dead," I said, inciting a chuckle from Doppelganger. "And two, you did the work, you get credit for it. Send the information to Aurora to compile for the Council." Chameleon stared at me, dumbfounded, and I snapped my fingers in his face. "Chop, chop. Now's not the time to dawdle."

"Uh, right." He put the device away, and before my eyes, his and Doppelganger's bodies fused into the wall.

But before they fully disappeared, Doppelganger reached into his jacket pocket and tossed me a key. "Safe house key. One Nineteen Callus way."

I nodded. "Oh, and for you, stop skipping leg day."

Chameleon chuckled, as if he had also said the same thing to his friend, and Doppelganger rolled his eyes. "I don't skip leg day!"

The two were then swallowed by bricks before any more conversation could be had. I turned to deal with the last issue at hand. With Doppelganger no longer slowing us down, we could get out, no problem. *At least, I think…*

I pulled a cloaking watch out of a pouch attached to my hip and made myself appear like a jogger. I used my armor cloth to make leashes for the two dragons. I whistled to them and they abandoned their posts, noticing the leashes in my hand. "Time to take a new shape, boys."

They looked at each other, shrugged, and then shifted into dog forms; Raikidan his typical Alsatian, and Corliss a golden retriever. Both had their armor create collars, making it easy for me to clip the leashes on them and get moving.

We made it three more blocks before soldiers spotted us and approached. They weren't hostile, but they made it known they weren't in a friendly mood. Raikidan went on alert, but wasn't aggressive, and Corliss decided to act dopey and friendly, as most retrievers would.

"Ma'am," a general in black armor greeted.

"Good evening, officer," I said, my words breathy from the jogging. "How can I help you?"

"We had some suspicious activity by the military post down the street," he said. "Can I ask you some questions?"

I nodded. "Of course."

"What are you doing out here?"

I smiled. "Getting some exercise. Ate way too much earlier and needed to burn some calories. My dogs were quite pleased I wasn't being a couch potato for once."

He chuckled. "Cute response. Why are you still out while the warning sirens are blaring?"

"There's only so fast I can run before it's suspicious," I said. "I learned that when I was a little girl. Some soldiers scared the daylights out of me with their questioning when warning sirens panicked me into a sprint home."

The general eyed me. "Have you seen any suspicious people?"

I shook my head. "You're the first signs of life I've seen for about an hour."

He nodded. "Very well. You wouldn't mind an escort home, would you?"

"Of course not," I said, sending a silent prayer of thanks for the key Doppelganger gave me. "I live on Callus way, so whoever goes with me won't have to go far."

He nodded and then ordered a soldier to accompany me. The soldier approached and pet both disguised dragons. They each reacted happily to the attention. I thanked the soldiers, wished them luck in their search, and then started jogging off again. The soldier followed me, not striking up conversation, and we made it to the safe house within fifteen or so minutes.

Several lights were on in the house, and a part of me became concerned the key I had been given was a poorly-chosen prank, but didn't allow my concern to show. I thanked the soldiers after I jogged onto the front porch and went to unlock the door, only for it to unlock itself and swing open. The smiling face of an athletically-built man with short black hair, lavender eyes, and olive skin met my gaze. *Ezhno?*

"Dear, I'm so glad you're home!" Ezhno said, opening his arms wide to me. "I thought I was going to have to come looking for you."

I smiled and gave him a hug, playing the part. "Sorry I worried you. Got caught up because some hooligans are causing the military problems again."

"Well, I'm glad you're okay." He gave Raikidan and Corliss an affectionate pat when they begged for his attention, and then he focused on the soldier who had followed me. "And thank you for making sure she got home safely."

The soldier nodded. "I would suggest you both stay home for the rest of the night, until this situation is resolved."

Ezhno grinned at the man. "You don't have to worry. We'll be sure to stay home where it's safe."

The soldier nodded again and left, leaving Ezhno to escort me inside. I breathed a heavy sigh of relief when he shut the door and slid the bolt. The boys shifted to their nu-human shapes, though their collars remained, and I couldn't help but laugh at them. They immediately removed the leashes so the armor cloth collars would go away.

I smiled at Ezhno. "Thank you for the assist."

He shrugged. "I'm used to people randomly showing up at my house."

My brow rose. "You live here?"

He nodded. "Yeah. Aurora is the only one who lives in the Underground. I prefer to live alone, as it gives me the peace and quiet I need sometimes to get work done."

"I can respect that. Though I'm still sorry for coming over uninvited." I handed him the key I carried. "I was told it was a safe house."

His brow rose. "This is Doppelganger's key. How'd you get it?"

"He gave it to me."

"That's strange."

I chuckled. "I've had a strange night."

"Fair." He pointed to a door on the hall to our right. "That's the door to the basement. Passage to the Underground is in the far left corner."

I nodded. "Thanks. Boys, let's get out of here."

The two dragons agreed, and we thanked Ezhno again before heading home through the smelly sewers.

CHAPTER 11

A sigh escaped my lips, and I stood and held my paint gun at my side. The mural the client requested was time consuming, but also rewarding. There wasn't any part of this I didn't like so far, even if skulls and skeletons engulfed in fire weren't my thing.

Raikidan came over to stand next to me and look at my unfinished piece. The two of us hadn't made up yet, but today he had been a lot friendlier than in the past few days. I decided I'd be willing to talk to him, but there was no way things would go back to the way they used to be if we didn't have a serious talk about the argument that could have been avoided had he been willing to listen.

"How did you learn how to do this?" he asked.

I shrugged and removed paint respirator. "When I was in the military, my mother and I would visit Zane and the boys. He taught me how to use the spray guns, and I figured it out from there."

"So you just up and taught yourself?"

"Basically, yeah. Everyone has skills others may or may not have. They just have to learn to use them. My skills happen to revolve around artistic mediums."

"But your self-esteem is too low to accept that you're good in, as you call it, the arts."

"My self-esteem isn't low."

"You don't believe you're any good at what you do, even when you are good. Better than good."

"It's not what I'm meant to do."

"Eira, will you stop it? It's getting real annoying hearing you talk like that."

I shrugged and shifted my gaze to the ceiling when I heard something. "It is what it is."

He sighed and then gazed up with me. "What are you looking at?"

Shaking my head, I placed my spray bottle down so I could refill it. "Thought I heard something."

"And you call me crazy," he teased. When I refused to play along and mess with him back, he frowned. "All right, what paint do you need?"

"Paint…" My reply came out absentmindedly as I gazed up at the ceiling again, more noise from above distracting me.

Blaze pulled away from the car he was working on and attempted to look up at the ceiling. "Okay, what the hell is up there? It sounds like a damn bear!"

"Your mother sounds like a bear," I said, a smirk tugging at my lips.

Raid and Ryoko laughed hysterically, and Blaze looked at me funny. "What?"

"It's a squirrel. Go back to work," I said.

"There's no way that was a squirrel," Blaze insisted. "It's way too loud."

"It's called an echo. A fish could sound like a bear in this place," I said. "Now drop it and go back to work."

"Fine, whatever," he muttered.

When everyone went back to their business, I shifted my eyes up again, spotted Mocha hiding in the shadows of the roof, and held eye contact with her for a few moments. She watched me carefully. I held her gaze for a moment more before going back to work. Removing the paint container, I checked to see approximately how much paint I'd need. I turned to retrieve the premixed orange, but was nearly knocked off my feet when I ran into Raikidan. He caught me with one hand and helped keep me steady.

I rubbed my cheek. "Ow."

"Sorry," he said. "I didn't expect you to turn around."

I glanced at the mixing container he carried. "Well, I didn't expect you to be bringing me more paint."

"This is the color you need, right?"

I nodded. "Yeah. Do you mind holding the paint container for my spray gun, so I don't dump it by accident?"

"Sure," he handed me the paint and then held onto the spray gun paint container so I could pour paint into it. His eyes flicked to the ceiling before looking at me. "Why did you lie to the others?"

"They weren't ready to know."

"You're not surprised she's here."

I continued to pour the colored liquid. "She comes here a lot. She's just usually quiet."

"And you don't think the others should know?"

"No. It's best if they don't right now. It's why they don't know Chameleon and Doppelganger helped us out on that assignment the other day."

"All right, if you say so."

I finished pouring the paint and then took the paint container from Raikidan to reattach to my spray gun.

"Will you need any other colors?"

"Not yet. I need to let this color finish drying once I'm done before I go back to black."

He sat on the bench. "Okay."

Before I got the chance to go back to my paint job, Zane called out to me. "Chickadee, I need you and Raikidan to grab a few things for me if you can. List is tacked up on the office doorframe."

"Sure, no problem."

I walked over to the office and took down the paper with scribbles of parts and tools. Raikidan followed me to the back of the shop, and we collected up the items on the list—him taking the heavier items and me taking the rest.

"Hey, Eira?" Raikidan said.

I continued to search through the toolbox. "Yeah?"

"I'm sorry for yelling at you when I came back. I shouldn't have done that, and I should have heard you out."

I rummaged some more to wait for him to say more, but he didn't say anything else. "Well, thank you for the apology, but I don't accept it."

"W—why? I told you I was sorry."

I turned to look at him. "Because what you said really hurt, Raikidan, and the kind of apology you just gave doesn't cut it for what you did. I may not have a perfect set of emotions like everyone else, but I do have some. As much as I'd rather not…"

I walked away from him and delivered the parts I had collected to Zane. He and Raid both opened their mouth as if they were about to ask if I was okay, but I turned around and returned to my corner. I buckled my respirator to my face and went back to work.

Ten minutes later, I finished with the color, and removed my respirator as I surveyed my work. A little more black, and maybe some more red, and I could call it finished. *I need a break first.*

I headed for the front door. "I'll be back. Grabbing lunch for us."

"Bring back something yummy!" Ryoko called to me.

I smirked. "All right, I'll bring back gruel just for you."

"Laz!"

I laughed and went on my way. I dug my hands into my pockets as I walked, taking as many side streets as I could to avoid all the people.

"Why'd you do it?"

I stopped walking and turned my gaze on Mocha, who hid in the shadow of a building. "Does it matter?"

"You've known I was here daily. You know I've been watching all of you, and you act like you don't care."

"I don't."

She straightened a bit and tilted her head. "Why? Why didn't you tell them so they could spit on me? Why have you been letting me do this? Why aren't you going out of your way to make me miserable?"

"You act like I hate you."

Her eyes narrowed. "Because you do."

"No, I don't."

She hesitated. "Y—you don't?"

"Raynn is an asshole and can't run a team right. My problem is with him, not you. All of you have had a problem with us, so my team, and even myself, have reacted to that." I turned away. "I didn't tell the others because you deserve to know what a real team is like. If the others knew, they wouldn't show you because they don't trust you."

"Trust is for fools."

"Trust is for those who deserve it. It brings peace to a troubled mind."

"Eira, wait up!" I turned to see Raikidan running toward me. When he reached me, I glanced at the shadow of the building to find Mocha gone.

Raikidan took a few deep breaths before speaking. "You didn't wait for me."

"I didn't think you wanted to follow. I'm just getting food."

"I like food." I laughed and continued walking. He followed. "What's so funny?"

"You don't like our food," I said. "It's always a fight to get you to eat things."

"Yes I do. I'm just... picky."

I chuckled more and led us onto an unavoidable busy street. "So what is compelling you to want food this time?"

"You're picking it out." My brow rose and he avoided eye contact. "When you give recommendations... it always tastes good."

"Always?"

His nose scrunched and his lips curled. "Well, if you told me to eat an insect, I don't think I'd like that."

I laughed. "They're not bad."

He shook his head. "I still can't believe you did that."

I shrugged. My gaze wandered when a man walking on the other side of the road caught my eye. He wasn't doing anything out of the ordinary, but I'd recognize that bronze skin and multi-colored hair even if I were half blind. *My mystery shifter from that assignment I worked with Chameleon on.* Sure, there could be other people in the city that would dye their hair in a crazy fashion too, but it was him. I just knew it.

A truck drove by, and after it passed, the man was gone. I blinked and tried to look through the crowd to find him, but he was nowhere to be seen. *Where did he go?*

Raikidan regarded me for a moment. "Everything okay?"

I couldn't let him think I'm crazy. "Yeah, I'm fine. Thought I saw something. But it was just a figment of my imagination." There was no way I had imagined him. *He was there, I'm sure of it.*

"Oh, okay. So, would you make me something to eat sometime?"

My head jerked back and my brow creased. "Uh, what?"

"When you make food, and I mean make something and not grabbing an apple to last you a day, it always smells delicious, but you only make enough for yourself. I want to try some of it."

"Raikidan, it's not that great. Ryoko can cook much better than me. You should ask her."

"But your food smells better."

I shook my head. "No."

"If I buy lunch, will you?"

"What?"

"If I buy the lunch you were going to get everyone, will you make me something?"

"Raikidan."

"Please?"

I sighed in defeat. "It's not going to be anything special."

He smiled. "I don't care. I want to know what food tastes like when you make it."

I rolled my eyes. "Whatever. Let's just get lunch and get back to the shop so I can finish my paint job."

He swung his arm over my shoulder and forced me to walk closer to him. "Thanks."

"Yeah, whatever."

As we walked into the restaurant, I thought about what to make him and became worried he wouldn't like it. I really wasn't that great of a cook. Daren had told me I did well, but I could tell he didn't like it when I made anything. There was something about the way I cooked—no one enjoyed it. It was the reason I only cooked for myself. I liked it and that's all that had really mattered. But now I was getting myself all worked up and I didn't know why.

If Raikidan didn't like it, then it wouldn't be an issue. It just meant I'd only have to feed myself like always. So why was I so worried he wouldn't like what I was going to make?

The fog was thick and dark. I couldn't see much more than a few feet in front of me, and I wasn't sure if I should continue walking. What was the point? Nothing had changed as I walked. The fog's thickness even stayed the same.

I blinked when I thought I saw movement. I spun around when I sensed a presence behind me, but there was nothing. Not liking this situation, I moved forward and this time, as I did, the fog began to thin. I hadn't gotten far before movement caught my eye again, and when I looked in the direction, I could make out a figure.

"Hello?" The figure didn't move, so I called out to it again. "Hello? Is someone there?"

The figure moved away from me.

"Wait, don't go!"

To my surprise, the figure stopped moving, and I took the opportunity to move closer. I stopped advancing when the figure became clear enough to tell me this mystery person was male. I didn't want to scare him off. Something felt familiar about him.

"Who are you?" The figure took a step back. "Please don't go… I don't want to be alone here."

The figure didn't move, much to my relief.

"Who are you?" I nearly sighed when he didn't respond. "Can I at least see who you are?"

This time the man growled, taking me by surprise. The growl wasn't completely human, but it still carried some human trace in it. It felt… familiar somehow.

"Please… I just want to know why you keep appearing around me in this fog! Who are you and what are you doing here?"

The man snarled again, then ran. I held out my hand, but stopped myself from yelling out to him. There was no point.

CHAPTER 12

Shva'sika pulled on my arm. "C'mon, Laz, just come with us."

I struggled against her grip, but she held fast. Raikidan and Corliss had come into my room and told me they wanted me to go somewhere with them, but when they wouldn't tell me where, I refused. They didn't press the matter, but not long after they had left, Rylan had come in and asked. He also wouldn't tell me where we'd be going, and when I refused, he wasn't as easy to get rid of—though he, too, eventually left.

Now Shva'sika was trying to get me to go to this mysterious location, and she wasn't taking no for an answer. But their elusiveness made me wary. Why didn't they want to disclose this mysterious location to me?

"Shva'sika, I said I don't want to go," I insisted as I tried to pull away.

"Well, why not?" she asked.

"Because no one will tell me where we're going."

"Well, I don't know myself, so that's why I'm not telling."

My brow furrowed. "Then why are you trying to make me go?"

She shrugged. "Because it could be fun."

I let out an exasperated breath. "I just want to stay home."

"Well, that's too bad. You're going with us," Rylan said as we emerged from my room.

"And why should I when no one is telling me where we're going?"

Rylan's gaze drifted over to Ryoko, who was doing her own thing in the kitchen, and then he snapped back to me. "Do something spontaneous for once, will you?"

My brow rose in interest. Something was up. I yanked my arm free of Shva'sika's grip. "Fine, but it'd better be worth it."

He smiled. "It will, now let's go. We'll be back, Ryoko."

"All right, have fun." She acted as if she didn't care that she wasn't invited, which was unusual for her.

I followed everyone to the garage and hopped into the front passenger seat while Rylan took the wheel. I didn't say anything until we were out of the garage and cruising down the street. "So, now can I know what's up?"

"Ryoko's birthday is coming up, and I need your help with the gift," Rylan said.

My head tilted forward as I stared at him. "You need your memory checked. Her birthday isn't for another month and a half. We're still in our last month of summer."

"No, I remembered that," he insisted, "but I want to get her something special. She likes jewelry, so I thought I'd start there."

"I suggested we go to my brother's shop, Black Starlight," Raikidan said. "Corliss and I had made plans to make a trip over, so we thought we'd kill two birds with one stone."

Shva'sika sighed. "Did you need to use such a morbid metaphor?"

The car echoed with quiet laughter. Rylan glanced at me. "I remember Ebon saying he usually does custom pieces, so I needed someone more creative in that sense to give me a hand if he didn't have anything suitable in stock."

I nodded. "Okay, this makes more sense now. What are you looking for specifically?"

"Um… something that looks nice."

I pinched the bridge of my nose and Shva'sika laughed. "You boys are real winners."

Rylan's cheeks reddened. "I'm trying to learn, okay? Give me some credit."

"Oh, dear, I do," she said. "You making this effort to make her happy is far better than what I see a lot of non-elven men doing."

Rylan peered at her through the rear mirror. "Care to elaborate on your culture, then?"

"It's simple. Both men and women take great pride in the gifts we shower our partners with, though our men go to much greater lengths than our women. The lack of effort I see in other races is rather off-putting. It also made it amusing to watch my brother interact with Laz."

Rylan glanced my way. "I don't doubt it. How many gifts did you turn down?"

I rolled my eyes. "How many did I accept is an easier question to answer."

Rylan shook his head. "Ouch."

"Eira, you've acquired quite the list of suitors, haven't you?" Corliss teased.

I let a fake laugh. "Yeah, no. Just a couple crazies, and one of them got himself killed because of it."

Mortification blanketed Corliss' face. Shva'sika placed a hand on his shoulder. "My brother was a bit too stubborn for his own good, and ran into battle for her sake when he wasn't equipped to do so."

Corliss' eyes softened. "I'm sorry to hear it was your brother this happened to."

"Thank you."

Rylan pulled up to a rustic shop and cut the engine. It amused me how different the shop looked from the high-class Sector Eleven shops around it. Ebon really liked to make a statement.

The group of us walked down the tunneled entrance and entered the shop. Ebon stood at the counter, scrawling notes into a book. He glanced up the moment the bell on the door rang and smiled. "Ah, looks like my prayers for guests to arrive have been answered."

Raikidan rolled his eyes, though the rest of us found the comment amusing. The two dragons immediately went to speaking, and Corliss eventually joined in, while Shva'sika, Rylan, and I went to looking around. I quizzed Rylan to get an idea what he was hoping to pick out, and his choice came down to earrings. Unfortunately, as nice as the display selections were, none of us found them very "Ryoko."

"Not finding anything to your liking?" Ebon asked.

I shook my head. "No, looks like a custom design is in order."

Ebon's eyes lit up. "Wonderful! What would you like?"

I glanced at Rylan, who stared at me with fear-stricken eyes. I sighed. "Fine, I'll pick. We'll go with imperial topaz. She tends to favor those."

Rylan's brow twisted. "Imperial what?"

I smack my forehead. "You're hopeless. Ebon, could you spare me some paper and a pencil? I need to do some sketching."

Ebon took great interest in my request. "You? Usually my customers need me to do that. This should be interesting. I'll be right back."

He disappeared behind the doorway covered by hanging bead strings that led to the back of the building. Several moments passed before he returned, a bundle of paper and colored pencils in hand. "I know you asked for a pencil, but my curiosity has the better of me, so I have my sketching pencils for you."

I nodded my thanks when he placed them down on the glass display case. "I appreciate that."

Ebon pulled back and watched me for a few moments as I sketched, before continuing his conversation with the other two dragons. I didn't have anything specific in mind, so I drew what came to me. Most designs came out simple yet elegant, though none resonated as a "Ryoko" piece. I continued on.

I stopped sketching when one popped out at me. The topaz was the center piece, with several gems orbiting it on one side, and three gem-embedded flares branching off the other, giving the design a winged look. I stared at the design for a few moments before sighing and going back to my designing.

"That one was good, though," Rylan said.

"Not for her. They won't work well with her ears," I murmured. "This style would flow up the ear, which isn't good for her."

He sighed and continued to wait. I aimed for more extravagant designs to see what would happen, but it didn't go as well as I had hoped. I ended up designing necklaces instead, getting me strange looks from Rylan.

"That's an interesting headpiece," Ebon said. "May I see it?"

"Oh, this?" I glanced up to see Shva'sika taking off the circlet I made her. "Sure."

He took it from her and handled it with care. "This is lovely. It's elegant but simple. Where did you get this?"

"Laz made it for me," she boasted.

Ebon shifted his gaze to me, shocked. "You made this?"

My gaze flicked up to him briefly before focusing again on my piece of paper. "Yeah."

"By yourself?"

I shrugged. "Had a little help, but could have done it on my own."

"Very impressive work."

My ears and face began to burn. I didn't want the attention. "It's nothing, really."

Shva'sika shook her head. "We need to work on your praise acceptance."

I grumbled and continued designing. I was on the verge of a breakthrough, and I didn't want to lose these ideas.

"Thank you for letting me look at this," Ebon said to Shva'sika. "Would you be able to help me with something?"

"I can try," she replied.

"I'm aware you're a shaman—and I recently purchased something from one of the caravans, but the shamans who sold me this item wouldn't tell me who made it. I was hoping you'd be able to help."

"Well, it depends on the caravan and the item. If you show it to me, I could tell you if I at least recognize it, and we could go from there."

I didn't pay Ebon any mind when he left. I was curious about the item he was questioning, but I really wanted to get this earring done. It was becoming more of a pain than I had first thought it would be. I did look up, however, when he came back.

In his hands, he carried a wooden carving about the size of both his hands. From where I sat, I could only tell it was made from oak, and that it seemed to be well-crafted. Whoever had crafted it had put a lot of time and effort into making it, and had a lot of skill.

"I was hoping you'd be able to identify this," Ebon said.

Shva'sika took the item and only gazing at it for a moment. "Laz, isn't this yours?"

I put down my pencil. "Doubt it, but I'll take a look."

She came over and handed it to me to study, immediately finding the wood to be heavy and sturdy. The carving was of a large bear and two cubs tumbling around with each other. I traced my fingers over the carved and sanded marks.

I then turned it over, spying the fancy *LER* carved into the bottom. "I made this last week."

"You're sure?" Ebon asked.

I placed the carving down on the display case and went back to designing. "I'd recognize my carve marks anywhere."

"Well, that solves my mystery. But why wouldn't the men selling me the carving tell me it was you?"

"Because I asked them to keep it secret." The only possible indicator any of my statues had was the signature on the underside of the bases. The shamans insisted I at least initial my work, and since only a select few knew my full name, I figured using it in its entirety was the best course.

"Why? This is excellent work."

My ears started to burn again. "Because I'm busy, and only do them in my free time. I don't want people knowing I made them, because they'll bother me for more."

"Very well." He seemed to get that I wasn't going to take his compliments very well, and knew not to press.

I tilted my head as I took in my most recent earring design. I absently sketched it out while talking. I liked it—a hoop style with an omega back. Encased in the front half were small white gems. A heart-shaped orange gem, set in the same material as the hoop, dropped off the bottom. The setting had more white gems embedded into it that surrounded the larger orange heart gem.

I scribbled down notes. The metal, white gold; the large orange gem, imperial topaz; and the small white gems, diamonds or cubic zirconia, depending on what Rylan wanted. "There, done."

Rylan's mouth fell open. "That's perfect!" He smiled wide at me. "I knew I could count on you."

"Then that's what we'll do," Ebon said, clapping his hands together once.

Rylan blinked. "But you haven't even seen it to know if you can do it."

Ebon took the sheets of paper and examined my design. "Oh, I can do it. Course, I have no idea what you wrote for gems and metal type. What kind of language is this?"

A grin spread across my lips. "A special one. The materials are white gold, imperial topaz, and diamonds or cubic zirconia."

He nodded and then eyed the rest of my designs. "Using those materials won't be an issue. Do you mind if I keep the rest of these?"

I shrugged. "Sure. I don't need them."

Rylan leaned on the display. "All right, now that she's done the hard work, I have to do the painful one. I need to discuss cost and payment."

Stepping back, I eyed Rylan. As he focused on Ebon and discussed payment, I grinned and reached for two important items on his person. I pulled away when I had successfully removed them, noticing that only Corliss had caught what I had done. He smirked, but slipped back to a neutral expression so as not to give me away.

Rylan winced when Ebon gave him his final total, discount included, and the two worked up a payment plan. When I heard the amount, I also twitched. I hoped he either had saved up a lot, or was going to pull some heavy shifts these next few weeks to cover it.

They discussed a down payment, and Rylan reached for his money pouch, only to find it missing. He searched frantically until Corliss' snickering caught his attention. "What are you laughing about?"

Ebon started chuckling then, and Rylan looked between the two. When his attention was on Corliss, Ebon glanced at me, a knowing smile spreading across his face. Then it dawned on Rylan. He whirled around and stared at me.

With a huge grin, I held up his money pouch. "Looking for something?"

"Seriously?"

"You need to pay attention to your surroundings more."

He crossed his arms. "Well, it is the money I was going to use on Ryoko's gift, and it's not like you're going to run off with it."

I held up the car keys as I backed away. "No, but I would run off with this."

Rylan checked his person again and then stared at me. Corliss and Ebon also appeared surprised. Even they didn't catch that part.

"Well, we have a master thief in our midst," Ebon said.

I bowed graciously at the compliment. "At your service." I then tossed the bag to Rylan. "I'll let you handle that. I'm going to go sit in the car. It was nice seeing you again, Ebon."

He waved. "You too, Eira. Feel free to stop by any time."

I spun on my heels only, to be nearly smashed in the face when the shop door opened. "Oh, I'm sorry, Eira, I didn't mean to almost hit you."

I looked at the newcomer funny. He was an older-looking man, somewhere in his forties, and had short red hair and green eyes with a golden ring. I didn't know him, although his features identified him to me as dragon, and his scent told me his origins. *He's not from Zaith's clan, so how does he know my name?*

"*Beware.*"

"A friend of yours, Laz?" Shva'sika asked.

I continued to eye the dragon. "No, this one is from the North."

The dragon chuckled. "How'd you figure that out?"

"How do you know my name?" I asked instead of answering.

"Let's just say, word gets around."

I grunted and headed out of the shop. "You smell like pines and mountain water."

The dragon chuckled. "Cheery, isn't she?"

I was halfway down the hall before Rylan and the others caught up. But before we made it to the car, I stopped.

"Eira?" Raikidan asked.

I turned back around. "I'll be with you guys in a second. I forgot to do something."

"Laz, you'd better not change that design," Rylan warned. "I like it as it is."

I ignored him. I had something on my mind that was a little more important to me. It was something I had thought about on and off since Raikidan had given me my necklace.

No one was in the shop when I entered. There was a deep silence, and it made me uncomfortable. I chose to wait a few moments to see if Ebon would come back. When I felt I had given ample time, I turned to leave.

"Oh, Eira, I didn't expect you to come back." I turned back around when I heard Ebon's voice. He made his way through the beaded doorway. The other dragon from before was with him. The two spoke quietly, and then Ebon put his focus back on me. "How can I help you?"

"I just wanted to thank you for the effort you put into making the necklace Raikidan gave me. It took me a little while to figure out who made it, but when I did, I wasn't surprised."

He smiled. "I was glad to work on it. May I ask why you're not wearing it? Raikidan made it sound as though it'd be the only necklace you'd wear, and you're not currently wearing one at all."

"I have my reasons."

Ebon chuckled. "Meaning my brother did something stupid again. Sometimes I wonder about him."

"I also have something to ask you. When I sent you the letter, I thought you'd leave, but here you are. Care to explain?"

"Because I already knew I was allowed here because of my dual-colored heritage."

I nodded. "Very well. I'll leave you be, then."

"Wait. I'd like to request something from you."

I strolled over to the display counter. "I may agree, depending."

He leaned on the glass surface and kept his voice low, as if he was afraid someone would overhear. "I was hoping you'd be able to carve something for me. Well, for my mate, actually."

"What do you want me to carve?"

"To be honest, I'm not sure yet. I hadn't expected you to be the person I was trying to track down."

I snickered. "Then how do you expect me to figure out how much it'll cost?"

"Well, I was hoping I could offer up a trade. I saw how much panic your friend was trying to hide when I told him the price of the earrings. I can discount it even more if you are willing to carve me something."

The idea sounded all right. It meant the money Rylan was going to spend on Ryoko was going to go to something else.

I nodded. "Sure."

He smiled. "Thank you. She really liked the one I bought, so I thought I'd get her one, but I wanted it to be special—made just for her."

"I don't know why you're all excited over them, but it doesn't matter. What does matter is what you want this to be."

Ebon shook his head. "You should learn to take more credit for what you can do, but that's really none of my business. As for the carving, I told you, I'm not sure."

"Well, I'm going to need to know before I can start. Even choosing the right wood relies on knowing what the subject will be."

He ran his fingers through his hair. "Well, shoot. I don't know…"

I pulled away from the counter. "I'll let you think on it. Let Raikidan know when you think of something."

"No, I'll think about it right now, if that's okay. I don't know how long it takes you to make them."

"It depends on the piece."

"Exactly. If it's something complex, I want you to have ample time without rushing. I won't need it for a few more months, but I still want to make sure you have plenty of time."

I leaned on the counter again. "Think of something she likes the most. You can't go wrong there."

"The ocean." He didn't hesitate with that answer. "She loves the ocean."

I nodded. "Good start. Anything thing in the ocean in particular?" He shook his head. "All right, I'll take creative freedom then. How big do you want it?"

"Twice the size of the bear statue I purchased."

I pulled away again. "I can do that. Let Raikidan know when exactly you'll need it, so I know my deadline."

"Sure. Thanks for doing this."

I shrugged. "No problem."

Just then, Rylan burst through the front door. "Laz, we have to go."

My attention snapped to him. "What's going on?"

"We got an urgent call to get home. Can't say much else."

I nodded and bolted out the door, though my eyes did go back to the other dragon who had come into Ebon's store. I didn't know why I was so wary of him, but something told me to stay away from him. Maybe it was because he reminded me off—I shook the thought from my head. Those thoughts made me hope for something that never existed. For something that never would be...

13
CHAPTER

T he tactical map changed as Ven, the battle leader of Team Four, messed with the control buttons. I knew he was in a hurry, but I wished he'd let me look at it for more than three seconds. When we had arrived home, Genesis informed us of military activity in Sector Four. The Council wanted all hands on deck, some heading out to gather intel on the military's activities, while the rest of us waited in the Underground. What reports our spies were able to get to us were disturbing.

The reports claimed possible planned raids on civilian and even shaman homes to flush out rebels. A big cover-up story was sure to be used the next day, but we needed to act before they could begin their assault. The shamans had already been warned and many were readying themselves for a fight. Several shamans stood at the tactical table as well to get a better idea of the area we'd be protecting.

They claimed to understand they were not to act unless they felt they could justify to Zarda that they'd felt threatened, but I wasn't so sure they'd be able to hold back long enough, and worried they'd get themselves into trouble.

"Ven, will you cut it out?" I demanded. "No one can be of any use if you don't let us see anything long enough to take it in."

"Sorry. I'm just trying to find a better map that will help us more."

"There aren't any other maps. It's a city, and it hasn't changed much in the past decade."

"As in I'm looking for a more detailed map."

I blew out a breath. "Then zoom in, dummy."

He blinked. "What?"

"Oh, for the love of—give me that." I pushed him away and pressed the buttons that would make the map zoom in. "I've been gone over two decades and I still manage to know more than you. Why is that?"

Ven went to reply, but thundering footsteps kept him quiet. I tore my gaze away from the map when Ryoko and a few others came in.

"We need to go now," Ryoko told us. "They had a psychic that found all our scouts. Teams have already started flowing in and fighting back."

"Then we'll join them." I looked at the shamans who were still inspecting the map. "You know what to do."

They nodded and let us go. We ran down the hall and I poked my head into a room where Rylan and Argus were going over weapons with Corliss and Raikidan. "All right, ladies, get moving. It's time to work."

Corliss looked at me. "But I haven't had enough time—"

"Too bad. Get moving."

"But—"

I glared at him. "Move your ass."

He pulled back a bit. "Is she always that scary when she wants something done?"

Rylan chuckled and picked up his sniper rifle. "Only if it's important. You learn to ignore it."

"Or avoid it," Argus added. "I like not having any conflict between her and me and it works great for us."

Rylan tossed his head Raikidan's way. "What's his excuse then? He can't do either."

Raikidan grunted and the two laughed at him. I shook my head and kept going. *Men.*

I followed Ryoko out into the main room of the virtual training center and accepted the gun and supply belt Blaze offered me. He watched as Ryoko effortlessly picked up her rail gun and rested it against her shoulder. "Ryoko, how the hell do you do it? It took four of us to move that thing from the spot Seda had dropped it off at."

Her eyes glittered with amusement. "Maybe the four of you are just a bunch of weaklings."

"Hey, I'm one of those guys, thank you," Rylan voiced as they joined us.

"And your point?"

Rylan shoved her lightly, but Ryoko wasn't so inclined to do the same. Rylan fell over like he weighed nothing, and I could only laugh. He got back up and pushed her back and she chuckled. The two were cute, and I was glad Ryoko was starting to see herself in a better light.

I went to follow the group of people out into the sewer system to join the battle, but Seda pulled me aside. "What's wrong, Seda?"

"You need to be careful in this fight. Strange visions keep coming to me. I don't like the vibe I'm getting from them."

"I'm guessing the images aren't clear?"

She nodded. "Just be careful, okay?"

I placed my hand on her shoulder. "I'll watch everyone's back."

"I'm more worried about your back. Your voice is all I'm hearing— and you're panicking."

"Seda, I don't panic."

"There's a first time for everything."

"Don't worry. I'll be careful in this fight."

"Good. Call on me if you need my assistance. I'll be doing my best to keep an eye out as much as possible."

"Sure." I ran off to catch up with the others.

Raikidan was the only one to notice my return. He gave me a questioning look and I shrugged. Nothing bad was going to happen.

I ducked instinctively when a grenade went off a few yards away. This battle was far more intense than I had imagined, and I knew it was only a matter of time before the shamans would intervene. They hadn't yet, but I couldn't deny that we could use them right now.

Gunfire rang in my ears, and the sound of Argus crying out in pain made my blood run cold. Throwing out a blast of fire, I ran to his aid. Ryoko, Raikidan, and Raid came over to help, and made an attempt to push the army back as I inspected Argus. *Leg wound.*

The clunking sound of an approaching tank caught my attention, but before I could call out to Ryoko to handle it, the tank stopped moving. I expected it to fire, but it started creaking as if it were being bent. I blinked in surprise when the tank began falling apart. I figured someone had seen it before me and had hitched a ride to dismantle it, but as I watched, I noticed the parts weren't just falling off, they were flying off. There was only one person I knew who had the skills to do that.

I turned to see the one person I had wanted to stay far away from this city. A tall nu-human woman with ivory skin, long blonde hair and red tips, and green eyes moved her arms skillfully as she dismantled the tank. *Arnia*. Her fraternal twin, Jaybird, a green-eyed, ivory-skinned man, with blond, blue-tipped hair, came up behind her and threw out balls of air, pushing the foot soldiers back.

"Incredible talent they have." I looked at an approaching nu-human man with short black hair, tan skin, and lavender eyes. *Ven'lar*. I had sent Arnia and Jaybird away with him to the North Tribe to recover. He knelt next to me. "Once I determined they were well enough to wander around the village, they assumed it was okay brush up on their skills. I bet you can guess how astonished we were to know one could manipulate metal, and the other air."

"It surprised us, too, when it was first made known in the military," I said. "Better yet, we assumed they would have similar gifts because they were twins."

Ven'lar nodded. "That was a surprise to me as well. Now go back to your battle. I'll care for your friend here."

"Thank you. Once you're done, please make your way to the east side. They have the heaviest fire."

"Of course."

I patted Argus on the shoulder, who nodded in response, and threw myself back into the action. Ryoko, Raikidan and Raid spread out on my motioned command, but when they went a little too far, I found myself being the next target of the foot soldiers. Lucky for me, Arnia had my back. A large sheet of metal crashed on the ground in front of me, protecting me from the rain of bullets. Arnia joined me by my side as Jaybird forced the bullets back.

"Surprised?" she asked me.

"You should have stayed away from here," I said.

"You said we could come back."

"That didn't mean you should. You could have had a better life, Arnia. One without any fear or fighting."

She shook her head. "I couldn't just stay away. I couldn't let you guys fight this battle alone. I need to be of some use."

I watched as she pulled a metal drainpipe from a building and threw it at the army. I smiled. "You're getting better at that."

"You sending us away for a little while was the best thing that could have happened to us. The shamans have been really helpful. They were able to help Jay more, but they did their best with me."

"Metal shamans are rare. Wind shamans are scarce in their own right, but not as much as metal." I couldn't resist reaching out and running my fingers through a strand of her gorgeous hair before throwing some fire around our shield. It looked like it had never been shaven off. "Your hair came back fast."

"That's because they have this amazing hair growth serum they don't share outside the tribe. My hair grew like wildfire for the first month, but finally slowed down and acted normal again after that point. I'm honored they were willing to share it. I have a feeling it was because of Ven'lar. He's highly respected there."

I grinned. "You seem to like him a lot."

Her face flushed. "He's nice."

I chuckled and threw out some more fire. It wasn't my business to press.

"Grenades!" someone called in warning.

I ducked, and Arnia bent the metal shield over us, but the blast didn't come—at least, not in the way we'd expect. I peered around the metal shield to see Raikidan blocking the street in his large dragon form. He shook his head as if the blast had stunned him, and then breathed fire down on the army. I watched as he continued to assault the army, his flames becoming hotter, until they were turning white at times.

Arnia touched my shoulder. "It might be wise—"

"I know. We need to get out of here before things get worse."

"I'll go round up—"

My eyes widened when I heard a loud gun go off, followed by the most terrifying cry of pain I'd ever heard—and that cry wasn't human. "Raikidan…"

"Eira, look out!"

"Tannek, no!"

Before Arnia could stop me, I rushed over to where he laid. His breath came out heavy and labored, and he wasn't moving much. Crimson blood pooled everywhere.

"No, no, no, no, Raikidan." I couldn't believe this was happening. "Raikidan, c'mon, you gotta get up."

He didn't move, and I could hear the army advancing. If I didn't act fast, they'd finish him off and go for me as well. Without thinking, I retaliated and breathed as much fire as I could muster up. The army retreated from the flame, but when I stopped to fill my lungs with air, they advanced again. Anger boiled inside me, and I breathed more fire onto them. When they didn't advance after my attack ended, I took the opportunity to check on Raikidan.

"Raikidan, you need to shift. We can't move you like this." Panic rose in my chest when he didn't move. I didn't know what to do.

"Stay calm," the voice said. *"You're useless to him if you panic."*

Had this situation not been so dire, I would have questioned why it wasn't telling me to leave him to die.

"How is he?"

I set my worried gaze on Corliss when he joined me at my side. "I don't know… He won't respond."

Corliss placed his hand on my shoulder. "It's going to be okay, Eira. We'll get—"

The army began raining bullets down on us. I ground my teeth together. "Get him to shift."

I moved away from the two dragons and breathed more fire, this time with more power, my ability unhindered by my self-restraint.

"Eira…"

"Get him to shift back!" I shouted. I didn't care if he saw what I could do right now. I didn't care if anyone saw. It didn't matter. Fire spewed from my mouth again, and the army finally retreated some more.

Corliss looked at me when I turned to face them again. "You need to do this. He's not responding to me."

I shook my head. "I don't know what to do…"

Corliss moved away from Raikidan and touched my shoulder. "I'll create a poisonous cloud. That'll give us some cover."

"Poison?"

He chuckled. "Looks like I'll need to teach you the difference between the colors, since Raikidan has neglected to tell you everything. Now go help him."

"I don't know what to do! He won't respond to me…"

"He will, Eira, and when he does, feed him fire once he's shifted. That'll give him the energy to live."

"Feed him—Corliss, what—"

Corliss left my side and began exhaling a pale green smoke. There wasn't time to ask. I touched Raikidan's snout and my blood ran cold. *Cold scales and closed eyes…* I feared I had been too slow.

"Raikidan, you have to shift. You have to do something to tell me you're going to be okay."

"If, after all he's done, you really want him to live, you must try harder."

"He's been good to me," I told it as I tried to shake Raikidan's snout. *"We might not see eye-to-eye all the time, and we may fight, but we don't hate each other. I realized this is why he came back and stayed. Why I struggle to let go…"*

When Raikidan didn't stir, I threw myself onto him, the harsh stench of his ashy, sulfurous breath enveloping me. "Please, Raikidan… please don't be dead. Please shift, so we can get you help. Please… I… I can't lose you, too…"

I gasped when Raikidan stirred underneath me. I pulled away, watching him shift to his human shape over several painstaking moments. I brushed my bangs away from my face and leaned over him, checking his vitals. His heart rate was weak and his eyes remained closed. Now that he was in a human form, I could see the horrific damage the gun had done to him. *It's a miracle he's alive.*

I frantically thought of how I could help him more. At this rate, he wouldn't make it back home alive. Corliss told me to feed him fire, but I didn't understand—I blinked. I did understand. Grasping both sides of his face, I used my thumbs to open his mouth. Taking a deep breath, I pressed my lips against his. Exhaling, I breathed a strong fire into his mouth and prayed he'd be able to absorb it.

I pulled away and cut the fire just as Ryoko and the others were rushing over to help. I ignored them and stared at Raikidan, hoping he'd stir, but he didn't. "C'mon."

Corliss appeared by my side. "He's going to be fine, trust me on this. But we need to get out of here now. They've put on masks that are resistant to my poison."

Rylan touched my shoulder and then picked up Raikidan. "I got him."

I nodded and followed them. My heart leaped when I noticed Raikidan's fingers twitch. *It's a response—that has to be good, in some way.*

Someone's hand brushed mine. I shifted my gaze to find Corliss looking at me, compassion and reassurance emanating from him. He didn't appear concerned at all, as if he knew for a fact that everything was going to be okay. Why couldn't I be so sure?

Corliss left my side when we made it into the basement of the house and led the way upstairs. He pointed Rylan to my room, against several protests from Shva'sika and Ryoko, but Corliss was too focused to listen, and Rylan didn't argue.

"Rylan, put Raikidan down on the bed," Corliss instructed. "Shva'sika, I need you to heal Raikidan up as best as you can once Rylan gets him situated."

She nodded and then went to work. I waited quietly by the window. I just didn't feel right being any closer. *I'd just be in the way.*

Shva'sika pulled away from Raikidan. "All right, he's as healed as possible at the moment. You know how dragon bodies react to our hea—"

"Everyone but Eira leave," Corliss ordered.

I blinked, and Shva'sika stared at him, shocked as me. "What?"

"Don't argue with me." I opened my mouth to speak, but he raised his hand and held his ground. "Eira, trust me. Everyone but you needs to leave."

I remained quiet and waited for everyone to accept his decision and leave.

"You think Laz is going to be okay?" Ryoko asked as she shut the door. "She's awful quiet."

"She'll be fine," Seda reassured. "Everything is going to be fine."

"Eira," Corliss said in a soft tone. "I need you to feed Raikidan more fire. He's going to need it to finish healing and get back up on his feet."

I nodded and went to Raikidan's side. His breath came shallow, making me wonder if Corliss was right.

"I hope you understand what you're doing."

Taking a quick, decisive breath, I sat down on the bed and fed Raikidan another heavy dose of fire. When I pulled away, I waited. I would wait until he woke up. I wouldn't sleep until I knew he'd be okay.

I squeezed my eyes shut as light tried to force me to open them.

My mind was heavy, and all I wanted to do was continue to sleep. I curled up more, but when I remembered Raikidan and his condition, I couldn't sleep anymore. I had told myself I'd stay awake until I knew he was better. I needed to wake up now.

My eyes fluttered open, a tattered red shirt filling my sight. My eyes drifted upward until they met Raikidan's watchful gaze.

I bolted upright. "I'm sorry! I didn't mean to fall asleep on you."

He chuckled, his voice coming out in a husky rasp. "Eira, it's okay. Allowing you to sleep is the least I could let you do, after what I put you through last night. But I have to admit, I was surprised when I woke up."

I gave a weak smile, but it quickly faded and my gaze fell elsewhere. "I'm glad you're awake. I should go get—"

He took my hand. "Eira, wait." My eyes lifted to meet his. "I'm sorry for thinking you didn't care when you sent me away. I should have talked to you and found out your side, instead of yelling at you. I knew better than to do that, and it was seriously wrong of me to. I promise I won't ever do it again."

I felt the sincerity in his words. I squeezed his hand. "Apology accepted. And I'm sorry for not giving you a choice. You were right, you did deserve one, even if you didn't get your way in the end."

He chuckled, and then frowned when his attention fell on my neck. "Why don't you wear the necklace I gave you?"

My gaze turned elsewhere. "I had to put it away. Anything that reminded me of you, was too painful to deal with. I'd get distracted by the smallest thought of you, and I figured if I didn't have any physical reminders in sight, I'd be able to get over it all. But it didn't work as well as I had hoped, and I still found myself wondering what you were up to, how you were feeling, or what you'd think in certain situations. It's what got Ryoko and me caught the night you saved us."

Raikidan let go of my hand and reached for my face. My heat tinged my cheeks when he cupped my face and forced me to look at him. "I'm glad the reason you don't wear the necklace isn't because you don't care. I really thought it meant you were only wearing it because you felt obligated to."

I cradled his hand with mine and smiled. "I like the necklace. I didn't want to stop wearing it."

"I heard what you said to me on the battlefield. I don't ever want to lose you, either."

My heart thumped in my chest and my face flushed hotter. *Was that a—don't be stupid, Eira. Of course it wasn't.* I had to look away out of embarrassment, but Raikidan pulled my gaze back.

"I mean it."

I smiled, my cheeks still flushed, and pulled away as I climbed off the bed. His expression grew concerned as he misunderstood my action. I walked over to my dresser and rummaged around in my drawer.

"Did you seriously hide it in your underwear drawer?"

My cheeks heated some more, but for a different reason. "Yeah. I figured no one would go through it. Well, except for you. You're a brat like that."

He chuckled. "You like it."

I shook my head and pulled out the necklace. After putting it back on, I returned to the bed and sat down.

"Swear to me you'll never hide it away again," he said.

"I promise."

He smiled, and then his expression grew serious all of a sudden. "Eira, Corliss said you can breathe fire."

I averted my gaze. I knew this would come up. It was only a matter of time. "I don't want to talk about that, okay?"

"But I do." I let out a small breath and tried to speak, but he continued. "Why didn't you tell me? Why do you hide it?"

"Humans fear what they don't understand—they fear what's different. Firebreathing alienated me. It made me a freak. I taught myself how to hide it, and I refused to use fire until I figured it out. Once I did, the mockery stopped. The whispers and finger pointing stopped. I didn't stick out as much anymore—I didn't feel as alone and alienated."

I closed my eyes for a moment. "There is no other human like me. Del'karo told me it was rare to find others like me, almost impossible. He called it a gift, but it's been nothing but a curse."

"It's not a curse." He reached out to touch my hand, but I pulled away. "Eira…"

His stomach rumbled, and I took that as an escape route. "I'll get you something to eat. You'll need to gain strength."

"Eira, don't avoid this," he begged.

I slid off the bed and left the room. He sighed as I did, and I wished I could get him to understand. It was best this way. Fire breathing was a normal part of his life, of his kind's life. There would be no way he could understand.

I grabbed a wrapped piece of meat out of the fridge and headed back to the room. Had he been human, the choice would have been harder, but since he wasn't, this would be best for him. I sat back down on the bed and unwrapped a part of the meat. Raikidan tried to raise his hand to wait for a section to be ripped off for him, but I pushed his hand away and ripped into the meat.

"Really? Is this you trying to get back at me or something?"

"I seriously doubt you're going to be able to chew this."

"Oh no. You're not feeding me that. I'm eating on my own."

I snorted. "If you can take this from me, then I'll let you."

His eyes narrowed into a disdainful glare. He knew he didn't have that kind of strength. I bit off another chunk and chewed it up. Raikidan placed his fingers on my lips, the motion stopping my chewing.

"I'll only let you do this on one condition." I glared at him, but waited to hear him out. "There's nothing wrong with what you can do. It's not a curse. Just because no one else can do it, doesn't mean it's a curse. It just makes you a little bit different."

I looked away from him. I wasn't going to agree to this. He didn't get it.

"Eira, I'm alive because you can. I didn't think anyone else here could use fire to heal, let alone just breathe it. I took risks knowing that if I was seriously injured, that was it. No amount of shaman healing could save me, I told you that. Only fire could save me—specifically fire produced internally and expelled through the mouth. This type of fire carries traces of the user's soul. This property is what allows a firebreather to heal others, including dragons, even if the fire breather isn't dragon himself. Your supposed curse is my gift."

I swallowed the meat and regarded him. I hadn't thought about why Corliss had told me to give Raikidan fire. I had just done it because I didn't know what else to do. I never thought it could be the only way to save him.

Raikidan rested his hand on mine. "Promise me you won't try to hide it anymore."

My gaze fell to the bed. It wasn't something I could just do. Del'karo had tried to get me to see it as a gift. He tried to get me to not hide what I could do. But I couldn't. I couldn't stop myself from hiding it, and Del'karo eventually stopped trying to encourage me. He wasn't going to make me do something I wasn't willing to do.

"Eira, please promise me."

"I… I can't. I've already tried this once. I can't do it."

He pulled his hand away. "Then I won't accept food from you."

The corners of my eyes tightened. "Raikidan, you need to get better."

"And you need to promise me."

"You don't understand!"

"Eira, I do. You don't understand what you're capable of doing."

"I know exactly what I'm capable of…"

He narrowed his eyes at me. "Don't start twisting my words. You know exactly what I mean. Now promise me."

I wrapped the meat up before placing it on his chest. "I hope you have the energy you think you do."

I went to slide off the bed, but Raikidan grabbed my wrist. "You're not going anywhere."

"You don't have the strength to stop me."

"Eira, look at me." I didn't. "Look at me." The added sternness compelled me to listen. Warmth flooded over me when the strength and intensity of his stare snared me. "Do this. Promise you'll give it another shot. Promise me you won't go out of your way to hide this ability." Could I? "Please."

I exhaled through parted lips. "All right, fine."

Raikidan smiled. "Good."

"But that doesn't mean it'll last." I grabbed the meat and tore into it again. "Now we have a deal."

He grumbled. "Eira, don't make me do this. My mother was the only one to have ever done this for me and I was really young. It's not right for a grown dragon to have to put up with something like this."

"Deal with it. You're the one who wanted to play hero."

"Why don't you find this weird?"

"Because I've had to do it before and I've been on the receiving end a few times."

His brow rose. "You?"

I ripped off another piece of meat. "As hard as it is to believe, I used to be reckless once. It didn't take long for me to change my ways, but it was long enough to put me in unwanted predicaments."

He grunted and held out his hand. "Just hand it over so I don't have to deal with this for much longer."

I ignored his gesture while I continued to chew. When the meat reached the right consistency, I pushed his hand away and leaned over him.

"Eira, what are you—"

I cupped his chin to keep his mouth from closing and leaned close enough to him to pass the meat from my mouth to his. Even though my lips touched his, I didn't pull away until he had all of it. He needed this, and that was all I cared about right now.

I ripped into the chunk of meat again and watched Raikidan as he recovered from his shock and swallowed his food. I had to refrain from laughing when his face contorted, show his disgust. It wasn't going to be tasty, but it would give him the strength he needed to finally eat on his own. When I determined he was ready for more, I repeated the action and continued to feed him until he was full.

Raikidan closed his eyes and I ate the rest of the meat to satisfy my own body's needs. He looked peaceful, sending relief through me. I really thought I'd lost him. I leaned over and pecked him on the cheek. His eyes fluttered open, his brow raised. "Don't play hero again, okay?"

His lips spread into a cocky grin. "Well, if playing hero gets that kind of thank you"—he pointed to his other cheek—"I need to even it out, or I won't be able to fly right."

I jerked my head back and twisted my brow.

He chuckled. "My mother used to say that so I'd keep doing good things."

A smirk appeared on my face. "Well, then I guess you'll have to be good from now on, else this nurse won't be able to discharge you."

His eyes traveled down my body, slower than I would have expected from him; and then back up before settling on holding eye contact. "What'd I do to luck out and get such a perfect nurse?"

I chuckled, though my face turned a shade of red. "Played hero."

"Then I guess I'm playing hero again."

I rolled my eyes and repositioned myself on the bed. I squeaked when he reached out and grabbed me, forcing me to lie on his chest.

My cheeks warmed as he held me there in a firm grip. "R—Rai, what are you doing?"

"Please lay here with me. It makes me feel better."

"Like this?"

His grip tightened briefly. "Yes."

My traitorous heart thumped in my chest. "Okay."

The two of us lay there, each listening to the other breathing, and the activity going on inside and outside the house. One thing I did notice was that the voice in my head had been uncharacteristically quiet through this whole moment. *"Are you mad at me?"*

I didn't expect a response, but I got one, and the answer surprised me. *"I do not know what to make of the situation. I don't trust him, nor should you. You're too happy around him."*

"Why do you hate that I'm happy?"

"I don't. You're just on a path of heartache."

"What do you want from me?"

"To protect you."

A ripple of shock rolled through me. There was something strange about the way it was acting. The malicious tone it typically had wasn't there. Instead, it sounded concerned for me. *"Do you think he'll hurt me?"*

"I think you will hurt yourself if you're not careful. I do not want that."

"Why?"

Silence answered my question. I didn't understand this change in behavior. *What is going on with it?*

Raikidan began stroking my back. I fought the soothing call pulling on me for some time, but in time I gave in. I snuggled into him; eventually falling asleep without a care in Lumaraeon about the position I'd be found in if someone decided to walk in the room unexpectedly.

14
CHAPTER

I watched Raikidan as he slept soundly on the floor. He was doing much better, now that he'd had a few days to recover. Corliss had encouraged me to feed Raikidan more fire to help him recover faster, but Raikidan wasn't so willing to accept the gesture. I had to strike a deal in order to get him to agree so he'd heal enough to be able to shift again and give me my bed back. As accustomed as I became to his presence next to me, or when he wanted to be a pain, under half of me, I'd gotten to the point where I wanted my bed back for myself.

I grabbed the large bowl on my nightstand. There was barely a trace of use, but that was only because Raikidan had insisted on licking up every last drop. In order to get Raikidan to agree to the fire feeding, I had to promise I'd make something just for him when he was well enough to eat on his own. I had made him a stew, and he scarfed that down faster than I could blink and then asked for more. I had been so surprised. No one had ever liked what I made. It was why I only ever cooked for myself.

I sighed and slid off the bed. I needed to put this in the sink and talk to Shva'sika. Last night I had that strange dream again about the man in the fog. He still wouldn't come close enough to me, but he did speak this time. It was only to tell me to leave him alone, but I was still shocked to hear his voice.

I needed to know why I was having these dreams of him, and in the manner I was having them. He was remembering me as much as I was him, and I knew Shva'sika would know more about this dreaming business than me.

Leaving the bowl in the sink, I ventured over to her room and rapped on the door. I waited a few seconds, and when I didn't get a reply, I rapped on the door again. When she didn't answer again, I figured she may be still asleep, so I turned to leave, but stopped when I saw her coming down the hall. She appeared deep in thought.

"Shva'sika, I need to talk to you about something."

She lifted her gaze and blinked. "Oh, good morning, Laz. Sure thing. We can talk in my room." I followed her inside and sat down on the edge of her bed. "What do you need to talk to me about?"

"I need help figuring out a dream."

"You need help? This is a surprise," she teased.

"Shva'sika, this is serious."

"All right, sorry. What is the dream about?"

"It's simple, but because it's so simple, I don't get it. I'm in a dark, thick fog that doesn't get any thicker or thinner as I walk. Then, just as I feel like I'm lost and it's pointless to keep moving, I hear a noise. A figure moves in the fog. He notices me every time and runs away."

"How many times have you had this dream?" She inquired.

"Last night was the third time, but they're not exactly the same. The second time, I managed to get closer to the figure and figure out that it's a man. I tried talking to him, but he let out this inhuman growl and ran off. Last night was the strangest of the two. I managed to get just as close as before, but this time he spoke to me before running off."

"What did he say to you?"

"He told me to leave him alone. It's like he remembers me as well as I remember him, as if we're actually meeting and I'm not dreaming. That's why I wanted to talk to you about it and see if you might know what's going on."

She nodded. "I do. The two of you are meeting. Well, sort of. You're both having this dream and are able to acknowledge each other. You and I had a dream like this, remember? We both had dreams about each other, but because of how skeptical you were of me, your dream never progressed far, while mine did."

"So the dreams can be different?"

"Yes. If you accept these dreams and pursue them, they'll develop. If this mystery man doesn't, he will continue to see the same dream until he does."

"Why am I having these dreams?"

She shook her head. "I can't really say. I do know he's someone you will meet, and it's important that you do, but that's all I have for you. Once the dreams start progressing, though, you'll find why he's so important. Just don't rush it. If you can't gain his trust, you'll never figure this out."

"That's all you can tell me?"

She gazed at me with sympathetic eyes. "I'm sorry, Laz, but there isn't much else I can do. There are some paths only one person can take, and they must be done alone."

I sucked air through my teeth. I knew being frustrated with her wouldn't help, but I couldn't help it. I wanted to know the answers. "Well, thank you. I guess I'll go think on this."

"I am sorry. I wish I could help you more."

"It's fine." I left her room and headed down into the basement. I needed to think, but my current state wouldn't allow for it. I needed to work out my frustration before I could think about anything else.

My abs cried out in pain, but I continued to pull myself up. My legs hurt from the workout I had put them through. My arms hurt. My whole body hurt, but my frustration hadn't dissipated and I was running out of ways to work my body.

I heard footsteps coming down the stairs, but I ignored them. Based on the heaviness of the footfalls, I knew it was Corliss and figured he was here to fetch something, since he rarely came down here alone unless asked.

"Eira, can we talk?"

I let myself hang free from the pull-up bar I was currently using. *Guess I'm wrong.* "Sure, what's up?"

I went back to my workout and he sighed. "Without you doing anything else?"

My brow quirked up, but instead of questioning him, I reached for the key hanging around my wrist. Pulling myself up, I unlocked my ankles and lowered myself to the ground. "All right, now what's on your mind?"

"I'll be straightforward, because I don't like beating around the bush. I know who you are."

My face scrunched in confusion. "What?"

"Correction, I know what you are. I know what you're hiding from everyone."

"Be wary."

I headed for my worktable. "I don't know what you're talking about."

"Phoenix…"

I stared wide-eyed at my worktable, my breath caught in my throat. He didn't even have to speak the whole word to convince me he knew. I took a deep breath and continued to lean on the table. "How long?"

"Excuse me?"

"How long have you known?"

"I had my suspicions when we first met, but I only came to a firm conclusion the other day."

I let out a strained breath. "When we met. What gave me away?"

"It's the way you carry yourself. It's not obvious, but hearing the hushed whispers of stories from other races of this world, it was easier to piece together. Each story I've heard tells a different piece of the same picture. Each one brings a new light of hope."

My fingers curled. "If they knew who—what—I was, that hope would be gone."

"Eira, why—"

"My blood is tainted. I'll never be what everyone had hoped I could be. I'll never live up to that expectation. I can't accomplish what they hoped I could, because someone knew the other side of the stories. Someone knew how to flip it and use it to his advantage."

"Why do you hate things so much, Eira? Why can't you see a light in anything?"

"That's what happens when you're artificially created for the purpose of hurting others…" My hands clenched. "That's what happens when you're abandoned by the one who is the reason you are what you are. Abandoned by the one who gave others false hopes to cling to, and crushes the hopes of those he supposedly cared about."

"You're not talking about Zarda this time." He sighed. "Eira, you can't possibly think your father—"

The coldness of my stare him stopped him in his tracks. My gaze flicked away. "Never once did he come back. Never once did he try. He sent others. He sent them with false messages of how he'd come back and get us out of there. He kept sending them until we told them how fed up we were with the lies."

"That's why you don't tell anyone."

"He is dead to me, as is that side of me."

"Eira, you can't change who you are."

I took a slow breath. "No, but I can ignore it. It doesn't make me any less of what I am, but it makes it easier to go through life."

"Eira, you have my word—I won't tell anyone."

I regarded him with a critical eye. "How do I know I can trust your word?"

"Ebon thought he knew as well. He asked me to tell him if I figured it out." He knelt before me, gazing up. "I won't be telling him. I won't be telling anyone. I am loyal to you. Not Raikidan. Not your friends. Just you."

"Don't trust his words."

I held his gaze for several long minutes. This wasn't easy for me. So few knew, and all of them, human outcasts or halfling themselves. Trusting someone outside that, who I didn't know well and could very well cause me more harm... *I have to.* "I believe you."

"Don't!"

He smiled. "Good. Now what would you like me to do?"

"Go about your normal business and act like this talk didn't happen."

"Sure thing."

I watched him head for the stairs. Just as he started climbing up I stopped him. "Corliss."

"Yeah?"

"Some people in this house are aware of what I am. Some aren't. My question is, does Raikidan know?"

"Not that I'm aware of. I'm pretty good at figuring out what he knows and what he doesn't."

"Why not? Why were you and Ebon able to figure it out and not Raikidan?"

"Ebon and I are good at looking beyond the obvious. Raikidan has never been known to think past what he can see with his own two eyes."

"All right." I turned away. "It stays that way, then."

"Are you sure?"

"I don't want him knowing."

"Why?"

My hand clenched. "I just don't. But you're welcome to tell Ebon, since he figured it out too. That is, if you are sure he can be trusted with that knowledge. I'm giving you the choice—my trust."

"Thank you, Eira. I'll think on your offer and hope you reconsider your position with Raikidan. He can be trusted with this."

"No he can't."

I wish I could agree with you, Corliss. I really wish I could… I sighed when I was alone again. I had hoped none of this would come back to bite me.

15
CHAPTER

A smile crept onto my face. Ryoko had just given me the semi-good news. Twilight was now fixed up, and would be reopening tomorrow night. Even though I didn't like dealing with half of the customers there, it did mean more pay. There was only so much Zane could pay us, and if we didn't get customers, we didn't get paid. I sometimes wished he'd move the shop to a busier location, but he was too stubborn for his own good.

I shifted my attention to the basement door when it creaked open. I half expected to see Seda, since she had disappeared downstairs an hour ago without a word. But to my surprise, a tall, slender woman with long, wavy, forest-green hair and golden eyes appeared. Freckles splashed across her face and shoulders, creating a striking contrast against her light skin. I didn't know the woman's name, but it wasn't hard for me to figure out who she was.

"Who—"

I shushed Ryoko and signaled for to the woman to step back into the shadows of the door. She understood, nodding with a smile before hiding.

"Hey, Corliss, get out here!" I shouted.

The response I got was late, but it was of someone running down the hall. Corliss rushed into the living room. "What's up?"

He blinked and his nose twitched. I stop the grin from slipping up my face. He knew what was up. Before Corliss could react to what his nose told him, the woman giggled and came out from hiding.

Corliss' eyes widened. "Mana…"

She smiled and ran over to him. He embraced her in a tight hug and inhaled her scent thought her long hair. Raikidan, hearing the commotion, poked his head out of my room and became interested in Mana's presence.

"Mana, what are you doing here?" Corliss murmured.

"I was lonely," she said. "I didn't like staying at the lair by myself, so I contacted the psychic you used to contact me. She told me I could come and stay here with all of you."

"You mean Seda?" I asked.

Mana nodded. "Yeah, her."

Seda poked her head out of the basement. "Yes, that's what I was doing. I thought it best to show her the way in."

"Well we didn't need her getting lost," Ryoko agreed.

"Or caught sneaking in," I said.

"Mana, you shouldn't be here," Corliss scolded. "It would have been safer if you had stayed home."

"I'll be fine," she insisted. "And before you use the territory as an excuse, I already ask Enrek to take care of it all. He didn't have a problem with it."

I watched as Corliss' expression dropped to a scowl the moment Mana spoke Enrek's name. I looked at Raikidan, to find his expression had changed to one of concern. *What is the relationship with Enrek that causes such a significant difference in reactions between these two dragons?*

"Corliss, why don't you take her to your room and talk it over there?" I suggested. "This sounds more like a private conversation anyway."

"That's a good idea." He gestured toward the hallway. "Come with me, Mana."

"Okay!"

"Just don't break anything!" Ryoko teased.

I couldn't help but chuckle when Corliss' face tinted a shade of red. When they left, Raikidan went back into the bedroom, and I chose to follow. I needed to let him know about the club.

I shut the door behind me and he focused on me. "Need something?"

"I wanted to let you know the club is back up and running and we'll be working tomorrow." His lip curled as he grumbled to himself. I chuckled. "You were hoping it wouldn't be fixed."

"I don't like it there."

"Job pays well."

"Other places could pay better."

"But other places check for false identification cards, and the best paying places have better identifiers than the military posts. We can't work anywhere else."

He crossed his arms. "I don't want you waitressing anymore."

"Raikidan, I don't like to, either, but I have to do whatever job is open. Sometimes we have to do things we'd rather not."

"I'll talk to Azriel, then."

I chuckled. "You're not going to change his mind."

"We'll see about that."

I shook my head and decided to change the subject. "Mind answering something for me?"

"Depends."

"So, who is Enrek?"

"Corliss' brother."

"What is so wrong with him watching the territories?"

He rubbed the back of his neck. "Enrek is infatuated with Mana. Because of it, it's caused a rift between Corliss and Enrek. Corliss doesn't like it when Mana asks him for favors, because he's all too eager to say yes in hopes Mana will leave Corliss for him. Of course she's too dumb to notice."

"That's not nice," I scolded. She didn't come across as the type that deserved that kind of remark.

"She's the equivalent to the blondes you guys crack jokes about from time to time."

Oh… "Lovely. But that doesn't mean you should be mean to her."

"Trust me, it would have been better if she just stayed away," he said.

"You don't like her."

He crossed his arms. "I have my reasons not to."

I touched his shoulder. "Talk to me about it."

He tried to avoid eye contact, but eventually sighed and lowered his guard. "She's the reason Corliss and I don't get along like we used to."

"What happened?"

"He forgot about me." He sat down on the windowsill and I sat next to him. "He used to tell me family stuck together, and because we were family, we'd stick together and watch each other's backs no matter what. It only took one day for that all to change. It took the day she came into the picture for him to up and leave."

I lifted myself up onto the outer part of the sill and wrapped my arms around him to give him a hug around the neck. "And here I thought you'd say something that would make me think you were jealous."

He grunted. "Yeah, right."

I remembered the dream I had of when he first found out about the two of them. The despair he experienced made me unable to fully believe him. He believed he was alone and it wasn't fair to him that Corliss had someone. *But he's also afraid of who the gods have him paired to.*

Raikidan finally accepted my gesture and rested his head against mine. "Thank you for listening. It's nice to be able to have someone listen without having to give me advice about it."

Or just understands? I tightened my grip and then loosened it. "You don't need to thank me."

"I'm going to anyway."

I chuckled and gazed at the sky, the setting sun's colors blanketing the vastness in oranges and reds. I had to remember to finish Ryoko's birthday present. It was coming up fast, and the gift was taking longer to finish than I had anticipated. I also needed to get a good night's sleep to prepare for tomorrow's shift. The gods knew I needed it.

Amusement shone in her lavender eyes as she watched me inspect an empty vial. The open window nearby allowed a soft breeze to fill the lab room, blowing her long black hair with a single blue streak, and filling the room with a fresh scent of the spring weather outside, a welcome relief to the sterile-smelling environment the lab produced. As long as I was careful, I was allowed to look at anything she had laid out in this room.

I put the vial down when it no longer held my attention, and surveyed a strange string of symbols scribbled on a white board. "Jasmine, what is this?"

She stood next to me. "A formula I'm working on. I'm trying to understand how racial longevity works, to see if we can extend our race's lives. There are many races out there that live longer naturally, but it's still a mystery on how and why that is."

"We live a long time as it is," I said. "Why do we need to live longer?"

"Because most are afraid of death."

I nodded, trying to make sense of her formula, and process how she was treating me. Talking was still a new experience for me, after all these years of being unable to. Most didn't act like it was normal, but Jasmine, like a few others, took it in stride and acted as if I had been capable of speaking my whole life.

Jasmine looked at me, her eyes partially obstructed by her glasses. "I love you, my wonderful niece. Never doubt that."

I opened my mouth to say something back, but I never got the chance. The room around us darkened, the room changing to a long hallway, and she collapsed on the ground, an ear-splitting bang echoing through the hall, drowning out her scream of pain. The smell of blood wafted into my nose. Instinctively, I reached for her as she gazed up at me with pained eyes, but female hands grabbed my arms and yanked me back. My eyes snapped to the brown-haired, golden-eyed woman pulling me away from Jasmine.

"We have to go!" Ryoko shouted.

"But Jasmine—"

"Go!" Jasmine urged. "Just go. Don't look back."

I tried to reach for her again, but she struggled to her feet. "Go. I'll be right behind you."

I didn't believe her. I knew that sound—and why there was blood. Ryoko yanked on me again and this time I followed, but I made sure to grab onto Jasmine's lab coat. She stumbled and struggled to follow, her free arm holding her side. I cracked my neck over my shoulder when she slipped from my grip and lagged behind, but Ryoko refused to let me go.

Another gunshot rang through the hall, and my eyes widened in terror as Jasmine choked and then fell to the ground, unmoving, blood pooling out all around her.

"Jasmine! Jasmine, no!" Ryoko continued to pull me down the hall, now more forceful so I wouldn't run back. "Jasmine!"

My eyes snapped open and I bolted upright in bed. My breath came quick and cold sweat dripped down my skin. Raikidan lifted his large dragon head to look at me and then immediately shifted to his nu-human form. He rushed over and knelt on my bed. "Eira, are you all right?"

I took a deep breath and nodded, trying to get the horrific image of Jasmine's death out of my mind. "I'm fine. Go back to bed."

"Please don't lie to me."

"I'm going to be fine, Raikidan. I just… need to calm down. Go back to bed."

He didn't listen. I tried to force him away when he reached out to hug me, but he pushed against my strength and won our brief battle of strength and wills. An uncomfortable warmth and awkwardness crawled through my body as he held me close.

"Raikidan, this is awkward…"

"No, it's not."

I exhaled an irritated breath. "Yes it is. Please stop."

"With the way you woke up, you had another nightmare, didn't you?" he asked, ignoring my plea.

"Yeah. It happens."

"They weren't happening before you sent me away. At least, not so bad they woke you up."

"They came back when you were gone."

"That's not good."

I shrugged. "It's how it is. My dreams are my memories, and my life is one giant nightmare…"

Raikidan's grip tightened, but he said nothing—not that there was anything to say. I spoke the truth. How could it not be, with one look at my history?

"I will help make it better," Raikidan finally said. "One day at a time. I promise you."

Warmth flooded over me. "You don't have to waste your time trying."

He reached up and pulled my ear. "Don't say that. You're not a waste of time."

Before I could formulate a counter argument, Raikidan began leaning, and then the two of us fell back on my bed, him still holding me close. His presence engulfed me, sending my pulse racing. "R–Raikidan, what are you doing? This isn't very appropriate."

"I don't care," he said, his grip tightening.

My heart thumped hard in my chest. "But—" He hushed me and I sighed. "You don't have to baby me."

He stroked my head. "I'm not. I'm being here for you, even if you don't want me to be. You can tell me anything. You can trust me."

I chewed on my lip. I wanted to be able to trust someone—to rely on them more than to watch my back when I needed it. Raikidan could watch my back, better than anyone I'd ever come across, but I still wasn't sure he was that someone I could trust beyond that. Everything I'd witnessed—the betrayal I'd felt—the people I'd lost—pain pulsed in my chest.

"The dream started out nice," I whispered. "A memory of when I spent time with Jasmine in her small personal lab where she tested genetics on a small scale, and worked on several formulas. She was so smart, it fascinated me how she was able to make heads or tails of the formulas that were gibberish to me."

Raikidan continued to stoke my head.

"Then… it changed… to how she died…" I swallowed a lump that formed in my throat. "It's my fault she's dead. She wanted to get me out, and…" My hands clenched his shirt and I buried my face into his chest. "It's my fault."

Raikidan hushed me. "No it's not. She made her choices, knowing the risk. She risked it all because she cared more about you than her own life."

"She gave up her future—"

"You were her future."

"She was my aunt, not my mother."

"Doesn't matter. I see how Zane looks at you. How he treats you. He's your uncle, but also sees you as the daughter he doesn't have. You're his future, and I will bet my whole hoard Jasmine was the same way."

I tried to look at him. He'd bet his hoard on a woman he didn't know anything about? "How can you be so sure?"

Raikidan's grip tightened, burying me in his embrace. "Because you only surround yourself with those who care deeply for you, just as you do for them."

"You're here. And you hate me."

"No I don't," he growled. "I was upset—hurt from what you did. But I don't hate you. I care about you, Eira. Don't you ever think otherwise."

"Don't trust his words."

My heart thumped hard and I blurted out words without thinking, "I care about you, too."

"I know. That's why you said you didn't want to lose me." *That's right, he did hear me say that...* "And you know my answer, too. I didn't lie. I promise you."

I inhaled, taking in his strong scent. "Thank you."

He stroked my head some more. "Go to sleep. I'll be here if you need me."

"You going to let me go so I can sleep?"

"No, you can sleep like this."

"Don't let him trick you into staying like this. Move away from him."

I chewed on my lip and contemplated the pros and cons of this. More cons came up, but I said, "All right." *Why am I being so stupid? I know better.*

"You're not thinking! You need to protect yourself."

Raikidan continued to stroke my head, soothing me. My eyes grew heavy, and soon I was lulled into a deep sleep.

CHAPTER 16

The glass gleamed as I held it up to the light. I wanted to make sure it was completely clean before I put it away. Azriel was a bit of a neat freak when it came to the glassware, and it had rubbed off on me. When I determined it couldn't get any cleaner, I placed it in the row of matching glasses I'd already cleaned, and picked up a dirty one.

As I scrubbed the bar's surface, I scanned the club. I thought I'd never see a lull like this tonight. The moment the front doors had opened for the first time since this place was rebuilt, it had been absolute mayhem. We had large parties taking up most of the seating, citizens and soldiers alike who'd gotten drunk too quickly and got themselves thrown out, staff quitting during arguments with Azriel, and stock issues. Apparently, some of the most recent shipments we received earlier in the day had gone missing. Lucky for Azriel, we had a few staff members who were able to work some "magic" and get new stock after hours.

I held the glass up to the light and watched it sparkle. I liked looking at clean glasses—they were pretty. As I went to put it away with the others, the glass shattered, along with many of the other clean glasses and bottles of liquor, and I couldn't help but let out a surprised yelp. The club grew quiet as I stared at the mess around me, and then at my hand when I smelled something sweet, to find blood oozing from several cuts. *What the hell?*

When I heard someone laughing, I honed in on the source. *Amon and Sedo...* The two men who had jumped me in the alley that one day over the summer were laughing up a storm, clearly drunk, and one of them had a gun.

"Looks like I missed," he slurred.

My eyes widened and my body locked up. I couldn't get myself to move at all. *What is wrong with me? Move, Eira!* But before he managed to pull the trigger again, another gun went off and the glasses on their table shattered. The two men's reactions were sluggish, but they did jump from fright. I turned to see Azriel advancing toward the drunk soldiers, a pistol in his hand. *The hell? Does he carry that thing around with him?* Before I knew it, Rylan and a few other bouncers rushed over and pinned the two men to the table.

"Get these two out of here, now," Azriel ordered. "Keep them outside until their commanding officer comes to retrieve them. Before I decide to kill them."

"Order them to be killed for their treachery!"

"Eira, are you okay?"

I nearly jumped out of my skin and spun around to see Raikidan standing behind me. "You know not to sneak up on me like that!"

"I wasn't sneaking. I even ran into a chair when I rushed over here," he defended.

"Where were you anyway?" I asked, trying to hide my embarrassment for not being aware.

"Taking an early break. Now answer my ques—" He honed in on my bleeding hand. "Let me see."

I held my hand close and out of his reach. "Don't worry. It's nothing."

"Eira, let me see."

"Don't let him."

I began picking out the small shards of glass stuck in my skin. "I got it. You should see if the guys need help getting those two under control."

"No, let me see your hand."

"Seriously, I got this. It's nothing I can't handle."

He crossed his arms and watched me search for small shards I wouldn't have noticed on my first pick through. I stopped searching when I couldn't find anymore, even though it felt like missed one, and looked at Azriel when he jumped over the bar and took in the mess around me. "Sorry, Az, I'll clean it up."

He shook his head. "Why are you apologizing? You didn't do this."

"I know, but still…"

His gaze flicked to my hand. "I'll get you a med kit. We'll get you cleaned up before we work on this mess."

"Az, don't. I can—" My eyes snapped to Raikidan when he grabbed my hand. He handled me with care, but his intense inspection made me feel weird. "Raikidan, what are you doing?"

"Be careful. He's acting strange."

Azriel chuckled. "Maybe I'll get a mop as well. Save me a trip."

"Azriel, I can do—" My focus snapped onto Raikidan again when he slipped my index finger into his mouth. A flush ran through my face and burned my ears. *What is he doing?*

"And maybe a broom, too."

I didn't react to Azriel's comment or say anything when he left—I was too preoccupied with trying to think, let alone figure out what Raikidan was doing. I cringed when pain shot through my hand and arm. Raikidan removed my finger from his mouth and applied pressure to slow the bleeding. With his free hand, he reached up and pulled something small from his mouth. "This was still in there."

Interested, I leaned in. He had found the small glass shard, the one I could still feel but couldn't locate. I took the shard from him to inspect further, distracting me from another check he chose to do.

"He's strange all right, but I don't disapprove of him helping you. I still don't know how to feel about him, though. Continue to watch yourself around him."

I looked away from the shard when I heard someone coming up behind me. I turned and laughed at Azriel as he made the attempt to make this a one-trip deal. "Az, I told you I could have gotten that."

"No need, I got it," he replied as he placed the first aid kit down on the bar. "I see you two got that small shard out of your finger. Well, I supposed Raikidan gets the credit since you figured you were all set."

"How did you—"

"Eira, you know not to ask how I know these things. It's not easy to explain."

"Fine. Once Doctor Rai here gives me the okay, I'll wrap up my hand so I can help you."

Azriel laughed and Raikidan grunted. Raikidan let me go, allowing me to open the medical kit. I pulled out the supplies and Raikidan insisted on helping me patch myself up. Before we finished, someone rushed over to the bar. I glanced up, only to regret it.

Zo gazed at the chaotic vision of the bar and then at me. "Is this the mess they caused?"

"No, wogrons came in and shot at Eira." Azriel threw the broom down on the ground and I flinched. "Of course this is what they did, Zo, and I'm fed up dealing with this!"

I stepped away from Azriel. He didn't get angry often, but when he did, I never liked it.

"Azriel, please calm down," Zo said. "Eira, are you all right?"

"I'm fine," I muttered as I finished with my hand.

"Look, I'll make sure this doesn't happen again," Zo promised.

"You'd better," Raikidan threatened. "This isn't the first time they've pointed a gun at her."

"Rai!" I shrieked.

Zo narrowed his eyes. "What are you talking about, kid?"

I grabbed Raikidan's arm. "You promised you wouldn't tell!"

"Eira, what are you trying to hide?" Azriel asked.

"Those two jumped her while she was on her break one night," Raikidan told them. "I walked in on the situation when I was using the alley to get to the employee entrance, and my presence caused the situation to escalate. That's when they pulled a gun."

Azriel fixed hard eyes on me. "Why didn't you tell me about this?"

I crossed my arms. "Some soldiers were walking by and noticed the commotion, and took the two away."

"That doesn't tell me why you didn't tell me what happened, or why you made Ray promise not to say anything."

I worked my jaw. "Because I didn't want to cause any problems. Out of sight, out of mind."

"Had you said something, I wouldn't have allowed them step foot in here."

"He should have told sooner; as should have you. They deserve to pay with their lives!"

"I'll deal with them," Zo promised me. "Behavior like that isn't tolerated. You have my word—they'll be dealt with."

"Good, now get out of my club," Azriel said. "And take the rest of the soldiers with you."

"Excuse me?"

"As I said before, I'm done dealing with the bullshit all of you cause! I've never seen such unruly soldiers until this last generation of them, and they're starting to affect the older generations as well. Civilians come here to enjoy life. They don't cause any problems. They act normally, and my staff likes that. You and your soldiers come here to try to enjoy life, but cause problems as well. My staff quits on me left and right because of it, and I can't keep replacing them. I'm lucky to have any staff at all!"

"Azriel, calm down. We can talk about this," Zo tried to urge.

"Get the hell out of my club! I'll tell you in a week whether I've changed my mind."

I stared at Azriel in amazement. I couldn't believe my ears. He always told us he couldn't ban the soldiers because of the cuts to income. *I guess he's too angry to care this time.*

Zo huffed and then left, calling out to any soldier in the building. Azriel picked up the broom and began sweeping up the glass again. "Raikidan, take her home to rest. I don't need her going into shock."

"Az, I'm fine," I insisted.

"You're going home," he said in a no-nonsense tone.

"Can I at least help clean up?" I asked.

"No. Now go home." I sighed and he placed his hand on my head. "It's the punishment you were asking for."

I smiled. "I know. You're way too good to me."

"You were way too good to me in the past, so I guess this makes up for it."

"I guess so." Raikidan touched my shoulder to get me moving. "Sorry about the mess."

"Stop apologizing about the mess. Oh, and, Raikidan, it's your choice whether you come back or not."

"Then you won't see me come back," Raikidan replied.

"I figured as much."

"C'mon, Eira," Raikidan urged. "Let's get you home to rest."

I let out a tight breath. "Will you stop treating me like a child, please?"

"I'm not treating you like a child. I'm making sure you're going to be okay."

"It's just a small hand injury. You act like I was hit on the head or hit by a car."

"Stop complaining and get moving."

"Don't let him push you around like you're weak."

I exhaled hard and followed him into the back to get our things. At least I could go home and do something else, like finish Ryoko's gift. Her birthday was just around the corner and I was falling behind. Or I could sleep. Today had been stressful, after all…

The low light of the fire gleamed off my armor as I sat in the shadows of the trees. The other assassins did the same, but I stayed away from them. I didn't want to be near anyone. I watched the medic moving around and checking on everyone and it made me uneasy. I didn't want this medic to know about the injury I had, I didn't know him. "Last minute" and "one-time deal." Those were my mother's words, but I didn't trust it. Tannek, our main medic, was the only one I trusted to do that job. He knew not to push if I said no—other medics weren't so smart. But he wasn't here and this new one was.

I watched as the medic checked with the other assassins and then made his way over to me. His approach allowed me to take in more details. In doing so, I thought for a moment I'd been wrong about who he was. He looks a lot like Tannek.

I spoke before he could kneel down and start asking questions. "I'm fine."

The man chuckled and knelt to rummage through his medical bag. "My name is Azriel."

That certainly confirmed he wasn't Tannek, if his stupidity hadn't. "And you must be deaf, because I just told you to not bother me."

The smile on Azriel's face faded. "Look, I'm not stupid. I know you're injured. If you show me where, I'll fix you up and get out of your hair."

"And you are *stupid, because you don't get it. I don't want your help."*

I went to get up so I could get away from him, but he grabbed onto my wrist and yanked me back down. "Listen here. I know you don't want me here and that's fine. I don't care. But it's my job to see everyone tended to, whether they like it or not, and that's what I'm going to do. Now you can show me where you're injured and I can get this over with rather quickly, or I can make this very unpleasant. Your choice."

I stared at him and I knew others were, too. He had guts. I liked that.

I grinned. "You're a recent tank release, aren't you?"

Azriel frowned. "Is it that obvious?"

I chuckled. "Not many who have been around long have the balls to tell me what to do." I glanced over at one of the psychics, Telar. A tall, athletically built man with bronze skin and short black hair, he was only one of two psychics I trusted. He nodded ever so slightly. "Now let's get this over with."

Azriel smiled. "All right, then."

I removed my pauldrons and then my belt, allowing me to remove my breastplate. As I did, I revealed the sliced cloth designed to hide the weakness in the armor's design. I placed the breastplate down and winced in pain. Azriel shook his head the moment he got a good look at the blood-stained bandage I had wrapped around my torso. "You wouldn't happen to be the one who stole some of my pain relief serum, would you?"

I chuckled and averted his eye contact. "Guilty as charged."

I half expected him to be mad, but he surprised me by laughing. "You know, you had me second-guessing my counting ability. Now let's get this used bandage off of you and get you cleaned up." My hand flew up and stopped him from touching the bandages and he sighed. "I know what you're thinking, and I can assure you, you have nothing to worry about. Honest."

I held his gaze, until something clicked in my mind. Something deep in those dark eyes of his told me I didn't have to be so cautious with him. I wasn't sure what it was, but it felt familiar. It was strange. I needed time to build up trust, too many had broken it for me to hand it out so easily, but I could already tell, this man deserved it sooner.

I let his hands slip out of mine. "No funny business."

He chuckled and ripped my bandaging job apart. I watched as he shook his head at the sight of my injury. "Yeah, you're completely fine."

"Are you going keep mocking me, or fix it up?"

"I'm not mocking you. I just don't see how you believed you could only bandage this wound up. I'm going to have to stitch you. It's the only way this will heal well."

"You obviously haven't noticed my other scars."

He rummaged through his bag. "I have. You have a big issue with help, don't you?"

"I do better on my own."

He pulled out a small black container. "You may think that, but that may not be entirely true."

I watched him clean up the blood the best he could, then he applied the cream from the container. He put the container away when he finished, and pulled out a curved needle and thick thread. I took a few steadying breaths as he tied the two together and prepared to stitch me back up. The pain wouldn't be unbearable, thanks to the numbing cream he applied, but it wouldn't be painless, either.

"How long have you been out of your tank?" The answer interested me, and it would distract me from his task.

"Nine months."

"What company are you a part of?"

He didn't reply right away. "I'm not, ma'am."

I blinked. "You're not a part of any company yet?"

He shook his head. "You've never seen a medic assigned, have you?"

"Tannek is the main medic of our squad, and one of seven in our company. All were here prior to me joining."

He nodded. "Well here's how it goes, then. Medics are divided into teams differently than soldiers. There is no predestined squad or test to place us. We are trained for three months, and generals hand pick us to join their companies. But not all of us are chosen and placed. If we're not picked, we become floaters for any team that needs a last minute replacement or extra help on a temporary basis. That's what I am. I get moved around until someone chooses me, and it's why I'm here. Tannek went with your general and a patrol of foot soldiers from your company, and I was assigned to take care of the rest of you."

"Why are you a floater?"

He shrugged. "I'm new. The more experienced floaters are selected first. Generals don't want to look at the test results. Just the field experience results."

"You scored high then, during testing?"

"The highest ever recorded."

"Then the generals were dumb to overlook you."

He eyed me. "Are you sure?"

"Telar is masking us. Only he can hear what I'm about to tell you, and neither of you will tell another soul. I don't do needles. It's the reason why I have so many nasty-looking scars. Tannek couldn't convince me, even once, to put up with them long enough to get me stitched back up completely, or even try the healing serum guns." I glanced down at the stitched-up wound. "But you've made it so it didn't bother me. You've done your job better than any other medic, even the ones with decades of field experience."

Azriel stared at me for a few moments before smiling. "Thank you. Now let's get you wrapped up so I can get out of your hair."

I was patient with him as he grabbed a clean round of bandages and wrapped me. I watched at how careful he was, and how strangely he was acting. With the wound in the location it was, I would have had to worry about any other man, even Tannek, taking quick glances, but Azriel's eyes never faltered. I wonder...

He pulled away when he finished, and started putting his supplies away. "You're all set. Let Tannek know about the stitches. He'll be able to keep an eye on them and cut them once the wound is healed. Don't do anything that would rip them, though. It won't be too pretty."

"Well, with my line of work, I can't promise anything."

He chuckled and rose to his feet. "Very well. Thank you for putting up with me, uh—"

"Eira. Commander Eira."

The shock that ran through his eyes didn't escape my gaze. "Well, ma'am, thank you again for putting up with me."

I chuckled as I watched him go. He didn't seem like a bad guy, but there was definitely something different about him. My gaze stopped following him when I heard approaching footsteps. My ears told me they were friendly, so there was no reason to go on alert. Instead, I went about putting my armor back on.

Just as I finished, Amara, my mother, and the patrol came into camp. She gave a quick appraisal of our group before making a beeline over to me. Ryoko and Rylan started to follow her, but decided to grab some food instead. Tannek greeted Azriel and then looked at me and smiled. My mouth twitched, as if attempting to smile back, but the moment I noticed the action, I stopped it and focused my attention on my mother.

"Looks like the new medic is still alive," she said, a teasing smirk on her lips.

"He didn't do anything stupid."

She snickered. "Well that's a good thing. No problems on your end of the mission?"

"Minor. We accomplished our goal with no casualties or major injuries."

"What about you?"

"What about me?"

"Did you get hurt, dear?"

"Nothing Azriel wasn't capable of handling."

"You remembered his name—and you let him tend to you. He must have made a good impression on you."

I crossed my arms. "You told me to give him a chance. I didn't want you yelling at me."

She looked at me as if she didn't believe me, but she didn't press. "I'm glad you've chosen to listen to me for once. Now go sit with Ryoko and Rylan. I know you want to. We'll talk about the assignment after."

"Thank you, Mother."

"And keep an eye on Tannek. If he gets word you were hurt, you know he's going to insist on making sure Azriel did a good job of fixing you up."

I chuckled. "Thanks for the reminder. Don't forget to eat."

"I won't."

I left her side, even though I knew I shouldn't have. I suspected she wasn't going to eat again, and I knew why. I sighed mentally. I didn't get it. I didn't understand what was so great about having those feelings.

Tannek smiled at me again when I passed him, and my lips twitched again in response. I didn't get them at all.

CHAPTER 17

Raikidan offered the bowl in his hand to me and I took it, finding quite a bit of stew remaining. *He wants to share.* He had brought me a rabbit several days ago and asked if it would be enough for me to make something with. When I had told him I'd need at least one more, he left and came back with two more. Since then, he would bring me different meats so that I would make him something.

No matter how much I tried to figure it out, I couldn't understand why he liked what I was making so much. He was the only one.

To top it off, he started to insist I share it with him, and even eating from the same bowl. At first I had been hesitant because of what happened the last time I had shared food with him, but what happened then didn't end up repeating. He didn't react much at all, except becoming happier when I accepted the offer. Now it was normal for us to share. *If he's not going to get confused by it, then I'm not going to cause any issues between us by saying no.* Though that didn't mean I wasn't going to keep a close eye on him, just in case.

I stopped eating when someone knocked on the door. "Come in."

The door opened and Seda poked her head in. "Ryoko will be home soon—make sure you have her gift ready."

I nodded and swallowed the food in my mouth. "Already in a box."

"Wrapped up?"

"I don't do wrapping."

"Does it at least have a bow?"

"Made of string."

She chuckled and shook her head. "Well it'll make the gift deceiving, that's for sure. You know how she likes to think the package determines the worth of the gift."

I grinned. "You know that's why I'm doing this."

"You couldn't be nice to her even on her birthday?"

"It wouldn't be me if I was."

She chuckled again. "All right, make sure you're ready. She actually thinks everyone forgot, so this should be interesting."

"She always thinks people forget—every year."

"This is true."

"Don't worry. I'll be ready when she gets here."

"All right." She left and I handed the bowl back to Raikidan for him to finish the rest of the stew.

"What were you two talking about?" Raikidan asked.

"It's Ryoko's birthday," I said.

"Yeah, I knew that. But what are you two talking about with this whole gift business?"

"It's usually customary to give gifts during certain times of the year. Birthdays are one of them."

"You didn't get any gifts on your birthday."

"It's not a requirement to give them, and since I don't like getting gifts, no one gets them for me."

"Why don't you like gifts?"

I shrugged. "Because I don't."

"But it's free."

"Raikidan, I don't like them. End of story." I didn't need him knowing gifts made me uncomfortable. It meant I was the object of someone's attention, even for a moment, and I wasn't used to that.

"All right." He went back to finishing his food.

I slipped off the bed and onto the floor to grab the box that concealed Ryoko's gift. I checked the wrapping paper for tears, and then the green ribbon I had put on it to make sure it wasn't going to slip off and placed it on the bed. I looked up when someone came through my window, to find Mana smelling the air. "What's up, Mana?"

She ventured into the room some more. "I smelled something delicious and I'm trying to find it."

I chuckled. "So you came here?"

"The smell is coming from this room. I know it."

Corliss appeared in the window and he let out an exasperated exhale when he spotted her. "Mana, I told you to stop searching. You can't go into other's rooms like this."

Her lip stuck out into a pout. "But I want to find the source of that smell."

Raikidan chuckled. "She's smelling my food."

Mana blinked. "Is that what it is? It smells delicious!"

He held up the bowl, teasing her. "It is."

Corliss glared at him and the two began speaking in their tongue. My knowledge in their tongue was still poor, making any attempt to understand too difficult, so I decided to put away some clothes before Ryoko came home.

I sensed Mana watching me as I grabbed some clothes from my basket and carried them into the closet to put them away. *She really is as strange as Raikidan said she would be, if not more.* She was quite childish, and crazy enough, the most naïve individual I'd ever met.

"Eira, Raikidan won't share his food. Would you make me some?" she finally asked.

I stopped and stared at her dumbly. "What?"

"Mana, leave her be," Corliss warned.

"But I want to know what it tastes like," she whined.

I sighed. "Look. It's not going to be as good as you think it will be. Raikidan is the first to ever like what I've made." I glowered at Raikidan. "And it was supposed to be a one-time deal."

"You haven't exactly protested," he shot back before taking another bite of his stew.

"You gave me enough to feed two people and I wasn't going to waste anything."

"Still doesn't explain why you made the food in the first place."

"Like I said, I didn't want to waste the meat."

"You could have preserved it."

"And you would have cried about it like a little baby." I noticed Corliss watching us. "What's your problem?"

He shook his head. "I'm just listening."

I snorted and went to grab the last bit of my clothes, but Mana grabbed my arm. "Please?"

I blew out a breath and turned my gaze to Raikidan. "Can't you share some with her? She is family, after all."

Corliss folded his arms. "At least I'm not the only one trying to convince you."

That must have been what they were just talking about—or at least some of the conversation.

"It's my food," Raikidan said.

"Eira's scent is on the bowl, too, though," Mana muttered. "You shared with her."

Corliss' brow creased and he spoke to Raikidan in their native tongue again. Due to his reaction, I wanted to know what they were saying, so I made an attempt this time to decipher the words, but I only managed to understand some basic ones. I did know, as they spoke, that Mana was becoming unhappier by the second, as if she was coming up in the conversion—and not in a good way.

I suspected it was because Raikidan didn't like her very much, and she wasn't oblivious to the fact. It made me also wonder if his perception of Mana was the reason he wasn't interested in finding his mate. Did he assume all females were like her? Corliss and I had spoken a few days ago, when my curiosity about Mana's behavior got the better of me. He told me that as a young female dragon, she still had a higher curiosity level than an older female, but he also suspected that side of her wouldn't change too much as she aged. I could tell by the way he talked about her, he genuinely cared for her and embraced her traits, no matter how undesirable some others may find them. Why couldn't everyone be like that?

Raikidan sighed and held out the bowl to Mana. "Here."

She giggled and clapped before taking the bowl. She took a large bite and her eyes sparkled. I stared at her, my jaw slack, when she took another bite and then offered it to Corliss. "You have to try it. It's so good!"

Corliss took the bowl from her but didn't take a bite right off, as if waiting for Raikidan to protest. After waiting a few seconds, he finally took a bite. His brow furrowed and I began to relax. *Raikidan and Mana are just w—*

"This is good."

Or not. I crossed my arms and watched the three of them. Mana stole another bite before Raikidan took his bowl back and went back to eating his precious meal. Why did they like it so much?

"Eira, would you make enough for us too sometime?" Mana asked, her eyes pleading.

I shook my head and held up a hand. "Hold on, slow down. I'm still trying to wrap my head around the fact that you all like it."

Mana cocked her head. "Why wouldn't we? It's good."

"Because no one likes what I make. Everyone else thinks I'm a terrible cook. And now you three think it's the best thing since learning to fly."

Corliss chuckled. "I know of a few things that are a bit better, but this is right after them."

I shook my head again. "Okay. If I have enough ingredients, I'll make enough for the three needy dragons in this house."

Mana clapped her hands together. "Yay, thank you!"

A light rap sounded on my door, and then Seda poked her head in. "Ryoko is almost here."

"Okay, I'll be right out," I said.

She nodded and then disappeared. I abandoned my clothes basket and grabbed the box off my bed before making my way into the living room. Not wanting her to see the gift right off when she got home, I sat down on a barstool inside the kitchen and rested the box on my lap, where it'd stay hidden. Raikidan followed me and took up the stool next to me to finish his meal. I noticed him glancing down at the box, and I knew he was curious. No one knew what was in this—I'd made sure of it. And with Raikidan's lack of knowledge about birthdays, it only made his curiosity grow—not that this would be the last birthday he'd encounter.

Rylan's was next, and it wasn't too far away either, and although, like me, he didn't make a big deal over it, his couldn't be avoided since it was on the Winter Solstice.

My attention shifted from Raikidan to the front door when I heard someone touch the doorknob. They slammed the door behind them and stormed up the stairs, and from the heaviness of the feet, I knew it was Ryoko. She came into the living room, fuming as she headed for her room. I didn't speak to her until she passed me.

"Hey, birthday girl." I placed the gift on the counter and pushed it forward as she turned around. "Don't be grumpy."

Her eyes lit up. "You didn't forget!"

I chuckled. "Of course n—wait, don't shake it!"

Ryoko stopped mid-movement and then slowly brought the box back down. "You know I like to shake my gifts, especially if the package is this big."

"But it'll break."

"Oh—well, I don't want it broken, so I guess I'll make an exception."

She sat down on the couch and tore into the wrapping paper. Our other housemates made it into the room the moment she opened the box. Ryoko's eyes lit up in awe as she pulled out the jewelry box I had made her. The gift box clattered on the floor as she held the jewelry box in her hands and looked it over.

I designed it to look like an elegant miniature dresser made from red oak with white oak accents. Carved into the white oak were trees and other foliage, while the red oak had small wolves and some of her favorite animals carved into it. Ryoko smiled as she opened the top lid with hidden mirror underneath, and the front pull-out drawers revealing various differently-sized pockets for different types of jewelry, and then giggled when she discovered the hidden side wings. She had fun opening and closing them a few times.

When she finished playing, she ran her fingers over the carvings and then focused on me. "Thank you. This is the best gift I've ever gotten."

Not for long. I smiled in response. I was glad she liked it. Getting all the moving parts working right had not been an easy task.

Rylan sat down next to her and held out a tiny box. "Now here's my gift."

Ryoko took the small box and scrunched her nose. *Oh, Ryoko, so little you know.* After opening my gift, she'd have a hard time not seeing this box as something last minute, but looks were quite... deceiving. Ryoko shook the box, and then shook it again when it didn't make a sound. "This had better not be empty, or I'm going to kill you."

Rylan chuckled. "Just open it."

She shook it one last time before tearing apart the small bit of wrapping paper. Ryoko stared at the plain box curiously and then opened it as if she were expecting some practical joke to pop out at her. The box almost fell to the ground when she saw the pair of earrings inside.

Zane let out a low whistle. "Those look expensive."

Rylan leaned back on the couch. "Well?"

Ryoko, full of excitement, ripped her current earrings out of her ear and replaced them with the new ones. Seda levitated a small mirror over to her so she could take a look. Ryoko squealed and attacked Rylan with a tight hug around the neck. "Thank you! They're amazing."

"You're welcome," he wheezed with a small chuckle.

Ryoko let go immediately, realizing she was hugging him too tight. "Sorry."

"It's okay."

She turned her head toward me. "Sorry, Laz, but I'm going to have to bump your gift down to the second best gift ever."

I chuckled. "I anticipated that would happen. Don't worry about it."

Raid handed Ryoko a well-wrapped box. "Let's see how mine stacks up."

Ryoko smiled and took the thin box and shook it. Something rattled inside and her excitement got the better of her. She ripped the wrapping paper and yanked the top off the box. She gasped and pulled out an elegant diamond and sapphire necklace. "Raid…" She looked at him. "Please tell me you did not—"

"Cubic zirconia," he said. "I didn't want you to murder me for spending a lot."

She smiled wide. "Thank you! It's beautiful." She gazed at her three gifts. "Looks like this year is a jewelry-themed year."

Rylan glared at his brother while Ryoko was distracted. I tried my best not to react to the situation. Raid should have known better than to get her something like that. She wasn't single anymore. I understood he still wanted her to change her mind, but there were lines he still needed to stay behind.

Blaze glanced at the two men and then tossed Ryoko a small box to try to diffuse the situation. "Don't forget us now, not that they didn't show us up already."

She giggled and opened the box. Her brow furrowed when she pulled out a folded-up piece of paper. "You guys gave me a folded picture of a table?"

Argus chuckled. "No. That's what you're getting."

"Huh?"

Zane laughed. "Ryoko, you remember the engine we had to pull from your favorite car because it died and we couldn't find the right parts to fix it?"

Ryoko crossed her arms and pouted. "Yeah, I'm still pissed I had to replace it. I liked that engine."

"Well, we decided to send it out and have it turned into the glass table you see in the picture."

Ryoko's eyes lit up. "For real?"

"We figured you may need a new table in your bedroom," Blaze said.

She smiled wide. "You guys are the best!"

"Now, are you referring to everyone or just those three?" I teased.

"Laz, don't even start! You know the answer."

"Do we?" Rylan smirked. "It was kinda hard to tell."

"Guys, don't be mean to me on my birthday!" she whined.

"You'd worry if we weren't even a little," Zane said.

She huffed. "Fine, I'll give you that one. But I am grateful for all the gifts. Definitely the best birthday ever!"

Seda approached her with an envelope. "Now don't go saying that like it's over until I give you this. It's from Genesis and me."

Ryoko accepted the gift and tilted her head. I leaned forward so I could get a better look myself. Unlike the other gifts, Ryoko was careful in her attempt to open the envelope—not that I blamed her. Paper cuts hurt.

Ryoko's eyes lit up when she pulled a rectangular paper out and she squealed. "Spa day!"

The room filled with soft laughter, but mine was cut short when I noticed Seda making small motions to get my attention.

"What is it, Seda?"

"We have a visitor on the roof—and she's looking for you."

"Must be an interesting visitor if you don't want the others to know."

"It wouldn't be a good idea for them to know right at this very moment."

I slid off my seat and headed up the stairs, not caring if anyone noticed or not. Heading outside, I didn't need to look around to find this mysterious person. In front of me, sitting against the curb of the roof with her legs pulled up to her chest and a bag by her side, was Mocha.

I crossed my arms. "I was wondering when you'd show up."

She lifted her gaze to meet mine. "You knew I'd come?"

"Yeah, but I expected you sooner." I waved her over. "Let's get you inside and settled in."

"Wait, you're welcoming me in, just like that?"

"Well, yeah."

Her brow furrowed. "I don't understand."

"Because I know why you're here, Mocha. Now are you going to come inside or not? It's a bit chilly today."

She hesitated, but when I refused to wait for her, she picked up her bag and ran to catch up. I knew the others wouldn't be so welcoming, but this had to be done, and I'd make them understand that if I had to.

Everyone was laughing and having fun when I entered the living room, but it ended when Mocha followed me in.

Ryoko's eyes narrowed. "What is she doing here?"

"She's staying with us." I kept my voice calm but assertive showing there was no negotiating this.

Unfortunately, Ryoko wasn't having it. "Excuse me? Why weren't we involved in this decision?"

"Because there's no negotiating this," Seda said, standing. "I'll show Mocha to the room I prepped for her."

"Is this why you've been cleaning out one of the spare rooms these past few days?" Argus asked. She nodded in response and he nodded back. "All right."

"Why are you guys acting like this is no big deal?" Ryoko shrieked.

Argus shrugged. "Because it's not."

"How is it—"

"That's enough, Ryoko!" I snapped. "She's staying here and that's the end of it."

"But—"

I inhaled a tight breath and then exhaled, allowing thick, black smoke to stream out of my nose. The fire in my chest roared and begged to be used, but it wouldn't get its wish. Ryoko crossed her arms and sat back on the couch. Rylan leaned closer to her. He too didn't look happy—his unhappiness pulsing in the back of my head, thanks to the artificial bond the two of us were created with—but I expected this much from the two of them. I knew they'd take it the hardest, but they were going to have to live with it.

"Follow me," Seda instructed Mocha.

She glanced at everyone apprehensively and then followed. I stayed where I was and watched the two leave. I'd need to explain to everyone what was going on, so there was no point in leaving.

Once out of sight, I opened my mouth to speak, but Ryoko was faster. "What gives?"

"I'd like to know as well," Rylan muttered.

I exhaled. "Answer me this. What is her idea of a team? What is her idea of a *teammate*, for that matter? What has she been taught that you have?"

Ryoko blinked. "I don't understand."

"Nothing," Rylan answered.

I nodded. "Since she's been out of her tank, all she's known is what Raynn and the others have told her. What they've taught her. Raynn taught them all what it means to be on a team, but what is Raynn's idea of a team? What is his idea of loyalty? Mocha knows nothing of what I've taught you—what my mom taught us. That's what Mocha needs right now. She needs to know what a team means—what it means to rely on someone and be relied on in turn."

Ryoko nodded. "Okay, I understand, but why didn't you tell us? Why didn't we get a say in this?"

"Because I didn't invite her here. I've only been keeping tabs on her and the others. They've done their spying in their own way and I allowed it. They all figured out I knew, but I still didn't stop them. Doppelganger and Chameleon gave us a hand on an assignment without any of you knowing, and did so on their terms, to test the waters. Mocha came here on her own terms. She wants to know what it's like to have what we have."

Ryoko's ear drooped. "Oh. Well, if she's going to try, then I will, too."

Rylan nodded in agreement and soon everyone did as well. I let out a mental sigh of relief. It had gone better than I had expected. Ryoko slipped off the couch with her gifts and headed for her room. Rylan followed and shut the door behind him.

Zane clapped his hands together. "Well, looks like the party is over. Might as well get some work done."

Blaze chuckled. "It's over for everyone but Rylan."

I snickered and headed for my room and retrieved my digital planner.

Earlier in the day, Aurora had sent over some data for me to look over, and with a shift at the club later tonight, now was as good a time as any to review it. Powering it up, I looked over the reports.

New warehouses had been hit in the last week, upping our supplies, but there was no indication where our supplies as a whole stood. *Of course that'd be left out.* Team One, the rebellion's assassin team, had taken out key targets that would cripple Zarda's support, including a few from outside of the city. Moles had infiltrated several high-security facilities. More data would come in the future. There was a section about Zarda's defenses set up, but no data provided. *That's strange...* There was also a new function to try out. I read it over and smiled.

Someone had created a request form for assignments. It appeared the Council was looking for ways to fix the assignment discrepancies the teams were complaining about. I doubted it'd amount to anything, but I placed my requests anyway. *Can't hurt to try at this point...*

Once sent over, I figured it'd be best to finish laundry before my shift. I yawned. *And brew up some energizing tea.*

I tugged on my shirt as I tried to eat an apple. I had fallen asleep and no one had thought to check on me when Raikidan and Rylan left. I was not happy. Sure, I shouldn't have fallen asleep, but someone could have checked on me—ideally Raikidan or Rylan.

"You're having a lot of trouble with that shirt," Mana observed.

"I think it shrunk in the wash," I muttered.

She tilted her head. "Is your boss going to be mad?"

"About the shirt? No. He has a few spares lying around for workers to change into in case of accidents. Plus, it won't exactly hurt when getting tips. But me being late? Probably."

"What's a club like?"

I shrugged. "It's a place for people to hang out and have fun. You dance, drink, whatever you want. Or, close to whatever you want. Each club has its own rules to follow."

"It sounds like a fun place."

"I don't personally think it is, but you might. Ryoko will be stopping by later to have her own fun. You're welcome to go with her to find out firsthand what it's like."

Her eyes lit up. "Really?"

"No." We turned our gazes to Corliss as he walked into the living room. "Raikidan told me more about the place, in better detail, and I won't have it."

"But, Corliss—"

"I said no."

Mana sulked on the couch. "I just wanted to go and see what it was like. You never let me have any fun." Corliss looked a little upset with the way Mana was reacting to his decision—not that he didn't deserve it. Mana had been excited about the idea, and it wasn't like he had to right to dictate what she did. Before I had the chance to butt in, she spoke again, "You're like my father."

I winced. Even I knew that was not a favorable comparison, and I could tell Corliss didn't like it, as if she compared the two a lot.

"Fine. We'll go," he caved quickly, but with reluctance.

Mana perked up. "Really?"

He held up a finger. "But this will be the only time."

Mana jumped up. "Thank you! I'm going to go talk to Ryoko now."

I chuckled and shook my head. She knew how to play him. Maybe she wasn't as naïve as I once thought. Grabbing another apple for my ride over, I headed for my car.

I picked up the empty beer glasses and hurried back to the bar to get refills. Tonight hadn't gone as planned at all. Azriel did have a new shirt for me, but unfortunately I had been switched to waitressing because someone called out—again. I was getting sick of Azriel volunteering me to be the replacement, especially since he knew I liked working the bar.

I slid behind the bar and began filling my order. As I moved to head back to my tables, I noticed Ryoko, Mana, and Corliss sitting at the bar, but I had tables to get to, so couldn't acknowledge them before rushing off. I dropped off all the glasses I had, forced myself to flirt with some of the customers in hopes of getting some nice tips, and hurried back to the bar.

Mana's eyes lit up. "You came back!"

I chuckled, amused at her excitement over my presence. "You're acting like you expected me to never return."

"Well, you didn't notice us when you were here before."

"Because I'm busy. My job comes first." I glared at Azriel. "Of course, if someone hadn't changed what I was doing at the last minute, things would have been different."

"Will you stop being angry with me?" Azriel said. "I told you I was going to pay you extra."

I picked up a glass and began cleaning it. "You'd better."

Azriel blew out a breath between his lips and put away his clean glass to grab another to clean.

"So, Eira, what are we supposed to do here?" Mana asked me.

I shrugged. "You can try a few different drinks, order some food, and even dance on the dance floor."

"Oh, that last one sounds fun."

Ryoko grabbed Mana's wrist. "Then I'll show you the ropes."

"Hold on. I think I have a say in this," Corliss objected.

"Chill out, Corliss, and learn to have some fun," Ryoko teased. She slid off the barstool, Mana in tow.

Corliss sighed. "I guess I don't have a say."

"Lighten up, Corliss. She's safe with Ryoko." I put my clean glass down and went to go check on my tables. My checks were quick since my customers were happy, but when I arrived back at the bar, Corliss looked unhappier than before. "All right, talk to me."

"Don't worry about it," he muttered.

I picked up a glass to clean. "I may not be good at talking, but I'm pretty good at listening."

"I don't like Mana being out there with Ryoko. I trust her, but I don't trust the men on that dance floor. And with the way she is around people sometimes, she may not be able to handle their persistence."

"Then go join her. You can dance with her instead of someone else. Ryoko isn't shy about having to teach you if needed."

"I don't know…"

"It's just a suggestion. It would put your mind at ease, or you can sit here and sulk, too. Up to you."

His lips pressed into a thin line as he thought it over. "All right. I'll give it a shot."

I chuckled and left to check on my tables again like a good waitress. As much as I didn't like waitressing, I couldn't hate tonight. Customers were behaving, even the soldiers Azriel allowed back—

I spun around and struck a man when he grabbed my ass. The man stumbled backward, the dog tags around his neck jingling. *I knew it wouldn't last.* I stormed off, only to be grabbed by another drunk soldier, whom I also slapped. The man fell over from the force. I tore my gaze away from him as he struggled to get back up on his feet when I heard two sets of footsteps heading my way. Rylan and Raikidan approached.

"It'd be best to leave her alone," Raikidan warned the soldier.

"I'll do as I please," the soldier spat.

"I'll take care of him," Rylan muttered to Raikidan.

Raikidan nodded and came over to me as Rylan removed the drunken soldier. "You all right, Eira?"

I rubbed my ass. "Yeah. Small sting. Though if it's going to be like this the rest of the night, I'm not going to be okay."

"Talk with Azriel then. It would be in everyone's best interest if you don't kill anyone."

I chuckled. "At least I'm not the only one thinking that." I rubbed my ass one last time before walking back to the bar. Azriel was giving me a funny look when I got back to the bar. "What's your problem?"

He just chuckled. "What?"

He shook his head. "And here I thought there was nothing between you two. Who would have thought a little nu-human could have captured a dragon's heart?"

My brow rose. "What sort of craziness are you babbling on about? And how did you know what he was? I don't remember telling you."

"He told me the first day you two started working here. He figured I should know."

I grunted. "Figures. Now answer my first question."

"Don't go denying it. I know what I saw."

"Azriel, what are you talking about?"

"Laz, I saw him check you out as you headed back here."

I picked up a glass. "You're crazy."

"I know what I saw. It was obvious he was checking you out."

"You need your eyes check, Az. There's no way you saw what you think you saw."

"Yes, I did."

I sucked in a tight breath. "You know what? For this craziness you're spewing, I'm going to work the bar now whether you like it or not."

"Laz, I know what I saw."

"He may not be lying. Though I don't know why Raikidan would act that way."

I shook my head and cleaned my glass. He was crazy. So was the voice. Azriel didn't see what he thought he did. *There was no way Raikidan could have been looking at me that way... right?*

18
CHAPTER

The shirt I had in my hand dropped back into the drawer of my dresser as I search for another top. I was being picky about what I was going to wear for this assignment, and I couldn't afford that right now. It had taken me an extra-long time to get Raikidan out of my room and I didn't understand his problem. He knew I demanded privacy when dressing, and I thought he had finally got that through his head.

I let out a tight, frustrated breath and went to my closet, only to stub my toe on the leg of the dresser. I bit my lip in an attempt to prevent myself from howling in pain—but I failed and jumped backward as I held my foot until I fell onto my bed. I inspected the injured append-age and sighed when I saw the cracked nail and blood. *That's what I get for not paying attention. Now I'm going to have to take care of this, get dressed, and not fall behind on this stupid assignment.*

A knock sounded on my door, and as I turned, Ryoko poked her head in. "What's up, Ryoko?"

"Well, I'm a little confused," she said. "I heard your voice in Rai-kidan's room, and now you're in here and I know I would have seen you walk in here if you'd gone through the living room."

It was my turn to be perplexed. "I haven't set foot in Raikidan's room today."

"Um, okay, but I know I heard your voice in there. You were bothering him."

I got up and threw on the first tank top I could find before pushed past her. "Let's get to the bottom of this."

Ryoko nodded, and the two of us made our way over to Raikidan's room. Before I could knock, I heard voices talking on the other side. One was definitely Raikidan and the other did sound a lot like me, but I was right here.

"Eira, I don't know what's gotten into you, but you need to stop," he told her.

The person in there with him didn't respond, but it did grow quiet in his room and I didn't like that. Without knocking, I threw open the door and was taken aback by the scene in front of me. Raikidan was lying on the bed with his arms propping him up, and a woman who looked identical to me was sitting on top of him. The blank look in Raikidan's eyes indicated hypnotism of some sort, and that told me exactly who this imposter was.

The woman pulled away from him. "Looks like I took too long. Oh well. This makes it more fun."

"Don't let her touch him like that." The voice sounded uncharacteristically possessive. It had also been unusually vocal these past few weeks. I shook the thought free. I needed to deal with the matter at hand.

"Get off him, Rana," I ordered.

She slid off him, a devilish grin spreading across her lips, and shifted to her true self—a sultry, fair-skinned woman with raven hair. "Angry with me, Eira? Not happy that someone else was touching your pet?"

"You should be dead," I spat. Rana had attacked us while we had been raiding a supply warehouse. She'd disguised herself as Raikidan with her unique shifting ability and an attempt to kill me specifically. Lucky for me, Raikidan had my back, and with his help I killed her. *Or so I thought.*

"I would have been, had you actually checked to make sure I wasn't alive. You know me better than that, or, at least I thought you did. But it doesn't matter. You're all soon to be dead traitors anyway."

Before I could respond, she lunged at me. I deftly dodged and considered how I could dispose of her. I didn't want to make eye contact for too long, and I didn't want to get too close, due to one of her more dangerous abilities.

Rana came at me, but Raikidan pushed her back into the wall. I blinked in surprise. That wasn't something I had ever expected to see him do to a woman. "Don't touch her!"

"Faithful pet," she spat. "She has you trained well."

"I'm not her pet."

She chuckled. "No, you're right. You're the newest toy she has yet to become bored of."

Raikidan grabbed her by the throat and slammed her against the wall again. I watched in stunned silence.

"Laz, you're going to need this." I tore my gaze away from the two to see Seda standing in the hallway with an assassin's dagger.

She tossed the weapon to me and I sighed. *She's right.* I would have to do this. There had been a reason I didn't double check the last time we encountered her, and it was that reason—that weakness—that put us in this situation now.

"Raikidan, let her go," I ordered. He cranked his head over his shoulder, gazing back at me in question. "She's mine to deal with."

He looked at me a moment longer before throwing her to the floor in front of me. Rana struggled to her feet and lunged at me. I dodged, cutting her side with my dagger. She cried out in pain but came back at me. This time, I allowed her to come into range, and I thrust the dagger into her abdomen. Careful to not get any of her saliva on me, I withdrew the dagger and pulled back before she had the chance to cough up any blood.

She held her abdomen as she coughed, then glared at me through her hair.

I stared down at her. "You put this on yourself. You didn't have to do this."

"I hate you! It's all your fault!"

She lunged at me, but I was ready. Moving around her, I grabbed her by the hair and sliced the dagger across her back, then pulled her closer and plunged it into her chest. Knowing it would take a few minutes for her to die from blood loss, I spared her the agony and snapped her neck. Her body went limp and I let her fall to the ground. Pain clenched my chest as I stared at her still form. I sensed the audience that had formed outside the door. "Shva'sika."

"Yes?"

"I'm going to need your help forcing her to cross over."

"Laz, you know we can't—"

"We have to, or she'll come back."

"I don't know what you're talking about, but I'll do my best to help."

I sat down and forced myself into the spiritual plane. I didn't know what was going to happen, but I had to be ready for anything. I opened my eyes when my spirit merged with the spiritual plane and scanned the dark space around me. Shva'sika stood next to me, waiting.

That's when I heard it—a woman crying. I followed the somber sound until I came to Rana's spirit. She was on her knees, sobbing. "Why me? Why couldn't I have what you have?"

"What do I have that you don't, Rana?" I questioned.

"Freedom. A life."

"I have neither. I will never be free of what I am, and because of that I have no life."

"I didn't have any chance of one. You do!" she shouted.

"Then you don't know me as well as you think you do."

"I know you better than you know yourself."

"Why did you target them, Rana?" I asked. "Why didn't you leave my friends out of it?"

"Because they make you happy. It wasn't fair!"

"You had your chance and you threw it away."

"You never gave me a chance."

Now I definitely knew what was going on. "I never gave up on you, Rana."

"Yes you did!" she screamed. "Yes, you did…"

"You're the one who walked away. You're the one who looked for someone else to pass you to the next level of assassin training."

"Because you wouldn't do it! You passed everyone else but me."

"You weren't ready," I said. "You still had more to learn and you refused to see that. I couldn't pass you until I knew you were ready."

"Someone else passed me."

"He didn't have the same standards as me. I chose you, Rana. I saw your potential."

She was quiet for a moment. "What potential?"

I exhaled. "The potential to surpass me—to surpass Shyden."

Rana peered up at me. "You don't mean that."

I knelt. "Yes I do. You had skills we could never attain. You had a passion we didn't share. You liked doing what we did." My gaze lowered. "I didn't. I did it because it was the only thing I could do. You accepted what you were while I turned my back on what I am."

"Then why didn't you pass me so I continue to train at the higher levels? If you really had that much faith in me, why did you do it?" Her voice grew louder. "Tell me!"

"Because you wouldn't listen. If you couldn't listen, I couldn't teach you. You didn't want to know what I knew, so you chose to go to someone else who didn't have my knowledge. He passed you because you already knew more than him." Her anger melted away as I spoke. I let out a sorrowful breath. "I didn't want to have to kill you, Rana. You have no idea what that choice meant."

"Yes, I do." She looked down. "I'm sorry."

I pressed my lips together, preparing myself. "It's your choice. You have the ability to defy death and come back, or you can pass on."

Tears trickled down her face. "You know I'll never be able to have someone in my life. It's not possible. I've tried everything to make it so I could. I don't want to be alive if I'll always be alone."

"I can't guarantee you a happy ending if you come back."

"I'll move on then, and hope the gods give me another chance some other time to have a normal life."

"I'm sorry, Rana."

She shook her head as she began to fade. "No, it's my fault. I let my anger cloud my judgment, and that was the first rule you taught me. You were right, I did have a lot to learn still. I'm sorry for failing you."

"You didn't fail me."

"Could you burn my body? That way no one can get a hold of it and bring me back."

"Of course we can."

"Thank you—and good luck. I know you can win this."

She disappeared, and a weight lifted off my chest. Shva'sika moved to stand next to me. "You handled that well. It takes a lot of skill to persuade a soul of her type."

"Thank you, and thank you for being here. I know you didn't do anything, but knowing you were here in case it did go bad—that made this easier."

Her lips spread into a kind smile. "You're welcome. Now let's go back and check on Raikidan."

I nodded and closed my eyes, my body pulling away from the spiritual plane. Once my spirit was back where it belonged, my eyes snapped open and I stood.

"I'll contact some shamans to prepare her body so we can take care of it after your mission," Shva'sika told me.

I nodded. "Thanks. Raikidan, Rana's saliva didn't touch you at all, right?"

Raikidan blinked and then shook his head. "No."

"Good."

"Why?" Ryoko asked. "What's so important about her saliva?"

"Rana's saliva is toxic," I said. "It's the reason she stayed loyal to Zarda. She didn't see a life outside of what she already knew. She also has a hypnotic gaze, which is why Raikidan didn't have much of a say in all of this."

"How do you know that about her?" Raid asked. "How did you know it was her, for that matter?"

I sighed. "I trained her."

"What?"

"I chose her for her potential and trained her. Unfortunately, she didn't get as far as I had anticipated. She had the skills, but she lacked the ability to listen and control herself, so she came to hate me because I refused to pass her to the advanced levels of training. That's why she targeted us. She wanted me to pay for the wrong she felt I did to her." I left the room and headed for my room.

"That's it? No apology for getting you all mixed up in her mess?" Mocha questioned.

"That was her way of apologizing," Rylan corrected her. "By killing Rana she showed us she was sorry."

"I don't get it."

"Then I can safely assume you've never trained someone before."

"No, I haven't."

"Laz trained many assassins in her time. She was good at what she did and was very selective with those she took on. She's also been known to become attached to her students because she was so selective. So for her to kill her own student to keep us out of harm's way because of a mistake she made in her past, that's Laz's ultimate way of apologizing…"

I shut my door. I didn't need someone narrating how I felt. I entered my bath and cleaned off the bits of blood that had gotten onto my hand from my dagger. When I came out, I found Raikidan standing by my closed door. I didn't pay him any mind as I finished getting ready for the assignment I was now late for. I wasn't going to argue with him because it would only delay me further, as would changing the pants and shirt I had thrown on. Instead, I entered my closet to grab a jacket.

"Thanks for helping me," Raikidan mumbled out as I came out of the closet. "And I'm sorry about it being such an awkward situation."

"Don't worry about it." I fussed with the jacket as I headed toward him and the door. "It's just good Ryoko had been around to hear you talking to her."

"Well, had you not been able to step in, it wouldn't have mattered."

I stepped closer to him, invading his already-cramped personal space. Raikidan watched me. "You can smell her, can't you?"

My lip twitched, my nose catching whiffs of mint, orange, and jasmine. "I don't particularly like her smell. Just because I trained her doesn't mean I like the idea of her posing as me and getting her scent all over you."

He smirked. "She doesn't smell as nice as you. It's something she couldn't replicate. Of course I didn't realize it until she caught me with that hypnotic gaze of hers."

"Cover all of her scent with yours. Everywhere."

"Well, that's reassuring." My lip curled. "Her scent is concentrated in small areas all over you. Hovering isn't doing enough."

I pulled away. As I did, my hand reached out and grabbed him in the groin, though careful not to squeeze. Raikidan tensed, which I had expected him to do. I couldn't say why I needed to cover her scent; it would go away pretty quickly.

My back hit the wall when he spun around and pinned me against it. His breath was slow and almost sounded strained. "Don't do that again, you hear? Or I may do something we'd both regret."

I chuckled and leaned in close to him. "Did you tell that to Rana, too, or did you just let her do what she wanted?"

My boldness took him by surprise, his eyes going wide and mouth partially falling open. His grip loosened. I used this to slide out of his grip and around him to head out for my assignment. My words may not have been the kindest to say to him after his ordeal, but I never claimed to be a nice person.

19
CHAPTER

Dust fell on the coffee table as I sanded down my latest carving to be sold. I had made four today. Not a great number for me, but the shamans wouldn't complain. Word had come to me the other day that none of the caravans had any more of my carvings, and were running low on jewelry. Potential customers asked about new stock constantly, so while I had a tall order to fill, anything was better than nothing for them.

Mana and Raikidan sat around the coffee table and watched me with intent curiosity. Corliss relaxed next to Mana and watched me as well, but not with the same degree of interest as the others. Each time I finished a carving, they felt the need to look it over before allowing it to be left alone on the table.

I stopped my sanding when Raikidan's attention snapped elsewhere. His whole body went rigid and an ugly scowl spread across his face. My brow rose. "Something wrong, Raikidan?"

"We have unwanted visitors," he growled.

My eyes narrowed as I watched him and Corliss, who looked equally displeased, head for the roof. I turned my eye on Mana, who appeared a bit scared. Seda ran into the room, grabbing my attention. She didn't look happy, either. "You need to stop them. It won't end well if we don't step in."

I didn't need to be told twice to act. I nearly ripped the door off its hinges as I raced up the stairs. I had hoped the two of them hadn't gotten too far, but they were moving at a faster pace than I had anticipated. By the time I had caught up, the door to the roof was closing behind them. I pushed against the door and forced it back open.

The guys stood in front of me, blocking my view. Tension rolled off them in strong waves. *Whoever is here is just beyond them.* Then I realized they weren't just tense. They were speaking in their own tongue and readying themselves for a fight.

Taking a deep breath, I pushed through them. "What the hell is going on?"

Before me stood three people—a man appearing to be in his late forties, a woman who appeared to be in her early forties, and a young man looking to be in his late twenties. The two men had tan skin, piercing sapphire blue eyes, and short black hair. The older of the two sported a thin mustache and goatee and had a muscular build, where the younger one was clean-shaven and had an athletic build. Tall and also with an athletic build, the beautiful woman with them had mocha skin, almond-shaped sapphire blue eyes, and long wavy black hair. *Based on their features, and the way the dragons are acting, they have to be dragons as well. Black dragons, if I'm not mistaken.*

"Be careful."

I crossed my arms. "Who are you and what do you want?"

The older man looked me over, as if assessing me, a grin on his lips. I didn't like him; something about him felt oddly familiar, and not in a good way.

I ground my teeth together when the man started speaking in Draconic to one of the boys behind me. "I'm the one who spoke to you, not them. Now you'll address me or leave."

The man chuckled and spoke, a heavy northern accent coating his words. "You've got quite the attitude, with that mouth of yours."

"You have no idea. Now tell me what you want before I make you leave."

"Those are big words coming from a tiny human like yourself," he sneered.

Raikidan growled. "Watch it."

"Don't start challenging me, whelp," the man warned. "Didn't your red-scaled mother ever tell you to respect your elders?"

"Didn't your mother ever tell you how to treat a lady?" Corliss shot back.

"What mother?" Raikidan sneered. "You mean that over grown pond—"

"Silence, you impudent hal—"

My fist collided with his face, interrupting his insult. "Watch your tongue, Black."

The woman with him laughed. "Now that my mate has been put in his place, I think introductions are in order. My name is Salir. The dumb one you hit is my mate, Ambrose, and this is our son, Rennek."

I crossed my arms. She, too, had a heavy northern accent, but unlike Ambrose, I sensed she'd be easier to deal with. "Eira."

Salir placed her hands on her hips and eyed me. "From the rallying, I expected you to be friendlier."

My brow rose. "Rallying? What are you talking about?"

"If you let us in, we'll talk," Ambrose grumbled.

"Be careful." I could tell the voice didn't like him; I really didn't, either.

"We'll speak here." They weren't getting inside unless I knew exactly what was going on.

Salir sat down on the edge of the roof, remaining quiet. This made it clear she was done talking, and Rennek appeared more content to take in the scenery, as if he didn't want to be here either. It appeared I was going to have to converse with Ambrose if I wanted answers, even though I'd rather it not be him.

Ambrose crossed his arms. "Seems I'm going to be forced to speak with you."

"I'm not going to pretend to like this, either," I said. "Now get on with it."

"The clans and colonies are stirring. We've all hidden in the shadows where it's safe, but something has shaken everything up, and that something is you."

"Can you prove it?"

"The stir started with the Velsara clan under that whelp Zaith's leadership. They were the first to choose to fight against the pact forced on us for our species' survival."

"Anyone could have done that. It's not hard to kick a hornet's nest."

He growled. "Stop being stupid."

I narrowed my eyes, but Raikidan spoke before I could. "She isn't stupid. Give her the answers she wants and she'll return the favor. Maybe."

Ambrose snorted. "We know it's you. Your name is spoken enough. What we want to know is, why you?"

I chuckled. "If you figure it out, let me know, because I don't have the answer to that question. Hearing other clans are being stirred up is news to me."

"Then, can we stay to find out ourselves?" Salir asked.

I thought for a moment. *Did I want them here?*

"Tread carefully with this decision. They could be either useful, or a hindrance. Be sure to analyze all angles."

It was obvious Raikidan and Corliss didn't want them around. I didn't know their relationship with these three, and unfortunately, I couldn't find out at this moment. Putting that aside, more dragon allies could prove useful. The Council had been using Zaith's clan here and there, and the results were better than expected. I could only assume adding black dragons would add another helpful angle. And then there was another issue…

I exhaled. "In my oath as a shaman, I agreed to be hospitable as long as those seeking my aid show no hostility to me or my allies. You are welcome to stay here; so long you do not cause any trouble, understood?"

"Eira, do—" I smacked Raikidan in the chest to shut him up. He could argue with me after.

Ambrose grinned. "Thank you. We'll keep out of trouble."

I turned on my heels to head back inside. "You'd better."

Raikidan growled at Ambrose before following me. He was quiet as we walked down the stairs, but walked uncomfortably close.

Shva'sika greeted us when we arrived in the living room. "Seda is arranging some rooms for our guests. I'll bring them to the rooms for you."

"Thanks. I'm going to go meditate and reflect on my sanity."

"I'm sorry our customs put you in this situation," she said.

I shrugged and headed for my room—Raikidan still following close behind. The silence between us didn't last long when he closed the door. "Are you insane, Eira?"

I sucked in a slow breath through my nose to ensure I stayed calm. "I had to, Raikidan. I know you and Corliss don't want them here, frankly I don't either, but I had to."

"You couldn't have asked us before making the decision?"

"There wasn't time, and I have my own questions I need answering. Their leaving won't answer them."

He threw his hands into the air. "I don't care about your questions!"

"What, so now you're the only one who can have questions that matter?"

He narrowed his eyes. "Eira, don't you start with that."

"Then tell me, Raikidan, what exactly is eating you about this?"

He leaned against the door with his arms crossed and glared at some invisible object in another direction.

I walked over to him and placed my hand on his arm. "Rai, if I'm to know why this situation upsets you so much, you need to tell me. I'm no mind reader."

He sighed. "Ambrose isn't here for the reasons he's claiming he's here for."

"And how do you know this?"

He leveled his gaze with me. "He's my grandfather."

I retracted my touch in surprise. I had no idea. It would justify both Raikidan's and Corliss' actions toward him, but they didn't look anything like Ambrose. Even the two of them shared some similarities even though they were just cousins.

"You need to send him away," he insisted.

"Raikidan, I can't." I turned away. "I need to know the true reason he's here."

"Then I'm leaving."

My shoulders sagged. "I'd miss you…"

"But you wouldn't stop me."

I turned to face him. "I'm not going to make you stay somewhere you don't want to be."

"But you won't change your mind."

"Even if you told me the issues between you and your grandfather, even if I didn't want to know what he's up to, I can't send him away until he causes a problem."

"He's causing a problem by being here!" Raikidan shouted.

"No, you're causing a problem because you're not willing to give this a chance. He hasn't done anything except show up." Raikidan started to relax as he listened to what I was saying. "So why don't you be the better dragon and make an attempt."

"You don't know what he's done."

"You're right, I don't, and I'm not going to pry, but Shva'sika says the best way to get at someone you hate is to kill them with kindness. I've never tried it, so you're more than welcome to give it a shot to see how well that theory works."

Raikidan crossed his arms. "Doesn't that defeat you telling me to be the better dragon?"

"He's got a point. Wait… why am I agreeing with him?"

"Shut up," I muttered. Raikidan laughed at me, and I was sure the voice chuckled too. "Now are you going to leave, or stay?"

"I'll stay and try out this theory. As long as I can stomach it, at least."

I smiled. "Thank you."

He smirked and advanced toward me. I backed away immediately. For some inexplicable reason, I didn't trust him now. I thought I could hear the voice laughing, but it wasn't warning me about him. *That's not good.*

Raikidan lunged at me and grabbed a hold before I could get away. My struggling didn't stop him from throwing me over his shoulder and heading for the door. I found myself laughing even though I wasn't sure why. "Raikidan, what are you doing?"

The door flew open and he walked out of the room with me still over his shoulder. "You need to get back to work."

"I don't have to do anything if I don't want to."

"Then you wouldn't make any money."

"He has a point," Corliss agreed.

"No comments from the peanut gallery," I muttered. A yelp escaped my lips when he threw me down. I bounced on the couch a few times and then blew a quick breath upward to move my bangs out of my eyes when I stilled. "Not funny."

Raikidan chuckled. "To me it was. Now start carving. You could use the extra money."

I stuck my tongue out at him and grabbed a block of wood to inspect. I glanced up when I noticed someone standing in the hallway. It was Rennek. I narrowed my eyes. "What are you looking at?"

Rennek stared at me a moment longer without blinking and then turned and left.

"That was weird," I muttered.

"Definitely beats you on weirdness, Laz," Ryoko said, her mouth full of food.

"I don't know. I'm pretty weird."

She pointed her spoon toward the hall. "Yeah, but you've never done that before."

I stared at the block of wood in my hand. "True."

"So what are you going to make now?"

I shrugged. "Not sure."

"So you're going to stare at it until an idea comes to you?" I nodded and she chuckled. "Yeah, you're weird."

Raikidan sat down next to me to watch. I refrained from rolling my eyes. I wasn't sure who was weirder—me or him.

CHAPTER 20

I pulled myself up and ignored my abs pained cries. I only had a
few more pull ups to go, but that wasn't the end of my workout.
I'm far from finish—

I stopped when I heard the basement door open and Ryoko's
heavy boots came crashing down on the steps. "Laz, you're going to
want to come up here."

I cocked my head and then unbound my ankles so I could follow.
When I entered, I found everyone gathered in the living room around
Rylan, who sat on the couch.

He turned his gaze on me. "You've been challenged."

I approached. "Let me see."

Rylan held out his hand and I took the small black device he offered.
I turned the device on and it projected a hologram of a young man.

"Greetings," it played. "You, Eira, have been selected to participate
in *The Run* due to your specialized talents. You, along with dozens of
other competitors from cities around Lumaraeon, will compete along
a city-long course in a remote area to prove who of you has what it
takes to be called The Run Champion.

"Having entered in the past, this invitation does not have a recording
of the game rules and prizes for you to hear, as they have not changed
since the last time you entered. Use the device prompts to accept or

deny this invitation. You will not be penalized for not participating in The Run and are welcome to spectate instead."

"What is The Run?" Mana asked.

"It's a secret parkour challenge held every year," Rylan told her.

Mana tilted her head. "What's parkour?"

"It's a type of freerunning Laz particularly excels in," Ryoko explained. "You have to move through a course without the help of equipment, and although it was originally non-competitive, it's become a fun, competitive game banned in many cities."

Mana cocked her head. "Why is it banned?"

"Most governments see it as a threat," Argus said. "They believe it causes disorder and encourages rebellion in stricter areas such as our city."

"Which is the exact idea we've run with," Genesis said. "While to most, it's a fun competition with prizes, to those fighting against Zarda, it's a way to strengthen alliances outside the city and gain funding, as well as various other types of help. I expect, regardless of whether Eira participates or not, you will all attend to help with the cause."

"So what are you gunna do, Laz?" Ryoko asked, ignoring Genesis. "I know in the past, the outcome hasn't been favorable, but..."

"Enter it."

I nodded. "It's still worth trying again."

"You're acting as if she isn't going to win," Raikidan said.

Ryoko and Rylan exchanged glances before Ryoko spoke. "That's because she's never won before."

Raikidan's brow rose. "Say that again?"

"I've never won before," I said. "I've participated in The Run a few times but it wasn't in the cards."

"Then why try this time? You don't know if you're going to win."

"It's not always about winning. I enjoy the challenge." I pressed a few buttons on the invitation.

"Invitation acceptance received," the hologram said. "You are welcome to bring those you trust to spectate. Being a past participant, you are aware the penalties if they leak this out to those who would bring harm to other spectators and participants. Welcome to The Run."

"So, when is this competition?" Corliss asked.

"Tonight," Ryoko said. "Invitations only go out the night of the event."

"Which means if you're going to watch, get ready now," I ordered. "It's a long walk."

We set a quick pace through the sewers. More people decided to come watch than I had anticipated. Only Seda, Genesis, Zane, and Mocha decided to stay home. I half expected Genesis to force Mocha to come with us, but maybe she understood the woman's drive to stay out of sight. Even with so many different types of people attending the competition, who knew if any issues would surface around the way she looked.

"So is anyone going to tell us where this competition is being held?" Raikidan asked.

Ryoko hushed him. "We're not allowed to speak about its location. We can only show you."

"Can you at least tell us how long we'll be walking?" Corliss asked. "A few hours."

"A few hours?" Raikidan hollered. "Where the hell is this place?"

I spun around and hushed him. "Keep it down. If you don't want to walk a few hours, then go back to the house. No one is making you come with us."

Muscles flexed all over his body as if he resisted the urge to shrink back. "But I want to see this…"

"Then shut up and keep walking."

He sighed and continued to follow. Ambrose chuckled, but Salir silenced him with a scolding. They had only been with us for a few days and I already liked Salir. She was nice, unlike Ambrose, and it made me more curious about Raikidan and his kind. Raikidan told me so little about them, and I wasn't seeing everything he claimed.

"Why does it feel like we're going to that strange computer room you call the Underground?" Raikidan whispered to me.

"Because we are," I replied.

He shook his head. "I should have just listened and kept quiet. I'm more confused than ever."

I chuckled and continued walking. Everything would make sense soon enough.

We rounded a few more corners before arriving at the doors of the

Underground. Ryoko and Raid moved the large doors enough for us to squeeze through before closing them behind us. There were a lot of people here, but not as many as there usually were. *Not surprising, really.* Many of us were invited to either participate or spectate The Run. It was a huge event.

A mocha-skinned, crimson-eyed woman with shoulder-length black-and-red hair waved us over as we walked farther into the room. "I figured you guys would be going. Wanted to wish you luck, babe."

I grinned and bumped arms with her. "Thanks, Aurora, I'll need it. Safe to assume you're not going."

She shook her head. "I have too much work to do, but I did manage to obtain a virtual key so those who won't be going can watch from this room."

"And by *obtain*, you mean you stole it."

She crossed her arms. "I like to use the term 'strategically acquired,' thank you."

I laughed and patted her on the shoulder a few times before leading everyone to the back end of the room. When we arrived at a computer station that wasn't on, I moved around and opened a fuse box. Inside was a single switch and I flicked it to the *on* position. The sound of mechanical works came from behind the computer station and then the station slid to the side, revealing a large door behind it. The door was old, no less than nine centuries, made of several types of metal, and was decorated with intricate designs.

"Eira, what is this?" Corliss asked.

"The way to our destination." I closed the false fuse box and pushed the ancient door open. It didn't want to move at first, but eventually it gave into my demand.

Everyone filed into the small room and I shut the door. Even through the thickness of the door, you could hear the faux computer station moving back into place.

"Now what?" Ambrose demanded. "This is just a dark, cramped room."

A creaking noise was heard, and then the floor began to move as if it were lowering us.

"Patience, whelp," I said.

Ambrose snarled, but that was the extent to any possible comeback, as Salir smacked him in the shoulder and spoke to him in Draconic. Based on Raikidan's, Corliss', and Rennek's snickering, she was giving him a lecture.

The floor continued to lower us in darkness until light peeked out from around it and then opened up on one side. The light was a metal tunnel, lit with long, tubular blue lights. The floor reached the bottom of its descent and then moved down the tunnel on its own. The lights flashed by as our mode of transportation picked up speed. The platform continued its course long after the walls turned to earth and stone, and the lights turned to torches.

"How is it able to still move us?" Mana asked curiously from her spot in the center of the platform.

"If you're daring enough to take a look, the floor is still made of metal and mechanical works," I said.

She shook her head. "I'll stay right here and take your word for it."

I chuckled. I wouldn't have figured a creature that could fly would be afraid of moving fast. *Maybe it's because our feet are still planted on something solid.*

I braced myself as the platform suddenly slowed down. *We're almost there.* It was only a few minutes' walk after the lift dropped us off.

I couldn't help but laugh when Mana fell over the moment the lift came to a stop.

"Not funny. It stopped too fast," she complained.

A few of us chuckled as Corliss helped her up before jumping off the platform to continue on.

It wasn't long before Mana wasn't happy about walking so much. "Are we there yet?"

"Just a little farther," Raid assured her.

"Why do we have to travel such a long ways?" she asked.

"Because the competition is held in a secret location."

"Why couldn't that lift carry us any farther than it did?"

Raid chuckled. "Because it wasn't designed to go any farther."

"Why can't someone make it go farther?"

"Because it's ancient technology," Argus said. "No one knows how it functions on a technological level, and we don't want to break it."

"Mana, just be patient," Corliss said.

"But I'm tired of walking!" she complained.

"Well you can stop complaining," I called back to them. "We're here."

The others joined me at the edge of the cliff face. Below, clustered buildings forged of metal sprawled out around lakes and a river of lava, many buildings built right into the earth surrounding the city.

"Where are we?" Mana asked as she took in our surroundings, eyes wide with wonder.

"Ye be in the grand city o' Azrok, lass," a masculine voice told her.

Our attention turned to a stout man clad in armor. The armor made him look larger than he probably was, but his enormous mace and long, blonde beard did the opposite. His beard was braided, with metal rings and clasps with large decorative plates, and a large metal septum ring pierced his nose.

Mana blinked. "Is that a dwarf?"

"No, it's a pony," I replied sarcastically.

"Oi, lass, nobody be callin' a Thunderfist a pony," the dwarf warned.

"And what are you going to do about it, Vorn, throw me a mug of ale?"

"Dun be challengin' me, lass. Ye know ye cannae hold yer ale like me."

I pulled up my jacket sleeve. "And I can still make you cry 'uncle' in a brawl."

"Aye, let's be callin' it a draw then."

The two of us laughed.

I walked over to him and patted him on the shoulder, or at least the best I could without impaling my hand on the spikes he had on the pauldrons. "It's good to see you again, Vorn."

"Aye, ye too, lass. Been a long time. But we dinnae have time tae catch up, at least not now. Ye have a competition to go win."

"We have time."

"No, lass, yer late."

"Shit!" I took off down the path as fast as I could. If I didn't get to the sign-in post in time, I'd be disqualified.

Vorn's hearty laughter carried down the path as I descended into the city, as if taunting me. He then went about telling the others to follow him to make their way to their viewing station.

21
CHAPTER
(RYO'KO)

Vorn set a steady pace for us to follow. Rylan, Raid, and Argus chatted with him, and unsurprisingly, Mana reamed him with questions. Not many were given the opportunity to see a dwarf, let alone talk with one. Since Zarda's conquest for land and power, and the impending war looming over Lumaraeon because of it, most stayed deep inside their mountain cities to stay out of the conflict, and Azrok was no different. The dwarves weren't cowards, not in the least. They'd defend their mountains with their lives if the battles came too close, but they didn't seek out bloodshed. They were content with crafting and drinking.

Lucky for Mana, Vorn was a patient man and was more than willing to answer her questions. Of course, taking the form of a beautiful young woman didn't hurt her either. Even in the time that had passed since we had last seen him, the old dwarf hadn't changed a bit.

I gazed around as we passed through the city. It hadn't changed much, if at all. As usual, it didn't keep my attention long. I much preferred the thought of seeing Mount Azrok from the outside and not the inside for once. No doubt it was a beautiful mountain. I'd have to put it on my bucket list to come see it after this war was all over.

Vorn stopped walking when he came to a large platform. "Here we be. Ye know how tae operate the machinery, so I'll leave ye tae it. Tell ol' Eira if she wins, drinks be on me."

Rylan chuckled. "I'll make sure she knows."

Vorn slung his large mace over his shoulder and headed off. I jumped up onto the metal platform and ran over to the controls, excitement threatening to make me explode. It had been so long since we'd been here, since Laz was the only reason we needed to come and watch.

Below our platform, the metal city bustled with life. All the buildings were tall, making the residents even smaller than they really were. As I peered out, I could make out platforms from other spectators, but their platforms appeared at little different from ours. The big difference was the large, blue-green screens surrounding the platforms, which caused something in my mind to click. In order for us to watch the competition, since it was held in a more remote part of the city in order to keep spectators safe, we had to watch it through video feeds on these spectator platforms.

Not wanting to miss anything, I pressed a bunch of buttons until several translucent screens projected all the way around our platform. One of the screens showed two men in a booth. The slimmer and taller of the two, Den, had brown hair and blue eyes, and was from the east coastal city of Silvercrest, a city barely staying out of Zarda's clutches. Reynor was a muscular, tan man with blond hair and blue eyes from the south coastal city of Altaris, a city Zarda took over several years ago.

Den and Reynor were the commentators, and although the projection of them was convenient, it wasn't necessary since you could already hear them on speakers placed throughout the city and close to the spectator platforms.

"Wow, this video is really clear," Mana commented. "How does it come out so clear when the rest of the screen around it is almost transparent?"

"We're not sure," I admitted. "This technology is ancient. We've tried to recreate it, but nothing comes close to these machines. Like that lift, no one knows much about these particular machines. They just do what is needed without fail."

"That doesn't make any sense, woman," Ambrose said. "Someone would have to know something. These dwarves have to know. They live here."

I crossed my arms. "Does it look like dwarves know how to make this kind of stuff? It was already here when they got here. When they started digging into Mt. Azrok, they figured it would take some time, but they were completely wrong. It didn't take them long at all because large portions of this mountain were already excavated and the technology was already here."

"So this place was just abandoned?" Corliss questioned.

I nodded. "Yeah. The dwarves say there hadn't been a sign of life here at all, and looked like it had been abandoned for a long time."

"Do you have any proof of this?" Ambrose asked.

I placed my hands on my hips. "If you had half a brain, you'd know dwarves only pass their stories down by word of mouth. They'd don't write them down."

He growled when the guys laughed at him.

"So how do we see Eira?" Mana asked as she stared at the screen. "These two guys are boring."

I laughed. "We can't see them before everything starts, so you'll have to deal with Den and Reynor's rambling for a few more minutes."

"What's so important about them anyway?"

"They comment on what goes on during the competition."

"They do what, now?"

I snickered. "They talk about what's happening, and put their two gold coins in about everything and anything."

"Why? We can see it just fine, right?"

"It's a tradition thing the older generation of spectators enjoy. They can be quite funny sometimes, and every now and then, they even talk about interesting things."

Mana crossed her arms. "Well is there any place for me to sit while I wait?"

"Well... there's the floor."

Her nose scrunched. "That's not what I had in mind."

"Most people don't want to sit during these, so that's the only option."

She sighed and sat down on the floor. "This had better start soon."

"All right ladies and gents, looks like the contestants are all here 'n' on their way to the start, so it looks like—"

"It's time for The Run to start!" Den finished.

"Oi, I was going to say that!" Reynor said.

Den chuckled. "The only downside to it starting is that we have to listen to you more."

"You, mate, don't you what you're talking about."

"I don't?"

Reynor poked his chest with his thumb. "The girls can't get enough of this, mate."

Den rolled his eyes and pulled up a bunch of data-related widgets he'd use through the competition. "Let's just let everyone know who is in the running this time."

"Can we skip Lucas?" Reynor requested.

"He's the reigning champ. We have to talk about him."

Reynor rested his face on his fist. "Yeah, but the bloke is one cocky son of a bitch."

"He's undefeated for thirty years, and his city loves him for it. I think it's pretty justified. And look, here he is now in his ride up to the top."

We all turned our eyes to another part of our screen where a video showed an athletically-built young man with ebony hair standing in a poorly-lit elevator. It was definitely Lucas. I'd recognize that cocky look anywhere.

"Lucas may be the reigning champ, mate, but we have an old player coming back to shake things up," Reynor argued with Den. "'N' the girl looks like she means business."

Another video appeared next to Lucas' shot, and Mana squealed. "It's Eira! She looks so cool."

The video did show Laz, and she appeared pretty calm, but I noticed her fidgeting with her jacket sleeves. Don't be nervous, Laz, you got this.

"Yes, Eira coming back has made this game a bit more interesting," Den agreed.

"Maybe she can give Lucas a bit of a challenge 'n' spice this game up."

"It's possible, but not likely based on past games she's participated in. Eira has skills, no one can deny that, but she's never won a single competition. She has never passed the same part of the course twice. She can give Lucas a run for his money, but unless she's gained some sort of amazing skill in the time she's been gone, she isn't likely to succeed. I wouldn't bet my money on her."

Reynor chuckled as he peered at his screen. "It looks like everyone else has another opinion, mate. We've only spoken about these two wily competitors, 'n' we've already got bets piling in."

I stopped listening to the two and played around with the machinery so I could place my bet. Laz was going to win this time, I knew it.

"Ryoko, you can't bet that much!" Rylan hissed.

"Don't be silly, of course I can."

"We don't know if she'll win."

"I know she will."

He crossed his arms. "How?"

"I just do, okay? Besides, this is my money and I can do what I want with it. Don't like it, tough."

Salir chuckled. "I like her."

"An unruly, mouthy female is not something to be proud of being," Ambrose muttered.

Corliss and Raikidan snarled at him, and I smiled as I secured in my bet. Don't let me down, Laz.

CHAPTER 22
(EIRA)

I handed my invitation to the woman in front of me and waited while she checked to make sure it was legitimate. I took in my surroundings. Nothing had changed from the last time I had been here. *No surprise there.* The dwarves here were consistent. They didn't see a need to excavate the mountain more beyond mining purposes, and thanks to the materials used, the buildings required little more than basic maintenance from time to time.

"You are all checked in, Eira," the woman said. "You can go inside the building behind me. The Run will start in ten minutes."

"Barely made it," I mumbled as I made my way inside the building that looked more like a stronghold.

"Well what do we have here? Eira finally decided to join the party."

I gazed around until I noticed a young man around my age, with an athletic build and blue hair approaching. With him was a curvaceous woman around our age with blonde hair and dyed pink tips as well as a young girl with blonde hair.

I nodded in acknowledgement. "Alex."

A small grin spread on his face. "Still as formal as ever. You haven't changed."

The little girl approached and then circled me. "Is this the lady you told me about? She doesn't look that tough."

I chuckled and looked at Alex. "Yours?"

He shook his head and pointed to the woman with him. "No. Lexi is Lara's daughter."

"I didn't think they allowed kids back here."

"Lara is my extra help if I need it. We couldn't leave Lex—"

Someone's amused, cocky chuckle enveloped the room. I sighed. I didn't want to deal with this guy. "What do you want, Lucas?"

The ebon-haired man who approached grinned. "It's been so long, Eira, and this is the greeting you give me? You haven't changed."

"Wipe that smirk off his ugly face." Lucas had a rather nice-looking face, but the voice's insult amused me. Occasionally I liked that we were on the same page as far as the names on the hate list.

"Unless you have something useful to say, Lucas, I'd suggest you leave," Alex warned.

"I'd suggest you stay quiet, little Alex, unless you wish to find your loss much more humiliating than in the past," Lucas threatened.

"I'm not hearing a threat of foul play, am I, Lucas?" A wicked grin spread across my lips. "You know the penalty if it is. And I'd be more than happy to serve that punishment to you."

Lucas glowered. "What are you doing here, Eira? Do you honestly think you can beat me, with your poor record?"

"I've learned quite a bit in my absence." I walked past him. "So we'll see."

Lucas spat on the ground. "Cocky bitch. I'll wipe the floor with you."

I waved my fingers without turning to look at him. "You'll have to catch me first."

"I like her, Alex," Lexi whispered.

I chuckled, as did Alex, and I headed over to a hologram with a map of the course. The course changed every year to keep the game fresh, but it had been so long since I participated last, I could be running the same one and I wouldn't know the difference. *What's this?* My brow rose. *Elevators?* Sure enough, each course section now began and ended with elevators. This intrigued me. The dwarves were enlisting help to make these games more exciting. *I'll have to be on my toes even more now. Satria only knows what I'll run into.*

My eyes returned to the beginning of the course. It was new to me. The start was close to the end, right on top of it, really, and that confused me. *What do they have planned?*

"Be on your guard. I don't like the look of this."

"The beginning is brand new," Alex said as he joined me. "No one knows what it'll be."

"Interesting—that's what it'll be."

Alex chuckled. "Something is different about you, Eira. Others said you weren't the same, but I didn't believe them until now."

I continued to look at the map. "People change."

"But you never did. Nothing could change you."

"My world changed," I said.

"That could be an influence." He eyed me. "Or it's something else."

I knew where this was going. It's why I kept a formal attitude with him. If I didn't, these conversations would come up more often when we crossed paths. "No, I'm not going to join Team Four."

He threw his hands up into the air. "Oh, c'mon, Eira. You'd fit in with us. And we'd be great partners."

The drop in his vocal tone compelled me to glance his way. "I like my team."

"Just think about it."

"I have thought about it, and my answer hasn't changed since the last five times you've asked."

Alex glanced at the clock on the base of the hologram machine. "We'll talk about this later. Competition is about to start."

"There isn't anything to talk about," I muttered as I went over to the elevators.

Someone ushered me into an elevator and the door closed behind me. I crossed my arms and leaned against the wall. The one light in the box flickered and buzzed, and my nerves ticked up as unease fell over me.

The elevator lurched and then moved. I took a deep breath. *I can do this.* I could hear Reynor and Den going at it now, and I began to fidget with my jacket. This was it. I needed to get my head in the game and keep it together. I'd give it my best and that was all I could do.

Taking a deep breath, I closed my eyes until the elevator stopped. I opened them again as the elevator door opened. I ventured out and peered around, as did all other contestants. We were on top of a building, that much I was sure, but that was all I was sure of. The elevator behind me retracted back into the building as if someone thought we'd chicken out and try to head back down.

I watched several contestants walked around to figure out what to do. Even Alex was making an assessment. I walked to the center of the building and waited. I'd find out what to do soon enough.

On cue, Alex approached me. "There's nothing connecting the buildings. It's as if they want us t—"

"Ladies and gentlemen, our contestants are ready!" Den announced. "And I want to remind our viewers about some of the points to this competition, for those who are watching for the first time, or haven't attended for some time. All competitors are allowed help from two non-competitors at any point of the competition, but they are only allowed to use each help once. These helpers are also not to get in the way of other competitors directly. Competitors and competitive help are not allowed to use anything but natural abilities.

"In this competition, time is of the essence for these players, as competitors will be whittled down at the end of each part of the course by a limited number of elevators." *That explains the elevators.* "That is, if the toughness of the course doesn't do that first! And speaking of tough, this start is a doozy! I'm glad I'm not them."

"You're such a pansy, mate, this start ain't so bad," Reynor said.

Den chuckled. "Right. I'd like to see you jump off a twelve-hundred-foot tall building and get to the roof of an adjacent building at the same time."

"No way! I know I'm crazy, mate, but that's beyond my level. We're going to see competitors drop like flies far too early at this point. Who was the crazy bloke who thought of this idea?"

I tuned them out as I figured out how to get this part of the course completed. I knew what I had to do, but doing it was another matter. I made my way to the edge of the building. It didn't take me long to spot the elevator I needed to get to—and the height differences of the buildings didn't escape my eye, either.

The elevator ride up must have been fast, because this building was huge. Den may have said the height in numbers, but it didn't mean anything until I could visually see it myself.

We weren't on the building we had started in, meaning these elevators had the ability to go in more than one direction. Looking around, it appeared to be the tallest building here. I'd seen it in the past, but never learned about it.

"You know what to do. Just be careful."

I positioned myself just right and backed up. I closed my eyes and took a deep breath before opening them again. Other competitors in front of me jumped out of the way when I sprinted to the edge. I pushed myself out enough to not have to worry about hitting anything that may have been protruding off the building and slowing me from reaching the velocity I needed to gain.

"Is she crazy?" I barely heard Den yell through the wind battering my ears. "She just jumped right off that roof without a second thought!"

"'N' here I thought I was insane," Reynor said. "This girl is in a complete different game of crazy, though. I like it."

I tuned them out and narrowed my eyes as I plummeted toward the ground. I needed to time this right or I was toast. I continued to glance at the building with the elevators to make sure I was going to still have the right distance to perform my stunt and land safely. Finding my optimal opportunity, I flipped my body and then pushed off the building I had jumped from. I pulled myself into a ball to make sure I didn't cut my wind resistance, and prepared myself for my landing.

I rolled as I landed on my target building to absorb the impact, and used the momentum to get myself up on my feet.

"She made it!" Den yelled. "She actually made it!"

"Not only did she make it, but look at her walk it all off like it was nothing," Reynor said. "This girl is something else. Not only is she crazy, but she's also the first to make it to the end of this part of the course. Hell, she's the only one to have made an attempt! All the other competitors are still trying to figure this all out."

"Well, I can't believe I'm saying this, but I may have been wrong about Eira. She has the guts to get to the end. We may end up with a new reigning champ tonight, if that start is any indication."

"That's what I like to hear out of your mouth!"

"But this competition has only started, so I may change my mind."

"I'm going to hit you, mate."

I chuckled as I gazed up at the building I had jumped from and waved at a person I assumed was Lucas. I wasn't going to let him think he was going to win just because he had in the past for so long. Nothing was meant to last forever, and it was time someone dethroned him.

"Nice job."

I blew out a breath as I relaxed in my elevator and felt it move. A map projected in front of me to show what the next part of the course would look like. A control panel came out of the wall to allow me to input a few responses to prompts on the hologram. I made my choices carefully. I had to win this time. It didn't matter to the others if won or not, but it mattered to me. I needed to prove to myself I could do this—that I was different now.

23
CHAPTER
(RYOKO)

Laz ran as fast as she could and soared over every obstacle in her path, which wasn't difficult for her since the course wasn't all that hard right now. But Reynor and Den were acting like she was the most amazing runner they'd seen in a while. After her crazy yet amazing jump off that building, they couldn't stop talking about her—although they had fewer competitors to talk about now, since most couldn't make it down the building.

"Well, mates, it looks like we may be having a slight change in the course," Reynor announced. "We're getting notifications that hostiles who snuck into the mountain a day ago have moved onto the course, and at the pace this competition has been going, no one has had time to remove them. Our competitors better be ready for a fight, because there's no avoiding the area these hostiles have chosen to make their camp."

I bit my lip and watched, hoping Laz wasn't going to fall out of the competition too soon. Rylan sidled up next to me to watch, and his quiet nature helped calm me. If he wasn't worried, I should try not to be as well.

Hearing Reynor's announcement, Laz's expression changed. The change wasn't drastic, but I knew her well enough to know she was ready to fight her way through if needed. The worry I had been trying to suppress fought its way back up when I noticed the course closing in, making everything very linear. I couldn't understand why anyone would make camp in a place like that, but it didn't matter. They were in the way of the competition, and the only way to get any farther was to go through them.

Laz jumped into the air when something came flying at her. When she landed, she continued on as if it had been nothing—but that nothing didn't last long. More objects flew past her for about another minute before they stopped altogether. Laz slowed her pace, Alex and Lucas passing her. She came to a halt. I couldn't help but look closer at the screen in anticipation.

"What is she doing?" Raikidan hissed. "She's not going to win like that."

Ambrose grunted. "No wonder she's never won."

"Quiet, both of you!" I snapped. "If you were paying attention, you'd notice she's thinking. Lucas and Alex may have passed her, but they won't get past that blockade of people without a plan."

"She's right," Corliss said. "It wouldn't be like Eira to run in so rashly with something like this. Her aim is to win, after all."

"You don't suppose the girl is scared, do you, mate?" Reynor asked Den. "She's just standing there."

Den chuckled. "I highly doubt she's afraid of a few hostiles."

"What do you suppose she's doing, then?"

"Letting Alex and Lucas do the dirty work. I mean look at those two go, brawling it out down there."

"Hey, guys, looks like Laz is finally moving," I informed the others.

We stared at the screen as Laz moved to a full-out sprint. *Such an intense stare she has. Is she planning on running right through that mob?* When she closed in on the action, she leapt into the air and used a hostile that came at her as a foot hold as she came back down. She bounced off a few more people as she made her way closer to the wall. I held my breath as I tried to figure out what she was doing—I also worried about her safety.

When Laz was close enough, she launched herself at the tall wall. Her shoes melted away as she landed on it and ran across the surface.

"Are you seeing this, mate?" Reynor shouted.

"I sure am—and so are the sensors in those walls." I peered at a new screen Den displayed to us. It was a digital outline of Laz's fingers and they showed a slow-motion replay of tiny spines coming out of her skin and sticking into the wall for grip. "It seems Eira has tiny spines in her fingers and toes to help her grip! That's an incredible design, if you ask me."

Reynor's brow rose, an interested grin spreading across his lips. "I could think of a few more ways that could be useful."

He yelped out in pain when Den smacked him, and I rolled my eyes. These two were ridiculous. I watched as Laz made it to the top of the wall by jumping to the adjacent one a few times to keep her momentum, and then sprint toward the finish of this part of the course.

Rylan jumped up onto the platform and dished out the food he'd retrieved for everyone. I bit into my burger, relishing the delicious goodness. The dwarves knew the right way to make a meaty meal.

"So, find out anything while you were down there?" I asked, my mouth still full of food.

"Yeah, like manner lessons for Ryoko?" Blaze said.

I glared at him as everyone laughed.

"No, because they have worse manners than her," Rylan said. "But I did see Council members Akama and Enrée walking about, talking with some locals as well as others visiting for the competition. Couldn't catch what their conversations were about, but the two looked pleased, so I guess that's something."

"What about you?" Raid asked.

"I spoke to a few people about things here and there, but nothing great came of it. Seems people are a bit hesitant to help us beyond smuggling people out."

"I wonder why," Argus said. "It's not like we've done anything that would jeopardize them."

"Could be the poor pace we've set, dealing with Zarda," I said. "I mean it does feel like the Council isn't in any hurry to end this. It's why Laz is so twitchy about them."

I went back to focusing on the race. The competition was half over now, and Laz had set a nice pace. Only ten competitors remained. Alex struggled to keep his third place spot, and the competitors behind him weren't doing much better.

Joy overcame me and I squealed when Laz made it into the elevator. She was doing so well, and I hoped it stayed like this. We didn't get to see what each next part of the course was going to be until at least two eligible participants were in the elevators and heading to that course. *I hope the course she has trouble with isn't picked this year. It'd be nice for her to get a break for once.*

I turned my gaze away from my computer when I heard someone approaching our viewing platform. "What's up, Vorn?"

"Lookin' fer a lass named Elarinya."

Danika stepped forward. "That would be me."

He waved for her to follow as he turned away. "Follow me. Ye have been requested tae help Eira."

I looked at Rylan. "Laz, ask for help? Since when? That's not like her."

"Maybe she knows something we don't," Rylan said.

"But that doesn't change the fact that she's asking for help," Raid said.

Rylan shrugged. "I guess we shouldn't question it. If she's asking for help, then she has a better chance at winning."

"I know, but I still wanna know what's up." I turned to look at the screen and gasped at what I saw.

"What, what's wrong?" Rylan demanded.

"Look at what the next course is."

He leaned closer. "Ah shit."

"This is the course she does poorly on, isn't it?" Mana guessed.

I nodded. "I can now see why she asked for Danika's help."

"Let's hope she can," Rylan said.

"Can you tell us what's so bad about this course?" Mana asked. "It looks pretty straightforward."

"The layout of the course is as straight forward as it seems," Rylan explained. "But what the contestants have to do isn't. They become moving targets."

"You mean to tell us they purposely attack the participants of this competition?" Raikidan's eyes tightened, and the intensity of his gaze increased. Rylan nodded. "Who in their right mind thought up this course?"

I shrugged. "I don't know, but because the shots aren't intentionally lethal or maiming, they continue to use it."

Raikidan snarled. "So we have to sit here and watch. There's nothing we can do?"

I shook my head. "She agreed to the terms of the competition, so no intervention is allowed."

Raikidan spat on the ground and scowled at the screen. I could understand his anger, but the truth was there wasn't anything we could do. We had to abide by all the rules—and that meant we could only wait and watch.

"Looks like we're coming to the next part of the course, ladies and gents, and I won't be surprised if we see a large fallout of participants on this portion," Den announced.

"I have to agree, mate, this course is brutal, 'n' we may need to rethink how we see our star girl," Reynor said. "This is where she has always dropped out of this competition."

"I don't think I'm going to count her out just yet. I'm getting notification that not only is Lucas using his typical help for this part of the course, but Eira has opted for help this time, too."

"Mate, you'd better not be pulling my leg. We both know that's not her style."

"It might not have been in the past, but no one can deny she's changed. Her entire performance has done a one-eighty. We're dealing with a completely different Eira this game."

Reynor peered back down at his screen. "But we're not dealing with a different Lucas. The bloke is already out on the next part of the course 'n' his help is being the nice blockade we're used to seeing here."

"You're right, Reynor. Carlos is one hell of a Brute and makes one impressive shield. I mean look at how those bullets bounce off that stone-hardened skin of his!"

I crossed my arms. "So not impressive."

Rylan kissed me on the temple. "You're a much better Brute-class."

Mana's hand shot up. "And you're a whole lot prettier!"

I laughed. Carlos definitely had a face only a mother could love.

"And here comes Eira, everyone!" Den announced as Laz made it out of the elevator. "Looks like she decided to hang back for a few minutes for an unknown reason, giving Lucas a head start."

"But where is her help, mate?" Reynor questioned. "Is the bloke invisible?"

"Don't be stupid."

"Well, do you see someone with her?"

"No, but she does have a woman by the name of El–r–nya marked for help on this part of the course, unless it's a glitch in the system."

Reynor chuckled as Den played with his screens to check to make sure there were not glitches. "Mate, you butchered that name didn't you?"

"Shut up. It's an unusual name and it's not important. The location of her help is though. Why would she choose one and then not use it in the end?"

Reynor chuckled some more. "Don't worry about it too much, mate, Eira is doing fine right now. She's using that beautiful brain of her to take advantage of Carlos' presence! Look at how she's using him as her shield as well, even if it does mean she sacrifices whiz 'n' style points. I guess we now know why she hung back in that elevator."

"Is that legal?"

"Ain't rules against it."

"Well it looks like it's about to be short-lived because of us. Carlos has made notice and is trying to shake her while still staying in the rules he's bound to."

I watched as Laz was unable to keep her tactic up and was forced to push forward. Unfortunately, due to Carlos' lack of speed, this put her in front and in the direct line of fire. I watched with intense anticipation as she ran as fast as she could, which was an impressive speed, hurdling over obstacles while avoiding the gunfire. Then, the inevitable happened.

I stared in horror as Laz fell to the ground and clutched her shoulder. This was it. She wasn't going to make it any farther. Whatever she had planned, she couldn't put it in effect now.

"Well it looks like Eira is going to have to call it quits," Reynor said.

"Don't count her out just yet, Reynor. Look!" Den shouted.

Numb, I watched Laz rise to her feet and start running again. Obvious pain gripped her face but she wasn't going to let it stop her. I didn't know what she was up to, but hoped it wasn't going to cause her more harm than necessary. If she pushed herself too far, she'd lose a lot of blood.

"Now I know this girl is crazy," Reynor said. "Who would keep going after a blow like that?"

"Someone who is determined to prove us all wrong," Den replied. "She's got something up her sleeve and I'm dying to find out what."

I bit my nails. Laz used every possible hiding spot to her advantage as she made her way down the course. I glanced at Raikidan, to find his body tense and his teeth and hands clenched. *He's so furious.* I expected a negative reaction, but not even I could have predicted this look his eye. *He wants to murder whoever made this course.*

I gasped when Laz ran to her next position and was shot again, this time in the arm. She fell to the ground from the impact and held herself. Raikidan growled and Corliss attempted to calm him, but it didn't help. Raikidan's anger was making me feel worse.

"Well, it looks like Eira may be down for—what's this? Is she really getting back up?" Den shouted. "How many times does she need to be hit in order to stay down?"

"The girl looks determined. I don't think anything besides death itself will stop her," Reynor said.

"I just hope it doesn't get to that point. Even though those shots can't be lethally aimed, there's nothing in the rules to prevent contestants from pushing themselves too far, even to the point of death."

I stared at the screen as Laz continued on. Determination touched every corner of her face, but she couldn't take much more of this treatment. Unfortunately, the worst was yet to come. I watched with dismay as she fell to the ground once more, this time shot in the leg. And that's where she stayed. Lucas and Carlos passed her, but I was too busy splitting my attention between Laz and Raikidan. Corliss and Rylan struggled to keep him calm.

Then something amazing happened. She began to move, but her pain was apparent. Her movements were slow, however she eventually made it to her knees, and I could tell she wasn't stopping there. All gunfire ceased, and even the contestants behind her had stopped running to watch as she picked herself up.

"This woman won't give up!" Den yelled. "She's gone from crazy to absolutely insane! She should have just stayed down and accepted defeat."

"No, mate," Reynor corrected. "You're looking at a girl who has something to prove, 'n' she ain't going to let a few wounds get in the way. Even if she isn't capable of going beyond this course, she'll make it to the end of this one. To prove she can do it this time."

I shook my head as I watched her struggle to her feet. "You idiot, you should have stayed down. It's not worth it."

"That's where you're wrong," Ambrose said. "To you this may be a little game, but to her, it's a bit more. That annoying whelp is right. She has something to prove, and only death will stop her."

Raikidan pushed Rylan out of the way to get a better look at the screen dedicated to watching her. Anguish flashed across his face as he watched her limp down the course. I placed my hand on his shoulder. I understood his pain. It shouldn't have gone this far.

To my surprise, though, no more bullets were fired. No contestants behind her moved. It was as if her determination demanded their respect and earned her passage of the course. All I could do was watch helplessly as she limped closer to an available elevator. I didn't understand why she had called for Danika's help when she didn't even use it.

The elevator door opened before Laz was close enough to trigger it. Danika poked her head out, piquing my interest, and made an attempt to step out onto the course, but Laz motioned for her to stay.

"Well, Eira's help has finally made an appearance." Den scratched his head. "But what use is she at the end?"

"The girl could be here to give a hand at carrying Eira away," Reynor suggested.

"That would suggest Eira had planned on being this reckless, and until now, I didn't believe anyone would do that in a competition like this."

"Then let's see what we find out when she makes it to the elevator."

Laz collapsed into Danika's arms the moment she made it into the elevator. The doors shut them in and a new video appeared on our display screen of the two talking. Even though there was no audio, you could tell Danika was scolding Laz, although Laz laughed and smiled in response.

"I think that's the first time I've seen the girl smile." Reynor rested his cheek on his fist. "She's a real beauty when she does."

Den rolled his eyes.

As the two talked, Danika lifted her hands up and began healing Laz, and everything made sense to me. *Duh, Ryoko!*

"Whoa, what is going on in there?" Reynor asked.

Den played with one of his screens. "According to this data, Eira's help is a healer."

"So she's a medic? Ain't that against the rules?"

"Not in this instance. By these data entries, this woman is a natural healer. There are no rules against that."

"Well then, it looks like Eira did have something up her sleeve."

"As crazy as her idea was, she's heading to the next course like she wants—and I can only imagine what other surprises she has in store for us."

I smiled as I watched Laz stand up and act as if nothing had happened. I was glad she was okay, and a quick glance at Raikidan told me he felt the same. There were only three courses left. *You can do this, Laz. I know you can.*

CHAPTER 24

(EIRA)

My breath came fast and shallow as I continued to push myself. Lucas was still ahead of me—I wasn't gaining any ground on him, and that frustrated me. Sure, I had made it farther than I ever had before, but I wanted to win this one. It was a good thing I planned to pull out my last secret in the next course. It was the only way I knew to gain any ground, especially since the next course was the last and the longest. The rules stated that with this part of the course, any requested help could only assist the contestant through the first half, to make the last half that much more competitive.

I hurtled over a blockade and pushed myself harder until I made it to the elevator. I breathed hard as I rested against the metal surface, relief washing over me.

A familiar musky scent hit my nose a moment before he spoke, "About time you got here. Thought I was going to die waiting."

"Impatient whelp."

Raikidan leaned against the wall of the elevator opposite to me. The voice's chosen insult intrigued me, but I brushed it aside. "If you really want to take my place, be my guest."

"No, I'm good." He pushed away from the wall and handed me a bottle. "I thought you might need this."

I took the offering and drank the cool liquid inside. I hummed as it quenched my thirst. "Thank you. How are you liking this competition?"

"It's interesting, though you shouldn't be in second place."

"Give me a break. I almost didn't make it past one of the courses."

"Yeah, I know. I should smack you for that stunt."

I smirked. "But you won't."

"Yeah, well, I still should." I took another gulp of my drink and he dragged his gaze over me. "You look beat."

I rolled my eyes. "Thanks, that really boosts my morale."

His eyes narrowed. "Don't start with me."

I snickered. "You'd worry if I didn't."

"All right, fine, I'll give you that. Now, you going to tell me why you asked me to help and not anyone else?"

"Well, I was hoping you'd be able to give me a little boost."

"You want fire? You can make that yourself."

I laughed. "No, that's not what I meant, but that is a good idea." *I should have thought of that.* "I was hoping you could shift me into something that would be fast. I need to boost my speed to catch up to Lucas."

He chuckled. "I think I can help with that. I haven't worked on the forced shifting, so I don't know how long I can keep it up, but it should help."

"Any help is welcomed."

Raikidan looked around. "So where is the camera in this place?"

My brow rose. "Excuse me?"

"I know there's a camera in here so everyone else can see what's going on. I don't like feeling watched."

"Oh, that thing." I pointed behind him. "It's right there."

Raikidan turned around and then gazed up at the camera filming us. He took a deep breath and then melted it with a hot flame. I couldn't help but laugh, and it only increased when Reynor and Den reacted to it.

"Well, it looks like someone is a little camera shy," Den teased.

"I'm thinking it's something else, mate." Reynor said. "I mean, who wouldn't want to be alone with a beauty like that?"

"Can I kill him after I'm done helping you?" Raikidan asked.

I laughed more. "No."

"Please?"

"No. Just ignore him."

He made an unhappy grunt. "It's a little hard when his voice is everywhere."

"The competition is almost over. You'll survive."

"If dealing with that kills me, I'm going to haunt you."

I waved my hands in fake fear. "Oh, I'm so scared."

"Oh you'd better be, because if I can come up with ways to torment you while you're living, I can be even worse as a spirit."

"You're going to turn me into a bird, aren't you?"

He pointed at me. "No spoiling the surprise."

"Raikidan, you know I'm terrible at flying! You can't turn me into a bird."

"It's the fastest thing I can turn you into."

I crossed my arms. "Well if I can't do it, it's not very fast now, is it?"

"Do you want my help or not?"

"Turn me into something that can run. You'd be hindering me if you turn me into a bird. You're the one not helping!"

"Eira, calm down. It's a small bird, so it'll be easy."

I glowered at him. "Maybe for you. A little news flash, I don't fly often. And don't try to tell me I did fine last time." He closed his mouth and I continued, "Seda helped me that time. And even still, this is a competition. I'm not going to lose because you turned out to be unhelpful!"

He sighed. "Let me see the map."

I pressed a few buttons on the elevator wall. A map of the last part of the course projected.

He pointed to it. "Look how long this course is. There's no way I'm going to be able to keep you shifted for that long the who—"

I pointed to a thick line that split the course in half. "You can't help beyond this point. Competition rules for this last part."

"Even so, the first half is still long. I'll change you into a spine-tailed swift, and then when I can't hold that, we'll run a bit, and then I'll shift you into something with four legs when I can again. Does that sound fair?"

"No."

"Eira, I know birds best, okay? There are few four-legged animals that I know of that are faster."

"What's the fastest one you've seen?"

"A black-spotted, tan feline from the southwestern region on the west side of the Larkian mountain range. I've only seen it once, but it was fast."

I played with the database as I searched for an image of the cat he was talking about. I knew exactly what he had seen, but I wasn't sure if any images would be available. They were a rare sight these days. "This was it, right?"

He peered at the image I pulled up. "Yeah."

"That's a cheetah. I'm surprised you saw one, but I'm not going to complain." I tapped the image a few times. "Study it. I'll agree to your idea on the terms of that being what you change me to for the second go-round."

He smiled and then studied the picture. His studying didn't last long before the elevator slowed. I sent the holograms away and took a deep breath in preparation. This was it.

"You can do this. This plan will work."

"You agree with it?"

"I can see he wants you to win. I will trust him this time."

"All righty, folks. This is it!" Den announced. "We're at the last part of the course, and our last two contestants are nearing the end of their elevator ride. And yes, you heard me right. Alex dropped out during his trip, meaning this competition just got even more intense. Not only will it just be Lucas and Eira going at it, but with the length of this course, it's anyone's guess as to who will win."

"There are still two elevators at the end, so if this race gets closer than what it already is, we're going to be in for an exciting treat!" Reynor added.

I took my hair clip out of my hair and handed it to Raikidan. "Don't lose it."

He clenched it in his hand. "Don't worry." He then wrapped his strong arms around me. "I'll help you get going first before I shift myself. Just remember, the air is your friend here. It can help you—as long as you let it."

I nodded as I closed my eyes. The strange tingling sensation in my head that followed felt familiar, similar to the last time he did this, and I waited for it to stop.

"Okay, Eira, you're all set," Raikidan instructed.

My lids opened and I turned my new head. I peered up at Raikidan, and his gigantic size startled me. He was kneeling down, so in theory he wouldn't have been so big, had I realized he had planned to change me into such a small bird. Sure, he had told me what it was, but I had never seen one before.

"All right, hop on my hand, Eira," he encouraged.

I moved my feet to get used to them, and then made an attempt to jump up onto his offered hand, my wings flapping ungracefully in the process. He chuckled at my ungraceful landing and I pecked him. He grunted in pain but stopped making fun of me.

The elevator doors began to open, and my little heart beat faster. The moment the doors were wide enough for my liking, I opened my wings and took off.

"Whoa, what was that?" Den said.

"It looked like a bird," Reynor said.

My movements were fast, but jerky at best. This bird body was much different than the sparrow body. *He should have turned me into that.* I knew he turned me into a faster-flying bird, but at least I'd have had better control with the other bird body.

"Weird bird," Den said. "Doesn't look like it can fly right. Wait, what is a bird doing in an elevator? Wasn't that Eira's elevator?"

"I think it was, though I don't see her anywhere," Reynor observed. "I do see the bloke who is supposed to be helping her, though."

"What is he doing? Where is Eira? Did he just do what I think he did?"

"The bloke turned into a giant bird!"

"It's called a condor."

"Rack off."

If I could have chuckled, I would have. Those two really knew how to be stupid. Large wings flapped behind me, so I knew Raikidan kept a good pace, although I doubted it was hard for him. I was still having trouble.

"What is going on here?"

"Eira registered her help as a shapeshifter," Den explained.

"He's a what? Oh, my head hurts already."

"I'm just as confused, but we might as well sit back and watch, because they're covering some serious ground on Lucas, and the outcome of this competition is more important than a massive headache."

I zipped through the course and around every obstacle it threw at me as I closed the gap between Lucas and me. But my attempt felt futile—I never realized Lucas was so fast. Sure, he had time to get farther than me with some of my choices, but those alone shouldn't have put him this far ahead of me.

My altitude lowered involuntarily, and it became harder to control my wings. *Looks like my time is up.* It was for the best—I felt like I was paying more attention to my flying technique than the actual competition. Before I had much time to prepare, my body shifted and I fell to the ground. Luckily I was good at landing on my feet, and my landing was graceful enough.

Raikidan landed behind me and then caught up quickly. I could sense the energy rolling off of him and it perplexed me.

He grinned at me. "See, that wasn't too bad, now was it?"

I snorted. "If I wasn't under these time constraints, I'd smack you."

He chuckled. "I'll give you a freebie after all of this. Sound fair?"

"With the power rolling off you, you may owe me two."

"I need some way to keep up with you."

"We also need some way for you to shift me in a bit, and that energy is what does it."

"Don't worry, Eira. I'll have enough. The animal you chose can only run in a quick burst, so I'll have to time it just right, but that shouldn't be too much of an issue."

I narrowed my eyes and hurdled over and then under a few obstacles before responding. "We'll see."

Raikidan jumped in front of me and broke through a flimsy barrier with his shoulder, impressing me—and Den and Reynor. They shouted about his dramatic move and theorized about what he was. Most of their ideas were strange and absurd, and only proved to me that they really were as dumb as I thought they were.

"Eira, move closer to me so we can shift," Raikidan requested.

"Already, you sure?"

"You've set a swift pace, and this half of the course is more about speed than avoiding obstacles."

"Well, all right."

I closed the distance between us, and he placed his hand on my shoulder while placing my hair clip in his mouth so he wouldn't drop it. I hadn't thought to ask him how he was going to pull this off while moving. Raikidan's grip tightened suddenly and I felt the pull of the shift. Luckily it was fast, and I wasn't losing much ground from it.

"Whoa, did you see that?" Den shouted. "He changed them both in a matter of seconds!"

I shook my feline head and then bolted into the fastest run this streamlined body could put out. *This is fast!* I suspected the bird shape would have been faster than this, had I known how to utilize it. But running on feet was what I knew best, and sprinting on four feet wasn't much different than two. I felt so alive with this body.

Raikidan kept up with me well, his muscles rippling with strength in my peripheral. But it wasn't long before the shift wore off as the burst of quick energy plummeted.

"Easy come, easy go?" Den joked.

"That seemed quite pointless to me." Reynor said. "What was the point of that if it was for such a short time?"

"Just because it was short, doesn't mean it didn't help. Did you not notice the extra speed she gained from that? It doubled! Even for a few moments, that amount of extra speed helps in this competition."

"Then why not turn into that bird again? She went faster in that form."

"It may not have been as efficient. I can't really say, though, because the fact that these two can do this blows my mind."

Raikidan and I rounded a corner and I had to force myself to keep moving, even though my body said otherwise. At the end of the corridor stood a tall wall. *Tall is an understatement.* I estimated it to about five hundred feet high, though I was pretty sure that estimation was lacking.

This had to be the halfway point where Raikidan couldn't help me any further. It made sense, since on the map there had been a line separating the two parts of the map—but I hadn't expected that line to be a literal barrier.

"Eira, what would you say if I threw you?" Raikidan asked as he gazed up at the wall.

I cocked my head. "Excuse me?"

"That's a bit of a ways up, and I don't have the energy to shift us both into something that can fly—not that you'd be thrilled with that idea, but a boost couldn't hurt, and I can shift myself without any challenge."

"What will you shift into?"

"Something big."

I rolled my eyes. "That's real specific."

"Trust me, okay?"

"As long as you don't shift into a particular form that could get you into trouble, I will."

He chuckled. "I can't promise anything."

"Raikidan."

"Give me permission to go after that annoying guy with the weird accent when I'm done helping, and I can promise I won't, for now."

I chuckled. "Fine. Just don't do anything stupid or that could seriously hurt him. It won't look good on me."

He tossed me my hair clip. "Get ready, then."

I threw my hair up and watched as his form grew larger and darker. A trumpeting sound bellowed from his enormous body and the ground shook from the weight of his feet as they thundered on the ground. *An elephant? Well, okay.*

Using my speed, and timing everything right, I jumped up onto his back. Keeping balance as best as I could, I toed up to his head. When he curled up his trunk, I crouched low and stepped onto it. I prepared myself as we came closer to the wall. The strong muscles in his trunk tensed and then he launched me.

I flew high into the air and scrambled up the wall the moment I made contact. I jumped to a side wall when my vertical ascent became too difficult, and then bounced back to the main wall after a few moments. I repeated this process as I steadily made my way to the top. Raikidan had shifted into a hawk, and let out a loud screech above me when I made it to the top. Then he shifted back to his nu-human form. My heart skipped a beat at the sight of his free falling, but I didn't have much time to react to that. He exhaled a blast of fire right at me and then shifted back into his hawk shape.

"Whoa, what is going on?" Den asked.

Taking control of the flame, I swirled it around me as I jumped off the wall, and then fed it into my mouth. Energy flooded through me, revitalizing much of my exhausted state.

"Did she eat that flame?" Reynor shouted. "What is wrong with her?"

"It… it looks like it helped her," Den observed as I landed safely and continued on. "She looks better than ever!"

"This girl never ceases to—hey, that bloke just stole my jacket!"

"Well that'll teach you not to leave it on the table next time," Den said.

"No it wo—oh, lookie here. Looks like I have an excuse to go get it back."

"Great, what woman caught your eye this time?"

"Not just one girl, mate—two. Although, the green-haired girl he gave my jacket to did catch my eye first. Eira knows how to surround herself with some real beauties."

"Well, sorry to bust your bubble, bud, but it looks like they're already taken."

Reynor sighed. "Figures. Maybe those blokes are interested in sharin'?"

I rolled my eyes. *He's just as bad as Blaze.*

"You could set your sights back on the lady competitor you've been ogling over up until now."

"Mate, even I know no one has a shot with her. I can look, but I can't touch."

He was going to get punched at this rate. If I ended up encountering him before this night was over, I knew I would. Pushing the thought out my head, I focused on the competition. I needed to catch up with Lucas, and any hesitation would prevent that.

I gasped for air as I pushed myself to the limits. I had managed to catch up to Lucas, but at the expense of the extra energy Raikidan gave me with his fire, and Lucas wasn't making this easy on me. I flipped over obstacles and bounced off walls, but I still didn't gain any ground.

"Don't give up," the voice whispered. *"Prove them wrong. Prove you can do this."*

Lucas grinned at me, trying to rub it in. I wanted to punch him so badly, but the disqualification rule kept me in line.

"Wipe that smirk off his face!"

We jumped over a large gap in the ground and luck was on my side.

Lucas misjudged the leap and landed wrong, forcing him to recover and allowing me to pull ahead a little. He muttered insults and I smiled. *I can do th—*

Lucas caught up. *Dammit!*

The ending elevators came into sight and we fought for the lead. His breath came out in exhausted heaves like mine, but neither of us were willing to give this up. He had a title to hold onto, but I had something to prove.

"Look at these two go!" Den shouted. "I don't know who to root for anymore, and it's anyone's guess who is going to make it in first!"

"Looks like it'll be a photo finish," Reynor said.

I glanced at Lucas when my last bit of energy stores ran out. He wasn't struggling as badly as I was, and he pulled head. I needed to think fast. I needed to win.

"You have the energy to win," the voice said. *"Find it deeper inside you."*

"Why are you helping me?" I asked it.

"Because I want you to win."

Shock rippled through me. Not only was it responding to me, it wanted to help. It said once that it wanted to protect me… which I didn't get at all. I also didn't get why it wanted to help so much. It had been doing that a lot lately instead of saying awful things like in the past. I didn't understand its position—or its existence, really.

Focus, Eira. I could think about it later. I needed to focus on my win. Gritting my teeth, I searched deep for one last store of energy. For a moment, I thought I'd used everything up and this was it. But then, a warmth called to me and I reached for it. A surge of energy coursed through me and my pace picked up. I closed the gap between Lucas and me and pulled ahead, though the lead didn't last long.

I continued to push, my body crying out about my limits being reached. I'd hate myself later for ignoring those cries, but I needed to do this. I needed to win. I needed to prove I had changed and could do something on the unbloody path.

"Just give up now, Eira," Lucas whispered.

I narrowed my eyes. "No."

"You let me win and I'll give you the money."

"I'm not here for the money."

Lucas scowled and pushed forward. *I won't be outmatched by the likes of you, Lucas.* I ran until I slammed into the interior wall of the elevator, where I collapsed in exhaustion. My breath came out in ragged bursts and it hurt to breathe. I didn't know which of us had entered our elevator first, but right now, I was too focused on recovering to care much. I didn't even care to listen to Den and Reynor as they speculated who had won this. But something they said did catch my ear. There wasn't a camera in these last elevators, which meant they couldn't see my condition or what I was about to do.

I coughed out a pitiful ember, not worthy to be called a flame, and then ate it. Even though I was weak, I could convert enough of it to stabilize myself and produce energy at a stronger rate again. I sucked in a deep inhale when a burst of energy rushed through me. I then rose to my feet and fixed my hair. Win or lose, I'd still make sure I walked away with my pride intact.

The elevator stopped and I closed my eyes as I took a deep breath. The elevator made a strange scraping noise, which perplexed me. It wasn't the standard sound of an elevator door opening. It was as if the walls had slid down, or—

The spectators cheered with an excitement that echoed through the mountain at a volume I didn't expect. I opened my eyes to see that I no longer stood in an elevator. The floor beneath me still belonged to the elevator, but that floor was on a dais. *The winner's platform!*

"She did it! Eira actually did it!" Den shouted. "I can't believe my eyes, folks, but we have a new champion for The Run. And she's also set a new record! This is one hell of a day for us."

I did it. I shoved my hands in my pockets and listened. For once I didn't mind having all the attention on me. It felt good to have won this.

"Congratulations," the voice said. *"You deserve this win."*

"This is a day for the history books, mate," Reynor stated. "'N' look at how reserved she is. Most would be jumping around like a maniac, but she's soaking it all in quietly."

"Humility at its finest," Den agreed.

"Oi, lass, mighty fine run ye did."

I opened my eyes and smiled as Vorn walked up to the platform. "Thanks, Vorn."

"Now, get yerself down here. I owe ye an' yer friends a few rounds o' drinks."

I chuckled. "You're going to regret that."

His brow lifted. "Aye, maybe."

I hopped down from the dais and followed him. We walked through a maze of buildings until coming to an open plaza where all of the other contestants were gathered.

"I'll get yer friends, lass," Vorn said. "Dun get intae any trouble."

I smirked. "No promises."

A hearty chuckle rumbled out of him before disappearing into the shadows. Some of the other contestants waved at me, or nodded with acknowledgement and congratulations, but one small group approached me. *Alex and his friends.*

Alex smiled wide. "Excellent run out there, Eira."

I gave a curt, reserved nod. "Thanks."

"No really, you did amazing out there."

I shook my head. "My answer is still no, Alex."

"C'mon, Eira. Our assignments are geared around this kind of stuff." He wrapped his arm around my shoulders and grinned. "You'd fit perfectly with us."

"I told y—"

Someone grabbed his arm and pushed him away. "She said no, now back off."

My face twisted in confusion as Raikidan slid his arm around my shoulders in Alex's place. He did not look pleased with Alex at all.

Alex held up his hands. "All right, all right. She's yours, I get it. You don't need to get so physical."

Raikidan snorted and then shifted his gaze to me. "Let's get going. I don't know how long Rylan is going to be able to hold Ryoko back."

We started walking away. "That bad?"

"I swear she exploded earlier when she saw you on the winner's platform."

I laughed. "Oh boy. Nothing will stop her from crushing me with excitement, then."

"Then you might want to get ready now."

I looked at him funny when he pulled away. "Wha—"

A body crashed into me and squeezed the air right out of me. "You did it!"

I coughed. "Ryoko... I need to be able... to breathe."

"Breathing is overrated."

"Ryoko, please. I know you're excited, but I'd rather not die right now."

She huffed and let go, her lower lip sticking out into a pout. "Meanie."

Rylan came over and messed up my hair. "Nice job."

I swatted him away. "Stop it!"

He chuckled and I grumbled as I pulled my hair out of its hold. Placing my hairclip in my mouth, I played with my hair to smooth it out and then put it back up. As I was finishing, I noticed Lucas and his pals prowling our way, and he didn't look pleased. "What, going to be a sore loser?"

His lip curled up into a snarl. "You cheated."

I guess we're playing that game. "Excuse me?"

"You heard me. No one just wins after they've never participated in years."

Ryoko stuck her tongue out at him. "Your head just got too big."

"Quiet, woman!" he snapped.

Raikidan shoved him. "You're the one who needs to shut up."

Lucas sized Raikidan up. "And your help is another story. Healers and shapeshifters?" He spat on the ground. "Real, my ass."

Shva'sika chuckled. "Do I need to validate my lighting?" She snapped her fingers, triggering a spark. "I'd be more than happy to fry his insides to prove it."

Ryoko giggled with glee. "Oh, I like it when you're feisty, Danika."

"Make sure he's extra crispy," Corliss encouraged. "That's how I like assholes prepared."

"Even frying him that well won't make him taste any good," I said.

"Add barbecue sauce," Blaze suggested.

I shook my head. "You suggest barbecue sauce for everything."

Blaze held up his hands. "What, it makes everything taste better."

"Enough!" Lucas pointed at me. "You cheated and you will admit it. Especially with this one."

Raikidan growled when Lucas pointed at him, and I wasn't prepared for what he did next. He grew larger and darker as he shifted to his dragon form. Lucas backed up, his eyes wide and his hands shaking. Raikidan lowered his head and roared. Lucas fell over and looked as though he was about to wet himself any moment.

To add to the situation, Corliss and Mana exchanged a glance and grinned before shifting to their dragon forms. Although I had seen Corliss and Mana in that vision of Raikidan's past, this was the first time I had gotten the chance to see their true shape. *Impressive.*

Peridot green-colored scales covered Mana's body, the lower mountain city light shimmering off the polished surfaces as she moved. Two large frills ran down her back until they reached her tail. Dark green spikes grew from her front elbows, and her horns of the same shade were plated. Her horns were different than any other dragon's I'd seen before. Halfway up them, they branched, with the top half curving skyward like Raikidan's and the bottom half curving down and back toward her head. They reminded me a lot of antlers. *Actually, like Elder dragons.*

I'd never seen one, no one had in some time. They'd gone extinct long ago. But I'd found an entry once in the Eternal Library that had a painted depiction with brief description. *Interestingly enough, he had green scales too.*

Corliss, on the other hand, had darker scales, comparable to emerald, with ebony scales scattering his body like stars. Long, waved black horns protruded from under the plated crest on his head, and black spikes lined his cheeks, accenting above and below his eyes. A single frill raced down the center of his back to his spaded tail.

I couldn't help but glance at Ambrose to see his reaction. As I expected, mortification blanketed his face, while Salir and Rennek were surprisingly unfazed.

"Whoa..." Lexi, the girl I had met earlier, wandered closer and stared up at Corliss and Mana in awe. Her eyes sparkled.

Mana lowered her head and allowed Lexi to maul her face excitedly with her tiny hands. When she finished with Mana's face, she investigated her giant talons and ventured underneath them. Mana was careful not to crush the little girl.

Lexi finally poked her head with a big smile. "Mama, can we keep her?"

Lara chuckled. "No."

She kicked a rock on the ground. "Aw, man..."

I chuckled and flicked my gaze to Lucas. I found him trying to recover, although Raikidan made that difficult.

"Humiliate the ingrate."

It was time to rub salt in the wound. Leaning against Raikidan's leg, I crossed my arms and grinned. "Looks like you've been shown up by a child, Lucas."

Carlos moved forward and pounded his fists together while his skin hardened. "I'm going to make you shut your mouth, woman."

"Make him pay for his insolence!"

Mana moved herself around Lexi to keep her safe, although it didn't seem that Lexi minded, with all her giggling.

"Lass, here!" Vorn shouted.

I turned as he threw his hammer to me. I grabbed the weapon with both hands and was taken aback by its weight. I forced as much strength as I could muster into swinging the hammer around and crashing it into Carlos' chest. Carlos slammed into the ground as the hammer cracked the pavement when I let it fall.

I exhaled hard from the effort of swinging it. "Damn, this thing is heavy. What is it made of, lead?"

"Gold-infused titanium, lass. Gold-infused titanium."

"Damn…"

Vorn strode over to me and took the hammer, swinging it over his shoulder as if it didn't weigh anything at all, leaving us all dumbfounded. "Ye lads may want tae get yer friend tae a doctor. I doubt e'en he can take a hit like that without receivin' internal injuries. Now, lass, I promised ye a drink. Let's get tae the tavern, then."

25
CHAPTER

Vorn led us through the streets, each one as lively as the last. Races of all kinds mingled as if it were the most normal thing to do, and deep down, I hoped one day, it would be the norm up on the surface. I wanted Lumaraeon to go back to the old days, before the Great War—before the Purge—before the War of End—a time where everyone had a right to live, and live the way they deemed right for them.

Many civilians stopped to wave or shout out a congratulations to me. I nodded to them in respect, but otherwise tried to keep the attention to a minimum.

"Here we are," Vorn said. "The Molten Ale Tavern."

We all looked around. A large establishment stood before us, lively sounds coming from within. Around the back side of the building flowed a river of lava, and close by, several workshops. *I can see where it gets its name.*

Vorn threw open the door to the tavern. "Nordec, drinks fer Champion Eira an' 'er friends, on me!" Loud cheering erupted in the tavern. "Not any o' ye!"

I laughed when the cheers changed to disgruntled grumbling. Vorn led us to the bar where Nordec, a dwarf of dark complexion and long dark hair and facial hair, poured several pints. He slid them out to everyone and then poured a few drinks from a clear bottle filled with a pale liquid. He slid the mug to me and a few other ladies.

My brow rose. "Please don't tell me you just served me elven piss."

"Elven wine, lass," he said.

I pushed the mug toward Shva'sika. "Yeah, that's what I said."

Shva'sika scoffed. "Excuse you?"

"You know it's true," I said. "Your ciders are decent but your wines are disgusting."

She stuck up her nose and sipped on her drink. "More for me then."

Nordec chuckled and poured a pint of dark ale. "I like ye, lass. Drink up!"

I took a swig, paying close attention to the taste. *Bitter, more nutty than anything, with a taste of… chocolate? No… coffee.* "Let me guess… Rockyfist stout?"

"Ye be close, lass," he said. "Mountain Rock stout. Similar craftin' style."

"I like it. I'll have another after I'm done with this."

He nodded. "Just tell me when yer ready."

I turned around to find the others enjoying their drinks. Well, except Ryoko. She had grabbed the elven wine to try. "Not liking it, Ryo?"

She shrugged. "Meh. I've had worse, but I've definitely had better."

"Well, finish it off and get some dwarven brews. You'll be far happier with those."

She nodded and chugged the weak wine. Vorn chuckled. "Rather impressive, lass."

She held her thumb to her chest. "You're looking at an undefeated drinking champ!"

"Oh really?" he grinned. "Then I challenge ye. Been a long time since anyone outdrank me."

Ryoko threw her fist out at him in excitement. "That's what I like to hear. Bring it on!"

The bar erupted in excitement. Nordec went to pouring the Mountain Rock stout, and I brought them over to Ryoko and Vorn as they got themselves situated. Several other patrons wanted in on the contest, and the bets went in. When I noticed Nordec struggling to keep up with the needed order, I jumped behind the bar and poured.

He chuckled when I made my fifth well-poured pint. "Perfect head on those. I be impressed. If ye ever be needin' a job, there be one for ye here."

I chuckled. "I'll let my nightclub boss know so he pays me better."

Nordec belted out a hearty laugh and continued pouring. Rylan and Raikidan served the beers until they filled the large table chosen for the competition. Mana giggled with glee when Vorn selected her to start the little contest.

She raised her hand and waited for the last-minute entries before throwing down her hand. "Begin!"

Ryoko snatched a mug first and gulped it down as fast as she could. Vorn reached for two mugs and worked on one before working on the second and discarding the empty pint. I chuckled as he kept up this automation. *He's no stranger to these contests.* But Ryoko knew a pace that worked for her, and while this stout had decent strength, it wasn't as strong as some of the stuff she liked to compete with.

As I watched the other competitors, they too had their own way to go about their pace and many were holding out well. It was anyone's guess who'd come out on top, but I'd bet my money on Ryoko. I'd seen Vorn drink, but he'd never come close to what Ryoko did to her liver. Luckily for her, she didn't drink like this a lot, so I had a little less to worry about as far as her killing her organs just yet.

The room grew louder as patrons cheered and chanted. Many placed bets, and even I got in on the action, placing some down on Ryoko. As I drank my stout I noticed two psychics, a man and woman of fair skin and raven hair, watching the crowd. Well, the male psychic was getting rowdy; his sister just watched in amusement. I walked over and they shifted their attention to me. "Akama, Enrée."

They nodded and Akama spoke, "Congratulations on your win, Eira."

"Thank you. I assume it's added favor for us," I said.

She nodded. "Quite a bit, actually. You've allowed us to secure better funding, money that was going to another city fighting Zarda's occupation."

I snorted. "Fighting a symptom doesn't work well."

Enrée chuckled. "That's what we have told them for years, but we couldn't convince anyone to fund us. Our performances in this competition had an effect in that. They figured if we couldn't do well in this, we couldn't possibly do well winning against Zarda."

I took a swig of my drink. "We've done better than most, but whatever. As long as we get the funding now, that's all that matters. Everything else in order?"

Akama nodded. "The entry route we use to get here is still approved as a good smuggling route for both goods and people. And some of the other cities provided good intel, especially on strategic points for Zarda's forces and the type of supplies we all can work toward cutting free of him."

Enrée cheered and started chanting when three contestants dropped out of the competition, literally. Akama and I chuckled. "I never knew serious Council members could have so much fun."

Akama smirked. "We're among the few. No point to life if there isn't a little fun, though my brother does get a little overexcited sometimes."

"How could I not?" Enrée said. "If I could drink, I'd be joining these guys!"

Akama and I shook our heads. She then focused on me again. "Are you sure you don't wish to reconsider Alex's offer to switch to his team?"

My brow knitted. "Excuse me?"

"I know we'll never convince you to join Team One, but Team Four is geared around information relay. A transfer wouldn't be an issue after how well you performed today. That team could use someone like you."

My eyes darkened in irritation. "Or you could just give me some of those assignments and not play these team wars."

She frowned. "Eira, you must understand these teams are in place for a reason. We distribute assignments based on how the team lays out, to keep things organized. It's how we'll win against Zarda."

"Yeah, because you've done a bang-up job moving forward," I spat. "You're all so stuck in your ways you can't see how flawed they are."

"Eira, please don't—"

"I'm starting to wonder whose side you are really on. Might want to put that into consideration when making decisions, Council Member Akama." I turned and walked away. "Enjoy the celebration of my win, and have a good night."

I placed my empty mug on the bar and grabbed another before standing next to Raikidan. He chuckled when Blaze swayed as he finished another pint and struggled to grab another one. "How many more do you think he has in him?"

I studied Blaze for a moment. "He won't finish that mug he just grabbed."

"I hope not. I bet with Corliss that he'd be the next to drop out," he said.

I snickered and the two of us watched Blaze struggle to get through his stout. The guy next to him wasn't doing any better, and Corliss and Raikidan started to get a bit tense. Both Blaze and the other contestant stopped mid-chug and swayed. They looked at each other and I braced for what came next. They both bent over behind them and upchucked all the ale they'd just consumed. Many patrons retched or made displeased sounds. I had to turn away so I wouldn't lose what little I had in my own stomach. Corliss and Raikidan looked both disgusted and disappointed. Mana, on the other hand, jumped with joy, saying, "I win! I win!"

Both male dragons grumbled and handed her a few gold pieces. Salir laughed at the two men while Ambrose shook his head. Salir and Rennek appeared to be enjoying themselves, both choosing to brave a stronger dwarven craft than what was being used in the competition, and Ambrose, unsurprisingly, appeared displeased and tortured.

Contestants continued to drop out until only Ryoko and Vorn remained, and neither ready to quit. They each downed two more pints, not giving an inch.

"Anyone been keeping track?" I called out.

Mana raised her hand. "They're tied at twenty. Everyone started slowing down at about ten glasses, and most dropped out after that."

I could sense Rylan's concern at this point and I didn't blame him. The mugs may only be pints, and a stout wasn't as strong as some of the other alcoholic drinks Ryoko had consumed, but twenty in a single sitting was a lot for anyone. I cracked my knuckles. "All right then, let's kick this up a notch. Nordec, pour two steins of black dragon brew."

The tavern grew quiet and Nordec's eye bugged out. "Ye sure, lass? It be the strongest ale out there."

I nodded. "I think it's the only way we're going to find out who can handle more."

He shrugged. "All right, but I ain't gonna be responsible if yer friends die."

"Just pour."

Nordec pulled out two large ornate mugs with lids and poured an ebony-colored liquid into them—the low light of the tavern glistening off the dark surface, like you'd see on dragon scales. The dwarf pushed the steins forward and I retrieved them. I grinned at the two drunken competitors as I set a stein in front of each of them.

"Okay, ladies, drink up."

Vorn stared at me, his eyes crossing a bit. "Yer crazy, lass. Everyone an' their nana knows one pint o' those could put a full grown dragon down."

"Sounds like a fun challenge!" Ryoko slurred.

Vorn stared at her, mouth agape. "Ye both be crazy."

She picked up the stein. "You're right there. Now you gonna drink against me, or forfeit?"

Snickering, I backed up. Vorn grasped his stein. "Yer on, lass."

Patrons started rhythmically pounding their mugs on tables or slow clapping. Ryoko and Vorn each placed the rim of their stein to their lips, their noses twitching from the strength of the brew, and then guzzled down the dark ale as best as they could. Only a few gulps in, Ryoko pulled away, smacking her lips together. "Mouth feels funny."

We all laughed as the words barely came out as intelligible.

"That be the effect o' the black dragon brew," Nordec said. "Crafted strong like dragon scales and wi' a bite like black dragon lichtnin'."

A few patrons rolled their eyes, not believing much in the claim, but Nordec ignored them. Dwarves were among the few races who never believed in the dragon extinction tales from the Great War. Those who did believe the lie balked at them and labeled the dwarves either insane or skilled storytellers. Neither claim was too far off, even without their dragon knowledge.

"I like it!" Ryoko announced before downing more of her stein.

I glanced at Ambrose and found him now interested in the events going on. Raikidan leaned over and whispered in my ear. "He's interested in this brew. I thought he was going to have a heart-attack when you called out the name, but he calmed down once we got an explanation about it."

Ambrose let out a low hiss and the two of us chuckled. Vorn slammed his stein on the table, pulling all attention back to him. He breathed heavy with tense shoulders, clutching the handle of his stein. Someone leaned over him to peer into his mug and shook his head, indicating Vorn hadn't finished. *But he looks it.* I wasn't sure he'd be able to handle anymore. *But, Ryoko…*

She gulped the brew down, at a slower pace than she had with the stout, but still a steady one. The chanting started then, along with louder banging on the tables. Our half-wogron friend continued, spurred on by the encouragement, and Vorn watched in amazement.

The stein continued to tip up as she drank more of the strong brew, until it reached its maximum tilt. She slammed the stein down on the table, the wood cracking a bit. She took several deep, staggered breaths before letting the stein go and sitting up, a wicked grin plastered on her face. The room erupted with cheers and Vorn stared at her, dumbfounded.

"Well, Vorn, we going another round, or have you yet to finish yours?" she challenged.

Vorn pushed his stein forward. "I cannae believe ye did it, lass. I concede tae ye."

Ryoko jumped to her feet, nearly knocking the table over. "Oh yeah! Still undefeated!" She swayed. "Oh, that's not good." We all watched as she fell backward and hit the floor hard. The tavern grew still until her fists flew up into the air, both thumbs raised. "I'm okay!"

The room roared with laughter and Rylan ran over to help her. She complained about the room spinning, so he encouraged her to close her eyes and count backward.

"What's counting?"

Rylan couldn't help but laugh at her. Raikidan sipped on the Mountain Rock stout he was still working on, and the two of us watched as Ambrose approached the bar. When he ordered the black dragon brew I became interested.

Nordec chuckled. "I was wonderin' when ye be comin' over here tae try it."

Ambrose's brow rose. "What's that supposed to mean?"

The dwarf poured a pint of the dark brew. "I ain't no youngblood dwarf. I know what ye are. Easy tae tell when one o' yer kind cross me path."

Ambrose tensed and I slapped him on the back. "Lighten up, Ambrose."

He growled but I didn't care for his irritation. I took a new pint of the Mountain Rock stout and made my way back over to Raikidan. I yelped when Raikidan suddenly grabbed me, but became thankful when a body flew past us. We watched the man crash into a stack of chairs and then looked to find the culprit. I sighed when I spotted Blaze pounding his fists together. *He would get like this.* Others threw down their mugs, and an all-out brawl manifested on the other side of the tavern. Raikidan and I remained close, to stay out of the way. Well, until I realized he had a hand on the crook of my neck and another on my hip. I was acutely aware how well his hands fit against my curves, and the way his thumb pressed against my spine.

I pulled away and he immediately retracted his hands. "Sorry."

Sipping my stout, I shrugged, more to throw off the growing emotions in the pit of my stomach. "No worries."

The two of us watched the brawl take place. Nordec tried to quell it as best he could, but it didn't help much. Ambrose ended up liking the dragon brew. He seemed downright impressed by it, but refused to comment. Though we got a good impression from Rennek when he chose to give it a shot. According to him, it did a decent job simulating the *zing* lightning gave when breathed. It also had a potency that he agreed could put an adult dragon down with ease if he or she wasn't careful. His willingness to talk about it interested me. He'd been the quietest of the trio during their stay. I was going to have to keep an eye on him.

I gasped when someone was thrown into me and my stout spilled everywhere. Shoving the guy away, I cracked my knuckles, my eyebrows twitching. "Okay, someone is getting beat!"

I then jumped into the chaotic fray, ignoring Raikidan's protests.

I opened the basement door and helped Rylan with Ryoko as the two stumbled up the stairs.

Ryoko smiled at me. "You nice lady."

I chuckled and allowed her to fall onto Rylan once we were in the living room.

"Very nice lady," Rylan slurred.

"Someone had fun." I looked at Seda as she walked down the hall.

"Congratulations on your win. I wouldn't be surprised if the Council starts giving you more assignments specifically."

I snorted. "I won't hold my breath. My conversation with Akama has me skeptical."

She chuckled. "We'll see. I'll help everyone to a room. You go rest."

"I'll help," Blaze offered as he stumbled toward Ryoko.

Ryoko slapped him. "You not nice lady."

Blaze stumbled in a shocked daze and I laughed. "Thank you, Seda. I've had enough excitement for one night."

Argus hauled Blaze's arm over his shoulder. "C'mon you. Let's get your drunken ass to bed."

"Are there pretty women there?" Blaze asked.

"No."

"Then I don't want to go there." Blaze tried to push Argus away, but he was too intoxicated to succeed. I chuckled and headed for my room.

Taking off my jacket, I went into my closet and put it away. I left and pulled out some comfortable clothes to change into, but before I could head for the bath, Raikidan slipped in. I huffed. *Guess it's a shower night for me.* I left my room for to the bathroom to shower.

Water streamed out of the shower head and I hummed contentedly as the warm water relaxed my tense, blood-, sweat-, and ale-stained body. Once clean, I hopped out of the shower stall and dried off, listening to the silence of the house.

I hummed as I towel-dried my hair and took a wash cloth to the steamed-up mirror.

"You did well, I'm proud of you."

Just as I wiped a spot clean, a woman with long black and red hair appeared in the reflection behind me. I jumped and gasped, and then spun around, only to find myself alone. *What the—* I had seen her before, appearing to me in the same exact way, too.

I turned around back around, only to find her still there, reflecting in the mirror. I did my best not to jump and glanced over my shoulder, slower this time. I still found myself the only one in the room. *What is going on?* I stared into the mirror, studying the woman.

Her long hair was in fact black and red, though what I had interpreted as wavy hair, had been braided pieces. Gold metal and leather armor, with feather accents that looked more ceremonial than practical due to the excess exposed skin, framed her sultry form. An ornate golden circlet with a gemmed upward-facing crescent moon center decoration adorned her head. Her skin appeared as if it had been kissed by the sun itself, and large black wings folded behind her back. Her golden eyes pierced through me and she stood several heads taller, adding to her imposing figure.

Her expression changed from a welcoming happiness, to a twisted malice smile, and then back. This continued as I stared at her, which I found rather disconcerting. "Who are you?"

She continued to stand there, unmoving.

"Who are you?" I repeated.

"You already know. You just have to look deeper than the surface." She started fading away. "I am here for you, as hard as it is to be. Try to remember. It's important that you do."

I stood there staring at my shocked reflection in the mirror. *I drank too much, that's all.* Who was I trying to fool? Last time I saw her, I hadn't been drinking. But for her to talk to me... It was like the strange changes happening with the voice in my head. One moment it hated everything, and the next, it wanted to help. *She sounded a lot like the voice, actually.*

The voice I heard never really sounded like mine. I always told myself it was a twisted version of my own voice, but the more I lived with it, the more I realized it had its own tones and pitches. This mystery woman's voice reminded me of that. But the voice didn't come from in my head. *Or did it?*

I shook my head. I was just seeing things, and the voice was taking advantage of that. I needed to sleep. I dressed myself and looked in the mirror one last time to find the woman had returned, shaking her head. I rubbed my eyes and she disappeared. *Yeah, I'm seeing things.*

I entered my room to find Raikidan sitting on my windowsill. "How are you feeling?"

He shrugged. "Fine. I didn't drink much compared to the rest of you. How about you?"

I threw my clothes into my hamper. "I'm exhausted, but fine otherwise."

He nodded and I relaxed on my bed. "Hey, Eira?"

"Yeah?"

"I didn't get the chance to say this because of everything that happened after the competition, but congratulations on winning. I know it's a bigger deal to you than you're letting on."

I smiled. "Thank you."

"And I have something for you." I tilted my head as he pulled a small box from behind his back and held it out to me as he stood. "I had planned on giving it to you before, but never found the right time. Until now."

I slipped off my bed and took the plain box. I opened it and gasped. Inside was a pair of gold wing-shaped earrings with red and orange gems as well as small clear gems. *These are the earrings I designed when helping Rylan with Ryoko's gift.*

"Those are nice," the voice in my head said.

I gazed up at Raikidan. "But why?"

He rubbed the back of his neck. "I noticed how much you liked them, so I had Ebon make them."

I smiled. "Thank you. They're wonderful."

"Oh, and Ebon asked me to give you this." He held up a small pendant. "He said you'd know what it meant."

I took it and inspected the item. The metal was a polished ebony color, shaped into a three-taloned claw that held a red gem I guessed was a ruby. *What could this mean?* I continued to look at it, noticing some feathering detail hidden near the talons. I realized what it meant, but I wasn't ready for Raikidan to know. "I don't know, but I'll think about it. He wouldn't have said I'd know if I wasn't going to be able to figure it out."

"All right, I trust you on that. Ebon also told me that he needs the task he's requested of you to be done shortly before midwinter. What does he mean by that?"

I shook my head. "Don't worry about it. I know exactly what he's talking about with that one."

"Okay…"

I smiled and gave him a quick hug around the neck, his strong scent teasing my intoxicated brain. "Thank you again. I really do like the earrings."

He smiled and returned the gesture. "I'm glad."

"I'm going to go to bed now. I've had a long night."

He pushed me toward the bed. "That's an understatement. I still don't know how you managed to go through all that and not pass out before now."

I climbed onto my bed. "One of the many perks of being me."

He chuckled. "Goodnight, Eira."

"Goodnight, Raikidan."

26
CHAPTER

I sighed as I plopped down on a chair in Azriel's office. Tonight had been a real pain. Luckily, it was all over and I could go home. *I need a moment to sit first.*

"Eira, you can rest in the car," Raikidan said. "I don't want to be here any longer than I have to be."

I smirked. "What, don't want your biggest fan finding out you're off the clock and stalkable?"

He rolled his eyes. "Don't even start with that."

I snickered. The other employees gossiped about the female attention Raikidan received every night he worked. Even some of the workers had an eye for him. But none were as crazy as the one I met today. Apparently this one had a habit of selecting one of the men and creeping on them for a while before moving to the next. Azriel had to kick her out a few times due to questionable behavior, but she always managed to sneak back in.

Azriel had assured us he'd handle the problem, but no one believed it. If we couldn't keep her out by now, then we'd just have to deal with it. And unfortunately for this woman, if she pushed too far with Raikidan, she'd have me to deal with. I had fun teasing him about all the attention he received, since it irritated him when most men would love it, but I wasn't about to let one cause him actual issues.

Raikidan grinned. "You think we could convince her to pester one of your new fans?"

I laughed. "I don't know. We'd need to really put our heads together for that idea."

As much as I teased him about his fans, he wasn't the only one to have gained a few recently. I thought dealing with Zo would be annoying, but some real creeps had started to think I was a good target. There were some nice ones too, and they were easier to handle, especially when trying to extract a few extra coins in tips.

I stood, figuring I had rested enough. We left the office and headed for the employee door, only to stop when a voice I hadn't heard in a long time called out, "Hey, good looking, where you going?"

I turned to see a tall athletically-built man with bronze skin, a strong jaw, and short black hair and facial hair. A blue cloth with a golden hexagram painted on it was wrapped around his eyes. Azriel accompanied him.

"Well, would you look at who decided to show up," the voice said.

My brow furrowed. I had to be seeing things. "Telar?"

The man grinned. "Been a while."

I smiled wide and ran over to him and gave a tight hug around his neck, the slightest whiff of peppermint wafting off him into my nose. *His scent hasn't changed.* "I can't believe you're back."

He returned the gesture and then pulled away. "I can say the same about you. Heard through the grapevine you came back in the spring."

"Yeah, I've been back for a few months now. What about you?"

He shrugged. "Just got back last night."

"How's your sister doing?"

Telar's expression dropped. "No better. I can't find a single person who can help her."

"That's a shame."

I thought about his sister's condition—afflicted with an unknown illness on a military assignment. No matter how they tried, the scientists couldn't diagnose her. One had managed to get word outside the city to some contacts and they offered to care for her. It had been decided to smuggle the two out as it was her only chance. That had been about thirty years ago. "But no worse, right?"

He nodded. "Only thing we're grateful for at this point."

"Depending on how long you're back for, I might have another avenue for you to try."

"I was hoping you'd say that. I heard you had quite the adventure when you left the city."

I placed my hand on my hips and my face twisted. "That's one way to put it. How long will you be in the city?"

"As long as I'm needed. Avila wanted me to stay away a while since I was driving her crazy, so I thought I'd come and give everyone a hand."

"Let me guess, that's why you're here."

He nodded. "I picked up a task I thought you and your friend might be willing to help with."

"Agree to help." Telar had never done me wrong. On the contrary, he'd treated me better than most. The voice had come to like him, one of the few people it encouraged me to protect. Thinking about it, I'm sure its approval was why I trust him so quickly. Same with Seda.

I shrugged and smiled. "I don't see why I can't."

"Really?" Raikidan sighed. "Why can't we just go home?"

"You can go home if you want," I said. "I'm going to give him a hand."

"You haven't had enough of dealing with people after tonight?"

Telar snapped his attention on me. "Something happen?"

I shook my head. "Don't worry about it, Telar. Nothing I can't handle."

Telar frowned. I knew him well enough it would be best not to tell him what I dealt with on a constant basis. He'd go on a rampage that would get out of hand because he'd decide to show off.

"So, what do you need help with?"

"Infiltration and Recon," Telar said. "Nothing too major. We need to stock up on supplies from a nice little warehouse, and intel says someone I need to get some dirt on will be there."

"Two birds, one stone. Sounds simple enough. I'm in."

Raikidan let out a disgruntled exhale. "Guess I am, too."

Telar chuckled. "Good. I'll let you get home to change into something… more suitable for this. As good as you look in that outfit, it's not practical."

I shook my head. "You never change. Have the location coordinates sent to Genesis or Seda. We'll meet you there."

He nodded and turned to head out. "All right, don't take too long dolling yourself up for me, now."

I shook my head and encouraged Raikidan to follow me, saying goodbye to Azriel as we left.

Someone knocked on my bedroom door as I pulled on, my pants. I poked my head out my closet to find Telar standing in the doorway. "Moving too slow for you?"

A cocky smirk spread across his lips. "Well, when I said don't take long to doll yourself up, I wasn't kidding."

I shook my head. "Not my fault you gave me all of twenty minutes to get home and dressed."

"Well, I would have given you longer, had a change in the assignment not happened."

"Go on."

"We won't be doing any infiltrating tonight. My target moved locations unexpectedly, and he's more important, so the Council assigned a different team to the infiltration. I could still use your help, though."

I leaned on the doorframe of my closet. "Where is the target now?"

"On the move, but from what I know, he will be patrolling the Iron Hawk Mall."

I nodded. "I don't see why I couldn't help you. Military is more suspicious of psychics on their own than with a group, even in crowded areas like that."

Telar chuckled. "They've never been the sharpest bunch."

"Let me finish changing."

"What do you mean? You look fine."

I glanced at my reflection in my long mirror. "I still have half of my work clothes on, and only one sock on my feet. Not ready."

"Fine, fine. Just hurry up." He smirked. "Though, if I may make a suggestion, that black crop top you have stowed away would flatter you and go well with what you're wearing under those clothes."

"Right, forgot about that that part of his… personality…"

My cheeks burned, and anger mixed with embarrassment rose up in my chest. "Telar…"

Raikidan appeared next to the psychic and grabbed him roughly by the shirt. "You'd better not be using your abilities on Eira in inappropriate ways."

Telar forced Raikidan to let go. "Easy there, caveman. I didn't do anything like that. I happen to know what she likes to wear and decided to tease her about it."

Raikidan glared at him and then focused on me. "You sure you want to work with him?"

I laughed. "Calm down, Rai. Telar's mouthy but harmless."

Raikidan snorted in response. I slipped into my closet to finish changing, picking out the black crop top Telar mentioned because he wasn't wrong about it looking good, and grabbed a denim jacket to compliment my outfit.

"Grab those boots in the corner," Telar called out.

I grabbed sneakers instead. "Creeper."

"Hey, whoa, ease now with the name calling. I'm standing next to a strong, good-looking man here with a high protection drive. I don't want to be pummeled into paste before starting my first assignment back."

"You're the one who gave the advice out loud."

"I did? Oops."

I shook my head and strolled out of my closet, grabbing some gold coins from my personal stash in case I'd need it. I didn't like going to the mall because of all the people, but if I was going to be there and needed to blend in, I might as well buy something that caught my eye. "All right, let's go."

The two men nodded and the three of us left, but not before Ryoko called after us. "Bring me back something!"

I chuckled. "Sure."

Telar used his telekinetic abilities to open the car doors, and drove us to our destination. I played with his radio to irritate him, and he flicked my hand away several times until he used his abilities to keep my hands in my lap. "Now be a good girl."

I stuck my tongue out at him. "I don't know how."

He chuckled and focused on the road. "That you don't."

He let me go five minutes later, but I hadn't learned from my *punishment*. In the time it took to get to the mall after that, I managed to get under the skin of both men, Telar bound my hands again, and Raikidan threatened to pull me into the back seat.

Telar managed to find a parking spot at the enormous mall in the center of the shopping district in Quadrant Three. Even this late at night, the mall had life. I'd never seen it empty. The shops never closed and people in this city never slept, so there wasn't any time for there to be a lull in activity here.

"Is the guy here?" I asked Telar.

"Yes, but with so many people here, it's hard to get a good reading on him," he said. "We'll have to make our way closer."

I nodded and the three of us continued through the building, stopping at a few stalls and stores to browse so as to not to look suspicious. Telar stopped at a kiosk displaying sunglasses, and grabbed a pair with sharp arching edges and a nose guard. He placed them over his eye covering and looked at me. "What do you think?"

I laughed. "You look ridiculous."

He pulled them off his face and picked a white pair shaped as a single, unbroken strip. "What about this one?"

I laughed more. "That one doesn't look half bad, actually."

"Really?" He assessed himself in a mirror. "Yeah, you're right."

I rummaged through the sunglasses and found a pair of green sunglasses with oblong lenses that had a similar likeness to wasp eyes. I put them on and faced the boys. "Well, do I look fabulous?"

Raikidan hid his face in his hand with a groan and Telar laughed at me. "A bit too diva for you."

He sorted through the choices as he used his telekinesis to remove the pair I currently wore. He smirked when he found a pair of black sunglasses with fake gems around the circular rims and large fake gems on the upper corners as gaudy accents. He placed the glasses on my face. I posed in the most dramatic way possible, thinking of how Ryoko liked to act when trying on clothes. "Well, what do you think?"

Telar held his sides as he laughed. I changed my pose and he used the kiosk as a support when his laughter got the better of him. I smiled, glad I could be silly enough to get such a good reaction from him and looked at Raikidan to see how he'd react. His brow furrowed a bit at the sight of me, but when I did my best to look cute and pouty like Ryoko had drilled in my head for no reason, he sputtered a laugh and turned his gaze away, putting a hand on the hat kiosk as support.

I smiled in triumph, glad to have gotten them both to laugh. Telar had been warm to me this whole time, trying to catch up when we could, in between shop browsing and target hunting. But Raikidan had been far colder, almost annoyed when I paid attention to Telar.

I glanced back at Telar to find him composed and searching for his target. I studied his expression and frowned. Even after all this time he had spent away from this place, I could see the toll our forced military service took.

"Don't start thinking like that, Chickadee," Telar messaged telepathically. I put my glasses away. *"You know I hate pet names."*

"Yeah, well, Tannek picked a good one for you, so deal with it." He continued to scan the area. *"I'm glad you're able to laugh these days. I worried that time away hadn't helped you."*

Before I could reply, a pathetic sound of a complaint came out of my mouth when Raikidan placed something heavy on my head. Telar and Raikidan laughed as I reached up to understand what he did to me. I found myself wearing some sort of strange hat. I pulled it off and jerked back in surprise at the sight of the crazy thing. Purple-gray with one giant eye and some other eyes jutting off the top and sides. "What the hell is this?"

"Some sort of monster hat from the mini store behind you," Raikidan said. "I thought it was fitting."

I punched him in the arm and then Telar when he laughed at me. I put the hat back on the rack from the kiosk he took it from and found myself scanning the odd hats on display. A wicked grin spread across my lips when I found a pair of hats and placed them on the guys' heads, making sure the arrow for the "I'm with stupid" pointed to the other one. Both of the shop keepers of the kiosks near us laughed at them as they tried to figure out what was going on.

Telar, thanks to his abilities, figured it out quickly and removed the hat, glaring at me. "I'm not stupid."

Raikidan smirked and crossed his arms, indicating he wasn't going to remove the hat. I couldn't help but laugh now, and Telar swiveled his head between the two of us before realizing he took the wrong hat off. He ripped it off Raikidan's head and tossed them both at me. I blocked the assault and picked the hats off the ground, making sure they didn't get ruined, even though I wouldn't be opposed to buying them and making the two wear them. The shop keeper looked annoyed until I showed him things were okay, and he thanked me. I continued to peruse through the selection until I found one that I never thought I'd ever find, but was glad I did.

I pulled the fuzzy hat over my head and stuck my hands in the pockets of the long furry strips attached to each side. I then poked my head around the kiosk and lifted a single fake-pawed hand. "Meow."

The boys stared at me for a good solid fifteen seconds before Telar started laughing. Raikidan, on the other hand, knitted his brow. "What are you wearing?"

I grinned and held up my covered hands. "I'm a kitty."

"I can see that." He chuckled and walked over to me, tugging on the ears on the top of my hat. "It's cute on you."

"Ryoko keeps talking about these, but could never find one," I said.

"She's not a fan of cats, though," Raikidan said.

I pointed to the other hats like this, but of different animals. "There are more choices. I'm sure I can find one for her."

"What about you?" Raikidan asked. "You should have one, too."

I shook my head. "No, I don't need one."

Raikidan eyed me and then sifted through the other animal hats. He pulled out a white one with long floppy ears just as I was removing the cat one and placed it on my head. "Now you're a bunny."

I laughed. "Too bad I don't know bunny noises."

He poked me in the nose. "Wiggle that and you'll be fine." I made a failed attempt at wiggling my nose and he laughed. "That was adorable."

I hid my face in my pawed hands and he laughed some more. Little did he know, my actions mixed with him calling me cute and adorable, were flaring up true embarrassment, and I needed to hide my face so he wouldn't see. I wanted to make him laugh, so it was worth it.

Once Raikidan's laughter subsided and I got myself under control, I took my hat off and put it back. That's when I noticed a red and white hat with triangular ears. "That's the one!"

I grabbed it. It was definitely the one she'd want.

"What is it?" Raikidan asked.

"A red panda. She loves those little critters."

Raikidan looked at the tag. "Not a bad price if you want to buy it for her.

I nodded and peered at the rest of the selection before deciding on the panda hat. After paying for Ryoko's gift, we continued on. Telar not so subtly swiveled his head several times, trying to triangulate his target's location, and we moved in the direction he needed, pretending we were looking for a particular store or wanted to change direction for fun. We stopped in a few jewelry stores, many of which had lovely items to sell that even I would wear here and there, but I couldn't afford any, so we moved on.

"How you doing?" I asked Telar.

Telar smirked. "This guy has no idea I'm probing his mind. At this rate, I'll be able to complete this assignment in no time."

I nodded and then held my stomach when it rumbled. "Can we stop at the food court? I didn't get a proper dinner, and my body has liked the consistent meals I've been able to give it these last few months. It doesn't like it when I go back to my old eating habits."

Telar nodded. "Shouldn't be an issue. I have a good lock on him for now."

I turned my attention to Raikidan to make sure he was okay with the idea, but found myself looking at no one. I cranked my neck in several directions but couldn't find him. "Where did he go?"

"Uh, that's a good question," Telar said, looking around with me. "He'd been thinking about a few stores to stop in, but I didn't think he'd actually leave us to do it."

"I could have sworn he was just with us…"

"He'll catch up." Telar pushed me toward to food court. "I'll keep an eye out for him for you."

"Won't mess you up?"

"You have such little faith in me."

I chuckled. "More like concerned. It's been a while since you've been around this many people."

"I'm fine. I trained for this kind of stuff."

"You've been out of said training field for thirty years."

He sighed in aggravation. "Let's just get your tiny stomach some food."

I pondered over the various eating establishments, Telar having to translate all but one sign for me. Conveniently the only sign I could read was the place we settled for. *Éan Ag Eitilt*, claimed to sell "authentic" elvish food. Living with Shva'sika got me familiar with how authentic elvish food tasted. I had yet to find a place that could live up to their authentic claim unless they were elf or half-elf themselves. *I wonder if they even know their name means flying bird.*

Telar and I waited in line, me far more patiently than him. I studied the menu available, the options listed in Elvish with common translations under it. *I'm glad I can at least read enough Elvish to get by with this menu.*

"*You could always ask me for help,*" Telar messaged.

My cheeks reddened. "*I'm able to order food on my own.*"

"*Just an offer.*"

As I picked out my order I also kept an eye out for Raikidan. He still hadn't shown up or popped up on Telar's mental radar.

The two of us made it to the counter and were greeted by a brightly-smiling half-elf woman with black hair and blue eyes. *Maybe I was wrong, and this could end up being good food.* I then noticed the cook behind her. *Is that—*

The elven man with long black, silver streaked hair turned around, and the two of us stared at each other for a moment.

"Ayluin?"

"Eira!" He smiled wide. "You're a sight for sore eyes. How you been?"

"Uh, good. How about you? It's been, what, ten years?"

He nodded. "About that, yeah."

I looked around the food court. "Do I want to know how you ended up here?"

He chuckled and began prepping some vegetables. "Long story."

"Grandpa and I are hoping to be able to move into a real location soon," the woman at the counter said. "It'd be more fitting since we don't fit in with these faster-paced food venues."

I studied the girl. I had never met Ayluin's family, but I did know he had a son who had a daughter... "You must be Sumala."

She made a shallow curtsy. "That would be me. Grandpa has talked all about you, Miss Eira. It's a pleasure to finally meet you."

I smiled at her formality. "It's nice to meet you finally as well. Well, I should make my order, so I'm not holding anyone else up."

"I'm already working on it," Ayluin said as he finished throwing some chopped potatoes in a boiling pot. "I know what you like."

I chuckled. "You're the best. I'll need to order for myself and—"

"Your date there?" he asked.

My cheeks burned a bit. "He's not my date, Ayluin."

"Well why not?"

"Yeah, why not?" Telar said. "Raikidan ditched us, so it could be a date."

"Telar, knock it off," I muttered.

He chuckled. "You need to lighten up."

"This Raikidan fella, he going to be joining you too?" Ayluin asked. "Or did he really ditch you?"

"No, he went into a store to buy something. He'll be rejoining us for food," I said.

He chuckled. "Typical man. I'll make a good meal for you three."

"I'll tell you the total when it's done," Sumala said. "There's no way either of us are going to find out what he's making."

I chuckled. "Fair. Call me over when it's ready."

She nodded and then addressed the next customer in line while Telar and I found a place to sit. I continued to look around for Raikidan while Telar focused on his target.

"Any good information?" I asked him.

Telar relaxed in his seat. "Oh yeah. Access codes, hot spots, key people; it's all here."

"You luck out on the best contribution opportunities."

"Don't sell yourself short, hon." He grinned slyly at me. "You have some pretty amazing talents yourself."

I rolled my eyes. "It'd be nice if I could help you with this more."

"You're my cover. That's all I expect from you, since this is my assignment. It's the best help you can be for me in a situation like this."

Someone slipped into the seat next to me, startling me enough that I couldn't reply to Telar. I raised an eyebrow at Raikidan, as he sat next to me as if he had been there the entire time. "Where did you disappear to?"

"Just had to buy something," he said.

"What did you buy?" I asked, looking for some sort of bag to give him away, only to find nothing.

"Oh, you didn't buy that," Telar said.

"Buy what?" I asked.

"Seriously, you bought it?"

"Bought what?" I repeated.

"Did you have to ask that out loud?" Raikidan asked him irritably. "Now she's going to pester me."

Telar smirked. "Well, she should. What you bought is a pretty big deal."

"What did you buy, Rai?" I didn't like being the only one who didn't know.

"I'll show you later," he said.

I pushed on his arm and searched all around him, trying to find this mystery purchase. "No, show me now."

"Eira, stop being a brat," he scolded, pushing me away. "I'll show you later. I promise."

Telar chuckled. "You would want to show her that later."

Raikidan glared at my psychic friend and I let out an exasperated sigh. I hated them both right now.

Telar frowned and stood. "I'll be back. I need to figure something out."

"That's peculiar, even for him."

My brow furrowed. The voice was right, but Telar left too quick for me question him. "I hope everything is okay."

"I'm sure your friend will be fine," Raikidan said. "He does have a target to deal with."

"That's what I'm worried about," I said. "I hope he didn't lose the guy because of me. I'm supposed to be helping."

"You need to relax. It's going to be okay."

I sighed and tapped my fingers on the table while I waited. Telar still hadn't returned by the time Sumala called us over to receive our food. I paid the bill and gave a generous tip as Ayluin placed the to-go bags on the counter.

"So, if the other one isn't your boyfriend, this one is then." He gave Raikidan a good once-over. "Good pick, if you ask me."

I rolled my eyes. "No, he's not my boyfriend."

He shook his head. "One of these days you're going to have to tell me which one is your boyfriend. You can't keep that a secret for much longer. You know I'll find out."

"I don't have a boyfriend, Ayluin."

"Well, why not? You're beautiful and not getting any younger."

"Maybe she hasn't found the right one yet, *Seanathair*," Sumala said, trying to help me.

"I introduced her to plenty of nice young men and she said no to all of them!" Ayluin complained. I shook my head. I lost count after the fifty-sixth man he tried to introduce me to… in a single year.

"It took *Athair* almost three hundred years to meet *Máthair*, and that was after you introduced him to every available maiden you could find," she said. "Leave her be about it."

I found it interesting she chose to identify her family in Elvish. Not even Shva'sika and Xye did that.

Ayluin sighed and pointed at me. "Just you wait. I'll find a good one for you."

I shook my head and took the food. "Don't worry about it, Ayluin. I'm happy being single."

He snorted. "You keep thinking that."

"Take care, Ayluin."

"Don't be a stranger, and stop by again, but with a date next time. If you don't, I'll make sure you have one."

I chuckled, highly amused by his persistence, and walked back to our table with Raikidan. *He's something else.* Raikidan helped me figure out what Ayluin made for us, and we portioned out food for the two of us while keeping some aside for Telar once he returned. Except, he didn't, nor did he send me a telepathic message with an update. My concern grew and made it hard to enjoy my food.

"He has been gone a while without contacting you. It's not like him."

Raikidan let out a heavy exhale. "Let's pack up and find your friend. I don't need you having a heart attack."

"I'm not going to have a heart attack," I muttered as Raikidan took my food and stored it in a carrying container. "It's just unusual for him not to give me an update if things were okay."

"He's probably busy, but let's go check on him."

I followed Raikidan out of the food court, studying him. He seemed irritated and I didn't understand why. What was so wrong about concern for Telar? I knew he could handle himself, but it was still an assignment, and psychics did get hit with a lot of prejudice in this city.

Raikidan and I wandered around the mall for twenty minutes with no success on finding our missing psychic. At this point, Raikidan no longer showed signs of being annoyed with me, and understood my original worry. I chewed on my lip when ten more minutes passed with no sign of Telar. Raikidan grabbed my hand. I looked at him and he gave me a reassuring smile. I smiled back, but couldn't hide my concern. This wasn't like Telar. Even if he were in trouble, he'd find a way to warn me.

We walked by a security station and I stopped dead in my tracks when a familiar shape caught my peripheral. I backed up and my brow furrowed with concern when I spotted Telar sitting in a chair speaking to a few soldiers. I knocked on the window and held up my hands at him when he turned his head my way and waved.

One of the soldiers approached the door to the room and opened it to address me. "Can we help you, Ma'am?"

"Yeah, I want to know why you've got my friend in there," I said.

"We're just asking him a few questions. We'll be done soon."

The man tried to shut the door, but I stopped him. "Telar, what is going on here? We've been looking for you for thirty minutes!"

"Sorry, Eira, I didn't mean to disappear on you. These rooms are made with my abilities in mind," he said.

"Eira?" the familiar face of Zo leaned past one of the walls and came into view. "You really do know her?"

"Yeah, I was telling you the truth. When I moved out of the city after Lord Taric released us from service, my sister and I wandered a bit until we ended up in a small village in the mountains. That's how I met her."

I pushed the soldier in front of me aside, but not without protest. "Yes, Zo, I do know him." I approached Telar and crossed my arms. "What did you do?"

"Oh boy, here comes the real interrogation." He hung an arm over the back of his chair and reclined. "I didn't do anything. That's what I've been trying to tell them. A guy can't walk around a mall in peace these days."

"Except that's not what you were doing," Zo said.

Telar sighed and I looked at him expectantly. "I was following some guy who has suspicious thoughts—or I was trying to, at least. I was having a hard time pinpointing his exact location. I had planned to find him, tell someone, and then rejoin Eira and Ray for dinner."

I turned my gaze to Zo. "Is that really such a suspicious thing?"

He rubbed the back of his neck. "Well, sort of. We had several citizens bring up the concern your friend here may be up to something as it looked like he was stalking someone. Because of the amount of concern we received, we had to bring him here for some questioning."

"Some?" My brow rose in skepticism. "If that were the case, he'd be out of here already. So why is he here?"

"Well…" Zo rubbed the back of his neck and avoided eye contact.

I sucked air through my teeth and grabbed Telar's hand. "That's what I thought. Telar, we're leaving."

Zo stepped forward to stop me. "Eira, you can't just take him."

I held myself tall. "Unless you can give a legitimate reason to keep him any longer, I can."

Zo struggled to come up with something to say, so I pulled Telar off his seat and headed for the door. Telar held up his free hand as he looked at Zo, indicating he wasn't going to be stupid enough to fight me. The moment the two of us rejoined Raikidan, a security alarm went off. The three of us went on alert and looked around as the soldiers forced their way out of the security room.

Telar pointed to a jewelry store nearby. "Sketchy guy I was following finally struck."

We watched as a hooded figure ran out of the store and rushed through the mall, a backpack held in his arms. The soldiers immediately took off after the thief.

Zo focused on Telar as he exited the room. "Sorry for the accusations. Please excuse us while we deal with the issue."

The three of us watched the scene unfold as we played innocent civilians.

"Eira, you're the one who chose to hold my hand," Telar said without looking at me. "If you want me to stop holding on, you can say so instead of tugging away without words."

My brow rose and I held up my hand. "I let go already."

"That's my hand you grabbed, you *suvk nyekuvw dnyec*," Raikidan snarled.

Telar let go, but acted casual about it. "Oops."

Raikidan grumbled, and I couldn't help but chuckle with amusement, even though I suspected Raikidan had just used a nasty insult.

"We should head home," Telar said.

"You sure you don't need to stay longer?" I asked.

He shook his head. "My target is part of that chase. I learned enough, and I've pushed my luck for the night. That thief saved me, really. Had I not caught his thoughts, I wouldn't have had a good excuse to be on my own."

"Fair enough." I punched him in the arm. "That's for being stupid and walking off."

Telar rubbed his arm. "Ow, sorry. My target had some good info and was walking out of my range."

"Sure, sure." I headed for the entrance of the mall. "Let's get out of here before that thief makes it impossible."

Telar frowned. "Looks like we decided too late. Guy got away, so they're locking the place down. And no, I'm not going to help them this time. We found out what happens when I try."

My nose scrunched. "Fantastic. So now what? Finish eating?"

"I need to buy something for my sister," Telar said. "Can we get that out of the way first? I've been avoiding the store, but at this rate, I can't anymore, and if I don't get what she wanted, she'll kill me."

I shook my head. Avila may be a Seer, but killing her brother wasn't too farfetched of a claim. She could get pretty scary, though she wouldn't finish her brother off, as she wouldn't risk killing herself too. "What did you need to get her?"

He swallowed hard and started walking. "Just follow me."

"What's with that reaction?"

Raikidan and I exchanged a glance of confusion and skepticism but followed.

CHAPTER 27

Raikidan and I followed Telar as he set a slow pace to our destination. I watched the muscles in his jaws tense and then relax, and followed by his hands clenching and releasing. *What kind of store could get a Battle Psychic like Telar all worked up like this?*

We reached a store with mannequins in the display windows, dressed in different styles of nightgowns. My heart stopped. *By the gods, no.* "Telar, please tell me you're joking."

"I wish I was…"

"No wonder he's been a wreck."

I stared at the store front called *Silken Nights*, Avila's favorite lingerie store. I sucked in a deep breath and clapped him on the back. "Well, good luck."

He grabbed my wrist. "No, I'm not shopping for her. You are."

"Excuse you?" I shrieked. "I will not."

"I refuse to shop for such clothes for my sister. Girlfriend, sure, but… she's my sister, Eira, no! I don't want to know what she wears under her clothes, thank you."

"He's got a point. You could be nice this time. Repay him for his good treatment of you."

I shook my head and couldn't refrain from laughing. "Fine, I'll go shopping for you. Did she at least give you a list of what she wanted, and her size?"

Telar rummaged through his pockets and pulled out a folded piece of paper. "She said it was all on this."

I unfolded the paper and took a look to find it written in a way I could read it, and immediately understood why Telar didn't want to buy anything for his sister. She wanted some real racy things. "This shouldn't be too hard. She's quite specific on what she wants."

Telar held out a bag of money. "She gave me this, because she said they were costly."

I kept my voice low. "I'm going to take a wild guess and say that you suspected this assignment would get you sent to this mall, so you wanted me as backup for it."

He rubbed the back of his neck. "Yeah, well, I also wanted to catch up with you too, so, win-win."

I shook my head. "Wait here, and I'll be back with your sister's new wardrobe."

"Please don't say it like that," he begged. "Sounds like that's all she's going to wear, and I don't want that mental image."

I snickered and headed into the store. I searched for all sorts of items, from bras and corsets to babydolls and teddies, and even some fetish pieces, but I struggled to find the exact items on Avila's list—or the right size. I had to enlist the help of some sales associates, who only had a tad bit better luck than me.

"You should get this for yourself, Laz!"

I whirled around at the sound of Ryoko's voice, and my heart stopped as she held up a one-shoulder black lace teddy with cleavage cutouts. "What the hell are you doing here?"

"She's with me." I turned to find Seda not too far off carrying a pink silk babydoll with black lace accents and split down the center, creating a light ruffled look. It came with matching panties and a black lace choker. One of the cloaking watches clung to her wrist, hiding her psychic identity. "And I think this would be more fitting for her."

Well... she's not wrong.

I looked between the two of them. "What are you doing?"

"Seda needed some new lingerie, and I thought I should get some, too," Ryoko said. I eyed her skeptically. No way had it been that coincidental.

Seda hung her arm over me and kept her voice low. "It is, actually. I was getting restless sitting at the house, so the Council gave me an assignment similar to Telar's. Ryoko offered to accompany me, and only found out after we left that our target's location was the same as yours."

"And we just so happened to be in the same store?"

"I watched you come in. This is my favorite store. So, why not try this since you're in here?"

My cheeks reddened. "I'm here because Telar is too chicken-shit to shop on his sister's behalf."

Ryoko's eyes glittered with mischief. "Yeah, that's just a cover for you wanting to buy something sexy for your secret boyfriend."

If the voice had a face, I'm pretty sure she would have rolled her eyes. *"Here we go again."*

"Ryoko, don't you start with that!"

She grinned and held up the lace teddy. "C'mon, try it on."

"Well, I don't know about you ladies, but I think she'd look sexy in this."

My heart stopped when Telar spoke. *He did not come in here and start making suggestions on what I should wear.* I whirled around, and to my horror, Telar stood a little ways away from us, Raikidan next to him. Telar held up a blue and gold garter set. My face burned hot. "No way!"

He grinned. "C'mon, you'd look great in it."

"He's not wrong."

"Nope." I took a step back. "Nope, nope, and definitely no."

"I'm going to agree with her," Ryoko said. "Not really her style, though, Laz, you would look hot in that."

"No! And why are you in here, Telar?"

He continued to grin. "I said I wasn't going to shop for my sister. Never said anything about not giving you a hand, though."

"Top wouldn't fit her," Raikidan said before walking off further into the store.

Ryoko's brow rose as she looked at me. "I know he's right, but the fact that he knows you'd need a bigger size for the bra is pretty interesting."

"To be fair, Telar did pick a size that's more tailored to someone of my smaller size," Seda said. "It's pretty obvious Laz would need something larger."

Telar turned his head toward the bra in the set, then at me, and then back at the bra. "Yeah, I should have noticed that."

"You'd think as a man of his type, he'd have not made that mistake."

"So," Ryoko said. "Which one are you going to try on?"

"What?" I pulled back from them. "I'm just here to—"

"—get outfits Telar is too chicken-shit to buy for his sister. Yeah, you said that." A wicked grin spread across her face. "But since you're here, you might as well find something for yourself."

"Why would I need to?" I asked. Her eyes sparkled, and I couldn't help but roll my eyes. "No."

Just then, Raikidan returned, and in his hand he carried a red halter lace babydoll with a bow, and ruffled black silk along the split-style center. A pair of matching panties came with it. Ryoko squealed, her eyes lighting up. "That one!"

My face and ears burned. *What the hell is going on?* Why had Raikidan gone and pick something out? Was it some big elaborate joke?

Telar stroked his chin. "Impressive pick. You need to try that one, Eira."

I sighed, fighting the urge to pull my hair out. "Why?"

"Why not?" Seda asked. "It's just a bit of fun. You don't have to buy it, and it's not like you have to put it on and walk out here for us to see you in it."

I would have freaked out at idea of having to show them these outfits on me, but the boys' shocked red faces had us ladies laughing instead.

When Seda got herself under control, she handed me the garment she picked out and took Avila's outfits from me. "Have some fun and try at least one of them on."

"You should do this. Can't hurt to at least humor them."

My nose scrunched and I reluctantly accepted the babydoll lingerie. Ryoko grabbed the garment Raikidan had found, and even the one Telar had picked out, though not until he swapped it for the correct size, embarrassing that she'd up and tell him my measurements, and handed them to me, along with the one she selected for me.

"It's just to get you to learn how to loosen up," Ryoko said in a hushed tone as she ushered me toward a dressing room. "It's okay to do something out of the ordinary every once in a while, you know?"

"But why this?" I asked.

A teasing smile spread over her lips. "Because with you, we have to go to extremes."

I spoke to the sales woman instead of replying to her, so I could get a dressing room.

"Laz," Ryoko said when the woman had us sit until a room was available. "Tell me what's bothering you."

I shook my head. "Don't worry about it."

"I'm not going to make fun of you after this."

"Sorry, but I can't believe that." I shifted my gaze to find her in shock. "Nine times out of ten, you or Shva'sika have felt the need to point out things that you'd consider out of the ordinary for me. Because of this, I can't entertain the idea of doing something different without knowing I'm going to be judged. I'm doing this because you're making me do it, not because I want to try something new."

The sales woman came back and brought me to my dressing room before Ryoko had the chance to say anything. I hung each article of clothing on a provided rack and looked them over. I didn't feel comfortable trying on the piece Ryoko picked out, and I was mortified by the idea of trying on the set Telar chose. I decided on the babydoll Seda selected, and went about changing, my cheeks burning hotter the longer it took me to do this.

I can do this. I took a deep breath when I had it on and turned to face the large mirror, only to cover my face. *I can't believe I'm wearing this…* I took another deep breath and made myself look into the mirror. I turned my body and fussed with the nightgown in the front and the back, which was much shorter. Even though I wasn't trying on the matching panties, I had to admit, it did look cute… and sexy, even on me. My face reddened more at the idea of thinking I looked sexy in something. Not a word you would associate with me.

"Don't be embarrassed. You should feel sexy in this, because you are."

"How you doing in there, Laz?" Ryoko called from the other side of the door.

"Um, good I think. I'm about to try on something else."

"Can I slip in and see what you're in now?"

I chewed on my lip. "Uh, sure." I unlocked the door and she slipped in. She assessed me, her eyes wide with shock. "Well?"

"You look hot. Like… wow. I wish you had tried the matching panties, but it doesn't matter. Seda picked an awesome babydoll for you."

My eyes flicked away, embarrassment flooding over me. But when she grabbed my hand, I lifted my gaze.

"I'm sorry. You're right, I have unfairly made comments and it wasn't right. I shouldn't shoehorn you into a certain look. I should have realized my teasing had an effect on you. You look amazing in this, and had I not been so mean, you would have given something like this a shot sooner." She squeezed my hand. "I promise I will let up."

I smiled. "You can still tease every now and then. I'd worry if you didn't."

Ryoko grinned wickedly. "Good, 'cause I like seeing you squirm when I tell you to look good for your hunky boyfriend."

I slapped her in the arm and she laughed. "I don't have a boyfriend."

She looked me up and down, a sly grin firm on her lips. "Not for long, if you wear more clothes like this and he's still sharing a room."

My face flushed. "Ryoko!"

She laughed and considered my other options on the rack. "Seeing this on you, I don't think the one I picked out for you would suit you anymore."

"You should try it instead." I said. "Bet you could pull it off."

She giggled. "I was already planning a few, if you'd be willing to offer some opinions after you're done trying things on."

I grinned. "Rylan is in trouble."

"I was hoping you'd say that." She touched the garment Telar picked. "Do you want to try this one on?"

I scratched my head. "Well… I'm not sure I'm comfortable trying it."

Ryoko nodded. "Don't force yourself if you're not. Ruins the fun." She chuckled. "You could always come back and try it another time when you have the confidence." I glared at her and she smiled before pointing at the babydoll Raikidan picked out. "Let's see you in this one. I'm curious how well Rai picked."

"Watch it."

"Honestly… I'm dreading that one just as much."

Ryoko elbowed me. "Scared you'll like it?"

I chewed on my lower lip. "Full transparency, yeah."

"Is liking it the worst thing that could happen?"

"It's the idea he picked it out that's bothering me. And if it did look good, it…" I sighed, unable to finish the sentence. I couldn't allow myself to. It would mean I was hoping for something that didn't exist, and I told myself already it wasn't like that, so I needed to get myself under control.

Ryoko urged me closer to the nightgown before heading to the door. "Try it on and see what happens after."

"Be careful with this decision."

I stared at the nightgown when she left, and wrestled with myself until I opted for Ryoko's choice in lingerie. I got the thing on after a bit of struggling, and took it off almost immediately. I did not like the look of that at all. That left me standing nearly naked in the dressing room with two options, Telar's choice or Raikidan's. I could choose neither and get dressed, but that defeated the point of coming in here. *By the gods, Eira, stop being pathetic and wear the damn thing!*

I breathed out heavy through my lips and selected Raikidan's choice. *I might as well get this over with.*

"Be careful."

The soft, sheer fabric slid through my fingers as I removed the babydoll from the hanger and pulled it over my head. The loose garment flowed over me and the silk halter fit comfortably. I fussed with the nightgown for a bit before looking myself over in the mirror and was glad I kept my bra on. Between the sheer silk and the lace, this hadn't been designed as your average sleepwear.

I turned in the mirror and removed my hair from my hairclip and tossed it around and teased it. *What am I doing?* I chewed on my lip. I knew what I was doing. I liked it. It fit better than the one Seda picked out, and it fit my style a lot better. Sexy wasn't my thing, but cute, I could pull that off. *Did I really just think that?*

"You did. As you should. I hate to admit it, but it does look good on you. He has good taste... I guess."

Someone rapped on my door. "Laz?"

I messed with my hair some more, but in a way to make it look like I was just in the process of fixing it. "Yeah, Ryo, you can come in."

The door opened and she slipped in. In her hands I noticed she carried a few new garments, but before I could ask, her eyes lit up and she blurted out, "Seda was right, that looks amazing on you!"

I fussed with the silk ruffles. "Think so?"

"I know so." She messed with my hair. "And so do you, with the way you've been teasing your hair."

"I wasn't teasing it," I lied. "It came undone in my dressing and you showed up while I was fixing it."

"Even I know that was a horrible lie."

Ryoko chuckled. "You can't fool me, Laz. I know what's going through your head." She spun me around to face the mirror. "This has to go into your *must buy* pile. You'd be crazy to leave here without it."

"I don't know…"

She pulled me close to her and we gazed at our reflections. "Admit it. He has a good eye for your style, and you deserve something nice like this."

"I… I do like it, I just… don't see myself ever wearing it."

She half-smiled with one brow raised. "Laz, you know if you're nervous about seducing someone, I can always help you. I'm all for jumping in the sack with you once or twice."

I slapped her in the arm. "Don't start with that again."

She laughed. "Can't blame a girl for trying."

"I can when you know I'm not interested in women."

Ryoko winked. "Don't knock it until you try it."

"Rylan is so lucky you take monogamous relationships seriously, or he'd be in a lot of trouble."

"I don't know…" She giggled and held up one of the articles of clothing she carried with her. "He might find the idea pretty intriguing."

I blinked at the sight of what looked like some skimpy costume and then shook my head. "I don't want to know what you two do behind closed doors, thank you."

"We could always leave the door open." I smacked her in the arm again and she laughed. "But back to all seriousness, get this. It's perfect for you." She held up one of the other articles she brought in. "And you should try this one on next."

My brow rose in question as I examined the… I wasn't even sure what to call it. The top resembled a babydoll, but was much longer, going down the ankles, and had very little cloth to it. Small sheer strips of silk covered the breasts vertically like a bikini, and the long sections were also made of the same sheer silk material. The rest of the top though, were leather strings that crossed several times in the back and held the separate pieces of silk together in the front. The panties that went with it were a thong and made of the same leather string material.

"What the hell is this?"

Ryoko giggled. "Something sexy you need to try on. All of it. I need to know if it all fits, even though panties are hard to judge when you're wearing your own pair on underneath."

I shook my head. "No way. I won't wear glorified butt floss."

Ryoko belted out a hysterical laugh. "Glorified what? Oh man, that was such an amazing term for it."

I crossed my arms. "Well, it is."

"It's sexy."

"I don't see what's so great about a wedgie."

Ryoko shook her head, trying to keep herself composed. "It shows off more skin while giving them the satisfaction of taking something off you."

"I don't care, I'm not wearing it. This is something more fit for Shva'sika or Seda. They're taller and able to pull the length off more."

"Yeah, they can pull this off, but so can you." She handed me the hanger and clothes. "Now try it on. I'm going to give my options a spin."

I let out a loud, drawn-out sigh in protest as she left, warranting some laughter from her. I slipped out of the red and black nightgown and hung it up, finding myself glancing at it every now and then as I made myself try on the newest outfit Ryoko had just handed me. I struggled to figure out the top because of all the individual leather strings. Even the bottoms were easier to get on, and I was slipping those on over my panties for sanitary reasons.

The sheer silk flowed around me as I turned to face myself in the mirror. My first reaction, shock. My second, awkwardness. I chewed on my lips as I processed this look. *This isn't me.* I appreciated Ryoko's attempt, but this outfit was too sexy for me. *I just can't...*

"Looks good on you, Laz," Seda messaged.

"It's not a good look for me."

"Oh don't be like that. You look great. I could send in the guys to get their opinions."

I covered myself as if she were in the room with me. *"Don't you dare!"*

She laughed. *"You know I was kidding. I wouldn't send them in."*

"No, but you would leak a mental peek."

"Only if I absolutely needed to, like if you're too stubborn to see how good you look and need to see a man's reaction to get you to open your eyes."

"Seda!"

She laughed and left me alone to look myself over again. But the more I did, the more conflicted I became. I decided to take it off before I hurt myself in my decision making. It wasn't like it mattered anyway. I wasn't going to buy it even if I did look good in it. I had no reason to.

Once I had the garments off, I went to put my clothes back on, when my gaze landed on the garter set Telar had picked out. I sighed. *I might as well, since it's the only one I haven't tried.* Couldn't be any worse than the outfit I had just tried on, and I didn't need the others calling me a chicken.

The whole setup confused me, but I managed to get it all on, only to feel uncomfortable in it. The bra design barely kept my breasts in, and the panties were more glorified butt floss. I took the garment set off. No matter how I looked in it, this wouldn't be going home with me.

"Telar is going to be so disappointed when he finds out you're not going to buy that," Seda said.

"Well it's not like he knows what it looks like on me."

"No, but I did tell the two of them you looked good in it."

"Seda!"

She chuckled. *"And I also said you looked good in the one Raikidan picked out, but neither knows your personal feelings about each pick."*

I was quiet for a moment. *"How are they reacting to not knowing?"*

"Curiosity is killing them." I was pretty sure I could hear her grinning. *"And I'm being extra sure Telar can't sneak a peek."*

"I don't even want to think of him making that attempt."

"He's a guy, you're attractive, and you're trying on teasing clothes—expect the worst, from even him."

"She has a point." The voice in my head couldn't help adding its two cents.

I dressed quickly out of paranoia, and stepped out of the dressing room. Ryoko sat on a chair with some clothes in her hands. "I'm guessing I'm not helping you with your picks?"

She grinned and ignored my question. "Seda showed me what you looked like in those outfits."

"Of course she would," I muttered.

"You could seduce any guy you chose if you wanted to give it a shot."

"She's not wrong."

I rolled my eyes and we both laughed. "So, which one are you going to get?"

"None of them."

Her brow furrowed. "Why?"

"Because I don't have a reason to buy any." I went to hang the lingerie on a return rack, but Ryoko stopped me.

"Pick one."

I groaned as I threw my head back in exasperation. "Why?"

Her eyes twinkled. "Because I know you liked one of them and you should treat yourself—even if you won't wear it much. At least then you have it in case you do want to wear it at some point."

I considered at my choices. I did like the red and black babydoll, but picking it was such an awkward choice since Raikidan chose it for me.

Ryoko nudged me. "Don't think about who picked it out. Just choose the one you like."

"Be careful."

I hesitated, the worry about what others might think seeping into my mind, but I let it go as soon as I had the strength to. I needed to pick one. I needed to stop being so hesitant about these kinds of things. If I was to take control of my life and do what I wanted, I had to stop worrying about other's opinions the way I claimed to do.

I put away all but the black and red babydoll and Ryoko squealed. "I knew it!"

"You're walking a dangerous path."

I stuck my tongue out at Ryoko and then flicked my gaze to her selection. "What are you getting?"

"Several different *sexy* articles." She winked. "All of them things you're not ready to start attempting to wear."

I shook my head. I didn't want to know about the details of her sex life, especially not with Rylan. Feeling the bond go nuts when they were alone was torture enough for me, especially since it was starting to affect me in ways I didn't like.

New clothes in hand, the two of us left the dressing room and tracked down Seda. The boys weren't with her, but before I could ask their whereabouts, Seda pointed to the door of the store. "They decided to wait outside." She turned her head to the babydoll and smiled. "Glad to see you picked that one. You pulled off that one the best."

My cheeks warmed. "Thanks. Where are the clothes I found for Avila?"

"I took care of the purchase and handed them over to Telar." She grinned. "Hence Telar's absence. I made him stand there while I paid so he knew exactly what his sister was getting."

Ryoko and I laughed. She grabbed onto me when she almost fell over, and I laughed some more.

"I wish I'd seen the look on his face!" she said.

Seda snickered. "Priceless, that's the only way to describe it. Laz, you picked out some good choices."

I held up my hands and grinned. "I try."

When the sight of the nightgown flashed in my peripheral, embarrassment flooded over me and I hid it behind my back. The girls giggled, but gave me a look of understanding. I wanted to break out of this mold I had been pressed into—embraced out of safety—but it'd take time. I just had to keep trying.

Seda shopped around some more for herself and tried on a few outfits, Ryoko and I giving our two cents when she asked for opinions, and then we all paid for our things. The boys looked up from where they sat on a bench.

"About time you ladies finished," Telar said. "I thought I'd have to come do a rescue mission."

Ryoko wagged her finger at him. "Patience. The right outfit doesn't just jump out at you." She eyed me. "Takes a few tries to find the right one."

Telar turned his focus to me. "I see you bought something."

I held my head high. "I did—what of it?"

Telar held his hand out to Raikidan. "Pay up."

Raikidan grumbled and dropped a few gold pieces into Telar's hand. I shook my head. "Really?"

"I didn't think you'd buy anything," Raikidan said. "Even if you liked it. You're weird like that."

"He's... not wrong... I guess."

Ryoko placed her hands on the sides of my shoulders and pulled me close. "She almost didn't, but we convinced her to splurge on something different."

Telar chuckled. "Well thanks, ladies; I'm glad you could help me win this bet."

A thought came to me. "Oh! Rai, where is the—"

He held up the bag with the hat I bought for Ryoko. "Right here."

I smiled my thanks and handed it over to Ryoko. "Since you asked me to get you something, and you came here anyway…"

Ryoko's eyes brightened and she peered inside. Her head tilted as she pulled out the fuzzy hat, and then got excited when she realized what it was. She threw the hat on and stuck her hands into the paw pockets. "Laz, you're the best!"

I smiled wide. She looked adorable. "I'm glad you like it. I figured it was fitting for you." She nodded and played with her fuzzy paws. I turned my gaze to Telar. "Can we leave yet?"

He shook his head. "Afraid not. The guy is still—"

We all peered down the thoroughfare to see a young man in a baggy sweatshirt sprinting toward us with a backpack on his back. He threw panicked glances his shoulder several times before a few soldiers finally rounded a corner. The thief picked up his pace, but I could see this chase had his stamina worn down. Unless he could shake the guys and hide, he'd be a goner in—*Three, two, one.* I stuck my foot out as he passed us. The man tripped and tumbled, his backpack slipping off and sliding a few feet.

"Nice one."

"Bitch," he muttered as he pushed himself up and tried to run off.

Raikidan lunged out of his seat and grabbed the guy by the arm and back of the head. "Didn't your mother teach you how to speak to a lady?"

"Piss off," the man said. "Go f—"

Telar threw out his hand and the man cried out in pain. "Don't you dare say that about her."

"He's so good to you." Based on the tone, I was starting to think the voice wanted me to pick Telar as a partner, which was a rather weird thought.

"Please… please let me go," the man begged. "Please…"

Telar levitated the backpack and brought it closer to us. "Sorry, but I can't do that."

"Psychic freak, let me—" He screamed in pain again.

I went to stop Telar, but Seda held me back. *"Just let the boys be protective of you. It may be extreme, but it's how they show they care for you."*

"*Very well.*" I relaxed and waited for the soldiers to show up.

It didn't take them long, and they were grateful for the help. Once their thief was in custody, the leave ban was lifted, allowing Raikidan, Telar, and me to leave. Ryoko and Seda still had some surveillance to do, so our two groups went their separate ways.

Telar drove us home without much more incident than me messing with the stereo some more, resulting in Raikidan pulling me into the back. I laughed the entire time.

We climbed out of the car when we made it back to the house, and Telar handed me a box with the Silken Nights logo printed on the top. "Before you ask, Ryoko bought it. She wanted me to say I did, but I'm not that crazy."

I took the box from him. "Well, thank you. I suspect I know what this is, so it's a good thing you were upfront about it. I won't keep you since it's late. Don't act like a stranger, okay, Telar?"

He chuckled. "I'll try not to." His head shifted enough for me to tell he was glancing at Raikidan. "Though, with the way your boyfriend has been acting all night, I don't know if I'll be safe."

My cheeks flushed a light shade of red and Raikidan looked taken aback by the comment. "He's not my boyfriend, Telar."

"You sure?" I gave him a long serious look and he chuckled. "All right, then cool. Means you're still fair game to me."

"Telar!" My face felt hotter, and I hated it.

He laughed. "I'm joking, calm down. No, but seriously, it'll be nice to catch up with you sometime."

"*Well, he wouldn't be the worst pick in the world.*" That confirmed it. "*But he's not ideal for you. I won't allow you to get hurt by some man. Not again.*"

My heart twinged and I focused on the conversation at hand with Telar. I nodded while smiling. "I'd like that. I'll contact you when I get some news about how to help your sister."

"I appreciate the effort. I'd like to see her back on her feet again."

I nodded. Telar and his sister had an odd relationship for psychics. With her being a Seer and him a Battle Psychic, they should have some sort of rivalry going on, but there was none of that with those two. I liked seeing that, and wished other psychics would learn from their example.

Telar waved at me before climbing back into his car and driving off.

"You're real chummy with him," Raikidan said.

"Someone sounds jealous. Wait, why would he be?"

"Yeah, and?" I challenged. "Telar is a good friend. Has been ever since he gained my trust back in the day."

"Was there ever anything between you?" he asked.

I turned my head a bit as I looked at him funny. "What?"

Raikidan shrugged. "Just a question. You don't act like that with many people, especially not males, and when you were playing that truth and dare game, I overheard you may have cared for someone deeper than you want to admit these days."

"He did not go there."

Pain pulsed in my chest and my gaze darkened. I held up a finger to him. "Don't ever bring that up again, you hear?"

Raikidan stepped back, surprised by my change in mood. "What's wrong with what I—"

"Don't." I spun on my heels and headed inside, my chest still reeling with pain. I didn't know what got into him just then, but he knew better than to bring up that topic.

I almost jumped when Genesis spoke the moment I entered the living room. "How did the assignment go?"

"What are you doing up still?" I asked. "It's two in the morning."

She shrugged. "Couldn't sleep."

I nodded. "As far as I know, it went well. Telar said he got a lot of good information."

"Did you have any problems since he chose to go as his normal self?"

I laughed. "Yes. It's because of him being his normal self that he walked off alone and had to deal with unneeded questioning."

"Sounds about right. Would you have any issues if I included him in your assignments more if I can?"

"Not at all. I like working with him."

She smiled. "Good. Several teams have requested him, but the rest of the Council knows how well the two of you work together, so we get first pick if he's not already on an assignment."

"This pleases me."

"Sounds fair to me."

"Well, I'll let you get some sleep."

"Thank you. Have a good night, Genesis." I entered the kitchen to put our leftovers away and then entered my room, noticing Raikidan sitting on the edge of my bed instead of the windowsill. "You attempting to steal my bed or something?"

He chuckled. "No, but that's not a bad idea. This is a comfortable place to sleep."

I pointed to him as I headed for my closet. "Don't you dare try to break it. I will make your life miserable if you do."

Raikidan grinned and bounced on the bed. I grabbed a pencil from my dresser and tossed it at him. He chuckled as he protected himself with his arm. "Watch it, or I won't give you your gift."

My head tilted. "My what?" He grinned but said nothing more. *Could this be the purchase he and Telar were arguing about?* I put my bag down and walked over to him. "Where is it?"

He held up a small rectangular box. I looked at the plain container and my curiosity got the better of me. Even though I didn't have a love of receiving gifts, each time he gave me something, I couldn't complain about the gift itself. He always put a lot of thought into it. *His destined mate is a lucky woman...*

The box almost fell out of my hand when I removed the top and stared at the sparkling contents. "R—Rai, what is this?"

"Do you like it? I saw you looking at that one a lot, so I bought it for you."

I placed the cover back on the box and handed it back to him. "I can't take this."

He pushed the box back to me. "Please. I got it for you."

"It was expensive!"

"And? You deserve to have nice jewelry like that."

I sighed and gazed at the sapphire and diamond necklace again, the low light of my room sparkling off the faceted gems. "You spoil me too much, you know?"

Raikidan smirked. "You should be spoiled more. You deserve it and it means you smile more. I like it when you're pleased."

I shook my head, a smile on my face. "You have a strange way of wording things. But no matter what I say, you won't take this back, so thank you."

"You shouldn't do that."

I headed for my closet to put it away with my other jewelry, and to store away the new nightwear I'd never wear.

"So, what did you buy?" Raikidan asked when he watched me pick up the Silken Nights bag.

My brow rose. "Why do you ask?"

He shrugged. "I'm just curious."

"Well, sorry to tell you this, but that's my secret."

He frowned. "All right." I slipped into my closet and he called out to me again. "Can you tell me something? Did you at least like what I picked out?"

I poked my head out. "Why *did* you pick something for me?"

"Because everyone else was, and none of it looked like anything you'd be willing to wear. Well, except Seda's choice. It was similar to what I found. So, did you like it?"

"Careful how you answer."

I contemplated telling him I bought it. I didn't have to. I could simply not tell him anything, or I could tell him I liked it and end it at that, but a part of me wanted him to know how much I liked it. *Eira, watch that road you're on!* I slipped back into my closet without saying anything and chewed on my lip.

"So you liked Telar's choice more, then?"

A bit of shock rippled through me at the sound of sadness in his voice. "Why would you think that?"

"Seda said you liked one of the choices over the other. If you didn't like mine, then you liked his."

She said she didn't tell them I had a preference of one over the other... Now the need to tell him tugged hard on me. I pulled the babydoll out of the box.

"Don't do it."

"I didn't think you'd like something like that. I guess—"

"You should give me more time to work things out before jumping to conclusions." I grasped the nightgown by the hanger and held it out for him to see, making sure he couldn't see me at the same time. "This isn't the one Ryoko bought me. I liked this one the most."

Silence enveloped the room. I pulled the nightgown back to me. *I shouldn't have said anything...*

"You going to put it on?" Raikidan asked.

My face burned. "W–what?"

He chuckled. "I'm glad you liked it enough to buy it, but are you going to wear it?"

"Um…" I chewed on my lip some more. Was I going to have the guts to wear it? Raikidan appeared in the doorway of my closet and rested his arm high on the frame. I peered up at him through my lashes, my gaze struggling not to take in the sight he presented—corded muscles flexing down his long arms; under his taught shirt—my face burned hotter. *Oh boy, I'm in trouble…*

"Be careful!"

"Is that a yes?"

"I'm curious why you want to see me in something so revealing," I managed to say.

He stiffened, piquing my interest. "It's not because it's revealing or anything. I want to know what you look like in it. Seda said it looked good on you." I wrestled with the idiotic turmoil inside me, smothering it with logic, and slipped over to the other side of my closet to put the gown away. "So, no?"

"I'm not ready to wear something like this so freely."

"What do you mean? It's just clothing."

"He can't be that stupid, can he?"

I chuckled and faced him after hanging the nightgown up. "Rai, do you ever pay attention to what I wear?"

"Well, yeah. You have a unique style that you like and wear well."

He thinks it's unique? I tilted my head. "Unique is one way of putting it. But if you think about it, it doesn't match the style of this nightgown. It's out of my element, so it's harder for me to wear it so openly in front of someone."

"I don't understand why it's out of your element. It looks like something you could wear well, and Seda said it looks good on you, so how could it be that strange to wear?"

I tilted my head. "If I didn't know any better, I'd say you wanted to see me in clothes like these."

"Well, I'm… uh, just curious, that's all."

All lingering awkwardness disappeared and I walked closer to him, being sure to lock eye contact and keep my movement fluid. "Is that so? You're trying pretty hard to rationalize why you want to see me in it, when the whole purpose of this type of clothing is to be sexy and seduce another person."

He hesitated, then backed up and pointed to my room. "I–I'll drop the topic and let you wear what you want. I'll be out there."

Raikidan disappeared into my room. Now my curiosity was fully engaged. What got him to flip like that? Did he not understand the purpose of the nightgown until I said something? Or did I do something to freak him out?

"Doesn't matter, he finally gave up. He shouldn't have pressed to begin with."

I shook my head and went about changing into my normal sleep wear. It didn't matter. At this point in time, I wouldn't wear the gown in front of anyone. I glanced at the box with Ryoko's purchase. *I'm definitely not going to wear whatever is in there, either.* I didn't trust it and didn't even bother taking a peek. The box went into a corner and I walked out of my closet. Raikidan sat on the windowsill his gaze flicking to me immediately.

I smirked. "Sorry, but no nightgown tonight."

"Will I get to see you in it at any point?" he asked as I situated myself on my bed.

I turned my head with interest. "You're being really stubborn about this. Didn't they have a picture display with a model wearing it?"

"Yeah, but she wasn't you."

I was taken aback for a moment. "Fair, but I'm sure she looked better in it than me."

He shook his head and held eye contact. "I seriously doubt it."

"He's lying. He doesn't believe that."

It was my turn to look away. "Yeah, well, you may get the chance to see, you may not. All depends on if I can even get myself to wear it again in private, let alone in front of someone else."

"Well, you should. I'm confident you'd look cute it in." And with that, he shifted into his dragon shape, leaving me unable to continue this conversation.

"Did he just—" the voice didn't finish the sentence, not that I blamed it.

I watched him as he settled himself for sleep, thinking over the last ten minutes. Did he really want to see me in it that much? *He's acting as if—no, Eira, don't go down that road. You know better…*

28
CHAPTER

I shoved my hands farther into my pocket as Raikidan and I walked on the stone path, leaves crunching underfoot. Our mission was surveillance, disguised as ourselves. Unfortunately, everything but work interested me. The equinox was around the corner, and the trees and ground showed it.

The cast of reds and oranges captivated my eyes and melted the dreary feel of the city. I inhaled deeply to take in the crisp air.

"You need to focus."

Raikidan glanced my way. "You don't want to do this, do you?"

I caught a leaf as it fell. "Nope, you?"

"No."

"Then let's not do it."

His brow rose. "Who are you and what have you done with Eira?"

I laughed. "It's my life, right? Why shouldn't I have a little fun when I want?"

"Now that's the Eira I know. So what do you want to do?"

I picked up a handful of leaves and tossed them at him. He blinked furiously, and I couldn't help but laugh. When he came out of his shocked state, he grinned and tossed a handful of leaves at me in return. I shoved him and took off.

"Hey, get back here!"

I laughed and continued running. I decided to leave the path, kicking up a pile of leaves in my way. Raikidan did his best to keep up with me as I zigzagged through the trees, but I eluded him in the end—or so I thought.

I peered around a tree but couldn't find him. I knew he had to be hiding, like me, but the question was where? He wasn't small, so it should have been easy to spot him, right? Cautiously, I ventured away from my tree. Big mistake.

Raikidan came out of nowhere and grabbed onto me. A squeal escaped my lips from the surprise and it soon switched to laughter as he spun us around. My laughter stopped, though, when he slung me over his shoulder. I had no idea what he was doing, but he was purposefully walking somewhere, and I didn't like the feeling I was getting. "Raikidan, put me down."

He chuckled. "All right, suit yourself."

I yelp when he threw me. *Jerk! Throwing me on the—* My body bounced as I landed in a large pile of leaves, the musky-sweet scent invading my nose.

Raikidan laughed at me. "Your face was priceless!"

"That wasn't funny!" I grabbed a handful of leaves and tried to throw them at him, but they were too light to go far, making Raikidan laugh at me more. I crossed my arms and huffed.

His laughter ceased and he sighed. "Here, I'll help you up."

When he stretched out his hand I grabbed it and then smirked. His eyes widened as I pulled him with as much strength as I could. As he fell, I kicked my legs up to help me propel him over me and onto his back in the large pile of leaves. The moment he grunted from his landing, I was laughing—I couldn't help it. He'd fallen for it so easily.

He tossed a few leaves on my face from where he lay. "That wasn't fair."

I lobbed some leaves back at him and laughed more. "Yes it was."

He chucked more leaves my way and I retaliated. Before I knew it we were having some strange leaf war and I couldn't stop laughing. I didn't know what had gotten into me today, but I was having fun for once, so I didn't want to question it. It actually felt normal to laugh and have so much fun.

"Will you stop throwing leaves at me?" he asked finally.

I continued my assault. "You started it."

"Doesn't mean you have to finish it."

"Yes it does!"

"Nope, I will," he flipped over and shoved a bunch of leaves on me. "By burying you."

I sat up. "No, you won't!"

Raikidan grabbed onto me. "You're supposed to lie down and let me bury you."

I grabbed his arms and tried to wrestle him down. "No, *you* lay down so I can bury *you*."

"You're not strong enough to fight me."

I laughed. "No, but I can sure as hell try."

I fought him with as much power I could muster, but his strength was far superior, and before I knew it, I was on my back with Raikidan pinning me down. As compromising as the position was, I couldn't stop laughing.

"Hey, lovebirds, knock it off!"

My laughter died, my ears burning when I heard Ryoko's voice. Raikidan released me and we both sat up. Rylan and she were standing a few yards off, but Raid was nowhere in sight.

"You're just upset you're not having fun," I said.

She gave me a smug look in response and I stuck my tongue out at her. When I noticed a team of soldiers approaching, I sucked my tongue back in, especially since Zo was with them. What did they want?

Ryoko looked at them expectantly. "Any luck?"

"I'm afraid we still haven't found your dog, Ryoko," Zo told her.

Her ears drooped. "Oh, well thank you for trying."

My head cocked to the side. "What's going on?"

"After you guys left for your walk, Rylan and I figured it'd be a good idea to walk Raid, but he broke off the leash when he saw a squirrel. I called you so you could help keep an eye out, but you didn't answer. I left you a message, too."

I pulled out my communicator from my satchel. Sure enough, there was a missed call light. "I didn't hear it going off, sorry. But we'll help look. He can't be too far."

"I seriously doubt it," a soldier remarked.

Ryoko's ear drooped, and Zo smacked the soldier for his insensitivity.

Raid knew he wasn't to leave the park so we could find him, but the park was big and he could have wandered off anywhere. Of course if we didn't find him soon so we could continue our assignment, I'd ream him.

I sighed mentally. Here I was talking about getting an assignment done, and I wasn't doing mine myself. I got to my feet and dusted off the leaves that clung to me before calling for Raid.

"That's not going to work, ma'am," a soldier tried to tell me.

I ignored him and called for Raid again. If he was within earshot, he'd come to my call without fail.

"Here he comes," Raikidan said.

I stopped calling for him and watched as Raid came barreling toward us. He charged through the pile of leaves Raikidan and I stood in, jumping around excitedly. I couldn't help but laugh and try to razzle him. He did well playing a real dog.

"So much for your theory he wouldn't come to her call," Raikidan taunted the soldier.

"Something isn't right. There's no way you could have found him so effortlessly," the soldier muttered.

"Why, because it proves you wrong?" I said. Raikidan chuckled. "It's just our luck that he was in this part of the park. I didn't think he'd actually come when I called, but it wasn't going to hurt to try."

"Kid, let it go," Zo said. "The dog is back, and that's what matters."

The side of my lips twitched in fake appreciation for his backup. Ryoko called for Raid and he immediately ran over to her. "Don't you run off on me like that again, you hear?"

He barked at her and wagged his tail as Rylan secured the leash around his collar. "There, that should hold you this time. I hope."

"I hope so, too," Ryoko murmured.

"All right, now that they have their happy ending, let's go," Raikidan whispered in my ear.

I nodded and he slung his arm around my shoulders. I wanted to sigh. I knew he was doing it because Zo was here, and it annoyed me. What was his deal?

Two people walking through the park caught my eye, pulling my attention away. They weren't doing anything out of the ordinary, so I couldn't figure it out until I noticed both had strange multi-colored hair. *It's him.* It was the mysterious shapeshifter again. I wasn't seeing things the other week.

The man looked at me and winked a kaleidoscopic eye just as Raikidan and I passed a large tree. But when it was out of the way, the two people had disappeared. I cranked my neck in several directions but they were nowhere to be seen. It was like they vanished into thin air. But they had definitely been there. *That guy even winked at me.*

Raikidan took notice. "What is it?"

"Nothing."

"You're interested in something," he said. "What is it?"

"I thought I saw someone I knew."

"Who?"

I shook my head. "I don't know his name. Chance and brief meeting."

"Do you want to go talk to him?"

"That's the thing... I don't see him anymore. It's like he wasn't actually there."

"Don't tell me you're seeing things."

"I'm starting to wonder..."

Raikidan nudged me. "I'm teasing."

I chewed my lip. "It's not the first time I've thought I've seen him..."

He patted my back. "Don't let it get to you. I don't doubt you saw him. He's probably just slippery. Don't beat yourself up over it."

The fact he wasn't telling me I was crazy surprised me. Most would think I was seeing things, but he just accepted it.

As we made it back onto the path, I decided I didn't want to walk anymore. "Carry me."

Raikidan grunted when I jumped on his back. "You're such a pain."

"Oh, you love it."

He chuckled as he carried me down the path. "I thought you didn't like help."

I rested my arms across the back of his shoulders, and lay my head on them. "I don't. I'm just being lazy. There's a difference."

"You, lazy? Since when?"

"Since now."

We laughed, and I had to admit, it was nice.

"You're not watching the boundaries."

My laughter quieted down, and an emptiness rose up, choking out all the fun and joy in me. Raikidan was my friend, yes, but he had a life to get back to after this. He wasn't going to be around forever, and I shouldn't fuel anything. But it was hard not being able to get along with someone who somehow got along with you so perfectly. I couldn't think of one person I could get along with as well as he could with me.

Raikidan tilted his head to look back at me. "You're thinking too much again."

I blinked. "What?"

"You have that look and it's soured your mood. What are you thinking about?"

I shook my head. "Nothing. Don't worry about it."

He came to a stop on a bridge and let me go, forcing me off his back. He leaned against the railing, and I did the same to look out at the lake. "You shouldn't think of things like that. It ruins the fun you're having, and you should be having fun. It's nice… hearing you laugh."

A small smile appeared on my lips and I had to look away. His words were honest and friendly enough, but the way they made me feel was another story. I gazed out at the park in front of me instead, in hopes it'd bring me back to reality.

"You miss it, don't you?" he said.

"Huh?"

"Being outside the wall. You miss it."

"Yeah…"

"Is it the freedom you miss, or—"

I shook my head. "Running with an eye over your shoulder isn't freedom. It's the smells—the sights—everything. Here, I can still see all the buildings and smell the city. The park is a good replica, but that's all it'll ever be."

"Do you hate me for bringing you here?"

I took a glance and saw the soldiers Raikidan must have spotted. "No, I don't hate you. I honestly can't think of a better choice, except maybe going to that harbor city instead. I just wish we weren't forced to stay here. I miss having a choice."

Raikidan wrapped his arm around me and spoke low. "Soon. I promise."

I looked up at him. "Don't break it, okay?"

"I won't."

I smiled and gazed out at the lake again, the color of the trees reflecting off the surface. *Pretty, even for a man-made city lake.* It was going to be the closest I'd get to seeing the mountains during this time of year. That was the area I missed the most. The cleaner air. The change in the trees as time passed through the year. The trees here all carried that nursery grown, uniform appearance.

A weird sensation turned in my stomach. It wasn't something I had experienced before, but I'd been told about it. *Homesickness.* But I didn't understand why thinking of the mountains made me feel that way. The city wasn't my home, but neither were the mountains. The shaman village wasn't by any real mountains—a large valley, sure, but no mountains, and that was the only home I had ever really had. So what was it about the mountains that made me feel like they were my home I needed to get back to?

29
CHAPTER

My heart pounded to the beat of the music as I bussed the bar and my heeled boots clomped on the floor. My teeth ground together when my boots caught on the stupid skirt I wore. It was the night of the equinox, and instead of being home with Zane and the others to have fun and help hand out treats when the occasional child came by, I was stuck working.

While a good percentage of the city's population would be celebrating at home or at friends' houses, Azriel threw some of the best parties at the club, and that meant I had to dress up like everyone else. Azriel had picked out what I was wearing, but I wasn't sure if I should be grateful or not. While I could never have selected anything good out, what he picked wasn't something I had in mind as a costume.

The skirt he gave me was a bit weird. It started under my breasts and hugged my body until it reached my hips, where it draped in layers to one side. The non-skirted side showed off my thigh-high boots and spandex shorts. A tight corset covered my torso.

Ryoko supplied the jewelry adorning my body, and allowed me to go out with a light makeup treatment instead of the original torture Shva'sika had planned. Of course, the required decorative mask helped, and allowed me to feel far more comfortable and unrecognizable.

Zo pushed through the throng of people and sat down at the bar. "Hey there, Eira."

I tried to hide my disappointment. *Okay, not unrecognizable.* "Hey, Zo. What'll you have?"

"Scotch for now."

I nodded and prepared his drink.

"You know, I expected a little more leather on you." Zo had left me alone lately beyond our chance meetings in the city, but I could tell he was testing the waters again, and I was going to have to play along.

I turned around with his drink and wagged my finger at him. "You know that's our little secret, Zo."

He chuckled and took his drink, eyeing me in a way I wished he wouldn't. "That's right. Thanks for the reminder."

I started to bus the bar again when Raikidan came over. "What's up?"

"Beth asked for a bit of help." He handed me a piece of paper. "She was hoping you could make all this and help me deliver it. She's a bit swamped."

"Sure." I took the list, noting he'd translated the order.

"Good man."

I smiled and filled the order, Raikidan helping occasionally. When I finished, Raikidan took one tray while I grabbed the other two and he led me to where Beth worked. Maneuvering around all the people wasn't the easiest task with two full trays, but I managed, and Beth was more than happy to help me before Raikidan.

Once everyone was content, I headed back to the bar and cleaned the trays. I went to take Raikidan's, but he held onto it. "I'll help."

I tugged on the tray. "Rai, it's fine, I got this."

He stepped closer with the tug. "C'mon, Eira, let me help."

I chuckled and pushed him away. "Go back to doing your job."

He smirked. "My job today is to help where needed, and you look in need of help."

I kicked him in the rear. "Git!"

He chuckled and turned to leave. Raikidan's and Zo's eyes met, their faces twisting into sour expressions. I didn't miss their tense exchange, but before I had a chance to think on it, Azriel showed up. "Eira, I need you."

I put the tray down. "Um, okay, for what?"

He held out his hand. "Just come with me."

I eyed him but took his hand. He tucked my hands under his arm and led me away without a word, puzzling me further. "Azriel, what is going on?"

"I need a dance partner."

I stopped dead in my tracks. "Oh no. You know I can't dance."

"Can't"—he smirked—"or won't?"

"Az, please, you promised."

"I promised you'd only ever had to dance with me after I taught you," he corrected. "And I'm in need of a dance partner now."

"What, you couldn't work your magic and get a guy to volunteer?"

"As much I toyed with the idea, I need a woman for these dances, and you're that woman."

"Az…"

Azriel got the DJ's attention and made a motion with his finger that the DJ somehow understood. I gulped when the music changed. *I'm really going to have to do this.*

My body moved on cue, Azriel's drilling back in the day not something I could forget. Azriel spun me around and then pulled me in close. I didn't miss a step and performed my part flawlessly.

A firm hand grab onto me. I looked to see Rylan grinning at me. "My turn."

My eyes widened. "Wait, what?"

Rylan pulled me away from Azriel and took his place as my new partner. I was so confused, but I went with it—I couldn't do anything else. I couldn't get myself to stop dancing and go back to working.

Azriel stole me back from Rylan, but Rylan cut in again. I started laughing as I continued to dance. I was starting to see what was going on. As the two shared me, I got into it more, and my movements showed it. But Rylan threw me for a loop when he stopped taking me from Azriel. "Where'd he go?"

"Ryoko showed up on the dance floor," Azriel said. "I don't think I have to explain it any further than that."

I laughed. "No, I can figure that out for myself."

Azriel pulled me close, but I pushed him away with a grin and expected to dance by myself for a few seconds, but someone new grabbed me and forced me into a spin before pulling me close.

I blinked when can face to face with my new partner. "Raikidan?"

He smirked. "My turn."

My face twisted in confusion. "Since when do you know how to dance?"

"Since Big Boss there forced me to learn," he admitted.

I laughed. "That's awkward."

"You have no idea."

As we danced, his ability surprised me. When did Azriel have the time to teach him?

"When did you learn to dance like this?" Raikidan asked. "I remember you trying to convince Ryoko those months ago that you didn't know how to dance."

"Azriel promised no one would know," I muttered.

"You were forced to learn, then, like me?"

I blew out a breath. "It was for an assignment back in my military days."

Raikidan spun me around so I faced away from him and then pulled me close. "Well it's a good thing he taught you. Otherwise I wouldn't have such an excellent dance partner."

"And you can't have her," Azriel said as he took me back. Raikidan didn't look pleased and I couldn't help but laugh. This was meant to be fun, and I had to just let myself go and have fun.

I grinned and pushed Azriel away from me when the tempo picked up. The energy of the music coursed through me, and I couldn't help but enjoy the feeling. I felt so alive.

As I danced alone for a few moments, someone grabbed a hold of me, and annoyance flared in my chest. The unknown person spun me around. I scowled at the masked man with two-toned red, unsupported mohawk before me. "What are you doing here, Zaith?"

"You invited me here, no?" His words were thick with an accent usually heard in the south marshland areas of Lumaraeon, like the Sarget Morass.

"One, your clan was to stay away from the city, but you didn't listen to the warning. And two, I meant, what are you doing here, in this place?"

"Lookin' for you. Hopin' to… talk."

I pushed him away, only for Raikidan to grab me. He looked almost as angry as me. He tried his best to dance with me while keeping me out of Zaith's reach, but it didn't last forever.

"Reconsider my offer, and be my mate," Zaith whispered in my ear once he was able to get me back from Raikidan. "I'm a much better choice than him."

"Not really." The voice sounded about as disgusted as I felt.

"Raikidan isn't a choice. But if he was, I'd definitely choose him over you, in a heartbeat." I pushed him away again, but more aggressively this time, in hopes he'd get the hint and allowed Raikidan to take me back.

Raikidan tried to keep me close, but unfortunately, the music changed to a faster tempo that required me to move away from him, giving Zaith the opportunity to snatch me again.

"Think about it," Zaith said. "I can give you whatever you want."

I pushed him away. "No, you can't."

Raikidan took me back, but within moments, Azriel grabbed me. "You're a popular choice tonight."

My nose scrunched. "I wish I wasn't…"

"You should see it as a good thing."

"Zaith is still making his intentions quite clear, and I want no part of it."

"I see."

I pushed him away as a natural part of the dance, and Raikidan took me back under his lead. The two switched several times more before Zaith made another attempt to hold onto me, but I wasn't having it. I assertively pushed him away. I expected to return to one of my usual partners, but landed in the arms of a woman. "Uh, hi, Ryoko."

She smiled. "This should be fun."

I chuckled. "You lead."

"I like the sound of that!"

The two of us danced together and, even though I felt quite silly, I enjoyed myself. Ryoko tried to protest when Azriel stole me away but my dance with him didn't last long either, thanks to Raikidan snatching me. I laughed every time one of them stole me. Ryoko bowed out after I'd been passed around a few times, and Azriel and Raikidan battled for the position of my lead dance partner. As this continued, the tempo of the music continued to pick up.

Then suddenly, Azriel backed out of the dance, giving me to Raikidan fully. I didn't know what he was up to, but I wasn't going to stop to find out. With me being able to focus on Raikidan and his level of dance ability, I was able to get a smoother dance out, unlike when I was passed around.

The music picked up to the point where I knew the dancing was going to stop soon. A part of me was disappointed. I should have been uncomfortable dancing like this. Even dancing with Azriel was uncomfortable in a way. But dancing with Raikidan, all of that was gone. Nothing else mattered—just the music, him, and me.

Raikidan had just pulled me close to him when the music came to an abrupt halt. My hands clenched his shirt while one of his hands held my leg up against his, and his other hand cupped the side of my face. His heavy, exhausted breath tingled my lips and his heart pounded strongly through my hands as I stared into his eyes and struggled to breathe.

His grip on my face tightened little by little, and I was vaguely aware of myself leaning closer to him. I found myself unable to rip my gaze away. I didn't have control over any part of me as my breath became slower and my eyes began to close. My lower lip quivered as my lips parted.

"You guys were great!" Raikidan and I jumped when Mana popped in out of nowhere. "It was so much fun watching you guys dance so well together!"

I pulled away from Raikidan immediately and messed with my skirt. "Thanks, Mana. If you two will excuse me, I have to get back to working. Drinks won't get made themselves."

I dashed off—my ears feeling as though they were burning off.

"Um, did I say something wrong?" Mana asked.

"No, don't worry about it," Raikidan said. "We do have to go back to working. Excuse me."

I couldn't believe what almost happened. *That was too close of a call, Eira.*

"Yes, it was close. But you were enjoying yourself for once. You looked... happy..."

I slipped behind the bar and grabbed a glass. I needed to make Mana a drink, as a small token of gratitude for saving Raikidan's and my friendship. Handing the sweet drink to a waitress to deliver for me, I went to cleaning glasses, in hopes of distracting my racing mind and thundering heart.

30
CHAPTER

Water streamed from the watering can as I tipped it over some plants, but the water didn't last long. I peered inside the can, finding it empty again. With a sigh, I made my way over to the spigot and filled it again. *I need to work on fixing the sprinkler system.*

I stopped filling the can when the greenhouse door opened and closed. Placing the can down, I moved around the tables of plants to look at the front of the building, only to find no one there. Growing suspicious, I snuck around until I found my mystery guest.

I stood as he inspected a flowering plant with great interest. "I thought black dragons shunned curiosity."

Rennek jumped and stared at me in horror, clearly not expecting me to be here. "I, uh… um…"

I chuckled. "It's a hibiscus. This particular species grows in the tropical areas in the southern region."

His gaze went elsewhere and his voice lowered. "I know…"

"Do you know what this is?" I asked pointing to a fan-like crown flower of blue, orange and red colors.

"It's… a bird-of-paradise."

"You're ashamed you know so much." He didn't answer or look at me. I pulled some dead leaves off of a nearby plant. "There is nothing wrong with curiosity. It's how we learn and grow."

"I'm not used to someone encouraging me to learn," he said.

"I'm human. We're curious by nature. We've evolved to understand by learning, and in order to learn, we need a drive to do so. That drive is curiosity."

"Ambrose tried to drill it into my head that curiosity was a weakness." He shook his head. "I never understood how you could learn without it."

I tilted my head. "You don't call him your father—why is that? Even Raikidan refers to his father with that title, even though he has a deep hatred for him."

Rennek blew out a breath. "Because I'm not his son."

My brow rose. "Salir had another mate before Ambrose?"

Rennek shook his head. "No, I'm adopted."

That wasn't something I was expecting to hear. "I didn't know dragons adopted."

"It's not common, especially for dragon pairs, but some clans and colonies will do it."

"So, why were you so lucky? Ambrose doesn't come off as the hospitable, adopting type."

Rennek's voice lowered again. "It was because of Salir. She had three failed clutches before she found me, which was only days after she lost the last clutch. So the moment she saw me wandering around helplessly..."

He trailed off and I understood. "Her instincts took over."

He nodded. "She took me under her care and wouldn't allow Ambrose to say otherwise. I know the only reason he didn't kill me when she wasn't looking was because I have no signs of being of mixed color, even though he believes my personality would indicate otherwise."

"From what I've gathered during your stay here, Salir is quite caring. It's a stark contrast to what I'd expect from a black dragon."

"She is. Ambrose tries to blame me. He claims she wasn't like that before I came along, but I know better. She was always that way and he just doesn't like it." He sighed. "She deserves better."

"Do you know why she's so caring?" I asked.

"You were told black dragons were mean and nasty, right?" I nodded and he chuckled. "Well, that's true for most, but there are quite a few who aren't, and it's believed to be because they are descendants of mixed colors, even if they don't show it anymore."

"Care to explain a bit better?"

"A long time ago, when there were more of us, each dragon color had their own set of distinct personality traits. But when the colors started to mix, so did their personalities. Those personality traits remained even after single-color blood diluted the other color, even when there were no outward signs of mixing in the first place."

I nodded. "That's because when it comes to genetics, you can't fully get rid of a trait. You can dilute certain aspects, but it will always be there, no matter what. That means even if the scales don't show any signs due to dilution, traits, such as personality, will still exist."

Rennek blinked and then smiled. "Humans have always interested me because of what you just said. For creatures that are so small, you make up for it with your intelligence."

I chuckled and plucked more dead leaves from a plant. "Only some of us are that smart. The rest of us take the information when it's handed to us."

"But you've still learned in some way, and by truly learning it, you can remember it as you wish. That is still a type of higher intelligence."

"You didn't tell me why Salir is so kind," I said.

"I don't know for certain, but I believe she is a descendant of a mixed dragon pair."

"She won't tell you?"

"It's possible she doesn't know that far into her lineage, and it's possible she does and wants to keep it to herself. Regardless, I don't care. She took me in instead of letting me die, and I'm grateful for that."

"Do you call her mother?"

He nodded. "I don't see a reason not to."

"I can assume you never found out who your real parents were or why you were abandoned?" A risky question for me to ask, but I was curious.

Rennek shook his head. "There were no pairs or colonies of dragons near our territory, so it remained a mystery."

I nodded and headed back to another part of the greenhouse. "You're welcome here, Rennek. That is, as long as you're careful."

"I will be. Thank you."

The door to the house opened and Ryoko walked out onto the roof. She spotted me and waved me to join her. I gave Rennek one last glance to find him looking over some plants.

"What's up?" I asked when I exited, not bothering to close the pane glass door behind me.

"Genesis is calling for a group meeting," she said. "Said we have an update on our progress against Zarda."

"Let's hope the update is better than the last few we've gathered for." I rolled my eyes at the memory. "I don't know about you, but 'no update' would have been better than the runaround she tried to relay."

Ryoko laughed. "She also mentioned something about an assignment."

I nodded. "Good. Hopefully it'll be something more hands-on than the last one."

Ryoko snickered, her eyes dancing with mischief. "What, going on a date with Raikidan and Telar and picking out sexy clothes isn't *hands-on*? I never thought you were that type of girl, but we all have our dirty secrets."

My eyes narrowed into slits. "Don't you start."

She giggled and then headed inside. I was soon to follow, with Rennek not far behind. *What reason could he have to follow?* By the time the three of us made it inside, the others in the house were already gathered. Rylan, Argus, Raid, and Shva'sika sat on one side of the large curved couch. Genesis and Seda sat in the middle, and Blaze, Corliss, and Mana sat on the far side. Zane took up a seat on a barstool and Raikidan sat on the windowsill, his arms crossed, but his expression gave away his curiosity. Mocha stood in the hallway, keeping a close eye on everyone, and Salir and Ambrose were nowhere to be seen. *No surprise there.*

Ryoko and I took up a seat next to Seda and Genesis, and to my surprise, Rennek sat down next to Zane. *What's he up to?* I knew I shouldn't be suspicious due to how well we'd communicated earlier, but I couldn't help it right now.

"Okay, now that everyone is here, I have a status update for everyone," Genesis said.

"Is it a real update, or just a 'no update' update?" Blaze asked.

The room echoed with laughter, but Genesis cut it short with a stern look. "It's a real update, thank you. Someone found out about Eira's snarky comment to two of the council members after The Run, and rumors began to spread. It forced the Council to reveal many things."

"Wow, Eira, you must be pleased your mouth actually did something good this time," Blaze said.

I held my head high. "If I wasn't so proud of myself I'd hit you."

He smirked and held out a hand. "You love me."

"Yeah, sure."

Genesis cleared her throat. "Focus. Now, I'm going to discuss a few small things before getting into why the Council has been keeping things under wraps. Our supplies are decent at the moment. Weapons are in abundance, ammunition is getting low but satisfactory for now, and medical supplies are the biggest concerns. Several teams are already on the hunt for these supplies, along with working with the shamans for physical treatments to help operatives get back on the field faster. Even with the shamans helping, we're going to be seeing more assignments around supply retrieval and drops soon. We need to prepare, and there are several warehouses we can target. Due to Eira's outburst, this team will get quite a few."

"At least it's something," I muttered.

Genesis shook her head but didn't argue. "New information on some technology in the works has filtered in, and Team Six is eagerly digging into what we have to see if anything can be used to our advantage. This will pull on our supplies, another reason more supply runs will go on." She let out a slow breath through her nose. "Now for the big piece of information, and biggest problem—Zarda has increased his defenses."

Several of my housemates groaned, while others hung their heads. I frowned. This wasn't good, but for the Council to hide this kind of information, it didn't help us in any way. "So, what caused this change, and how are we going to get around it? Has what we've been doing been a waste of time or helped with this issue?"

Genesis took a deep breath. "We think our efficiency on learning defense weak points has accelerated their technology use to keep us at bay. Reports also indicate Zarda is still experimenting on himself, which we believe is connected to them bolstering their defenses."

"So, we were too slow on acting in their weakened state," Rylan said.

Genesis remained still and then hid her face in her hands. "We thought we weren't making a dent, but we now know…" She went quiet and then she hit the coffee table. "We were almost there!"

Several of us jumped. It wasn't like her to lose her cool like that. "We were so close and it slipped away…"

I looked around at the others and watched their morale drop before my eyes. *Not good.* I stood and paced in front of the TV. "All right, so hindsight is twenty-twenty. Whatever, it is what it is. But we can't sit here licking our wounds wishing we had done something different. What are we going to do about it? What do we have to counter this? That's what matters now."

Genesis stared at me and then smiled. "You're right. We haven't gotten enough information on the tech they're using in the fortress just yet to know exactly how to combat it, but we're working on it. In the meantime, I have an assignment for many of you—to infiltrate a compound for two key items."

I sat back down. "Lay it on us."

31
CHAPTER

A search light flashed over the opening of the alley and I shrunk back to avoid detection. When the light passed, I waited several moments before poking my head out and looking around. *Coast is clear.* I waved for the others to follow me into the street across from us. Once everyone had made it, we moved down the street. I swiveled my head, looking out for movement as I stayed alert.

Genesis had warned us this place would have high security, and that anything could jump out at us. We had always avoided Compound Fifty-Two because of its busy nature, but as she claimed in the meeting, they held two items of key importance. One, intel showed they were testing prototype tracking devices here that needed to be destroyed or remade to our own purpose. And, two, they had taken an operative captive after a failed infiltration at another facility earlier today. Getting both done without issues wouldn't be easy, but there wouldn't be a way to get them done at separate times. Luckily, we had two new cards to play that would aid us in this assignment.

Rennek, listening in on the meeting, offered his services. The offer surprised me, but I happily accepted. Another shapeshifter would be useful in a sticky situation. The other trump card was having both Telar and Seda. Having psychics on the team would make this much easier. Of course, we had to find Telar first.

"Hey, Sweet Thing," a voice hissed.

"Found him."

I spun on my heels to find Telar in the shadows of a side alley, leaning against a wall. I rolled my eyes and snuck my way over to him. "Between you and Zo, I'm loving 'Chickadee' more and more."

Telar grinned. "Well then, I guess 'Sweet Thing' is staying."

"Lovely…"

"What's with the owl?" Telar asked. "I can hear its thoughts."

I glanced at the little screech owl perched on my shoulder. "This is Rennek. He's a shapeshifter like Raikidan."

Telar nodded. "That explains a lot. And it'll be handy. This place is crawling with enemies. We'll have to be careful sneaking into any buildings."

Ryoko peeked around a corner and quickly pulled back. "No kidding. How are we supposed to get this job done?"

"By splitting up," I said. "We have two jobs, and they are on two separate sides of the compound. With Seda here, we can place her in one group, and Telar in the other group."

"How do we want to split everyone else up?" Raid asked.

"The team going after the target should be small. It'll make it easier for us to get in and out. I'll lead that team—"

Telar rested his arm on my free shoulder. "I'll be going with you."

I nodded. "Okay, then Seda will go with the other team. I had thought it would be best since she's smarter and better equipped to help Argus get any information he needs far better than you could."

His face twisted in offense. "Hey!"

Seda giggled. "At least I'm not the only one with that thought."

We all ducked and waited in silence when a spotlight swept over our hiding place.

"Ryoko and Rylan will also be with me," I continued when I figured the coast was clear. Rennek will also come with us, so Raikidan I want—"

"I will be going with you," he said.

I frowned. "Rai, that's not—"

"I agree with him," Argus said. "He'll be of better use to your group. While it's true the larger the group, the harder it is to move around unseen, my group doesn't need to carry someone back. You'll need all the manpower you can get. I'll take Seda, Blaze, and Raid."

Raid opened his mouth to protest, but then thought better of it. This wasn't the time to argue or try to be paired with the person you're infatuated with.

I nodded. "We'll go with that plan. If you have any issues, contact us immediately."

Blaze, Argus, and Seda nodded at me and then each other before slipping away into the shadows.

I addressed everyone left. "We need a better understanding of the layout of this place. We have a rough idea of where our target is being held, but we need to find out if we can get a better pinpoint and how to get there unseen."

Rennek took flight and Telar pointed after him. "He's going to get an aerial view. I'll be able to tap into his sight to help relay."

I looked at Raikidan. "Can you help out?"

He nodded and shifted into an owl as well. Rylan took point at the entrance of the alley to keep watch, while Ryoko sat down to conserve her energy. Telar leaned against the wall again to concentrate, and I remained still, keeping an ear out for anything that sounded suspicious.

"As I thought," Telar mumbled. "Several psychics walking around. There will be more inside if that's the case. I'll be too busy keeping them unaware of our presence to be of much other use."

I smiled. "That's a lot to ask for, so I'll be grateful for that contribution."

Telar nodded and went back to analyzing. Minutes passed before he spoke again. "Found a good entry point. It's not ideal, but it's our best shot and will have underground access to the building we need."

"Finally," Ryoko said, jumping to her feet. "I thought I was going to fall asleep."

I shot her a scolding look, only for it to be cut short when Rylan ran back and motioned for us to hide. We took up hiding positions as best as we could, and Telar covered the rest. Patrolling soldiers walked past, a flashlight beaming our way briefly before they moved on. It flashed up into the air when a form flew over, the form of a small owl lighting up, and then disappeared as the soldiers found no need to worry about the bird. The tiny creature perched on the eaves of the building above us and screeched a few times. Another owl appeared and landed near it. My eyes narrowed. *Boys, I'm going to kill you.*

Telar motioned for us to come out of hiding when the coast was clear, and we acted quickly. Who knew how long it'd be before those soldiers came back and made our infiltration harder. He led the way through small streets and alleys until we came to a fence. Raikidan came out of his owl form and helped me melt the metal chain links. We all slipped in unnoticed, and stuck to the shadows of the buildings inside the compound, avoiding lights and guards as much as possible. Those soldiers we couldn't avoid were knocked out and hidden.

I picked the lock of the door for the building we needed to enter, and slipped down the long corridor. The only sounds coming from us were a few footsteps and the muffled bouncing thuds of our weapons. Rennek rested on my shoulder, peering around intently. Prior to us arriving here, he had warned me his stealth abilities weren't anything to brag about, so he would be most useful in shifted forms. I had appreciated his honesty, and outfitted my gear to accommodate small forms he could take.

I poked my head into a room, to find it dark and empty and we moved on. The next few rooms did have occupants, but we managed to sneak past, Rylan now keeping a closer eye out in the rear. The corridor began to split off into different hallways, and Telar used his abilities to tap into the minds of surrounding soldiers to find the correct path to follow.

"There are soldiers coming, Sweet Thing," Telar messaged telepathically.

I let out a short breath of annoyance and motioned for everyone to duck into one of the dark rooms near us. Raikidan followed me into one, while Ryoko, Rylan and Telar found another. We hid behind a stack of boxes and waited. A pair of soldiers strolled past our room, unaware of our presence. I went to move away from my spot to see if we could move on, only to trip on the corner of the box stacked in front of me. The tower wobbled and then, to my horror, the top box fell, its contents spilling out.

"What was that?" one of them asked.

"I don't know, but it came from back there," the other said.

"Better hide quick, Sweet Thing," Telar messaged. *"I can't help you with this since I'm already stretching myself thin with some psychics on a floor above us."*

I scanned the room frantically. *Where can we hide?* Everywhere I looked, I couldn't find a good enough place. *Damn boxes!* I stopped and stared at the box I knocked over. It appeared large enough for—*That's it!*

Raikidan lurched when I grabbed him by the wrist and lifted the box enough for me to shove him under. I climbed in next and made sure Rennek was with us. The fit was a squeeze and I found myself sitting on Raikidan's lap with him holding me close, but it was our only option at this point.

I held my breath as boots hit the floor outside the room. Another pair clomped on the tiles. Two people entered and a beam of light moved around the room.

"What's that?" one asked.

"A box, dummy."

"I know that. But why is it on the floor like that?"

"Based on the contents all over the floor, it fell."

"But why?"

"Hmm, why not look around and see—this room is filled with these boxes, and they're all stacked too high. It was bound to happen."

"I don't trust it."

His companion sighed but let it be.

"Telar, can you hear me?" I thought in my mind.

"Yeah, what's up, Sweet Thing?"

"Will you stop calling me that?"

"Oh, you like it, don't lie."

I rolled my eyes. *"The three of you should get moving while these two buffoons are distracted by us."*

"Are you sure?"

"Yeah, we'll catch up."

"All right."

Rennek wiggled in my hands and I loosened up my grip, worried I had been squeezing him by mistake, but soon found out I was wrong. His body shape changed to something thinner and longer, and his feathers changed to coarse fur. My brow rose when a hairless tail brushed my wrist. *A rat?*

He jumped off my hands and scratched at the bottom of the box, squeaking a bit here and there. *Rennek, what are you doing?*

"What's that?"

"It's coming from that box."

I pulled a dagger and readied my finger gun as the two approached. *I am so going to skin a dragon after this.* The clomping stopped and the flap of the box lifted up. The moment a gap appeared, Rennek bolted out and the man screamed. I held my hand over my mouth, biting back laughter.

The soldier's companion laughed at him. "Seriously?"

"It's a rat!"

"What are you, a girl?"

"Shut up. You freaked out over a spider yesterday."

"You said we'd never bring that up!"

"Yeah, and we're not going to bring up my issue with rats, right?"

His companion grunted. "Fine. Let's get moving. Nothing suspicious about a rat making a tower of boxes fall."

The two left, but I remained still. Raikidan, on the other hand, squirmed beneath me. I smacked him in the knee to get him to stop, but it continued. Then his presence disappeared and I was left sitting on the tile floor. I jumped when a tiny nose with twitching whiskers poked me in the arm. Raikidan, now in a rat form, climbed over my leg and sat in my lap looking up at me. I smiled and scratched him in the head. Unlike most, I thought rats were cute.

Raikidan poked the box with his nose in silent request. I listened for sounds and only caught Rennek scurrying around. I lifted the box and Raikidan took off. Rennek followed him out the door and down the hall.

I slipped out of the box and over to the doorframe. Peering out, I found the hall empty. I took a step out, but pulled back when clattering echoed through the corridor. Someone swore but no one came running. I peered out again to find the hallway the same as before.

"Telar?"

"Yeah?" His voice sounded strained.

"How does my path look?"

"It'll be a slow go, but follow your rats, they'll lead the way."

I nodded, even though he couldn't see me, and let him be. I didn't need to cause him trouble. I glanced back at the box I had hidden in and thought about its use. Could it be used to my advantage? I decided to give it a go. *Eira, you're getting weird ideas from Argus' videogames.*

I cut out some hand holes near the flaps and brought the box with me. A rat scurried around a corner and then stopped moving when it spotted me. For a split second I wondered if it was Raikidan or Rennek, but the curiosity faded quickly. It didn't matter. The rat twitched its nose and then ran back the way it had come.

The little critter led me down the hall and met up with another. The two continued on together, poking their heads into open doors as we passed them. Every time we came to an occupied room, a tail would twitch and the other would look back at me. I could hear the rooms were being used, most of the time, but I appreciated the heads up.

I stopped moving when I heard voices echoing down the hall. Neither were in sight, but I could see a side hallway a few yards up. They laughed and gossiped, clearly not interested in their patrol. *One male, one female.* I cranked my head around but found no rooms for me to hide in. I glanced at my box and shrugged. *Let's see if this works.*

I slipped under it, and positioned myself next to a wall. One of my rat friends squeezed through the hand holes, and the two of us waited. The two soldiers rounded the corner and came my way, their boots visible through the hand holes in the box.

"What's with the box?" the female soldier asked as they neared.

"Probably someone not doing their job," her comrade said.

"Should we move it?"

No you definitely shouldn't!

"Nah, not our job."

"Okay."

I let out a silent relieved breath as they continued on. *Guess this wasn't so stupid of a decision after all.*

"Wow, your poor disguise worked. I'm surprised." I hated how little faith the voice had in me, but to its credit, this shouldn't have worked.

My rat friend peered through the hole on the other side of the box and then looked up at me and nodded when the coast was clear. I lifted the box up and scurried down the hall, the box still held close on my back just in case. I turned a corner and picked up my pace when my rat friend ran off.

"You're close, keep going," Telar said.

"How are you all doing?"

"We found the room. We're trying to get in."

I smirked. *"Need help?"*

"Well, we wouldn't say no to it."

I chuckled and continued on until my rat friend caught up with our other rat friend, who was scurrying around in a circle squeaking in a dark room. My brow rose, but since I couldn't speak rat, I had no way of communicating with him. He stopped running and continued to chatter at me, but I cocked my head in confusion. I was pretty sure I heard him sigh. Just then a figure appeared in the dark room and I aimed my finger gun out of instinct.

The figure held up his hands. "It's me, don't shoot."

I released a tight exhale through parted lips. "Rylan, don't do that."

"Sorry, I was told to stay here," he said. I slipped into the room and he glanced at my box. "Do I want to know?"

"Trust me, it came in handy. Where will I find the others?"

"Just down the hall and around the corner. They took out the guard to the cell they have our target in, but they're struggling with the locking mechanism."

I nodded and discarded my box. "I'll give them a hand. Rai and Rennek are running around as rats. Be careful where you step."

He sighed. "I hate rats."

"Maybe he should be a good little doggie and get rid of them." I snickered at the voice's crude humor and moved on.

Peering around the corner when I reached it, I found Ryoko fiddling with a door while Telar held an unconscious man up with his telekinesis. I snuck over to them. "Need help?"

Ryoko gasped and jumped. "Don't do that!"

Telar chuckled. "Keep a better ear open then. She wasn't exactly quiet."

"I was too!" I hissed.

He smirked in response. I shook my head.

Ryoko gasped again and jumped away from the door. In her place stood two rats.

"Relax, it's just the dragons," I said as I shooed them away to take Ryoko's place.

"I don't care." Ryoko's nose scrunched. "I don't like rats. They're gross!"

I jerked my thumb back at Telar and went back to fiddling with the lock. "Less gross than him."

"Hey," Telar protested. "I bathe every three days, thank you. More than you can say about other men."

Ryoko fake-retched. "That is so gross. Don't even joke about that." She pointed at the dragon-rats. "Change into something less gross." The two rats looked at each other and then shifted back to their nu-human forms. Ryoko grinned and placed a finger to a cheek while shifting her weight to one side. "Yeah, that's much better."

I shook my head and continued my task. *Click!* The locking mechanism released the bolts holding the door shut, and I opened the door to peer in. Only a single dim light lit up the room, illuminating a man tied to a chair. I scanned the space bit more, found no one else, and entered the room, the others following. Dried blood clung to the man's skin, and his breath came out labored and in pain.

"He's unconscious," Telar said. "Though we need to get him out now, or it'll be worse than that. They've been harsh with him."

I nodded and cut the ropes that bound him. He slumped over, but Ryoko caught him.

"What do we do with the guard?" Rennek asked.

"We do this." Telar lifted the man into the chair and bound him with the ropes. "I can disguise him as the prisoner for a bit. Should be long enough to get us out of here."

Ryoko lifted our man onto her back and nodded to me when she had him secure.

"Telar, how are Seda and the others doing?" I asked.

"They're on their way out," he said. "So if we set off any alarms, we won't put them into too much danger."

"Your vote of confidence in us is reassuring," I muttered.

He chuckled. "C'mon, my little sparrow. Let's get our man out of here."

I held up my hands. "Sparrow now? Why not just stick with chicka-dee?"

"Because sparrow is more fitting."

Raikidan grunted and moved past us. "Butterfly is still better."

"No way," Telar argued.

"They're far more beautiful, and more deceivingly deadly."

Telar thought this over and nodded. "You're right, it is a better name. I like it."

"No, you can't call her that."

Telar held up his hands. "Rude."

My eyebrow twitched in annoyance, and Rennek leaned closer to me. "Are they always like this?"

"Seems like it's going to be the trend," I muttered.

Rennek's brow arched in question. "I'm guessing they're not around each other much then?"

I shook my head. "No. This is only the second time."

He nodded and then pressed on. I made sure Ryoko headed out before taking up the rear. We reconvened with Rylan, and Raikidan and Rennek returned to rat forms to scout up ahead as we moved out.

Getting around unspotted with our extra body proved difficult, but manageable, thanks to Telar taking on the extra stress for the team around a few close calls. We made it three-quarters of the way through the building before the lights turned red and began flashing while warning alarms blared.

"We've been found out, let's move!" I shouted.

Our pace quickened, but it didn't last long when soldiers found us. I used my gun to stall a few while Rennek and Raikidan surprised a few more by taking new, more battle-useful shapes. Ryoko rushed in and knocked out the remaining untouched ones before going after the injured ones. With that squad taken care of, we pushed on.

We encountered three more groups, each larger and stronger than the last, but we prevailed, though not without issues with the last group. One of the soldiers got me in the leg, sending Telar and Raikidan both into a rage, shedding even more blood in one of the most gruesome assaults I'd ever witnessed. I had never battled alongside a Battle Psychic before, and honestly I was glad. I couldn't help but stare at all the blood splattered on the walls and ceiling as we moved on.

"*Sorry,*" Telar messaged to me. "*I never wanted you to see that side of me...*"

"*We're all plagued by the darkness of our past,*" I said. "*I wouldn't have expected a much different outcome.*"

"*Still...*"

I shot him an understanding look and encouraged Rylan to pick up his pace as he helped me down the hall while I placed pressure on the wounded area of my leg. The bullet hadn't shattered bone, so that was good, but the damaged tissue did make this inconvenient.

We finally made it outside, and took off through the compound toward our hole in the fence. Because of my injury, Rylan lagged behind everyone else to stay with me, until he offered to carry me on his back. I accepted, knowing this situation was too dire to argue my walking ability, or lack thereof.

"We need to split up," Rylan said when we finally made it to the other side and hidden in an alley, breathing heavily from having to carry me.

"I agree," Telar said. "Ryoko, I'll take our man. It'll be easy for me to get the two of us underground. The faster I do, the quicker he gets medical attention."

She nodded and handed the injured man over. Raikidan approached Rylan and me while the exchange happened.

"I'll take Eira," he said. "You won't be able to carry her the whole way, and I have a better way of getting her out of here."

Rylan hesitated, but I patted him on the shoulder. "It's okay. You get out of here with Ryoko." He nodded and set me down. I removed my gear and handed it to Ryoko. "This will slow me down."

She nodded. The two took off out of the alley and into the city. Telar smirked at me and then he and the injured rebel disappeared from sight. I listened and heard the sound of running feet leave us. *Smart.*

I looked at Raikidan. "So, what am I going to be today?"

"Well with that leg of yours, I'm thinking an owl," he said. "It'll be easier to get out of here by air than by foot."

"I wish you wouldn't encourage this type of behavior with him. But you do need to get out of here... so I'll allow it."

I ignored the voice and nodded at Raikidan. "All right, let's do this."

Rennek put his hand out. "Whoa, wait. You're not going to try that shifting technique, are you?"

"Of course we are," I said. "We've done it before."

Rennek crossed his arms. "This I have to see. No one has been able to do this in six hundred years."

Six hundred years? That's a pretty specific number. I narrowed my eyes. "We used the technique during my competition."

Rennek's face reddened and he scratched the back of his neck. "I, uh, fell asleep halfway through that."

I stared at him in disbelief. "Wow."

Raikidan wrapped his arms around me. "Ready?"

I took a deep breath and closed my eyes. "Yep."

The alley grew still as Raikidan concentrated. *One minute. Two minutes.*

Several more passed before the familiar tingling sensation fell over my body. Then, my body felt smaller and my senses distorted. I opened my eyes and blinked a few times to get used to how these new eyes worked. I swiveled my head around. Not surprisingly, Raikidan chose a small owl form. It would be easier for us to get away, and easier for me to get used to.

Rennek towered over us, his mouth hanging open. "I can't believe you did it."

Footsteps thundered through the connecting street and he immediately shifted to an owl form as well. This wasn't the time to go over the legitimacy of this ability.

Raikidan tapped me with a wing and then took off. I unfolded my wings and moved them around to get used to their weight, while being mindful of how much my leg still hurt in this form, and then took to the skies. Rennek followed shortly after. We cleared the restricted area, only having a close call one time, and made our way home in the least direct route as possible to keep our suspicion levels down.

I left the kitchen, dishes recently cleaned and put away, and looked around. The mid-afternoon sun filtered in through the window of the living room. Seda and Genesis were off at some Council meeting, and Zane and most of the boys had gone to the shop. Ryoko sat on the couch, enjoying her day off reading some *steamy* romance novel she had picked up at the store the other day—Rylan reading over her shoulder. *Trying to pick up pointers, eh, Rylan?*

Corliss and Mana lounged nearby on the couch watching TV, and Raikidan was settling down near Ryoko after helping me out with the kitchen chores.

The door to the basement opened, and before I could actually see anyone come through, a mass of black and red scales barreled out toward me. *Rimu?* I barely had time to brace myself for the inevitable impact.

I fell to the ground with a *thud* when he jumped on me—he was much bigger than the last time I had seen him. He let out strange noises that sounded like squeals of happiness as he rubbed his head against me, and I chuckled. "Hi to you too, Rimu."

I glanced up at a woman with light skin, flaming red hair, and bright green eyes standing in the doorway of the basement, a tall man with tan skin and ebon hair behind her. *Xaneth and her mate, Anahak.*

Xaneth's eyes softened. "I'm sorry, Eira. I was hoping to keep him calm and managed, but the moment he caught your scent, he got too excitable to control well."

"It's all right," I assured as I moved Rimu so I could sit up. "No harm done." Rimu tried to climb in my lap again but I pushed him away. "No, Rimu, you're too big now to be in my lap."

He snorted as I stood. I barely had my balance when he perched on his back legs and attempted to latch onto me.

I sighed. "Rimu, you're too big."

"Too big is an understatement," Rylan said. "He's the size of a small horse. I'm surprised he didn't crush you."

"At around five years old, dragonlings have a large growth spurt," Corliss said before looking at Xaneth. "He is about that age, yes?"

She nodded. "Yes, though, he's grown far more than any other of our offspring."

Mana pressed a finger to her lips. "He does look larger than most five-year-olds."

"He was also smaller than his siblings the last I remember," I said.

Xaneth nodded. "He was, that's why his growth is a bit perplexing."

"It's nothing to worry about," Anahak assured. "It happens."

Ryoko moved over on the couch so she was closer me. "Big, small—whatever, he's adorable."

Rimu chirped and made his way over to her, propping his front claws up on the back of the couch to look at her.

Ryoko smiled and then rubbed his head. "His scale pattern is fitting too."

I took a good look at Rimu. "He lost more red scales. And they came in black again."

His scales had changed quite a bit since I had last seen him. Red remained his predominant color, but black scales covered his entire underside, and a long trail of black scales lined under his eyes. Black scales also ran around his ankles, creating a band around each, and some black scales along his hips.

Xaneth nodded. "We're still not sure why that is."

Corliss's brow rose. "His scales shed to a different color?"

"Yes," Xaneth said. "It started when Eira paid our clan a visit."

Corliss rubbed his chin. "Odd. I've never heard of that happening. Have you, Mana?"

She shook her head. "Nope."

"How about you, Raikidan?"

Raikidan nodded. "Happened to one of my brothers. My parents also knew a few others who experienced it as well. It's rare, but it can happen. Nothing bad will come of it, I can assure you that."

Xaneth smiled. "Well that puts my mind at ease a little." Her nose twitched and her smile fell to a frown. "Why is that scent here?"

Scent? Which scent?

"Because he's here," Raikidan muttered.

Anahak scowled. "Why?"

Raikidan's gaze flicked to me. "Because she wouldn't send him away."

I rolled my eyes, understanding what was going on now. "You're all going to have to deal. They agreed to not cause any trouble, or else they'd be thrown out. This applies to all dragons who step foot in here. Don't like it, leave."

Xaneth blinked. "Well, okay. If you've gotten him to comply to that, I guess we don't have an issue."

"I don't trust it," Anahak muttered.

"He's been real good so far," Mana put in.

"But Zion only knows how he'll react once he finds out these three have shown up," Corliss said.

My head tilted a bit at the mention of Zion. *Who is that?* I'd never heard the name before, but for some reason it had a familiarity to it.

Raikidan stared down the hall. "We're about to find out."

Ambrose came around the corner and stopped dead in his tracks, Salir running into him. The air grew still as all the dragons had their stare-down. Well, that was until Rimu, completely unaware of what was going on, chirped and wandered into the line of sight of Ambrose. He snorted in disgust and continued stalking down the hall. Salir and Rennek followed, but kept some distance between themselves and Ambrose.

Rimu took one look at Ambrose and scampered away, though not to his mother. Instead, he came to me. *Probably for the best right now.* Rimu pressed against me and rubbed his head on my torso. I watched the tense scene unfolding, rather than paying too much attention to the little dragon.

Anahak took a position in front of Xaneth to protect her, while

Corliss and Raikidan blocked Ambrose from coming any further into the living room. Mana pulled her legs up to her chest as she shrunk down on the couch to avoid bringing attention to herself, and Ryoko moved to her side to keep her calm, and herself out of the way, too. Xaneth looked torn between protecting Rimu and herself, and her mate's honor. Salir hung back, concern clear in her eyes, and Rennek stood in front of her to keep her safe, though it was clear neither were intending to back Ambrose up. I needed to diffuse this before we had a dragon fight in the house.

"Ambrose," I said, keeping my voice stern, but diplomatic. "Need I remind you that you are here solely under the grace of my hospitality, and any issues you cause will result in your immediate removal by any means I deem necessary?"

He pointed at me. "Stay out of this, human."

"Oh, he did not."

I took in a tight breath through my nose, my posture straightening, and I forced Rimu off me. "You dare challenge me?"

"Know your place," he warned.

"Teach him his place!"

Rimu sunk low to the ground when I stalked toward the dragons. Raikidan and Corliss glanced at each other, contemplating if they should stop me. Deciding it best not to, they moved aside for me to approach Ambrose.

I squared off in front of the older dragon and locked intense gazes with him. "Only warning. Don't you ever think you can tell me my place, you uncultured wyrm."

Ambrose's eyes flashed in anger at the insult. "Watch your tongue, Maiden. I lead—"

"You lead a band consisting of your mate and a single offspring; both of whom show no signs of backing you up. I am a commander, rebel battle leader, and ranked shaman with allies who will stand against anyone I deem an enemy. You posture but you have no weight behind you. You address me as *human* but you have no idea what kind of human I am."

Ambrose turned up his head to look down on me and sneered. *"Sevugozemuty pumxr. You have no nyez gongily. You eny synyza an enmuduxuez xnyemuiv. You gilmony to ruky your finmrzyllvyll."*

"Oh, he did not just say that."

My chest tightened. I may not have known their language well enough to translate much of that, but deep down, I knew it was a low blow. It didn't help that every dragon in the room was now tense with anger, and even the voice acted as if it knew.

"Ambrose, that's gone too far," Rennek warned.

My hands clenched into fists. *"Mrul finmrzyll xnyemuiv has detin of Zion. What pzylluvw kiyl your dunyzyll lxezyl have?"* The Draconic words tumbled out of my mouth, even though I knew few of the words, let alone their common translation. But whatever I said, I startled Ambrose as well as the other dragons in the room.

Then my anger got the better of me. I slammed my forehead into his chin. Pain pulsed through my head, but I shrugged it off as Ambrose stumbled and fell to the floor. Blood dripped out of his mouth while blood trickled down my brow.

"Push me too far, take my hospitality for granted"—I used my thumb to wipe the blood from my forehead and licked it off—"and I'll rip you limb from limb and scatter your entrails to the crows." I cocked my head and sneered. "Shouldn't be too hard, since I've seen bigger lizards at a pet shop. So, *Ambrose*, you can be civil, or you can continue to act like a mindless beast that needs to be put down."

Refusing to be submissive, he locked gazes with me as he wiped away the blood on his face with the back of his hand. Minutes passed as neither he nor I backed down in our power struggle, creating massive tension in the air. I wouldn't allow this dragon to think he owned me like some faithful bitch.

Ambrose's gaze lowered. "We will be civil here."

"Well done."

"See that you do." I spun on my heels and headed for my room, making a motion to Rimu to follow me. The little dragon, who had remained hunched down during the altercation, perked up and scampered after me.

I sat down on my bed with a sigh and watched as Rimu checked out the new room. He followed scent trails and tried to get into places he shouldn't. I laughed when he managed to open my bra drawer in my dresser and got one stuck on his head. I slid off my bed and struggled to get him to sit still long enough to get it off him.

"Cute little thing."

"He is, isn't he?" A thought came to me, my attention drifting enough to allow Rimu to scamper off and get into something else. The voice's behavior had been peculiar as of late, and with it now showing it understood Ambrose... It had me wondering a few things. *"Hey, you sounded like you understood Ambrose's language. What did he say?"*

"You have better things to do than worry about the machinations of some pretentious, big-headed, narcissistic, xifenkza dragon."

I cringed when Rimu knocked over my small metal trash bin and rummaged through it, for the gods knew what reason. Xaneth's amused chuckle pulled my attention away from the little dragon. "You've opened a can of worms allowing him in here."

I went to clean up after the little whelp. "I'd rather deal with him than the stupidity out there."

She smiled and welcomed herself into the room. "I don't blame you."

"Rimu, don't you do that!" I scolded when I caught him rubbing his cheek against the windowsill. "You're not allowed to scent-mark my room."

Rimu stopped, glanced my way, and then continued. I released an exasperated breath and Xaneth laughed. "Nice try, but it'll take more than that to get him to stop."

"Apparently."

She regarded me for a moment. "You picked up on that quick. Most humans would have seen that as him scratching his face. I'm impressed."

I shrugged. "I have several dragons living in my house. Slight bump into something they would have normally missed; touching a surface when there's no need to; entering a room for a moment so their scents mingle; I see it happen all the time, specifically with the men."

She nodded. "Yes, males do it more often. We females don't have as much of a reason to." We watched as Rimu went from scenting the windowsill to rubbing his body against the floor. Xaneth chuckled. "I get it now. Raikidan spends a lot of time in those spots, doesn't he?"

My brow rose. "Yeah. What does that have to do with this?"

She smiled and pointed toward the door. Just then, Raikidan appeared and focused on Rimu. Raikidan snorted, in what sounded like a warning, and Rimu briefly regarded the older dragon before continuing his scent-marking without a care. Raikidan approached the baby dragon and snorted again. Rimu stopped and bared his teeth with a growl, surprising me. I glanced at Xaneth, only to find her calm. *What is going on?*

Raikidan put his foot on the little dragon's head and pushed him back several inches. I went to scold him, but Xaneth held up her hand to stop me. The look she gave interested me, so I chose to listen and see what happened.

Rimu grumbled and backed up a bit. My eyes widened, realizing what he was about to do. The little dragon then charged Raikidan, ramming his head into the older dragon's shin. Raikidan grunted in a bit of pain, but otherwise acted as if Rimu had no strength behind the attack. The little red-black dragon tried to use all his might to push Raikidan back, but couldn't succeed against his heavier opponent.

Raikidan pushed the little dragon away, and moved into the room some more, taking an arching path around Rimu, and closer to me. Rimu scampered from his spot and surprised me when he climbed halfway onto my lap, putting himself between Raikidan and me. The little dragon bared his teeth. Raikidan's calm but stern, demeanor changed then. His expression darkened into a scowl and he grabbed onto one of Rimu's horns.

From the corner of my eye, I watched Xaneth tense, as if she were fighting her maternal instincts to step in and protect her child. This perplexed me more. If Raikidan's actions weren't acceptable, then she needed to step in.

Raikidan began speaking in Draconic. *"My mnyelony. You xevvim have. I gnimyxm her."* Though I only knew a few of the words he spoke, Xaneth obviously knew them all, and her expression changed to surprise as he continued. *"She is suvy."*

"He doesn't mean that... does he?"

My brow rose when I recognized part of that phrase. *He said that phrase to Ergren.* He'd also spoken something similar to me, though wouldn't tell me what it meant. *What did it mean?* I thought hard, but the translation wasn't turning up. *Gods, why do I have to be so terrible at languages!* And why did the voice know when I didn't?

Rimu shook his head, disagreeing with Raikidan, and attempted to speak back, but his words were broken and rough. Much like me when I attempted the language. *"No. Suvy. Mnyelony."*

I remembered Raikidan telling me dragons didn't start learning to speak until Rimu's age, so it made sense for his speech to be so broken.

Raikidan pulled Rimu off me and towered over him, but didn't speak. Instead, he used his size and posture to force the little dragon to give in. At first, Rimu stared back in defiance, but after several minutes passed, he started to shrink down. Though not ready to admit defeat, he pressed against my leg and spoke again. "*Mnyelony.*"

Raikidan exhaled and Xaneth giggled. "That's as far as you're going to get with him for now, Raikidan. He doesn't understand yet."

"I'm aware," he grumbled. He stared down at Rimu for a minute longer. "*My mnyelony.*"

He placed his hand on my shoulder, clearly trying to scent-mark without being invasive, and then stalked out of the room, closing the door behind him, but not before he scented the doorframe with his shoulder. As if acting in defiance, Rimu started rubbing his head against my leg. I grunted. *Males.*

"*I concur.*"

Xaneth tapped a finger against her lips. "That went a lot differently than how I had been expecting."

I looked to her for answers instead of bothering with Rimu's scenting. "What exactly was all that?"

"Well, let me figure out how to word it so you won't misunderstand."

I waved her off. "Say it the way you know. I've been getting used to how different our species think and express ideas and feelings. As long as we talk it out after so it translates eventually, I'll be good."

Xaneth chuckled and sat down next to me. She pointed to Rimu with one hand and pointed at the door with the other. "These two were fighting for their claim on you."

My brow rose in question, but I knew better to hear her out than start jumping to conclusion.

"Have you been told about our hoarding tendencies for living beings?" I nodded. "Well, by doing so, we treat them as a hoard treasure for us to protect. This is what has happened to you. Both Raikidan and my son have claimed you as a treasure, but that causes a conflict. Because the two have separate hoards, they have to determine their dominance hierarchy and decide who gets to keep you." She smiled. "Luckily, Raikidan currently sees Rimu's claim as harmless and a non-threat, but he still has to establish his dominance now, or else Rimu could prove to be quite a challenge for him once he grows older."

"But if Rimu isn't a threat, did Raikidan have to be that aggressive with him?" I asked.

"He wasn't all that aggressive, to be clear. I know you noticed my reaction, but that shouldn't hint at the level of Raikidan's aggression. I want to protect my offspring as much as I can, but I also know they need to learn, as well. Raikidan went easy on my son, knowing he's so young and doesn't understand, though I am surprised by that."

"Why?"

She tilted her head. "How much of our tongue do you know?"

I shrugged. "Very little. I'm doing my best to learn, but language has never been my strength."

She nodded. "Well, from the way Raikidan worded it to Rimu, your level of importance to him is high. We rank our treasures, and the more important a treasure is to us, the more we'll fight to keep it. If your ranking is as high as I'm guessing it to be, Raikidan has to have a lot of control over himself to have treated my son as well as he did."

Rimu chirped and nudged my hand to get my attention. I smiled at him and gave him a good scratch on the head.

"Are you okay with this information I gave you?" Xaneth asked.

I nodded. "I am. I understand your species' possessive nature well, and I know it's far different than ours, so I'm good. Thankful you told me, though."

She smiled. "Good."

I had been honest with her, mostly. I was okay with what she had told me, though my reasoning wasn't exactly honest. Yes, I did understand their possessive nature, but I still dealt with my human thoughts about possession. This time was different, though.

"I'd tell you to be careful, but you won't listen to me."

"Hey, Xaneth, can I ask you something?"

"Of course," she said. "What's on your mind?"

"Why didn't your clan leave the city when I sent a letter to Zaith?"

She smiled. "Because we already knew about the treaty. We chose freedom over an agreement that controlled us with fear. I want my offspring to know what a real life is. So we stayed and worked in secret so you wouldn't get upset."

I nodded and went to speak, but someone knocked at the door. It opened and, to my surprise, Salir peered in. "My moron of a mate is off licking his wounds now. May I come in and chat?"

"Uh, sure." Though her desire to mingle confused me, I wasn't going to be rude and send her away.

To my surprise, Xaneth acted friendly toward Salir and the two embraced in a quick hug. "It's good to see you, Salir."

"You as well, Xaneth," Salir said. "It's been too long." She looked at Rimu, who wasn't sure how to react to the new female dragon presence. "I can't believe it's been five years. I remember like it was yesterday that while I had come for a visit, you had said his clutch would hatch any day."

Xaneth gazed at her son. "My guess was correct, too. The following day, all seven eggs hatched. Rimu was the last."

"All seven," Salir said in an awed breathy voice. "Such an impressively-sized clutch to begin with, especially for a first-time mother, and for all of them to make it, it's so wonderful to hear."

"Uh, because I'm a bit confused, and curious, what is going on here?" I asked. "You've been pleasant during your stay, Salir, but from what I've witnessed about your situation, I find it hard to believe you'd want to be in this room with us."

She smiled at me and then knelt to touch Rimu. He pulled away; unsure about the unfamiliar female, but it wasn't long before his curiosity convinced him to stretch his neck out. Salir rubbed his face with her thumbs before speaking. "Unlike my mate, I could care less about the colors of our family. I only care that they're all healthy and happy."

I smiled and nodded. I grew quiet again as the two female dragons spoke in their tongue for a private conversation. I thought about what Salir said, and it pleased me each time I ran it through my mind. It showed, even with predispositions to particular tendencies and mindsets, they had the ability to make their own choices, free of instinct and genetics. I reflected on it and found myself happy with this realization. It made me a bit hopeful for—I stopped immediately in my mental track and shook myself of the idea that had been forming. *No, Eira. Don't trick yourself into believing that. You know better.*

Rimu rested his head on my lap again and made himself comfortable. With a smile, I scratched his head, and then any part of his face, when he twisted and leaned to get different spots. When he had enough, he shook his head and then rested it on my lap again, looking up at me with wide eyes.

"What?" I asked. He snuggled his head into my lap more and continued to look at me. I chuckled. "What is it?"

"He wants you to agree to be his treasure instead of Raikidan's," Salir said. I raised a brow in question and she smiled. "I heard the conversation. Our tongue travels."

That's good to know. Would have been nice if Raikidan had told me that. I may not be good at their language yet, but I'd like to know if I could have private conversations or not.

I rubbed the scales between Rimu's eyes. "I'm no one's treasure."

Rimu snapped his jaws while making grumbling noises. I shook my head. He may not have liked my answer, but I wasn't worthy of being a treasure.

"That's not true."

Rimu pressed his head into my lap some more, and then tried to climb right up into my lap. I laughed. "You're too big, buddy." He grumbled and continued to try anyway. "Rimu, stop being so stubborn. You can climb onto my bed, just not on me."

Rimu stopped and stared at my bed. He reached out and tentatively touched it, clearly never experiencing a mattress before, and tilted his head while chirping as he pressed down on the mattress. He snapped his teeth and then jumped up on the bed, though rather clumsily. I helped him, when it looked as though he'd fall back, and watched as he walked around and tried to understand the springy, soft surface. The two female dragons giggled and watched him for a bit before going back to their private discussion.

I lifted my hands up when he wobbled over to me and laid down, pushing his head under my arm and draping his tail over my legs. The position was much like what Raikidan had done with me several times when we slept near each other. I pet Rimu's head as I tried to understand what he was doing, and he curled in closer.

"Raikidan is going to have quite the handful, dealing with him," Salir said in common. My brow lifted in question, but she only smiled and headed for the door. "I should go check on Ambrose and make sure he's not causing Rennek any issues in his anger. It was good to catch up with you, Xaneth. And I agree. *I too pyzuyty she will lety us. And Raikidan is lucky to py wutyv her."*

Xaneth chuckled. *"If ivza he will listen, and get his gnuinumuyl lmneuwrm."*

Salir glanced at me, confusing me more, on top of their sudden use of Draconic. "*I do not think fy will have to worry epiom mrem.*"

She then left.

"*She may be right… but I'm not entirely convinced.*"

I looked to Xaneth for answers. "I don't like to pry, but I'd be lying if I said I was comfortable with such a sudden language change with obvious glances at me, and Raikidan's name also being thrown in there."

She smiled and sat down. "It wasn't about you directly. More about Raikidan's actions lately; some of them revolving around you. Don't worry about it." *Why does it feel like she's not telling me the whole truth?* She patted my hand. "Would you be willing to do me a favor and watch Rimu for me for an hour or two? One of my clanmates is watching my other offspring, but Anahak and I haven't had much time to ourselves since the clutch hatched, and—"

I grasped her hand with mine. "Go spend time with him. There are plenty of things for couples to do in the city, or you could just spend that time alone in private. Rimu listens to me well—most of the time—so I don't think I'm going to have a situation where I have to tell you I lost or killed your son somehow. Keeping an eye on him is the least I could do for what your clan is willing to risk to help us take on Zarda."

"Thank you. I'll try to not be too long."

"Take your time. As long as I don't have him for several days, we'll be fine."

She smiled and slipped off the bed. Rimu looked at her and chirped. She spoke to him in their tongue. "*I will be pexc. Be wiik for Eira.*"

Rimu stared at her for a moment longer, then at me, chirped, and then laid his head back down and snuggled close.

Xaneth sighed. "Words, Rimu, you need to start using words."

I chuckled as she left. Like a human child, he was going to push his mother's buttons to the fullest. I listened as Anahak greeted Xaneth and then immediately went into questioning her when she told him they were leaving. Raikidan walked into my room, though he was watching the pair head down the stairs.

"Hey, do you know wh"—he stopped when he turned and spotted Rimu lying around me—"why is he still here?"

33
CHAPTER

I smirked, knowing full well my answer would annoy him. "I'm babysitting, hence Xaneth grabbing her mate and escaping."

He shut the door and let out a terse sigh. "You shouldn't let him lie around you like that."

My brow rose and then I looked at Rimu, who appeared comfortable. "Why not?"

"Because it's not a good idea."

"Well, that's not a good enough reason, and until you tell me why it's not a good idea, I don't need to listen to you. How does that sound?"

The voice chuckled but didn't give any input. Raikidan frowned and came closer. Rimu snuggled into me more in response. Raikidan snarled and spoke in his tongue. "*My mnyelony.*"

My eyes narrowed. "Yeah, we're not doing this shit." I pointed to him. "You are banned from speaking your tongue in here for the rest of the night."

Raikidan's brow rose. "Excuse me?"

"You heard me. You're not going to bicker with a child in a tongue I still don't know well." Rimu made sounds as if he was snickering, and I thumped him on the head. "And you both play nice, or I'm sending you both to a corner."

Raikidan sucked in a tight breath and ground his teeth together. I held firm, and he sat down next to me on the bed. Before I knew it, he reached around me and pulled me tight into his chest. *"My mnyelony."*

"Raikidan, I said no Draconic," I warned.

Before I could continue, Rimu grumbled and tried to climb on Raikidan to force him to let go. Raikidan growled and pushed the little dragon away with his shoulder. Rimu, determined as always, rebounded and tried again.

"Okay, that's it." I managed to escape Raikidan's hold. "Both of you—into a corner!"

"I'm not a child, Eira," Raikidan argued. "You can't—"

I grabbed him by the ear and yanked him off my bed. He complained about the pain, but I continued to drag him to my door and forced him to stand, facing the corner behind it. "You stay there."

I spun around and pointed to Rimu and then the corner by my bath. "Over there, now."

Rimu sunk low on the bed and shook his head. I inhaled a slow tight breath and Rimu sunk lower. He slipped off the bed and crawled to the corner, facing it.

"Now you two will stay there until I've told you otherwise," I said.

Ryoko's giggling came from the other side of my bedroom door. "I was going to come check on you, but it sounds like Momma Laz has her hands full with two children."

"Yeah, that about sums it up," I muttered as I sat down on my bed.

"Well, I'll let you do your job, then. When you're done scolding them, I'd like to play with the baby in there."

I snickered. "Which one?"

She laughed. "The little one, of course. If I were single, then my response may have been different."

I laughed. Only she would still be open about how attractive she found Raikidan, regardless of species. "All right, if things calm down enough."

"Thank you!"

The room grew quiet and I watched the two dragons. They stared at the corners but eventually their gazes drifted to each other, and neither were being friendly. I let out my best attempt as a dragon-like disapproving growl. I sounded pretty stupid, but it turned out to be not too terrible of an attempt, because Rimu immediately ducked down and stared at his corner. Raikidan was another story, at first at least.

He continued to look Rimu's way a little bit longer, but even he turned his gaze back at his corner. "That wasn't too bad of an attempt... I guess..."

"Don't lie, hunky dragon-man. She got you."

"Did... you just call him hunky?"

I received no response, but in the end it didn't matter. I had actually done it. My attempt wasn't great by any means, but I had managed to even get a grown, stubborn dragon to listen. I was getting better at this dragon communication thing. *Well, maybe not, but I can pretend.*

"I can't believe you're making me do this," Raikidan grumbled.

"Well if the two of you would behave, neither of you would be in the corner," I said.

"I am behaving."

"Oh? Care to tell me what's going on, then? Because to me, you're both far from behaving like civilized creatures."

Raikidan turned around and held my gaze. Several times, he seemed to have an answer, but stopped himself from saying anything. Eventually he did speak, but it wasn't directed to me or in common. *"She is suvy, whelp."*

"Raikidan!" I scolded. "I said common only. I'm not kidding here."

He sucked in a deep breath and glowered at me.

"My mnyelony," Rimu said.

Raikidan held his hands out at Rimu when I didn't scold him. "You're letting him speak?"

"He doesn't know common yet, stupid. Draconic is the only way he *can* speak. And even if he did, you drilled it into my head that dragons don't have the ability to articulate common in your natural state. So you can say what you have to, in a tongue I understand."

Raikidan took a deep breath but didn't say anything. Conflict flickered across his face, and I didn't understand why. *Why can't he just say things around me? What do I do wrong that makes him unable to be upfront and honest?*

"I was starting to think I'd been wrong about him. Guess I was right."

Rimu turned his head toward Raikidan. *"See. She not pyzivw to you. She my mnyelony. I myzz her if xiozk. You not. You not xeny yviowr. You elresyk. I not."*

Raikidan's eyes widened and my brow rose. He looked shocked to the core. What had Rimu said that could shake Raikidan so badly?

"Or, based on that reaction, I'm still wrong…"

"Rai, what did Rimu say?" I asked. *And what does this voice know that I don't?*

Raikidan focused on the little dragon instead of answering me. "You're right. I'm being stupid." Rimu snorted with triumph, but it was short-lived. "But she's not your treasure." Raikidan came over to me. He wrapped his arm around my waist as he laid down, pulling me with him. He held me tight against his chest. "My treasure."

Xaneth was right. He was calling me that. "I'm no treasure."

His grip tightened. "Don't say that. You are, and you're my treasure. Mine to protect, even if you don't want me to."

I tried to push against him so he'd let go, but his grip stayed firm. "You told me once, if a dragon saw a living being as a treasure, that dragon would protect them with their life—"

"And I will."

"Why? What's so great about me?"

"Everything. You may not see it, but I do, and I will value that even when you don't."

"You're wrong."

Raikidan chuckled when Rimu jumped on the bed and chirped. "He sees it, too. So there."

I huffed. I didn't understand what could possibly be so great about me to qualify me as some dragon's treasure.

Rimu laid his head on my hip and spoke, *"Mnyelony. Lreny?"*

Raikidan sighed. "Fine, we'll share."

"Excuse you?" I said.

"I don't share my treasure," Raikidan said. "But for him, I'll make an exception. He's just a whelp anyway, and it means he'll stop being annoying."

I chuckled. "You don't know kids, then. Annoying is what they're made of."

"Lovely."

I tried to push against him again. "Could you let me go now? Please."

"Only if you promise not to run away."

"I want to lie on my back."

Raikidan reluctantly let go and I rolled onto my back, Rimu rolling with me. I chuckled and rubbed his exposed belly. He chirped and wiggled up closer to me so he was able to lay his head on my chest.

"Raikidan, what did he say to you that got you to talk to me?"

"He accused me of being ashamed to claim you as my treasure. He said if you could understand, he'd tell you without hesitation."

"Well, he—"

"He was wrong. I'm not ashamed to say it. I'm just always concerned how you'll react. I don't want you to misunderstand and react negatively when you shouldn't. I don't like it when you misunderstand and pull away from me." I looked at him. *He sees that?* "It hurts when you do."

My heart almost stopped. "I… didn't think you cared when I did that. You never acted like you did."

"I do care when you do that. I don't feel like an adequate friend—like I've let you down."

My cheeks warmed. "Well, for the record, you are more than an adequate friend." My eyes drifted. "Sometimes, you're better than I deserve…"

"That's not true," he argued. My eyes lifted back to him. "You deserve better than what I can give on my best day. I wish you'd see that—and see why you're my favorite treasure."

My eyes widened and I stared at him. The longer I did, the warmer the sensation grew that flowed through me.

"He can't mean that… can he?"

I frowned and smacked his chest. "That's not funny."

"Ow." He rubbed the "injured" area. "What are you talking about?"

"I'm trying to be serious here, and you turned it into a joke."

"Eira, I am being serious."

"Rai, you mean to tell me of everything you own, combined, I'm supposed to be the best?"

"Yes. And I'm not taking it back. I don't care if you don't believe me. I speak the truth—you're my favorite. I'll fight for you more than I would the rest of my hoard. You're worth more."

I frowned and tore my gaze away. *Jackass. I thought we were actually communicating on some level for once.*

He growled. "Eira, don't make me bite you."

"You wouldn't dare."

"Oh yeah?" Raikidan grabbed my head to pull me closer to him, and lightly latched onto my nose.

I flailed in my attempted to get away, but Raikidan held strong. "Raikidan, stop being so weird!"

He chuckled as released me. I wiped his saliva off my face and smeared it on his shoulder. "You're my favorite treasure, Eira, and I don't care if you believe me or not."

"He sounds sincere enough, and is willing to fight a child for his claim. Maybe I have been wrong about him."

Rimu chirped then and tried to pull my attention away from Raikidan, which wasn't too hard, after what he had told me. I didn't believe him. There was no way I could possibly be worth that much to anyone, let alone a dragon. *I know better than to believe that, even if it would be nice if it were true...*

I razzed Rimu, and he made all sorts of happy sounds. Occasionally I made funny noises at him to get him riled up, and other times I'd kiss his snout, which he loved.

As I continued to pay attention to the little dragon, I realized how quiet Raikidan had become. I stole a glance, in hopes I hadn't hurt his feelings somehow, and was taken aback by how intently he watched me. I found myself unable to look away. My mouth dried up. I swallowed, but it did nothing to help.

"Everything... o–okay?" I managed to ask.

"Yes," he replied without blinking.

"That intensity... Maybe he really is..."

My brow rose. *What's with the odd behavior?* Both he and the voice were now acting weird. "You're not jealous I'm paying attention to Rimu now, are you?"

Raikidan snorted, this time breaking his intense stare. "Please. I'd never be jealous of the whelp."

I grinned. "Liar. I can tell you want this." I reached up and rubbed his cheeks with the palms of my hands. "There, how does that feel, weirdo?"

He laughed as he tried to push my hands away. "Eira, I'm going to bite you again."

"Careful, I might like it this time." He immediately stopped and stared at me with shock and confusion, and I laughed, rolling from my side to my back again. "I'm kidding! By the gods, your reaction was better than I expected."

He leaned over and nipped my nose in warning. "Don't be a brat."

I poked his cheek and then went to massaging Rimu's face, who looked on the verge of melting into a puddle from the touch.

"*My mnyelony.*" Raikidan mumbled as he poked my forehead.

I pursed my lips. "Mnlony… wow, that attempt sucked."

He chuckled. "You've had worse attempts." He had a point. "Try again."

"Mnyeny… Melny… Mnyeny…" I sighed.

"Almost, try again. *Mnyelony.*"

"*Mnyelony,*" Rimu said in an attempt to help… or tease. I wasn't sure with him.

I took a deep breath. "Mnyelny… *Mnyelony.*"

I smiled and looked at Raikidan, who nodded. "Very good. Now you'll need to practice."

I nodded. "Another word."

"How about"—he chuckled—"Sit and stay."

I noticed his quick glance at Rimu before suggesting the words. "Don't be mean."

"Well you have to learn them at some point."

"*He's not wrong.*"

"But not for the reason you think I should. Teach me something else. Teach me a long word. I like those. They're more rewarding since they're difficult."

Raikidan shook his head. "All right, if you say so. *Lmneuwrm.*"

I opened my mouth to try, but then shut it when I didn't even know where to start. Rimu attempted the word, but his attempt didn't end up being any better than my lack of trying.

"Dragon got your tongue?" Raikidan teased.

I snorted. "I need a minute with these longer ones. Doesn't help that you picked a word with sounds very similar to each other."

"You say that about most words."

"That's because it's true! What's the translation?"

"Straight."

I threw my hands up. "Seriously? Why is your language so complicated?"

He chuckled and waited as I made several poor attempts at this frustrating word.

"Lem–nyvn… Lemnu–wyrm…"

"*Lmneuwrm,*" Raikidan said.

Rimu made a second attempt but it came out as guttural gibberish and Raikidan laughed. The little dragon's eyes narrowed and he tried again.

I licked my lips as Rimu continued to try the word. The first part made the word the most difficult. I needed to focus on that. "Lne… lene… *lm… lmn… lmne…*"

"Good," Raikidan encouraged. "You're getting it. Keep trying. *Lmneuwrm.*"

I took a deep breath and tried again. *Lmneu…* lmneuwrym…" *Almost there, Eira.* "*Lmneuwrm.*"

Raikidan smiled. "Good."

Rimu made his attempts and, to my surprise, Raikidan corrected him in the same way he would me. Rimu chirped when he nailed the word finally, and then repeated it several times. I couldn't help but laugh a bit. Dragon, elf, human, didn't matter. All children had similar tendencies.

"Next word," I said.

Raikidan lifted in eyebrow. "Going to be one of those nights, then, huh?"

I smiled. "I like learning your language. I told you that. It'll also benefit Rimu. The quicker he learns words, the better for a lot of us."

"All right, what word do you want to learn?"

Before I could answer, my door swung open and Ryoko entered. "Okay, I want to play with the baby!" Her eyes danced. "Means you two can have some time alone."

"Ryoko…" I warned.

She giggled. Rimu perked up and watched Ryoko as she rushed over and fussed over him. The little dragon ate up the attention and squealed with delight. Her high energy had him jumping off the bed and running around. The two chased each other in and out of my room several times. Raikidan and I watched with amusement.

Ryoko stopped her chasing to take off her boots to make it easier to run around, but that proved to be a mistake because Rimu grabbed one and ran off with it. "Hey! Get back here with that."

Raikidan chuckled. "She's good with him."

"She likes kids and dogs," I said. "Rimu is a mix of the two. Perfect match."

He laughed. "Since the whelp is gone, do you want to continue your lesson?"

I nodded. "Of course."

"Pick a word, then."

"I'd like to know a few in a phrase you've used. You said it by accident around that gang member Ergren, and again tonight when fighting with Rimu."

Raikidan's brow furrowed. "*Lry ul suvy?*"

"Yes, that one," I said. "You told me the translation, but I've forgotten."

"Translation is 'she is mine.'"

I nodded, my memory coming back to me. "That's right, now I remember." My brow furrowed. "But wait... You said it meant—"

"Context gives it two meanings," he said. My eyes narrowed. *He was a bit too quick to get that answer out before I could finish speaking.* "*Suvy* means 'mine.' It's used in two ways, to stake claims on something. One is the way I told you, which is as a mate. The other is claiming as a treasure. This second meaning is the one I meant this time."

"*Suvy. Lry ul suvy.*" I looked at him. "Right?"

He stared at me, his mouth agape. "Y–you said that so well this time."

My mouth twitched. "Is that a bad thing?"

"No, of course not. I'm just... accustomed for you to take longer with words; even simple ones."

"Maybe I'm finally getting the hang of this."

"*Lreny,*" Raikidan said.

"*Lreny,*" I repeated.

He grinned. "Maybe you are. It means 'share.'"

"This is what Rimu asked you to do with me, yes?"

Raikidan nodded. I nodded back and then thought of something to ask, but mulled it over so I wouldn't push him away. As much as we talked about how I interpreted meanings wrong, Raikidan wasn't much better sometimes. "Raikidan, the phrase you taught me... is the dual meaning the same as the one you've directed toward me before?"

Raikidan froze and stared at me. He looked terrified to answer.

"Maybe I have been wrong this whole time..."

Shit, I didn't do this right. Fix it, Eira! "You've taught me *aio*, which means 'you,' and you've now taught me *suvy*, which means 'mine.' I don't know the word you used between the two, though it does sound familiar, but I'm smart enough to guess it means 'are.' I'm just curious if I'm right, since you said I didn't need to worry about it when you said it to me, not once, but twice."

Raikidan relaxed and chuckled. "You're too smart sometimes, you know that? I should have known it was only a matter of time before you brought up that memory and pieced things together."

"Well, am I right?"

"Impatient, aren't we?" *Well yeah, I want you not to freak out over my question.* He chuckled. "Yes, you're correct. *Aio eny suvy* means 'you are mine,' and I used it in the same context as the other phrase I used today."

"*Aio eny suvy.*" I stumbled over the new word, due to how awkward it was to say, but managed.

Raikidan nodded. "Good. Even though a simple word, *eny* trips up most dragons when they learn it due to the sounds needed to form it. It's why I skipped over it before in a prior lesson. I wanted to work with you on what I thought were more important words. Your attempt was much better than I expected."

I smiled my thanks. "Another. I'm on a role."

He chuckled and leaned closer. "*Cull.*"

"*Cull,*" I repeated.

"You are on a roll."

"What does it mean?"

He cupped my chin, his thumb caressing the corner of my mouth. Heat rushed to my cheeks when his eyes flicked down to my lips for a brief moment. I opened my lips to speak, but the words caught in my throat when he leaned over and pressed his lips to my forehead. "It means 'kiss.'"

The voice gasped. *"That... wasn't unpleasant... I guess."*

Ryoko's giggling pulled our attention to my door. She stood with Rimu cradled in her arms as if he didn't weigh a thing. *Gods, I wish I had her strength sometimes.* Her eyes danced with mischief and excitement. "I'll keep him away a little longer."

"Ryoko, it's not—" She ran off before Raikidan could finish correcting her. He let out a heavy exhale. "She's a piece of work."

I poked him in the cheek. "Your fault. You should know better. She'll use anything she can for ammunition against us. I could smile at you and she'd try to twist it."

He chuckled. "Like I said, she's a piece of work."

"Teach me more."

He sighed. "Fine."

I frowned. "Do you want to stop?"

Raikidan's eyes widened. "What? No, of course not. I was messing with you."

I half smiled. "Okay."

"I'll teach you *wikkyll*," he said.

I opened my mouth but drew a blank. "Looks like my streak is over. What?"

He laughed. "*Wikkyll*. It means 'goddess.'"

"Such a strange word for something so important."

He flicked my nose. "Is not. Now practice."

My nose scrunched and I made several horrible attempts until I finally got it right. Raikidan introduced another long complicated word, and this led into quite the language lesson, long into the night.

My eyes snapped open and darted around. *What time is it?* My light was off, the room dark, and my bedroom door was open, allowing a dim light from the living room to filter in. The last thing I remembered was finishing my language lesson and curling up with Rimu. Rylan had returned him to us when Ryoko fell asleep before the little dragon had grown tired himself, and he had joined in the lesson until I noticed him fighting his exhaustion. I had only planned to lay down with him until he fell asleep, but apparently I had succumbed to sleep, as well.

Wait, where's Rimu? I whipped my head around in a panic but couldn't find him, or even Raikidan. I stumbled out of bed in my half-awake state and ran for the door, crashing into a warm, hard body when I made it to the doorframe.

"Whoa, easy." Raikidan grabbed my arms so I wouldn't fall over. "What's the rush?"

"Where's Rimu?" I asked.

He chuckled. "Is that what this is about?" He pointed into the living room. I peered out to find Anahak carrying Rimu. The little dragon's head hung over his father's shoulder as he snoozed away. "He's going home now."

"Why didn't you wake me up?" I asked. "I was supposed to be watching him, not sleeping."

"He was also sleeping, not much to watch there." Raikidan turned me around. "Now go back to bed."

Xaneth came out of the bathroom. She waved to me and spoke in a hushed voice. "Thank you again. He's early to rise, so we thought it'd be best to take him instead of you having him through the night."

"Though I doubt by his current state he will be this time," Anahak said.

"I'm accustomed to odd sleep schedules," I said as I rubbed my eyes. "I wouldn't have minded."

Xaneth came over and gave me a hug. "You watching him for a few hours was more than enough for us. I'm grateful. Besides"—she peered past me at Raikidan—"making him put up with my son any longer would cause you more of a headache than I'd like to give."

I rubbed my bleary eyes and noticed her slightly disheveled state. I could see she tried to get herself looking presentable before arriving here. I gave her a knowing smile. "Trust me, he can't make my headaches any worse than he already does."

"Hey!" Raikidan protested.

I ignored him. "If you need me to watch Rimu again, I'd be happy to."

She smiled and gave me another hug. "Thank you. Now, I should let you get back to bed. Have a good night."

"You both do as well."

The two headed down into the basement for the secret passage and I shuffled myself back to bed. Raikidan pushed me onto the soft surface and I groaned in protest.

"That's for calling me a headache," he said.

"You are a headache, jerk," I said, my face half squished into my bed.

"And you're a brat, so we're even."

"Yeah, yeah."

He smiled at me. "Goodnight, Eira."

I pulled myself over to my pillows and snuggled down. "Night."

"What, not going to say goodnight to me?

I woke up. *"No, but I do have questions for you. How do you know Draconic when I don't?"*

"I know many things you struggle to know."

"So I was right. This odd behavior from you lately… You're not my subcon—"

"Bingo. You're finally figuring it out!"

"What the hell are you?"

"You already know."

I wanted to groan, but I didn't need Raikidan to know about this strange mental conversation I was having. *"That's real helpful. Just tell me."*

"I cannot right now.

"Why?"

"You'll find out soon enough, but know, I mean you no harm."

"Yeah… like I haven't heard that before."

"Answer me this… have I ever done anything to hurt you, or steer you wrong?"

"Well… no… but—"

"I have said horrible things in the past. I know. But I only want to protect you. I may not have done so in the correct way, but your protection was my only intent. So let us leave it at this; you will find out soon. I promise."

"Are you the woman I saw in the mirror?" Silence met my question. I clenched my teeth. *"Fine, but I expect real answers soon. You got that?"*

The voice still refused to comment, leaving me to my chaotic thoughts of unanswerable questions. *What the hell is going on?*

34
CHAPTER

The heavy bag swung back from another blow as I kicked it. I paid close attention to its ceiling support so I didn't knock it out and have to stop my workout early to fix it. I needed this workout—I had been slacking and that was bad. I didn't need to let myself get out of shape and become a liability to the team and our mission.

Someone came down the stairs but I didn't pay them any mind. If they were here to talk to me, they'd have to wait. If not, then it wasn't my business what they were doing down here. The mystery person was male, and I could hear him breathing heavily behind me. "If you want to chat, you'll have to come back later. I'm a bit busy."

"Give it back to him," Ambrose growled.

I stopped hitting the bag and cocked my head with a raised brow. "Give what back?"

"You've stolen Raikidan's heart, maiden. Give it back to him."

"Maybe she doesn't want to. It's nice... strong... caring..."

I blinked and then laughed. "You're joking, right?"

His brow furrowed. "Excuse me?"

"You seriously think I've stolen his heart?"

He growled. "Don't mock me, maiden. I know you have, and I won't allow you taint our blood any more than it already has been."

"Stop calling me maiden. I have a name."

He ignored my request, irritating me further. "Give him back his heart."

"I haven't stolen anyone's heart!"

"Then why is he here? Why has he chosen to call you friend? To stake treasure claim on something... like you."

"Oh, he did not just say it like that!"

My eyes narrowed. "I don't know. Why don't you find out from him? He's the one who saved me without asking. He's the one following me around like little puppy."

"A strong... muscular... puppy... I mean—forget I said that."

"It's because you bewitched him and stole his heart."

I took a deep breath. "Human hearts are fragile and short-lived—too much so for a dragon. What use does a fragile heart have for a dragon's? What use does a dragon have for something so weak?"

He stared at me, unable to come up with a good response. I took that as a cue to leave before this nonsense continued. I headed for the roof, as it would be the only place I could escape him for now. I needed to wrap my head around what he was raving about with this 'stealing hearts' business.

Ignoring the cold, I sat down on the ledge with a sigh. My mind was going a million miles a minute with questions and I didn't have answers for any of them. I could ask Raikidan, but I knew he wouldn't tell me, and then he'd go and confront Ambrose about the issue, keeping me in the dark still.

I looked up to the sky when I heard the flapping of large wings. A hawk blocked out the sun as it descended, and from the look of the canister strapped to it, it was a messenger hawk. The raptor landed on the ledge next to me and stared. I reached for the canister, breaking the element-protected seal, and took out the paper rolled up inside.

> *Laz'shika,*
>
> *A situation has come to my attention that I believe you can aid us in. Or, more specifically, your psychic friend, Seda. Would you two be able to spare a moment tomorrow to meet with us?*
>
> *Tla'lli*

Tla'lli? It had been a while since I had contact with her. As the chieftain's daughter of the West Shaman tribe, and main face for dealings with Zarda on the tribe's behalf, it was hard for the two of us to find time to be around each other long enough for anything more than a brief hello.

I flipped the parchment over in hopes of finding more to the request, but found the back side blank. *That's strange...* Something big must be going on if she was being so secretive, even when using a secure seal.

I glanced up from the note when the roof door opened. Corliss poked his head out and scanned the open space. "What's up, Corliss?"

"Even though it's cold out, I was looking for Mana up here. Have you seen her?" He his brow creased. "And have you seen your jacket?"

I laughed and shook my head. "I'm fine, really. Cold is doing me good. As for Mana, I haven't seen her. She may have gone out with Ryoko and Shva'sika. They said something about shopping earlier."

"Hmm, maybe. I'll look for her again, but you may be right."

He went to leave but I stopped him. "Hey, Corliss?"

"Yeah?"

"Um, can I talk to you for a moment? It won't take long."

"Sure, what about?"

"Something Ambrose said to me a little bit ago."

"Fantastic, what crazy nonsense is he raving about this time?"

"I'm not one hundred percent sure. That's why I'm asking you, in hopes you do."

He shivered from the cold before coming over and sitting next to me. "All right, what's going on?"

"Ambrose interrupted my workout to accuse me of stealing Raikidan's heart. From what I gathered from his raving, he's saying Raikidan is in love with me, but not willingly. Am I right to come to that conclusion?"

"He what? Oh, fantastic. I knew he had theories, but that wasn't one I thought he'd think of."

"That doesn't help me at all."

Corliss didn't answer; he was too deep in thought. I waited a bit longer, but he continued to think instead of clarifying. I sighed and walked off. "Forget it. I should have known you'd be no different than Raikidan on this."

"Hey, Eira, hold on," he called. I stopped to face him with my arms crossed. "I was just thinking. Don't go comparing me to Raikidan over that." When I didn't answer, he blinked. "Eira, how much has Raikidan told you about us?"

I shrugged. "Not much."

He stood and waved me to follow. "We'll talk about this in your green house. It's warmer in there."

I nodded and had the messenger hawk climb up on my arm before following, ignoring the pain the hawk's talons caused. If Corliss was going to be more willing than Raikidan to talk, then I wasn't going to say no.

Corliss didn't speak right away when we were inside, allowing me to get the hawk situated.

"I should start with the stories," he finally said. "It'll help you understand. I know many of your human stories, so this will be easy on us both."

"Are we going to talk about maiden sacrifices?"

He laughed. "As a matter of fact, yes."

"Fantastic."

He laughed again. "It's not as obvious as you may think. In your stories, maidens were sacrificed to dragons, right?"

"Well, yeah. People believed in order to keep a dragon from stealing their livestock and burning their villages and homes, they had to offer a maiden. They believed the dragon would eat her and it would appease him for a long period of time, leaving the village in peace."

Corliss nodded. "Yes. That's how our stories start off as well, but they don't end the same way. Dragons don't eat the women, not even black dragons, believe it or not." I didn't believe it, but I kept listening nonetheless. "When dragons took the offered maiden, they made one of two choices. The first, and most common choice, was to bring the maiden to another village for her to live out her life. The other choice was to bring her back to his territory and care for her. A dragon would make this choice due to the large possibility the maiden would be driven out of the new village if they found out about the contact she had with him. But this choice usually caused complications."

I blinked slowly and listened. This was interesting already, and he hadn't gotten to the part that answered my initial question.

"It's said that in caring for the maiden, the dragon who had taken her would start to see the woman as more than just a human and more like a companion, and eventually something more than that. The dragon, in the end, would give his heart to her, throwing out any regard to a possible dragon mate. Many dragons see this as some sort of magic only humans can perform, and this is what Ambrose is referring to when he says you stole Raikidan's heart."

I shook my head. "So, in the most long-winded explanation possible, you're saying I'm right."

Corliss chuckled. "Yes. The two of you have a strange type of closeness that Ambrose could misinterpret as bewitching and heart-stealing."

"Who's to say you did the bewitching? He's got some strong… charisma."

I snorted. "If anyone does any of the bewitching and heart-stealing, it's dragons."

"What?"

"There are human stories that tell of dragons disguising themselves as humans to mingle amongst them to find maidens who could sing. Once found, the dragon would bewitch her and steal her heart so she'd leave with him, making it so he could have her voice to himself."

"Maybe the real answer is that both stories are two parts of one whole," Corliss suggested.

I smirked. "Well, it does take two to tango."

He chuckled. "That's true. But back to what I was explaining—another thing that is true is the possibility of heart-stealing based on color, which would also fuel Ambrose's thinking." I waited. This sounded a bit promising. "Red dragons, as you may have figured out, would be most susceptible to having their heart stolen because of their social nature. But they're not the only ones who have a high susceptibility. Half-colors are just as likely to give their hearts away."

"Why?"

"Because they're more accepted by humans and other humanoid creatures. Full colored dragons usually don't want half-colors around, and all we want is acceptance. This means, if a half-color can get the human to care enough to accept him for who he is, he'll give his heart away if it means she'll stay. So with Ambrose seeing Raikidan gaining acceptance from you, he's going to worry."

I chuckled. "Well this explains a lot, though for a full-color who doesn't like half-colors, he does a whole lot of caring about what they do with their lives."

"That's Ambrose for you. One of the biggest hypocrites I know." Corliss scratched his head. "I don't see why Raikidan hasn't said anything to you. It's not like we have something to hide."

"He's always reluctant to talk about you guys. He prefers to not answer, or he changes the subject."

"I thought you were his friend."

I sighed. "Yeah, me too… But I guess not, since he doesn't trust me."

"I don't think we have the whole story to come to that conclusion." Why the voice showed favoritism to Raikidan suddenly these past few days, I couldn't begin to fathom.

"Do you trust him?" Corliss asked.

I knew what he was hinting at. "Not with everything, but I don't trust the others with everything, either."

"Fair enough. How much of what you know about us is from what you've figured out?"

"Prior to this conversation, just about everything I know about you guys is based on things I've figured out on my own, or read in the Library, and that wasn't much on its own. Raikidan has told me very little in comparison."

Corliss placed his hand on my shoulder. "Well, I'll tell you what you want to know whenever you ask. There's no need to hide anything from you."

I blinked. "Cor, why are you so much more trusting of me when he seems to be unable to?"

"Raikidan is a lot like you in the respect he doesn't trust often. It's hard for him to because of his experiences in life. This is especially true for humans."

"See, I told you there was more to the story."

"This is why I had to come here—to see you for myself once he told me where he had been after he disappeared. I hadn't been able to believe he'd try to help you since you were human."

I smiled. "Well I'm glad you enjoy human company. Makes it easier on me."

Corliss laughed. "I'm going to be completely honest with you, Eira. I wanted to call you out when you said Raikidan didn't tell you anything. The way he acts around you, it's as if he has told you everything and it's allowed him to connect with you in a way I never could. I feel like you understand him more than I do at this point."

I rubbed the back of my neck and avoided eye contact. "I said he didn't talk about your kind as a whole. I didn't say anything about him, though."

"So he does talk to you about himself."

"In exchange."

"In exchange for you talking about yourself?"

I looked at him through my lashes and gave a demure smile. "Yeah."

Corliss burst out laughing, which surprised me. "And yet he still knows nothing. The denseness of his brain still astounds me."

"And I'm thankful for that denseness," I mumbled. "I don't need too many knowing my secrets."

"He can't be trusted with that knowledge... yet."

Corliss shook his head, but didn't say anything. I knew he would have liked to argue with me, but he respected me enough to let me make my own choices about this very personal situation. "So, did I help you at all?"

I nodded with a smile. "Yes. And thank you. I now know that my answer to Ambrose was the truth."

"You tell him he was crazy?"

"In a nutshell."

He laughed and grabbed the door handle. "All right. Well I'm going to go look for Mana one last time before giving up my search."

"I'm surprised you let her out of your sight," I teased.

"She has free will." I tilted my head and raised an eyebrow. With the way the two acted, that definitely wasn't the full truth. "And she's pretty sneaky. I have a hard time keeping track of her when she doesn't want me to know where she is."

I laughed and paid attention to the messenger hawk, allowing Corliss to leave before heading into the house myself. I needed to find Seda and tell her what was going on so we could give Tla'lli an answer. And I wasn't about to give one without Seda's input.

35
CHAPTER

The shadow of a building kept us hidden while we waited. Genesis had told us we weren't allowed to complete the assignment until two more rebels came to help us, but she didn't say who they were or how long we'd have to wait, and I was starting to get impatient. This area was guarded and it had taken us a while to find this safe and secluded spot, but I didn't know how long it would remain that way.

Mocha fidgeted next to me. In the short amount of time she'd spent with us, I'd learned quick how patient she could be. So if she was getting tired of waiting, then we were waiting far too long for these two people to show up.

I jumped to a defensive stance and both Mocha and Ryoko had to stop themselves from screaming when a body dropped down next to me. I stared at Aurora as she crouched next to me with a smile. I had no idea what she was doing here.

"Hey, babe. Sorry I kept you waiting," she said. "I had to take care of some things the Council assigned to me before this assignment, and getting around the guards wasn't that easy."

Ryoko's brow furrowed. "Wait, you're the one the Council sent to help us?"

Aurora pointed up at the flat roof above us. "And Nioush, too."

We turned our gazes up at the fair-skinned, athletically-built, blond-haired man with matching goatee standing on the roof and in plain view of any guard in the yard. Nioush, Seda's psychic twin brother, and polar opposite. I assumed he had a telekinetic cloaking field around him. Not even he would be stupid enough to give away our presence.

"We're doomed," Mocha muttered.

"Shut up," Nioush spat. "It's not like I enjoy the idea of having to work with any of you."

"Then leave," Mocha said. "You're not welcome."

"I never said I wanted to be, house cat."

Mocha hissed. "Don't call me that, freak."

"Enough!" I barked. Mocha flinched and Nioush grunted. "I don't care what problems you two have with each other or with anyone here. This assignment is under my orders and my rules, and you will work together whether you like it or not. Do you understand?"

Mocha huffed and nodded but Nioush didn't respond. I glared at him and he still didn't respond. "Nioush, you will agree to this or we stay put and then you can tell the Council why we didn't get to complete this assignment."

His arms remained crossed and he was quiet, but I stuck to my guns. The team remained quiet until he finally spoke, "Whatever."

That was the best response I was going to get. "Now we—"

"Hold up," Ryoko interrupted. "Before we get to the assignment, I wanna ask Aurora something."

"Ryoko, we need to get this assignment done," Raikidan insisted. "Can't it wait?"

Ryoko crossed her arms. "No."

Aurora chuckled. "What's your question, babe?"

"Why are you here? You're a technician."

"The Council has decided that any technician with battle experience needs to help out when they can. So that's how I got assigned to this, though I wish they had picked someone who wasn't so out of practice."

Ryoko laughed. "Oh yeah. It's been so long since you've been out in the field that I forgot you ever were."

"So, what are we doing here anyway?" Aurora asked. "The Council didn't tell me."

Pulling out a hologram map, I brought up our location and pointed to a building. "We need to infiltrate this warehouse. It contains ammunition supply. You're aware of our ammunition shortage, yes?"

She nodded. "Yeah. I remember some of the other techs trying to search out new sources since ours are drying up."

I nodded. "They're drying up faster than they should. It's believed Zarda is cutting us off, so we're going to take it all by force. We've brought plenty of bags, and we're going to carry whatever we can, no matter the weight. Due to the number of guards, we're going to have to split up so we're less likely to be seen."

"Okay," Aurora agreed. "I'll go with you, if that's all right."

I nodded. "Mocha, you're also with me. Ryoko and Raikidan will travel as a pair, and Rylan, Raid, and—" I watched as Nioush hovered into the air and flew toward the target location. "Okay, looks like Rylan and Raid will be the last group. Anyone have any objections?"

"Aren't we going to stop Nioush?" Raid asked. "He could be seen."

"The asshole is cloaking himself," Mocha muttered. "Of course, I can't say he's doing the same for us."

"Figures," Raid muttered.

"Never mind him," I said. "We need to focus on getting to that warehouse without getting caught."

"What if we do get spotted?" Mocha asked. "Do we kill them?"

I shook my head. "No. We don't need blood on our hands tonight. Incapacitate anyone who gets in the way."

The others nodded and we broke off into our groups. Mocha and Aurora followed me as I set a quick pace toward the warehouse. I sunk low when I heard a soldier making his rounds, and peered over the edge to watch him. He stopped walking and looked around. I waited in hopes that he would leave, but he didn't. He sat down on a crate to relax. I ground my teeth together. We needed to get to the building across from us, but he'd spot us from where he sat.

I noticed Aurora fidgeting with her jacket. I shot her a questioning glance. She shook her head as if to tell me everything was fine, but I wasn't buying it. Slinking back into the shadows where she and Mocha hid, I moved to her side. "What is it?"

"Nothing," Aurora mumbled.

"Aurora, I know you better than that."

She sighed and peered at me through her lashes. "I'm hungry. I haven't eaten properly for the past few days because of the workload I've had. Don't worry about it, though. I'll get my nourishment when we're done with this assignment."

I placed my hand on her shoulder. "Go take care of that guy below us. You need—"

She shook her head. "No. I don't—"

"Aurora, just do it. We need to incapacitate him anyway. We can't move on until he's out of the way. It's a win-win."

She took a deep breath. "All right."

"We'll wait for you two buildings down, okay?"

She nodded and crawled out of our hiding place. Mocha looked at me curiously, but I didn't give her any indication of what was going on. I listened for the moment Aurora grabbed the guard below. When she knocked him out, I motioned to Mocha to follow and jumped to the next building. I headed to the next, but I stopped when Mocha stopped following me. She was heading back toward the alley.

I grabbed her by the arm and pulled her back. "We'll wait for her on the next building."

"Why not here? What's going on?" Mocha questioned.

"Don't worry about it," I said. "Let's just get to the next building."

"You're hiding something. What aren't you telling?"

"Mocha, it's not my place to tell. Please stop asking me."

"I don't understand," she said. "Is she doing something wrong?"

I shook my head. "The topic is a sensitive one, particularly for Aurora. She's a bit more sensitive than she likes to let on. Out of respect for her, I can't tell you what I've told her to do."

Mocha nodded. "All right."

I motioned for her to follow, and she complied this time without a fuss. Once on the next roof, we waited for Aurora. We didn't have to wait long.

"Better?" I asked her when she crouched next to me.

She nodded and kept her voice low. "Yes, thank you."

I nodded, a small smile on my lips, and then slunk out of the shadows to continue on. Once we finally made it to the target warehouse, I searched for the others. Ryoko poked her head out from behind a corner and waved to me. I nodded, and she and the boys came out to sneak over to us.

"Run into trouble?" she asked.

I nodded. "A small issue, but nothing we couldn't handle. Where is Nioush?"

She pointed at the roof. "Inside already, but from the sound of it, he's not doing anything but standing around."

I grunted. "Figures. Let's get inside and get what we can."

She nodded and jumped down onto a grate below. Once she opened a window, we all descended and climbed inside, onto the stacked crates below. Turning on a flashlight, I motioned for everyone to spread out and get to work. Climbing down to a group of unmarked crates below me, I took out my favorite dagger and shifted it into a crowbar. Prying the crate open, I peered in to take a look at the contents. The crate was filled with weapons, and I lost interest immediately. We were here for ammunition, not weapons, so I only had room in my bag for that. Opening the crate next to it and peering in, I found similar contents, so I decided to move elsewhere, hoping to be a bit luckier.

I passed Mocha as she pulled out rounds of rocket launcher ammunition and stashed them into her bag, purring away with glee. Rylan and Ryoko were near her, helping each other pull out ammunition of their own, and Raikidan was around a corner taping grenades before storing them into his bag. Nioush stood near the wall of the warehouse on top of some crates, doing absolutely nothing. I didn't expect much else from him.

Coming across a secluded spot, I pried open a crate to have a look inside. Grinning, I pushed the lid aside and pulled out small boxes of ammunition. Although they were small, they were still something we could use. Aurora made her way over to my location and helped me.

As we worked, I noticed she was acting funny, as if she were on edge. "Something bothering you?"

She glanced up at a window and then went back to working. "It's getting lighter out."

I placed my hand on her shoulder. "Don't worry. We'll be done with this before the sun comes—"

The sound of the warehouse doors creaking open echoed through the building. I crouched down and snuck around the crates to see what was going on. I made a retreat when I heard two male voices and their heavy footsteps entering the building. I didn't need to see them to know they were soldiers.

Aurora helped me slide the lid back onto the crate before we sunk low into the shadows. I found myself holding my breath as the two chatted and made their rounds.

"Hey, what's this?" one suddenly asked.

"Looks like an opened crate," the other observed. "I thought you said you didn't let anyone in here while you stood watch outside."

Aurora and I looked at each other with alarm in our eyes. This wasn't good.

"I didn't." I heard the sound of a gun being loaded. "Keep your eyes open."

I listened as the two searched, and wanted to smack my head when they found more crates. *How is everyone this careless tonight?* Aurora grabbed onto my shirt and pulled me back farther as the soldiers came around the corner. I heard them push open the lid of one of the crates and curse as they realized how much we had managed to take.

Aurora tried to take a peek, but I pulled her down and shook my head. We needed them to think we were gone.

"Let's keep looking back here," one advised. "I get the feeling we're being watched."

Aurora and I backed up more as they proceeded to continue our way. Normally I would have tried to move around them to take them out, but it was far too dark to guarantee a flawless execution.

"Looks like your friends are coming to help," Nioush messaged.

My brow creased. Why was he being helpful all of a sudden? Aurora's sudden retreat caught my attention. I followed her until there was nowhere else for us to go. The warehouse wall prevented that. Aurora leaned against a crate and exhaled. I watched her. She had something on her mind, but I couldn't tell what it was.

A loud smashing noise caught my attention and forced me to try and peek over the crates. I couldn't see what had broken, but it had caught the soldier's attention, because they were heading back the way they came. Unfortunately, from what I could see, that put Ryoko and Raikidan right in their line of sight the moment the soldiers rounded the corner.

Sinking back down, I tried to think of something. Nioush had told me about the others coming to help, but I couldn't be sure he'd feel so inclined to tell the others about the soldiers' change in direction. I didn't get him.

Aurora tugged on my shirt to get my attention. I noticed something odd in her eyes, as if she had just finished some sort of unseen battle. She leaned closer to me and whispered in my ear. "I know what we can do, but I need your help."

"I'm listening."

"I need you to make a big enough fire that it'll project my shadow on the warehouse wall."

I understood what she was getting at. "Are you sure about this?"

She nodded. "Very. It's the only way to keep these two soldiers distracted enough for the others to grab them. We're in no position to do it ourselves."

I nodded. "All right, I'm ready when you are."

She took a deep breath, as if fighting with the desire to back out of this choice, and moved back. I openly spit out an ember into my hand and forced it to grow until it illuminated Aurora's figure and a large shadow cast up onto the wall. Just as the soldiers took notice of the light, her back and arms began to convulse as she stood. Her fingers shaped into strange claws and longer hair began to grow on her hands. Her face distorted in areas and her back seized, large wings springing forth.

Terror rooted the soldiers in place. Their knees trembled and voices quaked in their failed attempts to speak as Aurora's new shape projected against the warehouse walls. To make the situation worse for the two, I took a deep, concentrated breath and let an inhuman hiss escape my lips. Then, the two men were jumped and taken care of. Aurora started to shift back to her normal look.

Just as she finished, Raikidan came around the corner to check on us. He didn't ask any questions when he noticed we were fine, and he remained uncharacteristically quiet as he waited. Picking up my bag of ammunition, I slung it over my shoulder and led the two back out into the open to regroup with the others, who were clustering near the two unconscious soldiers.

Before I could manage a word, Ryoko started asking questions. "Aurora, was that you that did that?"

Aurora shoved her hands in her pockets and avoided eye contact. "Uh, yeah…"

"That's cool! How'd you do that?"

Aurora, surprised that Ryoko reacted so positively to the news, didn't respond right away. I knew she was quite sensitive about this topic, but I wished she had a bit more faith in some of us. "Well... I'm part bat."

Ryoko blinked. "That's an odd animal for them to try. So, you're like Rylan then?"

"Sorta. I'm a little older than him, so my design is a little less per-fected."

"Not that mine was perfect, either," Rylan added.

Aurora shrugged. "More so than mine. At least you can take the shape of an animal. I'm only able to go into an in-between metamorphosis."

"Hmm, I can't picture that," Ryoko admitted. "But that doesn't matter. What ty—"

"That's enough, guys." I stepped in. "We need to get moving. We have a little of what we need, and this assignment is now compromised thanks to these two soldiers."

"But I wanna ask Aurora one more question," Ryoko argued.

"No. We're leaving now. We need to get out of here undetected, and once they realize these two are missing, they'll search for them and then everyone will be on high alert."

"There's a house just beyond this area we can go to," Aurora informed. "We recently acquired it, so it hasn't been attached to the underground with a tunnel system yet, but we can hide out there until it's safer."

"Why would the Council buy a house this close to a military loca-tion?" Raid asked. "That doesn't make sense."

"Actually, it does," Mocha objected. "The military has a tendency to not see things right under their nose, so why wouldn't they put a house next to a place like this?"

Raid thought this point over, but I wasn't going to let him think too long. "All right, enough talking. Aurora, you're leading us to this building."

She nodded. "Okay."

Aurora made sure her bag was secure and everyone was ready to follow before she led us up a stack of crates and out the window we had come in through. She set a quick pace against the rising sun. Our pace quickened when sirens bellowed. *They found the soldiers.* Unfortu-nately, we were still inside the compound.

"This way," Aurora ordered as she veered off our current path.

We ran behind a corner and she had us wait in the shadows. Several soldiers ran around below us. They finally went away, but we remained where we were until we were sure they were gone. Making it to the fencing that lined the boundary of the compound, we slipped through the hole we had made on our way in and followed Aurora down a small alley. She made several turns until we stopped at a back porch of one of the many houses.

Lifting up the mat, she grabbed a key and unlocked the door. She put the key back under the mat and ushered us inside. The moment she locked the door behind us, everything went quiet. The military would soon start to search the alleys, and any sound would prompt them to search inside.

We made sure all blinds were pulled so they couldn't look inside the house. I sat down and waited for the sirens to stop. That would be our sign we were in the clear, and until then, we were to wait.

Minutes turned to hours before the sirens finally stopped. *They really wanted to find us.* We had heard many groups of soldiers check around the building, but luckily, none found reason to barge inside. Raid, curious, split the blinds and peered out to check how safe it really was. The action allowed the morning sun's light to peek inside.

Aurora stepped out of its path as it headed for her. "Fantastic."

Raid looked at her. "What?"

"The sun is out," she grumbled.

His brow arched. "So? Sure, it'll make it harder for us to get around, but you act as if it's the end of the world."

"Because I can't go out in it."

Ryoko gasped. "Do you have vampire bat in you? Does that make you like a vampire and you'll burn up in the sun?"

I stared at her. She was all too excited over this idea of hers. While I was trying to figure how to feel about this, Aurora, on the other hand, laughed up a storm. "Babe, you have such an overactive imagination! You've been watching way too many movies. I'm just allergic to the sun."

Ryoko blinked. "What?"

"If I'm exposed to the ultraviolet rays the sun gives off, I break out, and if I'm exposed for too long, it can cause serious health problems that could ultimately kill me, although very slowly."

Ryoko scrunched her nose. "That's not as cool. That kinda sucks, actually."

"And burning in the sunlight is cool and fun?" Raid teased.

Ryoko's eyes narrowed at him but he only laughed, with Rylan joining in with him after only a few moments.

Aurora knelt and rummaged through her backpack until she pulled out long gloves and a shirt. "Luckily I came prepared just in case."

I watched as she removed her jacket and threw the shirt on over her cropped one, tucking it into her cargo pants. She then pulled the gloves over her hands and secured them with the built-in belts before she shrugged her jacket back on over her shoulders. She reached into her bag again and pulled out a necklace with a sun pendant before slinging the bag over her shoulders.

I started to stand up when I recognized the necklace. "Is that—"

Aurora nodded. "Argus and Seda worked hard to produce a bunch of these illusion devices. They had them distributed for testing and Seda gave me one personally, knowing this may happen. I'm pretty sure I'll stick out like a sore thumb like this."

I chuckled. "It's autumn. Sure, your fashion choice is yet to be desired, but the cold could make a number of people dress funny for warmth."

Aurora chuckled and pulled a long, cylindrical object out of one of her pants pockets. She pressed a small button on the side, extending it in length. Once fully extended, the top fanned out until it reached itself again. "That might be true if I wasn't using an umbrella on a sunny day."

I nodded. "Point taken."

Securing the necklace around her neck, Aurora twisted parts of the pendant until it changed her appearance. Her skin altered to a pale tone, and her hair grew longer and changed to an ebony color. Heavy, dark makeup covered her eyes, and red and black lipstick covered her lips. Her jacket was now black and made of fur, and her shirts and pants changed into a black and red corseted dress with lace and ribbon and connected collar. Tall knee-high black boots with spikes covered her feet and long, flowing, red and black arm sleeves with lace covered her arms. The bag on her back disappeared, and the metal umbrella she held was the last item to change, transforming into a dark decorative parasol of cloth and lace.

"I'll take a few of your bags back with me," she offered. "The field around me, thanks to this device, will make it easier to get these back."

I nodded and held my bag out. "Good idea. We'll have to hang out here for some time, if not until night fall to get out of here."

Before Aurora could take the bag, it flew out of my hands and into Nioush's. I took a keen interest in his behavior, but he didn't acknowledge me. He took a few more bags from the others and held them in one hand. In a blink of an eye, his appearance changed. He now wore a suit and his cloth blindfold was now gone, bright blue eyes left in its place. The bags he held now appeared to look like a suitcase, and I wasn't sure how he was doing this. I hadn't seen him put an illusion device on.

Without a word, he opened the front door and left. Aurora blinked. "Okay, that was weird."

Mocha grunted. "I'll bet my money that he's trying to get more credit than he deserves."

I shook my head. "I don't know. Something was off about him just now. But it doesn't matter. Aurora, you should get going."

Aurora nodded and took the remainder of the bags we had. "I'll let the Council know you'll be hanging around here. They're planning on sending in the renovation crew soon to fix this place up, so I'll just have them do it today so the crew can bring you disguises to get you out of here before the day ends."

I smiled. "Thanks."

She smiled and headed for the back door. Once out on the porch, she gazed up at the sky and sighed before walking off. I sat back down and waited for help to arrive. It was the only thing I could do.

36
CHAPTER

Blaze shoved Argus, who fell into Ryoko, who shoved them both into the slimy wall. Raid and Mocha chuckled as they complained and I rolled my eyes. Winter was nearly upon us, the first signs being freezing rain for days, so assignments were few and far between. It was like this every year. The Council never wanted to risk losing any of us to the harsh winter weather. This meant our skills tended to suffer from lack of use, but we had the range in the Underground to help curb that. Although it was only virtual training, it was still better than nothing, and it saved the limited supply of ammunition we had.

Ambrose, Salir, and Rennek hung back at the end of our pack and watched us. I kept an eye on them as always, but I wasn't sure why I still felt the need. Aside from the tension between Ambrose and Raikidan and Corliss, and the incident when Xaneth came for a visit, nothing bad ever happened. The three were always quiet, and most of the time you ended up forgetting they were around.

Ryoko and Rylan opened the large doors of the Underground, and the moment we stepped inside, we were hit with all the chaos. There were people shouting and machines were broken everywhere you looked, but the first thing that caught our attention was the large crowd in the middle of the room. There was a fight going on.

Aurora ran over to me. "Thank the goddess you're here. It's complete chaos in here!"

I ducked when a metal chair flew at us. "I can see that. What the hell is going on?"

"I don't know!" she shouted. "It happened so fast we were barely able to get people out of the machines before they started to get smashed up. I would have called you for help, had I been able to."

"How long has this been going on?" I questioned.

"About three hours," she admitted. "We only have my and Ezhno's computer stations left in one piece, and Ezhno, the other techs, and the only psychic here are having a lot of trouble keeping those safe."

I sighed. "Fantastic. I guess I'll go break up the party."

"Want me to help?" Ryoko asked as she pounded her fists together. "You might need some muscle behind you."

I exhaled a puff of smoke from my nose as I started to stalk off. "No, I have a good idea how to handle this."

Exhaling a flame into the palm of my hand, I held onto it tightly and used the broken objects around me to get off the ground and high into the air. The fight was a messy free-for-all, and looked to have no purpose behind it. As I came down in the middle of the crowd, I forced the fire to grow and slammed my hand into the ground as I landed, forcing those fighting to fall back from the heat of my flame.

"That's enough!" I scanned the crowd and watched as many tried to figure out how to react to my presence. "What are you, a bunch of wild animals?"

"Adra's team started it," someone called out.

"We did not!" another person yelled.

"The hell ya didn't!" someone else yelled. "Y'all strut yer stuff and think ya can tell us what to—"

"Enough!" I barked. The flame in my hand flared with my anger and then died just as fast. "I don't care who started this, or for what reason, it ends now!"

"Who are you to tell us what to do?" someone challenged.

I grunted. "I'm nothing more than the sane in this mass of insanity. Look around you! Look at the mess you've created. The chaos you've fed. You act like the wild animals Zarda believes us to be! You're nothing but rats in the sewers for his game of cat and mouse. Are we not better than that? Are we not better than him?"

The crowd started looking at each other as they started to think about what I was saying.

"This is exactly what Zarda wants! He wants us to fail from the inside out. One weak point and we fall apart. This chaos needs to stop, now!"

Murmurs of agreement started to echo around the room.

"So, the question is, are we men, or are we mindless beasts? Do we not have a purpose? Do we not fight a greater fight than ourselves?" I heard quiet answers, but that wasn't good enough. "I'm sorry. I didn't hear you ladies."

The crowd around me responded louder but still not loud enough.

"Don't make me repeat myself another time, civilians."

I received a full salute from the surrounding crowd and a booming answer. "Yes, ma'am!"

"Good. Now get your sorry asses moving and clean up this mess! You're all making me sick." I stalked off for Aurora's computer station. The dispersing crowd moved out of my way to allow me passage.

"Excellent job."

As I headed for the station, I noticed Ambrose's heavy gaze on me. I wasn't sure what he was thinking exactly, but I thought I caught a hint of admiration in his eye. Of course, I could have been seeing things, which was more likely the case.

I sat down in the computer chair with a sigh. Aurora walked over with a smile and handed me a drink. I took it gratefully.

"Thanks for doing that," she said. "I don't want to think of what would have happened if it had continued."

I waved her off. "Someone had to do it, and brute force wasn't going to work."

"So what are you guys going to do now?" she asked. "You can't use the range until everything is fixed and tested."

"We could help clean up," Ryoko offered.

"Or just go home," Mocha stated. "We shouldn't have to clean the mess they made."

"We shouldn't have to, but we will," I stated as I stood. "The faster things get put back together, the faster things go back to normal."

Some of the others grumbled, but they all went to give a hand anyway. Salir and Rennek followed Ryoko and Rylan, but as expected, Ambrose stayed out of it. I rolled my eyes and went to help. I couldn't wait until he left.

I lifted my gaze from my book when someone knocked on the door. "Come in."

The door opened and Corliss poked his head in. "They're leaving."

"Who?" I asked.

"About time," Raikidan muttered.

"Oh, them."

Corliss tilted his head in a motion to follow. "Salir wanted to say goodbye to both of you."

I nodded. "All right."

Raikidan grumbled before following. I wasn't sure what his issue was. He'd been in a decent mood until Corliss came in with the news, and I wouldn't have thought saying goodbye to Salir would be such an awful experience for him. Maybe it was because he had to see Ambrose. The two had been acting funny around each other earlier when we had gotten back from cleaning up the range.

We followed Corliss up the stairs, to the roof where everyone else was waiting. Rennek nodded to us when we arrived, and Salir smiled. Ambrose, of course, looked like he just wanted to leave, and Salir had tricked him into staying or something.

Salir came up to me and wrapped her arms around my neck for a hug. "Thank you for allowing us to stay."

"You're welcome," I replied.

She pulled away and turned to walk over to Raikidan and Corliss, who had wandered onto the roof a little further than me. She held Raikidan's face and rested her forehead on his, and Raikidan responded by placing his hands on her shoulders. She murmured something to him before performing the same gesture with Corliss.

"*You pimr keep her ledy. She is usginmevm. There is something lgyxuez epiom her.*" Salir murmured in their native tongue. She glanced back at Ambrose. "*Even he lyyl it.*"

Raikidan and Corliss gave a curt nod, their expressions serious. A part of me wanted to know what they were talking about, since I understood a few words, but I knew I shouldn't even be eavesdropping, and it was best not to pry.

She finally pulled away from them and joined Ambrose and Rennek.

Ambrose was the first to shift into a common bird, so as not to draw any unwanted attention, and he took off without uttering a word or sign of acknowledgement. Salir smiled and waved her fingers before following.

Rennek nodded to me and spoke a farewell in Elvish. *"Until we meet again."*

I was taken aback by the saying, but responded with the appropriate response. *"When the sun rises once more."*

He smiled and then followed his parents. The others filed back into the house, but I didn't follow right away. I waited, in case they came back for whatever reason. I ended up heading in when Raikidan placed his hand on my shoulder and encouraged me to follow.

I was glad Ambrose had finally chosen to leave. The tension in the house would finally die down and go back to normal—or at least, that was the theory.

37
CHAPTER

I gazed around the park as Raikidan and I strolled down the stone path, my arm tucked in his. The sun shone bright, and the birds sang a whimsical tune that carried through the park on the light breeze. Genesis had sent Ryoko, Rylan, Raikidan, and me out to monitor a day recruiting, the former two paired together, and Raikidan and me paired for another location. Recruiting others to our cause was by far one of the most important assignments out there, but to do so out in the open, during the day, went against our standard protocols for safety measures. *Last time one happened, the recruiter and the person being recruited both died.*

The Council assured us they had deliberated on the choice extensively, but the fact that they had agreed to go through with it at all surprised most of us. I would have requested more deliberation, or put in more of an opinion on the matter, had I not been preoccupied with the role assigned to Raikidan and me.

We were to act like a couple on a date. I was pretty sure this had been Ryoko's idea, especially since she and Rylan hadn't gotten assigned anything remotely similar. Of course I couldn't prove any of it, and it didn't matter how I felt—the assignment had to be done.

"We'll get her back for this."

I blew out a slow breath through my lips when my stomach growled.

This assignment involved a two-part process for the two of us. We were to keep a low profile and look out for anyone who might catch on to the recruiting happening down by the lake. When given the assigned signal, Raikidan and I were to leave the park, heading for the café across the street of the main park entrance to monitor for the same type of suspicious activity. Other assigned monitoring groups had similar orders. This location rotation, for all groups involved, assured our assignment would go with few interruptions—or worse.

"Do you want me to try to find you something to eat?" Raikidan asked. "That was the third time your body has told you to feed it."

I shook my head. "I'll be fine for now. We shouldn't have to be here much longer, and the café has better food than the food stalls here in the park."

He nodded, a smile on his lips, and patted my hand before looking around some more. I wasn't sure how he did it, but this fake date was far less awkward than I had expected it to be. We had kept up casual conversation when needed without issue, and the close contact required while walking and sitting didn't bother me like I would have thought.

My communicator attached to my satchel flashed once, and I glanced at Raikidan, who nodded. With the signal to move to the next position, I could finally get something to eat. *Thank the gods.* The two of us strolled out of the park and to the café across the street. After ordering and waiting on the painful prep and cook time for our meals, we sat down at a small table with an umbrella and clear view of the park.

I bit into my sandwich and hummed happily as it quelled my body's incessant grumbling. Raikidan ripped into his overstuffed sandwich and I smiled at his obvious enjoyment of it. I had let him order first, and he chose the sandwich I had planned to order, so at the last minute, I changed my choice so we wouldn't have the same food. *It would have been weird if we ordered the same food on a date, right?* As much as I knew it was a fake date, and I could have ordered the food I wanted, the urge to make this appear as real as possible tugged at me, even if that meant I didn't get to eat what I wanted. "How is it?"

"Good, yours?" he asked.

I took another bite of my food. "It's yummy."

He held his sandwich out to me. "Want some? It looked like you wanted this one until I ordered it."

"Be careful with that offer... we both know what happened in the past."

I shook my head. "I'm happy with my choice."

Raikidan scanned the area and then leaned closer to me and kept his voice low. "It's not a big deal, Eira. I'm willing to share. You shouldn't have changed your choice because of me."

"Raikidan, I don't think it's a good idea," I said. "Sharing food, with your instincts—"

"It'll be fine," he said. "We've shared food before. The first time took me by surprise, but the other few times, I prepared myself. Seda gave me a rundown on how dates work, so I knew to give myself that same prep time. Nothing weird will happen."

I gazed at his sandwich and struggled with the right choice. He may have been fine last time, but I didn't trust his instincts to not pull a fast one on the two of us.

"Be careful."

My stomach rumbled. "All right, fine, I'll take a bite."

Raikidan smiled and offered one of his sandwich halves to me. I reached out to grab it, but he pushed my hand away. "Take a bite. You don't need to take it away from me."

I rolled my eyes and did it his way. My eyes lit up, the delightful mix of tastes danced on my tongue. I regretted not ordering this sandwich myself. "So delicious!"

Raikidan chuckled. "I guess yours is rather plain, then?"

I held up a sandwich half. "Try it."

Raikidan took a bite and chewed for a few moments. "Not bad, but mine is definitely better."

I nudged him. "Yeah, yeah, rub it in."

"How about this, you let me try the yellow food you have in that bowl, and share your sandwich with me, and I'll share mine with you."

I looked at my bowl, filled with pasta and liquid cheese. "I'll only agree to that if you only take one bite of my mac and cheese."

"You must really like it if you're only willing to give me one bite."

"I don't know how they make it so good here, but Ryoko and I would fight to the death for the last bite if we had to share a bowl."

"All right then, let me try this, uh, 'to-die-for' mac and cheese."

I smiled and scooped up a spoonful and fed him some. Raikidan chewed the cheesy pasta a few times before realizing they were tender enough to swallow without needing it.

He sat there for a moment and then abruptly stood. "I'll be right back."

I laughed as he walked back into the café. At least I wouldn't have to share mine. I took in my surroundings as I ate my cheese-covered pasta, careful to watch out for any odd behavior. Soldiers were always a concern when recruiting was going on, but it wasn't the ones you could see that you had to worry about. If they caught wind of a rebellion recruiting, they'd try to be sneaky about catching us. It's what made such open recruiting so tedious and involved.

And there we have one. I attached my communicator and dialed it to the reporting signal.

"Hi, this is Starla, how can I help you?" a feminine voice answered.

"Hey, Starla, were you ever able to find that *guy* who left the *green shirt* on those folded-up *blue denim pants* the other day?"

"Um, describe the guy better for me? I returned a few pieces of clothing to some customers," she said.

"Short black hair, nice black boots. Rather short and bulky."

"Oh yes, him! Yes, I did. Thanks for checking in."

"No problem." I cut the line and went back to eating. *One suspicious character reported.*

I smiled at Raikidan when he came back with a bowl of mac and cheese for himself as well as a large slice of chocolate cake for us to split... well, large enough for me to give him a tiny bite of it and hoard the rest.

"C'mon, Eira, share the cake," Raikidan said, trying to grab some with his fork.

"No, it's mine." I said as I defended my delicious treasure with my fork. "Now stay back, you foul beast!"

Raikidan took on the challenge, and the two of us fought over the cake with our forks. In the end, I came out victorious and happily ate my prize. Though he managed to sneak in a few steals and I did relinquish the last bite, surprising him.

"You sure?" Raikidan asked.

I nodded. "I wouldn't be offering if I wasn't sure."

He smiled. "Thank you."

Raikidan devoured the last piece of the cake and then cleaned up, not allowing me to lift a finger in the slightest. This perplexed me, but nothing seemed off about him, so I figured it might be him trying to play his undercover part as well as he could.

He sat back down when done, and laced his hand into mine, and leaned closer. "What are we supposed to do now? We can't keep sitting here doing nothing. It'll look suspicious."

"Well, we can't up and leave our post," I said. "But I'm too full to eat, and we know how *great* I am at holding conversations."

Raikidan gestured to my satchel. "Your communicator is flashing."

I unhooked the device from my bag. Placing the device on my head, I answered. "Hello?"

"You two are having fun, I see," Ryoko teased.

I sighed. "What do you want?"

"Wow, no need to be so rude. I'm just checking in with you."

I lowered my voice. "All has been quiet, and we're running out of ways to stay at this table."

"Oh, that's bad. Um, let me call you back."

She hung up the line and I waited. As I did, Raikidan's grip on my hand tightened a little, and he placed his free hand over our joined ones. My brow rose in question and he smiled back in response.

Ryoko called back and she kept her voice low. "I got the okay for you to move back to the park. This whole thing is winding down soon anyway, so it'd be a perfect time for you two to look like you're leaving in order to maintain your cover."

"Thanks." We hung up and I shifted my focus back onto Raikidan, putting on my best civilian cover. "I need to go home. Something's come up."

Raikidan nodded. "All right, I'll bring you home, then."

The two of us headed for the park, our hands still intertwined. I couldn't help but glance down at them. Raikidan had been adamant about not holding hands up until this point, though he never said why. His grip tightened, and I grew concerned.

"Raikidan, is everything okay?" I asked.

He didn't reply and I frowned. What could have happened to make him act this way? I reached out with my free hand to touch his arm, and he pulled away. "Please don't."

"Oh, okay, sorry…" Now I really didn't understand. With that kind of reaction, it was as if I had done something wrong to cause this.

"This is a strange behavior, even for him."

I glanced around the park to keep an eye out for anything that could cause issues for the rebellion, but my mind couldn't let go of Raikidan's behavior. He was fine until just before we left the café.

"I'm sorry," Raikidan murmured. "I thought I could prepare myself so this wouldn't happen. I was wrong."

My eyes widened and my heart skipped a beat. *The food sharing caused this?*

"Nice going."

Raikidan let go of my hand and wrapped his arm around my lower back and forced me to walk close to him. "Forgive me. I need you right here until this calms down. I'll try not to allow this to get out of hand."

My heart raced. "O—okay. Let's just focus on getting to the car."

My paced quickened, and Raikidan matched it, though his grip on my hip tightened as the minutes passed. When we reached the car, Raikidan made it impossible for me to immediately climb in. He reached around with his free hand and pulled me into a tight hug. His strong musky-ash scent overpowered me, as if it'd gotten stronger in his state.

"Raikidan, let go," I said. "I can't get into the car unless you do."

"I'm sorry," he said. "This is just really difficult. It's far worse this time, and I don't know why."

"I noticed."

A minute or two passed before Raikidan was able to let go. He opened the car door and I slipped into the passenger seat. Once situated, he shut the door and then ran to the other side and jumped behind the wheel. The car started up easy for him, and he whipped out of the parking space a bit too recklessly, though I didn't complain, as I was aware of his tight grip on the wheel.

"Will rolling down the windows help at all?" I asked.

"I don't know. But it can't hurt to try."

I hit the window button and he did the same for his. The wind whipped through the car and blew my hair in all directions, but if it'd help him get himself under control, I could deal with it.

"Thank you for this suggestion," Raikidan said when a few minutes passed. "This has helped a bit. Do you mind if I stop at the store?"

"If it's required for you to get your head on straight, then yes, that's fine."

He nodded, and changed our route. Once parked, he sat there for several moments with his hands gripping the wheel until he managed to convince himself to let go and head into the store. I let out a sigh and slouched in my seat. That had been far too tense of a situation for me. I had been so worried of triggering a bad reaction that I didn't try to engage in conversation.

And now that I was alone, I couldn't help but blame myself. I knew I shouldn't have allowed us to share food. He wasn't human, meaning his instincts were far different. I had gotten so caught up with how normal and, well, fun that had been, that I had I ignored what kind of problems I could be causing him. *I'm such an idiot.*

"Eira, you okay?" I jumped and looked at Raikidan, who was now sitting in the driver's seat. He held up a hand. "Sorry, didn't mean to startle you."

I shook my head. "Don't be. I was just lost in thought. You didn't take long."

Raikidan held out a candy bar. "I only needed a moment. I got this for you, though."

I smiled and accepted the gesture. "Thank you."

"Are you sure you're okay?" he asked.

"Yeah, I'm fine. Let's get home."

He regarded me for a moment longer and then started up the car. We drove in silence for about ten minutes before he spoke, "Eira, I don't want you to blame yourself for any of this."

"It's not your fault," I said. "I should have been more cautious than I was. I sometimes forget you're not human and I need to stop that."

"It is my fault for putting you in this position. I should have known I'd need to handle that differently than I did." He reached over and laced his fingers in with mine. "I'll do better next time."

"There won't be a next time, Raikidan."

"I wouldn't count on that. As long as this rebellion continues, situations like this have a potential to come up. If not with you, then with someone else I'm paired with. I can't let this get out of control."

I stared at our hands. "That break didn't help you, did it?"

"No. I think it's just going to need to run its course."

I bit my lip. "What does that mean?"

"Means I need to be close to you until my instincts calm down. I'll be abnormally close and, like I said before, I'll try to not let it get weird."

I chuckled. "You don't know what a personal space bubble is anyway."

Raikidan grinned. "I do. I just like to pop yours."

I pulled my hand out of his and smacked his shoulder. "Jerk."

He chuckled and focused on driving while I went back to thinking.

Water dripped out of my hair as I wrung it one last time. I then tossed it behind me and fluffed my hair to help it air dry better. Making sure my towel was secure, I left my bath and slipped into my closet to find something to wear. Raikidan and I had been the first to return, and since Raikidan was doing a little better than before, I convinced him to allow me to bathe. For a while, he hung out in my room, but when I chose to take extra time to relax without him invading my space, he had wandered off somewhere.

After pulling a tank top and comfortable sweats on, I walked out of my closet as I towel dried my hair, only to run into Raikidan. "Ow..."

"Sorry, I was distracted by a scent, and didn't realize you were leaving your closet," he said.

"It's fine." I maneuvered around him. "What scent put your brain into a bigger fog than it already is?"

Raikidan reached around and placed his hand on my stomach, stopping me in my tracks. My heart thumped in my chest as he drew closer and it then raced when he reached up and touched my hair and inhaled deeply. "Your hair... are you using something different in it?"

"N–no," I managed to say. He smelled my hair again, and the uncomfortable feeling in me grew. "Raikidan, you're acting weird."

"I know," he said. "But trust me, if I wasn't in control, you'd be under me on that bed."

My heart stopped and my body warmed. I knew that's where his instincts were trying to lead him, but for him to put it into words... *This day can't end soon enough.*

"I'm sorry for putting you in this situation, Eira," Raikidan said before inhaling my scent again. "I know you're uncomfortable."

"Well, as long as this doesn't get much weirder, it's really no different than when you help me with my issues, right?"

"I suppose." He wrapped his other arm around me and pulled me closer. "At least, for one of us it is." I swallowed hard and my cheeks flushed as he continued inhaling my scent, but this time closer to my neck. "Sorry. I thought it'd be best to stay as honest as possible about this."

"You're right, it is," I said. "I'd much rather know exactly what's going through your head or why you're choosing a particular action, instead of guessing. But if I can ask, is it necessary for you to grab onto me like this?"

"I need to be physically close to you. As long as I have that, I will be satisfied."

I thought for a moment and came up with an idea that would keep him from holding me. "Go sit down on the bed while I dry my hair. I have an idea, but I don't want sopping wet hair."

Raikidan hesitated, fighting his instinct to stay close, and his logic to listen. After several moments, he slipped away and sat down on my bed. I fluffed my hair with my towel and then warmed up my hands with fire heat. Teasing my hair with warmed hands, I dried it. I turned around to find Raikidan reclining on the bed, staring at me. Normally he was hard to read when he watched me, but this time, he clearly enjoyed watching me. *Yeah, that's not weird at all.*

I put my hair up in my hairclip, and then rummaged through my dresser until I found the bottle of massage oil. I held it up so Raikidan could see. "I figured since you need to be uncomfortably close to me, and you haven't had your back worked on since the first time I did it for you, I could kill two birds with one stone."

Raikidan looked uncertain. "I don't know if that'd be a good idea."

"I'll only get your back," I said. "Since you aren't facing me, nothing surprising can happen."

"And after the massage?" he asked. "You can't do that all night."

"We'll think of something when we get to that point."

Raikidan thought about the option and then nodded. He removed his shirt and lay down on his stomach, folding his arm under his chest to rest on them. I climbed onto the bed and seated myself over him before pouring the massage oil into my hand and going to work. But as before, Raikidan made my job difficult.

"Raikidan," I said in a quiet voice. "Please relax. This is difficult with you so tense."

"I know, I'm sorry. I'm just worried if I relax too much, something bad will happen."

I pushed my hands up his spine and then crossed my arms when I reached his shoulders and leaned on him. "I trust things will be fine."

He glanced up at me and I smiled. Even though his action before had me all out of sorts, I felt fine now. No awkwardness in the least, even as I leaned on him like this. *On the contrary; this makes me feel rather confident. But why?*

Raikidan exhaled and relaxed slowly. I pulled away, my hands gliding over his skin and his muscles reacting in turn. I then went to working on specific muscle groups and paid attention to Raikidan's reaction to his pampering. Most of the time he sighed contentedly, but occasionally he'd grunt if I did something to cause him discomfort.

Abruptly, as I was using my arms to put a bit more pressure on a portion of his back, my door flew open and Ryoko came in. "Laz, we're back and need to"—she spun on her heels—"never mind. Debrief can wait."

Raikidan and I laughed when the door shut behind her.

"I didn't expect that kind of reaction from her," Raikidan said. "She left without a fight. Not even some sort of tease."

"In her own way, it was a tease," I said.

Raikidan shook his head and then glanced up at me. "I think I've had enough of this massage. As much as I enjoy this, I can tell you're running out of areas to work on."

"All right." I pulled away and placed the bottle of oil on my nightstand. As I did, I went over the next course of action of dealing with Raikidan's issue. While I had been giving him the massage, I ran a few thoughts through my head, trying to come up with the best one to satisfy the pull he experienced, as well as keeping things from getting too weird. The best idea I had, would fulfill the first requirement, but the second was a bit iffy.

I'll do it. I had to. He did so much for me, I needed to suck it up and do this for him. *It's not as if he's acting like this because he feels this way about me...*

I climbed off him, and before he could say anything, I lay next to him, crossing my arms and laying them on his shoulder and back, using them as a pillow.

"Eira?"

"Is this okay?" I asked. "I thought we could lay here until things went back to normal."

"Yes, this is perfect."

Minutes passed and the two of us lay next to each other until the fire escape creaked. I pulled away to look out my window and Raikidan started to growl. At first, they were Draconic words. But then, they changed to irritated, wordless growls.

"Corliss, is that you?" I asked.

"Yes."

"It'd be best if you came back later," I said.

"I gathered that from Raikidan's unneeded hostility," he said. "Are you going to be okay?"

"I'm fine. Don't worry."

"All right, but if you need another dragon to set him straight, yell."

I chuckled as he headed back up to the roof and then flicked my gaze to Raikidan. "Did you have to be so rude to him?"

"Yes."

I shook my head and lay back down, but this time, I repositioned myself since my neck had started hurting with the last position. My new position had one arm stretched out over his back and my head resting directly on the back of his shoulder, while my other arm folded with his. Raikidan mumbled something about liking this change and no weird actions came from him. Me, on the other hand, that was a different story.

As we lay like this, my thumb on his back began rubbing his skin, and then before I knew it, my hand moved until I could play with his hair or rub the back of his neck. *Eira, watch yourself.* I knew I shouldn't do this—it was wrong to do, but I couldn't get myself to stop. The action soothed me—made me feel a little less alone. Of course I knew that was wrong. *Nothing can come of this. I need to get myself under control.* But no matter how much I struggled mentally, I couldn't get my body to listen. *I like being this close to someone... even though it's the wrong someone...*

"This satisfies it," Raikidan murmured sleepily.

"Good."

Raikidan's eyes hooded and his muscles loosened more as I continued to stroke his head and neck. Before I knew it, he was asleep—or, appeared to be asleep. Being a dragon, he would have shifted to his natural state had he fallen asleep. This was something else.

"You put him in a trance," Corliss' hushed voice said. "Nice job." I tried to turn and look at him, but he stopped me. "Whatever you do, don't stop. The moment you do, you'll break the trance, and since he doesn't want me in here, we'll have some issues."

I kept up with my action. "Thanks for the warning."

"I'm curious what got him in this state to begin with."

I bit my lip and my cheeks warmed as embarrassment flooded over me. "I made the mistake of sharing food with him again. I know what it means for you guys to share, and at first I was hesitant, but since nothing went wrong the last time we shared food, I didn't see how it'd go wrong this time. Turns out, it could go very wrong."

"You did nothing wrong," Raikidan said, his voice breathy. "It was my fault."

"Hmm, looks like he wasn't in as deep a trance as I thought," Corliss said.

I hushed Raikidan. "Rest."

"Who else is here?" He began to stir. "Corliss, I told you to get away."

"Raikidan, stop," I said. "We're just talking."

"No."

I flicked his ear. "Regardless of what state of mind you're in, you don't order me around like you own me, got it?"

A serpent-like hiss escaped his lips and I pinched his ear. The hiss stopped and he glowered at me. I met his gaze and eventually he lowered his eyes in submission. With a triumphant smile, I pulled away so I could sit up, but Raikidan didn't like that. He reached out and hooked his arm around my waist. I squeaked when he pulled me down. My heart's pace quickened as he held me captive against his muscular chest.

"R–Raikidan, this is n–not okay," I managed.

"*Mine,*" he murmured in Draconic.

Oh, this is really not good. It didn't matter if there was a dual meaning to that word. I knew what it meant in his current state. I tried to squirm away, but Raikidan's grip tightened. Corliss snickered.

"Shut it, peanut gallery," I warned. Unfortunately, acknowledging Corliss only triggered Raikidan to further tightening his grip. "Rai-kidan, please let go."

"No…"

I struggled against him more and managed to free an arm and scoot my body a little closer to my headboard. Raikidan held on tighter. "I'm not leaving. I want to sit up."

"No."

I let out an exasperated breath and fought more, but only resulted in having the front of my tank top pulled down far lower than I would have liked. I struggled to fix that as the two dragons chuckled. *I should have worn a T-shirt.* "Not, funny…"

"Silly human," Raikidan said. "If you're too busy worrying about your clothes, you're never getting away."

"I told you, I'm not trying to get away."

"You're just saying that so you can get escape."

I let out an exasperated sigh. This was getting me nowhere.

"I'm surprised you're not making any comments." The voice had been uncharacteristically quiet for this event.

"Oh, you did this to yourself, and I'm enjoying every minute of it."

Of course she'd enjoy my torment. And it looks like I'm acknowledging this voice as a real entity now. The voice always sounded like a woman, but since I had associated it to be a part of me, I had never thought it strange, until my talk with her the other day. Whoever and whatever this entity was, I suspected I'd never be rid of her if I'd been stuck with her this long. I had to discover more about her. In time.

An idea came to me dealing with Raikidan. It would be rather embarrassing, but this whole situation was, so I might as well go with it.

I wrestled against Raikidan's grip until I managed to free my other arm. Displeased, Raikidan held on even tighter. I sighed. *He's something else…* Squirming to test the tightness of his hold, I found it loose enough for me to turn my body so I faced him. This took him by surprise, but this was nothing.

Taking a brave, quiet breath, I wrapped my arms around his head and shoved his face into my chest. He froze and Corliss couldn't stop himself from laughing. My ears and cheeks burned hot and the feeling grew worse when Corliss left up the fire escape to continue laughing.

Raikidan's grip didn't loosen like I hoped, so I stroked the side of his head in an attempt to send him back into a trance. As luck would have it, it wasn't long before he snuggled up to me more and lulled into the sleep-like trance. I continue to stroke his temple until I was sure I'd have enough time to move, and then sat up.

Raikidan's trance broke instantly and he latched onto my lower body for dear life. "Don't leave!"

His plea was filled with so much distress, it hurt. "Raikidan, I'm not leaving. I just wanted to sit up."

"Lay back down," he mumbled. "Was better that way…"

I shook my head. "I'm sitting up right now."

He grumbled but gave in and rested his head on my lap while he held onto my lower body. I stroked his head again, and it sent him back into a trance. *He's something else.*

When I was sure Raikidan was in a deeper trance, I shifted my gaze toward my window to find Corliss had returned and taken a seat on the windowsill.

"I apologize for laughing," he said. "But to be clear, I wasn't laughing at you. I never thought in my life I'd ever see my cousin like this, or have that kind of move pulled on him."

"Don't lie, you were laughing at me too."

He grinned. "Okay, maybe a little. It took me by surprise."

I looked down at Raikidan. "You're not the only one."

"You're handling this very well," Corliss said. "I'm impressed."

"He's helped me a lot, so the least I could do is put up with this. It was my fault to begin with."

"That's not what I mean. His actions are extreme for something as simple as food sharing."

My brow rose. "Come again?"

Corliss smiled. "Well, food sharing is a big deal to us, but when it's family, it doesn't cause us to go nuts. Sharing with non-family causes confusion, though usually our heads stay on. Raikidan's, as you can see, isn't."

"Wait, you said 'usually.' What do you mean by that?"

"You sure you want to know?"

My eyes narrowed. "Don't do that. You started telling me, now you'd better finish."

He smirked. "All right, you asked for it. Those who go a bit overboard usually do so around their unclaimed mates or a dragon they're so close to, they might as well be mated with—or in this case, a human."

I pointed a finger at him. "Don't you dare go there."

He held up his hands. "You wanted to know. We struggle to keep ourselves under control around our mates, especially when we're not mated yet."

"A, not going to happen, and B, not like that."

Corliss grinned. "You two are too stubborn. You both might as well admit it. We all see it, and I know you two do as well. You just like lying to yourself."

"Go screw your mate."

He chuckled. "Already planning on it."

I pointed at the window. "Get out."

He grinned but left without a fuss. I gazed down at Raikidan. Was Corliss right? *Of course he's not, Eira, don't be stupid.*

I stopped stroking Raikidan's head, figuring he had spent enough time in his trance, and his eyes fluttered.

"You feeling any better?" I asked.

He glanced up at me. "Yes. My instinct's pull is still strong, but not as bad. Thank you for putting up with me."

I smiled. "You're welcome. Anything I can do more for you?"

Raikidan stared up at me for a while longer in silence before speaking, "Would you lie next to me?"

"Sure."

I scooted down the bed a bit so we'd be at eye level with each other and then lay next to him. Raikidan smiled and rested his hand on my shoulder. We gazed into each other's eyes, time slipping away. The deep blue—the attentive nature—the softness of his gaze—I couldn't look away.

His hand left my shoulder and found my cheek. My hand found his, but I didn't stop his thumb from caressing my skin. I should have, I knew it wasn't right to allow it to happen, but I didn't want him to stop. Then, before I knew it, he leaned closer and his warm lips touched mine. Shock rippled through me, but I couldn't find the strength to want to stop him.

My lips parted and accepted the embrace. Seconds, or maybe it was minutes, passed, before Raikidan suddenly pulled away and put a few inches between us. "I—I'm sorry. I said this wouldn't go that far. I—"

I reached out and placed a finger on his mouth. "On a normal day, I'd smack you. But due to the circumstances, I'm not going to." My gaze faltered and my cheeks warmed. "And I can't say it wasn't a pleasant experience."

"Really?"

"Yeah…" I tried to look at him but failed. "I guess."

Raikidan pushed himself over to me, taking me by surprise, and claimed my lips again. The momentum sent me on my back with him hovering over me. My heart raced, heat seared my body, and his intoxicating scent numbed me to any thoughts of reasoning. It only lasted a moment.

Our lips parted again and he rested himself beside me, his head on my chest, and his arms pulling me closer. "Thank you."

Flushed face and swimming head, I could only rest my hand on his head. My thumb caressing his temple and he relaxed even more into me. I stared up at the ceiling. *What just happened?*

"Wow," the voice almost sounded breathless, like I felt. *"He's good."*

"I like the sound of your heartbeat," Raikidan murmured. "It's so beautiful… like you."

More heat spread through me. *He doesn't mean that… right?* Raikidan snuggled into me more. *Maybe he does.*

I wondered if there was some truth to Corliss' words. *Is there some truth in Ambrose's accusations too?* No, I didn't steal Raikidan's heart. But even if I had, and he did, for some crazy reason, care for me that deeply, it wouldn't matter. Raikidan belonged to someone else, and dragons and humans couldn't be. I couldn't make him happy in the long run. I knew that, and that's just how it was. Once Raikidan's instincts calmed down, things would go back to the way they were supposed to. I just had to wait out the rest of the day.

I smiled and looked at Raikidan as I stroked his head. *But until then, I can let myself enjoy this a little.*

CHAPTER 38

A yawn escaped my lips as I rubbed my eyes. I hadn't slept well at all, but it wasn't because of the usual issues. The temperature had plummeted, and the house heater decided not to kick on, but I was too stubborn to go under my blankets. Raikidan, on the other hand, had slept so well that tripping over his face didn't even stir him.

After the incident the other day, things had gone back to normal for us. Well, sort of—as normal as it could be after the line we had crossed. I broached the subject to make sure he was okay. Heck, who was I kidding? I brought it up because I couldn't quite get it out of my mind. Raikidan went out his way to apologize, and make certain we hadn't damaged our friendship. I assured him we hadn't, but even as I spoke those words, I feared it hadn't been the truth.

My fingers grazed my lips. *I can't forget—Get a hold of yourself, Eira! It was just a kiss. You've been kissed before, it's no big deal.*

The voice inside my head chuckled. *"Yeah, right. You keep telling yourself that. We both know you crossed the line I warned you about. Now you're reaping the consequences."*

She was right, I knew better. I caught myself touching my lips again. *But that feeling... that look he gave me...* It'd been so long since—

I sat up when someone pounded on my bedroom door. "Laz,

Raikidan, wake up!" Ryoko shouted as she pounded on the door again when she didn't receive an answer right away. She tried to open the door, but Raikidan, who was still fast asleep, was in the way. "Raikidan, wake up and move your fat ass!"

I chuckled. "Hold on, Ryo. Let me wake him up."

She huffed but waited. Sliding off my bed, I walked over to Raikidan and patted his nose. "Raikidan, wake up." He didn't respond. I patted him again and then tried to shake his large head as best as I could. "C'mon, Rai, wake up." When he still didn't respond, I growled in aggravation and punched his nose. "Raikidan, wake the hell up, you stupid lizard!"

Raikidan snorted and jolted awake. He peered up at me with groggy eyes and then attempted to go back to sleep.

"Wake up!" I said. "Ryoko needs to get in."

He exhaled and shifted. He looked exhausted. He stumbled over to my bed and flopped down on it. I raised a brow and stared at him. This was not like him at all.

Ryoko burst through the door and nearly barreled me over. She went to speak, but then noticed Raikidan. Her face contorted. "What's with him?"

I shrugged. "Your guess is as good as mine."

"Okay. Whatever." She started bouncing. "Look outside!"

My brow rose. "Um, okay." I figured I'd at least humor her, so I made my way over to the window. Peering out, I blinked in surprise at the sight of white stuff falling from the sky. "Is that—"

"It's snowing!" she squealed. "Get dressed, so we can—"

My synthetic armor cloth changed into winter weather wear before she had a chance to finish. She squealed more and barreled out of my room, nearly knocking Rylan on his face.

She giggled. "Oops, sorry."

Rylan only laughed and handed her a jacket and gloves. "You're going to want these if you're going outside." She smiled her thanks and threw them on. Rylan turned his focus on me, then furrowed his brow. "Where's Raikidan? He's going to miss out on the fun."

I pointed behind me after I fixed my unruly bedhead. "Sleeping beauty is hibernating, I think."

"That's a pretty good way to sum it up." I shifted my gaze to the hallway where Corliss stood. He rubbed his bleary eyes, with Mana trying to wake up behind him. "We're a bit sluggish during the winter. Raikidan has a habit of sleeping through most of it."

I snorted. "Well, I hope he doesn't plan on sleeping through the winter while he's still living here. He's going to be in for a rude awakening otherwise."

"If it's like the rude awakening you just gave me this morning, I'll be ready." I turned around to see Raikidan rubbing his face.

I grunted. "Trust me, that was nothing."

Ryoko groaned. "Who cares? Let's go outside! It's been snowing like crazy since early this morning. There's bound to be a ton on the ground!"

Before I had a chance to think about the possible accumulation, she grabbed me by the arm and yanked me down the stairs. Letting go as she opened the door, Ryoko jumped into the snow. It was only a few inches deep, but she jumped around in it like a child seeing it for the first time, and I couldn't help but laugh.

Moving away from her and bending down, I scooped up a handful of snow and packed it together—glad it was a wet snow. Grinning, I threw the snowball at her and nailed her in the back of the head. Ryoko yelped and spun around. She glared at me as I laughed. But in my laughter, I forgot to pay attention to her, and missed the chance to block the snowball that flew at me.

The two of us laughed and prepared another snowball just as Rylan opened the door and stepped out. Rylan blinked in confusion when the two of us grinned and he barely had time to shield himself from the flying snowballs.

He chuckled. "All right then, have it your way."

Bending down and packing a snowball, he threw it at Ryoko. She squealed and dove out of the way. I bolted and slid behind a car parked on the street for cover. Packing up a few snowballs first, I peered around the car to see Rylan and Ryoko going at it.

"Get them while they're distracted."

Grinning, I pelted them with my stocked ammunition. Unfortunately, my attack opened me to retaliation, and I had to duck down and re-arm myself.

When I peeked around again to figure out who would be the easiest target, I spotted Blaze taking his first steps outside. I smirked when the others took notice, too, and readied themselves. I wasn't going to be left out on this, so I packed my snowball extra tight and pelted it at him.

"Shit!" he yelped as he balled up in an attempt to shield himself.

The three of us laughed and went back to our three-on-three fight. Argus joined us in time, allowing Blaze to feel a little more confident about taking us on, and it wasn't long before the dragon trio became curious about our "strange" choice in activity. Raikidan enjoyed watching us act like fools, as he put it, and Mana, of course, wanted to join in only moments after watching us. It took a few tries for her to get the concept of making the snowball, but once she'd gotten it, she was good. She had a good arm, and managed to nail the guys a few times while practicing.

Corliss, on the other hand, wasn't as thrilled out about our game. To his credit, I could see why. It was oddly easy for me to see through his eyes and how he viewed this. The game was competitive, and to an outsider, rather violent. A big no-no for dragon females. But Mana didn't care what he thought. She enjoyed herself regardless.

"Good for her."

I stopped participating when I caught a brief glance of Mocha watching us before retreating from the window. Ryoko also took notice, which caught everyone's attention in a snowballing effect.

"Why won't she come out here?" Mana asked. "It looks like she wants to."

"Because she doesn't look like us," I said. "She sticks out, and it tends to lead to unwanted attention for her."

Mana's nose scrunched. "Humans are so judgmental."

Ryoko crossed her arms. "Welcome to our world."

Ryoko got her share of comments and stares because of her ears, so she could understand, more than most, what Mocha went through.

I watched Argus head inside and cocked my head to the side. What was he up to? The others all looked at each other, hoping someone would have an answer, indicating I wasn't the only one questioning his behavior.

It wasn't long before he was back, but nothing was any different. He wasn't even carrying anything in his hands.

"All right, what did you do?" Blaze asked.

"You'll see," Argus said as he bent down and packed a snowball. Just as he finished, the door opened again and a young woman with short black hair and creamy skin poked her head out.

My brow crinkled. "Mocha?" She certainly did look similar to her, only, less cat-like.

The woman I thought was Mocha moved outside completely and eyed Argus. "Are you sure this thing isn't going to malfunction?"

"No," he admitted. "I can't be sure any of them aren't going to at one point. But they've been heavily tested, especially that one, so it shouldn't."

Mocha, okay with his answer—probably due to his honesty—relaxed and gazed around. I could only assume this was her first time outside during the day since her days in the military.

"Now think fast!" Argus called as he chucked his snowball at her.

She shrieked and ducked. The snowball sailed through the air. I doubled over with laughter when it hit its new, unsuspecting target. Raikidan wiped bits of snow off his face and shoulders and zeroed in on Argus. Argus, unsure of how Raikidan was going to react, watched him carefully.

Raikidan bent down and packed a snowball, acting far too casual for anyone's comfort, and Argus readied himself to block. I was a bit confused as I lowered myself to the ground in preparation. *He's going to throw it, he's not hiding that fact. So what is he playing at?* Suddenly he grinned and threw it, but not at Argus. The snowball smashed into the back of Corliss' head and I laughed. He was the last person I would have expected he'd throw that snowball at.

Corliss, stunned by the attack, stood still for a few moments. When the shock finally wore off, he turned on Raikidan and tackled him to the ground. The two wrestled around until Raikidan managed to get the upper hand and whitewashed Corliss. The whitewash was relentless until someone pegged Raikidan in the back of the head with a snowball.

I laughed raucously before looking to see who was the new player in this. To my surprise, I saw Mana packing another snowball. She didn't look angry that the two had been wrestling. On the contrary, a mischievous grin spread across her lips, showing she only wanted in on the fun. Just as she had her snowball ready to throw, she squealed and dove into the snow to dodge Raikidan's lunge as he tried to grab her.

Raikidan spun around with a grin and went to snatch at her again, but a snowball slammed him in the head. He stumbled and turned to face Mocha, but then was nailed again in the back of the head. I couldn't help but laugh as Ryoko made another snowball and hit him in the face this time, just as he turned around. I looked at the snowball in my hand and grinned. The snowball flew through the air and smashed into Raikidan's face just as he finished wiping away the snow from his prior attack.

I laughed when he grunted, and then more when the ladies started pelting him with snowballs. The guys hung back and made their enjoyment at his expense known, but their fun didn't last long when they started to get hit as well. I tossed another snowball at Raikidan, but he caught it and I blinked.

"Oh you're in trouble."

He grinned. "You'd better start running."

I didn't hesitate. I knew that was no idle threat. Unfortunately, I didn't make it far before he tackled me to the ground. We wrestled around and I tried to get the upper hand, but his dragon strength far outclassed my assassin nu-human build. He pinned me down, and for once, while rather uncomfortable, I was finding it hard to hate this. *Not good.*

Luckily, Ryoko was on my side and more than willing to save me. She hauled Raikidan off of me and tossed him aside before jumping on him. I didn't hesitate to grab a handful of snow and dump it on him, although it was not as effective as Ryoko's whitewashing.

Our attack stopped when a wave of snowballs assaulted us. The attack forced us to slide behind a parked car and duck down. Mocha and Mana joined us soon after. The guys had ganged up on us. Snowballs flew all over the place and before I knew it, this war had gone from a battle of the sexes to a free-for-all.

I found myself on the other side of the street and doing more dodging than throwing. I turned to take cover behind a car but was nailed in the head by a hard object, falling over from the force.

"Got you, Eira!" Mana laughed. "Um, Eira?"

"Ow..." I rubbed my head and I pulled myself to my knees. Whatever she had thrown, it had really hurt.

"Oh, did I pack that snowball too tight?"

"Yeah, I think so, that one really hurt."

"Are you sure you're okay?"

"Why aren't you calling for blood like you usually do when someone harms me?"

"Because I know she didn't mean to."

"Hasn't stopped you in the past."

"I've learned... from my... mistake."

"I'm so sorry! Let me see." Mana rushed over to me and fussed, especially after she found blood. I protested as much as I could, finding her worry charming and amusing, but she wouldn't have it. Not until Shva'sika poked her head outside.

"Mana, why don't you let me take a look at her?"

"Yeah, I guess you're right..."

Mana helped me up and insisted on following me inside. I understood she felt bad, but there was no need to be glued to me. Shva'sika sat me down and checked me over, giving me a little healing to close up the small wound. As she did, I noticed Genesis standing by one of the windows, staring out and frowning.

"What's wrong, Genesis?"

"I hate it when it snows," she said, not looking at me. "This snow is really going to hinder our progress."

I released an aggravated sigh. "Seriously? Is that all you think about? I understand that the rebellion is important, and this conflict needs to end, but you need to lighten up sometimes. Have some fun for once. It won't kill you, just like this snow won't kill our progress."

Her shoulders sagged, but she didn't reply. I frowned. *Does she know how to have fun?*

"Believe it or not, she's having trouble adjusting to this body of hers," Seda messaged. *"As a child, she couldn't do much. Her body was too young, and with her mind constantly battling two ages, it took its toll. And even after the initial age fix, it took time for her mind to adjust. Now, everything is clicking together, but she doesn't know what to do. She doesn't want to bother anyone, so doesn't say anything."*

My frown turned into a scowl, and Shva'sika and Mana exchanged confused glances. *"Seda, get me a jacket and gloves for her."*

She chuckled. *"Leader Laz to the rescue. Give me a moment."*

A minute or two passed, the room quiet, before Seda showed up with a puffy jacket, hat, and mittens. I got up and took them from her with a smile, and faced Genesis. "Okay, mopey, put these on."

Mana clapped when she realized what I was trying to do, her eyes sparkling. Genesis turned and looked at me with a cocked brow. "What?"

"You're going outside with us."

She shook her head. "Eira, I didn't mean to make it sound like I—"

I held up the articles of clothing. "Come over and put these on. Now."

"I don't"—she resigned with a heavy exhale when I gave her a hard look, and Mana came up next to me to give a pleading one—"Okay, okay."

She pulled the jacket on, and then the hat and mittens. Mana clapped excitedly and dragged Genesis to the door. We remaining ladies couldn't help but chuckle. I tried to encourage Seda and Shva'sika to join us, but they were adamant about not joining our rough snow game, both preferring to build with snow rather than get hurt by it. I accepted their reasoning and headed back outside.

As I got there, Blaze opened his big mouth to Genesis' presence. "Oh look, her highness chose to join us peasants."

I shot him an icy stare but Genesis didn't acknowledge him. She was too busy gazing around at the winter wonderland, her eyes wide with wonder. "It's beautiful out here…"

"You've never been outside when it snows?" Mana asked.

"Well, I have," Genesis responded. "But it's been some time since I went into hiding. I forgot what it was like beyond the windows."

She held out her hands and let the snow fall down onto her mittens. When a small flake landed and didn't melt immediately, she inspected it, like a child trying to see the unique shape. I grinned wickedly and scooped up an armful of snow. The guys started snickering when I crept up behind her, but by the time she noticed, it was too late. I dumped the snow all over her and she squealed.

Before she could recover, Raikidan ran over and hauled her over his shoulder and then threw her into a soft snowbank. Ryoko and Rylan fell over laughing when she screamed and complained about the cold, and I didn't last much longer when she jumped up and did a snow jig because it got into the back of her shirt and pants.

"Not funny!" she screeched. Her face twisted into a scowl when we continued to laugh at her. She scooped up some snow and tried to pack it into a snowball before pelting Raikidan with it.

It wasn't well-made, and fell apart before it hit him, but the chunks still managed to meet their mark. Raikidan turned his head and gave her a curious look and she pouted. "I've always sucked at making snowballs."

"Can you at least throw?" he asked her.

She placed her hands on her hips. "Duh."

Raikidan, skeptical, packed a snowball and handed it to her. She took it, and without hesitating, nailed Blaze in the head.

"See!" she said, proud of herself as everyone laughed at the resident playboy.

"Why did you hit me?" Blaze complained as he rubbed his head. "Raikidan was right in front of you. And Eira is the one who dumped snow on you."

"Eira is already on the ground, and Raikidan was kind enough to make me the snowball." Genesis held her head high. "You, on the other hand, decided to insult me, so as queen I punished you."

Blaze gave her a dumbfounded look, and Argus and Corliss grinned at each other. The two came up to him and restrained him.

Raikidan bowed to Genesis. "M'lady, what would you have us do to this peasant?"

She stuck her nose up and waved her hand dismissively. "Whitewash him."

Raikidan nodded to the two men; Blaze struggled and panicked, but failed to escape his punishment. The rest of us roared with laughter.

"Yes, this pleases me so."

A window opened above us and Seda stuck her head out. "I'm brewing up hot cocoa for anyone interested."

Ryoko gasped, her eyes lighting up. "With whipped cream? And sprinkles?"

Seda chuckled. "If you so desire." She face twisted in confusion. "What are you all doing to Blaze?"

I gazed up at her from where I sat. "Her highness deemed him worthy of punishment."

"Her... highness?" She started laughing. "Oh, well—if adequate punishment is required, then allow me."

She flicked her wrist for flair, and a large pile of snow lifted into the air. Corliss and Argus immediately let Blaze go and jumped out of the way.

Blaze, not realizing his new fate, breathed with relief. "Not cool, g—"

Seda dropped the snow, burying him. Those who had been standing no longer were, as their laughter took over. Genesis was the first to collect herself—around the same time Blaze unburied himself—and smiled at Seda. "Thank you, fair Seda. Your contribution is appreciated."

Seda gave a flourished bow. "Of course, your majesty."

She then pulled back into the house and closed the window. I picked myself up off the cold ground in time for Genesis to run over and hug me.

"Thank you," she whispered. "I needed this."

I smiled. "You're welcome."

She pulled away and held her head high. "But you must still be punished."

I took a step back, not knowing what to expect from her, but without her making a movement, a pile of snow fell on me. It was my turn to do the snow jig, as the snow made its way into my jacket and down the back of my shirt. The others laughed at me, but Raikidan's voice rang out the loudest as it came behind me.

"Get him!"

Once I got the snow issue taken care of, I whirled around, and without warning, launched myself at him. Taken aback, he didn't have enough time to prepare, and almost fell over. I wasn't heavy enough to take him down right away, but I grabbed a hold of his arm and yanked enough to get him down. Of course I fell with him, but it was worth it. We laughed, and Raikidan called me weird. I whitewashed him for it, and Genesis announced it pleased her.

I liked how she had been so easily pulled into the fun. She needed this, like the rest of us. The rebellion was important, but without fun, we'd lose our morale—and our effectiveness.

Raikidan wiggled out of my grasp and hauled me over his shoulder. "Okay, my face is numb enough—"

"Like your nuts?" Ryoko called out.

"Nice one."

I sputtered out a laugh, as did everyone else. Raikidan pointed at her. "Watch it, or I'll tie you to a sled and make you learn the all the proper pulling terms."

She winked at him. "Promise?"

Raikidan's brow twisted in confusion, much to Ryoko's disappointment, and my laughter increased. Only Ryoko could be that bold and have her comment go wasted on someone so clueless about human copulation.

Rylan rolled his eyes and steered Ryoko toward the house. "I think we should head inside."

"I'll second that motion," Blaze announced, his face red from all the cold. "I've had enough of the snow for one day."

"Hot chocolate time!" Ryoko cheered before running the rest of the way, Rylan barely able to keep himself upright due to her sudden disappearance.

Mana and Mocha chased after her, and it wasn't long before we were all going in to warm up, Raikidan still carrying me over his shoulder like some caveman.

"Just be glad it's not some weird mating ritual."

"Don't even joke about that." At that moment, I was glad my face was already red from the cold. I didn't need the others knowing about my little mental conversation with... whatever this voice was, and the chaotic feelings she stirred up again.

Raikidan put me down and allowed me to change into dry clothes. As I did, I noticed a cardboard box poking out from under my bed. I realized it was the carving I'd worked on for Ebon. *Oh shit, I was supposed to deliver that today.* In my fun, I had completely forgotten I had completed it last night.

"Nice going."

I finished changing and pulled the box out as Raikidan entered, carrying two mugs. "Ryoko was trying to hoard the... hot chocolate, so I got you some."

I placed the box down on my bed and accepted the mug. "I appreciate it. Everyone thinks I'm bad with chocolate, but between her and me, she's the one you have to watch out for. And when Seda makes the hot chocolate, it's even worse."

"That good?"

I nodded and sipped my drink. "I make it pretty well, one food item

I can make halfway decently, but she has a special touch that no one can beat."

Raikidan took a sip, and then another. "Well, this is my first time having anything like it, so all I can say is it's good."

I chuckled. "You were missing out."

He shrugged and I shook my head. Finishing off my hot drink, I pulled out the wooden box—it was decorated with carved ocean motifs including fish, waves, even the extinct mermaid. Hidden inside and wrapped in dark blue silk was the carving Ebon had commissioned. The piece had been my most intricately-designed one to date, having several types of sea creatures and plant life carved out of multiple selections of wood. I had never seen these creatures in person before, but thanks to a few books, I had managed.

I went about checking the clear coat of the carving, to be sure no imperfections decided to pop up last minute.

Raikidan noticed the large piece and took immediate interest. "What's that?"

"Keep it a secret, just to annoy him."

"A commission I've been working on for a while."

"You're no fun."

He came over and peered over my shoulder. "You don't take commissions."

"I do when my friend needed a little help paying for something special for his girlfriend, and the supplier he got his special something from needed something special."

He eyed me, showing he had gotten a little lost in my purposely-wordy answer. "This is for my brother?"

I nodded. "It's the super secret project I've been working on for him. Well, for his mate actually."

Raikidan's brow rose. "Nyoki?"

I shrugged. "I guess? It's a surprise for her, so I never thought to get a name, especially since he didn't want her name engraved on it."

Raikidan took the piece from me without asking, and inspected the carving. "Well, she's going to love it. Nyoki won't shut up about the ocean. Ebon let it slip with me that he recently obtained a small island for her down south. He hasn't told her yet, so he can build a few things first."

"An entire island?" I whistled low. "Man, I wish I had that kind of money."

"Well, if you focused on making more of these and your neat jewelry, and didn't help your idiot friends out, you would."

I smacked him. "He's not an idiot."

"He is when he tries to get something he can't afford."

"He could afford it." I took the carving back. "I just wanted to give him a hand. I owe him that much."

Raikidan watched me as I did yet another look over, and then stored the carving away in its custom-carved box. "Are you dropping it off to Ebon today?" I nodded. "Can I come with you?" When I cocked head in question and he shrugged. "I'd like to see him."

I smiled. "Sure. We'll head out when you're ready."

He finished his hot chocolate and collected my empty mug as well. Slipping on a dry jacket, I placed the carved box into a cardboard carrying box to keep the gift discrete, just in case, and slipped it into a backpack for extra safety. *I don't need this breaking now, of all days. Not with the solstice only days away.*

Weeks ago, Ebon had told me of the needed date. Two weeks before the solstice. I thought it was cute he wanted it for that specific date. Unfortunately, I had missed my deadline due to an issue with some of the wood I'd chosen, and it needed to be replaced. Ebon hadn't minded when I told him of the issue, but I didn't like missing my deadline. No artisan did. *Did I really just call myself that?*

"Well, that's what you are. Even if you don't do this full-time like you should."

Raikidan met me at my door, his jacket already on, and he handed me a scarf. "So you stay warm."

I smiled. "Thanks. We'll be driving, but I appreciate the thought."

Ryoko tilted her ear back from where she sat at the couch. "You two *love birds* going somewhere?"

"We who are *friends* are going to visit Raikidan's brother," I retorted. "We'll be back in a bit."

"Be safe with the snow," Rylan said. "I know you're good at driving in it, but still—"

"Yeah, *drive safe*, you two," Ryoko said with a wink.

I shook my head. "I'll *drive* the *car* safely in the snow."

She huffed, but didn't have another overly aggressive hint to throw at me.

Heading down to the garage, Raikidan and I walked to my car and jumped in. Starting it up, I typed the coordinates to Ebon's shop into my map before shifting the car into gear. I knew where the shop was, but Argus had installed the map a few days ago, and it would be best if I tested it out.

I took it easy on the roads with the snow, though Raikidan couldn't help but make snide comments every now and then. I offered to let him drive, but he quickly declined. I gave a snort of mild contempt. *That's what I thought.*

The map worked well, but glitched out a few times. I made a mental note and had Raikidan write it down in case I forgot. Roughly twenty minutes later, we arrived at Black Starlight and I pulled up into one of the snow-covered parking spaces.

Before I could grab the backpack with the delivery, Raikidan snatched it and held it protectively. My eyebrow rose, but he exited the car before he noticed my non-verbal question. I shrugged it off and joined him outside in the cold. Raikidan smiled at me and then led the way inside the rustic little shop. *Is it me, or is he acting a little strange?*

"No, he's definitely acting weird, even for him."

At least I wasn't the only one seeing it. Of course, with some weird voice or entity agreeing with me in my head, that didn't really make me feel much better.

I expected to see Ebon, or an unmanned store when we entered, but to my surprise, there was a lovely, slender woman standing behind the main display and cleaning the glass top. She had mocha skin, almond-shaped eyes, ebony hair, and piercing sapphire eyes. *This has to be Nyoki.* Neither Raikidan nor Ebon had made mention what color dragon she was, but it only made sense.

The woman looked up when the doorbell above us rang. "Can I help you? Oh, Raikidan, it's good to see you."

He nodded at her. "It's good to see you too, Nyoki." *Ah, I was right!* "We have a delivery for Ebon."

"We?" My brow rose. "You mean, I do. You're just tagging along like a little puppy."

Nyoki laughed. "Still trying to take credit from others. You never change." Raikidan snorted and the lovely woman opened a book. As she thumbed through it, her brow creased. "That's strange… I don't see that he ordered any new supplies recently. Not even from an individual. Well, no matter. I'll sign for the delivery on his behalf."

"I'm afraid I have specific instructions to only allow him to take this delivery." I couldn't risk her finding out about the surprise.

She narrowed her eyes as if she didn't believe me, and then glanced toward Raikidan suspiciously. "All right, I'll go look for him."

Nyoki disappeared behind the beaded doorways, and Raikidan leaned over to me. "Watch out. She was not pleased with that. I think you're now on her bad side."

I chuckled. "Like I couldn't see that?" His brow twisted in confusion and I shook my head. "You're so clueless."

I wandered over to a display and scanned the jewelry inside. While I had never been one to go crazy about jewelry, the pieces Ebon made always caught my eye. The style wasn't consistent, ranging from everyday styles you'd find in any jewelry shop to the style of my necklace, but they still carried tiny trademark similarities that hinted Ebon was the crafter.

"You seem to like this side of my store." I jumped at Ebon's voice. "Sorry, didn't mean to scare you."

"You're just as quiet as Raikidan," I muttered as I rose to an upright position.

He chuckled. "You might want to get your hearing checked. I wasn't being very quiet. I even ran into the wall when I greeted my little brother."

"I've told her that, too," Raikidan said.

He laughed raucously and I frowned. When he finally quieted himself down, he smiled at me. "All right, so Nyoki told me that you were here to deliver something—and she made it clear she wasn't happy with the fact that you wouldn't let her handle it."

I smirked and motioned for Raikidan to hand me the backpack. Rather than do as I requested, instead he unzipped it and pulled out the delivery. I gestured to the carrying box. "I finished last night, finally. Sorry it's so late."

Ebon's eyes sparkled. "I told you not to worry about it. You finished before the day I needed it, so it's all good."

Nyoki came from out back and tried to peer over Ebon's shoulder, but he wasn't having it. He took the box and tucked it under his arm.

"I'll go take a look at it now. I'm too curious to wait. Raikidan, can you come out back with me? I need to talk to you about something anyway."

Raikidan nodded. "Sure."

Ebon cupped Nyoki's chin. "Keep Eira company for a few minutes, would you?"

Her brow creased, offended by his request, and the two of us watched the brothers walk into the back. She took a deep breath and faced me. "So, you're Eira."

I nodded. "That would be me. For better or worse."

She chuckled. "You're exactly how Raikidan described you."

My brow rose and I leaned on the counter. "He talks about me? Hopefully nothing bad comes from his mouth."

"He won't shut up about you, like you're some obsession of his. It's cute, really."

"She's lying!" came a shout from the back.

She ignored Raikidan's call-out, and grinned. "And I can't blame him." I rolled my eyes and she laughed. "Just the response I expected. This pleases me. While strange to me, I'm glad a human can be such a good friend to him. He deserves that much."

"Well, you may rethink that when I tell you he's never told me anything about you."

She placed her hands on her hips. "That little garden snake!"

"I am not!"

The two of us laughed. She then looked me over again. "No, you're not as bad as I thought. I quite like you."

"Uh, thanks, but I'm not telling you what I delivered."

She threw up her hands. "Why not?"

"Because my lips are sworn to secrecy. You'll have to ask Ebon about it."

She crossed her arms and sulked. "It's not like him to keep secrets…"

I tried not to show the pity I felt for her. Watching Corliss and Mana, I knew it wasn't common for dragon mates to hide things from each other. Corliss struggled to keep a surprise hidden for more than a few hours.

"It's not your business to feel bad."

The two male dragons returned, Ebon looking ecstatic. "It's perfect, Eira!"

I grinned. "Good. I was going to hit you if you hated it."

Ebon was taken aback and Raikidan chuckled. "Told you."

Nyoki's eyes flicked to me, then the two men, and then back at me. She crossed her arms. "Ebon, what did you get?"

"I'll show you later," he said.

"No, now."

Ebon sighed. "Later."

She shifted her gaze to Raikidan, but he only held up his hands and ducked his head, indicating he wasn't going to get into it. She huffed and stared her mate down. A wicked idea came to my mind.

"Oh, that's evil. You should do it."

"Psst, Nyoki. Look at your beautiful self and think for a moment. Feminine wiles. You have them, use them. He is your mate, after all."

Ebon held up his hands. "Oh, c'mon, Eira. Playing both sides? That's just dirty and wrong."

I winked at him. "I'm only ever on one side—my side."

"It's usually the winning one," Raikidan added. Ebon stared at his younger brother, clearly not happy about the lack of support.

Nyoki's eyes glittered with amusement. "Oh, yes. I'm really starting to like you. Raikidan, you'd better keep her around."

"I'm liking her as well."

Raikidan chuckled in response and joined me by my side, ready to watch the show.

Nyoki cracked her knuckles and faced her mate, her posture immediately switching to a softer one and a few of her fingers lightly touching her lips. "Please tell me, Ebon."

I bit my lip. When she played, she played hard. *Ebon, you poor soul.*

"Oh, you love it."

"Every second."

Ebon stared at me in distress. "You females don't play fair!"

I smirked and spun on my heels. "Have *fun*, Ebon. It was nice seeing you again. And nice to meet you, Nyoki."

"Come by any time, sweetie," Nyoki said. "I'd like to get to know you more. Of course, make sure it's much later, after I've dealt with Ebon."

Raikidan and I both laughed while Ebon made several nervous sounds. We left the pair to sort out their issues and jumped into the car.

"You know, you're really horrible," Raikidan said. "She's going to win. He struggles saying no to her. It's the whole reason she will now have an island just for her."

"You're all so good at spoiling your partners," I said, admittedly a bit jealous.

"Yeah, well, when you care about them, you want to give them everything." I eyed him and he stammered out a defense. "T–that's what Ebon and Corliss say, at least."

"Lying piece of shit."

"Right…" I punched the coordinates of the house into the map and pulled out of the parking space. "You're reconsidering your stance on this mate business, aren't you?"

"No." He said it far too quick. I eyed his and he sighed. "All right, maybe a little. But I'm not convinced it's the right thing for me."

I chuckled. "We'll if you'd stop running from it, and actually think about it, you'd know exactly what you want."

He heaved a heavy exhale. "It's not that simple."

I gave a sidelong glance when he didn't continue. "Don't want to talk about it?"

"It's… complicated. I'm not ready to talk about it."

I nodded and focused on the road. "I'll respect that. Just know, my stance, she'd be lucky to have you."

"Yeah?"

I nodded. "Yeah."

"Well… thanks. Maybe I'll think that way, too, some day."

His response intrigued me. *Is his issue based around self-doubt?*

"Sounds like it might be. You should press more at a later time."

"Why do you want to know?"

"Sick curiosity, like you."

"Hey, Eira," Raikidan said. "Can we go to the park instead of going straight home?"

I chuckled. "Is that really why you gave me the scarf?"

His cheeks tinted a slight shade of red. "And why I tucked some gloves in my coat pocket."

I laughed. "With that kind of response, how could I say no?"

He smiled at me and I smiled back. Realizing I needed to pay attention to the road, I quickly focused on driving.

"Yeah, sure that's the reason."

"Shut up, it is."

The voice chuckled, but left me to my driving and thoughts about how nice it'd be to walk through the park with Raikidan, without an assignment looming over my head or anything weird happening between us. *Gods, please don't let anything weird happen.*

39
CHAPTER

I flipped another page of the Eternal Library book as I sat on the couch in the living room, the book continuing to read out information on ancient Elven culture in my mind. I had learned a lot about the current culture during my stay with Shva'sika and Xye, but they didn't live the same way their ancestors did millennia ago. It was fun comparing the two and figuring out how the changes happened while others remained the same.

Raikidan walked out of the kitchen and into my room. My eyes narrowed when I remembered how much of a pain he had been earlier. While speaking with Genesis about some rebellion-related task, he had tried to insist he needed my help right that moment. After arguing with him for a good five minutes, he left, but when I finished with Genesis and checked to see what he needed, he had completely forgotten what it had been all about. *Sometimes I wonder about him...*

"He's a man who has more brawn than brains. What's there to wonder?"

Shva'sika walked into the living room and made her way over to me. From the look in her eye, I could tell she had something to speak to me about, so I closed the book. But just as she sat down, someone knocked on the front door.

"I got it," Ryoko offered, leaving her spot at the bar in the kitchen.

When Shva'sika chose to stay quiet, I knew what she wanted to talk to me about wasn't for others' ears.

"Eira, you have a visitor," Ryoko told me as she came back into the living room."

I turned back to look, and saw Zo standing by the stairs. "Oh, hi, Zo."

"Hey," he greeted. "I'd like to speak with you for a minute, if that's all right."

"Um, sure." I moved over the back of the couch to save time getting over to him. "So, what is it you want to talk to me about?"

"Well, it's more of a question than anything," he admitted. "There's a party tonight, and I'd like you to go with me. I know it's last minute, so if you have plans, I understand. I'm bad with dates and forgot about this, otherwise I would have asked you sooner."

"Don't go anywhere with the slimeball."

"Well, um…" Genesis' stare burned into my back. As much as I wanted to say no, I didn't have anything planned, and Genesis would probably want me to do some spying. "I can't think of any plans that I have, so I don't see why I can't."

Zo smirked. "Excellent. I'll pick you up at seven."

I nodded and watched him show himself out. When he was gone, I sighed and turned to face my audience.

"I thought you were going to turn him down," Genesis admitted.

"I would have if you hadn't been here," I muttered.

"Well, then it's a good thing I was here."

Shva'sika lifted a finger. "Actually… Laz, that party is what I was going to talk to you about before he showed up. The shamans were invited to that one as well."

"Nice going."

I smacked myself in the forehead. "Fantastic!"

Shva'sika frowned. "I thought you were going to turn him down. I would have said something, had I known you were going to accept."

I shook my head. "It's fine. Not your fault. We'll come up with a realistic excuse for my absence as shaman, what with me being elected as Ambassador."

She tapped a finger to her lips. "Perhaps I was too quick to worry. You're not expected to show up to all of them. It's known you're quite busy with shaman-specific matters, and the matters between the shamans and this city are not your main priority. We'll have Raikidan stay here. This will make it look a bit more believable that you're busy since he's your personal Guard, and, if Ryoko wants to, she can go in your stead as a shaman from the tribe."

Ryoko squealed. "Of course I will! I love pretending to be you guys. It's fun."

We laughed at her enthusiasm. At least someone was going to enjoy the night. Me, on the other hand, I definitely wasn't going to, and I had a feeling Raikidan was going to be quite unhappy, too. He acted strange when Zo was around or came up in conversations.

I sighed and motioned to Ryoko to follow. "I'm going to need your help."

Her nose scrunched. "Why? It's a party date with Zo. It's not like you wanna look your best like you do when you're with Raikidan."

"I still want to look presentable, and I'm a lost cause when it comes to dresses and shoes."

Ryoko nodded. "True. Guess it's time for us to play dress-up."

I twirled my finger around in fake enthusiasm. "Whoopee."

She laughed before hooking her arm into mine and leading me into my room.

I brushed my bangs out of my eyes before taking Zo's offered hand. He grinned at me as he led me to the limousine. Just as I went to climb in, I noticed Raikidan watching from the living room window. The cocky grin Zo gave Raikidan, and Raikidan's scowled response, didn't escape my eye. I suppressed a sigh and climbed into the car. *Why me?*

"Is that you acknowledging something?" the voice teased.

"No, of course not."

"You can't lie to me."

"It's not like that between us…"

"But you want it to be."

"Doesn't matter what I want…"

I found an area of seating that was empty and away from the other occupants, and stared out the window. Zo slipped in next to me and snaked his arm around the back of the seat, although I didn't pay him any mind. The city was more exciting than him, and I didn't need to encourage any unwanted behavior.

The car ride had started off quiet, but it hadn't stayed that way. I refrained from engaging in most conversations, only answering direct questions.

I internally sighed in relief when the car pulled up to our destination. I could tell by the landscaping, before even looking at the building, it was the same location they had hosted parties in the past. At least they were consistent. It made me think we could predict what the military did every once in a while.

Zo helped me out of the car and led me up the steps. When I tripped for the second time, he grinned. "I could carry you the rest of the way."

Of course you would offer to do that. I put on a fake smile. "No, it's all right. I'm just not used to walking in heels this big."

Zo chuckled. "You're pretty tall as it is. I'm surprised you're wearing them."

"When it comes to fashion, you don't fight Ryoko on what may be right or wrong. You're never going to win."

"I'll take your word for it."

We finally made it to the doors, after I nearly killed myself another two times, and Zo wasted no time grouping up with his comrades. They joked around and tried so show off in front of their dates, Zo being the worst culprit, making it difficult for me to stay invisible.

"He's so… weird."

My attention left the group's conversation in intervals, my eyes wandering around. Small packs of shamans arrived and began to mingle about. From the styles of the cloaks, most appeared to be from the North and East tribes, and I began to wonder who would be showing up. Since I wasn't here as a shaman, Shva'sika had never told me who to expect to be here.

One of the soldiers chuckled. "Looks like Talon and his village girl have finally shown up."

"Oh, this better not be going where I think it's going."

"I don't see how he can actually like hanging around them," another said. "They're nothing but primitive savages."

"Wrong thing to say."

"The only primitive savage I see is the idiot standing in front of me," I spat. I was not going to stay quiet while he insulted them.

The soldier blinked. "Excuse me?"

"Drop them off in the middle of nowhere with nothing but their clothes, and they could make it without an issue. Throw you in the same situation and you'd be dead in a matter of days. You have no idea what it means to truly live."

"How dar—"

"Take it easy, Eira," Zo tried to calm. "He's not insulting you."

"I lived like them! I lived in a village that survived off the land, with its own customs that are far different than this city, that would come across as primitive or savage. How am I not supposed to take insult to his comment?"

Zo held up his hands defensively and tried his best to think of something to say back, but before he could, I stormed away.

"Zo, I'm sorry," the soldier said. "I didn't know she wasn't from around here. She sure does know how to blend in."

"Yeah, well, 'sorry' doesn't rectify this situation," Zo said. "Now I have to go chase her down and hope she doesn't want to leave."

I searched for a place to seclude myself so I could calm down. I wished I could have beaten him up. Being a commander in the military gave such privileges, but I wasn't a commander anymore. I was a fugitive; an outcast who hid in the shadows. He could say what he wanted in front of me and get away with it, because there was nothing I could do.

"There's always something you can do."

"Eira, hold on," Zo called to me.

I sighed and came to a halt so he could catch up. He'd follow me if I didn't. "What?"

"Hey, calm down," he pressed. "He didn't intend to insult you."

"That doesn't matter, Zo. He was still insulting someone, and had I not said anything, you would have encouraged it, which you actually did by telling me to 'take it easy'!" Zo backed up a little bit and appeared a little worried, as if he had an idea of where this was going. "I thought you were above that. I thought you were better, but I guess I was wrong. I don't like people who are two-faced."

I turned and stalked off again. Now maybe I could be free of him for good. There was no way he'd be able to change that side of him.

The voice in my head, however, had a different opinion. *"Anyone can change. You have."*

"Not really."

"Oh, yes you have. Think about it. You're constantly battling with yourself over some male who manages to get you to genuinely smile. You're not as adamant about you not having emotions to protect yourself. That's not the old you."

"Yeah, maybe you're right."

"Oh boy, looks like someone has angered our little chickadee." I rolled my eyes, a slight smile on my lips giving me away. I turned around as Zane came up and took my hands so he could spin me.

"So who was stupid enough to piss you off this early into the night?" Argus asked.

"Yeah." Blaze pounded his fist together. "Whoever it is, I'll give him a good wallop or two."

"Please do, Blaze. I'd enjoy it."

I laughed. "Don't worry about it, guys. It's nothing that you three need to worry yourselves over."

"Oh, c'mon! You can't say you wouldn't love to see Blaze make Zo's ugly mug prettier."

"Zo isn't ugly, though. Just... a creep."

Seda, disguised as her psychic alter-ego, Crystal, wrapped her arms around me. "You sure? I don't mind throwing someone over the balcony."

I laughed some more. "No, it's fine. I especially don't want to get you into trouble, Crystal."

She shrugged. "It'd be worth it."

I chuckled again and shook my head. My better mood soured again when Zo showed back up.

"Well, based on Eira's reaction, I would say you're the problem, Zo," Argus said.

"I told you to stay out of it," I muttered.

Argus crossed his arms, but showed no signs of wanting to be friendly with him.

"Cheer up, Chickadee. You're supposed to be having fun," Zane tried to encourage. Unfortunately, he chose to mess up my hair.

"Zane!" I shrieked. "It took Ryoko thirty minutes to get it the way she wanted, and now you've gone and messed it up."

Zane held up his hands. "I'm sorry! I didn't think you'd mind."

"I mind because I had to sit still for that long against my will," I muttered as I fussed with my hair. Unfortunately, I wasn't succeeding in fixing it. I had a feeling I was making it worse.

"Dear, let me help you." I blinked at the familiar voice and feminine touch as she helped me with my hair.

When she was done, I turned and faced Shva'sika. "Thank you."

She smiled. "You're welcome."

Ryoko and Rylan also appeared, and the three struck up conversation. Zo acted eager to talk to them, as if he genuinely wanted to strike up conversation, but I knew his game. He was just trying to get me back on his side. Therefore, I stayed out of the conversation, to let him believe I was still in a foul mood. It also made it easier to pay attention to others in the room. It wasn't like I was here on leisure.

Shva'sika stopped her conversation short when someone approached us. I did my best not to react when I realized it was Raikidan. He wore a new style of guard clothes Shva'sika has made for him for the winter months, and because it was so new, I hadn't recognized him at first.

What is he doing here? I stressed the importance to him the need to stay at the house. I kept my mouth shut, but Shva'sika surprised me when she didn't act shocked by his presence. *Did she tell him to come after I left?* No, that didn't make sense. She was the one who suggested he stay.

Shva'sika wagged her finger at him. "You're late."

Raikidan grunted. "Don't blame me. Laz'shika was being stubborn and uncooperative, like usual."

Thanks, Raikidan. I'll remember that when we get home.

Shva'sika crossed her arms. "Well, it's her fault she couldn't be here. If she hadn't been so reckless with her training, then she wouldn't have broken her leg."

My eyes widened. "A broken leg can be pretty serious. Is she going to be okay?"

"Oh, don't worry, dear," she assured. "Once her pride heals, she'll let a healer take care of her and she'll be back on her feet doing something crazy again in no time."

I giggled. "She sounds like an interesting person."

"Interesting?" Raikidan snorted. "Interesting doesn't begin to cut it with her."

Shva'sika pointed at him. "I'm going to tell her you said that."

Raikidan crossed his arms. "As if she wouldn't expect me to say that."

Shva'sika giggled. "One of these days, you're going to get in over your head with her, and I'm just going to stand and laugh as you fail to get out of it."

Raikidan snorted, and I laughed. It was interesting, and fun, interacting with them like this.

Raikidan turned his gaze my way as if finding interest in me. "Were do you come from? You hold yourself differently."

My brow rose. "What?"

"Ignore the last part," Shva'sika said. "He's known for saying strange things."

Raikidan frowned, and I laughed. "I'm from the northwest region. I lived in a small village, at the base of a mountain I can't remember the name of."

"How can you not know the name?" Raikidan asked.

"I had an accident about three years ago, and lost a large part of my memory. I left the area soon after that, giving me no time to relearn."

"Oh, you poor dear," Shva'sika fussed.

"But why not stay there to remember?" Raikidan asked.

"It's... complicated."

Raikidan nodded and didn't press, as I had trained him. I glanced up when some of the lights dimmed, and then soft music followed. Argus led Seda away, and it wasn't long before Zane asked Shva'sika. Our large group was now much smaller, and it made me uncomfortable because I knew Zo was planning on asking me to dance.

Raikidan offered me his hand. "May I?"

I tittered. "I don't think that would be a very good idea. I have two left feet."

Raikidan flashed me an alluring grin. "I have two right, perfect match."

"Couldn't hurt. Would get you away from Zo."

"Well, with an answer like that, how can I refuse?"

I accepted his hand and he led me to the dance floor. I made sure to glance at Zo to see how he'd react, and I wasn't disappointed. He wasn't happy in the least. *He only has himself to blame.*

Raikidan held me gently as he led me around the dance floor. "It looked like you could use some time away from your date."

I let out a slow breath. "Yes, thank you."

"What did he do? You looked pretty angry."

"Usual stuff. I hate having to put up with it."

"Then end it so you don't have to."

I pressed my lips together. I couldn't do that. At least, not yet. I had a job to do, and until I got enough information from him, or he put me at risk, I needed to continue doing this.

"It's not worth it."

Raikidan didn't speak again until we were out of earshot of most people. "Eira, are you angry at me for not listening, and coming here against your wishes?"

I blinked. "No, I'm not angry. I half expected you not to listen."

"All right."

"Why are you here anyway?"

He didn't get a chance to answer as we came into earshot of other couples. I sighed, and then scowled, when Zo strolled up and tried to cut in. Raikidan allowed him to take me, but I wasn't as willing, at least, mentally I wasn't. I didn't put up a fuss when Zo took me in his arms, but I also didn't greet him like I should have.

"You were pretty friendly with him," Zo said when Raikidan was gone.

"Well, he's not a judgmental prick," I muttered.

He exhaled. "Eira…"

I turned my gaze away from him. I wasn't going to be the helpless little amnesia girl anymore. I was tired of playing that part and getting walked on. If I was going to have to play this game, I was making the rules.

"If you won't cease this pointless assignment, then I suppose I can go along with this reasoning."

The song ended, and thankfully, so did our dance. Zo led me off the dance floor and back toward our little group that had begun reforming, but I had no intention of stopping there. "Eira, where are you going?"

"To get something small to eat."

"All right."

I half expected him to say he was going to go with me, so I couldn't deny I was surprised when he didn't. Maybe he was getting the hint. But then again, this was Zo and he probably wasn't.

As I browsed the impressive selection of food that made my mouth water, I tuned in to the conversations around me, in hopes of catching something of interest. Unfortunately, most of it was boring and unimportant. But then again, this was a diplomatic gathering, and any hints of what was truly going on were going to be kept quiet.

I gasped when I tripped and was unable to catch myself. Luckily, someone was close enough to catch me. "Whoa, easy there. The food isn't going anywhere. No need to hurry."

I peered up at Raikidan with a sheepish smile. "Sorry. Not used to walking in heels."

He chuckled and helped me right myself. "I can tell."

Gee, thanks, Raikidan. "Well, thanks for catching me."

"Sure." I went back to surveying the food when he didn't say more. "Hey, Eira?"

"Yeah?"

"Do you really want to be here with him?"

I blinked. "What? No, of course not."

"Then why did you say yes?"

I sighed. "Raikidan, you know why."

He went to reply, but two well-dressed soldiers came up and positioned themselves on either side of me. Raikidan went about minding his own business, but that put me in a bad position. It was no accident these two did this. They wanted something.

The one to my right half-smiled as he leaned on the table. "Hey there."

"Um, hi," I replied.

"We couldn't help but notice you and Zo aren't getting along so well right now. Why don't you hang out with us for a little while instead? We're a bit more fun."

"Gross."

"Thanks, but no thanks." I went back to looking at the food.

He grabbed my arm. "Look, I don't take rejection well, so why don't you make this easy and say yes?"

I pulled my arm away. "Why don't you go jump off the balcony?"

He grasped my arm again, only tighter this time. "Don't say no."

I shoved him. "I said get lost."

"You should make him pay for his disrespect."

The soldier scowled and came at me again, but this time before he could touch me, I slapped him, which only pushed him over the edge. Luckily, just as he came at me again, Raikidan stepped in and pushed him back. "She gave you a clear answer. Back away from her."

"Get out of the way, shaman," the soldier ordered. "And mind your own business."

"I was—until you decided to get out of hand."

The other soldier went to step in, but a shaman Guard from the South Tribe came out of nowhere and stepped in, creating a shield in front of me. The soldiers' aggression continued to elevate, and Raikidan even had to shove one back to keep him away. Neither of the Guards attacked the two men, merely acting in defense when needed, which was for the best. If they had done anything aggressive, it would have reflected poorly on the shamans, even if the acts were in my defense.

Just when I thought things were about to get even worse, Zane and Blaze ran over and grabbed the two unruly soldiers. They forced the men back, and Blaze had no problem hitting one of them. The commotion drew unwanted attention, and I found myself shrinking behind Raikidan and the other Guard in an attempt to hide from their gazes.

"You should be beating the vital viscera out of them instead."

"Uh, no, I need to keep up a civilian cover."

The voice snorted. *"Not all civilians are weak—you even said it yourself. You didn't want to be seen as timid."*

"Baby steps here. Realistic ones."

When Zo finally came over to get involved, the two soldiers were quick to disappear. Unfortunately, that wasn't the end of all of this. Zane was so worked up that the moment Zo went to open his mouth to speak, he exploded. I couldn't help but stare at Zane as he yelled at Zo. I had never seen him so angry. Zo was just as taken aback by this new side of Zane. I watched as he struggled to defend himself.

While Zane was taking care of Zo, Raikidan turned to face me. "Are you all right?"

I nodded. "Yes, I'm fine, thank you. I just want to go home."

Zo sighed and rubbed his head. "Okay, I'll take you home, then."

I glared at him. "You can stay the hell away from me! I'm so sick of soldiers thinking they own everything and can do whatever they damn well please."

"I'll take you home, then," Argus offered.

I shook my head. "No, you need to stay here, and it wouldn't fair to Crystal."

"I don't mind," Seda said.

I shook my head again. "I need to take a walk and clear my head."

"Okay, I'll go get your spare clothes from the car." I looked at Argus questionably and he shrugged. "Ryoko said she had a feeling you may need them. I guess she was right."

Shva'sika held out her hand. "Come with me. I'll show you where you can change in private."

I nodded. "Thank you."

I followed her, not even giving Zo a passing glance. Ryoko filed in next to me, and we accompanied Shva'sika into a room adjacent to the main gathering hall. I plopped down in a chair with an aggravated sigh as Ryoko closed to the door behind us.

"You going to be okay?" Ryoko asked.

"Yeah, I'll be fine. I just want to get out of here," I replied.

"Genesis isn't going to be happy."

I snorted. "Like I care. There's only so much I'll put up with. I'm about ready to tell Zo to go jump off a bridge and end this stupid fiasco for good."

"You should."

Shva'sika giggled. "By the way he reacted when you told him he couldn't take you home, you might already have."

"Good."

Ryoko opened the door when someone rapped on it. She accepted the offered backpack, then closed it again without uttering a word. She tossed the backpack to me and I dug into it to grab the clothes inside.

"I'm glad I thought to have the boys bring those," she said. "I didn't know things would go this way, but I thought it best to be prepared for anything."

"Well I'm grateful you did," I replied. "Had you not, I'd be walking home in this dress."

Shva'sika giggled. "I doubt the boys would have let that happen. But we should leave so you can get dressed."

I nodded and waited for them to leave before changing. I stuffed my dress and shoes into the bag roughly, not caring if they were ruined. After tonight, I wanted to burn them anyway.

I opened the door to find Ryoko waiting for me. She motioned for me to follow her and so I did, following her until we reached Shva'sika and the others.

Shva'sika made a gesture toward Raikidan. "I've assigned Raikidan to accompany you home."

I was taken aback by her offer. I had not expected her to suggest that. I shook my head. "That's not necessary."

"It's late, dear. It wouldn't be safe for you to walk alone. He won't bother you, I promise."

"Look, I don't want to bother any of you. I just want to go home and clear my head."

Raikidan crossed his arms. "You don't want to argue with Shva'sika. Trust me."

I inhaled through my nose. "All right, fine."

Raikidan motioned for me to follow. Slinging my backpack over my shoulder, I complied. We were both quiet as we left the building and walked the street. I became surprised when we were far out of sight of the building and he had still yet to say anything. I know Shva'sika had said publicly that he wouldn't bother me, but that didn't mean he wouldn't when no one was around to witness our conversations.

My confusion grew when we didn't take a street I had anticipated on taking. "Raikidan where are we going? We should have gone down that street to get to the house."

"You did say you needed to clear your head, right?" he said without looking back.

"Well, yeah."

"Then follow me."

"He's acting strange…"

I sighed and did as he asked. He was up to something, and even though I wanted to go home, I did want to know what it was. Then the park came into view and I knew exactly what he was up to. *He knows me well.*

"I suppose it's not strange after all."

I took a deep breath of the crisp air as we walked deeper into the park. It was still polluted, but it was cleaner than anywhere else, thanks to the trees. Raikidan looked back at me several times but didn't say anything. He was letting me clear my head at my pace, and I was grateful.

Coming up to a bridge, I stopped and gazed out at the frozen lake. No one was here this late, thanks to the cold, making it easier for me to enjoy the quiet and clear my head.

"You're not cold, are you?" Raikidan asked as he leaned against the railing.

"No, I'm fine. How about you? This is the first time you've had a chance to try out that new outfit Shva'sika gave you, and it doesn't look too warm."

He shrugged. "It's fine. Cold doesn't affect me much."

I nudged him. "Says the guy who has a habit of sleeping through the winter."

"Quiet, you."

I laughed. "I think my head is clear enough to go home now."

"Not enough to go back to that party?"

"Don't you start. You still have to go back, and I can have Seda make sure the rest of your night isn't fun."

"Can't I stay at the house? I don't want to go back to that party."

"Then why did you show up? We told you to stay home in the first place."

He pushed away from the railing. "Let's get you home."

I blinked. *Why doesn't he want to answer that question?*

"You know why."

"It's not like that."

"How long are you going to deny this?"

"Why are you encouraging it all of a sudden?"

"Because I see what is in front of us. Denying won't change that."

"No, but it keeps me safe."

"Then why look for the answers that are already in front of your face?" I refused to answer this. *"You want to hear it from him. I know you do. You want to justify how you feel."*

"Just shut up…"

Raikidan took a direct route to the house, and we made it in record time. He didn't say anything when he left me at the front door, confusing me more. My question seemed to flip his mood for some reason. Shaking my head, I went inside. I needed to rest.

I sat up in my bed when I heard noises coming from the living room. *Party's over.* Raikidan came in and closed the door behind him, removing his hood and sighing in the process. Besides the sigh, he appeared to be in a decent mood. "How'd the rest of the party go?"

He walked around the bed and sat down. "Slow."

"Anything good happen?"

"Besides Zo getting harassed by his buddies for scaring you off, not really."

"Well at least he didn't get away with it."

Raikidan relaxed against my mountain of pillows. "Trust me, things weren't made easy on him at all."

I smiled. That made me feel a little bit better.

He rolled onto his side. "So, are you feeling better now?"

I nodded. "Much."

"Good."

The smile on my face faded when I remembered that I wanted to ask him about his reaction to my earlier question at the park. I hadn't been able to sleep like I had wanted because I was thinking about it so much.

"Raikidan, why did you show up at the party after we told you to stay here?" He didn't answer and it frustrated me. I didn't like his reluctance to talk about this. "Well?"

He sighed and avoided my gaze. "It's just... I didn't want you there with him."

My brow rose. "Okay... I figured that much on my own. B—"

"Look, I'm sorry I didn't listen. I just couldn't keep myself at the house. I tried, I really did, but I failed."

I lay on my stomach and propped myself up on my elbows. "Tell me why you have such an issue with him asking me to go. I saw the look you gave him when he picked me up, and then you were reluctant to talk to me about this at the park. I want an honest answer from you."

He lay there for a moment and then sat up, running his hand through his hair. "I... I don't like him. The way he treats you... the way that foul *thing* looks at you... I want to rip his throat out, just like I do with Zaith. I hate them equally."

"Oh, I'd love to see that. Be a good boy and do that for us."

"But tell me why."

He looked at me and held my gaze for a good thirty seconds before reaching for me. Startled, I pushed myself away, not sure what to make of his actions. He grabbed a hold of me and hauled me into his lap. My cheeks burned as he held me tight and nuzzled his face into the nape of my neck.

"Because you're my treasure. You're precious to me." Raikidan growled. "Zaith... Zo... neither understand your worth. They don't know how to care for you properly. They are not worthy."

"Where is my say in this?" I asked.

He pulled away to look at me. "Y–you want one of them?"

I leaned back in his arms, knowing full well I shouldn't. "Well, no. But I want to make sure I get a say in all this."

Raikidan's grip tightened and he rested his forehead against the back of my head. "Of course you do. You get the final say, but that doesn't mean I'm not going to look out for your best interests."

"For once... I don't doubt his words."

"Thank you." Even though I didn't believe for a second I'd be worthy enough for a perfect match, I did appreciate him looking out for me.

Raikidan inhaled deeply. "You smell good."

My cheeks burned a bit. "Uh, thank you?"

He chuckled. "It's a good thing. Scent is important to a dragon. It tells us a lot."

"Like?"

"Like, the last time you showered." He laughed when I smacked him in the arm. "I can tell where you've been, who you've been with, who you're often around, and even tell your mated status, as difficult as that is with humans."

"That I don't believe."

"You can't determine all that, you liar."

He chuckled. "Okay, maybe I exaggerated a bit, but not all, and you know it, since, even though you're human, as a nu-human you have a very good sense of smell."

"You're right, I do." I leaned closer to him and turned half of my body so I could press my nose against his chiseled chest and inhaled deeply. "And I can tell you've been sweating a lot today."

He chuckled. "That's it?"

I inhaled again and then peeked up at him through my lashes. "You smell good, for someone who has been around a hundred or so people in the last few hours. Everything else is just the different layers of your own scent. We nu-humans are good at picking that apart when we're trained to."

Raikidan stared at me for a moment and then smiled. "All right, if that's all you smell, then so be it."

His grip on me tightened and then the two of us fell over. A pitiful squeak came from my mouth and I tried to squirm away, only to find that impossible. I did manage to untwist myself, but the end result was me facing him.

"*Treasure*," he murmured in Draconic as he exhaled into my hair again. My cheeks flushed. "Do I really have to stay like this?"

"For a little while; you can deal with it. It's not going to kill you."

I exhaled with fake exasperation and lay against him. Soon I found myself yawning and snuggling into him, Raikidan's thick musky scent blanketing me in comfort.

He rubbed my back. "Sleep. You'll always be safe as long as I'm around."

"Yes, I do believe that as truth now. That means he could possibly be…"

The voice's words trailed off as my eyes grew heavy, and soon, I was lulled into a deep sleep. *Thank you, Raikidan.*

40
CHAPTER

Seda steadied Raid as he made a desperate attempt to hang a decorative snowflake from the ceiling. The others were hanging fine, but this one just didn't want to stay up. Shva'sika, Mocha, and Azriel, who had come over for the occasion, worked together in the kitchen to finish making snacks for us to nibble on, and Genesis peeked over the arm of the couch and stared at the mound of gifts stacked in front of the TV.

I lounged on the couch and observed the activity. The winter solstice was upon us, as well as its effect on me. The searing heat of the flame in my chest burned as a mere ember, allowing my body to relax from the short reprieve. Corliss and Mana sat on the couch near Genesis, and Raikidan sat on the window sill, all three watching the activity. I wondered if they understood what was going on. By the curious looks they gave, they didn't seem to, but I couldn't be sure.

Rylan jogged into the room with a small gift in his hand and looked around, his brow furrowing. "Where's Ryoko?"

I shrugged. "I think she's still in her room. I haven't seen her all morning."

He glanced back at her room. "That's not like her. She's usually the first up on this day. I hope she's okay."

"I'm sure she's fine," I assured. "She probably was so excited she fell asleep late and hasn't woken up yet. We'll get her when everyone is here and ready."

Seda turned her head our way. "She's not asleep."

I blinked. That was odd. What could she be doing then?

Mocha left the kitchen with two mugs and handed one to me. "Figured you might want this."

"Thanks." I took the mug before she went to sit down. It pleased me to see her coming out of her room for this. Getting her to open up and trust us enough to interact had been a struggle. She had her moments, and I hoped this was a sign things were improving. I didn't want to push her too quickly.

"No, you want honey and tea," Shva'sika protested.

I glanced at my mug and its contents and then held it up. "Chocolate."

"Tea and honey," she insisted.

I held the mug up again. "Chocolate."

Rylan chuckled and sat down on the couch next to me. "I figured of all people, you'd know Laz would always choose chocolate."

Shva'sika shook her head and sipped her tea. "I do, but I always try to make her choose better."

"There is nothing better than hot chocolate." I hummed and my shoulders sagged when the warm, liquid chocolate touched my tongue. I stopped drinking when Ryoko poked her head out of her door. "There you are. What are you doing in your room?"

"Um... do you have some armor cloth I could borrow?" she asked. "I can't find mine."

The request raised some flags with me, but I wasn't going to cause a scene by inquiring further—yet. "Sure, let me go grab—"

My eyes flicked to Corliss when he handed me a piece of cloth. I tilted my head, but then noticed Raikidan as his shirt reformed. *I should have known.* Raikidan had a preference for using the synthetic armor cloth over anything... if he wore clothes at all...

Standing up, I walked over and handed it to Ryoko. She snatched the cloth and slammed the door closed.

"I know she's weird and all, but this is even strange for her," Mocha said.

I nodded a little as I came back into the living room. Leaning against the back of the couch, I sipped on my drink and waited. I suspected we'd find out what was going on pretty soon. As I waited, Azriel handed me a plate of sweets. I snatched two cookies and passed the plate off.

I looked at Ryoko's door when it opened again. She poked her head through but hesitated to come out. "Ryoko, what is up with you today?"

"I'm having an issue…"

"You're always having some sort of issue," Genesis teased.

She ventured out of her room and turned around. "Not one like this."

Azriel poked his head over the bar. "Well, that's different."

I cocked my head at the sight of the fluffy tail sticking out of her backside. "Is that… real?"

She nodded as she turned back around. "I woke up this morning and there it was. I don't know why, and I don't know how to get rid of it!"

I held up my hands. "Ryoko, calm down. It's not the end of the world."

Her fingers curled by her side. "But I need to know why. This has never happened before!"

I sighed. "Ryoko, I said calm down. You were on those pills for a long time. It's going to take time for your body to go through its changes to compensate. This may be one of those changes."

"But what if it's permanent?"

"What if it is? Would it really be the end of the world?"

Ryoko crossed her arms and shrugged. "I don't know."

I motioned for her to come into the living room as I headed to sit down. "Then don't fret over it right now. We'll figure it out later."

She released a long exhale and then nodded. I sat back down next to Rylan. Ryoko made an attempt to sit down on the couch, but struggled with getting comfortable.

Mocha set her mug down and waved Ryoko over. "Come here. I'll teach you how to do it."

Ryoko nodded and made her way over. I chuckled when I noticed Rylan staring as Mocha taught Ryoko how to tuck her tail. "Rylan, you're drooling."

Ryoko's face reddened at my comment, as did Rylan's. He glared at me. "I am not."

I grinned. "Then why is your face red?"

"Quiet."

The room echoed with laughter. I chuckled and leaned back to relax.

As I did, I noticed Raid still trying to get the decoration up. He wasn't laughing, although I wasn't too surprised. I had noticed a change in him in the past few weeks. His attempts to gain Ryoko's affection had plummeted, and his interaction with everyone in the house had also dropped. I had a sinking suspicion he was planning on leaving soon. He seemed to finally understand that Ryoko was with Rylan for the long haul, but that meant he didn't have an anchor to keep him here. He'd be wandering the streets again, and that wouldn't be good.

"Raid, just give it up," I told him. "It's not going to stay."

"It will," he insisted. "I'll make sure of it."

"It's a stupid decoration," I said. "It'll be coming down in a few days, so it's not worth it."

"I'm going to get it up there."

I rolled my eyes. "Too stubborn for your own good."

Ryoko focused on Mocha. "Hey, question. Out of curiosity, do you have real ears, too, or just cat-like ones?"

Mocha chuckled and brushed back her hair. Where ears of a human or nu-human would have been, there was nothing but flat skin and hair. "I only have the ears on the top of my head, adding to my freakish nature."

"You're not freakish."

"Says the experiment that still looks mostly human," Mocha muttered.

Raid looked at her. "You're trying to tell a bunch of freaks that you're more of a freak than them. Doesn't work very well."

I took another sip of my drink. "He's got a point."

Mocha crossed her arms and snorted. "I still stand by my prior statement."

"You don't know everything about us, Mocha," I reminded her. "There could be plenty of things we may be hiding, meaning you have more courage than any of us because you don't hide it."

"You can go outside whenever you please," she said.

"You could too, if you stopped caring what people thought of you."

Mana nodded. "And when this fighting is all over, you won't have to worry either. Things will be different."

"They don't become different overnight," Mocha said.

"No one said it would," I corrected. "It doesn't become different until you make it different."

Mocha blinked slowly as she thought about this. I leaned back to relax. I hoped the boys would be coming home soon so we could get things started. I didn't even know why they insisted on going over to the shop. It was snowing like crazy, and since this particular day was so important to most other people, no one would come to the shop for work.

I turned my attention when I heard someone opening the front door. When the sound of several footsteps rang through the hallway, I knew it was the boys.

Zane brushed the snow off his bandana while Blaze shook his head vigorously. "Well I don't suggest going outside. It's picking up out there, and I suspect it's only going to get worse."

Argus finally came up the stairs and swatted off his jacket with one hand. I watched him. He held his other hand in front of him as if he were holding something, or even hiding something.

"Or both."

My brow furrowed when his jacket moved in ways it shouldn't. "Argus, what do you have in your jacket?"

He chuckled and unzipped his jacket until a tiny kitten poked its head out. "I was hoping she'd stay calm a little longer."

Seda walked over to investigate the tiny ball of fluff that was now squirming in Argus' arms. When she held out her hands, Argus eagerly handed the kitten over and the moment Seda touched it, the kitten stopped squirming. Instead it stared at her with wide curious eyes. Seda smiled and scratched the kitten behind the ear, triggering its purring mechanism.

"You like her?" Argus asked.

Seda continued to smile. "Yes."

"Good, she's yours."

Her face lit up. "Really?"

He nodded. "Yeah."

"Thank you, Argus!"

"Hey, no gift giving until everyone is here!" Ryoko scolded. "Laz said Ryder was coming."

"I am here." Ryder poked his head into the living room. "They picked me up on the way. I couldn't come in until Argus gave Seda the cat, since I'm carrying her food."

Ryoko nodded. "Okay, I can accept that."

"Not that having Argus keep that kitten in his jacket for much longer would have been a fantastic idea to begin with," I said.

Ryoko thought this over and then nodded. "Good point."

Seda walked around the couch and sat down next to me, placing the kitten on her lap and playing with her. She was a fluffy cat with a beautiful brown, orange and white coat, long bushy tail, and crystalline eyes. Her ears were tufted, one having a small tear in it, and she had rather large paws for her size.

"Where did you get her?" I asked Argus.

He shrugged. "She just showed up at the shop the other day. She was real friendly, so I figured we could give her a home. Vet says she's healthy for a stray, and she hasn't gotten into any trouble at the shop, so I don't think she'll have an issue living here."

I grunted. "That's probably because you haven't let her in to that mess you call an office."

Zane's eyes narrowed at me. "The office isn't a mess."

Several of us looked at him pointedly and he muttered to himself. The kitten became antsy, and Seda let her wander and explore. Ryder put the bag of cat food in the kitchen and then came to sit down, as did Raid, giving up on his hopeless attempt at hanging that decoration.

Zane headed for the hallway. "I'll be right back."

Ryoko groaned. "You've made us wait this long already. Can't it wait?"

"I'll only be a minute. It won't kill you to wait a little longer."

She sighed. "Fine."

He chuckled and set a quick pace down the hall. Blaze walked over to the couch and flicked his gaze to Ryoko, his face twisting in confusion. "Why are you sitting so funny?"

Ryoko avoided eye contact. "I grew a tail."

"Really?" Typical of him, he sounded too interested, but also typical of Azriel, he smacked Blaze in the back of the head.

"I still don't know if I should be impressed by his consistency, or appalled."

Azriel placed a plate of cookies down on the coffee table and Ryoko's nose scrunched. "Please don't put those near me. I'll be tempted to eat them."

"So?" Azriel said.

"So, they'll make me fat."

"Not possible."

Ryoko glared at him and then grabbed a cookie. He chuckled and then found a place to sit down.

"You still don't look comfortable," Mocha observed as she watched Ryoko.

Ryoko shook her head. "This tail is uncomfortable. It's going to take some time to get used to it."

"Would it be such a horrible thing if it's permanent?" Mocha asked.

Ryoko shook her head. "I can't say it'd be super terrible."

"Then why were you so upset?"

"Because I'd have to modify my clothes."

Azriel chuckled. "That doesn't sound so bad."

I gave him a long look. "You've never seen her closet."

"That bad?" he asked.

"She donated seven gigantic bags of clothes a few weeks back and it didn't put a dent in her collection."

He laughed. "Okay, I can see the issue there, then."

I looked up as Zane came back into the room. In his hands he carried a small wooden statue. "Is that what I think it is?"

He grinned and showed me the wooden statue of an anthropomorphic woman that resembled the rare snow leopard species from the North Hyberia Mountains. The statue, while not ancient, did look old. "I always bring this out."

I cringed. "You still have that ugly thing? I thought it would be long gone by now. That's why I made a new one."

His eyes widened. "Where's the new one?"

"In the box under the coffee table."

Azriel reached under the table and pulled out a box. Opening it, he removed a wooden statue and placed it on top of the coffee table. Zane placed the old statue next to it, allowing everyone to compare the differences. Besides the higher quality wood, the carved woman stood taller, even in the different, more graceful position, and had an advanced carving technique used on it.

Rylan reached over and picked the two statues up. "Well I'd be lying if I said you hadn't improved in any way over these past few years."

Mana cocked her head. "Is that a carving of Solstice?"

I nodded. "You guys don't know what's going on, do you?"

She nodded. "We do, we're just not used to such commotion and extravagantly wrapped gifts."

"Dragons usually only give a gift or two to those who are closest to them," Corliss added.

"How come you guys go so crazy about it?" Mana asked.

"You know why we celebrate, yes?" I asked.

She nodded. "Yep!"

Ryoko pouted. "Darn. I wanted to tell the story."

"She's so cute."

Raikidan's eyes flicked back and forth between the dragons and us. "I'll fess up, I don't. We didn't do much with this day."

Corliss laughed. "That's right. Just about all of you would sleep through it!"

Raikidan smacked him, but this excited Ryoko and she bounced in her seat. "Yes! I get to explain after all."

She composed herself and held up her hands. *Oh boy, here we go with the dramatics.*

"When Lumaraeon was young, the four seasons we know now for certain regions weren't defined. Seasons could last from several months to several years, winter being the strongest and most prevalent season, and the people weren't happy. The change in the seasons made it difficult to live off the land."

Ryoko snatched up the statue on the table and held it up.

"Solstice, the goddess of ice and winter, and sole remaining Leocona, a naturally occurring anthropomorphic species, was happy to have the longest season. But she saw how unhappy the people where, and her kind soul couldn't handle that."

Ryoko's voice had lowered with the last sentence and she paused, both for dramatic effect, before going on with renewed excitement.

"So she spoke with Valena, the goddess of the earth, Tarin, the god of nature, Kendaria, the goddess of water, and Phyre, the god of fire, to think of a way to harmonize their wants with the people's. It was then they set up the seasons and made the climates different based on the regions of the land."

Ryoko's eyes widened and she threw her hands out into the air, almost throwing the statue by mistake.

"Solstice offered to give up a large portion of wintertime to make the people happy. For such an offer, the rest of the gods gave her the mountains to keep cold year-round. Grateful for her sacrifice, the people dedicated this day in thanks. This day wasn't randomly chosen, though. This day had always been the time where people gave gifts to encourage each other to keep going throughout the long, hard season of cold, and not to give up."

Our half-wogron friend held the statue to her chest, her large breasts nearly swallowing it. Blaze became visibly excited seeing this, but the dark look Rylan shot him ended that quickly.

"The gods chose to keep this tradition, and added to it by making this day the peak of winter. They called it the winter solstice. The sun would shine the shortest period of time, making it the darkest day of the year, before it slowly became spring and then summer. To this day we still celebrate. We give gifts to each other and we honor Solstice."

"Well, except Laz," Rylan commented.

I snorted. "Not only am I not a great gift giver, this isn't exactly my favorite time of year."

"It's a perfect time of year," he argued.

"Maybe for you, frostbutt."

"Do you want to go?"

I snorted out a cloud of smoke from my nose. "Bring it on."

Rylan blinked and then jumped to his feet. "I forgot something in my room."

The room erupted with laughter as he ran down the hall.

Shva'sika quieted her giggling down and smiled at me. "Nice bluff."

I grinned and relaxed. "Not as easy as it looked."

Ryoko cocked her head. "I'm confused."

"As Laz takes more control over her element and dives deeper into her training, the solstices affect her more and more." Shva'sika explained. "Tell me, Laz, how are you feeling?"

"Honestly, like I could sleep for days," I admitted. "I'd much rather be sleeping right now than up and doing this."

She chuckled. "Well, you can sleep after."

I fell over onto Ryder's lap and sprawled out. "Or I could sleep now."

"And I could go grab markers and draw on your face," Ryoko offered.

I glared at her and sat up. I then blinked when I noticed Raikidan staring at his feet strangely. "What's up with you?"

Mana peeked over the couch and giggled. "It's the kitten. She's rubbing against his leg."

Corliss cranked his neck over his shoulder. "What? Nothing likes him—well I'll be damned. Raikidan, it looks like we finally found a creature that isn't afraid of you."

"Wait," I said. "Raikidan said all creatures are naturally afraid of dragons. Is that not actually true?"

"Well, partially," Corliss said. "Many are hyper-aware of our dragon nature, even when shifted—particularly prey animals. But there are many others who are less wary, like predatory animals. That's why Raikidan is able to use your messenger hawk, and this kitten isn't afraid of him. Though Raikidan has an unusually high-threatening aura that tends to scare animals more than most dragons. So the fact this kitten is seeking out attention from him is rather surprising."

"Well, that explains a lot."

Mana giggled. "Raikidan, you're supposed to pet it."

Raikidan's brow creased. "How?"

She rolled a bit as she laughed. "With your hand, duh."

"Honestly, his lack of understanding is adorable."

My lip twitched, threatening to turn into a smile. *"I will agree with you on that."*

Raikidan stared at the little kitten a moment longer before reaching down to pet her. I could hear the tiny thing purring from my spot on the couch. Then the kitten suddenly scampered off, sliding just past the mountain of presents thanks to the slipperiness of the wood floor.

Rylan came back in the living room as she zipped around and tripped him. He stumbled, but caught himself. "Seda, what are you going to call that thing?"

She chuckled. "I'm still thinking on that, though I'm starting to get a few ideas from watching her."

He shook his head and set the package he carried down with the rest of the packages. The box was long, far bigger than any of the other boxes, and my curiosity about whom it was for had a tight hold on me. Unfortunately, I couldn't find the tag from where I was sitting.

"So are we going to start this or what?" Blaze asked. "I think Ryoko is going to explode if we don't."

Rylan chuckled and sat down next to Ryoko, pulling her into his lap. "We have all day."

"No we don't!" she argued. "We only have a few hours until it's nighttime."

I chuckled. "Okay then, pick out a gift, Ryoko, so we can get this started."

"The one with the red bow!"

"Ryoko, there are at least seven gifts over there with red bows." I said with an obvious lack of amusement.

"Then pick any one of those!"

Azriel chuckled and grabbed a package at random, not caring if it had a red bow or not. "This one is for you, Mocha."

Mocha blinked. "Me?"

"Well, your name is Mocha, isn't it?" Ryoko teased.

"I can't accept this. I hadn't planned for you guys to celebrate this day, let alone give me something," she said.

"You guys didn't celebrate?" I asked.

Mocha snorted. "Asix and Doppelganger are the only ones who are all buddy-buddy, so they gave each other something every year, but that's it."

"Who is Asix?" Ryoko asked.

"Oh, sorry. That's Chameleon's real name."

"And here I thought he had one of the strangest names out there. What about Doppelganger?"

"No, his real name is Doppelganger."

Ryoko cocked her head. "Huh, interesting. So, have you ever been given a gift before?"

Mocha's face scrunched. "Only if you'd consider a knuckle sandwich a gift."

Azriel held up the gift. "Then here you go, a real gift."

Mocha took the gift and stared at it for a moment before ripping the wrapping paper, revealing a plain box. After a moment of hesitation, she peered in and pulled out three small clay pots, a bag of soil, and a few packets of seeds. She examined the unmarked seed packets and her nose scrunched up. "This isn't catnip, is it?"

Shva'sika laughed. "I'm not that mean."

"Then what are they?"

"Grow them and you'll find out."

Mocha smiled and nodded her thanks. Azriel grabbed a large package and handed it to Ryoko. She squealed and wrapping paper flew everywhere as she tore into it. The squealing got louder when she opened the box. "New boots!"

"Fantastic." I rolled my eyes. "Just what she needs, more shoes."

Just then the basement door flew open and Telar entered, his hands held up. "The party has arrived."

Azriel lounged on the couch. "Sorry, but I'm already here."

The two stared at each other and then laughed. I rolled my eyes. "You two are ridiculous."

Telar pointed at me. "Watch what you say, or you won't get a gift from me."

I crossed my arms. "Fine. Your gifts aren't anything special anyway."

To my surprise, my words looked to have hurt him a bit. "Really?"

I shook my head. "I was kidding."

He relaxed. "Don't be mean to me today." He held up two small boxes. "Especially since I only had enough money for two gifts, and they're for two out of three of my favorite ladies."

The boxes levitated in the air and shot over to me and Ryoko.

"All right, I'm a favorite!" Ryoko cheered. She tore into her gift and pulled out a thick strip of paper. "Score! Spa day!"

Rylan chuckled. "You did enjoy the one you went on for your birthday."

"Spa days are the best."

I eyed Telar for a moment and then opened my gift. Inside I found a simple yet elegant amethyst pendant. I smiled as I removed it from its box. "It's lovely, Telar. Thank you."

He smiled, pleased that I liked the gift.

Shva'sika giggled and then pointed to a thin box. "Azriel, grab that one. It's for Laz."

He nodded and handed the box to me. Telar found a spot to make himself comfortable as I accepted the next present. "Oh, boy."

Rylan's brow rose. "You act as if you know what's inside."

"Well, since Shva'sika asked for this specifically, it could only be one of two things. A weird knitted sweater—"

Shva'sika pointed a finger in my direction. "I never give you those."

"They always had your name on the box."

"Xye put my name on the box and you know it!"

I chuckled. "Sure, we'll go with that if it makes you feel better." I gazed at the box. "Or something far more bizarre than a weird sweater…"

Ripping the wrapping paper, I cracked open the box on one side to peek, and shook my head at the sight of lace. *I knew it.*

"She's so predictable."

"What is it, Laz?"

I took a deep breath and held up the black and pink lace lingerie shaped like a monokini. "One of Shva'sika's famous family traditions."

The room boomed with laugher. A mix of "I can't believe she gave that!" "Is that really?" and "That's priceless" were heard through the laughter. In the past, this group reaction would have had me running for my room to hide, but things had changed. Now, I laughed with them.

I focused on Shva'sika when I got myself under control. "You surprised me with this one. Every year you picked ones with less and less material. This one might have the most coverage to date."

"There are more?" Ryoko said with disbelief.

"Twelve, to be exact," Shva'sika said. "One for each year she was with us."

Rylan shook his head. "Do I want to know why?"

"It's just a tradition in my family for women to give to each other, regardless of marital status. Some of the articles given have been quite interesting."

"Sounds like my kind of family," Telar said, a smirk tugging his lips.

"So how has it affected you, Laz?" Ryoko asked.

I snickered. "Glad you asked. Az, can you grab those six boxes in the corner with the shiny wrapping paper?"

Azriel's brow rose in question but he did as I asked. He gleaned the names on the tags and handed them out to the ladies in the room. All but Shva'sika looked at each other, and then me, concern clear in their eyes.

"Well, go on," I said.

"I'm not going to lie, I'm a bit scared," Ryoko said.

Seda chuckled as she ripped her wrapping paper. "Might as well get this over with."

The girls opened their gifts while everyone else watched on. Well, all but Shva'sika. She remained relaxed in her seat with her gift on her lap. Ryoko and Seda were the first to pull their gifts out and they laughed. Both Rylan's and Argus' faces went red at the sight of the leather teddy lingerie with breast cutouts. Mocha and Genesis were next, and were almost too embarrassed to pull their garments out of the box, but after some egging on, they did, revealing garter sets. Mana was last, and appeared confused when she pulled out the green babydoll nightgown with a bow in the center of the breasts, much like the design of the one Raikidan had picked out for me.

"I don't understand," Mana said, her innocence on clear display. "What's so crazy about this that everyone is acting weird?"

"Oh, her naïvety is so cute."

Corliss took a shaky hand and had her put the nightgown away. "I'll explain later."

I grinned, and it remained on my face as I noticed the reactions from all the men in the house. Some were shocked, some interested. Azriel was the only one laughing, completely unaffected by it all. Even Raikidan seemed conflicted, though I couldn't interpret the exact emotions he felt.

"Are you sure you want to?"

"Mom, did you really have to do this?" Ryder asked, discomfort clear in his voice.

"All of you act like you've never seen lingerie before," I teased.

"I'm trying to figure out when you ladies are going to show these off for us," Blaze said.

Mocha hit him in the head with a box. "Knock it off, you."

He chuckled. "Hey, you can't wave all of those in our faces and not expect at least one of us to want that."

"He's right," Telar said. "Eira has some good picks here. Of course, hers was rather nice, too."

"Well, for those who aren't as vocal about their desires, they just know better and stay quiet," Azriel said.

Mocha hit him with the box next, but he only laughed. I laughed, too, because I had a feeling he was close to the truth. Most of the men tried to be respectful and controlled, but this was a bit much for even them. Had the shoe been on the other foot with the ladies in their position, we'd have a nearly mirrored situation. *Though with some of the women here, I'm pretty sure it would have been a more vocal reaction.*

"I can't disagree with you there."

I glanced at Ryder and couldn't help but be amused by his awkward, embarrassed look. Poor kid was the only one really out of his element. I didn't know what he had been exposed to now that his body matched his adult age, but I had kept him hidden from a lot of things.

"Danika, how come you haven't opened your present?" Ryoko asked. She grinned. "Because I know mine is a bit different."

Everyone focused on her and she opened the box, revealing a frilly garment.

Ryoko sputtered a laugh. "What the hell is that?"

Shva'sika chuckled. "This would be Laz's counter to my gifts. She figured if she was going to get revealing clothing she'd refuse to wear, then I'd get the most conservative clothing I'd never wear." She held up the long, lavender nightgown with frilly sleeves and bib-like collar for all to see. "I present to you Laz's famous *grandma gown*; name courtesy of my brother."

Uncontrolled laughter echoed through the room. Ryder clung to me to keep himself from falling off the couch, and Ryoko wiped away her tears in vain, as they failed to stop rolling down the sides of her face. Even Mana laughed, though I could tell with her, it had more to do with the contagious nature of laughter than her understanding the joke.

"You two…" Zane pointed at Shva'sika and me as he tried to get himself under control. "You two…"

"Need to do this every year!" Azriel said through his tears. "Please. This has been the most amazing celebration yet and we haven't even gotten started."

"This trumps the ones I've had with my sister, and we get creative with the town we stay with," Telar admitted.

"I agree," Ryoko said. "This is better than the gag gifts we do."

Mocha tilted her head. "Gag gifts?"

Ryoko nodded. "Yeah. We try to make sure we get some silly presents in. Gives us all a laugh and makes sure we don't get too serious with each other and ourselves."

Mocha looked unsure. "Forgive me for being a little unsettled by the idea."

"We're not like your former team," I said. "They really are in good fun."

She didn't look convinced, but I expected as much. She needed more time to understand how this team worked compared to what she was used to. We had shown her a lot, but there was a lot of time to undo.

Zane pointed to a box with blue wrapping paper and a silver bow. "Azriel, pass that one out."

Azriel grabbed it and read the tag. "For me from... Laz and Ryoko." He glanced up at the two of us. "This should be interesting. Laz must be feeling evil—or generous—with all the gift giving."

I held my head high with crossed arms. "I said I suck at gift giving, not that I'm completely incapable of it."

He chuckled and tore into the wrapping paper, being careful not to ruin the bow. Ryoko passed me a sly grin as he opened the box. Azriel laughed and pulled a handful of flimsy books out of the box. "And to go with today's theme, lady magazines."

Most of our housemates laughed, including myself, glad Azriel was a good sport about these things.

"I'm confused," Mocha said. "What's so funny?"

"Love, I'm gay," Azriel said as he flipped through one of the magazines. "And these are not geared for gay men."

She started to giggle. "Okay, I get it."

"This is what we mean by gag gifts," I said. "Convenient one showed up so soon, but now you see how harmless they are."

She nodded. "I'll try to be open-minded tonight, then."

Ryder sat forward and pointed at the pile. "Azriel, when you're done drooling over those ladies, grab that one." Azriel chuckled and reached for a blue wrapped box with red ribbon. "No, not that one. To your left. Your other left. Yeah, that one."

Azriel tossed me a package wrapped in red paper, and I looked at Ryder funny when I caught it.

"Just open it," he said.

I examined the package. "I'm more curious about where this came from. You didn't bring it in with you."

Ryder's eyes crinkled into upward slants as he laughed with amusement over my confusion. "I brought it over a few days ago, when I had some free time. You were at work."

I smiled and opened the gift. My smile grew when I pulled out a lightweight dagger designed perfectly for throwing. I twirled it in my fingers for a few seconds to test out how balanced it was, and I wasn't disappointed. "Thank you."

A smile on his lips, he nodded. Azriel grabbed more gifts, and little by little the pile dwindled in size and the room got louder. Everyone who had been planned to be present had received nice gifts and a few gag gifts. Ryoko, Rylan, and Raid all got dog toys, and Mocha was given a cat toy and collar with a bell. Zane received a blonde wig with large curls, to fulfill his "desire" to have long golden locks, and Blaze got a stack of *gentlemen's* magazines catered to gay men, which he managed to convince Azriel to trade his magazines for. But per Azriel's nature, he made Blaze go through every page of them before the swap, Telar egging on the whole situation while casually flipping through Azriel's magazine and making comments to Blaze how he was missing out. His face didn't angle once toward the pages, so it was difficult to determine if he was actually looking at them or not.

Ryder also received lady magazines, which we had a good laugh about when he immediately put them away and wouldn't hold eye contact with anyone. The dragons got a heat lamp each, all of whom found the gag lacking due to their sluggish nature during the season, and Seda and Genesis both received sex toys—Seda's was far less tame than Genesis', but each one elicited similar embarrassed reactions. Others in the house also reacted to the reveal, making it that much funnier.

Argus opened a box filled with books titled with several different topics "...*for dummies*," and I received three very different gag gifts, because no one coordinated for mine. In one box, I received books to teach me how to read and write. In the second box, some women's romance novels. And the last box contained a guide on how to capture and force a man to love you. I suspected the last one was a combined effort from Ryoko and Shva'sika. Only they'd be creepy enough to find a book that condoned Stockholm syndrome.

All the ladies also received lingerie from Shva'sika, completing this year's... *interesting* theme.

"This theme pleases me greatly. I enjoy the mixed reactions."

Rylan pointed to the box he had brought in before we had started all this. "Azriel, get that one. I need to see that one opened now."

Azriel grabbed it and peered at the tag, and then handed it to me. I blinked and took the gift, realizing quickly that it was heavier than it looked. Although I had been curious who it was for, I hadn't expected it to be for me. Before opening the package, I shook it in hopes of hearing something that would give it away. Nothing came out of that attempt so I ripped open the wrapping. My eyes grew wide when I opened the box. Inside was a pair of long, outward arching blades attached to long leather gloves. Picking one up, I inspected it.

I found the blade well-balanced and, although heavy, it was surprisingly light for the appearance of the design. Inscribed on the blades were sayings in various languages, most of which I wasn't able to make out. It didn't take me long to recognize signs Ryder had a hand in making this. It pleased me to know the two had worked together, even if Ryder still didn't know the truth yet. *I should probably rectify that.* I was seeing less and less of a reason to keep that knowledge from him.

I slipped my hand into the leather glove, the suede interior caressing my skin. My thumb slid through the empty hole created for it, while my other digits were mostly covered, the lower half of them exposed, along with the entirety of my palm. My guess was that Ryder had designed them so I could control fire with a little less concern about damaging the glove if I lost concentration. A long metal plate rested against the back of my hand and along the arm, but the leather between it and my hand kept my hand protected. On closer inspection, I found the blades forged to the metal plate, the gloves tailored around it to conceal that part of the design.

Ryder moved away when I almost hit him with the blade. "Easy with that."

Before I could apologize, two people walking up the front door stairs caught my attention. My brow rose in surprise when Ebon and Nyoki stepped into the living room. They carried a few gifts in their hands, so it was pretty obvious they had planned to visit.

"Nice to know you know how to knock first," Raikidan said.

"Don't be a brat," Nyoki scolded. "We were invited in before we could."

My gaze flicked to Seda, who smiled. "I figured I'd save everyone time."

I waved the two dragons in, careful of my blade and Ryder's proximity to it. "Come on in and join us."

Nyoki immediately rushed over to me and gave me a huge hug. "Thank you for the amazing work you put into that carving. It's gorgeous!"

I chuckled. "You're welcome."

"Wait, you carved something for someone?" Telar said. "Not fair."

I pointed to Ebon. "He paid."

Telar frowned, and then the new sculpture of Solstice I'd made shot off the table into his hands. "Fine, I'll take this."

"Telar, that's not for anyone to claim!" I said. "If you're going to be that much of a brat about it, I'll make you one."

"Not me, Avila. To this day, she doesn't shut up about wanting one."

"Fine, for her, I'll make something." I figured I could make an intricate one of Tyro and Sela, the psychic god twins.

"I think that'd be a nice gift. You should do one for Telar, too."

"Maybe I will."

Ebon walked up to the couch and held up the gifts in his hands. "Ladies first."

"Why don't we find out who this one is for?" Nyoki suggested as she held up an oddly wrapped box. "One of your friends was about to drop it off when we arrived. He didn't say who it was for, just asked us to give it to the recipient, and there's no tag."

"How do you know he was one of our friends?" Ryoko asked.

"He sneezed, and a copy of himself popped out," Ebon explained. "We kinda figured you knew him."

Ryoko looked at Mocha. "Sounds like Doppelganger had a gift for you."

Mocha pursed her lips. "That doesn't make sense. They never give me anything." She thought it over for a moment and her nose scrunched. "Unless it's some sort of prank."

Nyoki held out the gift. "Well, you won't know until you open it."

She handed the package off and it was passed around until it finally came to Mocha. She stared at it for a moment before opening it. She was definitely convinced it was a prank, because when she knocked open the top of the box, she flinched as if expecting something to pop out at her.

When nothing happened, she sifted through the tissue paper inside the box. Her eyes grew wide just before she pulled out a beautiful necklace. "I can't believe it…"

Ryoko whistled. "That looks nice."

"And expensive," Telar said.

"I've wanted this necklace for years." Mocha held the jewelry up to her neck. "I never expected them to actually get it."

"Well maybe that would explain why they never gave you anything in the past," Raid suggested. "They would have had to save for a while to get you that."

Ebon let out an exasperated sigh. "Great. They couldn't have waited another year?"

"Don't be like that," Nyoki chided. "A woman needs variety in her jewelry."

Mocha's brow rose in confusion and Ryoko giggled. "Ebon is a jeweler. It's not that hard to guess why he only has gifts for us ladies."

Ebon pointed at her. "I said ladies first, not ladies only. I have something for the men, too."

Mocha put her necklace down so she could catch the gift as Ebon tossed it to her. Once the women of the house had their gifts, Ebon handed out boxes to the men; no one was missed. *How did he know how many would show up?*

"I told him," Seda messaged telepathically. *"He contacted me and asked how many were expected, and I told him to bring a few extras in case."*

"Smart move."

Mocha stared at the neatly-wrapped package for a moment, as if she wasn't sure if she should ruin the wrapping. I didn't blame her. As I peered at my gift, it looked like someone had put a lot of effort into wrapping the small box. Finally deciding it was worth ruining the paper, Mocha opened the box and peeked inside. Her eyes grew wide with awe as she pulled out the beautifully-crafted necklace.

Holding up the other necklace she received, she compared the two. "I... I don't know what I like more."

"Choose mine," Ebon whispered.

Raikidan bent over and kept his voice low. "Choose the other one... just to piss him off."

Ebon pointed at his brother. "Quiet, you."

Raikidan stood, pulling his shoulders back to make himself more imposing. "And who's going to make me?"

"Oh, our little puppy is showing off now."

"Our?"

"Yes. Our."

Before Ebon could respond, Seda's little kitten barreled back into the room. He watched the kitten as it scampered around the couch. I cringed when I heard the sound of the kitten's claws grabbing onto denim. Raikidan bent over and bit his lip to prevent himself from howling in pain.

Ryoko giggled. "Apparently, she is."

Raikidan swatted at the kitten, who bolted off, her tail fluffed out behind her, and nearly slammed into a wall as she lost traction on the wooden floor. Mocha took the cat toy she received as a gift and tossed it for the small feline to play with. The kitten jumped on the toy and went to town.

Raikidan shook his head and sat back down. "I'm never going to understand you humans and your damned pets."

Ryoko's eyes squinted as a teasing smile tugged her lips. "You're only upset she's hyper and chose to make you her climbing target."

"Just… open your stupid gift," he muttered.

She giggled and did as he said. The rest of us ladies did as well, eager to find out what Ebon had worked on for each of us. Genesis and Seda received matching bracelets, while Ryoko received a wire-wrapped ring that fit her fingers surprisingly well. Shva'sika opened her box and pulled out a beautifully crafted gemmed circlet that was definitely a special-occasion piece, and not an everyday piece like the other circlets she had acquired since she had been here. The guys also opened their presents, to find leather bracelets with metal and gem accents.

Ryoko pointed to the one Rylan received. "Those look like something you made recently, Laz."

Ebon rubbed the back of his neck. "I actually got the inspiration from her when I came across some pieces at a caravan last week."

Ryoko narrowed her eyes. "Thief."

I wagged my finger at her. "Not a thief. Craftsmen gain inspiration and techniques from others all the time. I'm not the first to come up with the idea to mix leather and metal."

Ebon held out his hand to me in thanks and Ryoko grumbled. "Just open your gift. You're the only one who hasn't."

I chuckled and removed my arm-blade before tearing into the well-wrapped package. My eyes grew wide at the sight of the stud earrings inside. I pulled them out to look them over. They were by no means small, made of large rubies, and styled similarly to my necklace.

"Those earrings are awesome-looking," Ryoko said. "Wanna trade?"

I enclosed my hand around the earrings and pulled my arms away. "No."

"Aw c'mon, please, Laz?" she begged.

I stuck my tongue out at her and she did the same in response.

"Well I think I should have them," Zane said. "They'd look better on me."

I chuckled. "Oh really? Let's find out."

Zane took the earrings and grabbed his new wig. Putting the wig on, he held the earrings up and batted his eyes a few times. "What do you think? Do they match my eyes?"

The room roared with laughter. After giving him a few moments of his fun, I held out my hand and he gave them back. Azriel went about handing out the last few gifts, and Shva'sika slipped into the kitchen and brought out drinks for everyone. The moment I tasted the alcohol, I knew it wouldn't be long before this night got even more interesting.

I put my gifts away, making extra sure to store the nightgown Shva'sika gave me with the lingerie Ryoko had bought me. I had deemed it my *Do Not Open* box.

"I still find it interesting that the one you purchased willingly isn't in that box."

My face tinted red for a brief moment. *"Shut up."*

For a day I wasn't usually fond of, I had fun. The alcoholic drinks had loosened everyone up some more, and the guys ended up rough-housing, nearly breaking the couch and Mocha in the process. Surprisingly, she ended up taking it well, even with them almost destroying the music player and specially-designed ear buds Argus had given her.

Mocha was acclimating well here, and to my surprise, everyone was taking to her just as well. I had thought it would have taken longer than it had, especially with Ryoko and Rylan, but I was glad to be proven wrong. She needed a team, although by the way she had talked about Doppelganger and Chameleon, I wondered how broken the team really was.

My gaze lifted when Ryder knocked on the door of my room. "Everything is all good."

I smiled. I had asked him to make a call to find out if he could stay here. The storm had picked up, and I didn't want him going out in it. It had been decided that Azriel, Ebon, and Nyoki would stay the night as well. However, Telar chose to head back to the Underground instead of staying in a spare room. "Good. At least they won't make you go out in that storm."

"I'm more worried about my walking ability," he admitted.

I laughed. He did have a bit too much to drink. "Just go get some rest."

He nodded. "Good-night, Mom."

I smiled some more. "Good-night, Son."

A tingling sensation ran down my spine. It had been so long since I had been able to say that to him. A dark pain pulsed in my chest. It had been far too long and I wished I could say it more often to him.

"You will have that moment again."

"I just wish I hadn't missed out on so much."

"We all have regrets. But they don't change the present. You must focus on making a future so you have new memories to build."

"Yeah, you're right."

I went about getting ready for bed just as Raikidan showed up. He didn't have any gifts in his hands, so I assumed he had put them away in his room. *His room. Why can't he sleep there instead of taking up my room with his... large self.*

The voice chuckled. *"Don't be like that. You know you want him here. I'm surprised you haven't asked him to be your cuddle buddy."*

I did my best to keep myself from physically reacting, especially in the face. *"Oh, shut up."*

The voice laughed some more, but otherwise said nothing.

"Hey, Eira?" he asked.

I didn't turn to look at him. "Yeah?"

He hesitated. "Do you, uh, want me to give you anything?"

I lifted my brow. "What do you mean?"

"Well everyone else gave you a gift, even my brother. I feel like maybe I should, too."

I chuckled and waved him off. "Don't worry about it. You didn't know about the celebration, and I don't normally give gifts myself. I only did a few this year as it was, so I don't expect anything in return."

"All right." I resumed my task, but he went back to being typical Raikidan and asked another question. "Is today really that hard for you?"

"The only reason I'm still up is because of the high energy everyone put out for the past few hours." I said as I headed for my bed. "It'll wear off in a few minutes and I'll be completely useless."

He came over and easily pushed me onto the bed. "Looks like it's already wearing off."

"Jerk," I muttered as I curled up.

He chuckled before bending over and kissing me on the temple. "Good-night, Eira."

The gesture both shocked me and sent a rush of pleasant emotions through me, though because I shouldn't feel them, it made me a bit uncomfortable. The gesture also shocked the voice. I heard her gasp, but she didn't make a comment like she normally would. Raikidan moved to his typical spot and shifted just as I recovered. I sat up, but he settled himself and closed his eyes.

"Why did he do that?"

I yawned and pushed the confusion and rush of pleasant emotions away. *"It's because he's weird, nothing more."*

"I don't know…"

I lay down and smiled. "Good-night, Rai."

CHAPTER 41

I flattened myself against the icy metal roof when I spotted soldiers patrolling the street below. I shivered as a cold breeze blew by and I listened, counting their steps. *Three feet… Five feet… Seven… Twelve…* I peered over the eaves when I calculated them to be twenty feet away, and watched as they turned a corner and continued on. I swiveled my gaze to the other size of the street and found the coast clear. I glanced back at the others and nodded. Raikidan and Rylan approached, and looked around to be sure I hadn't missed anything that could give us away. Ryoko approached more slowly, with Telar next to her, the latter with a cocky smirk on his face as usual.

The Council had swapped out the other psychic we were to work with for Telar when he found out about the assignment. According to Seda, they wanted him to stick with the other team he had been assigned to work with, but he put up enough of a stink that they gave in. She said he had a preference for working with our team over any other, so it wasn't a surprise when it happened. Of course, when Ryoko teased him about it, he denied everything. No one bought it.

Telar held out his arms, and my body levitated off the ground, as did Ryoko's. He continued to grin as he also lifted into the air. "We'll see you two on the ground."

The three of us moved so fast, it startled me. I knew Battle Psychics had extraordinary psychic power, but rarely had it been used on me like this. Even with my past with Telar, I didn't allow him to use his gifts on me often.

Telar set us down on the ground. "What do you think of that trick, ladies?"

"That was so cool!" Ryoko said in a hushed excitement, being sure not to attract too much attention.

I nodded in agreement and glanced up at Raikidan and Rylan, who stared down at us. Rylan appeared confused, and Raikidan… well, he looked irritated. To prove it, he shifted into an owl and flew down to us. Raikidan landed on my shoulder and hissed at Telar.

My brow rose in silent query. *What is his problem?*

"Hmm… I wonder…"

Telar chuckled and move to the opposite side of me, placing a hand on my lower back. "Got a problem, little bird?"

Raikidan jumped off me and shifted to his nu-human form. He removed Telar's hand from my person but didn't say anything. Telar smirked and went about keeping watch, Raikidan close behind. Rylan landed next to Ryoko and me. He arched an eyebrow in our direction but we shrugged. I couldn't even begin to guess what was going on between those two. Raikidan had acted weird when Telar was around, but this was a new level for him.

"You do know."

"That's an illogical assumption."

"It's the only one that makes sense."

Telar waved us on. "Ladies, move your cute asses. Coast is still clear. Let's move."

"Hey, what about Rylan, he's here with us," Ryoko said.

Telar smirked. "I did say ladies, didn't I?"

I held my hand over my mouth as I muffled the laughter I couldn't stop. Rylan glowered and I had to make myself move on so I wouldn't give away our position.

I looked both ways before bolting to the adjacent street. *Mom would be proud.* The others followed and we quietly continued on. Well… as best we could, with Ryoko humming spy music she'd picked up from her most recent movie binge. No matter how many times I told her to quiet down, she'd ignore me and keep on going. She even started to sneak around as if she were a spy in a movie. *She and her overactive imagination are going to get us caught!*

Then, suddenly it stopped.

"There, that should keep us from being spotted," Telar said.

My eyes flicked to him and then at Ryoko, to find her failing her arms at him. "Did you mute her?"

He held his head high. "More than any mute individual in Lumarae-on."

I shook my head. "You could have just asked her to stop."

"You did, but she didn't."

"She never listens to me."

Ryoko held her hands out to me. Telar sighed and released his hold on her. She let out a relieved exhale. "Thank you, Jerkface."

Telar chuckled at the childish insult and moved on until thumping footsteps sounded around a corner. We all ducked into the best available hiding places and waited. Two soldiers passed the street, unaware of our presence. Once we were sure they had moved on, we pushed forward until we reached the building we needed to infiltrate. Telar and Raikidan stepped aside for me to fiddle with the lock. The lock was an intricate one, and took some time to crack, but I finally won out and the locking mechanism gave way. The five of us slipped into the building and scanned our new surroundings. This part of the building showed no signs of life.

"Currently, the working bodies are on the other side of the building," Telar whispered. "Most are too comfortable and took breaks at the same time."

"Perfect timing we have," Ryoko said.

"Yes, but it won't last long," I said. "We need to move fast and find our target room."

I led the way through the halls, checking every room for a large computer system. We didn't find it, and when we came to a forked hall, we stalled.

"We should split up," Ryoko said.

"Is that wise?" Rylan asked. "We don't know what we'll run into in here."

"We're not just here for that computer," Ryoko said. "Remember, Genesis said the computer has physical back up files stored in a vault. We need to destroy both to make this infiltration work."

"There she goes, using her brain again," I teased.

She smacked me in the arm and I snickered.

"I'll stay here and keep an eye out for activity," Telar offered. "I'll keep everyone posted regarding our finds and potential trouble."

"Smart."

I nodded. "Good idea. Ryoko, Rylan, you head out together. Raikidan will come with me."

The three nodded and we split off. Raikidan stuck close and thankfully kept his noise down. He was the worst at stealth out of everyone, and his wet shoes didn't help him any, but at least he had other useful skills to make up for it.

"Yeah, keep pretending those skills will be useful when he gets you caught."

We passed several rooms before coming to a locked one. I pressed my ear against the door and heard the ticking of computer works. *I think we found it.* I listened more to make sure I couldn't hear anyone inside before playing with the lock. It clicked open. *That was easy.* I opened the door and peered in. A grin spread across my face at the sight of the large computer station, and I waved Raikidan to follow me in. He closed the door behind us as I rushed over to the machine and plugged in Argus' portable computer. I dialed my communicator to his signal and waited.

"I'm here," Argus said when he picked up. "Let's see if this is the computer we're looking for."

I chuckled at his parodied movie reference and let him take charge of this computer data stuff.

"Yep, this is the one, and it's networked with another computer, so I'll wipe them both, just in case."

"Do you want me to take any of the data for us?" I asked.

"Nah, I got it. I don't think much will be of use, but you never know."

"Okay." I watched as the portable computer buzzed to life and destroyed data in rapid succession. *"Telar, how are the others doing?"*

"They know you found the computer, so they're focusing on finding hidden vaults," he said.

I glanced over my shoulder at Raikidan. "Check the room, in case they're stupid enough to hide the safe in here."

"Or smart," Argus said. "It's usually too obvious of a place, so most wouldn't look for the backups in the same room."

"Yeah, Zarda might do that, but only because he wouldn't put a lot of logical thought into it. Those running this building, on the other hand, would know paper files and computers don't do so hot when it comes to fires. The vault may be heat resistant for a while, but they'll want to minimize the risk of losing all the data."

"Fine, be smarter than me."

I snickered. No way would I be smarter than him, but I appreciated the joke anyway.

"Ryoko and Rylan found the vault," Telar messaged. *"But they're having trouble. It's locked by a computer system."*

"Thanks for the heads up. I'll come back that way ASAP." I shifted my focused to Raikidan, who was examining a wall. "You can stop your search. The dogs sniffed it out."

Raikidan snickered and walked over to me. "Well I'm glad you didn't let me keep looking like an idiot."

"Would have been more amusing if you had."

I grinned. "I thought about it."

He pushed my head and then eyed the computer I held. "Almost done?"

"I don't know. Argus?"

"We have about a minute to go," he said. "They didn't secure these files at all."

"Well, it's a good thing the guards have big heads. This keeps getting easier."

"Too easy," Raikidan voiced.

"Well, the vault is computer locked, so there's that."

Raikidan sighed. "Of course it is."

"You're all set," Argus said. "If you need help with the vault, let me know. But this computer I gave you has a lock decoder built in, so you shouldn't have too much issue."

"Thanks, appreciate it," I said as I unplugged the computer.

I tucked it away in my satchel and Raikidan made a hasty retreat back the way we came. When we met back up with Telar, he waved us on. "I'll give you directions, and I'll stay here. There's a bit more activity now, so I want to make sure I have this place covered."

"But with your abilities, you shouldn't have any problems with following us, even if we're caught," I said. "Just throw the attackers off and we keep moving."

"I guess Genesis didn't tell you. They're using a prototype telekinetic blocker here. It's why we're doing what we're doing. The scientist defected to us last week, but he realized they still had some of his ideas. You just disabled the computer holding his important files; you've also emitted the signal for the blocking field, so the pressure in my head is letting up, but it'll be a while before the field has completely dissipated."

"That would have been nice to know."

I knitted my brow. "Why didn't you say anything before?"

"Because it's not a big deal." He pushed me forward. "Now get moving. I'm strong enough to handle this nuisance of a field. Get rid of the paper trail so they can't reconstruct the project."

I nodded, a frown on my lips, and ran off looking for Ryoko and Rylan. Telar messaged me directions and warnings until we reached the room Ryoko and Rylan were camping out in. A soldier sat unconscious in a corner and I couldn't help but chuckle.

Ryoko waved me over to a wall with a large vault door. "Over here. They didn't make any attempts to hide this."

"That's suspicious," I said as I walked to her.

She nodded. "I know, but I'm pretty sure this is it."

I pulled the portable computer out of my satchel and plugged it into the computer lock. "We'll see if we're right."

The computer went to work on the lock, the screen on the lock switching through numbers like crazy, but when it took longer than I had anticipated, I began tapping my foot. *Some amazing program...*

The screen on the lock went nuts and then stopped on a random set of numbers. *Click.* The lock mechanism released the door and it popped open. My heart slowed as we waited for something crazy to happen, but the door remained ajar. I unplugged the portable computer and stored it away before touching the door of the vault.

Blaring alarms sounded in the room, and soon throughout the entire building. Ryoko and Rylan swore, and I threw open the vault door to find it empty. "It was a damned trap! Everyone out!"

Rylan and Raikidan bolted for the door, while Ryoko grabbed the knocked-out soldier. I looked at her questioningly. "Trust me, he could come in handy."

I shrugged and followed the boys out. We set a fast pace the way we came, but when Telar ran around the corner, we stopped.

"What gives?" Ryoko asked.

"We don't want to go that way," he said. More soldiers than you want to count."

"It's like they were expecting this," Rylan growled.

"Maybe they were," I said as I started us moving back the way we had come. "They probably knew the scientist wanted his data back."

"Damn, you're right," Rylan said.

"There's another exit we can use," Telar said. "We have to hurry before it's blocked off."

I quickened the pace, but before we even made it to the room with the fake vault, we heard the sound of rushing footsteps coming our way. I skidded to a halt and looked at the others, but no one knew what to do. If the defensive mass was big enough to get Telar moving, we wouldn't be able to fight our way out of this. *This is bad…*

Ryoko threw open a door to a utility closet and grabbed Telar's arm. "In we go."

Telar tried to protest, but she overpowered him. I was next, then Raikidan. Ryoko and Rylan forced their way into the small space and shut the door.

My cheek burned as I was squished between Telar and Raikidan, but it wasn't the pile-up that had me flustered. I had two pairs of hands on me in very inappropriate places, and the lack of space meant they wouldn't be moving.

"Have fun with this."

"Laz, you okay back there?" Ryoko asked.

"Oh yeah, I love being sandwiched between two men and having my lady assets grabbed by them in a dark closet."

She sputtered a laughed. "Oh, Laz, I didn't realize you were *that* kind of woman. Had I known, I would have given you three your own private closet."

"Will you two shut up?" Raikidan hissed. "You're going to get us caught."

Ryoko snickered. "You're the one who was lucky enough to get a handful of boob, weren't you?"

Raikidan remained quiet, refusing to answer, but Telar sold him out. "Yep, I'm the one who gets to feel this nice ass."

"Telar…" I muttered.

He chuckled. *Cocky son of a bitch.* Neither he nor Raikidan had an actual hold on my body, as much as it was unfortunate placement due to the rushed nature of our hiding, but Telar liked playing things up.

"Yeah, well, Ryoko, how's your captive doing?" I asked. "You did make him go limp."

Telar and Raikidan chuckled. Ryoko gasped. "How rude! A beauty like myself never has that effect on men."

"This one is probably into men," Telar said. "He's drooling all over Rylan."

"Shut up," Rylan said.

"Wait, is he really drooling?" I asked.

"Yes," Rylan grumbled. "It's gross."

We quieted down when the storming footsteps drew closer and then were upon us. People remained outside the door for some time, interesting me, but based on the conversation, our hiding confused them. When they started to think we had gotten away, I became hopeful. It would be difficult to get out of here still, as well as find the missing vault, but at least we now had a chance.

Minutes passed and the hallway seemed to remain empty. Telar started moving around a bit, his hips grinding into me. I twisted the skin on his shoulder. "Knock it off."

"I'm not trying to be obscene here," he said. "Something square is driving into my back."

"Oh man, guys, wait until you're in private," Ryoko teased.

Raikidan's hand moved from my chest down to my stomach and he pulled me closer to him. *Okay, this is getting ridiculous... Wait...* "Telar, what kind of square?"

"Uh... lumpy?"

"Ryoko, where did you find that soldier?"

"Outside this door actually," she said. "Kinda weird. He was just standing here."

"I suspect it's no coincidence." I did my best to reach my flashlight strapped to the back of my pants.

"Whoa, watch where you're grabbing there, Sweet Thing," Telar said.

"Don't even start with me," I warned.

"Oh don't be like that. It'd only be natural to want to cop a quick feel for someone in your situation."

I finally managed to get my flashlight removed and held it around Telar. I flipped the "on" switch, making sure to pick the lowest setting. A muted light reflected through the room and I pulled away from Raikidan to peer around Telar.

Telar grinned. "You know, for someone who's been sandwiched between two sweaty men, you smell wonderful."

"Well, if a primadonna like you isn't going to smell pleasant, then I might as well," I said.

He chuckled and tightened his grip on my ass, only to let go immediately when I conked him on the head with my flashlight.

I continued to look behind him and found there indeed was a square box behind him that didn't look like anything in this closet. "I think we found our vault."

"What? No way," Ryoko said.

"I'm positive this is it. Why else would anyone have a box with a key pad on it in an inconspicuous room that is being guarded?"

"Oh for the love of Satria!" Rylan said. "Seriously? What kind of ass-backward thinking is that?"

"A clever one," Telar said. "None of us would have thought to look in a utility closet for a vault."

"He's right."

"Now I just need room to get it open…" I said.

"Give it a few more minutes and we can open the door," Telar said. "Things are calming down out there."

About fifteen minutes passed before Telar gave the okay for the door to open. Rylan did, but was sure to be cautious, even with our drooling captive leaning on him. Everyone filed out when he confirmed the all-clear. Once Telar was out of the closet, I re-entered and took a look at the box. This one had a much more simple locking mechanism and wouldn't allow for the portable computer to be attached to it.

I called Argus. "I'm projecting the vault. Computer won't hook up to it."

"I see that. Give me a few minutes to figure out the best combo of numbers to try." I waited while I listened to the sound of keys clicking. "Okay, try seven-six-two-eight." I tried it, but it didn't work. "Try nine-eight-eight-one." That one also failed. "Four-eight-two-one."

I gnashed my teeth when that one failed as well. "Are you just guessing? Because I can do that."

"No, these are strategic numbers based on the most commonly-used combinations."

"Maybe you should try something uncommon," I said.

"Hmm, all right. Leading zeros aren't common, so try zero-nine-two-six." The door popped open. "Wow, it worked. You sure you didn't take my brain for a bit?"

I let out a fake laugh as I opened up the vault. "If it had been up to me, I would have been trying random combinations and praying they'd work. And if that didn't work, I'd go up the number count in chronological order."

"Well at the rate I was going your choice would have been better," he said.

I filtered through the papers inside the vault. "True. Does this look like the files we're looking for? I'll destroy them either way, but I want to get out of here."

"Oh yeah, those are it. I'll let you take things from here. Good luck getting out."

He cut the line and I lit a powerful fire in my hands. Not caring if anything else caught on fire, I tossed it inside the vault and slammed the door shut. Smoke billowed out of the seams, but I didn't stay to watch the fireworks. I grabbed Raikidan's wrist as I exited the closet and pulled him down the hall, calling out to the others. "Let's go!"

The others didn't hesitate. We made it about twenty yards down the hall before the utility closet exploded and the alarms went off again, as well as emergency sprinklers. Ryoko dropped the body she carried and we continued. Telar directed us around the correct turns, and before anyone could catch up to us, we were bolting out of the building and into the city.

Telar and I left the Council chamber and reunited with the rest of the group. Debrief had gone well, and my little explosion had done a bit more damage than I had expected. A nice added bonus for me and my review. The Council as a whole was usually far more critical about successes than when evaluating their team in private, so when they scored our team higher than normal, I took it with pride.

Before I could say anything to anyone, Telar's hand smacked me in the ass. "All right, Sweet Thing, you get home now."

"Oh my…"

I froze up and the hall grew still. Telar moved away slowly. "Oh, shit, sorry, Eira. I didn't mean to—"

"Three…" My eyebrow twitched. "Two…"

He sprinted down the hall.

"One."

I pulled a flame from my lips and tossed at him. Telar took a sharp turn around a corner, but my flame control allowed the fire to follow, and soon after, he yelled out in pain.

A shaman walked around the corner and smirked at me. "Caught his hair on fire."

"Good. Jackhole deserves it."

Raikidan advanced, cracking his knuckles. "Not good enough."

His reaction pulled me out of my irritation and I tilted my head. "Uh, Rai?"

"Oh, this is interesting."

The group of us watched Raikidan turn the same corner.

"Whoa, wait, hold on!" Telar yelled out.

I flinched when the sound of Raikidan hitting Telar echoed through the hall, and then ran after the two men. When I turned the corner, I found Raikidan holding Telar by the shirt, ready to throw another punch. I grabbed Raikidan by the arm. "Rai, stop!"

Raikidan glanced back at me. "He deserves it after what he just did."

"Overprotective lap dog never ceases to disappoint."

"Rai, this isn't like what happens at the club. Let him go." I didn't understand why Telar didn't fight back. It wasn't like him. "Please, Raikidan."

Raikidan held eye contact with me for some time before sighing and dropping his prey. I went to Telar's side and looked him over. Beyond the singed hair, he had a nasty mark on his face from Raikidan's punch, but otherwise seemed okay on the surface.

"You okay?" I asked.

Telar rubbed his face. "Yeah, I deserved all that. I really need to think before I act. Sorry."

I chuckled. "As long as you learned from it, we're even."

"Oh, just tell him you liked it. You know you did."

"Good," he said as I helped him up. "Now I should leave before I do something else that's stupid."

I waved goodbye, and then shifted my gaze to Raikidan, finding him glowering at Telar's retreating form. "You could stand to chill, you know?"

"He shouldn't have done that."

"There's a reason I only singed his hair."

Surprise flicked over Raikidan's face. "You controlled yourself?"

I place my hands on my hips. "Duh. Telar and I have a strange friendship, and sometimes he can go overboard. I'll discipline him in extreme ways to compensate, but I'm not out to kill him. I had it covered. I didn't need you to jump in like I'm some damsel in distress."

"That's not"—he sighed—"I'll try better next time."

I hit him in the forehead with my palm. "There's your reprimanding. Next time I won't be so lenient."

"I'll help you come up with a… more fun punishment next time."

"Don't start turning into Ryoko on me."

"We know where you stand, so there's no point denying you'd like it."

"Why are you encouraging this all of a sudden?"

My question was met with silence.

Raikidan chuckled while rubbing his forehead. "At least I got off easier than your psychic friend."

"So, can we go home now or are you two going to continue to act like children?" Ryoko called out.

I shook my head. "Let's get home."

T he channels on the TV changed as I absently flipped through them. I was more focused on Shva'sika. She had been acting strange today, and every time I asked if something was wrong, she'd insist she was fine, but I wasn't convinced.

"I agree with you, something isn't right."

"Will you stick to one channel, please?" Ryoko begged. "If not, could you give the remote to me?"

I tossed her the remote. "Have at it."

She caught it and started punching in a number to get to a specific channel. Her tail had finally gone away, but not before she transformed into a wogron again. It led me to believe it may happen again in the future.

Ryoko finally got to the channel she wanted, but before she was able to enjoy her program, our attention was pulled to the kitchen when something smashed on the floor.

"Shva'sika!" I shouted. I jumped over the couch and rushed into the kitchen, where I found her unconscious on the floor. "Shva'sika? Shva'sika, wake up."

Suddenly the house was full of commotion. Everyone crowded in to see what was going on, and Azriel had to push his way through in order to get over to me. "What's going on?"

I shook my head. "I don't know. She just collapsed."

"Well, it's a good thing Genesis had me stop by today to chat. We need to move her, but not too far. Without knowing what's going on, I don't want to risk anything."

"Pull out the coffee table extensions and move her there," I ordered to the others.

Ryoko and the boys went to work immediately. Raikidan and Corliss stood and watched together, out of the way, while Mana watched from the hallway with Genesis. Azriel scooped Shva'sika up and carried her over to our little setup. He set her down, and went to work checking her vitals and seeing if anything could give him a clue to what was going on.

"Was she acting strange at all today?" he asked me as he worked.

I nodded. "Yeah, but she insisted she was fine. So I'm not sure if she was hiding that something was wrong, or if she honestly didn't know something strange was up."

"I suspect a little of both."

He nodded. "Let's hope it's the latter. I have no idea what is going on, and I'd hate to think she'd purposely not tell us if something was wrong with her."

Seda stepped up. "I'll see if I can search her mind. With her being unconscious, there's a high likelihood I won't be able to connect t—"

"But it's better than what we have now," I said. "Go for it."

We all waited as Seda knelt, with her hands hovering around Shva'sika's head. After a few moments, she released a slow exhale and let her hands drop. "I'm sorry. I'm being repelled."

I placed my hand on her shoulder. "You tried, and that's what matters." I glanced over to the three dragons when I noticed them speaking privately. Although I wasn't able to pick out much, I could understand enough to know the topic needed to be open to all of us. "What?"

"Raikidan might be able to help," Mana said.

Raikidan gave her an ugly scowl and I narrowed my eyes. "Raikidan, right now isn't a time for your little secrets. If you know a way to help, then do it, or the gods help you, I will rip you limb from limb."

"If you won't, I will."

Corliss looked at Raikidan. "If you won't do it, then I will."

"No, I'll do it," Raikidan muttered. "We don't need you hurting her with your inexperience."

"Not that you're much better," Corliss shot back.

Raikidan grunted and took Seda's place. I watched as he made himself comfortable and rested his hands on the sides of her face. After taking a deep breath, he closed his eyes and his breathing slowed.

Ryoko knelt and cocked her head, gazing at him intently. "He's asleep! How is—"

I shushed her and watched, extremely curious.

Then suddenly, Raikidan's breathing returned to a normal rate and his eyes snapped open. "She's a bomb."

Ryoko blinked. "What?"

"She said she hasn't been practicing."

My time spent with Shva'sika ran through my head. Living with electricity running through your body wasn't easy, and it forced you into certain habits to keep it controlled. *Wait... that's it!* "There's a charge built up in her body." I pointed to the basement door. "Get her downstairs, now!"

Raikidan scooped Shva'sika up and followed me as I flew down the stairs.

I pulled the worktable out and pointed at it before going to look for something that would help us. "Put her down and get away from her. That build up could hurt you if it builds faster than expected."

He nodded and stepped away. I rummaged through the cabinets in hopes to find something that could help, but nothing was jumping out at me.

"What are you looking for?" Ryoko asked.

"Something to pull the electrical build-up out of her body and store it elsewhere."

"Well, we have a few dead batteries we could use," Blaze offered.

I grunted. "A few batteries won't cut it. We'll run out before we put a scratch in that buildup."

"Is it really that bad?" Ryoko asked.

I nodded. "The only charge that can out-power a Shaman of the Dancing Lights is the lightning produced during a storm."

"Whoa," she murmured in awe.

"Then you'll need the generator from the shop," Argus said. "It's in need of a new charge, so we brought it back for me to work with. I'll go grab a few tools to rig it up to draw out her power. Azriel, come with me in case I need your help."

I nodded my thanks while Ryoko and Blaze went to grab the generator and Azriel followed Argus back upstairs. Ryoko and Blaze wheeled the machine out just as Argus and Azriel returned and went to work, my anxiety dissipating as I watched them.

I noticed Zane watching Shva'sika with worry. "Don't worry, Zane, she's going to be okay."

"You sure?" he questioned. "She seemed a bit out of sorts earlier."

I nodded. "It is pretty common for this to happen. Shva'sika is usually good about keeping her buildup down, but with everything going on these past few months, I'm guessing she forgot. The reason I freaked out was because when it does happen, other Shaman of the Dancing Lights are able to draw the buildup out. Since there isn't anyone else here, I wasn't sure if we'd be able to help her in time. Now that Argus has a way to do that, I'm confident she's going to be okay."

"Do you want me to call some lightning shamans in case it doesn't work?" Seda asked.

"You can try, but I'm not sure how many are in the city," I admitted. "That's why I didn't think about that option first."

"All right, it's all set up," Argus said. I blinked. *That was fast!* "Just tell me where to hook her up, and I'll start it up."

I nodded and showed him the best positions on her body to draw out the buildup. Once Argus had Shva'sika hooked up, he ran the generator and we waited. It didn't look like anything was happening, but the gauge Argus had set up said otherwise.

The generator made a strange noise, and Argus checked on it. "This isn't good."

"*Oh no.*"

"What, what isn't good?" I demanded.

"The generator is just about full already," he explained. "I thought it could hold more."

"Don't worry," Seda encouraged. "The shamans are looking for help."

"Let's hope we've taken enough for Shva'sika to hold out that long," I said.

Argus shut down the machine. "That's it. It can't take anymore."

I sighed and started biting my nails.

"*Stop it.*"

It was something I had picked up in my attempt to stop my pacing habit. Now I was a nail biter and a pacer. Seda used her telekinesis to stop me and I gave an appreciative look. Just as I did, I noticed a strange light forming behind her. *A portal!* Relief washed over me when it stabilized and several shamans stepped through.

"Where is she?" one asked.

"What, you can't see the woman on the table hooked up to a generator?" Blaze asked sarcastically.

I glared at him, and then stepped aside so the shamans could finish what we started. Everyone ended up stepping back when sparks began to fly about as they drained what was left of the buildup.

I let out a sigh of relief when they pulled away. "Thank you."

One of them nodded. "I'm glad we could help. I have to admit, I'm surprised at the degree of buildup she had. I was told she had been partially drained already."

I pointed to the generator. "That was empty before we hooked her up to it."

"That's either a long time for her not to keep the buildup in check, or she has a lot of power," he commented. "Regardless, it's good you knew what to do. I suspect she wouldn't have lasted much longer if you hadn't jumped in."

One of the shamans wandered over to the generator and started looking at it inquisitively. He even poked it with his metal glove, which looked like it was made in the Eastern Tribe. "Fascinating hookup you have here. You put this together on the spot?"

Argus nodded. "Nothing major. Just some simple alterations, and reversed the output mechanism to draw energy in instead."

"That's impressive work for most in such a short time," he complemented. "I use the electricity I build up to power up my inventions and get them to work."

"That would explain the gloves."

The shaman chuckled. "They're not much of a fashion statement, I know."

"Nerds."

I checked on Shva'sika and touched her forehead. She felt feverish, but I knew from experience that would go away as she rested, now that she was better.

"I'll take her to her room," Azriel offered.

I nodded and followed him upstairs after he scooped her up, after thanking the shamans one last time for their help. As I reached the living room, Azriel encouraged me to take a nap. I tried to protest, but he insisted it would be beneficial and since he was my doctor, per se, I couldn't really deny him.

Throwing myself down on my bed, I waited for Raikidan to show up. He had some explaining to do, and I wasn't going to sleep until I got it. Unsurprisingly, he didn't come in right away. He wasn't completely dumb. He knew I had questions, but I wasn't going to give in and I knew if I left my room, Azriel would have a fit.

"He's a coward."

"No, not a coward. Just a pain in the ass."

When Raikidan finally came in, he had a nasty scowl on his face.

"Who spit in his food?"

"All right, start asking so we can get this over with," Raikidan muttered.

I propped myself up with my elbows. "Wow, I'm sorry, I didn't realize lying down would put you in such a foul mood."

The voice snorted but made no actual comment.

Raikidan sighed and sat down on the windowsill. "Sorry. The others, they"—he scrubbed his face—"just ask me your question."

"You know what I want to know."

He took in a deep breath. "Promise no freaking out?" I nodded. "I'm a Dreamwalker."

I sat up and cocked my head. I knew that word. That weird dream I had, where there had been two different versions of him, I had heard that word in that dream. "What is that?"

"It means I can walk into other's dreams."

I nodded in thought. "Corliss can do this, too?" Raikidan nodded in response. "How about Mana?"

"No, it's a black dragon ability."

"So, you can just walk into anyone's dream?"

"Full black dragons, yes. Sentient beings who are capable of dreaming have created something call a *sentinel* to combat the ability, but it's only effective against half-colors. This is because half-colors are less adept at dreamwalking due to their mixed scale nature. A half-color can get past the sentinel if they're crafty enough, otherwise, we need expressed permission from the being that dreams."

I pursed my lips. "So, what else can you guys do? Corliss has demonstrated that he doesn't breathe fire like you can, and you both can Dreamwalk when Mana can't, so obviously you all have all sorts of abilities that are unique."

Raikidan nodded. "We do. We have three abilities that are unique to our color as well as a unique sight ability. Red dragons breathe fire and can put up fire barriers, but can also heal with that flame. Their sight ability is the same as what you can do thermal sense... or *heat sense* as you call it." I chuckled at his jest. I knew the technical term was thermal sense, but *heat sense* was an old phrasing habit I never quite broke from.

He continued, "Green dragons breathe poison gas and have acidic saliva they can projectile spit. They can also help with plant growth and have a sight ability to see organic cell matter change. Black dragons have the ability to exhale lightning, breathe sleep gas, and walk dreams. Their sight ability allows them to see electrical impulses."

"So these abilities are another reason why mixed colored dragons are so frowned upon?"

He nodded again. "What abilities we inherit from our parents isn't set in stone. Take my brother and me, for example. I can Dreamwalk, and Ebon can't. But he can breathe fire and lightning. We also have different sight abilities; he can see the electrical impulse, while I have a thermal sense."

"So basically, they're jealous because you're less predictable," I said.

He furrowed his brow in thought. "I guess... I guess you're right in some way."

"So, how about the colored dragons that you said have gone extinct? Do you know anything about them?"

"Not much, to be honest. My mother told me a little about them, but her knowledge was limited, too."

"Why's that?"

"It's said the colors died off during the War of End, or so few of them were left that no one knew, or told, in fear it would start trophy hunts."

I knitted my brow. "But you told me they died off during the Great War."

He rubbed the back of his head. "Yeah, I know, but that's because at the time, I didn't trust you, so I told you something you might actually believe. The Great War did do a number to the rest of our kind, if that'll make up for it."

I shook my head. "How about you tell me what you know about the extinct colors, and we call it even?"

"There used to be seven colors in total. Blue, white, brown, and violet dragons were the ones who went extinct."

I nodded. "What could they do?"

"From what my mother could tell me, white dragons could control ice and snow, blue dragons commanded the water, and brown dragons had control over earth, but unlike green dragons, they couldn't do anything with plant life."

"What about these violet dragons you mentioned?"

He thought for a moment. "They were the rarest of the seven colors, and not much was ever known about them except their ability. They were masters of arcane magic."

I blinked and then laughed. "Arcane magic? Are you serious?" When he shot me a pointed look, I shook my head. "Raikidan, no one has been able to use major arcane magic since—" I stopped when I realized how long magic had been missing from Lumaraeon.

"Since the War of End," Raikidan finished. "That's because violet dragons were the ones who taught others, and with them gone and the world in need of rebuilding, no one was around to keep the knowledge going."

"This is all really fascinating," I admitted. "Why didn't you trust me with knowing any of this?"

"It's not that I didn't trust you," he said. "Well... it used to be that, but that changed, I swear! I... I just didn't think you'd understand."

"Raikidan, this is me we're talking about here. I may be impulsive and hard to handle, but I'm pretty good at understanding."

He sighed. "All right, I was also worried you might ask if I've ever—"

"Walked my dreams?" I guessed. He eyed me as if expecting me to start lashing out at him. "Well, have you? I know I haven't expressed any permission for you to, but you did say it's not always needed."

He rubbed the back of his neck and his eye contact waivered. "I have, but I swear it was on accident! Most of the time, if I wander into your dreams, I'm stopped by your sentinel. You have an exceptionally strong one."

"When you're in a dream, can you change them?"

"Sometimes," he admitted. "But when we can, the alterations can only be positive. We can't cause nightmares."

"Have you ever changed any of mine?" I asked.

"I've tried to. Sometimes it worked, others times it hasn't."

I smiled. Even though I should hate the idea of him changing my dreams, knowing he tried to make them better gave me a sense of comfort instead. "Is your ability why you like dreaming so much?"

He nodded. "And the reason I couldn't understand why you had such a hard time experiencing them. At least, until I got to know you better."

"Can you pull others into your dreams?" That dream I had about him not accepting me as I was made me want to know. It would mean I had met a sentinel, and that dream was his.

He shook his head. "Not that I'm aware of. But if it was possible, and I had done it once, I'd know. We're very aware of when we're dreaming and what goes on."

I nodded. "Well, thanks for sharing with me."

"Sure."

As I lay down for my nap I spoke again. "Hey, Raikidan."

"Yeah?"

"Um, you have my permission to walk my dreams."

"Are you sure?"

I nodded as I rested my head on my pillow. "Yeah. Maybe it'll help you understand me better, seeing as I find it difficult to talk about myself. And maybe it'll benefit me in some way some time."

"All right, thank you."

I smiled a little and then closed my eyes for rest. Hopefully, there weren't any nightmares in store for me, but if they were, maybe he'd make them better. Maybe this invitation would help me enjoy dreaming.

"You have been without even knowing it."

"You were quiet the whole time Raikidan and I spoke. What's up with that?"

"I already had that knowledge."

"How the hell did you know all that?"

"We've been over this. It's because I am not your subconscious. There is much that I know."

"And you didn't tell me?"

"I cannot."

I wanted to groan. *"Seriously? How about telling me what you are?"*

"Again, I cannot."

"Why not?"

"I don't know. Every time I try, I forget. Showing myself to you was taxing enough."

"So you are the woman..." Silence met my statement. *"What is your opinion on Raikidan walking my dreams?"*

"I am fine with it. I don't fear his ability, because I understand it and its limitations. Your sentinel won't be pleased, but no sentinel is when that permission is given."

"Are you unhappy I gave permission?"

"No. I'm glad, actually."

"Do you trust him?"

"I'm... not sure."

I found this doubt peculiar. Occasionally she would backtrack and wonder, but never had she ever openly admitted the doubt to me. *"Very well. I'll remain careful still. Thank you. Goodnight."*

"Goodnight, Eira."

43
CHAPTER

I turned up the speed of the windshield wipers as snow began to fall harder. I normally wouldn't drive in weather like this, but I promised the children at the orphanage I'd visit. Even Matron Lyra asked me not to come, but I was too stubborn for my own good. Even so, I had waited until midafternoon to see if the weather changed for the better before heading out.

"You should have stayed home."

Raikidan sat quietly in the seat next to me. While he went with me to the orphanage every time and dealt with the children well, I wasn't sure if he liked going. He refused to talk about it any time I brought it up, and that bothered me. If he didn't like going, I didn't want him to feel pressured into it. It wasn't like the Council sanctioned our visits. The other rebels would help with supplies, but in the end, this was something I liked to do.

The children deserved this kind of visit. They deserved families more than visits, but I couldn't give them homes, so this was the best I could do for them. It did help our position, though, with Matron Lyra knowing I was part of the rebellion.

I knew I didn't have to worry about her ratting me out. We showed more compassion for these children than any soldier ordered to check on them, and Matron Lyra was a kind woman and only took a neutral stand in the matter because she worried for the children; I couldn't blame her. If she were to be found conspiring against Zarda, there wouldn't be anyone to take over and care for the children. Even if I were to be found out for real and they suspected she knew, she could at least fake innocence. *She's good at that.*

I pulled over on a street and put the car into park. I glanced at the time and then waited. *I'm early.* Raikidan and I couldn't go to the orphanage without Raid, and this was where I was to pick him up. I remembered the night he left. It was snowing like it was today…

I put down my book when I heard someone out in the living room. From the sound of it they had shoes on, though it didn't sound like Ryoko's stride. Who would be up at three in the morning, besides me, and wearing shoes?

I slid off my bed out of curiosity, but when I reached the door, someone spoke.

"Raid?" It was Ryoko. "What are you doing?"

"I'm, uh, heading out," he replied quietly.

"What? It's the middle of the—what's with the backpack?" She gasped. "Raid, you're not leaving, are you?"

"Yeah, I am," he admitted. "And I didn't plan on saying goodbye because I knew you guys would try to stop me."

"Because you should stay!"

Raid sighed. "I can't."

"Why not?"

"Forget it. It's not important anymore."

He walked toward the stairs, but Ryoko stopped him before he reached them. "Don't do that. Tell me what you have to say."

He was quiet for a moment. "I was here because of you, Ryoko. I'd thought that by now, you had finally given up on my brother, and I finally had a shot with you. I thought I could show you that I'd been there for you this whole time, even when he wasn't. I can't stay because I can't be okay with seeing you with him right now. I want you to be happy, but I wanted you to be happy with me."

"Raid, I…" She sighed as the words died on her lips. I knew guilt gripped her when it had no business to surface.

I chose to open my door then, to make sure neither of them made a bad decision, and caught the tail end of Raid kissing Ryoko on the forehead. He pulled away from her and shifted his gaze to me.

"Be careful," I said.

He nodded. "I will."

He gave a small wave before heading out. I looked at Ryoko when the front door shut, tears brimming her eyes...

Someone knocked on the window of the rear door of the car, pulling me back to the present. I glanced over my shoulder to see Raid outside. I unlocked the door and he climbed in.

"Sorry, didn't mean to be late," he said as he brushed snow off his head.

"No, I was early." I pulled away from the curb. "With the snow, I wanted to make sure I didn't make you wait."

He chuckled. "Thanks."

I glanced at him through my rearview mirror. "You know, I could have picked you up at your new place."

He shrugged. "I've been out all day, so this worked well."

"You still don't have a place to live, do you?" I said.

"No, I do. They're pretty cool, too."

"He's lying."

"Raid, don't lie to me."

He exhaled, hard. "Look, I don't want to talk about this."

"You know the only reason I'm bringing this up is because you left in the middle of winter. Had it been warmer out, I wouldn't be bothering you, even though we both know you'd get in trouble for being a vagrant."

"I'm fine, Eira."

"You can't live on the street in the winter. You'll freeze!"

"I'm fine. My temperature runs higher than most, and I can shift if it gets too cold. Really, stop fussing."

"Stop making her worry," Raikidan muttered.

I eyed him. That was the first thing he'd said all day.

"No one needs to fuss over me," Raid murmured.

"They don't need to, or you don't want them to?" Raikidan asked.

Raid sunk back in his seat, unwilling to talk anymore. I shook my head and continued driving until we came to the large house the orphans and Lyra called home. Pulling up, I cut the engine and climbed out of the car to grabs supplies from the trunk. While I was retrieving what I needed, Raid removed his jacket and shifted, and waited for Raikidan to get a collar and leash on him. The two jumped out of the car just as I shut the trunk.

"Here, let me help with some of that," Raikidan offered.

"I got it," I said. He gave me a long, stern look, and I rolled my eyes. "Really, I got it. Go up and knock on the door for me."

He held out his hand. "Hand me the blankets."

"Rai, I got it," I insisted.

"Eira."

"You two are both too stubborn for your own good."

"Will you two please stop it?" Raid muttered, careful to not look suspicious. "My feet are going to get cold standing around, and you're going to just outright make me sick." Raikidan and I looked at him funny and he huffed. "You two are ridiculous. Let's get inside so I can be mauled by happy children."

My lips spread into a smirk. "You sound so miserable."

"I told you before, I like kids," he said. "I want some of my own someday." I eyed him curiously and he took offense. "What? That's not weird at all, okay?"

I laughed. "Never said it was. I just never pictured you wanting kids."

"Why, because of my brother?"

I shrugged. "I don't know if he wants them."

"Really?"

"Yeah, he's one of those people where it's hard to tell, and he doesn't exactly talk about it."

Raid looked at the snow-covered stairs as we walked up them. "You know, I don't know the answer to that, either."

Raikidan rapped on the door and then stole some of the blankets I carried. I huffed and was caught in the act when Matron Lyra opened the door.

She was an older woman, near the end of the typical nu-human lifespan, but she had aged gracefully, only appearing to be in her mid-fifties. She had long blonde and gray hair, crystal-blue eyes, and alabaster skin.

She giggled. "I'm guessing Ray took those blankets from you, yes?"

"Yeah," I muttered.

She giggled again. "You're too stubborn for your own good. You should let the man help if he offers. Hard to find that kind of man these days. Not even soldiers are that helpful anymore." She laughed when Raid attempted to nose his way past her legs, attempting to sniff out the children's location. "Looks like someone is eager, as always. Why don't I let you all in before we all freeze."

I nodded and we all followed her in. I could hear the children laughing as they played, but could tell they had no idea we were here yet as we removed our winter clothes and put them away.

Matron Lyra took the blankets Raikidan had and then noticed the basket I carried in one of my hands. "What's that, dear?"

I smiled and pulled back the cloth covering the top, revealing a mound of pastry goods. "A friend of mine thought you and the children could use a sweet treat. They were made with allergy-free ingredients, just in case."

Matron Lyra smiled wide. "Oh, that's so thoughtful. Thank you so much!"

Raid whined and pawed the floor, and I giggled. "Okay, okay. Let me unhitch you."

The moment the leash was gone, he took off into the orphanage. We knew he'd found the children when they squealed out his name. Amusement had Matron Lyra and me giggling and then went to see the children. When we came to the room, the sight before us was too cute—Raid was belly-up, getting a belly rub any real dog would die to have. He ate up the attention the children gave him. *What a ham.*

One of the girls who was rubbing Raid's belly noticed our presence, and squealed when she spotted me. "Eira!"

I knelt and gave the girl a hug when she ran over to me. "Hey there, Elara."

"I'm so glad you came!" she beamed. "Jakcel said you weren't, because of all the snow."

I pulled away while chuckling. "Well, everyone told me to come another time, but I couldn't do that to you guys. You'd be so disappointed."

Elara nodded. "Yeah! It's fun when you come by." She tilted her head when she noticed the basket. "What's that?"

I smiled. "A treat for all of you."

The children cheered and ran over to me in hopes of seeing the treat. Raid huffed at his lack of attention, but soon after, a little girl with wavy ebony hair latched onto him, making him forget. Her name was Myra, and out of all the children, she adored Raid the most. She never wanted to go anywhere without him when he was here.

"What did you bring us?" A young boy with sandy-blonde hair asked.

"You'll find out in a second, Kelcen," I told him. "But first we need to make sure the table is cleaned off and everyone is in a seat."

The children ran off to the dining room. I headed for the kitchen, while Matron Lyra and Raid went to the dining room to help the children. Raikidan placed the blankets he was carrying down on a chair and followed me into the kitchen.

"Rai, can you grab some plates for me?" I asked as I placed the basket on the counter and searched for napkins.

He didn't respond verbally—just did as I asked. I watched him from the corner of my eye; I couldn't understand what was up with him. *"His behavior is peculiar."*

Without saying anything, I took the plates from him when he returned. I placed napkins on the basket and headed into the dining room. I smiled at the sight of the older children helping the younger ones into their seats at the table before sitting down themselves. *"How precious."*

All of these children were good. They deserved homes with families that loved them. In a perfect world, they'd have that. Then again, in a perfect world, this place wouldn't be needed and people would be happier.

The children gazed at me eagerly, and I couldn't help but laugh. They acted like this was the first time I had ever spoiled them in the many times I came here. In an attempt to build their eager anticipation for their treat, I handed out plates and napkins slowly. And then, at a painstaking pace, I reached for the towel that covered their treat. But before I could reveal it, Raid jumped up on his hind legs, latched onto the towel, and took off with it under the table. "Hey, you brat!"

Laughter echoed through the room and I huffed. *He would do that.*

Elara squealed with delight when she realized their treat was now revealed thanks to Raid. "Sweet rolls!"

The children squealed and cheered, and I went about handing out the tasty treats. I watched as the children happily ate their sweet rolls, and even shared parts of them as if each roll was different in some way. Even Matron Lyra got to have one.

I looked down at Raid when he barked at me. He sat by my feet, wagging his tail and panting. He tilted his head, his eyes flicking to the basket. I chuckled, and then held the basket away from him. "I dunno…"

He lowered his head and whined while wagging his tail some more, but I didn't give in. It wasn't until he rolled onto his back and stretched that it became hard to say no. He whined and pawed at me in the air while wagging his tail, and I laughed.

"Okay, okay. You get one."

He flipped back over onto his belly and caught the roll I tossed to him. I turned to see if Raikidan wanted one, but he wasn't standing by the kitchen anymore. Setting the basket down on a small table, I went to look for him.

I didn't have to look far. I found him in the large room used for the children's bedroom, pulling the sheets and blankets from the beds. *Odd. He struggles to do that at home without having to be asked a hundred times.*

"Like I said, peculiar."

I watched as he piled them into a basket for a few moments before heading back into the dining room.

"Did you find him?" Matron Lyra asked.

"Hmm?"

"Ray," she clarified. "Did you find him?"

"Oh, yeah. He's doing laundry."

Her brow rose. "He does laundry?"

I laughed. "Sometimes. Though usually he has to be asked a few times."

"So, what's making him help out with the chores this time?"

I shrugged. "I don't know."

"You didn't ask?"

I frowned and rubbed my arm. "We haven't exactly spoken much today."

Concern registered on Matron Lyra's face. "Why not?"

I shrugged. "I don't know. I try to communicate with him, but it doesn't go anywhere. I think I did something to upset him…"

"Do you know what?"

I shook my head.

Elara peaked around her chair. "Don't worry. He loves you, so he won't act like this forever."

My brow knit and my head twitched to the side. "What?"

Matron Lyra giggled. "Elara, dear, Eira and Ray aren't together."

Elara frowned. "Why not?"

"Because we're just friends," I said.

"Why?"

"Well… because that's just how it is."

"Wow, that was bad, even for you."

"What am I supposed to say to a kid that age that will make sense to them?"

"You don't give them enough credit. They're smarter than you think."

Elara, unhappy with my answer, slid of her chair and left the room. I went to follow her, but Matron Lyra stopped me. "Let her do her thing. She may be able to get to the bottom of his behavior."

"You really think she's going to talk to Rai?"

She nodded. "I know these children. That's exactly what she's doing." We watched as several more children climbed off their seats and left the room. "Correction, what they're doing."

"Do you think it's okay for them to do that?" I asked.

"I don't see the harm. He's good with them, even if he doesn't think he is. So if he doesn't want to answer their questions, he'll redirect their attention to something else."

"He told you he doesn't think he's good with kids?"

She nodded. "I'm guessing he doesn't say anything to you?"

I shook my head. "He doesn't like to talk about how he feels about coming here with me."

Matron Lyra rubbed my back. "He'll come around. It'll just take time."

She helped one of the smaller children out of his chair when he was having trouble, and then escorted him into the living room. Sighing, I picked up the basket with the remaining sweet rolls and headed for the kitchen so I could put them someplace safe, to be eaten later. Raid followed me, though my mind was too preoccupied to pay much attention. *Why would Raikidan talk to her about his feelings regarding the children, and not me?*

"Hey, Eira?" Raid mumbled when we were inside the kitchen.

My eyes narrowed. "You know you're not supposed to speak while we're here."

He dipped his head. "I know, I just want to ask you something while it's still relevant."

"Okay, what is it?"

"Has Raikidan really not spoken to you much today?"

I nodded and searched for some plastic storage container. "The first time he said anything to me was when he wanted to take those blankets."

"Do you really think he's upset with you?"

I shrugged uncommunicatively.

"What would make you think that?"

"Because normally, he's real talkative with me when no one is around. He typically only goes quiet when he's upset over something I've done. But he could just have something on his mind. I don't know. Not like it matters. He has every right to not talk to me."

"But it upsets you, so it does matter."

I shrugged again and put the sweet rolls away. Raid leaned against my leg and wagged his tail. I chuckled and rubbed his head. "You're so weird."

I turned around when I heard a shuffling noise coming from the living room. I watched Raikidan carry a large basket of linens through the living room to the laundry room, and several children attempting to help by carrying or dragging linens of their own behind him. I couldn't help but giggle at the cute site.

"Adorable."

"You laughing at him or the kids?" Raid asked.

"Keep your voice down. The older kids are harder to convince they don't hear things." I glanced down at him. "But I'm laughing because of the kids. They're adorable." I smiled. "I mean did you see Elsa? She was carrying a blanket over her head and couldn't see where she was going so she held onto Nari's dress."

A little red-haired girl ran into the kitchen and started tugging on my shirt. "Come play with us, Eira!"

"One second, Levi. I need to finish putting these treats away so they don't go bad. I'll come out into the living room once I'm done."

"'Kay!" She then ran off.

"You know, for someone who says she wouldn't make a good mom, you do well with kids," Raid commented.

I stored the plastic containers in the fridge. "Being a good parent and being good with kids are two different things. You can be good with kids but be a bad parent."

"Yeah, whatever you say," he replied slyly as we headed for the living room.

The moment we entered the room, my hands were seized and I was pulled over to a couch.

"Play time!" Levi said.

I laughed. "Okay, what are we going to play?" The kids went quiet and I chuckled. Of course they wouldn't know what they wanted to do. I surveyed the room and I snapped my fingers when a thought came to me. "A fort! We'll build a fort."

Elara's face scrunched. "How?"

I tipped one of the couches over. "With the furniture and blankets, of course!"

Kelcen gasped. "We can't do that! Ms. Lyra will get mad."

I grinned. "Matron Lyra, we're going to make a fort out of the furniture!"

Matron Lyra poked her head out of the laundry room and smiled. "Okay, have fun. Just don't break anything."

I looked at the children. "We have permission."

They cheered. The smaller children ran around grabbing blankets and pillows, while the older ones grabbed chairs that were light enough for them to move. I dragged larger furniture around while Raid pretended to help by snatching blankets to drag around aimlessly.

Raikidan and Matron Lyra came out of the laundry room when I pulled the last remaining blankets over the top of the fort. Matron Lyra appeared happy with the results of our activity, but Raikidan looked quite the opposite.

"What's wrong, Rai?" I asked. "You look angry."

He crossed his arms. "I am. Why didn't I get the invitation to build this fort? You know I love doing that."

I giggled. "You did. You were just too deaf to hear it."

Raikidan blinked dumbly, and Matron Lyra laughed. "She yelled to me asking if it was okay for them to build it. You were only loading linens into one of the washing machines. You should have been able to hear her."

Raikidan hung his head.

Nari rushed over to him and latched onto his hand. "You come play inside now."

Raikidan's body jerked when she pulled him with surprising strength, but he didn't protest. I watched as he ducked inside the fort and then he grunted. "You don't have any flashlights in here."

"So?" Nari said.

"So, we can't have a proper fort without flashlights." He stuck his head out of the fort and focused on me. "Right?"

I snorted. "Don't look at me. I don't know where they are."

Matron Lyra giggled. "They're over here in the utility closet. I'll go get them."

The older woman pulled out a ladder and rummaged around on a high shelf of the closet in question. Raid trotted over to her and watched.

"I'm thinking you need a better place for those," I observed. "If the power goes out, that would be dangerous to do."

Matron Lyra shook her head. "It's the only place I can keep them. With the range of ages in this place, I can't risk some of the younger children getting at the batteries."

"She has a point."

My lips twisted and went to voice an argument, but just then, the lights flickered and then went out completely. I heard the ladder fall, and then two things hit the floor. Thinking one of those things was Matron Lyra, I lit a fire in my hand by pure instinct and illuminated the room.

As I thought, Lyra had fallen off the latter, but to my horror, the other falling object hadn't been a flashlight. It had been Raid. He'd shifted out of his dog form and caught Lyra as she fell, using his body as a cushion. "Raid..."

He smiled at me weakly. "Sorry. I reacted out of reflex."

I wasn't sure if I should freak out at him, or try to run with it and make whatever attempt I could to salvage this situation.

But then Matron Lyra started giggling. "Dear, it's okay. I'd already figured it out."

I cocked my head. "What? Really?"

She smiled. "Yes. About two months before you started volunteering here, we had a boy who had shapeshifting abilities. I knew the moment I saw Raid he was the same. I didn't say anything because I understood why you were keeping it a secret."

"What happened to the boy?" Raid asked as he helped Matron Lyra up.

"Some shamans came by and took him to their village to help train him and find him a family. I got a letter a week later, saying he had found the perfect family the day he arrived."

I nodded. "South Tribe. They're partially druidic. Doesn't surprise me they'd take him in."

I watched as Raid took interest in the children again. I could only assume he was hoping the children wouldn't treat him differently now that they knew.

"He won't have anything to worry about."

Like typical children, they took it all in stride. Elsa came over to him and grabbed his hand and pulled him over to the other children. The older children played fifty questions while the younger ones treated him the same as when he was a dog, making attempts to pet him to see if he would react. Of course, Raid, being his weird self, reacted like he normally would, enjoying any attention he could get.

The only child I could see who hadn't engaged with him was Myra. She hid in the fort, her hand clenching Raikidan's shirt as she stared at Raid. She was acting as if Raid was a stranger. It was typical of her to run or hide when someone came to the orphanage looking to find a new addition to their lives, but I never imagined she'd do this to Raid since she was so attached to him. I shifted my gaze to Raikidan in hopes he could give me answers, but he shrugged in response.

"Her reaction won't last long. You'll see."

"I hope you're right."

I went about helping Matron Lyra find as many self-powered light sources as we could, as well as extra blankets. The power issue didn't surprise me. The building lost power on a nice day, so during a snowstorm, well, I was honestly surprised the building had power at all when we first arrived.

When I deemed we had lit the building up enough, I extinguished my fire and observed the children. Most had gone about playing in the fort to keep warm since the heat was also not working, while some others were trying to find more blankets and pillows to help keep everyone warm.

Raikidan messed with the circuit board in another room. He had been convinced that was where the problem was, and wouldn't listen to reason from either Matron Lyra or myself.

Raid shifted back and forth between his human and dog form for the kids and Myra was still hiding, but this time behind a couch that was away from everyone. I was now rather concerned, and when I noticed Raid glance her way, I knew he was, too.

I decided it was best to go over to her and I knelt in front of the frightened girl. "He's not going to hurt you, Myra."

"I know…"

"Then why are you hiding?"

"Scared…"

My brow furrowed. "Scared of what?"

"Something… here…"

I tried to follow her gaze, but I couldn't tell if she was looking at Raid or at a room beyond him. "What do you mean, Myra?"

She shook her head and I frowned.

"Don't dismiss her fear. I'm not at all convinced something isn't up."

"What do you mean?"

"I'm not sure yet. I'm still sensing out the area."

"Do I want to know what that means?"

"I wouldn't be able to answer if you asked."

"Of course…"

I focused on Myra again. I knew she wouldn't answer the question if I asked again—fear had that effect on her, so I needed to redirect her behavior. "If you're scared, why are you alone? Why not go over to Raid? You know he'll keep you safe."

She peeked up at me, and then at Raid, who was now aware of what I was trying to do. Raid sat upright with his legs crossed and held out his hand to her. Myra didn't need another invitation. She ran over to him, latching onto his neck and burying her face into him. Raid chuckled and held her.

I smiled at the sight, but it didn't last long once a knock was heard at the door.

"I wonder who that could be," Matron Lyra mused before heading to the door. "Oh, good evening, General Zo. How can I help you?"

I rolled my eyes and groaned. *Really?* It was as if there were no other commanding officers who did anything around this city. I couldn't figure out why my luck was so bad.

"We got a report that the orphanage lost power, and it's the only one to do so in three blocks, so we thought it'd be best to check it out," Zo informed Matron Lyra.

"Oh, well that's very kind," she replied. "But this building is old, and it goes out even on a good day. But please, come in anyway. It's cold out and you four did come all this way in this weather to check on us."

"I know this will sound condescending, but did you check your circuit breakers, in case a fuse popped?" Zo asked as Matron Lyra led them into the living room.

"Yeah, I've been working on it for the past thirty minutes," Raikidan sneered as he exited the circuit breaker room. "Nothing is wrong with it."

"Told you so," I muttered as I headed for the fort to play with the children. Normally I would have chosen to scold him for being rude, but since I still wasn't willing to forgive Zo, I rolled with it instead.

Zo blinked. "Well this is a surprise."

"Not really," Raid said. "We come by a lot to volunteer."

"But in weather like this?" Zo asked.

Raid pointed at me and I chuckled before speaking. "I insisted we come. I promised the kids."

"And by insisted, she was going to come here without us if necessary, so it was only right that we came along," Raid explained.

Nari came out of the fort a little bit and tugged on my shirt. "I'm hungry…"

I looked down at her. "You're hungry?"

She nodded and some of the other children stared at me the same way.

"Well, it is around the time I'd start making supper for them," Matron Lyra said.

I nodded and stood. "All right, let's see what we can conjure up for dinner."

The children cheered and several chose to follow me into the kitchen to see what I'd make for them, while Matron Lyra told the soldiers to either make themselves comfortable or have a look around to find the source of the electrical problem. I wasn't sure if offering to make dinner was a good idea, but depending on what I could find, it might result in something good for them.

I opened a few cupboards and even the fridge, and frowned when I couldn't find much. Apparently, Matron Lyra was running low on more supplies than she was willing to admit—again. I was going to have to do something to fix that.

I smiled when I finally found something. I shook the box and poked my head into the living room. "Pancakes!"

The children cheered, as did Raid. The kids laughed at him and I shook my head with a smile.

"What? I like pancakes," he defended.

"I know you do. But you can't have any."

He sat up straight. "What? Why not?"

"Because you'll eat them all on the kids," I accused before heading back into the kitchen.

"Would he really eat them all?" Nari asked, her eyes wide with fear she wouldn't get any.

I laughed. "I doubt he'd be that mean to you guys, but Raid could eat pancakes for breakfast, lunch, and dinner for the rest of his life and he'd be the happiest man alive."

Raid held his head high. "Yes, I would!"

The children giggled and I shook my head as I went about getting the wet ingredients to make the pancakes.

"I help! I help!" Myra ran into the kitchen.

I giggled. "Okay, you can help."

I lifted her up on the counter and tossed the ingredients into a bowl. When I began mixing everything, Myra insisted on doing the task, but that didn't last long. I went back to mixing until Myra asked to be put down on the floor, but of course, she wasn't done just yet.

"Whisk?"

"In a minute," I told her as I resumed my task. "I need to finish this."

"Whisk!"

"Why do you need it?"

"Whisk!"

I sighed and handed her the whisk. Unsurprisingly she giggled and ran out of the room with it. "Myra, come back here with that!"

I chased her into the living room and caught her, but only because she'd came to a screeching halt, staring at the dark bedroom.

"Myra, what's wrong?" I asked.

Myra screamed, the whisk clattering to the floor, and flung herself into my arms. "Something there!"

"Myra, it's okay. Nothing is there," I said. "It's an empty dark room."

"No... something there..." she insisted.

"Myra, I—" I stopped dead when I heard the creaking of the floor-boards in the bedroom. Myra trembled and I stared into the empty room.

"Be careful!"

A tall figure appeared in the darkness and lumbered forward, some-thing not quite right with his gait. The figure appeared unbalanced, almost like it was drunk or hurt.

"Back up, now!"

"Guys..." I warned.

My call caught the attention of the others in the room, but no one reacted right away. I pulled Myra into my arms when the figure emerged from the room. The man in front of me was tall, built, and there was definitely something off about him. I couldn't tell if he was drunk or on some sort of drug, but that didn't matter. He was somehow inside the orphanage when he shouldn't be, and he didn't appear to be friendly.

Raid rose to his feet. "Who are you and what are you doing here?"

The man didn't respond to him and kept up his sluggish pace... toward Myra and me. My instincts were screaming at me, but not in the usual way. I had an innate fight instinct, but today, it was flight and I didn't doubt it was because I held Myra in my arms.

"Protect the children."

The moment I scooped Myra up and took a step away from the man, he picked up his pace and reached out at me with one arm.

"Kids... orders..." he moaned.

Before I could think to move, Raid plowed into the man in an attempt to get him away, but the man rebounded well and tossed Raid aside like a ragdoll.

I ran with Myra in my arms and the man pursued us. "Kids... orders..."

"Don't you touch them!" Raid roared as he got back on his feet and tackled the stranger.

The two of them wrestled on the ground while a soldier pulled me into a corner with Matron Lyra to keep us safe, and Raikidan ran to the kitchen to protect the children in there. Raid struggled to keep the man down until he managed to get him in a chokehold. The man struggled until he passed out, but Raid didn't stop. I watched as he continued to choke the man, and I realized he had relapsed. He had had such good therapy in the past that I had forgotten about his severe case of post-traumatic stress disorder.

"Raid, stop!" I yelled. "He can't hurt us anymore."

He didn't hear me.

"Raid!"

"Raid, let him go," Zo ordered. "We don't want him dead."

But Raid didn't hear us. He continued his hold. I had to do something. The military would need this man alive, and Raid, with the kind heart he had, would beat himself up for days if he killed the man, even if this man was threatening these children.

With no good plan coming to mind, I did something dumb. I ran over to Raid and wrapped my arms around his chest as I sat on the floor behind him. I pulled him closer to me and rested my forehead against the base of his neck. "It's okay, Raid. You got him. You got him. He's not a threat anymore." Raid froze and I continued. "The kids are safe because of you. Come back to us... please."

Finally, Raid came back to the present and immediately let go of the man he had been choking. He tried to push the unconscious body away in a panic, but I held onto him tightly and hushed and cooed to get him to calm down. Two soldiers rushed over and dragged the strange man out of the house, and I continued to calm Raid, while also looking over at the children in the fort and then the ones hiding behind Raikidan in the kitchen. Luckily, they were no worse for wear, if a bit shaken up over the encounter.

"I'm sorry..." Raid whispered. "I'm sorry... I didn't mean to."

I hushed him. "It's okay. It's not your fault."

"Poor kid..."

Myra ran over to us and latched onto Raid. He held her, and when I determined it was safe to let Raid go, I stood and assessed the situation. Zo sent off two soldiers to check the outside of the house, and Raikidan continued to stand guard in the kitchen.

Zo flagged my attention and motioned for me to approach. I complied, curious what he wanted. Zo's gaze flicked to Raid, who was now checking on the children in the fort. "Is your friend going to be okay?"

I nodded. "Yeah. If you check your records, you'll find that he's an older soldier who was discharged due to severe PTSD. What you saw was his first relapse in years."

"You don't think he should be removed from the children?"

I shook my head. "No, he's safe. Trust me."

He nodded. "Okay, I will."

Kelcen poked his head out from the fort. "Eira, can we come out now?"

I smiled. "Yes, it's safe."

Kelcen and the other children inside the fort ventured out and then stampeded over to me asking questions all at the same time.

"Who was that man?"

"What did he want?"

"Why was the man here?"

"Hey, easy, easy," I cooed as I knelt. "I don't know who that man was, and I don't know why he was here." I glanced up at Zo. "But Zo here is going to find out. His friends took the man away so they can question him."

The children peered up at Zo and he nodded as he knelt. "We're going to do what we can to understand what happened today."

The children thanked him in unison and then looked at me expectantly. I laughed. "Yes, I'm still making pancakes for dinner."

They cheered, as did Raid and Myra over in their little corner. My lips twisted to the side and I tilted my head forward. He laughed. "What? I'm still excited about having pancakes—and I think I deserve at least one."

"Yeah!" Myra cheered. "Puppy daddy needs pancakes!"

Zo cocked an eyebrow in my direction and I shrugged while laughing. "She just calls him that."

He nodded, accepting the simple answer, much to my relief.

I headed for the kitchen. As I did, one of the soldiers Zo had sent outside came running back in. Zo met him halfway and they spoke quietly. Of course, I chose to listen in.

"Someone cut all the wires to the house," the soldier informed Zo. "This was definitely something planned."

"That doesn't make any sense," Zo voiced. "Why would they want these kids? They couldn't hold them for ransom."

The soldier shrugged. "I'm not sure, sir. Helren thinks this man is on a type of drug, based on the way he was walking and talking. It's possible the drug and his actions are related. Of course, we won't know until we get him back to the command post and question him when he's finally awake."

Zo nodded. "All right. In the meantime, I'll have to assign someone to watch this place until we get to the bottom of it."

"No need," Raid said as he came over with Myra in his arms. "I'm staying here. The kids are safe with me."

Zo looked at him questioningly, but Matron Lyra stepped up. "Starting today, Raid had been planning to stay here to help me out. I'm confident he can handle any issue that may arise in the future. There's no need to waste any more of your time here."

"Good, she's going along with it. There's hope for his situation yet."

"Are you sure?" Zo questioned. "We don't know the intentions of this man. Even if Raid is here, that may not deter another incident."

Matron Lyra nodded. "I'm positive Raid can handle this task."

Zo nodded, though clearly reluctant. "All right."

"Yay!" Myra cheered. "Puppy daddy staying!"

Zo patted her on the head. "You're so cute."

I sent a silent prayer of thanks to the gods. Myra was just young enough for things she said to be dismissed by adults.

I focused on Raikidan when I entered the kitchen. He leaned against a counter and the children who were in here with him sat on the floor. "Everything okay in here?"

Raikidan nodded. "Yeah."

"Can we go play now?" Nari asked me.

I smiled at her. "Of course. I'll have dinner ready in a few minutes."

They herded out of the kitchen, and I moved further in so Raikidan could leave. He left without saying a word to me. I sighed as I stood in the kitchen alone. Figuring it was best to get dinner going, I found another whisk and finished mixing the pancake batter before heating up a gas griddle.

"Don't let it affect you."

"Here, let me help," Raikidan offered.

His reappearance surprised me. I hadn't expected him to return. "Don't worry about it. I got it."

He reached for the bowl and whisk. "Just let me help."

"Rai, I know I'm a terrible cook and all, but I do know how to make pancakes that everyone will like."

"That's not why I'm offering to help."

"I don't care about your reasoning. I just want to do this on my own."

He frowned. "All right…"

I watched him leave, and he sat down on the couch before I poured the pancake batter onto the gas griddle.

"How come you didn't want his help?"

I gasped and jumped, my heart lurching into my throat. "Don't do that!"

The girl next to me frowned. "Sorry."

I gazed at her, still startled. I didn't recognize the girl, which was surprising. I knew every child here, or at least I thought I did. She was a fair-skinned girl with long blonde hair, and incredibly unique-looking eyes. They were several colors of blue, red, and green, and they appeared to sparkle like stars in the sky. She appeared to be about thirteen or so, a rare age here, making it hard for me to believe I had never met her before.

The voice gasped. *"Her…"*

"So, why didn't you want his help?" the girl repeated before I could go about questioning the voice.

I flipped some pancakes. "I didn't need it."

"But you didn't need it when mixing the pancakes and you still let the other kids help."

"It would have been mean to tell them they couldn't help."

"It was mean to tell Ray he couldn't help you."

"Children and adults are different." I turned the pancake batter so it wouldn't settle. "Whereas adults know how to do basic things like cooking, children don't. They need us to teach them, so we involve them in the cooking process to learn."

"You're doing it to push him away, aren't you?"

My face screwed up. Something was off about this girl. "I just didn't need his help. That's the only reason."

"And if Raid came in and offered to help?"

"I'd tell him I didn't need it, too."

"Why do you insist on pushing others away?"

I placed my hands on my hips. "I'm not pushing anyone away. I'm making pancakes."

"The pancakes are irrelevant."

I stared at the girl. "Who are you?"

"You need to trust your champion, Eira. You guard your heart out of fear of pain, when you should be able to trust your champion. He is the only one who can understand you in the way you want. Believe that he'll do his job correctly."

"So, it's true then... he is..."

I went to say something, but the girl ran for the dining room. When she reached the threshold of the doorway, the air around her distorted and the girl morphed from a thirteen-year-old to a twenty-something-year old. She winked a sparkling eye at me and then disappeared. *Genesis...*

"Eira, is everything okay in here?" Matron Lyra asked as she walked in. "I smell burning."

"Oh no!" I had been so distracted I had forgotten about the pancakes. "Dammit, I totally spaced!"

Matron Lyra chuckled as I dropped the burnt pancakes on a plate and stared at it in disappointment. "Would you like to share what you were thinking about?"

"It's not really important," I lied.

She came over and poured more batter onto the griddle. "Some of the kids told me you were talking to someone, but they knew none of the other kids were in here with you."

"You wouldn't believe me even if I told you."

"It was Genesis, wasn't it?" Surprise flashed over me and she smiled. "As odd as it sounds, she comes here every once in a while. She likes visiting the children to tell them how important they are and how they'll do great things with their lives. It encourages them, and me."

"Doesn't sound too odd to me. Gods can do as they please, especially her. If she wants to make an appearance on the mortal plane, instead of staying on their immortal one, then who's to stop her?"

Matron Lyra smiled. "Fair. Since she didn't come to talk with the children, I'm guessing she had something to say to you."

I nodded and flipped the pancakes. "I'm not quite sure I get what she was trying to convey, because she was using the word *champion* to refer to someone."

"Champion? That's an old word," Matron Lyra mused. "But for a goddess, that doesn't surprise me."

"It's not the only time this person has been called a champion in my presence," I told her. "Someone else called him that too…"

"May I ask who they were calling a champion?"

I glanced back to the living and furrowed my brow. "What is Rai doing?"

Matron Lyra laughed. "Panga asked him to braid her hair."

My face lined with worry. "Was that wise to allow? Last I knew, he didn't know how to braid hair. The concept of pulling hair into a ponytail is hard enough for him. He's a handy man, but not an overly smart one."

Matron laughed again. "I can't argue that. He did try to tell Panga it'd be a bad idea, but she insisted he try."

I shook my head and removed the pancakes from the griddle. "I hope he doesn't ruin her hair."

"He's being careful, so I don't think we have anything to worry about."

"Speaking about worry, I need to talk to you about Raid."

"If you're worried I'm going to tell him to leave after he offered to stay to keep us safe, don't," Matron Lyra said. "I wouldn't dream of doing that."

I shook my head. "I didn't think you would. I'm actually grateful you're allowing him to stay. Full transparency—Raid doesn't live with us, not anymore at least. He's a vagrant and I'm concerned. He won't listen to anyone when it comes to finding a place to stay, or even come back home. And since vagrancy is against the law…"

Matron Lyra rested her hand on my shoulder. "I'll do what I can to keep him here as long as possible without him going back on the street."

I smiled. "Thank you."

"And speaking of home, you and Ray should get going. It's late and it's still snowing like crazy, so you'll need time to get home before the streets are too covered to go anywhere."

I nodded and turned the griddle off. When I came into the living room, the kids looked at me and then frowned when they realized what was going on. "It's time for Rai and me to leave."

Elara and Elsa ran over to me and clung to my pants. "Don't go!"

"I'm sorry, but we have to."

"You can stay, like Raid!" Elara insisted.

I shook my head. "Rai and I have to go home. We'll be back, though."

"When?" Elsa asked.

"I'm not sure yet. But Matron Lyra will be sure to let you know when I figure it out."

The two pouted and reached out for a hug, which I gladly gave.

"I'll need you to help me before we leave," Raikidan said as he shifted his gaze down at Panga.

He hadn't made any progress on her hair. I laughed. "Sure."

"I'll go clean off the car," Raid offered. "I need to grab my stuff out of the back anyway."

"Great, thanks," I replied as I took a seat on the couch and worked on Panga's hair.

"Are you sure you're supposed to do it that way?" Raikidan asked me.

"Coming from the guy who sat here for over five minutes unable to figure out how to start a braid?"

He groaned and let me work.

By the time Raid returned, I had finished, and Raikidan and I were putting our boots and coats on. "Good thing you're leaving now. It's picking up and there's quite a bit of snow on the ground. I doubt the plows will be by any time soon."

I nodded my thanks. "Good to know."

Matron Lyra left the kitchen, and Raid moved out of the entryway so there'd be room for her to say goodbye. "Be careful driving."

I smiled. "We will. Thanks again for letting Raid stay here. I'll speak to some people and get some supplies dropped off."

"Oh, you don't have to do that!" she protested. "I'm letting him stay here out of the goodness of my heart! Not because I want something in return."

I shook my head. "Lyra, I saw the pantry. If anyone in this blasted city needed more than what they're getting, it's you and these kids. You're getting more supplies."

She sighed and then smiled. "You have a kind heart, Eira. Just be careful it doesn't get you into trouble."

"Yeah, what she said."

I chuckled. "Don't worry."

We said our goodbyes and headed out into the snow. Once Raikidan and I were in the car, I headed down the street, aware of how often the car was threatening to fishtail. It was definitely a good thing we were leaving when we were.

"Eira," Raikidan said quietly. "Are you upset with me?"

I took my eye off the road for a minute to look at him funny. "What? No. Why would you think that?"

"Because you didn't want my help when you were cooking, and the kids said you thought I was upset with you for an unknown reason."

I shook my head. "One, I was *just* making pancakes. I didn't need help. Two, I wasn't sure why you were being quiet. You could have had something on your mind for all I knew, but everyone took that to mean that I was sure you were upset with me for something."

"Well, I was thinking. And I'm not upset with you in any way."

"Okay."

We were quiet while I struggled to get down a few streets.

"Raikidan," I started when I was on a street that was a bit easier to get down, "I'm going to ask you this question again and I don't want you to avoid it this time. Do you like going to the orphanage?"

When he didn't reply, I waited. I was going to get this answer out of him. I wasn't even sure why he couldn't say anything to me.

"It's complicated," he finally said.

"Oh boy… here we go."

"Complicated?" I replied with disbelief.

"You don't like that answer?"

"Of course I don't like that answer, Raikidan." My grip on the steering wheel tightened, and my eyes narrowed as I tried to keep my irritation in check. "But it doesn't matter… After all this time, if that's the only answer you can give me, there's no point in asking again."

"Why can't you be okay with that answer?"

"Because it means you don't want to go, but are making yourself and can't tell me, and the gods only know why." My teeth clenched, but I took a few moments to calm myself before continuing. "You don't have to come to the orphanage if you don't want to. I'm never going to make you go. I go because I want to—because these kids deserve homes, but all I can give them is attention. Because these kids are the future, and seeing how positively they reacted to Raid being a shifter, that gives me hope for the future of Lumaraeon."

I punched the garage door opener when we came down the street for the garage. At the end of the dead-end street a hole opened up, snow falling into it. I drove the car down the now-snow-covered ramp and into the spacious garage.

"You really think that's what my answer meant?" he asked as I pulled into a free spot.

"What else would it mean?" I said as I threw the car into park.

He frowned, knowing my answer tossed him back into the same position he was in before.

I grunted and noticed Ryoko waiting at the far end of the garage. "Just forget I brought this up."

Raikidan grabbed onto my wrist when I attempted to get out of the car. "Please don't be mad at me."

I held his gaze for a moment. "I wish you'd trust me, like you expect me to trust you. Like you seem to be able to with the Matron, from what she's told me. Friendship isn't one-sided." *Neither is… love.*

"Dear, please don't go down that road. I don't like it when you take that one."

I pulled my wrist free and climbed out of the car. Ryoko had disappeared, but I suspected she saw the conversation Raikidan and I were having and assumed we were fighting… again. So naturally, she'd leave for us to sort things out. I headed for the stairs leading to the living room.

"It's my instincts, Eira!" Raikidan called after me, but I continued on. His reasoning didn't matter anymore. He'd had his chance to be straightforward without me having to resort to all this, and he blew it. "I do like going to see them."

I paid him no mind. I didn't stop until he took one of my fingers gently.

"Please listen," he begged.

"Why should you?"

"I'm tired of listening to excuses," I said. "I don't see how you can expect me to trust you when you can't even trust me."

"I do trust you, Eira," he insisted. "I just…"

"Just what? If not lack of trust, what could possibly be holding you back from saying anything honest to me?"

Raikidan sighed. "You're not the only one who guards their heart from everything…"

"Oh my…"

My chest tightened. He continued.

"When I told you it was complicated, I was telling the truth. Your kind and mine do many things differently. You humans care about offspring, even if they aren't your own. You tend to care regardless of your mated status. We dragons aren't typically like this. We care for only our own offspring, and it's not common for us to adopt. An orphaned whelp is generally considered a dead one, if it doesn't figure out how to survive on its own. Even in a clan setting, it's up to the parents to care of their offspring, and found orphans may not be taken in. Other mated pairs may take interest in the whelps and help with the raising, or take in an orphan if they feel a strong need to, but unmated dragons will keep their distance.

"As a solitary, unmated male dragon, my instincts tell me to stay away from offspring. It tells me they're not my responsibility, even though they don't have parents to care for them. But I also think independently from my instincts. It's why, even though I struggle with Rimu, I tolerate him far better than other males would. And, while I was reluctant to go to the orphanage the first time because I wanted to follow my instincts, I liked being there. I liked helping the Matron since she deserved the help for doing what she does all on her own, and I liked being the reason these children smiled and laughed. I like going there, Eira. I really do. I'm just fighting myself half the time."

"I wish you had told me that from the start." My gaze dropped to the floor. "It hurts when you keep your distance and yet expect me to confide in you. I'm not a stranger to one-sided relationships…"

Raikidan reached out and lifted my chin, making me look at him. "I swear to you that's not my intent. I just know, if I don't word myself correctly, you tend to misunderstand and it ends up worse than if I had stayed quiet. Like you said, it hurts when you misunderstand and pull away."

I managed a small smile. "Then promise me you'll do your best to give me a full, honest answer in the future. Half answers and no answers won't be acceptable."

We stared at each other for a long time. I wanted an answer out of him on this, but he remained quiet, though I could tell it wasn't reluctance.

Raikidan reached out and grazed my cheek with his fingers. Normally I'd have jumped back, but I found myself locked into those eyes of his. Then he cupped my cheek and pulled me into a tight hug, taking me by surprise. "I'll do what I can if it means you won't freak out on me as often."

"We'll see," came my muffled reply. "But first, can you let up? Hard to breathe through this fluffy jacket."

"I could take the jacket off."

"Dealing with muscle wouldn't be any better." *And really I don't think I could handle that while staying true to my resolve...*

Raikidan reluctantly let me go, and I put space between us by heading for the stairs.

"Eira, I really was thinking about something today, making me quiet," he insisted as he followed. "I wasn't mad at you."

"I know. But if I may ask, what was on your mind?"

"Nothing important."

I shrugged. "Okay."

His brow creased. "Are you sure?"

"If it concerned me, you'd tell me, right?"

"Well, yeah."

"Then I have no reason to not be okay with that answer."

"You confuse me sometimes, you know that?"

I laughed and glanced up the stairs when feet clomped down them.

"Are you two finally done fighting?" Ryoko asked as she poked her head under the railing.

"We weren't fighting," Raikidan stated. "We were... miscommunicating."

Ryoko nodded. "Right. If that's what you want to call it, fine. I see Raid isn't with you, I guess you couldn't convince him to come back?"

I shook my head. "No, but I got the next best thing. He's staying at the orphanage."

Ryoko smiled. "That makes me feel a lot better. And Matron Lyra could use the full-time help. Oh, you're going to want to come up ASAP. Danika wants to know how much the kids liked her treat for them."

I headed up the stairs. "She'll be happy with what I have to say."

"You're talking about those sticky bun things, right?" Raikidan asked. "Are there any left here? I want to try them. They looked good."

I grinned. "Well I did try to offer you one, but you decided you wanted to do your own thing. If there aren't any left, you really missed out. Shva'sika makes the best sweet rolls in all Lumaraeon. Even her allergen-conscious ones."

Raikidan pushed past us. "There better be one left."

Ryoko and I laughed at him before following to find out if he'd get what he wanted or not. As we did, I realized how quiet the voice had been through the entire exchange I had with Raikidan.

"No comments from the peanut gallery?" Silence met my question. *"Hello?"* Still silence. This perplexed me. She had been so active lately. Something I wanted an answer to, but suspected I wouldn't be able to get.

"What? There *has* to be more!" Raikidan shouted.

Ryoko giggled. "Danika is so mean to him."

I snickered. I suspected this might happen. She had made a lot, and not all of them went to the kids. Our housemates could have consumed the rest while we were gone, but Ryoko's comment had me thinking otherwise.

I picked up my pace. I wanted to watch the drama with my own eyes.

44
CHAPTER

now swirled around in the air, a light breeze blowing it around
as it fell from the night sky. The path Raikidan and I walked on
was lit by light posts and decorated trees. I shivered and pulled
my hands under my arms to try to keep them a bit warmer.

I couldn't believe Genesis had sent us out to do a surveillance
assignment. I knew the assignments wouldn't completely stop because
winter had hit, but to send us out at night while it was snowing? That
was just uncalled for.

I shook my head free of the snow that had accumulated on it, noting my ears were numb, and grumbled quietly.

"You okay, Eira?" Raikidan asked.

"I'll be fine," I muttered. "Just cold."

"I'd offer you a hat, but I didn't even think of grabbing one for
myself."

I chuckled. "It's all right. I should have thought to wear one in the
first place."

Raikidan moved his arm behind me and grabbed onto the side of
my shoulder. "It's not much, but maybe this will help?"

The heat seeped through his coat and it made my body melt. "So
warm…"

He chuckled. "And you're so sensitive to heat."

"It's not always a good thing."

Raikidan gazed around. "Let's get out of this snow."

My brow creased. "But the assignment. We have to complete it. Rules of our accep—"

"You, follow the rules?" He smirked. "Since when?"

"I always follow the rules." I grinned. "My rules."

He laughed. "Well maybe your rules this time should side with reason. Our *valiant* leader shouldn't have sent us out here in weather like this if she really expected us to notice anything amiss."

I couldn't help but laugh at bit at the little title he gave Genesis. She could get overbearing sometimes with her expectations, even more so now that she was an adult and not an adult stuck in a child's body, but she meant well. *Just like the god.* Her sudden appearance at the orphanage still had me shocked.

"He has a point."

"Okay, where do you propose we go? You know she'll freak out if we get home too early, and I don't want to deal with that."

He pointed. "How about taking that?"

"Hmm, interesting…"

I peered in the direction he pointed, spying a large horse drawn sleigh under a lamppost waiting for new passengers. "A sleigh ride?"

He frowned. "You don't like the idea?"

"It's not that. I've just never been on one," I admitted.

"Me either, so why not?"

I laughed. "When you put it that way, how could I say no?"

He grinned and led me over to the sleigh. The driver nodded and Raikidan helped me in before paying the man and jumping in next to me. The driver hopped up on his perch and got the horses moving. I watched with growing delight as the park moved by us in the dim light.

"Hey, Eira?" Raikidan said quietly.

I turned my head to face him. "Hmm?"

"I, uh, have something for you," he said as he reached for his jacket pocket.

I tilted my head. "You have something for me?"

Taking my hand, he pulled out a small, plain white box from his pocket and placed it on my palm. I looked at him funny and he chuckled. "I know you told me not to give you anything on the Solstice, so I figured it was safe to give it to you now."

"Raikidan, I meant I didn't want any gifts at all."

"Just open it, please?"

I blew air through my lips and opened the box, only for my breath to catch. Inside was a stunning sapphire ring.

"Oh wow."

I closed the box almost immediately and tried to hand it back. "I can't take this."

"W—what's wrong? Why not?"

"Yeah, why not?"

"It looks expensive. I can't take another expensive gift from you."

He folded my hands over the box. "Please take it. I had it made for you."

"That's… really nice of him."

I gave him and exasperated look. "Why do you do this to me?"

"Do what?"

"Shower me with gifts. Expensive gifts at that."

"Someone should."

"But why you?"

He flashed an alluring smile. Even in my conflicted state, the expression made my heart skip. "Because I want to. Now keep it, please."

I sighed and nodded. He smiled wider and watched as I pulled the ring out of the box. I thought I could hear the sleigh driver chuckling quietly, but I ignored it.

"I didn't know your finger size, so I had to guess," he admitted as I attempted to put it on a random finger. "I didn't think about that part when I first had the idea."

I laughed as I continued to fail at finding the right finger. "Are you sure it's going to fit?"

"Ebon promised it woul—"

I snickered when he stopped dead. "I already figured he made it. I know this style."

He muttered to himself and shifted his gaze away. I wasn't sure what he was so upset about. It wasn't like knowing where he got it was a big deal, right?

I exhaled through my lips when the jewelry finally slipped onto a finger. "There, it fits on…"

"Oh my."

My voice trailed off and my eyes widened when I realized what finger it fit. Raikidan studied my hand. "It fits on your left ring finger." My jaw remained slack as I stared at the ring. He leaned closer and kept his voice low. "Is there a problem with that?"

I licked my lips. "For most human customs, that finger is usually reserved for engagement and wedding rings."

He thought about the meaning and then raised a brow. "Will it fit on your right hand?"

I shook my head. "Tried that side first."

"Why is it different?"

I shrugged. "Just happens sometimes."

Raikidan's shoulders sagged. "Sorry. I thought he knew a good size for you. I could see if he can resize it."

"It's not that big a deal."

"But it is…"

"It's only a big deal if you make it one. And besides, we both know you'd be perfectly okay if it did mean that."

"Don't start. It will never mean that."

"Then what's the problem?"

She had a point. I smiled and curled up to him. "It's okay. It's the thought that counts, and it's obvious you put a lot of thought into it. I'm okay with wearing it on this finger."

He lips twitched into a smirk. "You're just saying that so you can steal my heat."

"No, but I'm going to steal your heat, too." I curled into him more. "You're a nice little furnace."

He chuckled and wrapped his arm around me. I hummed, embracing the heat radiating off his body.

"I'll figure out how to pay you back," I mumbled.

"That's thoughtful of you."

"You don't have to, Eira."

"But I'm going to. You went through the effort of giving this to me, so I'll make the effort too."

He shook his head. "Fine, just don't go overboard."

I chuckled and thought about what to give him.

I bit my lip as I changed into my nightclothes in my closet. I had been thinking hard about what to give Raikidan, and the same two ideas kept popping up. Unfortunately, one of them was a little more personal than the other.

"Interesting idea. It'll work."

"You're not going to tell me I shouldn't?"

"You'll do it anyway, so why bother?"

I took a deep breath. She was right. It was something he wanted a lot, so why not give it to him? *He's gotten a few from me over the past few months anyway. Sure, the situations called for it, but they didn't mean anything. On top of that, he's promised to another, and that's how it is. This one will be the same as the ones before it… Meaningless…*

"Uh huh. Why continue to lie to yourself?"

"If I didn't know any better, you're encouraging this."

My accusation was met with silence. *Of course, she'd stop talking to me.* I started to wonder if her position on the whole situation was shifting.

I strolled out of the closet and looked at Raikidan, who sat on my bed with a book. For a dragon who claimed he didn't like to learn, he did a lot of it.

He glanced up. "Oh, I didn't realize you were heading to bed yet. Sorry."

He slid of my bed and placed the book down on my nightstand. I stopped him before he had the chance to shapeshift. "Wait, Raikidan, before you shift."

His brow rose. "Yeah?"

I scratched my head, my cheeks warming a bit. "I, uh, have something for you."

"What is it?"

"The first part of your Solstice gift," I said as I moved closer to him.

"Okay, where is it?" he asked, his eyes looking me up and down, as if expecting me to be hiding it somewhere in plain sight.

"Right here." I grabbed his chin lightly and pulled his face closer to mine until our lips touched. He tensed, but soon relaxed and rested his hands on my hips.

Several moments passed and I pulled away, struggling to look at him.

"Oh, don't be like this. You're good."

"It was nothing…"

"Look at how he's acting. It's not nothing."

His eyes fluttered open, as if it took him a moment to realize the kiss had ended, and then gave me a cocky grin. "I can't complain about that gift, though I'm curious what compelled you to give it to me."

My cheeks flushed more and I continued to look away. "Because you used to ask for that a lot before I chewed you ou—"

"Tricked me," he corrected. "You tricked me into a deal after you chewed me out—twice."

I thought I caught the voice chuckling. I rolled my eyes, the awkwardness fading with Raikidan's cocky attitude. "Loophole, if you want to get technical."

He shook his head while crossing his arms. "Whatever. So, you said that was only part one?"

I nodded. "The other part will take some time to work up. I just wanted to give you a little something sooner."

Raikidan grinned. "Well then, I guess I have to give you a part two, as well."

I shook my head. "No, you don't. Your gift was expensive and—"

His hand cupped my cheek and he made me look up at him. My heartbeat slowed as he and I held eye contact, and then it stopped when he leaned down and claimed my lips with his. My hand flew up and rested on his chest instinctively. His intoxicating scent filled my senses, and his strong muscles tensed under my touch, teasing me. My knees weakened, and the urge to press myself against him and slip my tongue between his warm lips crossed my mind. *I shouldn't... but I want to.*

Our lips parted, Raikidan choosing to pull away, and I had to fight with all the control I could muster to hold back from crossing any more lines.

"Oh wow..." the voice said in a breathless voice that would have matched my own if I could speak.

I tried to formulate a sentence, but my mind continued to blank. All I could do was admire him—his strong jaw—his well-sculpted physique—making me look like some pathetic, lost mess.

He chuckled as he turned away. "You're cute when you're flustered."

Flushed face, I managed to catch my breath. "I–I am not cute." I crossed my arms and looked away, my lips nearly formed into a pout. "Or flustered."

"Yeah, sure." He chuckled more and then shifted into his natural dragon shape.

I sighed when he nudged me toward my bed, but complied. After what had just happened, I didn't trust myself too close to him. I crawled into the soft mattress and stared up at the ceiling when I flopped down on my back. I needed the sleep, but it wouldn't come easy—not tonight—as I silently dealt with all the strange emotions whirling around the pit of my stomach.

45
CHAPTER

Taking a deep breath, I stepped off my platform and onto the smaller one in front of me. The Council had called a meeting to reveal their verdict on what would happen to Raynn's team. I had sent them several progress reports on Zenmar's status as he adjusted to his new life, and how well Mocha had transitioned into our team, even though she believe it to be temporary. But even with all of the data I had given them, I wasn't sure how this would go. They could give Raynn his team back even if I could lay out a good case against it, or they could do what I believed was the right move and take his team from him. I hoped I wouldn't have to fight for the outcome I wanted, but if I had to, I would, and I prayed I'd get some backing on it.

I barely gave Raynn a passing glance as our two platforms hovered near each other. We stood at attention when Elkron stepped forward to address everyone. I swallowed when I saw the clear look in his eye. They had made up their minds and there would be no room to discuss it.

"We have gathered you here to reveal our decision on Team Seven's fate," Elkron announced. "Our decision is based on information we have collected over these past few weeks. The information provided brought us to a unanimous decision." He stared at Raynn. "Starting today, Raynn's position as general is no longer recognized within the resistance, and his station as Battle Leader for Team Seven has been terminated."

Others murmured about the decision, many of them surprised. Me, on the other hand, I released a mental sigh of relief. I was so glad they had made this decision. Raynn, unsurprisingly, looked livid. I could tell he wasn't going to take that answer without fighting back as if his life depended on it.

"Sir, I'd like to know what information you're using to base your decision on." I was taken aback by Raynn's diplomatic response. It had been so long since I had heard him try to act so well in a situation as tense as this, I thought he had forgotten how.

"We have collected information from dozens of individuals about your past and how you've acted in situations," Elkron told him.

"How far back are we talking?"

"Since your promotion to captain while still in service under Zarda."

I tried not to show any physical signs of surprise. That was a long time ago and it was a lot of information to collect. But what got me was how far back they had gathered the information. That was just after—

"Sir, can you tell me what was specifically said of me?" Raynn asked.

"Summed up, you were described as 'an arrogant, self-serving narcissist who left comrades behind to die to save your own ass.'"

My eyes widened, jaw going slack. That type of response wasn't something I would have expected from a Council member. I could tell he was angry with Raynn, he wasn't hiding that one bit, but even Genesis would have given a more tactful answer.

Raynn, on the other hand, took it as an opportunity to get the upper hand on this debate. "Can this be proven? Besides by word of mouth? Is there physical evidence to prove any of this?"

"You left Zenmar to die."

"We were in a high-stress situation. Anyone could have left their own behind," Raynn tried to defend.

"Except you gave a direct order to abandon him," I shot.

Raynn glared at me and went to snap back, but Elkron held up his hand and addressed me. "Commander, you speak out of turn."

I bowed my head and lifted my hand up to my chest in salute. "My apologizes, sir."

"You are forgiven, but only because what you state is true. Several reported hearing this order. You failed as a leader, Raynn, and Commander Eira took that responsibility on herself to rectify that."

Raynn's eyes darkened in anger. "With all due respect, sir, I believe it's in everyone's best interest if you reconsider."

"Is that a threat, Raynn?"

"No, of course not, sir. I just feel there isn't anyone else capable of taking my position. I know this team. I have commanded battle for it longer than most battle leaders."

Elkron chuckled. "Commander Eira, why don't you recite to everyone the reports you gave us about Zenmar and Mocha."

I nodded. "Making the decision to amputate Zenmar's leg was not an easy one. I knew the consequences of doing so, but I trusted my highly-skilled medical practitioner on his advice to remove it. To my surprise, Zenmar has adapted quite well to his prosthetic.

"In the beginning, he had difficulties adjusting to it, and to the training program I set up for him. I feared even surveillance assignments would be too much for him to handle. But he has proven me wrong, and in these past weeks alone, his ability to adapt has shone through. Unfortunately, it's still unknown whether he will ever make a one hundred percent recovery. If he can, it could take years to do so."

"Could the situation have been avoided?"

"If Raynn hadn't screwed up the assignment so badly, yes." Small groups chuckled at my attack, but one swift glance from Elkron quieted them down. "That being said, if the assignment's failure was unavoidable, the outcome would have still been the same. Zenmar's accident was a result of the assignment's failure."

"Do you regret saving him?" Elkron asked.

"I do not, sir."

"Even with everything you've had to sacrifice for him?"

"No sacrifice is too great for one of our own, sir."

He nodded. "What of Mocha?"

I took a deep breath. "Mocha's addition to my team came as a surprise. No one coerced her to come to us, and no one forced her to stay. She arrived of her own free will, although it was obvious she had doubts on whether she was making the right choice. I wasn't sure if she would stay for very long, not that my team would have minded at the time. They had voiced their own protest about the situation, but I stuck by my decision to allow her to stay. I had reason to believe her choice was for the best, if everyone could put up with the idea."

I took another breath, to keep my reports correct and my head level.

"It didn't take long for her to fit in, though for the first few weeks she struggled to come out of her shell and trust us. After my team and Mocha put aside past differences, they were able to find similarities and get along. The team showed Mocha how a real team functioned, while including her. It was something she had never seen while under Raynn's leadership. Mocha adapted much better than I could have hoped for. And even if she doesn't stay on this team, I know she's learned something valuable. It is something she can bring to any other team she goes to."

Elkron had closed his eyes as I told Mocha's story, as if trying to envision my report. When I finished, he opened his eyes and then focused on me. "Can you tell me what she's learned that was so valuable?"

"I think that's pretty obvious, don't you, sir?"

"It still needs to be said. For the sake of this meeting."

Before I could speak, a familiar voice sounded from behind me. "I learned what it meant to be on a real team." I cranked my neck over my shoulder, spying Mocha, attention full on the Council. She knew better than to speak out. She could get into real—

Elkron chuckled, surprising me. "Go on."

"I've learned what it means to be on a real team," she repeated. "I learned what it means to be able to rely on someone other than yourself and know if you fall, they'll be there to give you a hand." Her gaze dropped, a tiny smile on her lips as if she were a little embarrassed. "I also have been shown true friendship. I've seen what it's like to not have to question or wonder if that friendship is real, or a face for someone else's personal gain."

Elkron nodded and then gazed down at Raynn, his eyes intense. "Will that be enough proof for you? Because of your incompetence as a leader, you failed to keep your team safe in more ways than one. You failed to have a true team. You are not worthy to be called a leader."

Raynn's fists clenched as he tried to control his anger. I waited to see what would happen. It wasn't like him to have so much control, at least, not anymore. A long time ago, before he had been promoted to captain, it would have been easy for him, but something had caused him to change, and he became the asshole we knew him as today.

Raynn exhaled slowly and his fists loosened. "Very well. All I request is that I be reunited with my team."

Elkron shook his head. "No. You will remain separated from them until we are sure you've learned from this."

My eyes widened a bit. I had no idea the Council had separated him from Mocha and the others. But it shed light on why Mocha had come to us, and why Doppelganger and Chameleon helped us on occasion with assignments. With Raynn removed from their lives, they would have more options to explore. It also explained the gift the two men gave Mocha during the solstice. The small camaraderie they had had grown in Raynn's absence, and Mocha's choice to leave altogether enabled them to think about what was important, and how important it was to openly show this in order to keep it.

I could see Raynn's anger boiling again, but he managed to keep it under control. "Then at least allow me to have my girl back."

My brow twisted in confusion. Who was he talking about? I'd never heard of him sticking with one woman more than a few nights at most.

Mocha mirrored my thoughts and spoke to herself, though rather loud. "Who is he talking about?"

Raynn turned to look at her. "You, of course."

"You're joking, right?" She laughed, but from the way Raynn reacted, it looked as though she'd pulled his heart out. "You mess around with other women and act like I'm a disposable convenience and you dare to claim I'm your girl? Yeah, I don't think so." She shifted her eyes to the Council. "I know you've made choices you've deemed best for the teams and our purpose, but if they will have me, I would like to become a permanent member of Team Three. I don't have to live there if it's not feasible, but just knowing I will be a part of a real team will make me happy."

"We will grant this if the Council member and battle leader of Team Three allows of it," Elkron said.

Genesis smiled. "I don't mind her sticking around."

I nodded. "I will welcome her."

Elkron responded with his own nod. "Then it's settled. Mocha, permission granted to move in with your new teammates. As for Team

Seven, we have chosen not to disband permanently, and a new battle leader will be appointed to replace Raynn. We will make accommodations for anyone who wishes to transfer to another team, within reason. This meeting is over."

"But, sir—"

Elkron glared at Raynn. "We are finished here."

Raynn glowered at me, but before he had a change to blame me, I turned away and headed back to my team. How he felt about the situation didn't matter to me. It was his fault and he got what he deserved. What did matter was how my team would react to Mocha's choice. Yet one look told me I wouldn't have to worry. They all appeared happy, although Ryoko by far surpassed them on the happiness meter by the death-grip she had around poor Mocha.

I was glad they had been able to put aside their past differences and see what great friends they could make when they did so. This was the future of Lumaraeon we all wanted. For everyone to put down their hate and grudges—to put aside their differences—and get along as one.

Pain twinged in my chest. How could I advocate for such a world when I struggled to put those kinds of issues behind me? I embraced those reminders so I wouldn't repeat past mistakes. *I'm afraid of repeating them...*

"But you can't know inner peace until you let go."

"I'm not sure I deserve inner peace."

"That's not true. I've been with you on this life road the entire time, and if anyone deserves peace, it's you."

"Why are you so kind to me now? What changed?"

"I can't form it into words. The answer is blocked. But know, your choices leading up to this have caused it. It is good. I'm here to help, and I hope to finally be able to guide you as I should."

"What do you mean?"

"I still cannot say. But I can say you deserve happiness. You shouldn't fear it. And while I'm not convinced of some things, the dragon you fawn over now and then isn't a horrible choice. He's strong, protective, if a little too much, and... easy on the eyes."

"Are you sure I'm the one fawning over him?"

"Oh, it's all you. I just appreciate his... assets."

"He's not the one for me. He has someone already."

"I'm not convinced we know the whole truth."

"Laz!" I blinked and came back to reality when Ryoko called my name and started waving at me. "Let's go."

I smiled and nodded. "Yeah."

Joining them on the platform, we waited for it to bring us to the entrance. As we walked down the hall, I noticed two pairs of people waiting in the shadows. The pair closest to us was Zenmar and Lena. The other, Chameleon and Doppelganger. I locked eyes with Zenmar and knew he wanted to speak with me. Doppelganger motioned for Mocha to come over to them, but she hesitated. I placed my hand on her shoulder and nodded. It was best if she went over and talked with them.

Mocha stared at me for a moment and then nodded. "I'll catch up with you guys."

"Same," I told the others. "I need to speak with Zenmar. We'll meet up at Aurora's computer station."

I went to meet with Zenmar before anyone could argue. As I made my way over to him, I noticed the cane he was leaning on. I had hoped he wouldn't have to use it the way he was by now, but I guess that was a bit much to expect at this point in his recovery. He held out his hand when I approached, and I happily took it in mine to shake. "It's good to see you."

He smiled. "You too, Eira. I won't keep you long. I just wanted to thank you for what you've done for me."

I shook my head. "You don't have to thank me for this."

"Yes, I do," he insisted. "Raynn may be a royal ass, but many of the other battle leaders would have also given up on me. Some may have saved me like you chose to, but none of them would have put all the effort in to helping me that you did. They would have forced me to go underground and wait for all of this to be over or somehow integrated me into the city and not allow me to come back to our cause. You've done none of that, and for that, I am grateful."

I smiled. "Well, you're welcome. I just wish there had been more I could have do—"

Lena hugged me tightly. "He's alive and recovering. That's all I could have asked for."

I wrapped one arm around her and rested my free hand on her head, but I didn't say anything. I didn't feel there was a need.

"We should be going now," Zenmar announced.

Lena pulled away from me and nodded. She joined him by his side and held his hand. "Thank you, again."

I only nodded as they turned and headed down the hall at a slow pace. I couldn't help but smile at Lena's patience. She had to care about him a lot to stick through all this mess. *He's a very lucky man.*

Remembering I had somewhere to be, I went to head to the range when I noticed everyone still waiting. I shot Ryoko a questioning look when I approached. "Didn't I say I'd catch up?"

She shrugged. "We figured it wouldn't hurt to stay put. Mocha!" Mocha glanced over her shoulder and waved a little. "Let's go home!"

She smiled and nodded. She said a few more words to Chameleon and Doppelganger before waving goodbye to them and rejoining us so. "Hey, Eira?"

"Yeah?"

"They're not sure on the decision yet, but Chameleon and Doppelganger are thinking about switching to our team. Not moving in or anything, just being part of the team. Would that be cool?"

I smiled at her. "I don't have an issue with it."

She smiled back. "Thank you."

"You aren't planning on leaving, are you?" Ryoko asked. "I mean the house, not the team."

"I'm not sure what I want at the moment," Mocha said.

Ryoko ears drooped. "Okay. Well, if you don't stay, you'd better visit! Like every day."

The group of us laughed. Even I did. The amount of joy I experienced due to her reaction was elating, but also daunting. It'd been some time since...

"It's okay to feel this way. You have that right to experience all emotions."

"I've spent most of my life trying to pretend... trying to embrace my design so I couldn't be a failure..."

"You're not a failure. You're far from that. Let the emotions in. They're confusing, but that's what it means to live."

I wasn't sold on the idea. Emotions caused pain as much as they caused happiness. I found myself looking at Raikidan, as the others pushed on at a quicker pace since Ryoko challenged a few of them to a foot race. He smiled at me, and a mix of emotions turned in my chest. *Emotions are confusing. Some even deceiving. And because of that, I don't know the right ones to follow...*

46
CHAPTER

Water splashed into the bucket as I wrung out the rag before wiping down the bar. We had been busy today, and it was finally calm enough for me to clean up. I looked up when someone approached. Seeing that it was Zo, I snapped my gaze back to the bar as if to appear like I was only taking a quick glance. The last time I had to deal with him was when I had been at the orphanage, and before that was the party. I wasn't keen on changing that now, but since I was working, there was no way to avoid it.

"What'll you have?" I asked as I dropped the rag into the bucket.

"Sidecar," he said as he sat down and placed his money on the bar. When I chuckled at his request, his face twisted in confusion. "What?"

"I took you to be more of a Typhoon or Rusty Nail guy," I said as I mixed up his drink for him.

He chuckled. "On a normal day you'd be right, but not tonight."

"Fair enough. Enjoy," I told him before going back to cleaning the bar.

"Who's the lucky guy?" he asked after several minutes of silence between us.

My brow cocked. "Huh?"

He pointed to my hand. "The ring. You're engaged now, right?"

I glanced at the ring and then laughed. "Oh, no! I'm not engaged."

His face lit up with a mix of surprise and excitement... for some stupid reason. "Really?"

I nodded. "Rai bought it for me as a friendship ring." A small smile spread across my lips as I touched the ring. "He really knows how to make a girl feel special."

"I see." I could tell he wasn't happy at all that it had been Raikidan who had given me the ring. *Like I care.* Then, all of a sudden, he became very serious as he stared at his glass. "Eira."

"Yes?"

It took him a moment to respond, but when he did, he looked up at me. "I'm sorry. For everything that happened at the party and how I've treated you. You're right, I've been a complete ass, and I'm sorry." I went to respond, but he wasn't done. "I'd like to make it up to you. I'd like to take you out tonight, after your shift is over. It's always been one of your shorter ones during the week, so I figured there would still be enough time left in the night to enjoy it. What do you say?"

My gaze fell away. "I don't know, Zo..."

Genesis was going to kill me if she found out I turned him down, but I couldn't make myself say yes. I didn't like going on dates with him, and I didn't like letting him believe he had some sort of chance with me.

I particularly hated the fact that Genesis thought I had the right set of skills for this type of undercover work. I didn't know how to use femininity and seduction to extract information. I wasn't alluring enough. Shyden, my mentor, and several other assassins tried to teach me to pretend such confidence, even resorting to certain types of drugs to attempt a state of mind change. Even with the induced help, I failed to look past what I saw, and they gave up, instead focusing on abilities I excelled in.

"I had planned on picking up an extra shift so I could buy something nice. And honestly, I don't know if I want to..."

"Please," he begged. "Give me another chance. I promise it won't be a disappointment."

I hesitated. Not only would Genesis kill me if I said no, but the way he was looking at me made me feel guilty. I sighed. "All right. One chance."

Relief and happiness burst from him all at once. "Excellent. I'll see you after your shift."

"Right after my shift?"

His brow twisted in confusion. "That's not a problem, is it?"

I half laughed. "I need to be able to change out of my work clothes."

"You look fine to me." I gave him a stern look and he exhaled. "Okay, okay. I'll pick you up at your place. How much time will you need?"

"Give me an hour total. That'll give me time to make it out of here, get home, and clean up."

He smirked. "It's a date, then."

I sighed mentally as he walked off. *I can't believe he conned me into going out on a date with him again.* I looked at Raikidan when he came over to the bar.

"Why did Zo look so happy when he left? And why do you look so miserable, for that matter?"

"I'm doing my job."

"You did not agree to go out on another date with him."

I resumed my cleaning. "I had to. I didn't have a good enough excuse to say no."

"Why not?"

"Because I couldn't think of anything. My excuse to pick up extra hours didn't work, and since I'm single, I don't have that backup plan. It's because I'm single that Genesis makes me do this, regardless of my inability to do it properly."

"What about the ring? You told me what it meant to have it there."

"And who would I say I'm engaged to? You? I wasn't going to put that kind of pressure on you. That wouldn't be fair."

"But it's not fair that you have to put up with him like this."

"It's part of the job, Rai. It's something I have to live with."

Raikidan growled and stormed off, surprising me. Not only did he not put up a fight, but acted like he disagreed with me on the position of pretending to be my partner. I knew he hated Zo, but I didn't think he'd be okay with acting as my boyfriend. *Well, Eira, that'd be fiancé, with the ring and all...*

"You should have assumed he'd be okay with the way he acts. Well, acting may not—"

"Don't you dare finish that sentence! I don't want to be fighting you about this topic either."

"We both know how you feel. You fight it on a regular basis."

"It doesn't matter how I feel. He's not mine to have. That's why I fight it."

"It's not the only reason."

"Just go away."

I rubbed my temples. This whole topic was causing a headache. It didn't matter how anyone felt about the matter. I had a job to do, regardless of whether I liked it or not, and that was how it was until this stupid rebellion was won. *Or Zo miraculously finds himself a girlfriend… who isn't me.*

I nodded my head and tapped my finger on the car console to the beat of the song on the radio while Zo drummed away on the steering wheel. He had a decent taste in music, I could give him that, and the date had gone a lot better than I had expected. He had made himself look nice, made sure the car was clean—well, had a car for that matter, and had treated me to a nice dinner. All of our conversation was pleasant, too. He asked simple questions that weren't too personal or invasive, and brought up topics that lasted more than a few minutes. It had actually felt like I had gone on a real date.

I blinked when Zo turned down the music and pulled the car to the side of the road. Looking out the window, I realized we were at the house. Again he surprised me. I assumed he would have tried to be sly and bring me back to the barracks in hopes he'd get lucky. Maybe he wasn't as bad as I was trying to make him out to be. He could be a great guy and just wasn't used to the whole dating scene, and that was why he screwed up so much.

Zo jumped out of the car and made it to my side to open the door before I could even unbuckle. I smiled my thanks and climbed out, tripping in the heels Ryoko made me wear. I had done that several time tonight, and it ended up sparking a strange conversation with Zo about shoes. It had to be the weirdest conversation I had ever had with a guy, especially since he knew more than me. Not that it was a bad thing, just that I wasn't used to such a situation. *Unless you're Azriel.* I was used to off-the-beaten-path conversations with him.

Zo walked me to the front door and I smiled demurely at him. "Thank you. Tonight was nice."

He stood tall, puffing his muscular chest out a bit too much in an attempt to impress. "I told you I'd make it up to you."

I nodded. "Yes, yes you did. Well, have a good night, Zo."

He placed his hand on the doorframe and the other on the wall of the house. "Wait."

I swallowed. *Not good.* "Um, ye—"

My eyes widened when he crashed his lips into mine. He didn't even have the courtesy of allowing me to finish my sentence. What made this worse was that my body locked up completely in defense, and he was trying for more than a quick goodbye.

"This is not okay!"

Finally, after what felt like hours, he pulled away and gazed down at me. I could tell from that look that he was quite aware I was not into what he was trying to do.

"Eira—"

"Good-night, Zo." I ducked under his arm and rushed inside the house.

He hit the house in anger and cursed at himself, but I didn't care. I ignored everyone in the living room as I stormed into the bathroom and slammed the door shut. I felt sick.

Grabbing for a toothbrush, I scraped it over every inch of my mouth in attempt to get the awful taste out of my mouth, trying desperately not to puke. It wasn't until the metallic taste of blood hit my taste buds that I stopped.

I released a slow breath after rinsing out my mouth and reluctantly left the bathroom, knowing full well what I was about to have to endure.

Blaze smirked my way. "So, how was that kiss that Zo stole?"

"Fuck off." It didn't surprise me that he was the first to say something. *He's lucky he isn't close enough for me to throttle.*

"Oh, it couldn't have been that bad," Ryoko said.

"He tried to jam his tongue down my throat."

She grimaced. "Yeesh. He tells you he'll prove he's good, and goes and does that. What an idiot."

"Hey, if I was in his shoes and was able to convince Eira to go out on a date with me, I'd be dumb not to try to kiss her," Blaze admitted as he leaned back on the couch.

Ryoko glared at him. "That's because you're an asshole."

"In the end, it doesn't matter," Genesis stated. "You still need to continue with this. We need any information that could come out of it."

"Like hell I will." I headed for my room. "I'm done."

"Eira—"

"I said no."

"That's not a request, Eira. It's an order!"

I stopped dead in my tracks and Ryoko gasped. The room stilled. No one ordered anyone to do anything in this house. It was agreed on due to our design. Even Zane, as old as he was, had a similar design built into him.

I chuckled, which confused the others. Unfortunately for Genesis, I had a new trick up my sleeve. "Screw you."

"E—excuse me?" Genesis stammered. "Did you just ignore that order?"

Shva'sika snickered from where she sat at the kitchen bar. "You won't be able to order her around anymore. I saw to that."

Ryoko blinked slowly, shocked by the news. "You broke her of it?"

Shva'sika nodded. "Laz had done most of the work already by the time she had arrived at the village, but I helped her with the rest. When I found out about your inability to ignore an order, I took action. If Maka'shi had found out about it, she would have made Laz's life a living hell. Besides, no one should live like that. That's not a fair life."

"B—but, how did you do it?" Ryoko questioned.

Shva'sika shook her head. "It's not easy to explain, and it's even harder to do. It's a rigorous and taxing process. I can help any of you if you're willing to put yourselves through it."

Everyone went to thinking over this option. I headed for my room. I closed the door behind me and made my way to my closet to change. The sooner I swapped clothes, the better.

When I finished and had my clothes put away to be washed, I came out of my closet to find Raikidan waiting on the windowsill. I would have tried to scold him for coming in while I was changing, but his stare prevented me from saying anything. It forced me to look away. He was concerned and wanted to know if I was okay, but I couldn't talk to him about it. I knew if I did, the truth would come out. I showed the others I was angry, but I only showed the one emotion. I didn't let on to any of the others raging inside me.

"Eira—"

"I'm fine." I headed for my bed. "I just need sleep."

He grabbed my wrist, stopping me, and then rested his forehead on the back of my head. "Please don't lie to me."

I stood there, trying to stay calm and figure out how to tell him I was fine.

He pulled away. "Turn and face me." I hesitated. "Please."

I did as he asked, and lifted my gaze hesitantly, unsure if I'd be able to keep my composure. My hand clutched my necklace for dear life. Raikidan reached up and cupped my face with both his hands, his strong fingers curling around the back of my head. Shock rippled through me when his warm lips touched mine, and my face flushed. The shock soon melted away into desire.

I no longer felt gross—like I was tainted. I released my necklace and rested both of my hands on his muscular chest. My heart raced and I wished it'd stop. This situation didn't mean what I hoped, but I couldn't even convince myself of that at this point. His intoxicating scent consumed me; made me crave for a touch that wasn't meant for me.

"I'm not so sure about that anymore…"

Our lips parted and Raikidan wrapped his arms around me in a tight embrace. "Sorry, but it was the only way I knew of to get rid of his awful smell. He tries anything like that again and I'll rip his throat out."

I snuggled deeper into his chest, forcing myself to sound as though none of that affected me the way it had. "You're the only one who gets it…"

Someone knocked on my door. "Laz?"

"Go away, Ryoko, I got this covered," Raikidan replied before I had the chance. My heart thumped in my chest. *His response sounded… possessive…*

I knew Ryoko thought so as well because she giggled. "Well, well, well. Looks like Eira's sexy dream man beat me to the punch."

"Ryoko, he is not!" I shouted. *Please don't pick up on the lie… please don't pick up—Eira, stop encouraging this thought for yourself!*

"Yeah, sure, you keep thinking that." She walked away before I could continue to argue with her through the door.

Raikidan looked down at me. "Completely honest here, I'm not sure if I should be offended by your comment." I stared at him, surprised and confused. But before I could formulate a proper response, he smelled my hair and growled. "You still smell like him. That needs to be fixed."

I squeaked when he lifted me up and carried me to my bed. He lay down and held me close. I wanted to ask him if this was necessary, but the tightness of his grip told me the answer. *I'm not sure who's more upset about the situation...*

Raikidan snuggled with me more, and instead of feeling awkward or out of place, I felt calmer... safer. I knew Raikidan would hurt Zo, if given the chance. My heart's pace picked up, and I did what I could to slow it down. This wasn't the time for it to be stupid.

"It's the exact time for most anyone to be stupid. Like you."

"Shut up."

"You should rest," Raikidan said.

"It'll be hard with you holding me."

"Try. I'm not going to let go yet."

My heart thumped hard and my cheeks and ears warmed. "Can you at least ease up?"

"No—now sleep, before I make you."

"Dragons have a maximum of three abilities. And I know all three of yours."

His chest rumbled as he chuckled. "Maybe I have more and can only have three active at one time."

I giggled. "You sound like a character from one of Argus' videogames."

His grip tightened for a moment. "Just go to bed."

I smiled and snuggled into him, mentally reminding myself this was just us being close friends. "Good night, Raikidan."

"Sleep well, Eira."

CHAPTER 47

Wood shavings fell to the floor as I carved into the wooden block. This was my sixth carving today, on top of the three pieces of jewelry, and I was growing bored. Seda had told us about a "surprise" inspection sweep, but unfortunately she wasn't able to figure out when. So I chose to stay here all day, and it was getting close to the time I'd go to bed. I wanted to work on some special projects that couldn't be done during the day for reasons of secrecy, and the others' habits of popping in on my solitude to check on me could ruin the surprise I had cooked up. Luckily I was close to finishing, and I wouldn't have to keep it up for much longer.

A light rap on the front door made me sigh in hopeful relief. Seda let our guests in, and they went about their business as always. As I carved away at the block that was now beginning to look like the cougar I had spotted in a book, I noticed the psychic they brought paying particularly close attention to me. I realized he was the psychic who had read my false memories. "Um, can I help you? Your staring is creeping me out."

"I'm sorry," he said. "I'm just interested in that carving. Would I be able to buy it from you?"

"Uh…" I looked down at it. "I don't think it's going to be done by the time you guys finish here."

He lifted his hand and I watched one of my carvings levitate off the coffee table. It flew over to him and he gave it a careful assessment. Of the carvings I'd done today, it was my favorite, of a male lion head. To ensure I got the creature right, I reference several images in various books. It was an impressive piece, even for me.

A tied bag on his side unraveled and levitated to me. "I hope that's enough."

I snatched the bag and opened it. "Looks to be a bit under, but I'll let it slide since you've been so nice."

He smiled. "Thanks."

I nodded and went back to carving. I glanced up when the soldiers returned, and the general with them came over to the psychic. "Don't tell me you stole that from her."

"No, I purchased it."

"Oh—well then, get moving. We're done here." The general faced us. "We apologize for any inconvenience at this hour, and please have a good night."

The psychic waved to me. "Thanks again, miss."

I smiled at him and watched them all leave. Once gone, I cleaned up my mess and headed for my room. Raikidan was already shifted and lying down for the night, and just as I went to close my door, Seda's kitten, Crystal, scurried inside. It had taken Seda a while, but she had finally settled on the name Crystal because of the kitten's eyes. I smiled when she curled up next to Raikidan to sleep.

Tiptoeing past Raikidan, I put my carvings down and then snuck back to my bed. Turning off the light, I sat in the dark for some time before deeming Raikidan to be completely asleep. Scooting to the edge of my bed, I reached under it and retrieved my void bag. Reaching in, I pulled out a large carving. I couldn't see the details well, even with the light filtering in through the skylight, but I could tell the clear coat I had applied didn't have any flaws as I ran my fingers over it.

"This was a good idea for a gift."

I smiled and peered over at Raikidan. It had been hard keeping this from him. Getting any alone time to work on this wasn't easy, especially when it came to him. I still wasn't sure if he understood what personal alone time was.

"Seeing as he watches you sleep in hopes—I don't know why, actually—I'm going to say no, he doesn't."

"I'm going to pretend I didn't hear any of that..."

I tiptoed over to Raikidan and placed the large carving down carefully so I wouldn't damage it or wake him or Crystal. I smiled at the sight of her all curled up beside him. She had really taken a liking to Raikidan. She tended to follow him around seeking attention, and didn't shy away when he shifted to his natural form. After a while, he even started to like having her around, though he tried to act like he didn't care. *He's adorable.*

"Yes, he is."

Now we couldn't get her out the room. Every night she'd come in, and I felt bad for Seda since it was her cat. Seda insisted she didn't mind, but it didn't change my opinion about the matter.

Backing away, I went back over to my bed and snatched the bag I'd pulled Raikidan's gift from. I crept over to the door and barely managed to pry it open enough for me to fit through, thanks to Raikidan's large head. I then slunk down the hallway to empty the contents of the bag.

I moaned as someone tried to stir me from my slumber. I rolled over in a sorry excuse of an attempt to flee. "Let me sleep."

Raikidan's familiar chuckle echoed through my ears. "It's almost noon. I've let you sleep in long enough."

I snuggled deeper into my pillows. "Sleep longer."

He chuckled. "Don't make me tickle you."

"I let you sleep," I muttered.

Fur brushed against my face and loud purring vibrated in my ear. Raikidan chuckled. "See, I'm not the only one who thinks you should wake up."

I pet Crystal for a moment and then snuggled back into my bed.

"Just get up. He won't stop being annoying until you do."

"I want sleep..."

"And you make fun of him for hibernating."

Raikidan sighed. "Please wake up."

I groaned reluctantly and sat up. Crystal rubbed against me again and I gave her the attention she asked for. Raikidan held up a large, intricate carving made of black oak, carved in the shape of a dragon with a man's head. Both the dragon and the man had a red stripe carved from red oak, which had been seamlessly embedded into the black oak. The carving was highly detailed, right down to the eyes, which were sapphire gems.

"Is this really for me?" he asked.

I nodded with a smile. "I told you I had another gift for you. It just took a little bit for me to complete it."

"When did you find time to do this?" he asked as he sat down on the bed.

I shrugged. "At night. It's the only time I could do it without anyone getting nosey. Plus, it made it easier to take in the details of your face since you're such a heavy sleeper."

He chuckled. "Well, thank you. I love it."

"Good, you'd better. She put a lot of hard work into it."

I smiled. "I'm glad."

He put the carving down and stood. "Now get dressed so we can go out."

I cocked my head. "Out where?"

"Just out." He took Crystal so I couldn't use her as an excuse not to move.

"What is he up to?"

I eyed him suspiciously, but slid out of bed and started to get ready for the day. Just as I finished and came out of my closet, he was shrugging a jacket over his shoulders. I pulled mine on and followed him out.

Leaving my sanctuary, I was nearly knocked off my feet by Ryoko as she latched onto me. "Thank you!"

I laughed as I tried to pry her off. "Welcome."

Raikidan observed the exchange. When Ryoko finally detached from me, she set curious eyes on him. "Did you get a little statue, too?"

"Uh, yeah."

"Everyone got one," I said. I had even made one for Telar and his sister. I just needed to find the time to get it to him.

Her eyes lit up. "I need to see what everyone else got!"

I chuckled and headed for the door. "You have fun with that. We'll be back in a bit."

"All right, have fun doing whatever you're planning on doing!"

I shook my head when she ran off. I was happy she liked the gift, and I was also glad she was so excited over it that she forgot to be nosey or tease us about us leaving. When Raikidan closed the door behind us, I noticed a slight frown to his lips. "What's wrong?"

He blinked. "What? Nothing."

"You thought you were the only one who got something, didn't you?"

He shrugged. "I don't know."

"Aw, poor thing is disappointed."

I smiled at him. "Well, just so you know, you're the only one with such an extravagant carving."

"What do you mean? What did the others get?"

"I gave most of them some basic carvings. I carved out a similar style of carvings for Ryoko and Rylan, but you're the only one who has a carving made of two pieces of expensive wood or gems."

"How expensive is the wood?"

"That's a craftsman secret."

"Why?"

I chuckled. "Because I said so."

"Then why tell me it was expensive?"

I grinned. "Because I can."

He pushed me. "You're being such a pain."

I smirked. "Payback."

"I'm not that much of a pain to you… anymore."

"Yeah, sure."

"Yeah, you keep thinking that."

Raikidan shook his head and hailed a cab. Why he was flagging one down, I didn't understand. If we needed to drive somewhere, we could have grabbed a car from the garage. We had plenty.

Keeping my mouth shut, I climbed into the cab. Raikidan told the driver to take us to a large outdoor shopping center in the second quadrant, and even though I wasn't sure why we were going there, I continued to stay quiet. Raikidan didn't try to strike up any conversation, which didn't really surprise me. The cab driver kept looking at us in the rear-view mirror, which I found creepy.

Once at our destination, Raikidan paid the driver and helped me out. His serious face faded and turned into a smile as I climbed out and the driver sped off.

"Yeah, this is weird, even for him."

I smiled at him before we headed into the shopping center. It was crowded, but neither of us minded as we spent the afternoon here. We'd go into a shop or stall and mess around, be goofy, and maybe even purchase something, and then go to another one. Just like the time we had been at the Larkren, which had been the only time I enjoyed shopping. With Ryoko and the other women, it was all business and what would or wouldn't look good on me. With Raikidan, it was about how much fun we were having, and it was easy to have fun with him. *This is really fun.*

Raikidan didn't care how stupid either of us acted. He didn't care what others thought when they watched us. He didn't care because he understood. He understood even though he was so different. Or was he? I watched as he haggled with a shopkeeper and how successful he was. I thought about how well he listened to me and how he was able to help in ways no one else was capable of. Maybe it was our differences that made us the same. Or maybe, we weren't as different as it seemed.

"Now you're getting it."

The two of us laughed as we tried on some funny hats. Luckily, the shopkeeper didn't mind. He actually enjoyed our spirit, unlike many of the past shop keepers. We stopped laughing when a loud noise echoed in the distance. *Sounded like an explosion.* For a moment, I thought I had been hearing things, except the shopping center had quieted. People looked at each other, murmuring.

People started pointing and frantically talking amongst themselves. Raikidan and I exchanged a glance, concern on both our faces, but before we could try to see what the other citizens found, something exploded a few blocks away. People shouted and many started to run, though others were too confused to figure out what to do.

"What's going on?" Raikidan shouted.

"I don't—" I froze when sirens blared.

"Oh no…"

"Eira?"

"We're under attack…"

"What?"

"Run! Run now!"

"Those are raid sirens!" I shrieked. "The city is under attack! We need to get underground."

At the sound of the sirens, people panicked. They swarmed and stampeded through the shopping center, trampling carts and people who got in the way. Raikidan tried to grab onto me as the flimsy temporary shop started to shake, but we were forced to run separate ways as it began to collapse and cave in as people trampled it.

I ran until I found a place out of the way of the stampede and searched for him. "Raikidan! Raikidan!"

There were so many people I couldn't find him. He didn't stick out well enough.

My ears pricked when Raikidan shouted my name. "Eira? Eira!"

"Raikidan!" I called back as I tried to find him. I saw a head bobbing and weaving through the throng of people. I flailed my arms in attempt to flag him down. "Raikidan, over here!"

"Eira!" He shouted when we spotted me. He forced his way through the mass in a line straight for me. I grabbed onto his outstretched hand when he came close and pulled him into my safe spot. "Are you all right?"

I nodded. "I'm fine. But you look like you were hit."

He rubbed the side of this face. "I was elbowed in the stomach and the eye. Nothing major."

"All right, if you're sure. We really need to get out of here."

"That's a great idea, but how? If you hadn't noticed, that mass isn't getting any smaller."

"We're going to have to brave it and find side streets to run through," I said. "The city is in a panic. All the main streets are going to be a mess, and more dangerous than side streets."

"The side streets will be dangerous?"

"Raikidan, we're under attack. The raid sirens only go off when a large-scale attack is on us. The only safe place is underground. These people won't stand a chance if they stay above ground."

"So why aren't we choosing to help them? I thought that was part of our purpose here. To save these pe—"

"Because it's mayhem here, Raikidan!" I shouted. "These people won't listen!"

"Yeah, use your head."

He grabbed my hand and pulled me into the mass. "Then we need to move."

I followed him, but began to struggle to keep up when people tried to push through us. Raikidan shoved someone and hauled me onto his shoulder. I'd have protested, but due to the situation, I allowed it so we wouldn't be separated from each other.

"Side street!"

His head snapped in the direction I pointed, and pushed his way over to it. I wasn't allowed to run on my own until he was sure we were safely inside, not that this side street was any safer. There were plenty of people here, too, and they ran around, completely disoriented. I called out to them to follow us, but no one listened.

We continued to run through street after street, explosions and gunfire in the distance pushing us forward, and as we did, the population on the streets started to dissipate rapidly. It was too fast a pace. I stopped running and took in our surroundings.

"This isn't right."

Raikidan skidded to a halt, staring at me in bewilderment. "What are you doing? Let's go."

"Raikidan." I looked around more. "Raikidan, we're going the wrong way."

"What?" he questioned.

"This is a main street, and it's deserted," I pointed out. "We're not going away from the invasion, we're—"

I dove to the ground when the corner of a building near us exploded. Raikidan jumped on top of me to protect me, and before I could make sure it was safe to move again, Raikidan yanked me off the ground and pulled me back the way we came. Unfortunately, we weren't the only ones here. We switched directions when several armed men dropped down, and then we stopped running when we found ourselves surrounded.

Raikidan and I shared a quick glance and focused on the soldiers. They didn't look like any city soldiers I'd ever seen. *Wait, I have seen this look before—or something similar. It's the way they hold themselves.* They looked a lot like the controlled men who had attacked that first party between the shamans and soldiers.

I couldn't believe I had forgotten about them and the possible threat they posed, but then again, I never imagined a full-scale assault on the city being the overall plan by whomever was controlling them. A good question was, who was controlling them?

Raikidan stole a dagger from my arm and pushed me behind him. I wanted to scold him for trying to protect me when it wasn't needed, but as I watched at him, he appeared to be doing it subconsciously. When they attacked, he went on the defensive and kept me behind him until they began attacking on all sides and separated us. Drawing a dagger from the sheath on my leg, I defended myself. I did fine until someone grabbed me from behind. I kicked and struggled, but he had a tight hold. *Oh, not cool!*

"Keep fighting!"

I slammed my head back into the person's face. They yelled in pain and released me. I took the forward momentum to swing around and kick him in the side while he held his face, and then aimed for his groin. He choked and then dropped.

"Nice shot."

"Thank you."

"You two, get down!" someone yelled.

Instinctively, I ducked as several guns fired. The soldiers around us fell to the ground. I turned to see a band of Dalatrend soldiers advancing, with Zo leading them.

"What are you two doing here?" he demanded. "Didn't you hear the raid sirens?"

Raikidan crossed his arms. "Yeah, and we thought we'd just take a leisurely stroll through a battlefield."

"Rai, don't," I warned before looking at Zo. "We ended up going the wrong way due to all the panic. When we finally realized it, we were ambushed."

"Well, you're lucky they didn't kill you on the spot," Zo said.

"Why didn't they?" Raikidan asked.

Zo's jaw tightened, drawing my interest. What didn't he want to reveal? *"Get the information, it could be important."*

"They were armed with guns, and chose to attack with blades or bare hands," Raikidan stated. "I demand an answer."

A young soldier stepped up. He had an air of familiarity about him. It took me a few seconds to realize he was the young kid who had sworn his allegiance to me when Verra went on her rampage over the summer. "We're getting reports that they're snatching up civilians."

"Kid," Zo warned.

"They need to know, General," he said. "There's no indication of why, or what for, or even if their targets are randomized or specifically targeted. Age and sex don't seem to matter, either. If you two are going to seek out shelter somewhere, watch your backs. You'll be easy to single out if you're running alone, and they have already taken an interest in you as it is."

"Go with them, kid," Zo ordered. "You know where some safe houses are that we're hiding civilians in. Get them there and help protect those locations."

The soldier nodded. "Yes, sir." He motioned for us to follow. "This way."

I complied without a fuss and Raikidan followed after, but not before he and Zo shared a tense exchange . I stayed alert as we passed through the roads. The kid took an odd interest in me and I found it a bit disconcerting. "What?"

He shrugged. "Just observing. In the heat of battle, you did well with making yourself look like a civilian, even with that impressive hit to the man that grappled you. Even now, you are alert, but still keeping that act up."

"Takes a lot of practice," I said. "Standard training that is mandatory for assassins. It's definitely not something you learn in the course of a day."

"I can tell," he said. "I know I haven't received any training like that."

"Hopefully you won't be in this mess long enough to need it," I told him as I eyed the rooftops. "Hey, what's your name anyway? I never caught it."

"Oh, that's right. My name is Arlon." His brow furrowed when he realized I was still paying attention to the rooftops. "You're really expecting them to jump us."

"We're being watched," Raikidan said as he scanned the street. "I can smell them."

Arlon's brow rose. "Smell them? What are you, exactly?"

"That's on a need-to-know basis," Raikidan replied.

"And I don't need to know." He sighed. "I'm told that a lot."

I chuckled. "Get used to it, kid. It's how life works."

The three of us stopped dead when we heard something crash in an alley. Readying our weapons, we waited. I exhaled and lowered my dagger when an alley cat poked its head out. The other two did as well.

"Look out!"

Large hands grabbed my arms and something was thrown over my head, plunging me into darkness.

"Fight!"

I struggled, but the arms were too strong. Raikidan called out my name in distress, sending me into a greater fight response, but my assailant had help, and my hands and feet were bound. I felt completely helpless as I was hauled onto someone's shoulder and carried somewhere.

"Why did you stop fighting?"

"Because it's a waste of energy. I wouldn't be able to get far with my feet bound."

"Fine."

Minutes felt like hours. Our captor's boots clomped on the asphalt. I heard metal doors open, and my captor's boots landed on a concrete floor. It wasn't long after that my captor put me down on the ground and forced me to kneel. I could hear people breathing all around me, and many of these people sounded scared. *The captured civilians.*

My eyes fluttered to adjust to the dimly lit room when my head covering was removed. Looking around, I observed the other captives. Most had their hands bound and were huddled together in fear. Others, who I could only assume had been more rebellious, either had their feet bound as well, or were bound around the torso so they wouldn't move. I did notice there weren't just ordinary civilians here. There were also shamans. They remained quiet and calm, but as I made eye contact with some of them, I knew they were just biding time, trying to figure out what these men were up to with these hostages.

"Smart idea on their part."

The man who had carried me reached down and stole the other dagger strapped to my leg so I wouldn't be able to use it to remove my restraints. He smirked as he attempted to taunt me by spinning both daggers in his hands, but I didn't react in the way he had hoped. I stared at him as if I didn't care, angering him. He raised his hand as if to strike me, but another soldier grabbed him by the arm and shook his head. The soldier snorted and turned to leave, but not before spitting on me. Before I could even flinch, Raikidan rammed into him.

"Oh, yes personal body guard. Teach him a lesson."

"Your friend has a lot of guts," Arlon whispered.

Before I could reply, a soldier came up and punched Arlon. "Quiet."

The soldier Raikidan had rammed jumped to his feet and tackled Raikidan to the ground. Raikidan attempted to fight back, but with his arms bound to his body, he didn't fare too well. That's when I noticed that Raikidan wasn't bound by ropes like the rest of us. *Are those... metal rods?* Another soldier came up to the pair and bound Raikidan's feet with the same material as his arm bindings. *They are! Why did they choose such a binding for him?*

The soldier holding Raikidan stood and grabbed Raikidan by the jacket. He dragged Raikidan over to me and dropped him off at my feet. The man sneered when I bent down to make sure Raikidan was okay. I noticed some strange reddening around his skin where his bindings touched him. *Does this metal have—*

"I think it does."

"How do you know about that?"

"How do you, when you outwardly claim to know so little about dragons?"

"I know some stuff."

"What you know isn't public knowledge, though."

I almost narrowed my eyes as if she were actually in the room with us. I focused back on the thought we both had. If we were right, it explained Raikidan's current powerless situation. This room wasn't large, so shifting into a dragon shape would be idiotic. His size would have this whole building come crashing down. Not to say stupid choices were beyond him, but he could try to shapechange into a small creature to escape his bindings at the very least. But if this metal around him weakened him, he wouldn't be able to shift to another form at all.

Raikidan chuckled, souring the soldier's mood again, and he pulled himself up into a kneeling position. At the same time, he managed to move himself behind me so our backs touched. The maneuver impressed me.

"I'm impressed, too."

I turned my head a little to look at him when he grabbed my hands. He was already trying to look at me, and the amount of concern expressed in his eyes upset me. With a reassuring smile, I laced my fingers with his and wiped the spit off my face with my shoulder to show him things were going to be okay.

"Considering the circumstances, his attempt to protect you was admirable."

I eyed a soldier as he came over to us, but when he noticed we weren't doing anything suspicious, he kept walking by and checked on the other captives. I noticed these soldiers didn't talk much. When they did, their voices were low and only to the same middle-aged man with black hair and ashen skin. And, even from my distance, I could see the blue lines of veins. He didn't look well.

"Why… Something is familiar about him."

"What do you mean?"

"I'm not sure yet. But look for strange marks if he comes close."

"Clarify."

"On the skin. By his neck."

I glanced at Raikidan again when he pulled his fingers from mine and began playing with the rope around my ankles. He gazed at me as he normally would, and his movements were slow enough to make it appear as if he wasn't doing anything at all. I turned my gaze away and continue scanning the room.

"I like this plan."

That's when I noticed the soldiers were starting to group up. They huddled around the single man dressed a bit differently. He held a communicator in his hand. *He's either their assigned leader, or the one pulling the control strings.*

Once he decided enough soldiers had gathered, he searched for a signal on the communicator and then pressed a button on the side. The visor slid back, and as the man held the communicator up, a beam projected an image onto a wall. It seemed our city had also started working with the video feeds for the communicators, and these invaders had gotten their hands on one. On the other end of the feed was a squad of Dalatrend soldiers.

"General, they're calling us again," one soldier said.

The soldiers parted and Zo came into the feed. "What do you want?"

The enemy leader's lips spread into a wicked grin. "An answer."

Zo scowled. "I gave you an answer. It's still—"

"You may want to reconsider." The leader chuckled. "Bring the woman over here."

I snapped my head back and forth when two men grabbed me and dragged me over to the group. *Why do they want me?*

"Be on guard."

Zo's expression changed to surprise when I came into view of the feed and the enemy leader grinned. "We know more than you think, General. We know a lot, and we know she's pretty special to you. So give us what we want"—The soldier who had taken my daggers pulled my head back and held a dagger to my throat—"and she lives."

I heard Raikidan try to move and then get tackled to the ground. *In your state, Rai, I wish you'd use your brain.* I wished I could tell him to stay put, but I knew it was best to stay quiet until the right opportunity presented itself. Instead, I did my best to look for any marks on the leader of this group. *There.* On his neck, he sported a tattoo with a black shield and red tear drop. *Is that symbolism for blood?*

"It can't be…"

Zo's brow creased as he struggled to come up with the right decision. Unfortunately, these soldiers weren't in the mood to wait any longer, because the enemy leader pointed at something and two soldiers left the group. My eyes widened when a woman and child screamed in fear.

"Elizabeth!" a Dalatrend soldier shouted.

"His wife and child will be next," the lead enemy soldier stated coldly.

Wife? That wasn't something I expected to hear. Child, sure. Accidents happened, but a wife? I hadn't realized soldiers were now taking that risk.

"Despicable! To stoop this low…"

"You know if you hurt any of them we'll send a special force after you," Zo told the leader, calmly, but with authority.

The leader chuckled. "Yes, but I also caught one of your underlings giving you away. This special force isn't controllable and would more than likely attack these civilians, too."

Zo scowled. *Are they talking about my clones?*

"I believe so."

"Zo, have you found her?" a woman called on Zo's end.

Oh no. I knew that voice and if she saw what was going on, she wasn't going to act civilly.

"This is going to get interesting."

"You called me to tell me you sent her somewhere safe and then tell me you can't find her at all!" Ryoko pushed her way through the throng of soldiers. "Zo, are you—Eira!"

The enemy leader laughed at her as she shoved Zo aside to get a look at the feed, but his laughter only made the situation worse. I watched as her horror and fear switch flipped to anger in seconds. Her eyes dilated, and a strange aura emanated around her. *Not good.*

She snarled. "If you hurt her, I will find you and scatter your entrails over your mother's grave!"

The leader laughed at her threat. "Why don't you go chew on a bone, halfling." Ryoko was taken aback by his insult. "Yes, that's right. We know about you as well. We know all of the halflings here. Many are in this very room." He glanced down at me, a sickening grin on his lips. The sheer malice in his glance ran my blood cold. "That's why we're here. There are too many of you disgusting pieces of filth crawling around Lumaraeon and in this nu-human city. This city should never have allowed it, and it will be razed as punishment. Unless, of course, our demands are met."

He knows. He has no intention of letting any halfling here live. Including me.
"He won't get away with this. Not again."
"What do you mean by again?"

Ryoko's anger returned, a vicious growl tearing through her throat. Rylan pushed his way through the soldiers and attempted to calm her but failed.

"Ryoko," I stated. "That's enough."

She blinked and calmed a bit. "But—"

I smiled and threw in a tiny giggle for an added effect. "It's all right. These bone-heads have already screwed up anyway."

The soldier who held the dagger to my throat pressed it against me harder. "Shut up."

I chuckled and looked at their leader. As I did, I allowed the other side of me to slip through for a brief moment. It was brief, but enough that my eyes gave me away. "Never underestimate a captive."

As if on cue, large double doors to the room burst open, and two muscular men rushed in. Another man, of a slighter athletic build, came in behind them. The first two men, while both burly, had about a two-inch height difference. They both had light skin and blue and red hair. The leaner man was a few inches shorter than them and also had light skin, but had violet hair. My eyes widened. *Are they—*

Civilians screamed, and a captive fire shaman took advantage of the situation to throw out a blast of fire as best as he could from his bound hands. The enemy soldiers scattered, and the dagger held to my throat disappeared, as did the grip on my head, when the soldier holding me hostage became distracted. Rolling back, I pulled my arms under my legs to get them in front of me and pushed myself up with my bound hands. I kicked two soldiers in the face, and as I did, the rope binding my legs came undone, thanks to Raikidan's meddling earlier.

When I landed, my eyes snapped down to the communicator the enemy leader dropped, and I smashed it. The leader glared at me and I grinned back. Now I didn't have to hold back.

Spitting out an ember onto the rope around my wrist, I broke free of my bindings and went for the soldier who'd stolen my daggers. After all, they were mine.

I maneuvered around the soldier as he tried to stop me, and I took him out without much effort. He wasn't all that tough when all the cheap tricks were gone. Spinning my daggers, I went for the leader and found him trying to run through another door. *Oh, no you don't!*

I took off after him, Raikidan yelling to me, "Eira, wait!"

"Eira, be careful. He's dangerous."

"Don't worry."

The man rushed down a hall, but I was hot on his heels. He knocked down some boxes and even a beat-up locker; slowing me down. He turned a corner, and the sound of a door opening and slamming closed echoed down the hall. I pursued, finding the door, and recklessly ran through it. I skidded to halt and scanned the spacious room. Support pillars and broken lockers blocked much of my view, but I couldn't hear anything. Slowly, I ventured on, listening for any clues and looking for any exits. *Nothing. Where is he?*

"I don't sense him."

"That's not possible. There's no exit other than the door I came in."

"Wait, behind you!"

I spun around when I sensed a presence behind me, and sliced my dagger through the air to defend myself, but the man behind me seized my wrist. "Wait, it's me. I'm not going to hurt you."

I stared at the young man before me.

"Wow. A near spitting image of you. If, you know, you were a guy."

The only thing missing were freckles. *Doesn't surprise me in the least.* Zarda didn't like freckles. He saw them as an imperfection and sought to eliminate them when possible.

"We need to get you out of here," he said.

I glanced back into the room. "My quarry is still at large."

I looked at him when he placed a hand on my shoulder. "He got away, Sis, it happens."

My eyes widened. "You do know…"

Someone ran into the room, pulling our attention away. My brother tensed, but my eyes widened at the sight of the olive-skinned elven man with the black-and-red mohawk and various tribal-like tattoos, piercings, and gauged ears with feather earring attachments. "Del'karo?"

A smile spread across his face, his chestnut brown eyes crinkling, adding lines to his middle-aged face. "You're safe."

"Well, yeah. I'm capable of handling one guy."

"Don't underestimate him. He's more than he appears."

I approached him. What business did my shaman mentor have with this city? He wasn't a tradesman, and due to his large family, he took many shaman jobs that pulled him all over Lumaraeon to feed them. "What are you doing here?"

"Well, I came looking for you." He smiled. "I found out from Ne'kall I had missed you when you visited his tribe during the summer, and I wanted to see how you were doing. Looks like I chose a bad day to come for a visit."

I laughed. "I can't believe they were able to capture you."

"I'd like to say it was all a part of some elaborate plan, but I'd be lying. They jumped me from behind. To be honest, I'm just as surprised to see you here."

"They did the same to me."

He patted me on the shoulder. "Oh well, such is life. Let's get back to the others. Your friend is struggling with his bindings and the two that came with this man here"—he gestured to my brother—"don't seem to know how to handle panicking people. I've got the shamans handling that part."

I glanced over to where my clone had backed away. He struggled to keep eye contact with me. "We're not good with people."

Del'karo shrugged and then gestured to the door. "We all have our vices. Now let's go."

I took one look back into the room, hoping to find the man I pursued, but found nothing.

"Don't worry. He won't get away with this."

"How can you be so sure?"

"Trust me."

The three of us ran down the hall for the room the civilians were held in. "Oh, Del'karo, congratulations on the new baby. He's lucky to be born into a family with a father like you."

He smiled. "She."

My eyes widened and my gait faltered. "Really?"

He continued to smile. "Yes. We're finally having a baby girl."

My eyes lit up as a rush of joy flooded through me. Before I knew it, I was wrapping my arms around his neck. "I'm so happy for you."

"Tell him I am as well. This is exciting news."

"I'm not going to sound crazy in front of him."

"Fine, be that way."

"And you'll be happy to know she'll be our last." I pulled away and cocked my head. That wasn't something I was expecting to hear. "The only reason we had so many children was because Alena wanted a daughter, so we agreed to have as many children as it took until we had one. Had I realized it was going to take so long, I wouldn't have come up with the idea. I'm not sure how many more her body could have handled."

I smiled. "Well I'm glad the gods finally blessed you with your wish. She's got plenty of older brothers to look after her too."

He chuckled. "We're hoping she'll be just like you."

"Oh, that's quite the honor."

I blinked. "What?"

"Sister, we need to get out of here!" My brother called. I noticed he had kept running when the two of us stopped.

Del'karo lifted a brow in my direction. "Sister?"

"Yeah…" I rubbed the back of my neck as I continued down the hall. "New development these last few months. It's a bit complicated right now."

He nodded. "Sounds like we have a lot to catch up on. On a better day, of course."

I laughed as we reentered the captive room. My two large brothers stood off by themselves watching as the shamans corralled the civilians. Raikidan sat on the ground fighting his restraints and a shaman attempted to give him a hand.

Raikidan gazed up at me and smiled, relief washing over his face. "You're safe. You're not hurt, are you?"

"Aww, his worry makes me sick."

I ran over to him and knelt. His skin had reddened more, and had a texture to it, like an allergic reaction. "I'm fine, don't worry. But we're not out of the woods yet. He got away and we still have a battle raging outside."

To emphasize my last point, something outside the building exploded, and the building shook. The civilians whimpered but remained controlled.

"Del'karo, give us a hand," I said.

My mentor knelt and the three of us pulled on the bindings, to no avail. We continued but the combined strength didn't do us any good. I let out an exhausted breath, my face red from the effort. "What the hell is this shit?"

"A pain in my ass," Raikidan grumbled as he continued to struggle. I noticed the difficulty he had in his attempt, and I was worried about this metal's effect on him.

I looked over to one of my brothers. I pointed to the largest of them. "You. You look like a Brute-class. Come help."

He exchanged a glance with his brother before nodding and came over. My Brute brother grabbed onto Raikidan's bindings but they didn't budge much. His brow creased and he tried again. The metal creaked but it didn't move enough for Raikidan to escape.

I ground my teeth together. "Rai, your back is about to get hot."

"Whatever is needed to get this stupid thing off me."

I took a controlled breath and discreetly exhaled a flame into my hands before applying it to the metal. It glowed red after a few moments and I nodded at my brother. He nodded back and pulled on the metal again, this time, it bowed and Raikidan slipped out.

Raikidan took in a deep breath, as if he had been holding it, or been suffocating, and then fussed with his leg bindings. I shook my head and forced him to stop so we could melt the metal.

I helped him up once he was free and touched his reddened skin, only to find it uncomfortably warm. "Are you okay?"

Raikidan brushed it off. "Don't worry about it."

"But—"

He placed a finger on my lips. "We have more important things to worry about right now."

He's right. I pointed to my brothers. "You three head out and make sure a path is clear for everyone. We'll handle the civilians."

They shared some sort of silent conversation with their eyes, and my Brute brothers did as I asked. The leaner one's gaze lingered on me for a moment, and then Raikidan, before he too left. I sent Del'karo to help the shamans line the civilians up so we could get them out.

Raikidan glanced my way. "Were they..."

I nodded. "Yep."

"You know about them?" Arlon said.

"We do." I focused on him. "What do you know?"

"That in theory, they shouldn't be listening to you." He looked me up and down. "They're usually more savage around people. When they came in, I knew they'd been released out of desperation, even though General Zo made it seem like they wouldn't use them. I prepared to be dead at that point. How are you able to order them around?"

Raikidan chuckled. "She's got a way with people."

I rolled my eyes. "Let's focus on the people here and get them to safety."

"Once we figure out where we are, I can get us to a guard post," Arlon said.

I nodded. "Take point then. Del'karo, we're getting everyone out of here."

He nodded and readied the civilians. Arlon led everyone out, Raikidan and me bringing up the rear.

Raikidan placed his hand on my back. "Are you sure you're okay?"

I smiled. "Yeah, I'm fine. Stop worrying."

"Yeah, no need to fuss over this independent woman. Even if you are... strong... and handsome enough to protect her."

He glanced at the throng of people before us. "Your clones... can we trust them?"

"Good question."

"I don't know..."

I wanted to be able to trust them. I mean, after all, they were my brothers. One even came after me to help, and they all listened to me. From the rumors, and what Arlon said, they should have instead killed all of us outright. But I didn't have enough information to make a logical decision whether to trust them or not.

"I hope we can. They may be clones, but they are still family, and family is important."

I peered up at Raikidan when he touched my arm. Worry lines creased his forehead, so I smiled to make that look go away. I didn't want him to fuss over me. I didn't need anyone to. I could handle whatever outcome came my way. If one of our friends betrayed us, it'd hurt, sure, but I'd do what it took to stop them from halting our goal.

"That is a good resolve to stick to. I will help you if needed."

The hall lightened, and we followed the crowd outside, through some holes in the walls that looked like they were made by people. *Did my brothers do this?*

"That's my guess."

Arlon did well with keeping the civilians calm and following him, until gunshots rang out and several buildings exploded and crashed to the ground. People screamed and scattered. Arlon and the shamans tried to calm them, but it was a futile effort. I yelled for them to cease the pointless attempt and get somewhere safe. The shamans nodded and ran off, Del'karo going with them, and Arlon waving us to follow him. Raikidan and I didn't have to be told twice, but I didn't get far when I noticed a woman holding a child, shrinking back by the building, trying not to be trampled. *Elizabeth.*

I ran over to her and grabbed her hand. "Let's go."

She nodded and followed, her daughter shaking in her arms. The group of us took off, a few civilians with their heads still on noticing our movement and following. We ran for some time before Arlon pointed ahead of us. "There's the guard post!"

Relief rushed over us, but it was short-lived when armed soldiers took aim. We exhaled as one when they realized we were civilians and waved us in.

"Eira?" I flicked my gaze to my right just as Ryoko barreled into me. She wasn't crying, but I could tell from her hug that she had been worried and was trying her hardest not to shed the tears.

"Elizabeth? Lilly?" someone called.

Elizabeth looked around; her daughter did as well. "Daddy?"

The man I had seen on the projection pushed his way over and wrapped his arms around his wife. "Thank the gods you're both safe."

His wife murmured something and he nodded. "We're going to go somewhere safe. I promise."

Zo approached me. "I'm glad you're safe. I was a bit worried when I saw that our special task force was released before I'd ordered."

"They were a great help," I said. I could tell he was lying, but I wasn't going to fuss and it would paint my brothers in a good light since the opportunity presented itself. "Give my thanks to the person who did send them."

I could tell Zo was surprised, but he did well hiding it. "Good to hear. We're going to get all of you into a secure place until we're no longer at war. Follow me."

I complied without fuss.

Ryoko took interest in my behavior. "You all right?"

I nodded. "Just tired now."

"That's to be expected after what you've been through," Zo said. "You can sleep in the vehicle."

I nodded again and followed as he and several other soldiers made their way over to a convoy positioned beyond the small post. A soldier opened a door to one of the vehicles and ushered Raikidan in first, and then me and Ryoko. Lilly tried to protest to her father about not wanting to go into a different vehicle than us, and before her father could point out there wasn't any room for all three of them, Raikidan pulled me into his lap and Ryoko had scooted over. Normally I would have protested, but I was too tired and it made the girl happy.

"Rest. You deserve it after today."

Yawning, I rested my head on Raikidan's shoulder and found myself drifting off just as the convoy moved out.

48
CHAPTER

I filled several more glasses with as much finesse as I could, in order to impress the intoxicated customers at the bar in an attempt to squeeze out some extra tip money and still rush to fill table orders. With everyone calling out because of the attack on the city a few days ago, we were shorthanded today, which meant I had to assist with running the bar while working tables. Even bouncers were making an attempt to help out with tables and still balance out their main job.

It had taken the army the entire day to rid Dalatrend of the invasion, and they kept people inside the following day, too, just in case. Shva'sika and the shamans had done some digging into this mysterious group, especially after I mentioned the man who had gotten away. What they found sent chills down my spine, even now.

The Crimson Sanctuary. They believed pure blood to be the only acceptable blood out there, and to mix them was the ultimate crime. They had been formed with the discovery of the first halfling, though records struggled to pinpoint exactly when that was. And they had caused a great deal of trouble for halfbreeds and halfbreed supporters.

Shva'sika revealed to me that the previous shaman Ambassador, a proud halfling woman, had fallen victim to this faction during the *Purge.* I'd heard of it, but knew nothing about it. The voice, on the other hand, hadn't liked it one bit, and I had a physical reaction of intense discomfort. I had an unusual reaction to the word "purge." Every time I heard it, my stomach turned. But when she mentioned this purge, the discomfort I experienced was far more intense, so I had done some digging. I almost regretted what I found.

The Library accesses told of one of the most gruesome genocides Lumaraeon had ever witnessed. The victims had all been halflings. The Crimson Sanctuary slaughtered any halfling they found, along with anyone who sympathized with them or anyone they suspected was halfling, even without proof. The Purge lasted ten years uncontested, but after that, war broke out. This was the war we knew as the Great War. I found the description of the war fascinating, but mainly because it was far different from what I had been told. *Zarda really does like to mess with the information we know.* Arcadia, the goddess of the spiritual plane, had told me about his tampering, and this cemented that reality.

The Great War ended when the faction all but disappeared. That was about five hundred and fifty years ago. Many believed they had finally been vanquished because of this. Of course, the war had taken its toll on alliances, and many races saw an enormous decrease in numbers. The tension left over from this war was still present to this day. *One Zarda is exploiting.*

The shamans were keeping a close eye out for any more activity with this faction. Many still bore ill will for what had happened to the Ambassador, even those who had come along after her time.

I rushed around and delivered the drinks on my tray, making sure to apologize to them for having to wait, and making a failure of an attempt to flirt with the men for any tip I could manage to get. As I rushed back to the bar to take my position there, someone grasped my arm. I turned to face whoever it was and demand release, and was surprised to see it was Zo. Zo himself being here wasn't the surprising part of the situation; it was the fact that he had grabbed me. He'd never been so bold in an attempt to get my attention like that. "Zo?"

He grinned. "Hey, Eira."

"Look, I don't mean to sound rude, but I need to get back—"

"I know you're busy, but I was hoping you could... I don't know... dance with me?"

I swallowed. *This boldness is not good.* "Zo, I can't. I have to work."

"C'mon. I won't take a lot of your time."

"Zo, I'm on the clock, and we're short-staffed on a busy night."

"I doubt Azriel will mind. You'll be with me, after all."

"I said no."

He blinked. "What?"

I exhaled and tried to pull away. "I don't want to."

He wouldn't let go. "Why not?"

I managed to wriggle myself free. "Because—"

"She doesn't have to explain herself." Raikidan came out of nowhere and put himself between us. "So back off, Zo."

Zo held up his hands. "Calm down, Rai."

Raikidan pushed him. "I told you before, it's Ray. Only Eira calls me Rai."

Zo narrowed his eyes. "Whatever. Just get out of my way so I can continue my conversation."

"What conversation? All I see is you thinking you're Zoltan's gift to women and feeling the need to bother Eira."

"Guys, please stop," I begged. I knew this was going to escalate if I didn't stop this now.

My plea fell on deaf ears as Zo pushed Raikidan. "You know, I'm getting pretty sick of you, kid. You get in my way all the time and think you can tell me what to do."

Raikidan shoved him back. "And I'm getting sick of you thinking you can do whatever you damned well please, especially with Eira."

"Guys..." I didn't know what to do.

"Just let them fight over you."

"They are not."

"Don't play stupid with me."

"Take it outside, boys." I shifted my gaze to Azriel upon his approach. "I have enough to deal with right now."

"He's right," Zo said. "We'll handle this outside like men."

"Fine by me."

"Guys, don—"

Azriel stopped me. "Eira, don't get involved."

"But, Az..."

He ushered me toward the bar. "They're bullheaded men, and nothing you say is going to stop them from settling this in such a manner. Besides, with the amount of aggression that's built up between those two, it'll be good for them."

"I don't want them fighting because of me."

"You mean over you?"

"See?"

I gave him a stern look. "Az, I'm being serious here."

"Laz, you can't be that naïve."

"No, she's just being a pain in the ass about this."

"No one would fight with someone else over someone like me."

"Lies."

"Shut up."

"Stop being stupid and I will."

Azriel sighed in aggravation and ushered me behind the bar. "Work. Everything is going to work out, so don't worry about it."

I huffed and cleaned a glass. I was going to worry, and I wasn't going to be able to work at my best until I knew the outcome.

I glanced toward the front door again, hoping to see Raikidan strolling back in. Ten minutes had come and gone, and I was having a hard time not going outside to step in between the two meatheads.

"Laz, calm down," Azriel told me. "He's going to be fine. Raikidan can handle himself."

"I know he can," I spat.

"Oh, someone is getting testy."

Azriel smirked. "Then, do you care to tell me why you're so worried about him?"

"I'm not worried." I turned to face the glass rack. "I just think it's stupid that he's doing this. It's not worth it and I could have handled it."

"Meaning you're worried."

"I'm not worried! He's making a stupid decision."

"You're not a stupid decision."

"Well, now you can tell him how stupid you think he is."

I spun around to see Raikidan making his way over to the bar—and there was no doubt he had been hit pretty good a few times. I didn't see Zo anywhere, and I had suspected the outcome. My stomach did a few flips and I wished it hadn't.

"Don't push it away."

"Don't encourage this!"

"Eira, I need to tell you—"

I grabbed him by the shirt and pulled him into the bar. "Sit."

"But, Eira, I need to—"

"I said sit down!"

"Listen to the mother hen."

"I'm not a mother hen."

"Mother dragon, then?"

"No!"

Raikidan immediately sat down on the stool we kept behind the bar. I rummaged through different boxes and supplies to get the right healing aids for him. I assessed his condition before grabbing a cotton cloth. "Hold this on your mouth, you're bleeding there."

"Eira, please, just—" I glowered at him and he did as told.

"Good boy."

Azriel chuckled. "Laz, I'll go take care of your tables while you tend to him."

I ignored him as I grabbed some gauze to get the cut right above Raikidan's eyebrow. "You're really stupid, you know that, Rai?"

"Eira—"

"You could have gotten seriously hurt!"

Raikidan grabbed my hand to stop me from touching his face. "It was worth it."

I slipped out of his grip and dabbed his cut. "No, it wasn't. It was stupid." I exhaled through parted lips. "I'm glad you're okay, though."

"You worry too much. I had it all under control."

"You didn't know how strong Zo was. You can't gauge a soldier's strength by his looks. Look at Ryoko."

"If it makes you feel better, I gave Zo a good thrashing."

"It doesn't make you any less stupid!"

"Eira, I knew what I was doing."

I paused for a moment. "And what were you doing?"

"Putting him in his place, like I promised you I would. He shouldn't bother you anymore, or at least not as much."

"How do you know that?"

"Well that's what I've been trying to talk to you about."

I pulled away and folded my arms across my chest. "I'm listening."

He looked apprehensive, as if he were afraid to tell me, and based on how his eyes darted around, wasn't okay with others overhearing. My heart slowed and a tingling sensation pricked my fingers. *What did he do?*

He took a deep breath. "Well, I sort of told Zo that you were supposed to be my wife before you *lost* your memory."

He gave me an awkward, forced smile and I stared in horror. "Y–y–you what?"

Raikidan held up his hands. "Eira, let me explain."

I couldn't think straight. "W–why would you do that?"

"Eira."

"What were you—"

"Eira."

"Rai, how could y—"

He grabbed my hands and pulled me closer so I was forced to look at him. "Shut up and listen to me so I can finish."

"Yeah, no kidding. This isn't like you."

I stared at Raikidan for a moment and then swallowed hard to calm myself and nodded.

"Zo had questioned why I was so protective of you. He insisted it wasn't needed, so I told him the first thing that came to mind that was also justifiable. It was the only thing I could think of that would get him to believe me and leave you alone."

"Rai—"

"Let me finish." I frowned and nodded. "I also told him that you don't know. I told him I needed you to make that choice again, not feel obligated to tell me yes. I'm revealing all this so you'd know what I did. I didn't want it to be a real surprise to you if he slipped up and said something."

"See, no need to panic."

I pressed my lips together and dabbed his eyebrow with gauze again. I needed to think this over. While the damage had been done, I wasn't sure I was okay with this idea.

"Well, why not?"

"Please... just... don't start right now..."

"Eira..."

Raikidan sighed and sat still. The cut bled profusely. *Too much for it to heal on its own.* I rummaged through the medical supplies until I found thread and a needle.

"Eira, don't you dare," Raikidan warned.

"Well, if you weren't so stupid, I wouldn't have to do this!" I snapped. He shrunk down and stayed quiet.

"Smart choice, valiant protector… She's a chaotic mess right now."

I threaded the needle and held his face to restrict his movement. He flinched and complained, but it stopped almost immediately when I stared at him with cold, hard eyes.

Azriel's amused chuckle rang through my ears. "Rai, you must have pissed her off good if she's not use a numbing agent. Laz, I'm putting your tips in a jar back here."

"Fine." I was too busy concentrating to say much more.

He served some patrons at the bar before heading out again. When I finished stitching Raikidan, I disposed of the needle properly and then held his chin as I finished wiping his face clean. I checked the rest of him over after that. There was no more blood, but there were plenty of bruises.

"Eira—"

I pressed my lips against his, his taste tempting me. "Thanks, Tiger." He blinked with stunned silence and then flinched when I smacked him in the head. "And that's for being so stupid."

"Was that really necessary?"

The bar patrons laughed at him as I cleaned my hands. I shook my head at some of their comments and sanitized the bar, wiping it down before cleaning some glasses Azriel had brought back. A few people came to the bar for drinks and I mixed some of them up before cleaning more glasses. When I realized Raikidan hadn't moved, I looked at him with a knitted brow. He was leaning back and watching me, with his classic stupid grin on his face. "What do you think you're doing? You have work you should be doing."

"I think I'm due for break after all that."

"He's not wrong."

I shook my head. "Not here. Go take your break somewhere else."

"Why? Means you could stare back at him."

"Stop it."

His grin stayed in place. "No, I'm good."

I shook my head and did my best to ignore him as I went back to cleaning, but a bubbly sensation in my stomach made it difficult.

"He sure liked that kiss a lot. He's not hiding it one bit. But who can blame him?"

I tried to make sure my face didn't flush a shade of red. *"Shut up."*

"What? I'm just stating a fact. What good-looking man wouldn't want a kiss like that from such an attractive woman?"

"One that's essentially betrothed to some other woman. Besides, they'd be looking for something from a more attractive woman than me, like Ryoko."

"I'm not hearing denial on your end of the attractiveness scale, though."

I remained quiet for a moment. *"Yeah, so?"*

"Praise the gods, we have a break through! Let's go tell Ryoko so we can party. Maybe you'll get drunk enough to confess your undying love for your faithful dragon guard."

"Not going to happen! Don't even suggest that."

"Oh, don't be like that."

"Just... shut up already."

She chuckled, but let me be. Of course, that left me to deal with the idiotic smile on my face. Her suggestion didn't exactly displease me.

49
CHAPTER

Laughter filled the living room as embarrassing stories of the past were shared. Candlelight flickered against the walls of the dark room, and snow whipped around beyond the house windows, the blizzard making its presence constantly known. Ryder walked out of the kitchen with a plate of cookies Shva'sika had just finished baking, and both Rylan and Raid, who had stopped by for a visit, made sure to steal a couple the moment the plate came into reach.

Ryder set the plate down, only for it to levitate and shoot over to Telar before I could grab a snack. I held up my hands. "Cookie hog!"

He smirked. "Say please and bat your pretty eyes, and I'll let you have some."

Azriel leaned back and batted his eyes. "Please, Telar? I'd be most appreciative."

Rylan and Raid sputtered a laugh, but we were all roaring when Telar shrugged and handed the plate to Azriel. Even the voice got her kicks from all the shenanigans. She hadn't had any input for stories, but at least she was amused and not bothering me.

Ryoko clapped her hands. "Oh, oh! How about that time Blaze nearly blew up the shop."

Blaze groaned. "You guys can't let me live that down, can you?"

I cocked my head. "What did he do?"

Rylan laughed. "He wasn't paying attention, and grabbed the wrong liquid components to put in a car. He was lucky he was doing a remote start."

"I'm telling you, the bottles weren't labeled correctly!" Blaze tried to defend. "Someone switched the liquids!"

Ryoko giggled. "Yeah, you keep telling yourself that."

"Aright, how about that time you bumped into the wall of the shop and smashed it open?" Blaze shot.

Ryoko laughed. "That was bad. I'm surprised I didn't give that old woman that was walking down the street a heart attack."

I chuckled. I was glad Ryoko took that memory so well. Seeing her accepting her extreme strength and other abilities now was refreshing.

Zane chuckled. "Or how about that time Seda scared Argus shitless."

Argus laughed and Seda buried her face in her hands. "That was so embarrassing!"

I was greatly interested in this. "What happened, now?"

Seda sighed. "It happened a few weeks after I was taken out of my tank. I was being trained in mind reading and instead of reading the mind of the soldier in front of me, I managed to get into Argus' head."

Blaze held his gut as he laughed. "Best part about it all, we were on the opposite side of the compound!"

Argus chuckled. "It was a bit of a surprise, though her incessant apologizing was what made it funny."

Seda pressed her fingers together in front of her face. "I felt so bad."

"Not as sad and pathetic as Eira's little foul-up," Telar said.

My brow furrowed and then my eyes went wide. "Do not tell that one."

"It happened... four decades ago. She and I had been assigned to go out and scout a fortress for weak points to assault. I didn't feel like hovering over the ground to stay quiet, so she nagged me about my elephant feet. In her nagging, she failed to keep her eyes open for the protruding tree root in front of her."

Ryoko started giggling. "Please tell me she ate dirt."

He grinned wickedly and my eyes glittered, malice intent surfacing in my mind that I intentionally projected toward him so he wouldn't miss it. "She fell face-first in mud."

Everyone laughed, making fun of my blunder. I sat with my arms crossed and my eyes narrowed at Telar. "At least my blunder isn't as bad as yours."

Telar's expression dropped. "No."

Seda giggled, catching pieces of my thoughts. "Oh, that's a good one."

Telar's jaw tightened and I gave him a smug smile. "The night we returned from our assignment, Telar thought it'd be a good idea to go check on his sister, only to find her sporting some sexy leathers with two men happily tied to her bed."

Telar's cheeks reddened as everyone laughed at his expense.

"No wonder that shopping excursion was so painful for him when he got into town," Ryoko said.

I hadn't thought of that. *But she's right.*

Ryoko turned her gaze on the three dragons who had stayed quiet except for their laughter. "How about you guys? Have anything to share?"

Corliss shrugged. "I can't think of anything worth sharing."

Mana giggled. "I've been enjoying your stories too much to think of my own."

Raikidan chuckled. "I do have one to share."

Ryoko burst with excitement. "Well, spit it out!"

"This happened when Mana was still new in the picture—"

"Don't you dare share that!" Corliss hissed.

Mana giggled again. "Oh, calm down, Corliss. It's not that big a deal."

"Not that big a deal? I thought you'd gone missing!" He blinked and then his face reddened when he realized he gave it away anyway.

I chuckled. "Rai, you might as well tell us."

Ryoko nodded. "Now I really want to know."

Raikidan snickered. "Well, as I was saying, this happened when Mana was still new in his life. He was always paranoid and needed to know exactly where she was at all times. He came to me in a frantic mess because he couldn't find her. It had been about an hour, and that was the longest he'd dealt with up until then. Come to find out, she was in the cave the whole time."

"Oh, that's bad."

I let out a boisterous laugh. "How the hell does that happen?"

Corliss' face reddened. "I didn't check the entire cave."

Mana smiled. "I came from farther up North, so I hadn't adjusted to the hotter climate of our territory—I moved further into the lair than normal to stay cool."

The room filled with laughter, and Corliss hid his face in his hand. I didn't blame him for being so embarrassed. That was silly of him.

Shva'sika quieted herself down and smiled. "That reminds me of the time Laz went missing for three days."

"Oh no. Not this story."

I groaned and hid part of my face with my hand. I knew where this was going. "That sucked."

Ryoko was eager to hear something about me. "What happened?"

"Well, when she went missing, we didn't think much of it. She had a habit of going off on her own for a day or so, so nothing seemed out of the norm for her. Until Mel'ka came back into the village on that third day, in a frantic mess."

I chuckled. "That poor man. I would have rather been stuck for another three days than have him find me."

"Who is Mel'ka?" Mana asked.

"He is one of the elders in the village," I explained. "At that time, his mind was starting to go, so he had quite the imagination."

"When he had found Laz, he came back to the village as fast as he could, claiming the village was under attack. We weren't sure how to take his message, and that's when Valene finally fessed up."

"Fessed up about what? What happened to Laz?" Ryoko shouted. She wasn't happy we were dragging the story out.

Shva'sika chuckled. "Laz was stuck in a tree."

Ryoko blinked. "What? Why didn't you jump down?"

I chuckled. "No, Ryoko, I was literally stuck inside the tree."

"What? How did that happen?" she asked.

I chuckled some more. "I had taken Valene out for some training. I figured a quieter environment with more plant life would help her, since she was struggling. I was having her practice a technique when a tree grabbed me out of nowhere and pulled me inside. She freaked out and ran off, and was so ashamed and scared she didn't tell anyone."

"She's lucky she only covered your mouth, and not your nose, too." Shva'sika stated.

I nodded in agreement and Ryoko blinked. "Is that why it took them so long to find you?"

I nodded again. "I couldn't yell out for help. I was lucky Mel'ka even stumbled upon me, but I still wish it had been someone else. The poor man was a mess for the next few days."

Ryoko clapped her hands together. "What about that time you first introduced the guys to Azriel?"

My brow furrowed. "The first time? Nothing happened the first time, or at least that I knew of. I thought he was being pretty decent."

Azriel nodded. "I'm not pulling up any bad behavior memories from that day, either."

Rylan chuckled. "I think she's thinking of the second time, when—"

"Don't you dare bring that up!" Blaze nearly bared his teeth. "That was not a good day."

Ryoko giggled. "Yeah, for you."

Azriel's eyes lit up. "Oh, that day!"

"Yes, that day. That day amused me."

I smirked. Now I knew which memory Ryoko meant. Shva'sika tilted her head. "I'm pretty interested in what happened."

"Oh, I hope so," Azriel said, his eyes still wide, showing his joy of the memory. "It's a good one."

"The first time I brought Azriel to meet the guys, I asked him to be on his best behavior," I explained. "He was, so when I brought him back a second time, I didn't think I'd have to say anything, but he had other ideas." I glanced at Azriel. "Apparently, he didn't like how Blaze had treated me during that first visit, so he decided that he'd make Blaze as uncomfortable as possible by hitting on him."

Shva'sika giggled. "That's it?"

Argus chuckled. "This is also Blaze we're talking about. He's as straight as a pole." He started laughing as he remembered the event. "And Azriel wasn't exactly going easy on him either. He was quite aggressive, to the point where he was starting to try to touch him inappropriately."

"And none of you stopped it?"

He shook his head. "We were enjoying his torment too much. It just so happened that before they showed up, Blaze was being a pain in the ass, so it didn't feel right to stop it."

Azriel leaned closer to Blaze and winked. "I can always repeat that day if you like. I know you liked it."

"Be a dear, Azriel, and please do."

Blaze reeled back and tried to put as much distance as he could between him and Azriel, but Ryder grabbed onto him, a grin firm on his lips. Azriel reached out for Blaze, and with Ryder's assistance, grabbed a hold in a tight hug. Blaze struggled and struggled, but he couldn't break out of Azriel's grip. Our resident playboy complained by making distressed sounds when Azriel mentioned he smelled "wonderful." Everyone got a kick out of the display—and the situation gave me pause for another story to share about Azriel.

"I remembered another one for Azriel, one from back in our military days." All attention fell on me, eager to hear my story, although Azriel looked confused. "We were out in Lumaraeon, playing soldier, when we stopped in a controlled town for the night. At the local bar, Az decided he'd hit on some guy, only to find out he had an overprotective beefy boyfriend already, who wasn't keen on sharing. It took three of us to keep the guy off him, and two more of us to shut Azriel's mouth because he didn't know when to quit."

I was pretty sure everyone just about died, as many struggled to stay upright as they laughed. Even Azriel showed his amusement with the memory.

"Oh, what a memory it was."

"Well, you couldn't blame me. He was a nice catch, too." Azriel winked at me. "But after things calmed down and we patched things up, I was introduced to two marvelous men by said overprotective boyfriend, and what a night that was."

I rolled my eyes. "Didn't need to know that, ya pain in the ass."

Shva'sika giggled. "Speaking of being a pain in the ass, I remember a time when Laz was practicing an advanced fire technique and Maka'shi interrupted. She spoke so suddenly Laz lost concentration and lit Maka'shi's hair on fire."

I burst out laughing. "And then she had the gall to accuse me of doing it on purpose when I had also caught my own clothes on fire. Like I'd purposely do that. I only wish I had thought to do something like that to her on purpose. Would have made some of my days better."

"I'm glad my misfortune still amuses you."

My laughter ceased and I cranked my neck to look over my shoulder toward my bedroom. An open portal pulsed in front of the doorway, a hooded figure standing in front of it, the only visible features being her feminine chin painted with a blue stripe and long white-blue hair spilling out of her cloak. The figure pulled down the hood with pale hands, revealing her half-elf features. My eyes narrowed. "Maka'shi."

"You know they have a door," Shva'sika stated. "You could have at least been less rude and knocked, instead of inviting yourself in."

Maka'shi went to speak, but I snorted and spoke up faster. "Skip the manners tutorial, just tell us what you want so you can go on your way and back to your perfect life."

"Don't get defensive. Let her speak."

The others were perplexed by our rude behavior, but I wasn't going to start explaining it in the open—at least, not yet.

Her ice-blue eyes flashed with what looked like pain. "I came here to apologize." I sat up straight, interested in knowing the reason behind such an unexpected overture. "I deserve every bit of retaliatory anger you just threw at me. I deserve it because you didn't deserve the unjust hate I put on you…"

"Why are you apologizing now?" Shva'sika asked.

Maka'shi took a deep breath. "Because I finally came to terms with what happened in the past. When Zarda forced us to sign the treaty, Va'len, my husband, was the leader of the tribe, and he refused. We were neutral parties and weren't going to be forced into taking sides." Her lips quivered. "Zarda had him killed to force our cooperation, and because I didn't want anyone else suffering the same fate, I agreed to his demands. It's why our tribe didn't have to offer anything to him when the pact was signed. We had already paid a price. Because of what happened, I hated him and his soldiers. I let that cloud my judgment as your leader, and I forced my anger and mistrust on you, Laz'shika. And for that, I am sorry."

Shva'sika's brow creased and a pained expression fell over her. "But you said Va'len's death was due to a training accident!"

"We decided that all shamans who hadn't been there to witness the event were to be told it was an accident. All those who had witnessed it agreed to keep their mouths shut. You were gone visiting family up North with your mother, so the two of you were told this lie, although your father ended up telling your mother the truth a few days later."

"But why not tell all of us the truth?" Shva'sika shouted. "It wasn't right to lie to us!"

"She's not wrong."

"It doesn't matter why," I said. "It is done, and knowing the reason why won't change the past. Nothing can change the past."

Maka'shi stared at me. I could tell she was afraid I'd reject her apology, but what she didn't know was that I had always suspected her prejudice against me had to do with a past event. The first day I arrived at the shaman village, she knew my origins by looking at me. It wasn't a coincidence.

"I accept your apology," I said.

"Good for you."

The tension drained from Maka'shi's face. She sighed with relief and smiled. "Thank you. Now, someone is dying to see you, and I suggest you stand on my side of the couch."

I lifted an eyebrow in confusion, but did as requested. As I did, Maka'shi disappeared into the portal and came back a few moments later with a young woman with long brown hair that curled in ringlets at the end. Vined flowers branched out all throughout her hair. "Valene…"

Valene squealed and rushed over to me, her bright blue eyes sparkling. I took her into my arms and squeezed her. "I missed you!"

I smiled in her hair as I took in her scent. "I missed you too."

"I missed her too!"

She pulled away and smiled at me, her eyes gleaming. I feared our forced parting would have damaged our kinship, but she looked so happy, I had nothing to fear. Valene turned her gaze to the others and waved. "Hi."

The others gave her a warm greeting and I didn't miss the strange look in Blaze's eyes. He showed great interest in Valene's presence, but it wasn't the typical playboy look he had when he found interest in women. *I'll have to keep an eye on him.*

"You don't have to worry about him, trust me."

"Do I want to know?"

"You'll get overprotective if I explicitly say anything."

"Excuse you?"

The voice refrained from responding, irritating me.

Ryoko crawled her way over the couch to us and gazed at Valene. Valene, unsure of what she was doing, flicked her gaze to me and then back at Ryoko.

"Your eyes are amazing," Ryoko said.

Valene laughed. "Thank you. For a second there, I thought you were going to make a comment about me being an ordinary human."

Ryoko pointed to her own ears. "Though your ears are different than what I'm used to seeing on an ordinary human, I could care less about that."

Valene shrugged. "My mom always told me it was because faeries snuck into my room and pulled on them in an attempt to steal me away when I was a baby. Course, that's not true since faeries don't exist, but she never told me the real reason before she died." Valene cocked her head to the side. "Are you really a clone of Ryoko?"

Ryoko nodded. "Yeah, why?"

"Because you don't look like the depictions I've seen."

"Really?"

"Yeah. The ones I've seen, she had hair that curled like mine and it was said to be black, and her boobs were far larger than yours."

Ryoko blinked. "That's weird. All the ones we've run into, I've looked exactly like her. And we've always heard she had brown hair."

"It's been two millennia since they've been alive," Corliss said. "Depictions change over the years when they're passed around in stories and legends."

Mana nodded. "Even Pyralis' and Reiki's descriptions among dragons aren't the same."

"And don't forget statues of gods," I added. "Besides Solstice, all gods in nu-human temples are depicted as nu-human when it wouldn't have been possible for them to be one that long ago. Depictions of people can change based on the desires of the storyteller."

"It's true."

Valene nodded. "I guess that makes sense."

"So, are you really an earth shaman?" Ryoko asked Valene.

She nodded. "Yeah, I'm a plant-based earth shaman. Laz says you're an Earthshaker. Is that true?"

Ryoko's nose scrunched. "A what?"

I chuckled. "Yes, she is."

"What the hell is an Earthshaker?" Ryoko asked, her brow furrowed.

"It's exactly what it sounds like. You shake the earth," I said. "With you, you can stomp your foot on the ground and create small earthquakes."

Ryoko avoided eye contact. "Yeah... but I don't do that often..."

"You should!" Valene encouraged, her eyes sparkling. "Earthshakers are cool!"

"I concur."

"You think so?"

Valene nodded with enthusiasm. "My mom was one."

"As well as a plant-based shaman," Shva'sika added. "Unique shaman for sure."

Valene nodded again. "Yeah she was. I kinda wish I got that from her."

I rubbed her head. "You're perfect as you are." My action stopped when I felt a lump on the back of her head. My brow creased. Taking a closer look, I found the bump to be the source of all the branching plants in her hair. "Valene, what's wrong with the back of your head?"

She avoided eye contact. "Umm..."

"Oh dear..." Shva'sika said.

I stared Valene down. "What is it?"

"Well..." She wrung her hands together. "I was trying to create a fast-growing plant that can grow in any environment and on any surface... and... well... I had an accident with one of the seeds..." I stared at her in horror. "But it's nothing lethal! I promise."

I snapped my attention to Shva'sika. "You knew?"

She nodded. "Yes."

"When did this happen?"

"About two months after you left."

"Oh, you should have known better than to keep that from her."

"And you didn't think to tell me?"

"I knew you'd overreact."

"Overreact? I'm not—"

She held up a finger. "You are. The result of the accident isn't lethal, and she ended up finding out how well these seeds work."

"You can't be sure it's no—"

"We already had three healers take a look at her," Shva'sika explained. "They all confirmed that the roots are growing in a specific spot on her skin and are showing no signs of damaging her skull at the present time, or in the future. There's nothing to worry about."

I crossed my arms. "Well, I'll be getting my own medical professional's opinion on the matter. I gave Valessa my word I'd keep her safe, even from herself."

Azriel rubbed his hands together. "Oh, goodie. I get to play doctor. Let me go get some tools from downstairs."

Most of us laughed. Even Valene and me, despite the tense situation.

When she calmed down, Valene turned her gaze to Maka'shi. "Now that she's done freaking out at me, can I stay here until the ceremony?"

My brow furrowed. "Ceremony?"

Valene's brow rose. "Didn't Maka'shi tell you?"

"Tell me what?"

Maka'shi laughed. "I actually forgot."

Valene's face scrunched. "How could you forget? She's the whole reason it's happening."

I waved a hand. "Hello... Will someone please tell me what's going on?"

"Tonight, you're going to become a full shaman!" Valene beamed before Maka'shi got a chance to say anything.

"Well it's about time!"

I fixed Maka'shi with a surprised stare. "What?"

"Over the summer, I was told you had finished your pilgrimage and I was to perform the ceremony to make you a full shaman. But because of my harbored feelings, I didn't do it. So, you're a little overdue for joining our ranks."

My brow furrowed and I pursed my lips in thought. "I didn't go on a pilgrimage."

"Oh, yes you did."

"Laz, the pilgrimage is just a rite of passage that you complete while away from the village you train in," Shva'sika explained. "And you've been away from the village several times, each for long periods of time. There could have been a number of events that could have been counted as part of your pilgrimage."

I thought this over. *Over the summer...* Could it have been the incident I had on the spirit plane? Could that be what finished my pilgrimage? It was possible. I had put that off for so long out of fear of facing my past. I had to get over everything in order to move on as a shaman, making me grow in certain ways. Plus, Arcadia hadn't brought me to hell until I had faced all of that. "So, you said it's tonight?"

Maka'shi nodded. "The ceremony will be held on sacred shaman grounds, but the celebration will be held here in the city."

I eyed her. "Zarda's doing, no doubt."

She chuckled. "You know Zarda well. He tried to hold a meeting with us leaders, to bolster our 'alliance,' but we had to decline for obvious reasons. He tried to stick his nose where it didn't belong, and attempted to insert his presence into the affair. Once he realized he couldn't force his way into such a sacred tradition, he requested soldiers be allowed to attend the celebration instead. We were granted permits to use the park if we agreed. That way we wouldn't have to do a great deal of traveling to and from the city for a one-day event."

She grinned. "We agreed to the terms, seeing the benefit of holding the celebration close to our current point of... interest, though we did so only under the condition the portal ban be lifted for a twenty-four hour period and that we be allowed to hand-pick the soldiers, as the celebration was still very important and we didn't want any ruffians ruining it."

"So, you picked only rebels in uniform to go." I chuckled. "You're good."

"We also have shamans working hard to use the weather to our advantage to keep unwanted eyes from viewing from a distance."

Ryoko held up a tentative hand, concern clear on her face. "So, we can only go to the second half?"

"Oh, Ryoko, you're so cute."

Maka'shi smiled. "As close friends to Laz'shika, you are privileged to go to both the ceremony and the celebration after."

Shva'sika held up a finger. "As long as you don't speak to anyone else about it after. As Maka'shi said, the ceremony is sacred to us."

"And if we tell?" Blaze asked. "Even on accident?"

"I'll erase your memory," Seda stated.

Shva'sika giggled. "Well that means I won't have to."

Zane chuckled. "Watch yourselves. That's a team I don't think anyone wants to go up against."

Telar crossed his arms. "And they're being nice. I'd dangle a rat upside down over a building for a few hours." He smirked. "Or in the case of Blaze, force him to watch some gay porn and set off all his pretty pleasure centers." The room filled with laughter, except Blaze. He had a look of horror and disgust on his face.

"I'd love to see that."

"That's creepy."

"Oh, don't be an old maid."

"A what?"

Maka'shi cleared her throat and the room quieted down. "I should be going now. I still have quite a few things to prepare before the ceremony. Valene knows when to bring you to the ceremony site to get ready."

I nodded. "See you then."

She spun on her feet and faced the portal when a red mass barreled out of it. I blinked when I noticed it was a baby dragon. Well, baby was a bit of an exaggeration, mostly due to his size. The dragon swiveled his head until it laid eyes on me. Realizing it was Rimu, I readied myself as he came barreling toward me. I fell to the ground with a thud when he jumped on me.

I laughed as he rubbed his scent all over me. "Hi to you too, Rimu."

"He's so adorable!"

I looked up when someone rushed through the portal. It was Xaneth, and it wasn't long before Anahak exited the swirling vortex as well. Xaneth took in the room, and the moment she spotted Rimu and me, her expression changed to an apologetic one. "Sorry, Eira. He somehow realized where that portal was going and ran through it faster than I could think to stop him."

"It's all right," I assured as I moved Rimu so I could sit up. "No harm done." Rimu, unhappy with being moved, snorted and tried to climb in my lap again, but I pushed him away. "No, Rimu, you're too big now to be in my lap. You know this."

He snorted as I stood, though he didn't stay put. I barely had my balance when he rose on his back legs and attempted to latch onto me.

I exhaled slowly. "Rimu, you're too big."

"I think too big is an understatement," Mocha said. "He's the size of a small horse. I'm surprised he didn't crush you, Eira."

I grunted. "Trust me, it felt like he did."

Ryoko giggled. "Well, it's a good thing he's so cute."

Rimu chirped and made his way over to her, propping his front claws up on the back of the couch. Ryoko, like before when she had first met him, happily rubbed his head. She then focused back on Valene. "So, you going to tell us anything about this miracle seed you've made? That's all I can think about right now."

"Yes, I'm interested in this as well."

Valene giggled. "When Laz said you and I were a lot alike, I thought she was joking."

Ryoko blinked. "What's that supposed to mean?"

"I doubt you're as strong as Ryoko, though," Rylan said.

Shva'sika chuckled. "Don't dismiss that idea too quick."

A devious grin spread across my lips. "Of course, we could have the two hug him to test it out."

Rylan held up his hand. "No, thank you. I'll take your word for it."

Shva'sika and I laughed.

"I'd also like to hear about this amazing plant Valene has come up with," Argus said. "Sounds pretty interesting if it works as well as it seems."

"I'd like to hear about this amazing plant, too." I turned to find Azriel leaning against the hallway wall. "I just wanted to make my presence known. And I want you to know, Laz, how much I'm excited for this party of yours. You know I love parties."

"Of course you are, Azriel."

I snickered. "Your whole life is a party."

He smirked. "Don't be hating. Now, are we going to talk about this seed now, or"—he held up a small silver cylindrical object—"or can I play doctor?"

I laughed, but Valene let out an exasperated sigh and looked Maka'shi's way. "Help me out, will—Maka'shi?"

I blinked. She was gone, as was the portal. In her place stood Anahak.

"Where did she go?" Valene asked.

"She had to leave," Anahak said.

Valene's face twisted in slight distress. "But I don't have a portal to get us back!"

"I have a few," I said. "I don't use them, so they have plenty of power."

She smiled. "Well that's a relief."

"Wait, Laz, do portals run out of energy?" Ryoko asked.

I nodded. "They're an ancient form of transportation that only certain families of shamans know how to create. The creation process is difficult, and a lot of energy is put into them so they can travel anywhere in Lumaraeon. That lack of limitation comes with a price, however. The more you use them, and the longer the distance you travel, the less energy the portal has to maintain itself when in use."

"Wow, that's neat."

"She'd call it more than neat if she saw them being made like we have."

"Should I question this 'we' part?"

"You'll only get a headache if you do."

I focused on Valene. "Now, let's have Azriel check your head."

"Can we not?" she begged. "I told you already, it's not deadly."

"Sweetie, let Eira be your overprotective adoptive mother and get it over with."

"Shut up."

I gave Valene a pointed stare and she huffed. Azriel chuckled as he walked over. "It'll be painless, I promise. Just sit on the back of the couch."

She sighed, but did as told. Azriel pressed a button on the side of the cylindrical object he carried, and used both hands to pull it apart. Thin rods of metal on the top and bottom connected the two parts and a hologram projected in the center. He held the object up to her head. The hologram distorted and displayed an x-ray view of her head.

"Oh, where are my manners? My name is Azriel. I'm your doctor for this evening."

Valene giggled. "I know. Laz talked about you a lot when she was staying with us. That's how I knew who Ryoko was."

He glanced at me with playful accusations. "Well I hope it was nothing bad."

I crossed my arms and smirked. "Of course it was."

Valene giggled at my dishonesty. "She didn't have anything bad to say about you guys. Well, except playboy over there." She motioned her head toward Blaze, who took slight offense to her honesty. "But even with him, it wasn't that bad. Oh, where are *my* manners? I come here unannounced and don't even introduce myself. My name is Valene."

Azriel smiled. "Nice to meet you, Valene. Now just sit still while I look at this x-ray."

Everyone waited as he used the portable x-ray device and snapped pictures of her head. The voice got impatient after a while and started humming a tune. Interestingly enough, Ryoko started humming the same tune when she got tired of waiting. *These two are something else.*

"I resemble that statement."

"You mean resent?"

"No."

Azriel pulled away from Valene and flipped through the x-rays. "Very interesting. Did anyone tell you there's a plant growing out of the back of your head?"

Valene laughed at his joke and I smacked him in the arm, though not in anger. He snickered and continued to look over the images. Unable to resist, I peeked over his shoulder. Even Rimu, curious as ever, propped himself up on me so he could take a look at this strange new technology.

"I'm not seeing anything worrisome here," Azriel finally said.

Valene held her hands out at him while looking at me. "Told you."

Azriel went to a particular slide that he favored during his evaluation, and Valene hopped off the couch to take a look. "The plant's roots are in the skin, but are localized. There's also no skull penetration. From the looks of it, this will continue to remain the case, so we don't have to worry about it getting to the brain."

Valene nodded. "That's what I was hoping for."

Azriel looked at her with interest. "It might be best to explain everything in detail to us now, as this is quite fascinating, but I can understand Eira's concern."

"Yes, please do, dear. This sounds promising."

Valene nodded. "The plant got where it is on accident. As a plant-based earth shaman, I can accelerate the growth of a plan at any time, as well as a few other things. But not everyone can do that, so I thought I'd try to change the makeup of the plant's DNA to see if I could create a plant that would be useful to others such as faster growth, healthier and fuller production, as well as have the ability to grow just about everywhere without requiring a lot of space. I'd heard of this being artificially done in cities, but the plants have negative side effects to the environment that I'd like to avoid."

Mocha tilted her head. "You can do that without scientific means?"

Valene nodded. "Being plant-based, I understand the makeup of plants a lot better than most. It's an innate sense, something that's built into me. Because I understand it better, I also know how they can be manipulated by my abilities."

"So, were you successful?" Argus asked.

Valene weaved her head back and forth as if she weren't sure to say yes or not. "Sorta. Germination starts immediately and they grow a bit faster than regular plants, but not as much as I was hoping for. Though its ability to grow in any location was a success, as well as its lack of need to branch out its roots. I was able to get the three species of plants used in my experiment to grow easily on wood, metal, rock and, as you can see, skin."

"You're so smart! Eira, tell her I say that and encourage her to keep trying this."

"I'm not going to sound like a lunatic in front of everyone."

"How is that different from any other day?"

"So how did you accidentally get that stuck in your hair?" Xaneth asked.

Valene's cheeks tinted red and she rubbed her arm. "Well... I dropped a seed on the ground and bent over to pick it up. But when I stood back up, I bumped my head on my work table, and one of the seeds rolled off into my hair. Because of the nature of these seeds, I made it so that water was needed for the germination process to begin. My hair was still wet from the shower I had taken, so it had the means to grow. I'm lucky it was a vine-type plant that fell on me, and not one of the tree seeds I was also working with."

"So, can you not get rid of it?" Ryoko asked.

Valene shrugged. "By the time I realized it was there, it had grown quite a bit, so I didn't think it was a good idea. Besides, I'm able to use it to my advantage, thanks to my abilities, so it's not a major issue."

"It's probably a good thing she didn't try to take it out," Azriel said. "Looking at these scans, it's in there pretty good. Even if it were still a young plant, it'd need to be surgically removed to avoid any serious harm or scarring."

Valene snatched the x-ray machine and inspected the device with curiosity. "Hope you don't mind, but I'm really interested in this piece of technology."

Azriel chuckled. "You've never seen one?"

She shook her head. "Since technology is hard to come by outside of cities and large towns due to all the conflicts, I've seen a limited number of advanced tech. Laz told me about machines that could see inside a person's body but I never thought they'd be this cool!"

"And to think, that's just an x-ray," Mocha said. "I'd like to know how she's react to the images some machines can take that are much more detailed."

Valene blinked. "There are better—" She gasped and snapped her gaze to me "I forgot to tell you. Del'karo and Alena had their baby!"

I cocked my head. "Already?"

Shva'sika pursed her lips. "I thought she wasn't due until spring."

Valene giggled. "Yeah, about that. They got the due date wrong."

Shva'sika grunted. "That figures."

Azriel laughed. "It's been some time since I've heard of a due date being messed up. You guys really need better medical professionals."

"We do not! They're amazing." Valene's nose scrunched. "They just occasionally fudge up due dates."

Both Seda and Telar straightened and turned their focus toward the window, pulling my attention away from the current conversation. "What's wrong?"

CHAPTER 50

L ooks like we have a surprise inspection," Seda said.
"Perfect time, due to the weather," Telar added. He
pointed at Valene and Rimu. "Making them a problem."
I thought for a moment and then snapped my fingers
together when an idea popped into my head. "Valene, pull your hood
up and sit by Shva'sika. Shva'sika, you should go change, and Seda,
Genesis, and Mocha can use the hologram watches and necklace like
normal."

"But they already know I live here." Shva'sika objected. "Or at least
spend a lot of time here. Why do I need to go change?"

"Because shamans travel in pairs or more?"

She snapped her fingers. "Right."

"There won't be enough time," Seda said. "We caught them late.
They're almost here. She can use my watch. I can be Crystal."

I nodded. "It'll have to do. Valene, do me a favor and get Rimu over
to the coffee table while I go get something."

"Oh, I like this idea."

She peered over to the whelp, who was investigating Mocha with
great interest. "Sure."

Zane tossed me a flashlight as I headed for my room while Valene
coaxed him over to the coffee table. Digging through a drawer I

stored most of my sculpting tools in, I pulled out some items that I used during the finishing stages of my pieces and then headed back to the living room.

Everyone was in position; even Xaneth and Anahak were acting as casual guests as I made my way over to the couch. I sat down and patted the coffee table. "All right, Rimu, hop up."

Rylan's brow rose. "I don't think it'll hold him."

"It holds you," I shot. He looked at me unenthusiastically and I laughed, as did everyone else in the house. I patted the table again when Rimu showed hesitation on trying to climb up on it. "C'mon, Rimu, it'll hold you. Rylan was just being stupid."

Rimu stared at the coffee table and then place a leg on it. He tested it by putting a little pressure on it at first, and found out quickly that it was sturdier than it appeared. He hopped up.

"All right, now I need you to sit there and stay very still when our next visitors arrive, okay?" I told him. "If you don't, they'll take you away, and we don't want that."

"That's your plan with him?" Raikidan let out a contempt snort. "You would have been better off trying to hide him in a closet. You should have used a portal and gotten rid of him that way."

I glared at him. "Shut your mouth." I gazed at Rimu. "I know you'll be able to do this for me. I trust you."

Raikidan sneered. "You're going to get us all arrested."

I pointed at him. "One more word out of you and you're either going through that window, or I'm giving Telar and Azriel permission to go full unholy shenanigans on your ass. Whatever I decide in the moment."

Telar rubbed his hands together. "Please be the second choice."

"Yes, please!"

Azriel laughed, a deep and sadistic sound, but refrained from commenting.

Xaneth giggled and leaned over to Zane. She kept her voice low. "I have to know, is this normal for them?"

"If they didn't have at least one spat every day, we'd begin to worry."

She giggled more. "This is a spat?"

He nodded. "You don't want to see what happens when they actually fight."

Xaneth continued to giggle and Anahak snorted with slight amusement.

"In the end, this is the best choice," Seda piped in. "They're bringing a psychic with them with an affiliation unknown to me. I wouldn't be able to hide the portal from them, and then we'd have all sorts of issues if we couldn't explain that in a believable manner. This is the best choice Laz could have made."

I grabbed a container of polish and a rag I had brought into the room and began polishing the scales on top of Rimu's head.

"Um, Laz, what are you doing?" Ryoko asked.

"Making it look like he's the largest, most intricate carving I've ever made," I said.

"That's not a bad idea," Azriel complimented. "Though your choice in subject will catch them off guard."

"She's already had to explain why she has one on her bike," Rylan said. "She'll come up with a good excuse this time as well."

I smiled despite myself and continued to polish Rimu. To my surprise, he stayed quite still. I finished his snout and made my way to his cheek when someone knocked on the door. Ryoko left her seat and went to answer the door. Greeting the soldiers and apologizing for the lack of light due to the power outage, she led them into the house.

I turned my attention to them when they came into the living room to seem like I was slightly interested in their presence, and was a little surprised to see Zo amongst them.

When he noticed me, and then my "project", he crossed his arms and shook his head. "You and your choice in subject, Sweetcheeks."

I chuckled and turned away to go back to polishing Rimu. "No comments from the peanut gallery."

He chuckled and then addressed everyone. "We're just here for an inspection. We'll be out of your way real quick."

"Hope so," Blaze muttered. "We were having fun before you all showed up."

Instead of responding to Blaze's rudeness, Zo instructed several of the other soldiers to search the house. I ignored their search and focused on getting the scales behind Rimu's head. It wasn't as easy as it first looked.

"What the—" a soldier murmured.

"What is it?" Zo questioned.

"Nothing, sir. I thought I saw that statue blink," he admitted. "I'm seeing things."

"I'd say so."

"Don't go crazy on us now, Telan," a female soldier said as she came out of my room. "All clear in there."

Zo nodded and then focused on Telan again. "What is it now?"

"I'm not seeing things, sir. That thing is blinking."

Zo's eyes darted to Rimu and the back at Telan. "Are you feeling okay, kid?"

"I'm being serious!" he shouted. "There, it moved its head!"

The female soldier looked at Rimu. "I didn't see anything."

"This little one is being a shit. I love it."

I did my best to hide my amusement. He really was making small movements that only Telan noticed.

"I'm serious, that's no statue!" Telan insisted. "That thing is alive."

"Wait, hold on." I stopped working and focused on him. "Are you trying to tell us that there's a living dragon sitting on our coffee table and I'm just casually polishing him?" I laughed raucously as well as the rest of the room. "Azriel, you think you could check his brain or something?"

Azriel stroked his chin. "It might be a good idea."

"Stop laughing at me!" Telan shouted. "That thing is alive!"

Shva'sika covered her mouth with her fingers, trying to contain her amusement. "Sir, I believe you're mistaken. This is a commissioned piece for a client of hers outside the city."

"Is that why you're here?" Zo inquired. "I was honestly wondering about that."

Shva'sika nodded with a smile. "Yes. We sell a lot of Miss Eira's work for her. Many of which go to customers outside these city walls. She's quite popular and so far, hasn't found a piece she can't make."

Zo glanced my way from the corner of his eye. "Well it's good to know she's not squandering such a talent."

"They're lying, sir." Telan accused. "That thing is alive."

Zo turned to the psychic he brought in. "Well?"

The psychic shook his head. "It's a large wood carving. Nothing real about it, though the realistic nature of this piece is nothing to scoff at. How were you able to do it?"

I shrugged. "References."

"References? I've never heard of someone having photographs of dragons."

I chuckled. "Who said they were photographs?"

"I don't understand."

"Many of my clients, especially the ones outside the city, are particular about what they want, and in order for me to get it right I require references so they collect these for me," I explained. "They can give me anything from photographs to quick sketches someone made. The more high quality references I'm given, the better I'm able to create something for them. This particular client had many historical texts and scrolls with depictions I could use."

The psychic nodded. "Could we see these references?"

I shook my head. "Binding contract prevents anyone but the client and myself from viewing the references while the project is active. When I'm done, they go back to them, unless the client requests I keep them, which is when I can allow others look at them."

Telan ground his teeth together. "She's trying to distract you! That thing has been blinking this whole time and none of you have been noticing because she's been talking."

Zo released an aggravated breath. "Get him out of here. He's raving like a lunatic."

Several soldiers grabbed Telan and dragged him out of the house, but Telan was not interested in going quietly. I shook my head and went back to polishing Rimu, who now held himself still. I continued to work until the soldiers finished their search. Zo thanked us, then left with his squad without incident. Even though they were gone, everyone remained tense and alert until Seda gave us the all clear.

I sighed with relief and rubbed Rimu's head. "You're a little shit for pulling that stunt."

Argus laughed. "But you have to admit, he got that guy going pretty good."

"I appreciated the stunt."

Raikidan grunted. "Told you we would have been better off hiding him."

I shook my head. "He wasn't going to give us away. Just because he's young doesn't mean he's going to be a liability."

Raikidan snorted in disbelief, and I rolled my eyes and went back to working on Rimu's scales.

"I'm more impressed with Eira's persuasion skills," Anahak admitted. "I'm pretty sure she could easily convince me I'm a mouse."

Ryoko giggled. "Back in our military days, she convinced a guy he had chicken DNA when he didn't."

All the dragons laughed, as did a few others who hadn't been around for that fun day.

"Eira, I think you can stop polishing him," Genesis said.

"Well I can't leave him partially polished. He'd look silly."

"No kidding."

She giggled. "I suppose you're right."

"Let me help!" Ryoko exclaimed. "Two sets of hands are better than one."

"Make that three!" Valene said. "He'll be polished in no time."

I gratefully accepted their assistance. Rimu didn't mind either, and he remained still while the three of us worked.

I exhaled a relieved sigh and sat back on the balls of my feet when we finally finished. Seda, who left while we were working, returned with a large mirror. She leaned it against the wall and I encouraged Rimu to go check himself out. He didn't have to be told twice. He scampered off the table and examined his reflection. He chirped at the sight of his gleaming scales in the candle light.

"He's so cute."

"Rimu, she spoils you," Xaneth said.

Mana pouted. "Yeah. No one ever polishes my scales and makes me look that nice."

I laughed when Corliss promised to polish her scales and she squealed with delight. Rimu, finally done checking himself out, bounded over to me and gave me a gentle, happy head butt. I chuckled and rubbed his head, only for him to flop over and sprawl out over my lap.

"All right, Rimu, we let you visit, now it's time to go back," Xaneth announced.

He grunted and stayed put.

She held up a finger, and her eyes squinted as she grinned mischievously. "If you don't come with us, you won't be able to show your siblings the pampering you received."

"She would pull that card."

Rimu jumped to his feet immediately and scampered over to her. I understood his behavior. The last I knew, his siblings bullied him for having more red scales than black, so if they still were, he'd get to show off the pampering they didn't receive and make them jealous. Though, I wasn't sure Xaneth should be encouraging such behavior, even if it was to get him to listen to her.

"We'll see you all later at the ceremony." Xaneth waved before leaving through a portal Anahak opened. Valene huffed when she realized he had held onto one and didn't tell her, and he snickered.

When they were gone, I stood so I could put my supplies away and tossed Corliss the container of polish and a rag before grabbing everything else. "If you run out let me know. I have plenty more."

Mana squealed and yanked him off the couch before he had a chance to say anything. I only laughed as she dragged him down the hall to their room.

"She's too adorable for her own good, too."

"So, how much longer do we have to wait for this ceremony?" Rylan asked.

Valene pulled out a pocket watch as I headed for my room. "Well, the ceremony should be starting in about an hour, but Laz needs to leave in about ten minutes so she can get ready."

Dropping everything into my drawer to be organized later, I poked my head back out into the living room. "Why so much time for me to get ready? I already have clothes."

Valene shook her head. "You're getting new clothes."

I leaned against the doorframe. "Really? Why?"

"Because you need appropriate clothes for your new title," she said. "We threw your first pair of clothes together last minute, without thinking if they'd be a good choice for you."

"I've made some changes," I stated.

"Yeah, with the armor cloth," Shva'sika reminded me.

"That's because my original clothing was damaged. But I made real ones later."

Valene shook her head. "You're so stubborn. The new set won't be bad. I saw them myself; Alena and Tla'lli put it together for you. I know you're going to like it."

"All right, whatever. Do we at least have enough time for me to show you the greenhouse? I figured you'd want to see it, since you used to ask a lot about it in the past."

Valene's eyes sparkled and jumped to her feet. "Is that even a question?"

I chuckled, heading up the stairs leading to the roof and waving her to follow. As I made my way up, she pushed past me in her excitement. I laughed. I suspected I might be a little late to my own ceremony.

"More than likely."

I clasped my cloak around my neck and took a deep breath. As I had predicted, Valene had made me fifteen minutes late, but no one showed it bothered them. I was just whisked away into a room and several shamans went to work on me. I didn't even have a chance to figure out where we were. Tla'lli was now the only one left in the room, and she was being patient with me as I collected myself.

"You have nothing to worry about. You'll do great, I know it."

Someone rapped on the door and Tla'lli opened it. Xaneth strolled in, looking behind her.

"Looking for someone?" I teased.

"I'm making sure Rimu didn't follow," she admitted as she closed the door. "I did my best to sneak away when he wasn't looking, but that wasn't guaranteed to work."

I nodded in understanding and then noticed the satchel she carried. "What's that for?"

She held it out. "It's for you. Some of the other female dragons and I made it for you. Seda also grabbed a few of the things she knew you'd like to carry around if you could, so we put them in there, too. I was hoping I'd get here before you put your cloak on so you wouldn't have to take it back off to change."

I shook my head. "All of you have already contributed to my outfit; you didn't have to go and make this for me as well."

She smiled. "Well, this was just supposed to be from me. The others joined in. It's a thank you for being so kind to Rimu. I really do appreciate it."

Smiling, I took the bag and looked it over. It was a basic satchel, made of leather, but it had bones sewn into it in specifically chosen areas, as well as red and black dragon scales and a couple green dragon scale accents. I touched the scales.

"What a lovely gift."

"How is it that you're able to sew scales into these? They're so strong, I don't see how you were able to get needles through them."

Tla'lli shook her head. "It's not easy, trust me. I don't want to think how many needles we broke making the outfit, let alone the ones Xaneth broke making that satchel."

"But it was worth the hassle." Xaneth smiled. "It really was."

I smiled back. "Well, thank you for this. I appreciate the effort and it should be pretty helpful."

"It pleased me to do it. Now, I shouldn't hold you up anymore."

I nodded and watched her head out before turning to look at Tla'lli, who was slinging her quiver around her shoulders. "Anything else I need to do or know before you lead the way?"

"Well, since I'm not allowed to talk about the ceremony with you, no."

"How am I supposed to know what to do when no one will explain anything to me?" I exclaimed, exasperated.

She giggled. "You're not going to mess up. You're too good for that. Now follow me."

I sighed and complied.

"Stop fretting. This will be a cakewalk for you. Trust me."

Tla'lli led me down the hall, which then opened into a spacious room. It was well decorated and felt cozy. As I took in my surroundings, my curiosity was sparked. "Hey, where are we anyway?"

Tla'lli smiled. "I guess Valene forgot to tell you. We're at the East Tribe."

"Huh, I've never been here before. I'm a bit disappointed I never got to see much of the other tribes while I was staying at the West Tribe. Del'karo and I traveled to the North Tribe once, but that was it, until I showed up at your doorstep. So, what are we waiting for?"

"Us."

I peered down another hall to see four shaman leaders entering the room. Maka'shi, who had answered my question, led them. Following her was a tall elven man with dreadlocked black hair, tattooed dark skin, and white and blue face paint—Ir'esh, leader of the South Tribe, and Tla'lli's father, their shared golden eyes giving away their relation. The two other tribe leaders followed behind him.

Sha'hiri, the leader of the North Tribe, was an attractive, tall, porcelain-skinned nu-human with violet eyes and snow-white hair. Her cloak was pulled back across one shoulder, revealing her northern-style clothing made of high quality cloth, fur, and hand-crafted accessories. Several colors of paint dotted and swirled up her right arm.

Xa'vian, leader of the East Tribe, was an average-sized elven man with ebony skin, short dark hair with an unusual blue shine when light hit it, and crystalline blue eyes. A single white stripe of paint banded his nose. His cloak covered the rest of him, but with the crazy gadgets he had covering his face, I could only assume his clothes weren't much different.

I bowed my head.

Ir'esh turned his attention to Tla'lli. "We'll escort her from here."

She nodded and then spoke to me before running off. "I'll see you at the ceremony."

I focused on the leaders. "So, what am I doing?"

Maka'shi pulled her hood over her face. "Just follow us for now."

"What about Raikidan?" I asked. "I haven't seen him since I was sent to change."

"And you won't until your ceremony is over."

My brow furrowed. "Why?"

"Reasons I cannot discuss right now."

My lips pressed into a line. "You can't do that to either of us. I need to know what is going on so I know nothing will go wrong."

"You need to have faith in your Guard's abilities," Sha'hiri said.

"She did not just make assumptions."

"Don't." My eyebrow twitched and my fists clenched. "Don't you dare start assuming you know him better than me." The leaders exchanged glances. "Tell me what is going on, or I don't go anywhere with you. No me, no new shaman ceremony."

"Nice leverage. Stick to your guns."

Ir'esh rested his hand on his hips as he belted out a boisterous laugh. "Well, she passed that test real quick."

Xa'vian and Sha'hiri looked at each other with pleased smiles, and Maka'shi nodded. "I knew she would."

My expression dropped, with a lack of enthusiasm. *Of course they'd pull something like this.* Maka'shi knew my nature and my lack of trust, even for something like this. Shamans had secrets, which were revealed to shamans as they progressed in their studies and life. But for me to go into a ceremony of such importance with no information, even that went beyond cryptic for shamans.

Maka'shi gestured to Ir'esh. "Why don't you go retrieve Raikidan and the other Guards, while I let her know what she's allowed."

He nodded and walked back the way they'd come.

Maka'shi addressed me, pulling her hood down. "I cannot go into full detail for you, as some of this cannot be told. You have to experience it as it comes. But what I can say is that there will be a test on how you've grown as an elementalist."

That generally meant fighting. *Glad I put my foot down.* "If that's the case, I needed to talk to Raikidan about that."

She nodded. "He's a good Guard from what we've gauged, but still dragon. As you said, you know him best."

Ir'esh returned, and with him were Raikidan and Ken'ichi, the former showing clear joy at seeing me in the room. *That's interesting.*

The tribe leaders excused themselves to a far end of the room, taking Ken'ichi with them, and I motioned for Raikidan to follow me as I moved down the hall I'd come from with Tla'lli.

"If you two need a private room, there's plenty!" Xa'vian called out.

I shot him a dark look. Sha'hiri smacked him in the back of the head, turning my irritation to amusement. The two of them bickered and I couldn't bite my tongue. "You sure you two aren't the ones who need a private room?"

The other leaders and Ken'ichi laughed. Xa'vian looked taken aback by the call-out, while Sha'hiri appeared irritated. Raikidan chuckled and nudged me farther down the hall. This interested me. *Does he have something to talk about too?*

When we were out of earshot, we faced each other and Raikidan spoke before I could even open my mouth to try. "Ken'ichi said this ceremony could get tense. Whatever happens, I'm here. He said I'm supposed to stay out of it—that Guards aren't supposed to join. But I don't care about those rules. I'll help you however you need me to."

I smiled. His honesty was refreshing. "I'm going to need you to listen to him."

Raikidan's eyes widened in surprise and he opened his mouth to argue, but I continued speaking.

"From what I've been given for information on this ceremony, there is a sparring match involved. I know how you get with these situations." My eyes remained soft. "But your protective nature would only hinder me. I need to be able to prove myself to them."

Raikidan tried to speak again, but I placed a finger on his lips and rested my other hand on his cheek.

"Please promise me you will stay out of this unless it's is absolutely necessary for you to step in."

Raikidan held my gaze for a moment before sighing and placing both hands on mine, moving the one on his lips to his other cheek. He bowed his head. "I will do my best to fulfill this request. I do not like it, but if this is what will please you, then so be it."

I murmured a thank you and rolled onto my toes, planting a kiss on his forehead. I then pulled away from him and set a pace to the room the shaman leaders waited in. Raikidan ran to catch up, and when we re-entered the room, we found Sha'hiri holding Xa'vian in a headlock. An amused chuckled escaped my throat, alerting them to our presence. Sha'hiri immediately released Xa'vian and smoothed out her clothes. I remembered both Shva'sika and Del'karo hinting there was something between the two of them; Del'karo had even teased Sha'hiri a bit when we had visited her tribe, but I'd never been nosey enough to look into it. I suspected that at the very least, the two were close friends like Rylan and I were. *Same with Raikidan and me.*

"Don't be like that."

"We're ready," I announced, ignoring the voice this time. I needed to focus on the matter at hand.

Maka'shi nodded and pulled her hood over her head again. "Then follow us."

I pulled my hood up. Xa'vian and Sha'hiri also covered themselves, and Ir'esh opened a portal. He and Maka'shi took the lead, with me following them, and Xa'vian and Sha'hiri took positions behind me. Ken'ichi and Raikidan pulled up the rear.

Without making the others aware, I studied the portal. It was different from all the other portals I had used. This one didn't have as much swirling, and instead of being blue mixed with black, it was orange mixed with black. I'd never seen a portal like it.

When the portal's exit came into view, it took me by surprise. While portals greatly lessened the time it took to get from one location to another, the farther you traveled, the longer you had to walk through the portal. This walk was so short I wondered if we were still close to the East Tribe location. I shielded my eyes when we went through the exit, because it was so much brighter than your average portal. I blinked a few times when I was on the other side to get used to the dim light. I gazed around in awe.

We were outside, or at least it appeared like we were outside. Ankle-deep water covered the ground. Stone slabs, like the one we stood on, were scattered around the large gate that stood before us. Rocks and strange statues that looked like ancient spiritual tomb stones, with blue glowing lights emitting from holes carved out of them, were scattered about, illuminating the dark area.

Large trees with purple flowers and no leaves grew from the rocks that were scattered about in the water. Their foliage created a thick canopy that blocked out any light that could have shone through. Long talismans hung from the branches and gave off a protective, welcoming aura.

The large iron gate in front of us was intricately designed, especially where the four arched entrances were located, and had bright blue lights scattered about within the designs. Each entrance had two blue hanging lights built into either side to welcome anyone who entered.

In the center of all of this, where the canopy opened, stood a giant tree that grew on top of a boulder with blue lights glowing from within. Surrounding the tree and rock were more of the odd, ancient, spiritual, tomb-like stones. The tree had enormous purple flowers, similar to the others, growing from the branches, also with no leaves, as well as long talismans hanging from it like the rest of the forest around us—but the bark of the tree had symbols carved into it. As we traveled down the footpath made of individual, square stepping stones leading to the tree, the symbols became a bit clearer, but they remained unfamiliar to me. A few appeared shamanistic or druidic in nature, and a couple looked draconic, but I couldn't be sure.

Above the tree, where the canopy gapped, fluffy white clouds floated about in a bright blue sky. A tall, snowcapped mountain stood tall in the distance, but it carried a translucent look, as if it were extremely far away or not really there at all. This place reminded me of my trip to hell—just a lot less dreary-looking.

"It's been some time since I've seen this place. Quite different from the last time, but that's the beauty of it."

"What?"

My attention was torn away when more portals popped up on other stone slabs and people filed through them. Some I didn't recognize, while others I did. Unlike us, they remained on their stone slabs, rather than heading for the center tree.

"Can someone tell me where we are?" I whispered.

Maka'shi nodded. "We're on the *Plane of Between.*"

My brow rose. "This looks nothing like the Plane of Between. Shouldn't it look more lifeless, like the spiritual plane, and have elements of the living plane visible?"

"That's true when you have your spirit leave your body. But it shows its true form when you visit body *and* soul," Xa'vian clarified.

I noticed people beginning to appear out of nowhere, though not through portals. I guessed them to be spirits, as even though they took a physical form on this plane, living people couldn't appear out of thin air. I wondered which spirits would come to watch my ceremony. *Would Mom be here? Or even Jasmine?* I hoped at least one of them would, even if I couldn't see them. I knew they'd be proud.

"There are many who are proud of you."

I looked back when Ken'ichi told Raikidan to follow him, branching away from our path. Raikidan hesitated, struggling with having to leave me to handle this test alone, but eventually complied. *Hopefully his promise is what convinced him.*

Before the rest of us made it all the way over to the giant tree, Maka'shi motioned for me to stop following while the four of them took their place on small slabs spread out in an arc. That's when I noticed the path had stopped here and I was on a much larger stone piece than the one the path had. It was the same size as the ones each leader stood on and, interestingly enough, there were still two more stone that weren't occupied on both sides of their arc. *Who is supposed to stand there?*

"Just wait. You'll find out soon enough."

"How the hell do you know what's going on?"

The voice chuckled. *"I know much, remember?"*

"It's time," Maka'shi announced as she pulled down her hood.

As if activated by a magic word, a stepping stone rose up from the water near the two empty stones I was just considering. It wasn't long before two people were walking up the paths. I realized it was Del'karo and Shva'sika. *Makes sense, actually, with what Maka'shi revealed to me, though I'm not sure why they hadn't come here with us. I guess it doesn't matter.*

Maka'shi nodded at the two and then went to address everyone. "Today, we gather to welcome a new shaman, a new sister, to our ranks."

"Today, we gather to celebrate a new beginning to a life," Xa'vian said.

"Today, we find out how much our sister has learned," Ir'esh said.

"Today, we find out how much we can learn from her," Sha'hiri concluded.

"Laz'shika, you have learned much in these past decades," Maka'shi complimented. "You've learned to master the ways of fire. You've learned how to create new techniques that could not only benefit you but many around you. You've learned to overcome obstacles no one else will ever have to face. And now comes your final test. You must prove you are worthy of the shaman name I bestowed you. You must now prove you've learned everything we can teach you. It's time you face the two shamans who taught you everything you know, and it's time to prove to them you are ready to teach yourself from now on."

"He we go."

All four leaders stepped off their stones and backed up in the water. At the same time, Del'karo and Shva'sika exchanged silent words with their eyes. Del'karo stepped forward, but Shva'sika backed away down her path again. *Looks like I'm facing Del'karo first.*

"Hope his old bones can handle it."

I almost laughed. *"You and me both."*

As he positioned himself so he stood in front of me, the stones around us grew and formed into one large slab, and I found my interest in this place was growing. But there would be time later to sate my curiosity. Right now, I had a test to pass.

Del'karo removed his cloak and tossed it aside. "Are you ready for this?"

I smirked and unclasped my own cloak. "I hope you're ready, old timer."

51
CHAPTER
(RYOKO)

L az tossed her cloak and satchel aside, and stood in front of her elven teacher with determination in her eyes. Her mentor did the same. *Laz once said his name was... Del'karo... I think.* I brushed it off. Didn't matter right now. The two hadn't even started their duel, and they had me struck with awe. I also found Laz's clothes, while strange, quite fascinating.

Her top was the most surprising part of the outfit. Made of red dyed leather and decorated with golden metal along the edges, it was shaped like a bikini, but had a wide band wrapping around her back instead of tie strings, and a thick halter-like collar. What looked to be small black dragon scales ran up her breasts and around her collar in a pattern. In the center of her top, between her breasts, was a circular amulet that appeared to have a live fire burning inside it, and the necklace Raikidan gave her adorned her neck.

Feathers decorated her hair, which was styled as she normally wore it, hair clip and all. Her ears were also adorned with jewelry, old and new, and a spiral-style ring replaced the basic lip ring she always wore.

On her lower half, she wore shorts made of a thin, black, form-fitting material, and over that she wore a long skirt made of red cloth with intricate gold and orange embroidery that draped to one side of her body. An identical pendant to the one on her top clasped her skirt together on the open side.

Cloth arm sleeves, styled similarly to the ones she liked to wear on a regular basis, covered her hands and forearms. Layered black scales covered portions of the sleeves, as if simulating armor. Her daggers were in the typical place she always carried them, but they had new sheaths and bands that also carried a few throwing daggers each. *I wonder if she has the one Ryder gifted her over the solstice.* She carried it around with her more often than her usual daggers now, given it was easier to conceal than her usual carry choice.

Laz also still wore the ring Raikidan had given her on her left hand.

The last bits of her outfit that got my attention were her boots. They were knee high and plated in the front, with more black dragon scales layered in the same design as the ones on her top. Strapped over the top of each foot and ankle was a leather guard with a large amulet, with more living fire embedded into it.

The use of the dragon scales in her outfit intrigued me. There were so many. I would have thought, with the red dragon allies she'd made, that would be the color of the scales. *This color design makes her look like a reverse Raikidan.* The thought made me wonder if that's where the source of the black scales came from.

Del'karo had a similar appearance to the South Tribe shamans, with his mohawk, tattoos, and piercings. The only thing that set him apart from them was that he wore denim pants, as if he belonged in the city.

The two of them stood there, and the longer they did, the more my excitement built. I wanted to not only see this last trial, but I wanted to see her pass. I wanted her to prove to everyone that she wasn't the same woman she used to be. It had always been my greatest wish for her to no longer be alienated for small differences, and for her to have the life she deserved. For someone supposedly so full of hate and loneliness, she did so much for others. She put everyone else first without a thought about herself. And for this, I believed she deserved a better life more than anyone.

"Let's see if you remember what I taught you," Del'karo challenged.

Laz smirked. "Ladies first."

I couldn't help but laugh. It was nice to know she didn't treat her teacher any different than the rest of us.

Del'karo lifted his hand and then forced out a ball of fire toward her. She didn't move, much to my surprise. Instead, she lifted her arms up and dispersed the flames with ease when they came close. I blinked. She made it look so easy.

"That was weak, even by your standards. Something the matter, old man?" she taunted.

He grinned and threw out another flame, and then threw out another right after. Laz dispersed the first flame like she had done before, but when the second flame came at her, she did something different. She shifted her weight a little, and when the flame came within range, she made a small movement with her hands and then pushed them forward, and the flame switched directions. Del'karo moved to the side and dodged it.

Laz grinned. "My turn."

She made a swift motion with her hands in front of her face like she typically did when she didn't want to breathe fire from her mouth and then threw a blast at him. He dodged with ease, even though that flame went much faster than the ones he threw at her. To my surprise, he didn't attack her back, same as she had done when he started the match. I didn't understand why they were up to.

"They're sizing each other up right now. They'll start warming up in a second."

That voice is familiar. Turning, I was taken aback by the porcelain-skinned, aqua blue-haired woman who stood next to me. "A–Amara?"

She smiled, her green eyes sparkling with life. "Hey."

I blinked and failed miserably at trying to say something.

"Don't forget about me now."

I turned to look at the woman with milky skin and long ebony hair with a single blue streak, who was now on the other side of me. "Jasmine?"

She giggled and waved, her lavender eyes dancing with amusement behind her thin-rimmed glasses.

I yelped when strong arms grabbed me by the waist and lifted me up. "Zeek, put me down! Put me down! Put me—" I froze. "Wait, Zeek?"

I turned my head laying eyes on the muscular, bronze-skinned man. Zeek chuckled. "Hey there, Pipsqueak."

"Don't call me that! You know I hate it." I blinked and then shook my head. "I'm talking to a dead guy. I'm seeing dead people. My head hurts…"

Everyone laughed at me. I hated it when they did that. It made me feel stupid, especially when I knew I was missing something.

Amara quieted herself down and smiled. "Did you not see the other spirits?"

"Well I saw them, but I didn't think anyone could touch them!" I said as Zeek put me down.

She laughed more. "There's a reason the ceremony is held here."

"You guys can take a physical form here," Rylan guessed.

I couldn't see how he was so calm about this. It wasn't exactly normal to interact with the dead.

Jasmine nodded. "Exactly. And we're able to stay this way for the next twenty-four hours, even if we walk onto the living plane with all of you to attend of the celebration after the ceremony."

"Both here *and* the living plane? Isn't that dangerous?" I asked. "I mean, Laz said not all spirits are friendly."

Amara nodded. "Well that's true, but the worst people are in Hell, so there isn't a whole lot to be worried about. There are plenty of shamans, though, who aren't going to be here, so they can keep an eye out for the troublemakers just in case."

"But isn't this a big deal?" I asked. "Shouldn't everyone be here?"

She smiled. "There are far too many for everyone to come, so, only those who know Eira will attend."

Raid raised his hand. "Spirit knowledge of nothing here, why only twenty-four hours for corporeal forms? Pretty specific time frame."

Amara smiled at him, like one did a child. "It's not something we're at liberty to discuss. Let's just say... the why is because of this momentous day, and the how isn't up to us."

Raid frowned, and I couldn't help but find amusement in his disappointment. Laz had told us once there were things non-shamans couldn't know about spirits, and even things shamans weren't allowed to know. This seemed to be one of those times. "So, you all came to watch?"

Amara flashed such a happy smile it made my heart skip. "I've been waiting for this day for a long time. I wouldn't miss this, even if a new god ascended and had a party to celebrate."

Jasmine held up a finger, as I'd always known her to do when she wanted to add to a conversation. "Same here."

"I was made to come," Zeek said.

I crossed my arms and raised an eyebrow in disbelief, but before I could argue, a woman with pale skin and blond hair whacked him on the head. I blinked when I realized it was Jade.

"Don't be a jerk," she told him. "You were the most eager to come, though we all know it wasn't because of Eira."

My face flushed when she shot me a glance. Even though it wasn't a secret Zeek and I were a couple prior to his death, I was with Rylan now, and I didn't want to start complicating my relationship.

My attention went back to Laz's test when a large blast of fire shot past my periphery. The two were finally past the testing and at their warm-up phase, the effort put in, wasn't equal. Laz dodged or broke Del'karo's fire with little effort, only occasionally throwing fire back at him, and he definitely threw more weight into his attacks than he had during the warm-up.

I crossed my arms. "She's not even trying. I thought she'd at least make this interesting."

Amara chuckled. "Be patient. It just started."

"She could at least give it her all, right from the start."

"But that wouldn't be her, now would it?" she said. "Eira is conserving her strength. She is very aware that this test may take a while, and not because she's taking it easy."

I tilted my head and then went back to watching. What she said did make sense. Danika had been sitting back so far, and I was certain she would test Laz too, though I couldn't figure out when.

Laz finally put some effort into this, because she sent endless waves of fire in Del'karo's direction. At first, Del'karo had an easy time redirecting the flames into the water around them, creating thick clouds of steam that lingered in the air, but it wasn't long before it was apparent he was starting to have a difficult time. I wondered if it was because of his age, or if it was because Laz was just that good.

Then, out of nowhere, a young man who looked almost identical to Del'karo ran in and threw fire at Laz. My hand flew up to my mouth and my eyes widened. What was this man doing? Laz, on the other hand, wasn't fazed by this new curve ball. She dodged and evaded and acted as if he wasn't worth her time.

"You'll have to do better than that, Ne'kall," Laz taunted. "Not even when you team up with your father do you stand a chance against me."

Ne'kall didn't appear to be fazed by her words, and attacked her until he stood by Del'karo's side. The two barely acknowledged each other before creating a joint force against Laz. Laz, like before, easily defended herself against the onslaught and was able to push them back herself.

I turned my attention to the others for clarification. "What is going on? Why is that guy jumping in?"

"Ryoko, did you not hear Valene tell us that we could give Laz a hand or act as an opponent at any time during her test?" Seda asked.

It took me a moment to consider responding. I was too preoccupied taking in her appearance.

She wore a unique-looking outfit. It had a black, rather revealing bodice, with separate arm sleeves tailored tight to her arms until they reach the elbow, where they flared out, making it possible to hide her hands when clasped together. Golden cloth and thread decorated the ends of the sleeves in an elegant, almost regal design.

Tailored to the bodice was a black cloth waist cape, bustled just right to create a wide hip illusion on her leaner frame, as well as a cloak-like look in the back. She wore thin, tiny shorts to keep herself covered where the cape gapped in the front.

A large hood adorned her head and was attached to large, armor-like shoulder pads. Thigh-high black boots with a decorative, diagonally cascading cut at the top covered her feet and legs. She had switched out her blindfold for a new black one, decorated with golden thread in the same fashion as her sleeves and boots.

Telar stood next to her, wearing a similar outfit, though instead of a bodice and thin shorts, he sported a tailored vest and pants.

I had never seen either wear this outfit before, but Seda had explained they were outfits that psychics wore on special occasions. I had thought she was making it up, even though Telar tried to back her up, until we got here and several other psychics had similar garb.

"What are you talking about, Seda?" I asked.

She giggled. "I figured you might have missed—"

"I didn't hear her say anything either," Rylan said. "Don't single her—"

Seda laughed. "Let me finish, Rylan. When I said you, I was using the plural. Most of you were so interested in everything here, I didn't expect many of you to hear her say we could jump in before she ran off to check in with Raikidan."

I pursed my lips. *The people who jump in, I wonder how they'd affect her test.* "So, we can jump in at any time? There are no rules regarding who jumps in first?"

"There is no particular time that is best," Amara said. "Whatever the gut says, go with it. But only those who have had an impact on her life, like us and Ne'kall, are allowed to assist in the test."

"How has Ne'kall had an impact?" I questioned. "Laz never mentioned him before."

"Ne'kall is Del'karo's eldest son. He and Eira would spar all the time, but he could never come out on top."

I snorted. "So, he's using this as a type of rematch."

She nodded with a smile. "Pretty much."

"Well some of you can jump in," Blaze muttered. "Some of us would get our asses handed to us if they even looked at us."

I held up my hands. "Momentous moment! Blaze just admitted he's weak!"

Rylan laughed and Blaze glared at me. "You know that's not what I meant."

I snickered, a bitch of a smirk plastered to my lips. "Sure, you can keep thinking that."

He went to shoot off a reply, but something Laz was doing caught our eye. My eyes widened and my mouth hung open when Laz breathed fire straight from her mouth at the two shamans. Ne'kall appeared surprised by her ability as he dodged the attack, but Del'karo looked calm, almost happy even. *Did he know she could do this?*

He was her teacher, so it was a possibility, but Laz did everything she could to hide this side of her. She had been driven to hide it because she'd been picked on so badly in the military for it. The dragons had been real supportive of her ability when they found out, and it helped her come out of her shell a little, but with so many people around, I hadn't expected her to be so bold about it.

My ear pricked when I heard the whispering. Some of the soldiers were discussing how odd her ability was, but they were immediately hushed by the surrounding shamans. To my surprise, they were quite excited about Laz's ability. From what I could pick up, this talent was rare in fire shamans, and was considered a sign of power. Several of them, who I assumed were also fire shamans, sounded a bit annoyed that Del'karo had been chosen to train Laz instead of them. I refrained from giggling at their jealousy.

I glanced at Amara to see how she felt about this, and I wasn't surprised to see the glowing pride radiating off her. She had been so adamant about Laz not hiding her ability in order to fit in, it made sense that this pleased her. *I wish you were coming home with us after this…*

My excitement level rose when Laz used her impressive acrobatic skills to dodge a wave of earth as it rushed for her. I searched the expansive area to see who had joined the battle and was intrigued to see one of the shaman tribe leaders. I remembered his name being Ir'esh, or something like that. "What's his significance to Laz's life?"

Amara shrugged. "None. She formed the alliance with him first, but other than that, he's involved because he's the leader of the South Tribe. All the leaders will be involved at some point. It's an obligation for them."

I rubbed my chin in thought. There had to be more than that. It was the way he looked so eagerly at Laz.

"Laz'shika and my father also have a high volume of respect for each other."

This new voice took me out of my thoughts, and I smiled when I saw the newcomer. "Hey, Tla'lli."

She smiled. "Hey."

"So, is that why your father is really participating?" I asked.

She nodded. "He's been itching to have a match with her. Said she was a powerful shaman, and it had been some time since he had a match with one as strong as she is. I didn't understand what he was talking about until now. I had no idea she was a Firebreather."

"Your father didn't, either," Amara said. "He could just sense the power Eira was trying to suppress."

"You must be very proud of her," Tla'lli said.

Amara smiled. "I'd be proud of her even if she was completely ordinary."

"So, being a Firebreather is really that big of a deal?" I asked.

Tla'lli nodded. "Dragons aside, there have only been a handful of Firebreathers in the history of Lumaraeon. It's a powerful technique that is hard to learn, let alone master. Many Shamans of the Rising Sun have spent their whole lives trying to master this skill, only to never accomplish it. Those who have are never forgotten. How long has Laz'shika been able to do this?"

"I think it was three days after her tank release," Amara admitted.

Tla'lli's eyes grew wide. "W—what? Are you serious?"

Amara nodded with a smile. "And I believe it only took her two weeks to master it."

"A week and three days, actually," Rylan corrected. "And the only reason I remember is because that was when she'd set my fur on fire purposefully at that point."

I giggled. "Did she really do that?"

"When she was bored." He frowned. "Which happened to be a lot."

Tla'lli shook her head in disbelief. "She sounds like a handful when she wants to be, even now. Raikidan has to be sharp to keep up."

I laughed. "Sharp isn't a word we usually use with him. Stubborn and bullheaded is more him." Tla'lli laughed and I then scanned the area. "Speaking of Raikidan, where is he? I saw him arrive with Laz, but he walked away with someone else."

"Over there, with Ken'ichi and some other Guards who are keeping an eye on him." Tla'lli pointed, and I followed her finger until I spotted him.

No wonder I couldn't see him. He sat down on a stone slab, his arms folded over his knees. He rested his chin on his arms with narrowed eyes. *Is he pouting?*

I chuckled at the thought and went back to watching Laz's test. She was doing well as the three men ganged up on her. She acrobatically flipped and dodged all the attacks, her body never staying in one place for more than a few seconds. My eyes narrowed. *Too well...*

Anger boiled inside me. *She's not even trying!* She was toying with the three of them. I hated it when she did that. I hated when she didn't take certain things seriously. I tried my best to stay calm and keep my mouth shut. For all I knew, it was part of a master plan, but as I continued to watch, I could see she really was just messing around and I couldn't stay quiet anymore.

"Laz, put some actual effort into this! This is kinda important!"

The four of them stopped and stared at me. A stray fire from Ne'kall flew at Laz, but she pushed it away with ease without even looking at it, which only proved my point. But it wasn't just the four of them staring at me. Everyone in this strange place had their eyes locked on me. Well, everyone but Del'karo. He appeared unaffected by my outburst, as if he knew all along.

"You're joking, right?" Tla'lli whispered.

Laz grinned. "Why don't you make me?"

Tla'lli's eyes flicked back and forth between the us. "They're both joking, right?"

Amara chuckled and I narrowed my eyes at Laz. "Why can't you take this seriously? It's important."

"She is," Del'karo said. "We're not making it challenging enough for her." He shook his head, his voice lowering as if he were talking to himself now. "Nothing I throw at her is ever challenging enough."

Laz held up her hands. "You can jump in if you want, Ryo. You seem to really want to teach me a lesson anyway."

I glared at her, and before I knew it, I stomped my foot, sending a quake in her direction. Laz, of course, moved out of the way of the small chasm I created.

When the earth ceased shaking and trees stopped falling, Ir'esh ventured over to my chasm and then closed it up, but not before letting out a low whistle. "She hit the lava core."

Del'karo chuckled as if nothing could surprise him, and Ne'kall stared at me in wonder and disbelief, but I hardly paid them any mind. I was too focused on Laz. She stood there, taunting me. I took a short breath and ran in. If she wanted to go up against me, then fine. I'd test her, too.

To my surprise, Laz rushed at me. She was either doing this to fake me out, or she was taking this seriously and the three shamans really hadn't been able to give her a challenge.

As she came into close combat range, she tried her usual side-skirting technique, but I was ready. I knew her too well. I threw my fist to the ground and broke the earth again. She dodged, but I threw down my fist again, and the second time I managed to almost catch her, though I had also inadvertently sent the quake toward our friends.

"Hey, Ryoko, watch it!" Blaze yelled. "Not all of us are participating in this!"

Laz and I laughed, but I shouldn't have. Typical of her, she used my distracted state to throw a ball of fire at me. Luckily for me, I had enough time to harden my skin and I easily blocked her attack. Not wasting any time, I went at her and engaged in close combat.

Laz dodged and evaded, as was typical of her fight style, only occasionally blocking one of my swings or trying to throw off some fire at me, which I blocked. I finally managed to push her onto her back, but she recovered quickly and came at me with a vengeance. I was pushed back by her relentless waves of fire. Thanks to my toughened skin, though, none of it hurt. *This power. Annoying, but amazing how strong it is.*

"C'mon, Ryo, I thought you wanted to make me take this seriously," Laz taunted.

Taking a long, annoyed breath, I forced the fire away that she was throwing at me and ran at her. This move took her off guard, and she didn't react fast enough. I rammed my head into her forehead. Laz fell onto her back and held her head with a groan.

I blinked and then regretted what I did. "I'm sorry, Laz. Did I hit you too hard?"

Slowly she rose to her feet and then came at me, reciprocating and ramming her head into my forehead. I fell to the ground and held my face. That had actually hurt.

"No, you just fall for that way too easily," she teased.

I rested my hand on my forehead as Del'karo and Ir'esh laughed at the two of us. Blood dripped down from a cut she had created. She also had one, but the fact she had managed to do this to me was so crazy it was hard to believe.

I got back up on my feet, my excitement growing. She'd never been able to land a blow like that on me before. Not with my hardened skin on. *She's getting stronger.*

I always liked sparing with Laz. I felt so alive bonding with her, like I'd done it for many lifetimes. It sounded illogical, which is why I never told anyone before, but I liked the feeling. I liked the bond I shared with Laz, even if we were completely different people, down to our likes and dislikes.

We came into close quarters with each other and bare-knuckle-brawled it. Sometimes she'd "cheat" and use fire in her hands, but I "cheated" back with my hardened skin.

"Hey, so what's up with Mister Sexy Pouty Pants?" I asked her in such a casual manner, I became a hypocrite for accusing Laz of not taking this seriously.

Laz's brow twisted in confusion. "Mister what?" Her brows then relaxed and she laughed, before throwing a punch. "Is Raikidan really pouting?"

I dodged. "Yeah, it's cute."

"Damn, I want to see that. It's rare that I get to see him sulk."

I laughed and ducked under a kick. "So why is he sulking?"

"He's not supposed to join in." She threw some fire at me. "I didn't get a big explanation why, but Ken'ichi told him he couldn't join in for some reason. He didn't want to listen, but I told him he had to, otherwise he may get in the way."

My brow rose as I threw a punch at her. "And he agreed?"

She rocked her head back and forth, creating an illusion of being on me. "I told him the only time he could jump in is if I'm in big trouble."

I snorted. "At this rate, that'd be never."

She winked. "Explains the sulking."

I laughed and then grabbed her arm and threw her several feet. She landed on the ground ungracefully, but got back up. I stomped my foot on the ground, sending a quake her way. She barely managed to dodge my sudden move, and was even worse at dodging the next one I sent at her. She tried to stall me by throwing more fire at me, but I forced it away and sent another quake her way.

"Feel the earth around you."

I blinked as I threw out another quake. I had heard that voice before. Every once in a while I'd hear it, usually when I was having difficulties controlling my strength, or creating quakes when I had been in the military. But this time, it didn't come to me as a far-off whisper as if I were hearing things. It sounded like someone was behind me, coaxing me to do more.

"Bend it to your will. No amount of science can remove you from your true nature."

I'm not convinced. In my years of being out of my tank, I had never once been able to connect with the earth like Peacekeeper Ryoko, the woman I had been cloned from. The half-wogron woman helped saved Lumaraeon during the War of End, and had been known for her strength and impressive skills as an elementalist. When I was cloned, Zarda didn't want that earth ability in me. He wanted to keep playing god and determine the genes that enabled the ability, so I became his guinea pig, like many other unfortunate soldiers. *As far as I'm concerned, he succeeded.*

"He didn't. Trust me."

Oh what the hell. It wasn't like trying would hurt anything. I did my best to search out the presence of the earth from inside me, as this voice had encouraged so many times before.

"Feel it in your core and move it through your arms as an extension."

A strange sensation somewhere inside me pulsed. I did my best to force that feeling into my arm, though with little success. *I don't know what I'm doing!*

A pair of feminine arms extended out on either side of me. "I'll give you a hand."

The sensation grew stronger and forced its way into my arms. *What is this?* Using whatever this was to my advantage, I stomped my foot on the ground to create another quake, and then forced the earth to move and shoot out at Laz. I blinked slowly and then stared at my hands. I had moved the earth.

The person behind me giggled. "Try it again."

I nodded and felt for the earth again, and found it was easier than before. I then created another quake and forced the earth to move toward Laz in an attempt to hit her, since she was playing her dodge-and-evade game again. Determined this time to hit her, I went for another time, but I chose not to shake the earth. To my surprise, I successfully threw the earth at Laz, but she wasn't having it.

She dodged the wave and then rushed for me. Before I knew it, she was on me, but I wasn't to be her target. "All right, Peacekeeper Ryoko, you can stop helping *my* Ryoko now."

My eyes widened in shock. *Wait, what?*

Laz maneuvered around me and threw a punch at the person behind me. I whirled around, only to be shocked at the nearly-identical half-wogron woman Laz had targeted. There were two major differences; her hair, while as straight and long as mine, was styled a bit differently, and her clothes were something out of an ancient tomb.

Her clothes were shaman-like, like the wolf fur one Danika made me for the out-of-town expedition and allowed me to wear for this occasion, but hers were older and more primal. Large bone plating covered her neck, framing her face and making her breasts appear larger than I suspected them to actually be. There were large bones styled in a downward cascading fashion for optimal protection covering her shoulders, and underneath the armor were bone plates with large spikes protruding vertically. Decorating both the center of the neck plating and the sides of the shoulder armor were large gem-like spheres. Holding these all to her body were a few leather ties.

A short leather shirt covered her torso, though it left her belly exposed, and seemed nearly incapable of holding in her large breasts. Tied to her arms, under her shoulder armor, were long, flowing sleeves with an intricate design woven into them. A long cloth wrapped around her lower body, acting like a skirt. Strips of leather tied some gapping in the front to help keep it all from unraveling. Several animal skulls hung from two leather cords that were sewn into the left-top side of the skirt. She also didn't wear any shoes.

I blinked to make sure I wasn't seeing things.

"Aw, do you not want me teaching her something that might put you at a disadvantage at your own ceremony, Eira?" Peacekeeper Ryoko's eyes squinted as she teased.

Laz attacked her again. "I'd prefer you'd not."

I shook my head and decided to go sit down. My head hurt from my wound and all the confusion. I didn't understand any of this spirit stuff.

"Ryo!" Laz called.

I stopped and glanced over my shoulder. "Yeah?"

She smiled and waved. "Thanks for the good warm-up."

I chuckled and waved her off before heading back to the others. "Yeah, sure, whatever."

"You okay, Ryo?" Rylan asked with great concern when I was back by his side.

I nodded. "Yeah, my head just hurts. I need to sit and calm down."

The stone slab we stood on grew, and a small circular seat extended up out of it. I looked around to see Ir'esh giving me a quick wave. I nodded my thanks and sat down.

Rylan knelt next to me. "That was an impressive display."

"If it's all right with you, I'd like to not talk about that right now," I told him. "I need to process all of this."

He chuckled. "Sure, but for the record, I was referring to your control with the quaking not the other earth control you tapped into."

I smiled my thanks and continued to hold my head. It was still bleeding and my head was starting to pound.

"Here, let me help with that."

I peered up at the tall man with long blue-silver hair and half-elf ears standing next to me. "You're—"

The man smiled. "My name is Xye."

He then reached for my forehead and it healed up in a matter of seconds. "A healer, not bad."

He chuckled. "Not the best out there, but good enough to help you with that."

I smiled my thanks and then returned my attention to the test, to find Peacekeeper Ryoko bowing out. Laz was understandably unhappy about it. *I'd feel the same way in her shoes.* All the stories had said she was a formidable opponent, and knowing Laz, she had gotten all excited when she appeared, thinking she'd get a chance to face her. Laz, getting over her disappointment, chose to face off with her first three opponents before I intervened.

I scratched my head when I saw how much of a mess we had created so far. Large rock faces and shards protruded out of the ground, trees were on fire, and the small chasms I had made were allowing the water on the ground to escape within them. "We're kinda destroying your sacred ground."

Amara chuckled. "Not destroying, reshaping."

"Huh?"

She moved forward. "When each shaman is tested here, they change it. It becomes something new. The last shaman here was a plant-based shaman who had several water-based helpers. This test is quite interesting already, and it's just started. It'll be fascinating to see how it's shaped."

I cocked my head. "Amara?"

She chuckled and advanced toward Laz. "Now, it's time to see how much my daughter has remembered."

52
CHAPTER
(EIRA)

N e'kall threw another blast of fire at me, but as usual, it wasn't strong enough to do much to me. I pushed it away and hammered him with a wave of my own, pushing him back. Lucky for him, Del'karo had his back and was able to redirect the fire before his son was overwhelmed.

"Pup is out of his league."

"Ne'kall, why don't you just back down. Having your dad hold your hand through all of this is a bit—" A chunk of earth came flying at me, but I ducked down and threw a flame at Ir'esh in retaliation. "Hey, I'm talking here."

A feminine voice chuckled. "Well, if you have time to throw around insults, then they're not challenging you enough, now are they?"

I turned my gaze in the direction of Ryoko. My eyes widened at the sight of the woman advancing toward me. "Mom…"

She smiled as she stopped advancing and slammed her abnormally large great sword modeled after goddess Satria's Tamashi, into the ground. The weapon stood on its own. "You ready?"

"Oh goodie. I was wondering when this part would happen."

I smirked and lit a fire in both of my hands before readying myself. "For you, always."

She lifted her hands. The water around her swirled and I made sure I was ready. Mother was no easy opponent, and even though I had improved over the years, she wasn't going to make it easy for me. *Good. I need a challenge to prove to everyone here I'm worthy of taking on this new responsibility.* I wanted to prove to myself that I was able to do something good, but I wouldn't be able to do it unless someone pushed me to my limit.

"You're only seeing half the point. You need to look at this deeper."

"No, stay back," Del'karo told Ne'kall.

"But with four of us, we may actually be able to challenge Eira," Ne'kall argued.

"We stay out of this for now. This is between her and her mother, like it had been for you and me when you had been in Eira's place."

"All right, I'll wait and see what happens."

I stared my mother down as we faced off. Small bubbles of water floated around her, and my flame burned hot in my hands, but neither of us made a move. The others around us waited with bated breath as the tension between the two of us rose.

Then suddenly, Mother threw a water bubble at me. *Typical.* She was never as patient as me and had always initiated the first attack in the past.

"Give the woman some credit. She has power on her side that allows for first-strike attacks."

"But she doesn't have speed like I do."

I skirted to the side and forced a wave of fire at her. She used the water around her to create a shield, nullifying the flame, and then used the shield to keep her protected as she shot out more bubbles of water that came so fast they acted like bullets. I ducked, rolled, and did whatever I needed to in order to dodge her attack. I shot off blasts of fire when I could, allowing me brief reprieves from the water bullets as they were nullified.

Her attack stopped and gave me a few moments to assess my situation. I wasn't tired. No, I was far from that, but I wasn't sure if she could lose energy. Her being dead was another factor I needed to figure out. I didn't know her limitations anymore. Did she have any, or were they the same as when she had been alive?

My mother made motions with her arms, and the water around us began to move. She wasn't giving me any more time to think. From the look in her eyes, this was going to get very serious now.

She continued to move her arms and water began to swirl up next to her. Making quick motions, I forced the fire I carried to swirl around me in several differently-angled loops. Taking a deep breath, I watched her carefully. She had stopped pulling water and maintained the two water cyclones she had created, but she had yet to move. I knew if I waited too much longer to act, she may bring out more. They weren't something to mess around with. But I wasn't sure what she was doing. *Patience isn't something she's good at.*

"Death changes a person. Remember that rule."

With a quick, decisive breath, I sent some of the fire swirling around me at her. Mother grinned, as if I had done exactly what she hoped, and made her counter move. Skirting to the side to dodge my attack, she pushed both water cyclones at me. Evading them, I threw more of the fire around me at her, but she managed to use the water around her to wave up and block the attack. At the same time, she pulled the water cyclones back toward me. Not expecting them to come at me at such a rapid pace, I barely managed to evade them. Yet, before I could manage out a counter move she pushed the cyclones at me again.

I dodged and threw out another round of flames, but she blocked them, as I anticipated. While she was busy blocking, I built up more power into my flame and then threw it at her. I threw blast after blast at her, and although she blocked them, the water she used evaporated from the heat.

I kept up my assault, dodging the few cyclones she still managed to control, and continued my attempt to overwhelm her. It was an uphill battle, but slowly her moves became more defensive. I pressed my assault, not giving her a chance to go on the offensive again. She pulled her water cyclones in to help defend herself. *Those need to go.* I channeled more power into my flame, and shot off several more blasts at her, finishing by slamming my hands together and pushing out a large wave of fire. Unfortunately, my mother was ready for this move, almost as if she were expecting it.

"Remember, she knows you better than most. Such a move would be predictable to her."

With a large, swift motion, the water and the cyclones surrounding her swirled together and wrapped around her, lifting my mother high up into the air. I narrowed my eyes as she hovered up there in anticipation of her next assault. She cast me a quick grin, and then the fight resumed once more.

Mother pulled moisture from both the swirling waters around her body and the ground, sending it all rushing toward me. I jumped, rolled, flipped, anything else I could think of to avoid the massive assault, while trying to throw my own back at her. Unfortunately, my meager retaliation did little to help. Her wave was so strong that it snuffed my flames in small puffs of smoke. *She's just as strong as I remember.* A grin spread across my face. *Excellent.*

I liked the challenge she always presented. It made me think outside the box, and this time was no different. I needed to change my tactics. *How can I exploit her ability's weakness?*

I dodged and retaliated to bide more time. She couldn't utilize the water in the air, only pools and large bodies of water. *This testing field is a playground for her.* The cracks in the earth Ryoko had created drained the water, but not in any quick manner that benefited me. *I'll need to do the dirty work myself.*

"*Now you're thinking!*"

I took a deep breath and spewed fire from my lips, aiming in her general direction to mask my true purpose. My true goal was the water around her. I continued flinging flames from my hands to keep the deception going.

Mother chuckled and pushed a cyclone at me. "That isn't going to work, Eira. I've known you too long for you to pull that on me."

I didn't reply to her taunt. I kept up what I was doing while trying to dodge her attacks. Her knowing didn't mean the tactic wouldn't work.

"*That's the spirit!*"

She sent a wave of water at me. "Give up!"

I chuckled. "Not something I'm good at, Mother, you know this."

I exhaled a hot flame and dodged her attack, willing it to fan out into a protective barrier. Water slammed against the barrier and it evaporated on impact. With a deep breath, I forced the flame out and watched as it dispersed all the water it touched until it died.

I took stock of the situation. A lot of water had been evaporated, but there was still too much left. My attempt felt useless.

"*You're going to need to think of a better tactic.*"

My mother chuckled. "I told you it wouldn't work. Try something different, and fast."

She pushed another wave of water at me, but I sent fire through it, rendering it useless. An idea dawned on me. A thin smile spread across my lips, causing her to pause and cock her head at me.

"Fine, I'll just turn into a copy-cat." I took in a deep breath, and exhaled a large amount of flame, keeping focused as I willed it to spiral. Still concentrating, I spun it until it swirled into a huge flaming cyclone. While keeping it in place, I created two more like it.

"Oh, I like this plan. It's dangerous, but it can work."

Mother's eyes sparkled, her lips spreading into a wide smirk. "Well, this is new. Let's see how this plays out."

I grinned as I sent a fire twister her way, all water in its path evaporating on contact. Mother pushed a water cyclone at me in response and the two cyclones collided, sending a shockwave rushing through the air around us. The two cyclones, evenly matched, dissipated, leaving Mother and me watching each other.

Mother was the first to make a move. She spun another cyclone and sent it rushing toward me. I sent my two at her in retaliation, but didn't stop there. I formed continuous balls of flame in my hands, and pelted her with several rounds. She had to combine her last cyclone with the one already out to nullify the attack, maneuvering around the assault to come back with her own.

"Keep going. It's working."

As we continued to battle, the distance between us lessened. *Just a bit more. The queen is going to be dethroned tonight.* It wasn't long before the gap had closed enough. I prepared my lungs while dodging her attacks, then jumped into the watery cyclone she was using to help her. I forced the fire out of my lungs, along with the balls of flame in my hands.

"Good job!"

The cyclone's structure broke down, water flying everywhere. My mother fell to the ground, but somehow landed on her feet, immediately attacking again to keep me off balance. *Not this time, Mother.* I engulfed my feet in flames, and used them to kick the water away, followed by an assault of my own.

The two of us continued to go at it until a blast of lightning nearly crashed into us. We both jumped out of the way to avoid the strike, then spun in the direction from which it had come. Shva'sika, her cloak removed, advanced toward the two of us. I had lived at the shaman village for over a decade and trained with her for almost the entirety of that time, but had never seen her preferred shaman outfit. She had always worn a cloak or some elvish-styled clothing. I had to admit, her outfit was nothing close to what I had expected. It resembled a dancing uniform adorned with jewelry and tiny trinkets that had some sort of meaning, though I wasn't sure what.

Shva'sika smiled. "You two know how to build my static charge."

A thin smirk spread across my lips. "Does this mean you're finally ready to play?"

Shva'sika chuckled, and without warning launched a lightning bolt at me. I dodged the attack and threw my own at her, only to be caught off guard by my mother. *Looks like she's not going to back out.*

"That's fine. You can handle this."

"All right then." I chuckled as I pulled myself back onto my feet and then hurled a retaliation attack on her. She blocked and dodged my attacks, but to my surprise, she didn't try to create another body cyclone. She retaliated when there was a break in my attack.

She and Shva'sika worked together to put me on the defensive. Normally this would have annoyed me, but this time I embraced it. It gave me time to think about how to take them down. Del'karo and Ne'kall worked well as a team, but their power, even combined, was nothing compared to a combined force of my mother and Shva'sika.

A swift movement in the corner of my eye forced me to dodge as a large ice shard hurtled by. *That had better not be Rylan's doing. He's dead if it is.*

"Don't be so harsh. This is a test, after all."

I turned to face my newest opponent. Maka'shi and Sha'hiri both advanced on me, Maka'shi's arm still out, indicating the attack had come from her. *I should have known.* Ice shards were her specialty.

The conservative nature of Maka'shi's clothing surprised me. She never came off as that type of person. A little off to the side, Xa'vian also advanced. He adorned himself with metal, like all lightning shamans from his tribe, and that meant I was against two lightning shamans, two ice shamans, and a water elementalist. *This should be fun.*

"Stay calm. You'll be fine. You're even stronger than all of them combined."

"Yeah, somehow I really doubt that."

Maka'shi grinned. "I hope you're ready, because we won't be going easy on you."

A five-on-one battle wasn't something I had expected, but I was up for the challenge. "Let's see what you've got."

The five didn't waste any time attacking; I immediately went on the defensive. Their attacks were relentless, preventing me from attacking back. It didn't help that I had to block the water and ice attacks, while Sha'hiri froze the water around us. It made it harder for me to stand, but didn't hinder my mother.

Fire swirled around me as a defensive barrier, giving me a moment to think. Shva'sika and Xa'vian needed to be removed first. They posed the biggest threats, since I couldn't block their attacks. Maka'shi and Sha'hiri would then come next.

I swore under my breath when Xa'vian managed to slip behind me. Yet before his attack could find its mark, a giant ice shield shot up from the ground, shielding my body. The ice was so thick, the lightning barely made a scratch in it. There was only one person I knew who could make a shield like that. *Rylan.*

The trail of ice from that thick wall led back to him as he advanced across the arena. Ryoko strode close behind. My brow creased into deep furrows. "What gives?"

Rylan's eyes glittered with amusement. "We were told we could jump in at any time. No one said we couldn't give you a hand."

I chuckled. "Leave it to you to think of a loophole."

"Not that much of a loophole."

"Well, regardless, I'm not going to say no to your help. I know my limits."

Ryoko jumped in front of me and blocked a water attack Mother tried to sneak in. Her thick skin absorbing the brunt of it, Ryoko sent a thundering quake back my mother's way. At the same time, Maka'shi and Sha'hiri attempted to launch large ice shards our way, but Rylan shattered them in mid-air. Maka'shi, unphased by Rylan's counter, blocked my retaliatory strike. Sha'hiri was another story. She was caught by surprise, and unable to put up a defense, fell back when her ice shield shattered.

Maka'shi created a quick ice barrier to protect them both from my next attack, but before I could get off a third, Shva'sika and Xa'vian made their move. Rylan jumped in front of me, spinning a thick ice shield in their path, but it couldn't protect us from the surprise wave of earth that came from the opposite direction.

I braced myself for the painful hit, but it never came. Ryoko jumped in front of the wave and slammed her entire body into it, shattering it all the way back to its owner, Ir'esh. Ir'esh stared in astonishment as Ryoko wound her shoulder a few times to shrug off the pain.

I blinked when I heard her shoulder pop. Ryoko sighed with relief. "That's better." She nodded at Ir'esh in appreciation. "That was a pretty strong attack. I'm kinda excited he jumped in. I was hoping I might get a challenge."

"Yeah, but him jumping in makes this a six on three fight now," Rylan pointed out. "Five of them have been difficult to manage. We might not fare well for much longer at this rate."

"Wanna bet?" she challenged.

I chuckled. "You going to run home crying to mommy cause the odds are one person tougher, Ry?"

He snorted and attacked Xa'vian and Shva'sika. Our opponents reacted and fought back, but our experience as a team paid off. Rylan and Ryoko worked as shields, while I hung back and executed ranged attacks. The three of us combined easily kept the others in check.

Ir'esh turned his gaze to my mother. "They make for an impressive team."

Mother nodded. "They were the best of my elite. Shadow Phoenix, Shield, and Destroyer. Those were their codenames. No one could ever best them. All their team lacked was someone to heal their wounds in the heat of battle. With that, they would be an unstoppable force."

"Then they'll need to be separated."

"Easier said than done. I trained them and made sure that they knew how to stick together."

"I can help with that." My eyes flicked to Valene making her way onto the battlefield. She removed her cloak and then stopped advancing. She wore a plain halter that cropped high on her back, and low at a point in the front and a long skirt flowed around her legs.

I grinned. "Stay out of this, Valene. You're not experienced enough yet."

She smiled and then lifted up her hands. In the same instant, thick root and vine-like plants sprung from the ground around us. Ryoko and Rylan dodged one way while I moved another. I ground my teeth at how easily she had been able to separate us. *She's making us look like amateurs.*

Valene chuckled. "I had Tla'lli spread seeds around for me while you were busy fighting. You want to tell me again that I'm not ready?"

I grinned and cast a hot flame at her. A large root shot out of the ground, taking the blow. Valene giggled. My flame had no effect on the plant matter. At that point, she made her move, along with everyone else. Shva'sika and Xa'vian beat on Rylan's thick barrier, while Mother and Ir'esh worked on wearing Ryoko down. That left me to deal with Maka'shi, Sha'hiri, and Valene.

I melted the ice attack they sent at me and dodged a few more of Valene's vines. Catching a movement out of the corner of my eye, I spun around and blocked a blast of fire. Ne'kall and Del'karo had joined in on this battle once again. *Great, eight on three—just what I need. I wish I could have Raikidan in on this. He'd be helpful, with such odds. But I don't want to risk him getting in my way, either.*

"Do you have such little faith in him?"

"His instinct to protect me is strong. And he doesn't like that I fight as it is. In a high-stress situation like this, I can't be sure he'd not give into instinct and make it so I couldn't fight. And if I can't prove myself, I fail…"

"There are many ways to prove yourself. If you prove yourself a leader in the place of physical strength and element control, that would make up for his nature."

Blocking another blast of fire, I dodged another one of Valene's plants, and exhaled a breath of fire. Yet instead of attacking Valene, I shot the blast at Shva'sika, catching her off guard. She fell to the ground and cringed as her skin burned. Xye appeared next to her and healed her up. "Thanks, Xye."

"Of course, Sis." He then disappeared, allowing her to jump back in.

Ryoko and Rylan were pushed farther away from me. My mother forced me on a heavy defensive, but that didn't save me when Del'karo and Xa'vian teamed up with her. Intense pain shot through my body as fire scorched my skin. On top of that, the water acted as a conductor, intensifying the lightning strike. I fell to the ground writhing in pain. *I can't breathe…*

Raikidan's cry of distress carried its way across the battlefield. "Eira!"

"Hold still while I heal you," a familiar voice said, much closer to me.

My brow rose as a soft white-green light enveloped me. I hadn't seen a true healing light in some time, due to Shva'sika's inexperience. She had made progress, her healing aura now a green-blue, but it wasn't there yet. Not like her brother. "Whose side are you on, Xye?"

He chuckled. "Healers don't pick sides."

I snorted and jumped back into the battle. Rylan and Ryoko still stuck together, both too far for me to rejoin. An ice shard careened toward me and I rolled out of the way, but I wasn't able to get my bearings enough to dodge an incoming ball of earth. I braced for the inevitable impact, but someone jumped in front of me by a few feet and took the blow.

My eyes widened when I realized Raikidan had jumped in. The force of the earth pushed him closer to me, but he remained standing. His arms dripped with blood from the sharp rocks, and dark bruising would be sure to follow soon. *The fact he took that blow like that… without any protection, even from scales…* I smiled.

Ir'esh took great interest in Raikidan's presence and taking the blow for me. "You're not supposed to be here, Guard. You were told this."

"The hell with your rule," Raikidan snarled.

The tenseness in his voice made me acutely aware of his mental state. *He's in his protective mode. I'm going to have to be—*

He reached behind him and offered me a hand, though he didn't take his eyes off the battlefield. *Okay, his mind is clear. I think we'll be okay.*

"You should just trust him. Would be easier."

"My reasons for being cautious are valid, okay?"

"Yeah, yeah. Go finish your test with your 'not boyfriend.'"

I accepted Raikidan's gesture and climbed to my feet, taking a back-to-back position with him. "Thank you."

He glanced back at me. "Are you all right?"

I couldn't help but smile. "Now that you're here, yes."

"Then let's keep breaking some rules."

I chuckled. "I like the way you think."

Ir'esh came at the two of us, Valene tag-teaming in an attempt to separate me from everyone again. But Raikidan wasn't like the others. His drive to protect made him stick to me like industrial-strength glue.

"Next time try something more fun. Like chocolate. You won't regret it."

I tried not to physically react the *very* inappropriate mental image sprung into my head as I maneuvered around the combined attack against us. *"Don't even start with this."*

"Mental image too distracting?"

"Not in the way you'd hoped."

"Yeah, you keep pretending."

I threw out a flame that had no effect on the earth wall Ir'esh created. The wall came at us, but Raikidan took the force and unleashed a torrent of flame at our opponents. Xa'vian shot a bolt of lightning across the battlefield at Raikidan, but I managed to yank him out of harm's way in time. My choice ultimately helped, as the strike hit an unsuspecting Ir'esh. The shaman leader cried and doubled over, but didn't fall to his knees. After only moments, he righted himself, a big grin on his face. *Right, earth. Shit.*

The two of us found ourselves with more opponents, all of them clearly trying to punish us for breaking the rules. *Good thing I've got experience with this type of situation.*

"Little rebel you are."

I smirked and unleashed an onslaught of fury. Raikidan aided me, taking blows he could handle, and even some he shouldn't have tried to, while offering strong fire that impressed many of our opposition. After touching fire from multiple dragons, I became curious about their strength. In my research, I found dragon inferno was some of the strongest fire produced from any living being. It ranked close to what Phyre, the god of fire, could create. For me to be able to harness it, that was a feat in itself.

The two of us worked as a team—ducking, dodging, fighting back. Ryoko and Rylan got in their attacks where they could, but were kept back. Valene and Ir'esh continued to try to separate Raikidan and me, but we weren't having it. *I will remain with him.*

Then, the tides turned. Rylan landed a strong blow to Sha'hiri, taking her down, and Ryoko nailed a strong strike on Xa'vian with her new-found earth ability. When the two leaders made a motion that they were backing out, I focused on the remaining opponents. Shva'sika still posed a serious threat, and Valene was proving to be one herself. She had improved over these past months, and it wasn't only her skill—her confidence level was much higher.

I dodged another attack from Valene and shifted my focus to her. Unlike Shva'sika, Valene didn't need to charge up her ability. With all these plants scattered about, she had the ammunition to keep up with me. Raikidan noticed my focus and reacted accordingly.

As I exhaled flame on another plant, the two of us skittered around, searching for a weak point. Without warning, a plant wrapped around my leg and lifted me high into the air. Hot flame in hand, I grasped the vine and sent fire coursing through it. It disintegrated and I fell to the ground. Raikidan went to catch me, but another plant grabbed me by the ankle, as well as him.

I exhaled fire on it, causing it to let go, but then two more grabbed onto my wrist. Before I knew it, several more latched onto me and I was completely tangled. Looking to Raikidan for help, I found him in a similar predicament. The plants grew in thickness and wrapped themselves completely around me. I struggled, but they continued to constrict until I was engulfed and unable to move. *Well, this is great.*

"You should put that technique you've been practicing these past few years to the test."

"Well, I haven't perfected it, but I guess it couldn't hurt, given the situation."

"And this time, you can be the knight in shining armor for your damsel in distress."

I laughed. Raikidan was no damsel, but it wouldn't hurt to help him out.

Inhaling as deeply as I could, I breathed out a large flame. The roots were thick and mostly resistant to the fire, but hurting them wasn't my intent. With another deep breath, I willed the fire to engulf my body. It attached itself to my arms, legs, and even my face and clothes. It didn't hurt, but it did attempt to escape my control. Fire didn't bend easily to another's will—which was the biggest reason it was considered one of the hardest elements to master and manipulate.

I concentrated my will over the flames, until the roots around me began to burn, causing them to constrict and attempt to re-grow. However, their attempts were futile and the roots burned away, the added oxygen helping my inferno. It threatened to rage out of control, but I knitted my brow and kept the flames bent to my will. I cast a quick glance at Raikidan to find him entangled, but not in the way I had been. *He'll be okay for a few more moments.* I focused on Valene. She took a deep breath and grew more plants, planning a new attack.

Swelling with power, I pushed the fiery blaze toward her. Valene threw up a temporary plant shield while having another plant haul her away high into the air, yet I was ready for her. I threw out more flames, using the fire in my chest to force its way into my skin and replenish what I was using.

Valene tried to protect herself, using the roots from the one that carried her, but they weren't strong enough. In mere moments, her transporting vine burnt up and failed her. She fell to the ground and stumbled on her landing. Her breath came heavy, and her posture slumped, showing her fatigue, but she didn't look ready to give up. *She's not the only one, though.*

The others advanced to give Valene a hand, but I was determined to end this. Taking another deep breath, I drew in my will, my fire flaring even hotter than before. With a great effort, I forced it out in all directions. My opponents flattened themselves to the ground, struggling to protect themselves from the fiery onslaught.

I was aware of my flame's contact with Raikidan, and my chest swelled when it hit him, but absorbed into him, as if he were consuming it. Thick vines cracked and splintered, and a moment later, I heard Raikidan drop to the ground, landing on his feet.

Finally, my will gave out. The fire around me died, and I stood there, exhausted. *It still takes too much out of me.*

"Not as much as you may think."

"What?"

"You need to tap into your deeper reserve."

"I don't have a deeper reserve. I've used up what I've got."

"You need to look deeper inside yourself. All the answers, and more, are there."

Someone clapped behind me. I spun around. My eyes went wide as I fell to one knee, my breath coming out in heavy, ragged gasps. A god stood here, and not just any god—Phyre stood before me. Other gods appeared as well, mingling amongst everyone as if this were a normal occurrence.

Raikidan, head bowed, backed away from the advancing god and knelt beside me.

"Nicely done, Eira," Phyre praised as he his eyes swept around the area. I followed his gaze. The surrounding trees were all ablaze. I wanted to kick myself. I had been far too careless. "You've improved greatly since the last time we met."

My heart slowed as that memory flashed through my head. I had still been in the military and his visit had taken me by surprise. Back then, he had reminded me of what I had always tried to hide...

"But I'd expect nothing less from you." His eyes flicked to Raikidan. "Of course, the two of you could stand to listen to rules every now and then."

The voice snorted. *"Like he's any better."*

"But due to the impressive display, I'll overlook it."

"No, he just doesn't want to admit that he's glad you broke the rules."

Her comments intrigued me. *"It's almost like you know him on a personal level."*

"Now stand up," Phyre ordered. "Both of you."

I did as told, hesitant to look him in the eye. Instead, I took in his features. He appeared to be an ordinary human, with a muscular build, amber eyes, and dark tan skin. His hair was a fiery red, with a mix of orange and yellow, and I was sure there was some blue and white tucked away in there as well. His hair almost appeared to be a live flame, but I was certain it was because of the light fiery aura that surrounded him.

The statues that depicted him were spot-on with what he wore now. He looked like an ancient hand-to-hand fighter, or warrior monk, from a hot climate region whose preferred weapon type was tonfas.

Phyre extended his hand and offered me a flame. "Consume this so you can regain your strength. You're going to need it for the last part of your test."

I tilted my head. "Last part?"

He only grinned and continued to offer the flame.

Deciding it best not to refuse his offer, I willed the flame to come to my hands, which was not an easy task. *It's so strong!* I'd never touched a flame of this caliber before. Shoving it in my mouth, the raw power energized me faster than anything I'd ever experienced.

Phyre turned an intense gaze on Raikidan. "You went against the rules in helping your charge for the first half of the test. I overlooked it. But you must stand down and not intervene during this last half."

Raikidan opened his mouth to protest, but I cut him off quickly and quietly. "Please, Raikidan. For me."

His lips pressed into a line and he sighed with defeat. "Very well."

Glancing my way for a brief moment, he backed away. Phyre didn't address me again until he determined Raikidan had in fact left the battlefield.

"You've proven yourself as a leader, ally, and shaman." He lit a fire in both of his hands. "But let's see if you are worthy of the flame I've bestowed you."

I stared at him, wide-eyed. "You want me to face off against you?"

He chuckled. "This is your final test. You must prove to me you are worthy of the fiery burden you bear. Fail, and I will be forced to take it from you."

"You can do this. You're worthy. Trust me."

I back up and readied myself. It wasn't every day you were chosen by a god to test your worth. "All right then. Let's do this."

53
CHAPTER
(RYOKO)

I backed away, aware of each step I took alongside Rylan. *This isn't happening...* I couldn't believe the gods were actually involved with this process. I took my place in front of Zeek and watched Laz. Her breath came in controlled, but ragged breaths, and her hands hung at her side. Exhausted didn't adequately describe her state. This test had done a number on her.

Phyre held out a hand with a small flame. "Consume this so you can regain your strength. You're going to need it for the last part of your test.

There's more to this test? How much more punishment was Laz going to have to take before she could pass? Laz also questioned him but the god didn't explain anything. She stared at the offered gift and then took it. She swallowed it to convert it to energy. *Such a strange but incredible ability.*

Laz's energy sprung back, her posture improving, and a fighting flame returning to her eyes. Phyre's fire had to be strong in order for her strength to return so quickly.

Phyre then spoke to Raikidan, reprimanding him again for jumping in and ordering him to leave the battlefield for Laz to finish her test alone. Raikidan opened his mouth to speak, but Laz cut him off with quiet words.

Raikidan retreated to where he'd stood before joining in the match, a scowl of irritation clear on his face. *This must be really hard for him.* Of course it was. If he was willing to break rules to keep her safe, he wouldn't like being forced to leave. Even if a god ordered it.

The other Guards he had previously stood with nodded to Raikidan, instead of reprimanding him like I would have expected. *I guess he impressed them enough not to care he broke the rules. Phyre himself even admitted to being okay with it.*

I focused back on Laz and Phyre when he started to speak to her. "You've proven yourself as a leader, ally, and shaman." He lit a fire in both of his hands. "But let's see if you are worthy of the flame I've bestowed you."

My eyes widened. *What?* She was going to have to fight a god?

Laz exhaled and then backed up a few paces. "All right then. Let's do this."

How can she act like this isn't a big deal? Phyre looked formidable, a good opponent for any seasoned fighter to test his strength against. But to fight a god, even upon invitation, I couldn't determine if it was a great honor or a great sin.

"Do not hold back," Phyre said. "If you fail, I take the fire you breathe away from you."

My blood ran cold. Could he really do that? Would he do that? Sure, he was a god, but could he take someone's element away? How would it affect Laz? Would it change her? Would it hurt her in some way that would cause irreversible damage?

Laz grinned. "I guess I'll have to pass, then."

Phyre chuckled and then began his assault. Laz immediately went on the defensive and dodged his attacks. Seeing her choose this stance made me worry even more for her.

"Relax, Pipsqueak," Zeek teased. "She's going to do fine."

"But if she doesn't pass he'll take her fire away!" I shrieked.

He chuckled. "And you think she's going to fail? Do you have such little faith in her?"

"Well..." My ears drooped. "No, I don't. It's just... she's facing a god. I don't see how she can win against him."

"It's not about winning or losing." I shifted my gaze toward Amara as she began to speak. She appeared so calm, despite the fact that her daughter was facing a god. "It's about her proving she's worthy of the flame he blessed her with. She can lose this fight and still pass his test."

My ears perked up. "So, what exactly is he testing?"

She shook her head. "Don't know. Each test is unique. The only one who knows is Phyre."

I understood and went back to watching the fight, but the tension in the pit of my stomach remained.

"You're still worried." Amara observed.

I pressed my lips together and nodded. "We both know how Laz is. She'll see this as a fight where there is a winner and a loser. We also know she will go to great lengths to win just to prove she's worth something. I'm worried she'll take it too far."

"Then maybe that's the test." She smiled. "Phyre is no stranger to Eira's personality. He may be testing her to see how far she's willing to go."

I shook my head back and forth. "That doesn't make me feel any better..."

Raid slung his arm around my shoulder. "Relax and put some faith in Eira. She has a habit of coming out on top, even when evidence says it shouldn't be possible."

I gave him a curt smile and turned my attention back to the test, to find Laz still on the defensive. But I noticed the look in her eye and understood why. She was biding her time, trying to figure out how to get the upper hand without wasting too much energy, though Phyre looked all too aware of her plan.

"You won't win against me that way, Eira," Phyre taunted.

"There is more than one way to win a battle." Laz said.

He chuckled. "We'll see about that."

I held my breath. Laz sounded so confident, as if she wasn't afraid of losing her ability to harness fire. As I thought about it more, maybe there was a reason. Maybe she wasn't afraid. Maybe she didn't care if she could use fire or not. *No. That's not it. She's afraid, but like the strong, stubborn woman she is, she's hiding her fear.*

A strange thought came to me. *Is that the deeper meaning behind this test? Is it for Laz to come to terms with who she was? Is Phyre trying to show her it's okay to have flaws and to be afraid of things? That what she is, isn't a bad thing?* My chest grew heavy and my ears drooped a bit. *If he is, then he might as well take her ability now. If there's one thing Laz will never do, it's accept who she is.*

Laz suddenly went on the offensive, though it didn't affect Phyre. He continued his own assault and appeared to have the upper hand. Laz put everything she had into each attack, but Phyre deflected or controlled her fire and sent it back at her. Of course, Laz didn't let that stop her. I felt like I was standing on a precipice as I watched these two go at it.

I cringed when Laz took a direct hit and fell to the ground. She held her arm in pain, but didn't let it stop her from getting back up and going at Phyre again. *That burn is bad...* My chest tightened even further. Phyre wasn't going to take it easy on her, or worry about hurting her like the shamans and I had done. If she got hurt, he would keep testing her as if the pain didn't matter.

To my surprise, Laz was able to continue. It was as if she didn't feel the burn. I remembered hearing that Laz's pain suppression was nothing to sneeze at, especially related to fire wounds, but that was a bad burn. To ignore it was crazy.

My body tensed when Laz was hit once more, but she wasn't the only one. She managed to land a good hit on Phyre at the same time. Of course, he was unaffected, thanks to being an invincible god. *Cheater.*

Phyre didn't wait for Laz to get back up. He immediately came at her again, but that played right into Laz's hand. When Phyre got close enough, she unleashed her attack. Phyre blocked and dodged and tried to counter, but Laz was light on her feet. She deflected and dodged his counterattack with ease, while still managing to remain on the offensive. My eyes went wide. *Has this been her plan all along? Has she only been testing the waters to get an idea of how to battle him?*

Phyre chuckled. "You're doing quite well, Eira, but I want to see all your power. Stop holding back."

Laz narrowed her eyes, but kept her assault going.

Phyre chuckled again. "Could it be you've limited yourself so much that you've forgotten how to unleash your full power?" Phyre cocked his head to one side. "Or are you afraid of it? Afraid of hurting someone? Why do you hold back, Firebreather?"

Laz glared at the god who taunted her. "You want it? Fine, I'll give it to you."

She drew in a deep breath, and spewed a torrent of hot flame from her mouth onto the waiting god. My jaw dropped in amazement as their fight intensified, while Laz's flames grew in strength. It wasn't long before the flame changed in color from red and orange to blue and even white at times. It burned so hot, I could feel it all the way from here. I couldn't believe the intensity of her flames—I had no idea she had such a powerful connection with fire.

"You're still holding back!" Phyre accused as he dodged another attack. "

My brow furrowed. He couldn't be serious. I had never seen her use such strong fire before. Was he saying that she could still do more? I shifted my gaze to Laz, wondering if what he claimed was true. She appeared to be putting her all into those attacks now. There was no way she had more power to give.

Phyre changed his tactics and began a fierce assault on Laz. My throat tightened with fear as he put her back on the defensive. The tide had swiftly turned—she was losing the battle. My breath caught when he hit her with several strong blasts of fire. Laz stumbled and struggled to stay on her feet, but she was hit again and again until she cried out in pain.

I could barely breathe as I watched her stagger to her feet. Her skin was burnt in patches, her clothes singed and tattered. She was in pain, her breath coming in short, ragged bursts. The fact that she was able to stand at all was amazing.

Phyre folded his arms across his chest and regarded her with a deep frown. "You still hold back. Even after I expressly told you to use everything, you still hold back." The god of fire let out a deep sigh. "I had hoped this would have come out differently. I hoped you had grown in all this time. It seems I was wrong…"

Phyre unleashed another heavy assault on Laz. It was all she could do to protect herself. Yet that didn't last long. In a matter of seconds, she was on the ground again, struggling to get to her knees.

Phyre sighed once more. "I hoped this would have ended differently."

Eira's breath was ragged, but she held her head up off the ground. "I'm… not… done…"

Phyre stared down at her. "You can't even get to your knees. You held back, and this is where it placed you." Smoke sizzled from his hands, and then the fire appeared. "But if you insist on being this stubborn, I will show you where your stubbornness leads you."

He lifted a hand high above his head and I stopped breathing. *No, he wouldn't...*

But before he could attack, a blur of mass crashed into him. The god stumbled back and to my surprise, Raikidan stood in front of Laz, shielding her. *Well, honestly, I shouldn't be surprised. Anyone who'd think he would stand there and watch this go down is an idiot.*

Phyre narrowed his eyes at Raikidan. "I told you to stay out of this, whelp. This is not your test."

"If you think I'm going to stand here and listen to you try to force your expectations on Eira and then beat her senseless for not meeting them, you've got another think coming," Raikidan snarled out. *He's got a point.*

"You will know your place."

"This is my place."

I knew that possessive tone. Rylan had it in his voice a lot. *And here you two keep saying you're "just friends." Bunch of liars.*

Raikidan launched himself at Phyre, choosing close quarters combat. Phyre dodged most of his attacks, but Raikidan managed to land a few on his chest. The god grunted, indicating he wasn't impervious to everything, but retaliated with his own assault. He held nothing back against Raikidan, overpowering him quickly. He wanted to teach Raikidan a lesson, but there was a problem. Teaching him to abandon Laz wasn't possible.

Even now, as Phyre beat on our dragon friend, he kept himself between Laz and the god. Laz struggled to hold herself up, but wouldn't give in, as if Raikidan's bravery and loyalty gave her strength.

The god of fire slammed his fist into Raikidan's gut. Raikidan choked in pain, but threw a similar punch back, following up with punch to the face. Phyre stumbled back, lifting his fingers to his mouth. Pulling away, I noticed the crimson liquid dripping from his split lip. *No way.*

Phyre chuckled. "Not a bad hit. Too bad it'll be the last."

I gasped when he assaulted Raikidan. He hit so fast I would have missed them had I blinked. In seconds, Raikidan had been reduced to his knees, but he wasn't about to give in. Laz whispered his name and she continued to try to get up. *Man, I don't know who's more stubborn.*

Raikidan tried to stand, but Phyre swiftly kicked him and he crumpled into a heap. He didn't move this time, and my heart stopped. Everyone around me grew still.

Phyre shifted his gaze to Laz, but lit a fire in his hands and held it over Raikidan. "Are you happy now? Your stubbornness brought this upon the two of you."

That's not fair… None of this was fair. Laz didn't ask to be tested because she thought she was ready. She was told she was ready. It shouldn't be like this.

Just when I thought it couldn't get weirder, Laz chuckled. Then she spoke, but it was so low I didn't catch it. Yet Phyre's expression changed. It went from disappointment to intense interest. She continued to speak, her voice remaining low, until she heaved herself to her knees. At that point, her voice rose so I could hear what she was saying.

"I will use that strength to protect them. To show them their faith in me isn't in vain, you pompous bastard."

Out of nowhere, fire started pouring out of her body. Laz clenched her fists and rose to her feet. The fire around her swirled and grew, changing from red and orange to blue and white. *Where is she finding this energy?*

Laz's body warped and shifted, as if she were standing in multiple places at once. Even stranger was that some of the images didn't even look like her. They looked like a woman with long red and black hair, tan skin, and… *black wings?*

"Is anyone else seeing this?" I could barely get the words out.

Amara nodded. "Everyone move back."

My brow twisted. "Why?"

She pushed me back. "Just do it."

I went along with it, my eyes drifting back toward Laz. The multiple images had not gone away.

"Get, away from him, Phyre!" she screamed, the ground around her exploding and lava shooting up into the air.

"Hold your breath!" Zeek cried with alarm. "There's toxic gas in that."

"No need." Seda responded immediately. "Telar and I have a barrier set up around us. We're going to need it."

Their barrier was the last thing on my mind. My heart leapt into my throat as I watched Laz, or what she had become. The lava pooled around her feet, as well as Raikidan's form, but solidified as if the heat was being sucked from it before it could touch either of them. Fire continued to swirl around her body. Abruptly, the strange phasing around her body disappeared. *Did I imagine the whole thing? No.* Yet even though it was gone, I was still worried. *What and who was that other person with her? What in the blue-blazes is going on here?*

54
CHAPTER
(EIRA)

Ragged breaths escaped my lips as I struggled to get back up. Raikidan fought Phyre for me, protecting me from the physical harm, yet he couldn't protect me from the mental blows. Disappointment. Failure. Things I'd grown accustomed to. But I couldn't this time. I couldn't give up. *I can't fail him. Not when he's willing to give his all for me.*

"Let me help."

I ground my teeth together as I tried to ignore that voice and get up on my own, but to no avail. *I'm not done. I still have fight in me.*

"Eira, let me help."

"You can't help me."

"That's not true. I wish I could tell you why, but I can't. What I can tell you is, you have so much strength hidden away—so much potential—but with the limitations you put on yourself, your self-doubt, you can't access it without my help. Please, trust me… like you trust him."

I lifted my head just as Raikidan took a heavy hit that dropped him to his knees. "Rai…"

Raikidan made an attempt to get back up, but Phyre kicked him and he crumpled into a heap. He didn't move this time. *No…* Determination built within me.

Phyre shifted his gaze to me, his eyes narrowing. He lit a fire in his hands and held it over Raikidan. "Are you happy now? Your stubbornness brought this upon the two of you."

It's my turn to protect you for once.

"That's it. Use that to help."

"I also need you. You've been here for me the longest. I trust you."

"I thought I'd never hear those words… Thank you."

Power welled up into my chest. The power turned into energy and seeped out of my skin in the form of fire.

I chuckled. "I've never been able to live up to other's expectations. I stopped trying. Stopped caring about what they thought. Do you really think I care what you think?"

Phyre's expression changed to intense interest.

"But there have been some whom I cannot fail, no matter what I do. I have held onto that. Using it to make me stronger and push me farther than any disappointment could ever achieve."

A fiery hunger from below the crust called to me, and I grasped for it as I heaved myself to my knees.

"I will use that strength to protect them. To show them their faith in me isn't in vain, you pompous bastard."

A force rushed to the surface as I struggled to my feet.

"Get, away from him, Phyre!"

The ground around me exploded and lava shot up into the air. I didn't hold my breath, even though there were toxic gases released with the eruptions as I continued to fuel this new power I had tapped into, being aware of Raikidan's body and protecting him from the molten earth. Del'karo had taken me across the Larkian mountain range and even farther west to an area full of volcanic activity. He trained me under these conditions and helped me build up immunity to the toxic air.

Phyre smirked. "It's about time you showed me your power. Now, let's see if you can use it properly."

Lava erupted from the ground around him and I grinned. Not wanting to allow Phyre to take the advantage, I embraced the power of the lava surrounding me and sized up how it moved. It felt like fire, but it also like another element. A memory of my mother teaching me came unbidden.

"Out of everything I will teach you, if there is only one thing you can ever remember, always remember that water and fire may be opposite of each other, but they are almost the same in the way they are used."

I willed the lava to rush at him in two waves, evaporating all water in the way. Unfortunately, Phyre expected this and sent the same counter at me. The waves collided and sloshed together, spraying molten rock everywhere. Quick to react, I removed the heat from any bits of lava that came at Raikidan and me, so we were only hit with crust that crumbled on impact. *I will keep you safe this time. You have my word.*

While I focused on keeping myself from melting, Phyre took the opportunity to attack me with both fire and lava. Barely having the time to react, I whisked up a wave of lava to block his attack and then rolled away from his flame, cooling lava on the ground as I did so it wouldn't melt my skin. Not wasting any time, I flooded the ground in front of us with lava, controlling some to create a protective barrier around Raikidan, but Phyre didn't move. He let the lava rush around his ankles with a grin plastered to his face. *You have to be shitting me. How am I supposed to beat him if nothing affects him?*

"*You don't have to beat him. You just have do your best. That's all that has ever been expected of you, and that's all he expects,*" the voice told me.

"*Then why has my best never good enough in the past? What more did I have to do to prove myself?*"

It had no answer. *No surprise there…* I respected the gods, but I also resented them for throwing such a poor hand at me. If they just wanted me to do my best, the effort I put in before this entity helped me find this power—which I didn't even know I had—should have been good enough. My best, not my best assisted by something else beyond me, should have been good enough.

"*You don't understand,*" the voice said. "*You've always had this power. If you needed my strength, you'd go beyond even this. But you don't need it. You are strong. You are powerful. You are worthy of more than anyone has given you credit for—more than any of them will understand.*"

I breathed out a strong blast of fire as a distraction, then kicked up the cooling lava and reshaped the battlefield to allow me to get off the ground. Unfortunately, Phyre had other ideas, and shot blasts of fire to break up my ramps and walls.

"*But mother, how are they the same? They are used so differently.*"

"*Are you sure?*"

Throwing out fire and lava, I tried to push him back and use my ramps to my advantage. Sadly, it did the opposite. Phyre used them against me and managed to get the upper hand. I had a hard time keeping up with him while he used them as cover and means to sneak around.

"The elements are just an extension of our bodies."

"Mother, that doesn't prove that water and fire are the same."

"No, but the way they are used does."

I lost him altogether. My eyes darted around, cursing myself all the while. Had I not been so impulsive and thought this through, then maybe this wouldn't have happened. But I couldn't think about that right now. I needed to focus.

I heard a noise and hurled fire in that direction, only to have to block a blast from the opposite direction. Phyre chuckled. "You're making this way too easy for me."

I tried to pinpoint his voice, but it echoed around the area too much. Sighing mentally, I made my choice. Igniting my hands with fire, I began destroying the ramps and walls I had created. It was the only way to flush him out and get on more even ground.

Phyre's chuckle came from behind me. "Too bad I'm not over there."

"Fire can't be used the same way as water."

"Are you sure?"

I spun around, only to see a blast of fire coming at me. I instinctively threw my arms up in front of me, but the blast never came. Hushed whispers of astonishment and excitement passed my ears.

"Just because you haven't seen someone use them the same way doesn't mean it can't be done. It only means no one has seen it the way I have."

"Mother, what are you trying to get at?"

There was no more fire in front of me. Instead, steam fizzled in the air, along with what was left of the water that had blocked it. I stared at the falling water for a moment and then at my hands. *Did I do that?*

"I told you were worthy," the voice said.

My gaze drifted to my mother, who nodded with a smile.

"I am a water elementalist. I can't teach you to use your fire the way another fire elementalist would, but I can try my best to help you understand it and control it in the way I know best."

"Why?"

"Because one day, you'll be able to control both."

"That's crazy."

"This is crazy…" I murmured.

There was no way I had been able to tap into my opposite like she had predicted. Someone had to have seen some water that hadn't been evaporated away by the lava and stepped—

Phyre chuckled. "Well, well, well. You *have* learned a great bit since we last met. I have to admit, with the limits you placed on yourself, I wasn't sure you'd be able to tap into that side of you."

I stared at my hands. *I really did that?*

He chuckled again. "But it seems you're more surprised than anyone. Did you really doubt yourself that much?"

"I never... I never thought it was possible... for me..."

He smirked. "For you, Daughter of Fire, anything is possible."

"Except..." I closed my eyes for my moment and released a slow breath. "Except defeating you."

He regarded me with interest. "Does this mean..."

I bowed. "I concede this fight to you. I've given all I can, mind, body, and soul. I've done my best, whether anyone agrees or not. Judge me as you will, Father of Fire."

Phyre remained quiet for a long few moments and then finally gestured to Raikidan's hidden form. "Tend to him, and then meet me at the tree."

I didn't need to be told twice. I rushed over to Raikidan. He lay on his back, eyes open. He gazed up at me and smiled. I brushed my bangs out of my eyes as I knelt. "Hey."

"Hey to you, too."

"That was pretty impressive, what you did for me."

His eyes flicked to the hardened barrier I created. "You took my line."

I giggled and he joined in my laughter.

"How'd you do?"

"I'm about to find out after I'm sure you're okay." I produced some fire and handed it to him. "Here, take this."

Raikidan smiled in appreciation and consumed the flame. His face relaxed when the pain ebbed and made an attempt to get up. He cringed, reminding us both that it would take more time for the fire to heal him. I offered help, which he took without protest.

Supported by me, he looked Phyre's way. "Whatever happens, we're in this together."

I nodded and the two of us made it to the great tree, Raikidan's strength returning as we moved. Phyre's hard gaze bored into us, as if staring right into our souls. We remained quiet as we waited, but the anxiety rising up inside me made it difficult.

He then smiled and placed his hand on my shoulder. "You pass."

I blinked and laughed weakly as all the tension left me. The entire area erupted. Even the voice cheered. "I... I passed?"

He nodded. "You proved to me you are capable of change without losing who you are in the process. You pushed yourself farther than you have ever done before, to prove you were worthy even when someone may disagree. You still have much room to grow, but that will come in time."

The widest smile I could ever remember producing spread over my face. Raikidan's grip on my tightened as if trying to keep his composure for my sake. "Thank you."

"You don't need to thank me. You proved to me that I had chosen correctly. Truth be told, I had not doubted that for a second."

I gave him a look of skepticism. "Sure, you didn't."

"All right, maybe for a moment." He chuckled. "But only a brief moment."

My attention was pulled away when someone approaching caught the corner of my eye. Walking up to us was a tall woman with fair skin, white hair, and gray irises and pupils so pale they nearly melted into the whites of her eyes. I could only compare them to plate crystal. She carried what appeared to be a black cloak on one arm, and a wooden bowl in the opposite hand. A beautiful white wolf followed her.

I bowed. "Arcadia. Maiyun."

Arcadia smiled kindly, her voice coming out as hollow as Seda's. "You've done well, Eira. You've faced many trials and overcame them regardless of how impossible they seemed at the time. It's time for your mark and name."

Raikidan pulled away as Arcadia handed the bowl to Phyre, but he didn't dip his finger into the red paint it contained right away. I closed my eyes as he reached for my face, and I felt a rush of energy flow through me when his finger pressed against my forehead. I gasped when heat rushed out of my body. I gazed up as my inner fire, in the shape of a phoenix, took to the air. Its release hadn't been painful in the least, and it flew around majestically without me having to control it.

"Eira." I refocused my attention to Phyre, watching as he dipped his fingers into the red paint. "It's time."

I nodded and closed my eyes before waiting for him to give me my shaman symbol.

"Eira, you have shown us what you are capable of with your gift of fire." He announced as he touched my forehead and the bridge of my nose. "You have shown compassion to those who have lost much and shown them the path to peace." He touched the side of my face around my eyes. "You have proven to be capable of keeping a level head in most stressful situations and putting your comrades and allies before yourself, making you an excellent leader."

He dragged the paint down the center of my lips to the tip of my chin and then moved over so Arcadia could take his place. She reached out and touched specific spots on my face. As she did, her eyes began to glow. Energy rushed through my body the moment her last finger touched my face. At the same time, the damage that had been done to my clothes was mended.

"From this day forward, you will guide and mediate others toward the path of peace, Ambassador Laz'shika," Phyre announced. "May your brothers and sisters welcome you with open arms."

The area erupted with loud cheering and excitement, but I wasn't ready to rejoice. *The title he's giving me... was it...* I blew a breath through my lips. "Are you sure?"

The god smiled wide. "It's been a very long time since we appointed an Ambassador. You fit the qualifications beautifully. I'm sure."

I wasn't convinced. Arcadia pulled a mirror from her cloth belt and held it up. "Take a look."

I took the mirror from her and took in my reflection. The design was simple, but different than the one I imagined I'd receive. Two stripes started at the side of my forehead and flowed down to the sides of the bridge of my nose. Two more smaller stripes flowed down the center of my forehead, the four looking like symbolic sun rays. Another stripe came down from the corner of my face and flowed under my eye. A red streak trailed down my lips to my chin finishing of the design.

"It's perfect."

"It suits you," Raikidan complimented.

I smiled at him, my cheeks warming a bit. "Thanks." I focused on Phyre again, only to find him grinning wide. My eyes narrowed. "What?"

Phyre chuckled. "You're so suspicious."

Arcadia looked him up and down. "With you it's best to be."

Phyre shot her a displeased look and I couldn't help but laugh. They didn't act the way you'd expect gods to. "I'm not suspicious. I can smile if I want to."

"Except you're grinning like a peeping tom in a women's bathing house," she said.

I laughed as Phyre took offense to her accusation. He recovered after a few moments and focused on Raikidan. "Your turn."

My brow rose but my curiosity kept me quiet.

Phyre held himself high. "Raikidan, you disobeyed the rules to protect our young Ambassador, aiding her in her greatest time of need, even at the risk of your own life." He smirked. "I like that about you. It's what she needs. It's time you take your oath."

My brow furrowed. *What oath?*

"Did he really?"

"Did he really what?"

"You'll see, if I'm right."

Raikidan nodded. "I'm ready."

"Raikidan, you meeting our young Ambassador was no accident." Phyre's loud voice echoed through the area. "Nor was your choice to help and protect her. It is in your personal nature—your destiny."

I half expected Raikidan to look embarrassed or ashamed of what Phyre was telling everyone. But instead, he looked proud. *Does he really feel that strongly about protecting me?* Sure, he broke rules to protect me during the battle, but everyone thinks differently in the heat of the moment.

"He cares deeply for you."

I fought hard to stop warmth from spreading across my face. *"Stop playing with my head... and feelings..."*

"I'm not, Eira. He does care that much. It's obvious at this point, even to me."

"Just... stop. Please."

"Raikidan, you took the position of a temporary Guard, to help Laz'shika gain access to certain privileges. This help aided her on her quests in ways not possible otherwise. At that time, you pledged to protect her only when needed."

My eyes widened. *This oath?*

"Yes, this one. I told you he cared."

"Do you now pledge to permanently take on the position of her personal Guard to protect her?" Phyre asked.

Raikidan nodded. "I do."

"Do you swear to do so even at the cost of your own life?"

"I swear."

Phyre grabbed Raikidan by the arm roughly. "Then I hereby appoint you Main Guard of Ambassador Laz'shika. Failure to protect her with your life, no matter the circumstances, will result in immediate judgment."

Fire formed in the hand that he held Raikidan with. Raikidan collapsed to one knee as pain raked through him, but he refused to cry out. I stared, my eyes wide and my jaw slack. *What is Phyre doing?*

"Calm down. Everything is okay."

Fire engulfed Raikidan's arm and made its way to his clothes. My horror changed to curiosity and amazement when the fire burned his clothes into a new style. It appeared to be more armor than clothing, as if the fire were magical. Layered leather and black dragon-scale armor covered his left shoulder and upper arm, and a fingerless gauntlet of the same material covered the same side hand and forearm. Embedded in the gauntlet was a living flame amulet, identical to the ones on my outfit. A thick leather strap with dragon engravings secured the shoulder armor to his body.

Around his hips, on top of some cloth pants, he sported a cloth and black dragon scale waist cape, the cloth making up a majority of the piece of armor. An intertwined dragon and phoenix with the sharp pointed shapes of an amaranthine butterfly between them, was embroidered into the cloth both in the front and back side of the waist cape. Boots nearly identical to mine, living-fire pendant and all, covered his feet. The fire took to the skies in the shape of a dragon as if Raikidan's inner fire had been released. Phyre let go of Raikidan's arm, revealing a black tattoo of the same dragon and phoenix design from his armor. He then stepped back and allowed Raikidan to stand. "Remember your oath and never go back on it."

Raikidan nodded, and all I could do was take everything in. *He's... he's now my official Guard.* I was already having difficulty understanding why I was chosen to be the Ambassador of the tribes when there were far more qualified people, but now Raikidan was to stay by my side permanently? And to top it all off, Raikidan seemed to know this was going to happen from the start. *He's also okay with all of it.* Did he understand what this oath meant? Or was he putting on a show so neither of us would look bad?

"You know the answer. Don't start twisting it out of fear."

Arcadia stepped forward again and held up the arm with the cloak hanging over it. She and pulled it off her arm to reveal another one underneath. I took the cloak when she offered it to me, and Raikidan did the same. The cloaks were made of a black cloth and golden embroidery, with the same dragon and phoenix design from Raikidan's outfit embroidered into the back of the cloak.

"While all the shamans will know who you two are in time, these cloaks will identify you to those who aren't," she explained. "Wear them with pride and maintain peace amongst your brothers and sisters."

With a nod, I swung the cloak around me and clasped it together around my neck with the intricate clasp. Phyre held up his arms and announced, "Ambassador Laz'shika!"

Cheers erupted once more. Raikidan reached out and lifted me up into the air while spinning me around a few times, a large smile plastered on his face. A smile spread across mine, and I couldn't help but laugh with joy.

"Congratulations, Eira. I knew you could do it."

"Thank you."

Raikidan finally put me down and we smiled at each other, gazing deep into each other's eyes. A quiet chirp grabbed my attention. Looking down, I found a little black and red dragon sitting at my feet, gazing up at me. "Rimu?"

"Sorry, he got away again!" Xaneth called out.

Chuckles of amusement echoed around the area and I was sure to join them for a brief moment. Scratching Rimu under the chin and allowing him to lean against me as he enjoyed his attention, I watched Phyre as he surveyed the area with a smile.

"What's up with you?" I questioned.

"Just assessing the work we have to accomplish for one last task," he said.

I cocked my head in confusion. "Huh?"

He chuckled and lit a fire in both his hands. "You're going to want to stay still. Otherwise, you may get in the way."

My brow furrowed, I jumped back when he started throwing fire around. Raikidan stood close to me, and Rimu surprisingly stayed with us, though I could tell he was just as curious about the new activity.

Several other gods joined in. Valena, goddess of earth, a buxom elven woman, with long curly brown hair, began moving the ground while her lover, Tarin, god of nature, a muscular, dark-skinned elven man with medium length brown hair, started growing flowers and trees. Kendaria, goddess of water, a slim human woman with long, wavy blue hair, and copper almond-shaped eyes, began spreading water across the earth and Le'carro, god of lightning, a slim, light skinned elven man with long blue hair and crystal blue eyes, shot streams of lightning into the air. Solstice breathed frost onto many of the trees Valene and Tarin had grown, and Phyre ignited more with fire while splashing lava around into crevices Valena made as she moved the earth.

A crevice with lava formed near us, and Rimu chirped before diving in. He splashed around like a child in a bathtub and I almost panicked. "Uh…"

Raikidan held up a hand. "Don't worry. He's fine. It's good for his scales."

"Okay." *Good to know red dragons are immune to lava… at least in their natural forms.* "Hey, Raikidan?"

"Yeah?"

"You sure about this? Being my full-time Guard, I mean."

He nodded. "I made the choice prior to coming here. When Ken'ichi had me get ready in a different location than you, he told me if you passed, you were going to become the official Ambassador, and I would be chosen to become your full-time Guard. If I wasn't up for the task, I wasn't to be allowed to attend the ceremony."

"How long did it take for you to decide?" I asked.

He shrugged. "A minute? Maybe shorter? Definitely no longer than a minute."

"You really want to be my Guard?" I was having a hard time believing all this.

He smiled at me. "I'd give my life to protect you."

My heart stopped for a second. *He wants to protect me that badly?*

"Not many would give up their once chance at life to let others continue theirs."
"Would you?"
"At one time I had a reason to. Then things changed…"

"And what about your destined mate?"

"If I look for her, she'll have to accept this as the way things are," he said. "If she doesn't, then it's her loss."

"Means you can take him."

My heart's pace quickened. I smiled. "Thank you."

He nodded. "Sure. Oh, and those new clothes, they suit you."

I giggled. "Thanks. I'm definitely more comfortable wearing these than the others. You look good, too."

Raikidan went to say something, but the ground around us shook. We took that as a hint to move. Calling for Rimu, we backed up just in time for Valena to create a large hole around the great tree, and for Phyre to fill the gap with lava. The tree reacted to the lava's touch and changed. The bark charred and split, and within the splitting, an orange glow emitted that also carried through the symbols carved in the tree. The flowers glowed for a second, and I thought they might fall off from all the heat, but they remained after the glow faded.

I ventured a little closer to take a look at the lava pit to see if it would cool off and harden, only to find it remaining hot and molten no matter how long I watched it.

"It will never cool." I jumped out of my skin when Phyre spoke so close to me.

"Don't do that!" I hissed.

He chuckled. "I wasn't being quiet. You may want to get your hearing checked." I glowered at him and he chuckled some more before jerking his head back. "Take a look."

I turned around and gazed around in wonder. The terrain was no longer flat; tall rock cliffs towered over everything, and the forest diminished in these areas, opening up the sky. The water on the ground had receded and been replaced with lush grass and wild flowers, though the flowers were fire and ice in nature. The forest was now comprised of frozen trees, with fire flowers mixed with the same natural flowering trees that had been here when I first arrived for my test. Large stone half-arches with inscribed glowing runes reached across the cliffs, and water streamed down many of these cliff faces into pools below. Lava rivers flowed around these natural basins, connecting to the great tree in the center, and beautiful crystalline flowers and vines grew around the water and lava pools.

The ancient tombstones remained, though they were now reinforced by metal, and the glowing aura within them, along with the rocks with glowing lights, had been replaced by lightning. Stone and metal bridges arched over the lava pools, stone paths led from all-iron gate arches on the perimeter to these bridges and to the great tree, where the path circled the lava chasm the tree was nestled in. The opened sky allowed for more light to shine and glisten off the ice and water surfaces.

"It's beautiful."

I turned my focus on Phyre. "Why did you change everything? Why didn't you just fix what we destroyed?"

"Because it wasn't destroyed."

He smiled. "You and your friends didn't destroy anything. You only reshaped this area."

I tilted my head. "I don't understand."

"Nothing to us is ever destroyed, only reshaped. All actions change something, whether it be time or mass. But no matter the choice, it can never completely destroy something, and therefore can only reshape what was there to begin with. Your actions have accumulated allies of considerable strength and talents, and together you can reshape this land. And to show you how strong that power you hold is, we have reshaped this area between the living and dead."

"I see…" I closed my eyes and felt the warm breeze that rushed through. "Wind?"

"Anila brought some wind in because of your friendship with Tla'lli and Jaybird, and Jin put some metal around here because of Arnia." Phyre explained. "While we usually only reshape this area with elements used during the test, Arnia and Jaybird were needed to help with your celebratory feast, preventing them from testing you, so we made an exception."

I nodded in understanding. Raikidan's and my inner fires soared through the air together and it had me wondering. "Are we getting those back?"

Phyre shook his head. "No. They will remain here for some time before they rest in the mountains beyond, with all the other pulled elements from previously tested and passed shamans. It won't affect you, though, as they're not really your inner fires—just replicas."

"Ah, that makes sense, then, why it didn't hurt when it was released."

"You've acquired many allies and friends in these past years," he observed. "It may be time to rethink how you see yourself." I opened my mouth to speak, but he continued, clapping his hands together. "But we won't discuss this now. You have a party to attend, and what's a party without its guest of honor, my little phoenix?"

My eyes narrowed, noticing the insinuation behind the nickname. I chose not to dwell on it, and joined Raikidan by his side. As I did, a small crowed of people rushed over to us. In that crowd, two people stuck out to me—a young, umber-skinned elven man with long dark hair and brown eyes—Ren—and a young, fair-skinned nu-human man with short white hair and lavender eyes—Ral'ko. *Am I seeing things?* I hadn't seen them since the West Village had come under attack all those years ago. The two of them pushed their way to the front of the crowd and were all too inclined to act like no time had passed.

"Ral'ko, put me down!" I shouted as he grabbed me and hauled me over his shoulder. Ral'ko laughed and spun me around. "Ral'ko, stop!"

"Oh, you like it," Ren said.

"Shut up, Ren," I said. "Ral'ko, seriously, you're going to make me sick!"

Ral'ko huffed and put me down, only for Ren to embrace me in a tight bear hug.

"You two haven't changed a bit." I couldn't help but laugh. I was sure they had met the same fate as Xye. I had been so ashamed of what I had done that I never got around to finding out who had made it and who hadn't. The only reason I had known Del'karo was still alive was because of my conversations with Alena before my departure to deal with Zarda.

Ren chuckled. "You'd worry if we had."

"Yeah, yeah, let me go!"

"Nah."

Shva'sika laughed at us. "You three are a ridiculous trio."

I snorted. "It's all them."

She wagged a finger at me. "You don't make it any better."

"Well, biting off their heads didn't do much to them," I reminded her.

Ral'ko puffed out his chest and held his head high. "Nope, it made us stick to you more."

I grunted. "Yeah, no kidding. Not even an attack on the village could get rid of you two."

"Aw, now you're just being mean," Ral'ko whined.

Valene giggled. "And you expect anything less from her?"

Ren chuckled. "She has a point."

Valene grabbed my hand. "C'mon. Now that the lame serious part is over, it's time to have some fun!"

"Lame?" Ryoko laughed. "I thought that was all pretty exciting!"

I giggled. "Anything that has a serious nature is lame to her."

"Well that's because it is," Valene insisted.

We laughed and followed her to a portal set up beyond the iron gates. Raikidan forced his way through the crowd of people, taking up a position next to me. *When did he leave my side?* He handed me my previously discarded satchel, and I thanked him with a smile. *That explains that.*

"It was thoughtful of him, too."

My hand brushed against his as we walked side by side, the ring he'd given me snagging momentarily. I gave him an apologetic look, but he only smiled in response.

Now able to process everything that had gone on in this past hour or so, I was glad Tla'lli had place a temporary enchantment on my jewelry to save them from all the elemental attacks I'd endured. Non-lost magic enchantments weren't always easy to come by. The one shamans used, like the enchantment on the endless bag I carried, were hidden away, while the druidic one used on Raikidan's clothes, were visible to the public eye, as long as they could access the Eternal Library, that is.

I especially didn't want the necklace and ring Raikidan gave me to be damaged. I loved them and couldn't stand the thought of anything happening to them. Raikidan's hand brushed mine again as we walked through the portal. I knew I shouldn't like the gifts he gave, or accept them for that matter, as they complicated things for me, but deep down, I liked feeling special.

And even though I couldn't tell him, and it could complicate things when his destined mate came around, I was happy he wanted to be my Guard full-time. We had worked so well together through that test, even if we had broken rules to do so. I didn't want anyone else by my side… to protect me, of course.

"Yeah, you keep telling yourself that's what you mean. Because lying to yourself makes things so much better."

"Shut up."

"If you'd just tell him, you'd save yourself a lot of headaches."

"No, it'd make more, so drop it."

Coming out on the other side of the portal, we were met with a large clearing within a forest that was lit by a large bonfire. As I listened beyond the loud chatter of party goers, I could tell we were now back in the city, which meant we were in the park.

Valene tugged on my arm. "C'mon, everyone is going to want to talk to you."

I spun a finger into the air with fake enthusiasm. "Oh goodie."

While I wasn't keen for all the attention, I was looking forward to relaxing and having fun. *I will have fun for once.*

"That's the spirit."

"And then tomorrow, things will go back to normal, fighting Zarda. But this time, we'll be better equipped, both as individuals and a whole unit. And Raikidan and I will be in better sync with each other than ever before."

"I will also be with you every step of the way."

"We'll work together. And I will get to the bottom of who you are."

"I hope so."

My eyes fluttered open. The only sounds in the cell were of the others sleeping. I gazed at my hands, to find the fingers of my right hand lightly grasping the ring finger of my left, which no longer sported any jewelry. If only—no, it didn't matter. Knowing what would eventually happen wouldn't have changed my choices. I'd sealed my path long before making those decisions that night.

GLOSSARY CHARACTER

DALATREND

LEADERS

Taric – Former ruler of Dalatrend, nu-human, father to Zarda, deceased

Zarda – Ruler of Dalatrend, nu-human, son to Taric

MILITARY

Rana (*RAH-nah*) – Nu-human experiment, assassin, trained under Eira, vendetta against Eira, reformed ways, deceased

Rick – Nu-human experiment, general, deceased

Verra – Nu-human experiment, general, vendetta against Eira and Amara, deceased

Zo – Nu-human experiment, general, interested in Eira

REBELLION

COUNCIL

Adina (*ah-DEE-nah*) – Oversees Team 7, nu-human experiment, first Dalatrend shapeshifter experiment

Akama (*ah-KAH-mah*) – Oversees Team 5, nu-human experiment, first Dalatrend Seer experiment (not planned), twin to Enrée

Eldenar – Oversees Team 4, nu-human experiment, first Dalatrend war experiment

Elkron – Oversees Team 6, nu-human experiment, first Dalatrend elementalist experiment

Enrée (*EN-ree-ay*) – Oversees Team 2, nu-human experiment,
first Dalatrend Battle Psychic experiment (not planned), twin
to Akama

Genesis – Oversees Team 3, first nu-human, necromantic
abilities

Hanama (*HAH-nah-mah*) – Oversees Team 1, nu-human experiment, first Dalatrend anthropomorphic experiment

TEAM 1
Assassin based

Evynne (*Ev-een*) – Nu-human experiment

TEAM 2
Recruitment based

Dan – Nu-human experiment, former Lieutenant to Eira

Innon (*EYE-nin*) – Battle leader, nu-human experiment, former
commander

TEAM 3
Income based, former Brute and foot soldier mostly

Andariel – Nu-human experiment, double ear prototype,
brother to Azriel, former medic, strip club owner: Midnight

Argus – Nu-human experiment, inventor, partner to Seda

Aurora – Nu-human experiment, experimental shapeshifter:
vampire bat, Underground computer tech

Azriel – Nu-human experiment, double ear prototype, brother
to Andariel, former medic, night club owner: Twilight

Blaze – Nu-human experiment

Eira (*AIR-uh*) – Nu-human hybrid experiment, battle leader,
former commander, assassin, mother to Ryder, Shaman of
the Rising Sun. Alt names: Laz, Laz'shika (*laz-SHEE-kah*).
Interest in… complicated

Lena – Nu-human, partner to Zenmar

Orchon (*OR-con*) – Nu-human, bouncer at Twilight

Raid – Nu-human experiment, brother to Rylan, experimental shapeshifter: dog, interested in Ryoko

Raikidan (*RYE-ki-DAN*) – Black and red dragon, brother to Ebon, cousin to Corliss, son to Xephrya, Guard in training, promised mate to… unknown

Rylan (*RYE-lan*) – Nu-human experiment, brother to Raid, experimental shapeshifter: wolf, former captain, partner to Ryoko, artificial mental bond with Eira, ice elementalist

Ryoko (*Ree-OH-koh*) – Half-wogron experiment, clone of Peacekeeper Ryoko, Brute, former lieutenant, partner to Rylan, best friend to Eira

Seda (*SAY-duh*) – Nu-human experiment, psychic: Seer, twin to Nioush, sister to Saléna and Nyra, partner to Argus

Xantar (*ZAN-tar*) – Nu-human experiment

Zane – Nu-human experiment, uncle to Eira, brother to Jasmine and Amara, former soldier, mechanic, interested in Shva'sika

Zenmar – Nu-human experiment, crippled in a skirmish, partner to Lena

TEAM 4
Reconnaissance based

Alex – Nu-human experiment, Run competition participant, interested in Eira

Lara – Nu-human, mother to Lexi, Run competition help for Alex

TEAM 5
Psychic based

Avila (*ah-VEE-luh*) – Nu-human experiment, psychic: Seer, twin to Telar

Telar (*tell-ARE*) – Nu-human experiment, psychic: Battle Psychic, twin to Avila

Vek – Nu-human experiment, psychic: Battle Psychic, registered

TEAM 6
Research and development based

TEAM 7
Reconnaissance based

Chameleon – Nu-human experiment, molecular fusion ability, former assassin

Doppelganger – Nu-human experiment, temporary cloning ability

Ezhno (*EZ-no*) – Nu-human experiment, Underground computer tech

Mocha – Nu-human experiment, anthropomorphic: cat

Nioush (*NEE-oosh*) – Nu-human experiment, psychic: Battle Psychic, twin to Seda, brother to Saléna and Nyra

Raynn (*rain*) – Nu-human experiment, battle leader, former general, clone of Peacekeeper Raynn

MOLES

Arlon – Nu-human experiment, recent tank release, fan of Eira's reputation

Nyra – Nu-human experiment, psychic: Battle Psychic, twin to Saléna, sister to Seda and Nioush

Ryder – Nu-human experiment, son to Eira and Rylan

Saléna (*sah-LEY-nah*) – Nu-human experiment, psychic: Seer, twin to Nyra, sister to Seda and Nioush

Talon – Nu-human experiment, bone spike ability

MERCENARIES

Arnia (*ARE-nee-ah*) – Nu-human experiment, twin to Jaybird, metal elementalist, former mole, interested in Ven'lar

Jaybird – Nu-human experiment, twin to Arnia, air elementalist, former mole

SHAMANS

NORTH TRIBE

Fe'teline (*fey-TELL-een*) – Nu-human, Shaman of the Rising Sun

Sha'hiri (*sha-HEER-ee*) – Leader, nu-human, Shaman of the Frozen Waste

Ven'lar (*ven-LAR*) – Nu-human, Shaman of the Cleansing Spirit, interested in Arnia

SOUTH TRIBE

Ir'esh (*EAR-esh*) – Chief, elf, father to Tla'lli, Shaman of the Fractured Crystal

Ne'kall (*nay-CALL*) – Elf, son to Del'karo and Alena, father of four, Shaman of the Rising Sun

Tla'lli (*teh-LAH-lee*) – Elf, daughter to Ir'esh, Shaman of the Whispering Winds, interested in Talon

EAST TRIBE

Nela – Nu-human, Shaman of the Dancing Lights

Se'lata (*say-LAH-tah*) – Elf, spice merchant, Shaman of the Fractured Crystal

Xa'vian (*ZAH-vee-an*) – Leader, elf, Shaman of the Dancing Lights

WEST TRIBE

Alena – Elf, wife to Del'karo, mother figure to Eira, mother of Ne'kall and twelve other children, Shaman of the Cleansing Spirit

Daren – Human, Valene's adopted father, inn keeper, former partner to Valessa

Del'karo (*del-CAR-oh*) – Elf, mentor and father figure to Eira, husband to Alena, father of Ne'kall and twelve other children, Shaman of the Rising Sun

Ken'ichi (*ken-EE-chee*) – Nu-human, friend to Eira, Guard and Shaman of the Cleansing Spirit

Maka'shi (*mah-KAH-shee*) – Leader, half-elf, Shaman of the Frozen Waste, widow

Me'kunar (*may-COON-are*) – Elf, scholar

Mel'ka (*mel-KAH*) – Elf, elder, storyteller, Shaman of the Fractured Crystal

Shva'sika (*sh-VAH-see-KAH*) – Elf, sister to Xye, mentor and adopted family to Eira, Shaman of the Dancing Lights. Alt names: Elarinya (*ell-are-IN-yah*), Danika

Valene (*Vah-LEEN*) – Human, daughter to Valessa, Eira's and Daren's adopted daughter, plant-based Shaman of the Fractured Crystal

Valessa – Human, mother to Valene, former partner to Daren, Shaman of the Fractured Crystal, deceased

Xye (*zeye*) – Half-elf, brother to Shva'sika, attempted to court Eira, Shaman of the Cleansing Spirit, deceased

Ral'ko (*ral-KOH*) – Human, Guard

Ren – Elf, Shaman of the Cleansing Spirit

Va'len (*VAH-len*) – Former leader, elf, former husband to Maka'shi, Shaman of the Fractured Crystal, deceased

DRAGONS

Ambrose – Black dragon, mate to Salir, father to Rennek, grandfather to Corliss, Raikidan, and Ebon, great-grandfather to Anahak

Corliss – Green and black dragon, cousin to Raikidan, mate to Mana

Ebon – Black and red dragon, mate to Nyoki, brother to Raikidan, cousin to Corliss, son to Xephrya, grandson to Salir and Ambrose

Enrek – Green and black dragon, brother to Corliss, cousin to Raikidan and Ebon, infatuated with Mana

Mana – Green dragon, mate to Corliss

Nyoki (*NEE-oh-key*) – Black dragon, mate to Ebon

Rennek – Black dragon, adopted son to Salir and Ambrose, uncle to Raikidan and Corliss

Salir (*sah-LEER*) – Black dragon, mate to Ambrose, mother to Rennek, grandmother to Corliss, Raikidan, and Ebon, great-grandmother to Anahak

Xephrya (*zef-RYE-ah*) – Red dragon, mother to Raikidan and Ebon, deceased

VELSARA WILDS CLAN

Anahak (*an-ah-HAWK*) – Black dragon, mate to Xaneth, father to Rimu and six other offspring

Rimu – Black and red dragon, son to Anahak and Xaneth

Xaneth (*zan-ETH*) – Red dragon, mate to Anahak, mother to Rimu and six other offspring

Zaith – Clan leader, red dragon

GODS

Anila (*ah-NEE-lah*) – Goddess of air

Arcadia (*are-KAY-dee-ah*) – Goddess of spirits, daughter to Solund and Lunaria, sister to Phyre

Genesis – Goddess of time, partner to Zoltan

Gina – Goddess of health and healing

Halcyon (*hall-SEE-on*) – Goddess of the sea

Imera (*eye-MEER-ah*) – Goddess of literature and knowledge

Jin – Goddess of refined earth

Kendaria – Goddess of water

Koseba (*koh-SAY-bah*) – God of shapeshifting

Le'carro (*ley-CAR-oh*) – God of lightning

Lunaria – Goddess of the moon, partner to Solund, mother to Phyre and Arcadia

Nazir (*nah-ZEER*) – God of death and corruption

Phyre (*fire*) – God of fire, son to Solund and Lunaria, brother to Arcadia

Raisu (*RAY-sue*) – God of dreams

Rashta (*RAH-sh-tah*) – Goddess of judgement and rebirth, currently missing

Rasmus – God of love and fertility, partner to Savada

Satria (*sah-TREE-ah*) – Goddess of war

Savada (*sah-VAH-dah*) – Goddess of sex and seduction, partner to Rasmus

Sela – Goddess of psychics, sister of Tyro

Solstice – Goddess of ice and winter

Solund – God of the sun, partner to Lunaria, father to Phyre and Arcadia

Tarin – God of Nature, partner to Valena

Tyro (*TIE-roh*) – God of psychics, brother of Sela

Valena – Goddess of earth, partner to Tarin

Zoltan – God of matter, Partner to Genesis

MISCELLANEOUS

Alyra (*all-EYE-rah*) – Nu-human experiment, former soldier, partner to Lakon, mother to Eyri, musician

Ayluin (*eye-LOO-en*) – Elf, grandfather to Sumala, tries to find Eira suitors

Carlos – Nu-human, Run competition competitor help

Den – Nu-human, Run competition commentator

Devon – Nu-human experiment, former assassin, musician

Eyri (*EYE-ree*) – Nu-human, Lakon and Alyra's daughter, musician

Lakon (*LAY-con*) – Nu-human experiment, former assassin, partner to Alyra, father to Eyri, musician

Lucas – Nu-human, Run competition competitor

Nordec – Dwarf, tavern owner

Reynor (*RAY-nor*) – Nu-human, Run competition commentator

Rosa (*ROH-sah*) – Succubus, mated to Zaedrix

Sumala (*sue-MALL-ah*) – Elf, granddaughter to Ayluin

Voice – Mysterious voice that speaks to Eira inside her head. Once malevolent, now benevolent. May have an ethereal form. Goal: to protect Eira… so she says

Vorn – Dwarf, old friend to Eira

Zaedrix (*ZAY-driks*) – Incubus, mated to Rosa

SPIRITS

Amara (*ah-MAR-ah*) – Nu-human experiment, general, mother to Eira, grandmother to Ryder, sister to Jasmine and Zane, water elementalist, deceased

Anir (*ah-NEER*) – Black dragon, claims to know Eira, deceased

Jade – Nu-human experiment, former soldier under Amara, deceased

Jasmine – Nu-human experiment, aunt to Eira, sister to Amara and Zane, geneticist, deceased

Lazei (*LAH-zay*) – Human, ancient swordsman, protector of

the Eternal Library, deceased but active by use of spiritual crystal

Tannek – Nu-human experiment, double ear prototype, medic, deceased

Zeek – Nu human, Brute, former soldier under Amara, former partner to Ryoko, deceased

PEACEKEEPERS

Assar – dwarf, deceased

Pyralis (*PIE-ral-iss*) – Red dragon, former Valsara Wild Clan leader, deceased

Raynn (*rain*) – Human, deceased

Reiki (*Ray-KEY*) – Green dragon, deceased

Ryoko (*Ree-OH-koh*) – Half-wogron, Shaman of the Fractured Crystal, deceased

Varro – Elf, healer, deceased

ORPHANAGE

Lyra (*LIE-ruh*) – Matron, Nu-human

Myra (*MEER-uh*) – Nu-human, attached to Raid

Orphans (Elara (*el-ARE-ah*), Jakcel (*JACK-sell*), Elsa, Levi, Panga, Nari, Kelcen (*Kell-SEN*), Alson, Ellie)

GLOSSARY LANGUAGE

ELVISH

Elvish is an eloquent language, light on the tongue with an airy sound. Even the usual consonants of common don't hold the same harshness in Elvish. Many elves and other humanoids raised with Elvish as their mother tongue carry this light speech over in their common.

While not the easiest language to learn, Elvish is a favorite among the linguistically gifted. Those who seek to learn this language seek out elves before any other race and are taught by full immersion. Some elves will provide a few words for the humanoid to start with but it's not common to do so. The elves believe this technique is the best way to learn and creates a better understanding of the language for everyday use.

Written Elvish is just as elegant as spoken, usually written in script by native speakers. Non-natives tend to forgo the script, which is accepted by native speakers, though the handwriting is still expected to be neat, and flourished on important documents. Sloppy writing is considered an insult.

Phrases used in the series:

Éan ag eitilt – Flying bird

Go dtí go gcomhlíonfaimid arís – Until we meet again
Nuair a ardaíonn an ghrian arís – When the sun rises once more

DRACONIC

D raconic is a guttural language made up most of grunts and growls with the occasional tongue flick, exhales, or teeth clatter. It's difficult for a non-dragon to learn, as the formation of these words are foreign to most humanoids. Some sounds are impossible for non-dragons to create so other sounds are substituted as an alternative. Even dragons taking a humanoid form must make these changes. Rarely is a humanoid able to perfect the speech, even when raised among dragons.

Those attempting to learn are always taught single words before attempting sentence structures. Draconic sentence structure is similar to Common, but with a possessive edge due to the mindset of dragons. There are no contracted words in Draconic, as such, dragons who don't speak common often, tend to use the same sentence structures of their mother tongue when they do speak common.

It's not common for dragons to write in the current age but there is a basic written form of the language that was used more extensively in the past. This written form is comprised of glyphs easily created with dragon claws and easy to decipher for most dragons no matter the cleanliness of the script. Non-dragons find this writing easier to learn than the spoken language and most of the time will stop learning after they've master it.

Words Raikidan has taught Eira in the series:

Aio – You	*Diik* – Food
Aion – Your	*Dnyy* – Free
Aionl – Yours	*Duny* – Fire
Ayl – Yes	*Din* – For
Cull – Kiss	*Dinytyn* – Forever
Cyyg – Keep	*Dnis* – From

Dnuyvk – Friend
Eny – Are
Eun – Air
Ev – An
Evk – And
Ezfeal – Always
Femyn – Water
Finna – Worry
Frem – What
Fryzg – Whelp
Fulkis – Wisdom
Fuzz – Will
Gyexy – Peace
Gyelevm – Peasant
Gzyely – Please
Id – Of
Iddlgnuvw – Offspring
Ion – Our
Iv – On
Ki – Do
Keowrmyn – Daughter
Knewiv – Dragon
Lgunum – Spirit
Lisymruvw – Something
Liv – Son
Livw – Song
Lmneuwrm – Straight
Lmnyvwmr – Strength
Lreny – Share
Lry – She
Luny – Sire
Lulmyn – Sister
Lupzuvw – Sibling
Lxezy – Scale
Lynyvuma – Serenity
Lyy – See
Mi – To

Mii – Too
Mioxr – Touch
Mrevc – Thank
Mruvc – Think
Mryny – There
Mnyelony – Treasure
Ol – Us
Pnimryn – Brother
Pnyemry – Breathe
Pumy – Bite
Py – Be
Regguvyll – Happiness
Rel – Has
Rety – Have
Rl – He
Rosev – Human
Rovwyn – Hunger
Rul – His
Rus – Him
Ryn – Her
Ryzzi – Hello
Sa – My
Simryn – Mother
Siny – More
Suvy – Mine
Sy – Me
Semy – Mate
U – I
Ud – If
Ul – Is
Um – It
Vi – No
Vim – Not
Vyyk – Need
Wiikpay – Goodbye
Wik – God
Wikkyll – Goddess

Wym – Get
Xifenkza – Cowardly
Xivvexmyk – Connected
Yem – Eat
Yenmr – Earth
Ytyv – Even

Ziaeza – Loyalty
Zity – Love
Zoxca – Lucky
Zudy – Life
Zulmyv – Listen
Zutyl – Lives

Phrases translated to Eira in the series:

Ion cuvk – Our kind

Lazmira, sa xruzk – Lazmira, my child

Zity, gyexy, lgunum, ziaeza, lynyvuma, lmnyvwmr, fulkis – Love, peace, spirit, loyalty, serenity, strength, wisdom

LOST LANGUAGES

Throught the history of Lumaraeon, language has developed and died, but some have left a more notable impact on the races. These forgotten languages hold important information lost during the millennia of turmoil making them important topics for scholars.

OLD TONGUE

Old Tongue, also known as God speech, is the most ancient form of speech that was replaced by the various languages of Lumaraeon, ultimately dying out among the mortal races. Much of the language was lost during the War of End and with no one but the gods around to remember, the language was thought dead. Until a large find of books in the Eternal Library turned up after a new entryway was found, eight hundred years ago.

Scholars have done their best to decipher the old language and have since found new discovery sites all over Lumaraeon to help with their research. But while the tongue is researched, it is not know if the translations are quite right, and no one has thought to ask the gods, not even Imera, the goddess of literature and knowledge.

Words used in the series:

Mukarna – Makers

ABOUT
THE
AUTHOR

S hannon Pemrick, is a full-time USA Today bestselling author, and fuller-time geek and dragon obsessed. She also has too many novelty mugs, not enough chocolate, and a forbidden love-affair with all things shiny.

Shannon resides in Southern New Hampshire with her overly sarcastic husband and one too many pets who steal all her bed space. When she's not burning her fingers across a keyboard or trying to squeeze into a spot on the couch for movie night, she's rolling dice and getting lost in RPGs or searching for brides for her dragon overlords.

You can learn more about Shannon by visiting her website at:
Shannonpemrick.com

CPSIA information can be obtained
at www.ICGtesting.com
Printed in the USA
BVHW081723080121
597262BV00001B/19